Belle
City

Also by Penny Mickelbury

The Carole Ann Gibson Novels
One Must Wait
Where to Choose
The Step Between
Paradise Interrupted

The Mimi Patterson/Gianna Maglione Novels
Keeping Secrets
Night Songs
Love Notes
Darkness Descending

The Phil Rodriguez Novels
Two Graves Dug
A Murder Too Close

Belle City

Penny Mickelbury

Whitepoint Press
San Pedro, California

A Whitepoint Press First Edition 2014

Cover and book design by Monique Carbajal
Cover photo © iStockphoto.com/niknak99
Author photo by Peggy Ann Blow

ISBN - 13: 978-0-9898971-2-9
ISBN - 10: 0989897125

Library of Congress Control Number: 2014935036

Published by Whitepoint Press
whitepointpress.com

————————

For my unknown ancestors. Your journeys made mine possible, and

For my known Georgia ancestors:
Andrew Jackson and Mary Poe Shehee
James Oliver and Mexico Shehee Hembree
Arthur Jennings and Mexico Hembree Mickelbury

I am grateful, perhaps especially, to my father who, though Louisiana-born,
made his way to Georgia and made Georgia his home.

————————

Belle City

PART ONE

Carrie's Crossing

1917-1922

– 1917 –

L et me shoot him," Tobias whispered, settling the stock of the shotgun firmly into the soft part of his shoulder.

"No," Little Si said, shaking his head. "It's my turn, we do it my way."

"Shhhh."

"Shush your own self, Jonas Thatcher," Silas Thatcher hissed without moving a muscle. His feet were planted, left in front of right, a yard apart. His body was angled so that his left shoulder pointed directly at the deer which, at that moment, raised her head. In a single, fluid, powerful motion, Silas pulled the arrow back and released it. None of them saw it travel or even hit the deer. They knew she was hit when she collapsed.

The three boys stepped out of the dense underbrush, still moving quietly and cautiously but in a hurry to reach the felled animal to end her suffering if she wasn't already dead. She was. It was a productive day: A deer for each of their families, a brace of rabbits for Silas and Tobias to take home, three quail for the pots in Jonas's house because his mother didn't eat rabbit or squirrel.

"I sure wish you'd teach me to shoot that bow and arrow," Jonas said to Silas.

Tobias replied for his brother. "You got to be a Indian to shoot a bow and arrow, Jonas, and you ain't no Indian."

"You ain't neither," Jonas said, stung.

"Our Ma is, you know that," Silas said. He and Jonas were best friends, and he didn't want to hurt his feelings.

"You reckon she'd mind if you taught me how?"

Silas considered but again Tobias answered. "Our Pa would. He don't even want us playin' with you, just like your Pa don't want you playin' with us." At fifteen, Tobias was two years older than his brother and Jonas, old enough to understand the danger contained in the nuance of their family relations and old enough to hate it. They all were Thatchers, but Jonas was white and Silas and Tobias were Colored. Jonas and Silas had been best friends since they met in the woods foraging for wild strawberries years earlier—one of them illegally on the other's family's land—but neither had given much consideration to the fact of the sameness of their names and the difference in their color. They were friends, a relationship that Big Silas Thatcher, Tobias and Little Si's father, strenuously discouraged.

Tobias bent over the deer and yanked out the arrow, which he gave to Silas. "That was a good shot, Si. Make sure you tell Ma how good."

"I will," Silas said, savoring his older brother's praise and looking forward to that of his mother who was, in truth, only half Muscogee Creek Indian.

"How many people y'all havin' at your celebration?" Jonas asked, as much to have something to say to the other boys as to find out the answer.

Tobias gave him a strange look. "What celebration?"

"For your brothers. Beau and...I forget the other one's name. They goin' to the war, ain't they? Just like my brother Zeb's goin'."

"It ain't a celebration, it's just a dinner that the whole family's comin' to." Tobias tied the deer's front legs together, then the back ones, and hoisted the animal up and onto his shoulders. "We better get going, Si. We got a longer walk home than you, Jonas. Plus you ain't got to carry your deer, seein' as how you got a horse." Tobias was as tall as a man and almost as strong, and as he turned and walked off, Silas and Jonas looked admiringly at his back, the muscles rippling under the weight of the dead animal. He really was almost a man, Si thought, like his older brothers, Beaudry and Eubanks.

"Why ain't y'all havin' a celebration?" Jonas asked in the silence that was left after Tobias's departure.

"'Cause there ain't nothin' to celebrate," Silas said as he helped Jonas tie his deer's legs. "My Ma says they're all crazy, goin' way cross the ocean to fight a dang war."

"My Pa says my brother's gonna be a hero."

"Your brother ain't Colored. Now let's get this deer up on that horse." They lifted the deer as Jonas whistled for his horse, who came strolling through the brush toward them.

"What the hell?" Jonas exclaimed, almost dropping his end of the deer when the horse appeared wearing a daisy chain around its neck.

"Oh, Lord," Little Silas groaned as they hoisted the deer onto the horse's flank. Then he turned a full circle, looking up into the trees. He stopped, facing a giant oak, and squinted into the branches. "Come here, Girl," he said, and his eyes followed the almost imperceptible rustle of the tree's branches. The boys, both trained hunters, heard a soft thud, then the underbrush parted. Jonas inhaled.

"Who's that?"

"My sister, Ruthie," Silas said as the grinning girl walked toward them. She wore half a dozen daisy chains around her neck, and her inky black, waist-length hair flowed freely. She was as tall as the boys, reed-thin, red-brown colored, and she walked without seeming to move. She stood close to Si.

"Who's he?" Ruthie asked her brother.

"Jonas Thatcher. And how come you're spyin' on us?"

"Daddy don't want you playin' with him, and I wasn't spyin', I was fishin'."

Little Silas gave exaggerated looks all around, up and down. "I don't see no fish."

Ruthie smirked at her brother. "They're in the creek, keeping cold."

"Fishin' where?" Jonas asked.

"Carrie's Creek. Where else?" Ruthie said, looking at Jonas as if finally seeing him and uncertain what she felt about what she saw.

"There ain't no fish in that water. Not a single one."

Now Ruthie did look at him strangely. Then she looked at her brother. "What's he talking about, Si? The creek is full of fish."

"No, it ain't. Is it, Si? Tell her."

Silas fidgeted uncomfortably as his glance slid away from Jonas but refused to meet his sister's. Both were waiting for him to reaffirm their position, and he was caught between the truth and a lie, between his sister and his best friend. Ruthie grabbed his hand. "Come on, Si, we gotta go. Bye, Jonas." And they were gone, Ruthie and Silas, and Jonas watched them go, feeling...feeling something strange and different that he couldn't put words to, but knowing that he didn't want them to leave.

"What's that got to do with anything?" he called out. He couldn't see them—danged Indians could disappear into the danged air—but he knew they heard him. "Being Colored, I mean?" he called out, and waited as the sound of his voice reverberated in the dense forest. Then Ruthie emerged, silent and graceful. She walked toward him.

"Say what?"

"How come your brother can't be a war hero just 'cause he's Colored? What difference does it make?"

Ruthie gave him another one of her looks, but this one was different; this one was the kind of look that meant he'd done or said something stupid. "You don't know the diff'rence between bein' Colored and bein' white?" she said.

Jonas knew he was turning red because he could feel the heat rise in his face, but Ruthie didn't seem to notice. She was waiting for him to answer. "'Course I do, but that don't mean a Colored man can't be a hero. If he fights a good fight, then he's a hero."

Ruthie looked long and hard at Jonas Thatcher, remembering the times Little Silas had defended his friend in arguments with their Pa who would thunder, *Zeb Thatcher's a mean, nasty cracker and I don't want you playin' with his boy. Don't want you nowhere near him!* And Little Silas would respond: *Jonas ain't like that, Pa. Jonas ain't nothin' like that!*

"What you say is true, but everybody don't think like that, Jonas," Ruthie said and turned away from him.

"I wish I was Colored," Jonas said so softly that not even the wind could hear what he said, but she did and turned back to face him, the look on her face different this time. "If I was Colored" Jonas said, "I could marry you, Ruthie Thatcher."

"You'll get yourself killed six times you say that again, Jonas Thatcher."

He laughed even though there was no humor in her voice or in her eyes. Nothing there but deep seriousness. But he felt good talking to her, being near her. And besides, a thing could only die one time. He said that to her, then asked, "How'm I gonna get myself killed six times?"

"I got four brothers, a daddy, and Uncle Will, and each one of 'em'll kill you, you say something like to me again."

"Si won't hurt me."

"He'll kill you. Bye, Jonas." Walking silently but rapidly, she disappeared into the forest, and Jonas climbed on his horse and rode off in the opposite direction. Their houses were less than a mile apart through the woods and twice that by the dirt road, but the distance between them was the distance between white and Colored in Georgia in 1917, and that was a great, gaping chasm.

"What did he say, Ruthie, when you asked him?" Silas had retrieved Ruthie's fish from the stream, and, rabbits strung over one shoulder, fish over the other, he'd started for home, knowing that his sister would quickly and easily catch up.

"He said Beaudry and Eubanks could be heroes just like his brother... what's his brother's name?"

"Don't matter what his name is. He's either lying or he's crazy. Anyway, who you gonna believe: Jonas Thatcher or your own Pa?"

"How come he thinks there ain't no fish in the creek? And how can him and us be named Thatcher, but we're Colored and he's not? We some kin to them, Si?"

Little Si blew air through his lips. "Don't ask me stuff like that, Girl."

They walked quietly through the dense forest, Ruthie leading the way, holding low-hanging branches out of the way of her brother's face. There was a dirt road leading to their family farm but through the forest was faster and cooler. It was almost noon and the sun was directly overhead, but they were protected by the massive maze of tree tops. They'd beat Tobias home. Carrying the deer, he'd have walked the road, hoping for a ride, and if nobody came along, he'd just trudge along in the heat. "I can take the rabbits and fish, Si, if you want to go help Tobias," Ruthie said. Si stopped walking and without a word, he slung the rabbits and fish over his sister's shoulders. He knew that she loved being alone in the forest, that she loved being alone anywhere, especially when she had something on her mind. And he could tell by her stillness— the stillness that was inside of her—that she was thinking hard.

"See you at home," Little Si said and angled north toward the road.

"You're gonna have to stop bein' friends with him, Si."

Si stopped walking but he didn't turn around. He waited for her to say something more, but she didn't. He didn't, either.

Normally, Jonas would have been in a hurry to get home and show off his prizes, especially since they represented his going away gifts to his big brother. For reasons that Jonas couldn't figure out, Zeb seemed not to like him. More than once, he almost asked Si how it was that his older brothers liked him— taught him things and did things with him—but he'd been too embarrassed and hadn't wanted his friend to know how Zeb was always punching or pushing or laughing at the youngest of the Thatcher children. Shoot, Jonas thought, Si and his sister even liked each other, and Jonas's sisters hated him more than Zeb did.

The thought of Ruthie Thatcher caused a hitch inside Jonas, like something was hung up in there somewhere. He breathed in and out until it went away, to be replaced almost immediately by another hurty kind of feeling at the thought that Si would kill him. And he had no doubt that Si would, because Ruthie said so. And he had no doubt about anything that Ruthie Thatcher said. He didn't know why. He just knew that if she spoke, what she said would be the truth. Which would mean that there were fish in Carrie's Creek.

He saw the smoke dancing in the air from the cook stove in his house, and before he smelled the food, his stomach rumbled. It was almost time for dinner, and he hadn't even had breakfast. He'd snatched a piece of leftover from the bowl on the kitchen table on his way out that morning before dawn, but that was so long ago his body didn't remember eating it. Whatever his Ma had for the midday meal would be welcome, even if it was something he didn't like, like squash or okra. Then he had a mouth-watering thought: Maybe there was something left over from breakfast: biscuits and grits and gravy.

"Git up, now, Red," he said, urging his horse to hurry. He already was tasting leftover grits and bacon and biscuits. If Zeb and his Pa hadn't eaten it all. That thought made him hurry the sedate old horse even more as his house came into view through the woods. It was the rear view and his sister, Esther, was hanging clothes on the line. She turned at the sound of galloping, saw it was him, and turned back to her work. Esther hanging up clothes was not a good sign. It meant that his mother was feeling even more poorly than usual. Esther had gotten married the year before and lived several miles away in Spencerville. If she was back here long enough to wash clothes...

"Hey," he called out, riding into the yard.

"Don't kick up dust, Jonas."

"Ain't you got nothin' to say about my deer? And the hens?"

Esther looked at the deer and the quail, and then at her youngest brother, and she gave him a small smile. "You had yourself a busy morning, didn't you?"

"Sure did," he said, walking—not galloping—the horse around the side yard and down to the barn, where he knew he'd find the Zebs: His Pa and his brother. He called out to them as he got closer, and Big Zeb stuck his head out.

"Hey, Boy! I wondered where you'd got to." Still carrying the pitchfork, Big Zeb's eyes widened in surprise; he came to meet Jonas. "Well, now. Ain't this somethin'."

"It's for Zeb's goin' away celebration. A hero can't go off to war on a empty stomach."

"I reckon you're right about that," the old man said as he leaned the pitchfork against the barn and came to get a close look at Jonas's bounty. "These some fine lookin' animals, Boy. Where you get 'em?"

"North, over by the creek," Jonas replied and knew immediately that he'd made an error. His father's eyes narrowed and his shoulders tightened.

"You been with them niggers again?"

"They was huntin', I was huntin," Jonas said, hoping he sounded offhanded and relaxed, like Si's brother Tobias always sounded. Or like Ruthie sounded: Like the words were coming from God and nobody better give any back talk. He slid down off the horse, keeping his back to his father, and began to untie the deer and the quail.

"Big ol' woods and y'all just happened to be huntin' in the same place at the same time."

"Yes, sir," Jonas answered, though his father had not asked a question.

"I want you to stay away from them people, you hear me, Jonas? You done got too old to be runnin' through the woods, chasin' behind some niggers. Leave 'em be, you hear me?"

"What if they Indians, Pa, and not niggers?"

"Who tole you they was Indians? They ain't no more Indians than you and me. Anyway, ain't been no Indians in these parts for sixty, seventy years. Now, I said stay clear of 'em, you hear me?"

Jonas nodded and his pa slapped him on the back of the head. "Yes, sir, I hear you," Jonas said.

"Aw right, then. Let's get this hero food gutted and cleaned. I believe I'll salt the deer."

"Can I eat first, Pa?"

Zeb gave his son a surprised look. "Sure you can, Boy. You done all this huntin' and haven't et?" Jonas shook his head. "Then go 'head on in the house. And if ain't nothin' left from breakfast, tell Rachel to fix you somethin'."

Jonas's face fell. His sister Rachel hated him more than Esther did. Dang it. Why did Ma have to be poorly again? She'd be proud of him and happy to fix him some food. Rachel would just be mad at the extra work she'd have to do.

"Come on. I'll go with you and I'll tell her," Pa said with a sly grin. "I'll tell her she can fix you some breakfast or she can clean and gut them birds. What you think she'll choose?"

Jonas managed his own sly grin and followed his father to the house, trying to imagine never again being able to hunt and fish and roam the woods with Silas. "How come Ma is poorly again?"

Zeb Thatcher sighed deeply. "She lost another baby."

Jonas was shocked. He hadn't known she was carrying again. He snuck a look up at his Pa. The big man's weathered and lined face was scrunched up like he wanted to cry. Jonas wanted to say something but saying the wrong thing would earn him another slap up side the head, and the look on Pa's face said that just about anything would be the wrong thing.

"That makes five," Zeb said sorrowfully. "Another one'll kill her."

Five! Jonas knew about two: One last year and one the year before. He also knew enough about the process of animals giving birth to know that two miscarriages was a bad sign. But *five*. For sure the next one would kill her. Five miscarriages would kill a horse or a cow or a pig. His Ma should have been dead. No wonder she was poorly all the time. "Is she gonna be all right?"

"I hope so," Zeb said. "I pray so." He dipped his head as if praying.

They'd almost reached the house. Jonas saw that the lines were filled with clean clothes flapping in the gentle breeze, and as hot as it was, they'd be dry in another hour. He figured that Esther would stay long enough to fold the clothes and make sure Ma had food to eat—even when she was well, Corrinne Maxwell Thatcher was a picky eater—and only Esther would take the time and make the effort to prepare the food their mother liked. And what she liked, the food of her native Scotland, Zeb Thatcher called hog slop and refused to eat.

"Pa?"

Zeb slowed his long-legged gait and looked down at his youngest son, at the child who most likely would be his last. "What, Boy?"

"What's wrong with Si and his people that you don't like them? They got the same name as us."

Zeb slapped him up side the head. Hard. "That don't mean nothin', you hear me? A whole lotta niggers got the same name as white folks, and it don't mean nothin'. What means somethin' is how you act, and you been actin' like no son of mine, and you're gonna stop it right now." And Zeb slapped him up side the head again.

Now Jonas was mad. "Si's brothers are goin' to fight the war just like my brother. Don't that mean they're the same?"

"Somebody's got to dig the ditches and cook the food and slop the latrines. That's why niggers are goin' to the war, not to fight the...the...whoever it is we're fightin'." Zeb pushed him up the front steps to the porch, then snatched the screen door open so hard it slam-banged against the side of the house, knocking off some of the chipped paint. Then he pushed Jonas inside ahead of him with such force that the boy fell and skidded across the parlor floor.

"Well, it ain't right," Jonas said, halfway to his feet and halfway out of the room, headed for the kitchen.

"But it's how things are," his pa bellowed back, "and how they always been and how they always gonna be!" And Jonas knew right then that the difference between what was right and how things were would some day cause him bigger problems than a slap up side the head.

Tobias, Silas and Ruthie's mother, Nellie, was so proud that she cooked them a whole breakfast, even though she was in the middle of her dinner preparations, and she gave Little Si a whole roasted yam—his favorite food—for himself alone, he didn't even have to share with Ruthie, as congratulations for his bow-and-arrow prowess. "You do your People proud, Son," she said. "You all do. Them woods is your home, same as this house is, and don't never forget that." Nellie didn't make a point of emphasizing her fifty percent Muscogee Creek ancestry—there was no point to that since there were no Creek left in Georgia—but it was important to her, and her husband and children knew and respected that. Nellie also knew that the bow and arrow were not Creek tools, though she doubted that her family knew that, doubted that it would matter if they did. What mattered was that in Carrie's Crossing, Georgia, in 1917, a few Colored people had something that was theirs—had something that white people did not, even if that something belonged to somebody else. It would never have occurred to the white people of Carrie's Crossing that the Indians of Georgia—back when Georgia and Alabama and Mississippi and Tennessee still had Indians—would be different from the Indians of the Plains and the West, and that a left-behind Georgia Indian would hear about and relish the stories of those other Indians' bravery (savagery, the whites called it) and adopt the bow and arrow as her own, and then offer it to her children as something that they too could claim as their own.

"Jonas wanted to shoot with the bow, but I told him he couldn't 'cause he wasn't no Indian," Si told his mother. Since all of his attention was focused on peeling and buttering the roasted yam, he didn't immediately notice the change his words produced around the kitchen table: A mixture of pride and dismay in his mother, foreboding in his brother, and something resembling annoyance in his sister.

"Your Pa told you to stay away from that boy," Nellie said, her anger gentled by the gratifying sense of her child's pride in the ancestry that soon would be lost to history. "Y'all know better than to go against what your Pa says." She looked from one to the other of her three youngest children, her gaze lingering the longest on Ruth, the youngest, the only girl, her joy. But that's not why Nellie's eyes held Ruth's. "Did he do something to y'all?"

They all shook their heads and said, "No, m'am."

"He said something," Nellie said—a statement, not a question—looking at Ruthie.

"He said Beau and Eubie could be heroes too since they're goin' to the Army like his brother. He said it don't matter that they're Colored." Ruthie looked into her mother's eyes as she spoke, searching for proof of Jonas Thatcher's lie, but Nellie got up from the table, turned away from her, went back to the stove and her dinner preparations.

"You don't need nobody to tell you who you are or what you can be," Nellie said, her back to her children so they wouldn't see the anger in her face; she had never shown them anger, and she hoped to God she never would. "It's no good us believin' that some otherbody knows us better than we know us." Nellie turned to face them. "You don't need Jonas Thatcher to tell you nothin' 'bout your brothers. You known Beaudry and Eubanks all you life, Ruthie. Ain't that right? And ain't they already heroes to you?"

Ruth nodded. Her Pa and her two oldest brothers and her Uncle Will were more than heroes to her—they were gods: Strong, powerful, good, providers and protectors. She looked at her younger brothers—Silas and Tobias—and saw them the same way, only with more familiarity because they were closer in age and size. They were her friends too, Si and Tobias.

"If y'all are through with eating, you boys go on out and help your Pa and brothers and Uncle Will. And make sure to tell 'em what y'all brought home this mornin'."

Two chairs pushed back from the table, and two pairs of feet crossed the kitchen. The back door opened and slammed shut. Nellie came back to the table and sat across from Ruthie. "What else did he say?" she asked her daughter.

Ruthie knew better than to tell her mother that Jonas Thatcher said he wished he was Colored so he could marry her. Nellie would tell Pa and he'd tell Beaudry and Eubanks and Uncle Will and the four of them would go crashing through the woods looking for Jonas and kill him for sure. "He said there ain't no fish in the creek."

"He's right."

Ruthie looked toward the sink where the line of fish she'd caught in the creek was waiting to be cleaned, then she looked back at her mother. "Ma?"

Nellie gave her an odd smile, one Ruthie had never seen before. "There ain't no fish in Carrie's Creek for *him*," her mother said, in a tone of voice that was unfamiliar, too.

"How come?"

"'Cause Miss Carrie, she put a curse on it, that's why. Cain't no white people catch no fish in that creek. Not never."

Ruthie still stared at her mother, her eyes wide and questioning and confused. "Miss Carrie, whose name I got? Who is she? And that's her creek?"

Nellie nodded. "She was your Grandma and it sure is her creek."

From the Recorded Memories of Ruth Thatcher McGinnis

"Sissy, you said for me to just start talking, but are you sure that tiny little thing can hear me and see me? Well…if you're sure…my name is Carrie Ruth Thatcher McGinnis and I was born on the seventeenth day of May in nineteen-hundred and four in Carrie's Crossing, Georgia. And I want to tell how the place got its name because right now, today, there's a real estate developer trying to change the name to something more 'upscale' because, he says, Carrie's Crossing sounds backward and country. We can't let that happen. It's enough of a shame that nobody today realizes that Carrie's Crossing and Carrie's Creek got their name from a real woman: Carrie Thatcher, born a slave in eighteen-hundred and fifty. I know this because she was my grandmother. She and her brother, William, stayed on to work for Carney Thatcher, helping him farm, after the Emancipation in exchange for some land of their own. He gave them what he thought was useless land because a creek ran through it, a creek that flooded every time it rained, so the land was marshy and swampy and full of snakes and bugs. It was near a crossroads—trails, really, more than roads back then, trails in the woods, one of them leading to Carney Thatcher's farm and the part where the white people lived, and the other trail leading to the part that Carney gave Carrie and William. And it was because of them that other Colored people moved to live up that trail.

In the spring of 1890, it rained in Georgia like it had never rained before, swelling the creek on Carrie and William's little farm and turning it into a wild river that rampaged across the land, washing away everything in sight, including Carrie. William heard her screaming and calling for help and he ran out into the storm looking for her, trying to save her. He saw her bobbing up and down in the fast-running creek but he couldn't run that fast. On the opposite bank, close to where Carrie had grabbed a tree root and was trying to hold on, two white men with nets were scooping up fish. Carrie called out to them to help her. To save her. They stood there on the bank of the creek, watching William try to reach his sister, watching Carrie lose her strength and her grip on the tree root. William said Carrie's last words were, "You'll never catch another fish in this creek! This is my water now! My creek!" And she was swept away. William and the other Colored men from up the road spent the rest of the day and into the night looking for Carrie. They found her in a tree at the crossroads, holding on so tight to a branch they had to break her arms to get her down. She had died trying so desperately to live.

From that moment to this, Carrie's Creek and Carrie's Crossing bore the name of that slave woman who was my grandma. And from that day to this, no white person has ever been able to catch a fish in that creek. In Carrie's Creek. She cursed it and she claimed it.

Now, as to why the whole city and the area around it is called Carrie's Crossing: Once again, back then the creek ran past a junction in the road, though, like I said, back then they were more trails than roads. One of those trails led from the woods to the creek; the other led from Carney Thatcher's farm to the creek. After the Emancipation, the whole area started to grow. Small farmers like Carney Thatcher now outnumbered the big plantation owners because they no longer had free labor, and quite a few Blacks now had their own land, like Carrie and William. So, a third road came into being—and this one was a real road. It started at the point where the original two met and it ran south, down toward Belle City. Both Blacks and whites traveled this road, the Blacks turning right to go uphill when they got to the creek and the whites turning left. It became sport for whites to lay in wait and ambush Blacks, steal their sacks of flour or sugar or beans or whatever they had, and throw them into the creek. Until Miss Carrie drowned hanging onto a tree limb at that crossroads. From that time on, there was no more attacking or ambushing of Black travelers—nobody really knows why but everybody liked to think that she protects the crossing. So, just like the Creek now belonged to Miss Carrie, so did the Crossing. And that's how one of the most affluent communities in Georgia came to be named for a slave woman, and I'm not so sure sometimes that those of us who know the true story should tell it. That real estate developer wants to change the name because he thinks it sounds too low class for his gold-plated plans, but in a way, it might just be to his benefit—and ours—that he not know the true story. Why? Because secrets have power, that's why.

From the Diary of Jonas Farley Thatcher

Summertime 1917. Pa would surely skin me if he knew I was writing down everything like I do. It's called Keeping A Journal and its something imporant people do. Im not importnt yet but I aim to be some day. A teacher or a writer like Mr. Mark Twain or Mr. J. F. Cooper. I could write about the last Indian in Carrie's Crossing which is in georgia. It's my friend Silases ma. I don't know what kind of indian she is, but she surely is one. I don't know her name either. Maybe I'll ask Si and he'll tell me what kind of indian she is and what's her name. I'm not supposed to be playing with Si nomore. Pa said so and he hits me when he finds out if I play with Si. Pa hats Si. Pa hats all collard people tho I don't kno why. He saids they are lazy and nocount but Si and his Pa and brothers work all the time. I think his ma does allso. One time when I have climed up a tall pecan tree to look thru the woods at Si's house I saw his ma out in the fields. leasways I think it was his ma cause it werent Ruth. I surely know Ruth when I see her. She works in the field allso my ma and sisters donot work in the filds. They just cook and wash clos swept the yard. Ruth and her ma do that allso. I see then when I clim the big pecan tree. I want to mary ruth but I kno I cant. she sayd her brothers and her pa wood kill me. my Pa wood too. Ruthie's collard and we cant marry with them. But I wish we cood so I cood mary Ruthie Thatcher. She is the most butiful girl I ever saw.

Everybody leaned in closer to the glowing kerosene lantern in the middle of the table. It was turned up as high it would go, but even with extra light from the firepit and its flames' shadows dancing against the kitchen walls, they could barely read the lessons Nellie wrote for them on the lined pad with her stub of a pencil. She sat at the head of the table. Uncle Will and Big Si sat to Nellie's right, Tobias and Little Si to her left. Ruthie was in her father's lap. This was their Saturday night ritual, Nellie's reading and writing lessons. Late, well after dark, they closed the shutters on the kitchen windows so that the house would almost be in total darkness, and the six of them gathered around the table. When the weather was warm, the room got too hot too quickly, but the lessons were more important than comfort. This December night was pitch black and icy cold, but just as the heat didn't deter them, neither did the cold. It was a practice night: Everybody got a chance to write his or her name and *Carrie's Crossing, Georgia* on the paper, along with their date of birth. Uncle Will always wanted to be the last one, and when he finished, he grunted with satisfaction and everybody else clapped their hands.

"That's real good, Uncle Will," Big Si said. "Real good."

"You all keep this up and I won't have anything left to teach," Nellie said, taking one of Uncle Will's huge, calloused hands in both of hers and squeezing.

"Is mine good too, Ma?" Tobias asked.

"I forgot how to spell *Crossing*," Little Si said, reaching for the paper everybody had written on so he could check his spelling. "I left out a 's' and dang! I put the 'n' in the wrong place—"

He was cut off midsentence by a knock on the front door. For one brief instant, the six of them were frozen, like the Biblical salt figures. Then, as one, they moved, making no more noise than mice scampering across the floor. Nellie grabbed Ruth from her husband's lap with one hand and Little Si with the other and headed for the pantry door which Tobias already had open. Uncle Will and Big Si had their pistols in their hands. As Nellie and the three children disappeared into the pantry, Big Si closed the door and followed Uncle Will through the kitchen, into the front parlor, and to the front door.

They stood on either side of it as five more knocks sounded on the door in rapid succession, followed by a voice quietly calling them by name.

"That sounds like...that's Freeman from over in Belle City," Will whispered.

Big Si put his mouth to the crack in the door. "Freeman?"

"It's me," they heard whispered back, and they unlocked the door and opened it a crack, barely enough for the tall, thin man to squeeze through, bringing a blast of frigid air with him. He stamped his feet and rubbed his hands together, then blew on them.

"Go on in the kitchen and get warm," Will said, as he and Big Si threw the bolts back on the door, stuffed the rags back into the crevices around and beneath the door, then hurried back into the kitchen to release their frightened family from the pantry. "It's all right, y'all," Will said as Tobias emerged first, clutching a thick stick and looking both frightened and defiant. "It's all right," Will said, as Nellie and the younger children emerged and he alone saw the big hunting knife that Nellie returned to the deep pocket of her skirt.

Nellie turned up the lantern. "Mr. Freeman?" She said his name but made it a question: *What are you doing here?* it asked, though it carried no impoliteness or sense of unwelcome, merely the honest fact that his unexpected presence was unusual in the extreme.

He hurriedly removed his hat. "Miz Thatcher, Will, Silas. How y'all doing?" Then he looked closely at the pantry, and the question on his face was: How did they all fit inside?

"We all fine, Freeman," Will said. "What you doin' here this time of night?" he asked, the only one of them who could voice what they all were thinking.

"I heard the Army took your oldest boys—they been doin' a lot of that, usin' that draft to take the young men, knowin' womenfolk and old men can't keep up with all the work 'round the farm—so I brung somethin' to help y'all out."

It took them all several seconds to grasp the import of their guest's words. It was Nellie who reacted first, and the fury behind her words was frightening. "I told you, Silas, didn't I tell you? I told you it wasn't right, them taking my boys. The law said ages twenty-one to thirty-one was subject to that draft and my boys ain't but nineteen and twenty but they came and got 'em anyway. The dirty bastards. And now I know why: So they can steal the land, too. First they steal my boys, now they want to steal my land!"

Nobody, not even Silas, had ever seen Nellie so angry, but they all reacted the same way: Ruth wrapped her arms around her mother's legs and Tobias and Little Si each grabbed an arm and Big Si pulled the group of them into his embrace, and Uncle Will kept patting Big Si on the back, like he was trying to burp a baby. Nobody spoke until Freeman cleared his throat. "We got to get that mule and trap into the barn," he said.

The Thatchers broke their huddle, and confused murmurs of "mule?" and "what mule?" replaced the earlier frightful anger. Then Ruthie said, "What's a trap?"

Freeman gave her a long, hard look, then a wide grin. "It's a kind of wagon, Little Missy, and we need to get it out of sight, it and that mule. God knows we don't need no white folks knowin' you Colored folks got a mule and a trap." Then everybody was talking at once, and in motion, putting on caps and coats and brogans and filling lanterns with kerosene, standing in front of the cook stove to gather warmth before going out into the dark, cold night.

"You look hungry, Mr. Freeman," Nellie said as she threw several big chunks of wood into the stove. The flames rose and the room felt warmer immediately. "We got leftover rabbit stew and some roasted potatoes and some cornbread. I'll make some coffee and bake some apples and have everything ready by the time y'all finish with the mule and the wagon."

"Thank you, m'am, I 'preciate it 'cause I passed bein' hungry 'bout two hours ago back yonder on the road." He tightened his scarf at his neck and pulled his hat down over his ears. "Where them dogs? I'm surprised they let me get all the way up in the yard."

"We put 'em in the barn 'cause of the cold," Uncle Will said.

"Well, you gon' have to take 'em out," Freeman said, "'cause you know good and well dogs and mules ain't no friend to each other."

Uncle Will and Big Si got a good laugh from that one; Little Si, Tobias and Ruthie followed the men outside, demanding to know why dogs and mules weren't friends. Nellie followed them to the door and watched the children's awe-struck reaction to seeing the mule, watched her husband keep them well away from the notoriously cantankerous animal's deadly hooves, watched them all clamber into the flat-bedded wagon and drive toward the barn, watched and listened until she could see and hear nothing but the silent darkness. Surely having the mule would mean that Si and Uncle Will wouldn't have to work so hard—not having the two oldest boys, Beaudry and Eubanks, these last six months had indeed been a hardship—but Nellie would gladly give the farm away—and the mule and the wagon—to have her boys back. She'd never say those words to Uncle Will or Si, but they probably knew what she felt. But the mule also was a mixed blessing, for if any white person discovered its presence—well, best not to think about that. *Never trouble trouble 'til trouble troubles you,* her Ma always used to say. And right she was, Nellie thought.

She lit the wall lamps in the parlor and the logs in the fireplace so the room would be warm when everybody came back in. Then she got busy in the kitchen. First she hurried down to the root cellar and brought up half a bushel of dried apples. She washed them, laid them in a pan, sprinkled them with some cinnamon sugar, and put them in the oven. Then she set the kettle on to boil and put coffee in the pot. She got the kettle of leftover rabbit stew from the cold porch, filled a bowl, and put it in the warming oven along with the roasted potatoes and cornbread. Then she sat down at the kitchen table, grateful for the few minutes of quiet she'd have before they all returned from the barn.

Nellie never showed strong emotions to her family other than love. Feelings of anger or the rare hatreds she harbored she kept to herself. That she hated the white people who had taken her sons was something she had intended to keep to herself, but she couldn't conceal the anger and hatred that arose when she realized the reason for the theft of her children. It was almost as horrible as having children sold away during slavery time, to have them stolen away to serve in the army of a country that despised them, so that same government might more easily steal the meager legacy of their centuries of unpaid servitude.

She also needed the brief quiet period to assess her feelings about First Freeman. That was his name—the name he'd given himself after the Emancipation. This much she knew from Uncle Will who'd known him "back before," which is what the older people who had been slaves called that period of their lives. Most of them wouldn't discuss having been slaves at all, and when they did—when forced by family or circumstance—they never did so in terms of the stark reality that had been their lives. It was always euphemistical: Uncle Will's "back before," or "the old days" or "the old times" some of the other older Colored called it. Uncle Will always was vague about Freeman; had even been hostile to him when he first began visiting several years ago. Gradually he had softened to the point that he now would invite the man to share a meal and talk to him about his family and his life in Belle City, but he'd never speak of his former life in Carrie's Crossing, and Nellie thought that the fact of their shared slavery was only part of the reason. There was some other thing about First Freeman—not a bad thing, Nellie hurried to assure herself— for the man was kind and polite and generous. But even if Colored were doing good for themselves over in Belle City, nobody, white nor Colored, could afford to give away a mule and a wagon.

"And he can't be doing it looking for something back from us 'cause we ain't got nothing," Nellie said to herself now that she was back to herself; back to being calm and rational and thoughtful. So, what was there about First Freeman that Uncle Will wasn't telling them, and did it matter? Nellie wondered. Maybe it was enough that what the two old men knew about each other was all any of the rest of them needed to know; slavery was a word almost unspoken now, but oh, the meaning the word held.

The front door opened and Nellie stood up, hurried to the wood box and grabbed a few more chunks of wood to feed into the stove. She could feel the cold that rushed forward as fast as her children did.

"Ma! Ma!" The three of them calling her at once, talking at once, about the mule named Clem, about the wagon which could haul "everything we got." She hugged them to her, their cheeks and ears and noses frosty. She rubbed her face against theirs to warm them, rubbed their hands between hers, but she knew they were too excited to realize the cold. She listened to their excitement as she turned them toward the stove's heat, their voices as bright as their eyes. She would kill anything or anybody who ever threatened these children. They had taken two from her, the two oldest, but she wouldn't let it happen again, war or no war, government or no.

"Y'all go hang up them coats and hats and take off them dirty shoes."

"Yes'm," they chorused, trooping out onto the cold porch.

"And Tobias! Make sure them shutters is pulled tight. That wind sounds mighty strong."

"It is strong, Ma," he said, looking and sounding older and stronger than the boy he was. She knew he was trying to step up and be the big brother to Little Si and Ruthie and the oldest son to Big Si, but he was still a boy; he was still her child. She watched his retreating back. He would be tall and straight like his pa, like her pa, like Uncle Will, like all the men. Like all the women, too, if she thought about it, because she herself was taller than most women, and Ruthie was growing like a weed—tall and straight. And strong.

"Looks like we got ourselves a mule and a wagon," Big Si said throwing off his coat and heading for the stove's warmth. Nellie took his coat, and he sat down to begin removing his heavy brogans. "I want to ask Freeman why he's doing that—giving us things that cost more'n we could ever pay—but I don't want to seem...what's the word, Nellie?"

"Ungrateful."

"Ungrateful. 'Cause I'm mighty grateful. But why you think, Nellie? We ain't no kin to him. Why you think—" He was interrupted by the children tumbling back into the kitchen with the news that Uncle Will had put the dogs on the back porch out of the cold. Nellie held out Big Si's coat and shoes and the boys took them out to the porch to hang while Ruthie climbed into her father's lap. "Before we go to bed tonight, we better bring all them coats and boots in here—dogs, too—and stoke the stove real good, otherwise they'll freeze solid, clothes and dogs. It's gon' be mean cold tonight."

"It's already mean cold," Uncle Will said. He came into the kitchen followed by First Freeman. The two older men carried their outerwear, and Big Si and Ruthie took the coats and shoes from them to put out on the porch. First Freeman held on to a big bundle tied at both ends with rope that he put on the floor near the stove. When everybody came back in, the kitchen was too crowded.

"You children go sit in the parlor while I get Mr. Freeman some food on the table. Then later we can all have some apples and coffee."

The children clapped their hands and danced out of the room. The three men took seats at the table, all facing the stove and rubbing their hands together, their feet extended toward the heat. Nellie put more wood in, then got the food from the warming oven for their guest.

"I thank you, Miz Thatcher," First said. He bowed his head for several seconds, then raised it and reached for his spoon at the same time. He ate quickly and unselfconsciously. Uncle Will ate the same way, Nellie realized. She left to go check on the children and wasn't surprised to find them on the floor in front of the fireplace, arms wrapped around each other, almost asleep. She put more logs on the fire and a blanket over the children, which roused them.

"Is it time to eat the apples?" Ruthie asked sleepily.

"I'll go see," Nellie said. She returned to the kitchen to find Uncle Will taking the pan of baked apples from the oven, the scent of cinnamon pervasive. The children came running. Wide awake now, they crowded around the stove, inhaling the aroma and hopping from foot to foot in expectation. "Maybe we can put a little butter and cream on?" Nellie asked, looking at Si and Uncle Will. There wasn't much of either left, but hoarding it wouldn't make it last any longer while eating it would make seven people very happy.

"Go 'head then," Uncle Will said and, as big and strong as he was, he had to sit down quickly when the three children all jumped at him. He caught them, but just barely, and it's a good thing the chair was there for him to fall down on. Big Si got the butter and cream from the porch while Nellie put apples in bowls, thinking that Uncle Will had become an old man and grateful again to First Freeman for the mule. "And since we actin' like it's already Christmas, might as well eat in the parlor."

The adults on the room's four chairs, the children on the floor, the fire roaring inside, the wind howling outside, the baked apples swimming in butter and cream—it was, indeed, very much like a holiday, like Christmas, considering the gift of the mule and wagon. "We thank you again, Mr. Freeman," Nellie said.

First Freeman looked uncomfortable. He wasn't accustomed to expressing his own feelings, or having others express their feelings to him. "It ain't nothin', Miz Thatcher."

"It's a whole lot, Mr. Freeman," she said. "More'n anybody we know can afford to give away."

Freeman sighed deeply. "Things is a bit better for Colored in Belle City than in some other places. One thing, won't nobody stop you from tryin' to work if that's what you want to do. Most white people ain't gon' say you can't own a mule or a hoss or a wagon. Ain't nobody gon' say you can't paint your house or plant pretty flowers in your yard." This was a lot of words to be spoken at one time for Freeman, and he sighed again, stood up, walked into the kitchen and returned quickly carrying the big bundle he'd left in the kitchen beside the stove. "I got me a bizness, my own bizness. I got four mules and two hosses and wagons to hitch to every one of 'em, and I hauls things—people, furniture, garbage, food—whatever needs haulin', I hauls it. I got three other boys workin' for me and we works seven days a week, sunup til sundown. And..." He paused and looked into each of the six pairs of eyes that watched him. "...white folks well as Colored hire me for my work. White folks well as Colored pay me. They pay me what I ask for, and they pay me when I ask for it."

The only sound in the room was the crackling of the fire and the howling of the wind. Then Uncle Will spoke. "Why you tellin' us all this, Freeman?"

"'Cause I think y'all oughta move to Belle City. Sell your farm 'fore they steal it from you, and move 'way from here."

Will was on his feet. "Ain't nobody stealin' nothin' from me. This my land. I got the deed to it. Got my name and my sister's name on it. Cain't nobody steal it."

"They can if they want to, Will, and you know that. Evil and nasty as Zeb

Thatcher is, I'm surprised he let you hang on to it this long, 'specially with all the good growin' y'all doin' up here and him goin' broker and broker ev'ry day tryin' to grow a cotton crop."

"Zeb ain't got no idea what we growin' up here," Uncle Will said, sounding more like he was growling than speaking.

"What would we do in Belle City, Freeman?" Big Si asked. "Cain't but so many men haul things, and looks like you got the haulin' bizness all took care of. What the rest of us gon' do if we don't farm?"

"There's all kinds of work to do," Freeman started, but Will stopped him.

"Ain't nobody related to me goin' to work in white folks' houses cookin' and cleanin' and bowin' and scrapin' and I mean that. This fam'ly is through with that kinda thing."

"Don't have to work for white folks, Will. We got Colored hospitals and banks and insurance companies. And the schools! Colleges and universities! These children could go to college, Will. Could be doctors or teachers or preachers...could be whatever they want to be."

The logs shifted in the fireplace, as if the thought of Colored children going to college to become doctors or teachers or preachers was too much. It was one thing Nellie at the kitchen table teaching the alphabet and some few numbers—teaching as much as she had been able to learn. College was something else, something for people who maybe already lived in Belle City, but certainly not something for people who lived in Carrie's Crossing, even if they did own their own farm. The children of Silas and Nellie Thatcher had never given thought to becoming anything other than what they were— children of the farm, of the land, of the forest. That their parents may have dared to hope for more was merely that: A hope kept private, secret even, for what would be the purpose of expressing hope for what could never be? What good would be served by telling children they could be doctors and teachers and preachers when they could not be? After all, Silas and Nellie were the son and daughter of slaves. The best they'd ever hoped for their sons and daughter was that they wouldn't have to be the children of slaves. The children didn't know what to say or think, so they didn't say anything, but their eyes widened in wonder for they certainly would have things to think and talk about in secret from this time forward.

The logs shifted again just as a big gust of cold air blew down the chimney, and sparks flew past the screen into the room. The embers glowed on the polished, wood floor before several hands and feet smacked them out.

"You children go get them big coats off the back porch so we can hang 'em up here round this door and these windows, keep some of that cold air out where it belongs. These rags ain't much help." The three children scurried out as Big Si helped Nellie stuff the pieces of cloth deeper into the crevices around the doors and windows in an almost futile attempt to preserve the room's warmth. Hanging the heavy coats in front of the windows and the door would help, but nothing could stop the wind from howling down the chimney.

Big Si put more logs on the fire and the room became noticeably warmer. "It's time for you children to go on to bed," he said, then looked at his wife.

"Mr. Freeman can sleep up in Eubanks and Beaudry's room, Little Si and Tobias can sleep in Uncle Will's room, Uncle Will can sleep in Ruthie's room, and she can sleep with us," Nellie said, answering the unasked question.

"I don't mean to put nobody out," Freeman said quickly.

Uncle Will waved away the protest. "Ain't nobody gettin' put out. Everybody gon' be inside where it's warm and up off the floor too," and he laughed along with everybody else at the humor.

Then First Freeman took a knife from his pocket and cut the ropes that bound the bundle that seemed so precious to him, and unrolled it, looking all the time at Uncle Will. "I come across all kinds of things drivin' and haulin', things people throw on the junk heap, 'specially white people. I sells most of it 'cause I don't need it. Some of it, though, the good things, I keep. Like these things here. I want y'all to have these things." The bundle itself was a dark, thick carpet, almost big enough to cover the whole parlor floor, and inside it were clothes—men's clothes, women's clothes, children's clothes—and shoes and pots and pans and books. Nobody spoke. Six pairs of eyes moved about the bundle of goods, staring as if the entire contents of a dry goods store had been dropped in the middle of their parlor floor.

"Why you doin' this, Freeman?" Uncle Will asked angrily. "What you want?"

First Freeman was shaking his head back and forth. "Nothin,' Will. I don't want nothin'."

"Ain't you got no family, Mr. Freeman? No people in Belle City? Why you come all the way over here to bring these things?" Big Si asked. There was no anger in his tone, but there was deep puzzlement and no small amount of wariness. The rug and the clothes and the pots and pans, Si would be happy to have Freeman bundle back up and take with him back to Bell City. The mule and wagon, though...

Nellie walked over to stand beside Freeman and touched his shoulder. She could see all the similarities between him and Uncle Will. She also could see a difference, and it was a major one: First Freeman was a lonely man. "We are grateful to you, Mr. Freeman. These things, all of this—" Nellie ran out of words.

"You give things like this to your family. This ain't your family, Freeman, this MY family. You hear me? This MY family!" Uncle Will strode from the room. In the silence that followed, the bundle in the middle of the floor remained the center of attention, but there also now was the freedom to show interest in it.

"People give you all this?" Big Si asked.

Freeman shook his head. "Naw, they ain't give to me, not how you mean. They throwed it away. Told me to haul it off or left it on the trash heap."

"But ain't nothin' wrong with these things," Big Si said, sifting through the pile of shoes and clothes. He picked up a book, turned it over in his big hands, and squinted as he tried to read the cover. He passed it to Nellie. "It's about some land," he said, and Freeman gasped.

"You can read?"

Big Si looked embarrassed and shook his head. "Naw. I know some letters and some numbers but naw, I can't read. Not like you mean."

Freeman looked at the children who were looking at the pile of goods. "I ain't got no family, not no more. My wife, she been dead way long time ago. And I had four chil'ren. My three girls, they married and moved on away." He sighed deeply and shook his head. "I got me some grandchil'ren but I don't never see 'em. And my son, I don't reckon I know where he is." He sighed again. "I don't want Will mad at me. I ain't hardly got no friends left. The folks from the old days is mostly gone now. There's Will and me and Maisy Cooper and Zekiel Fordham—that's why I come over here so much, 'cause of Maisy and Zekiel. We all was raised up on the same farm and had the same name— Fordham it was—just like you and the Thatchers. Maisy Fordham she was 'fore she married with Sam Cooper, and Zekiel and a gal named Florence and one named Esther and a ol' boy named Fox, and me. We was all raised up together. Ain't nobody left from the Fordham place but me and Maisy and Zekiel, and Will's the only one left from Thatcher's." The old man sighed again and this time so deeply Nellie ran to the kitchen for a jug of water that had frozen. She poured a little of the coffee on top on the ice and was able to pour several inches of muddy but cool liquid into Freeman's cup. He drank it off and wiped his mouth on the back of his hand. "I hope Will let y'all keep these things." He looked at the goods in the rug like he was mad at them.

"You children," Big Si said. "Tell Mr. First thank you, then get you some things."

The children jumped up and down on First Freeman like he was a bed with big springs, then they pounced on the bounty, holding up articles of clothing and shoes to assess the fit. Nellie fought to keep the tears at bay. Her daughter had never owned a proper dress and none of her children had ever owned a whole pair of shoes—they always wore hand-me-down or, worse, cut down shoes. Big Si gazed in wonder at the pants, shirts and shoes that Nellie placed in his lap, and he laughed at a red Union suit that Nellie said would fit Uncle Will perfectly, along with two shirts and two pairs of pants. None of the clothes had holes or patches of different colors. Without these gifts from First Freeman, Nellie doubted her family ever would have had such nice clothes. Yes, they owned their own farm and most of the time they had more than enough to eat, but they did not have any money to go and buy things. And you couldn't grow clothes and shoes. You could trade greens and cabbage and tomatoes and turnips for a sack of flour or corn meal or a few eggs—or for somebody's old clothes. But nice almost new clothes like these?

Nellie took the pots and pans into the kitchen and when she came back, their new rug was spread out in the middle of the parlor floor just like it belonged there, just like it always had been right there. And it was beautiful.

- 1918 -

The sweat ran off Jonas like somebody had poured a bucket of water on him, and he would swear on a whole stack of Bibles that he could hear a sizzle when the sweat drops hit the roof: That's how hot it was. He wished somebody *would* throw a bucket of water on him. He'd dearly love to be cool, even if it only lasted for a few seconds, because that's about how long the feeling would last given how hot it was. Just two days ago the wind was howling and the rain was coming down in sheets and his Ma was so chilly she had him lay a fire in the living room grate. He used the last of the wood trying to keep his Ma warm, which made Pa mad as hell. Then the wind ripped off a section of shingles on the roof causing a leak so bad his parents couldn't sleep in their bedroom, and that made Pa even madder. He stomped about the house and cussed and hollered until it stopped raining. Jonas didn't know who was more grateful—he or his ma. They both were pretty sick and tired of Zeb's ranting and raving though neither of them ever would express that thought, Ma because she knew it wouldn't do any good and Jonas because he could get slapped up side the head for no good reason at all, so no need to furnish a reason. With his sisters married and moved away and his brother over there in Europe fighting in the War, Jonas was home alone with his parents. It was not a comfortable state of affairs.

The first thing Jonas had to do when it stopped raining was gather more fire wood. Not that any of the wood could be used because it was good and soaked, but he gathered it anyway and stacked it on the back porch, and then it was only pieces he could find in the woods that were the right length to fit in the stove or the fireplace grate. Pa had lost the axe—he didn't know where or when—and he couldn't beg, borrow or steal another one. At least he hadn't so far. Then Jonas had to dig around in the barn to find enough kindling and straw to light the stove so Ma could cook dinner. "I don't know what in the hell y'all were thinkin', burnin' up all that wood and ain't got none left to cook with," Pa yelled at them before he stomped out the back door, leaving it open, which the flies and mosquitoes took to be an invitation to come on in.

"Oh, Jonas! Close the door!" His mother hated bugs. She called anything with more than four legs or anything that had wings a bug; snakes and frogs were in a hated category all their own. "And light a piece of that damp wood. The smoke'll chase the bugs back out."

She was right about that; bugs didn't like smoke. People didn't, either, and, choking and coughing, Jonas headed outside too and up on the roof. His second task was to repair the hole in the roof and stop the leak in his parents' bedroom. He wasn't sure how to do that without shingles, tar and tools, for the axe wasn't the only item missing from the tool shed: The handsaw, the good hammer and chisel, and a carpentry knife also were gone. However, Jonas had no intention of asking about the tools or mentioning their absence. He'd make do with whatever was at hand—just as soon as he devised a plan for patching the roof that wouldn't require tools—and that could take awhile since he knew next to nothing about patching holes in roofs. In fact, according to his father, he was pretty useless all around since he didn't know anything about farming either. But he sure could hunt. And that thought gave Jonas an idea. He backed toward the edge of the roof and panicked until his feet found the ladder. He shimmied down and crept around the side of the house toward the back, careful not to let his father see him. He peeked around the house, toward the fields, and knew he didn't have to worry about Pa noticing him because Pa was too busy jumping up and down and waving his arms at the two Colored men he had just hired to work in the cotton fields. Jonas couldn't hear him, but he knew Pa was yelling and screaming at the two men. He also knew that sooner rather than later the two men would quit, no matter how broke they were, just like all the others before them, and Jonas didn't understand why his Pa didn't understand that you couldn't holler at people and call them stupid niggers and expect them to keep working for you.

Jonas's shotgun was in the barn in a secret place. If asked, he couldn't have explained why he'd hidden his most prized possessions, but deep down inside he knew it had do with the way things disappeared, especially tools. There was a shelf in one corner of the barn—Pa probably didn't even know the shelf was there—and this is where Jonas kept his special things: His shotgun and his store of buckshot and his pocket knife and his writing tablet and the two books that he owned. He hadn't had much time lately to read or write; until his Pa had hired the new field workers last week, Jonas had been the field hand and he didn't know which was worse—pulling a plow or crawling along a row on scraped knees, pulling weeds and inhaling dust and being eaten alive by every bug God ever made. He found himself hating bugs too, just like his Ma, and he wasn't even from Scotland like she was, where, according to her, they didn't have bugs.

Jonas grabbed his shotgun, buckshot, and a burlap sack that he had added a strap to and which he slung over his shoulder, and slipped through a gap in the planks of the barn's back wall. From there at a dead run, he was into the woods in less than a minute and almost immediately he was cooler. He stopped in his tracks and dropped to the ground. The forest floor was still damp from the rain and cool. Jonas lay flat on his back inhaling the musty scent of dead and rotting leaves. He loved the forest—its dimness after the glaring brightness of the sun, its coolness, and the privacy it provided. In here, he was away from his parents, away from his Pa's yelling and screaming and always being mad at everything and away from his Ma's sickness and sadness and always wishing they lived in a better place and had better things.

Realizing that he was more than just cooled off, that he was wet, Jonas got up, wiped the leaves off his back, gathered his belongings and started through the forest. A game bird or a rabbit or a couple of squirrels sure would make the turnips taste better. "Hellfire and damnation," he cursed and stopped dead in his tracks. There wasn't enough wood to build a cook fire hot enough to stew an animal. "Hellfire and damnation," he said again as his shoulders drooped. No point in hunting now. May as well go on back home to the hole in the roof. He'd thought that if he took home fresh meat for dinner his Pa wouldn't be too mad that he didn't fix the roof. Now, though, he surely was asking for trouble. So why was he walking deeper into the forest instead of turning back and heading home with some idea in his mind about how to fix that hole in the roof? Thank goodness he didn't need to provide an answer anywhere but in his own mind. The real question for him, though, was why he was so fascinated by Ruthie's people's farm and what went on there. Yes, he was mesmerized by Ruthie, and Si was his best friend, but it was more than that, he just didn't know what to call it, and there was nobody he could ask.

Jonas camouflaged himself high up in the pecan tree that provided him with a view of the Thatcher farm. He'd like to have been closer but that would be dangerous. He already was trespassing, and he also knew that the Thatcher's dogs patrolled the farm's boundaries in all directions, and if they got a scent of him they'd sound the alarm and he'd be in the same shape as a treed animal in a hunt: Caught.

Funny how he always thought of this place as 'Thatcher's farm' but didn't think of his own homestead in those terms. Maybe because this place really looked like a farm. He could see the fields in the distance, could see how straight the rows were. He couldn't tell what was growing because the fields were too far away, stretching almost to the end of what Jonas knew to be their property, but it sure wasn't cotton. He'd probably never know what the Thatchers grew because he never had, never would, indeed never could venture that far away from where he lived to the area where, he knew, all the Colored people lived, an area that began at Thatcher's farm and extended he didn't know how far. He gazed at the fields in the distance and suddenly realized something he either hadn't noticed before or hadn't recognized the importance of: There were a least a dozen people working in Thatcher's fields! Jonas risked standing up on the thick bough of the tree to get a better view so that he could count them. He lost count at seventeen. Seventeen people. How was that possible? His Pa could barely afford to pay two workers. And there was something else. How could he have missed it? There was a mule. They had a mule.

Jonas sat back down in the cradle the tree boughs made, comfortable and concealed, and thought about what he'd just seen. He could make no sense of it so he returned to watching the Thatcher house and saw in the near distance what he'd missed looking afar—Ruthie in the front yard of the house, but what in the world was she doing? There were pieces of wood and tree limbs spread all across the yard and Ruthie was turning them like pieces of bacon or corn fritters in a pan. Then he understood. She was drying the wood. He couldn't climb down out of the tree fast enough, and his hurry caused him to fall the last five or six feet. He hit the ground hard, and his shotgun landed on top of him. Good thing it wasn't loaded. By the time he got back home, the burlap bag on his back was filled with wood, and he carried an arm load. He was so busy imagining himself laying out the wood in the yard under the burning sun that he didn't see his pa bearing down on him.

"Where the hell you been, Boy?" the old man roared.

Jonas dropped the load of wood he was carrying, backing up and away from his father. "I went to shoot squirrels or birds." He was talking as fast as he could. "I thought you would like some meat for supper. Then I remembered that we didn't have enough wood to cook a stew. So I got all this wood and I'm gon' lay it out there in the yard under the sun and let it dry and I'll go huntin' tomorrow."

Zeb looked hard at his youngest child—youngest living child—then looked at the wood on the ground and at the bulging burlap bag on the boy's back and finally up at the bright and burning sun. Then he nodded his head. "That's right good thinkin', Boy. Lay the wood out in the sun, let it dry. And these pieces of wood you got, they ain't too thick. They'll dry in right good time, I 'spect. By the time you get back from huntin' tomorrow with squirrels or rabbits or fowls, your Ma oughta be able to make a right good fire under that kettle." He walked away, back toward the field, and Jonas started laying the wood out like he was laying bacon out in the cast iron skillet. He wished he could tell Pa about what he saw from his perch in the pecan tree, but he knew that he could not. He watched his father walk away and realized for the first time that he was an old man; that he was old like Si and Ruthie's Uncle Will was old: His head hair and his beard were white. But Pa walked slow and stiff, Jonas thought, while Si and Ruthie's Uncle Will walked like he was in a hurry to get somewhere.

Ruthie tried not to think about how she, too, was drying up from the heat of the sun as she moved the wood pieces around on the ground, turning them every half hour or so. There must be a thousand of them, she thought, maybe even a million. Uncle Will had said the storm a couple of days ago was a blessing, blowing all these good pieces of wood off the trees and down to the ground where she and Si could collect them. This was "free" wood, Uncle Will had said, a gift because it didn't have to be chopped before it could be stacked—and, best of all, he'd said—it meant they didn't have use their store of firewood for the weekend Juneteenth Celebration. All the wood that Ruthie was drying out would be used to cook the food they'd need, and there likely would be wood left over.

The men had dug six firepits for the Celebration, and spits hung over four of them. The pits were behind the house so that the smoke would blow either north or east—away from Zeb Thatcher's place. Uncle Will knew, and he'd told Big Si and Nellie, that Zeb was in a bad way, that his farm was producing next to nothing and that he was so broke he was selling off his tools. Uncle Will felt no sympathy for Zeb Thatcher, but he couldn't help but wonder at the man's stupidity: He actually believed he could force people to work for him without pay; he really did believe that he was superior to Colored people and that they were obligated to do his bidding. He believed that the laws that had replaced slavery still enslaved. Those laws might make it near impossible for a Colored man to earn a living or buy land or goods in a store even if he had money, but the laws didn't make a Colored man a slave again no matter what

Zeb Thatcher and others like him hoped for. That's why his farm was in ruins: Zeb was a worse farmer than Carney, his pa, and without Colored farmers who knew how to work the land, Zeb's farm would simply die.

"And won't nobody stay there workin' for Zeb," Uncle Will had said. "That last fella who come through here, the one told me Zeb was sellin' off his tools, he said Zeb don't do nothin' but stomp up and down the rows, cussin' and yellin' and wavin' his arms all around. But what's so crazy, he said, is that Zeb is cussin' and yellin' at the cotton, mad 'cause it won't grow, cussin' at the weevils, mad 'cause they eatin' the cotton!"

Ruthie looked up at Uncle Will who was staring at the dense forest as if he could see straight through the trees and all the way to Zeb Thatcher's farm. He wasn't thinking anymore about all the drying wood spread out before them on the ground being a gift. He was, as her Ma would say, 'way back somewhere in his mind.' He did that a lot these days, and it worried her Ma and Pa. 'He's a old man,' her Pa would say, sounding sad. 'But he's still strong, Si,' Ma would say, sounding like she was praying it was true. Right now, though, Uncle Will didn't seem very strong; he seemed as if he had stopped being. He still stood beside her, but only his body was there; his mind was in a different place. Ruthie's Ma and Pa told the children not to worry, that what happened to Uncle Will happened to a lot of the old ones. It was a thing they couldn't help. They just, now and again, went to another time and place in their minds, in their memories, and when that happened it was best not to bother them, even if they seemed sad or mad. "Best thing we can do," said Pa, "is make sure they know they're in *this* time and place and not that other one, that bad one."

"Uncle Will," Ruthie said, and the old man stirred. He inhaled deeply, and his eyes seemed to stop trying to look through the woods. His eyes looked all around until they looked down and found her. Then he smiled and put his big hand on her head. It always surprised her that his huge, rough hands could feel as light as her Ma's.

"Did I tell you, Little Miss Ruth, what a good job you done dryin' out all this wood?" he asked, looking again at all the drying wood.

"Yes, sir," Ruthie answered and leaned into him. Her head reached the middle of his chest, and she felt the hard knot of the leather pouch she knew that he wore around his neck—something his mother had given him when he was a boy. She didn't know what was in it, and she wasn't really sure what it looked like—she only got a glimpse of it in the hottest weather when Uncle Will and all the men removed their shirts, usually tying them around their heads to catch the sweat that poured off them like rain from the sky.

"Then did I tell you, Little Miss Ruth, 'bout all the fish Hiram and them bringin' back from the river later on tonight, and 'bout them chickens First Freeman bringin' from over in Belle City later on tonight, and 'bout how it's gon' be better'n Christmas when you wake up in the morning?"

Ruthie was hopping from foot to foot. "No, sir. You didn't tell me none of that."

"It's all true, Little Miss Ruth. We gon' have ourselves so much good food to eat at this Juneteenth Celebration, folks just might get tired of eatin'! Can you 'magine that?"

"No, sir," Ruthie said, dancing about Uncle Will as he started moving the wood pieces into a pile with his foot. "I don't think I could ever get tired of eating!" Especially, she thought, not tired of eating food roasted on spits over a fire or wrapped in leaves and roasted on rocks that were surrounded by hot coals. That was the best food ever—potatoes and corn and turnips and fish and chicken and squirrel and rabbit—all roasted until their outsides were crisp and crunchy and the insides flavorful and smooth and juicy. "I wish we could have Juneteenth all the time. Can we, Uncle Will? Can we have Juneteenth all the time?"

"You know we cain't do that, Little Miss. I b'lieve I tol' you why last Juneteenth when you asked, didn't I?"

"Tell me again, Uncle Will. Tell me again," Ruthie said. She knew that Juneteenth was important, and she knew that it made Uncle Will both happy and sad.

"Well," he said, digging his pipe and tobacco out of his pocket, "Juneteenth is the day when slaves got the news they was free. It was way long time after the law said they was free, but some folks didn't want 'em to be free so they didn't tell 'em. And since we couldn't read or write and didn't have no way to find things out other than what white folks told us, we didn't know the freedom had come 'til it was some time in June, 'round the thirteenth or the sixteenth. And way back then, bein' free for the first time, the freedom and the feelin' it give us, that was all we had to celebrate."

"But now, we got fish and chicken and yams to roast," Ruthie yelled.

"We surely do, Little Miss, and thank God for it, but don't forget we didn't always have food to eat, and don't forget there's a whole lot of us still ain't got food to eat." And, just like that, the sadness was back, covering the old man like a blanket.

"But you got food, Uncle Will. And you got us."

"And thank God for it," he said again, sounding like he was praying.

Jonas watched his Ma while she cooked. He liked watching her. He thought she was pretty, but mostly he liked watching her because he thought she was nice. Every now and then she'd look over at him and give him a small smile, or, when she passed by him, she'd touch his head or his face—just a small, gentle touch—but it was nice. He liked how it felt to be touched by her. He couldn't imagine a hug or a kiss because the last time he'd received that kind of attention from her he'd been a baby of two or three years, and he didn't remember it, and he'd never in his life received that kind of expression of sentiment from his father. Of course, neither had any of the other children—the son or the daughters.

"Why is Pa mad all the time?"

Jonas's mother looked at him, as surprised as he himself was that he had voiced his thoughts about his father. None of them did that—Zeb's children or his wife. She wiped her hands on her apron and tried unsuccessfully to return a strand of red-gold hair to the bun at the back of her neck. "I don't really know, Jonas, but if I had to guess..."

"What would you guess, Ma?" he prompted when she'd been silent for several seconds.

"He's disappointed. That would be my guess," she said, sitting down at the table by him.

"About what?"

"About his life, and how it's turned out."

Jonas was puzzled, confused. "Is somethin' wrong with Pa's life?"

She gave him a sad smile. "Your Pa is no good as a farmer, and he knows that, but he doesn't know why. He thinks because he has land, it should produce for him, and things don't work that way, Jonas. Remember that: Everybody has a talent for something, and we should do what we *can* do, not what we *want* to do." She got up from the table and, walking sadly, if it could be said that a walk was sad, went to the stove.

Jonas studied his mother as she returned to the business of making their dinner. That was another reason he liked his mother: She knew things. Things from books and things about people and even things about animals. She didn't like farming or the land, and she was fearful of most forest critters, especially snakes and bugs, but she always seemed to know things about them. She also knew enough to help him keep up with his reading and writing when he couldn't get to school regularly. He'd often heard his father say that his wife had married beneath herself, and while Jonas didn't really understand what that meant, he understood what 'disappointed' meant, but what was his pa disappointed about? Maybe because the cotton wouldn't grow on his farm and everything grew on Ruthie's farm? "Ma?"

"What is it, Jonas?"

"Do you hate Colored people like Pa does? You don't, do you?"

She sighed heavily and looked over her shoulder toward the back door, then craned her neck to look toward the front parlor, though they both knew that Zeb should be out in the fields. "You shouldn't be talking about that."

"Yes'm, I know," he said, and waited.

She sighed again and her shoulders drooped, and she shook her head. "I been treated too bad in my life to give bad treatment to another human being."

"Who treated you bad, Ma?" Jonas had raised his voice, and the final word was little more than a squeak. His mother looked up in surprise, then she crossed to him and rested both her hands on top of his head.

"My baby child is no more a baby."

"Huh?"

"Your voice, Jonas: It's changing. You'll sound like a man soon. You'll be a man soon."

"Who treated you bad, Ma?"

"Everybody until I met your Pa."

"Why?"

The sigh from his mother's chest was so deep this time that Jonas thought he could feel the pain that caused it. "Because I was a slave, too. That's not what it was called, but that's what I was. I was sold by my father to pay a debt, and the man who owned me brought me to this place, here to Georgia, when I was just a lass."

"From Scotland?"

"Scotland is where I was born, but I came here from England—the man who bought me was English, and he took me there first, and then he brought me here when he came looking for gold." She suddenly shook her head furiously causing long tendrils of hair to fly about her face. She brushed them away impatiently. "Seems that he didn't have any more money than my father, but he did have a title, which meant that he could demand payment of a debt from my father. I was that payment, and I remained his property until your father bought me from him."

Jonas didn't know what to say, in part because he didn't really understand what he'd just been told, but also because he couldn't imagine his father having enough money to buy anything.

"What's a title?"

"Something we don't have here in this country, thank the dear Lord."

"How much did you cost, Ma?"

Corrinne Maxwell Thatcher laughed, a high, sweet sound that Jonas had never heard before, and so delighted was he that he laughed, too. And then he hugged her. Tightly. And then he ran out the back door and across the yard and into the woods because he was crying and he didn't know why, but he did know that grown men didn't cry and his Ma had said that soon he would be a man, and she knew things like that.

The first thing Ruthie heard when she opened her eyes on Juneteenth celebration morning was First Freeman snoring. Her Pa and Uncle Will and her big brothers all snored, but it was nothing like the sound made by First Freeman: It would terrify a person who didn't know anything about snoring since it sounded more like a prowling, growling animal than a sleeping man. She and Tobias and Little Si had tried to stay awake the night before until the man from Belle City arrived, but as it got later and later, Ma finally made them go to bed. Knowing how late he had arrived and listening to him snore, Ruthie knew that he would not awaken any time soon. She also knew—she could tell by the otherwise quiet house—that everybody was awake, up and out of the house, except herself and First Freeman, and she jumped up from her pallet on the floor of her parents' bedroom. She rolled up her sleep things in a tight cylinder and shoved it under her parents' bed—she'd sleep in here for as long as First Freeman was their guest—and hurried into the bathroom, out again, into the kitchen to grab whatever was left over from breakfast, and out into the yard where preparations were underway for the Juneteenth Celebration.

If Ruthie had ever been to a fair, she'd think that the yard between her house and the fields looked like a fair grounds. Maybe a hundred people milled about, maybe more. Tents and lean-tos had been set up in a semicircle, and cloth and material of every color imaginable adorned the simple structures, giving them a magical quality. Some of the material blew in the breeze and if she'd known anything about flags, she could have thought that people were flying colors of kin or ancestors—red and yellow and orange and green. Half a dozen firepits had been dug and already the scent of smoking and roasting meat permeated the air.

Ruthie took her time leaving the immediate yard of her house, so mesmerized was she by the sight that stretched out before her. She realized that she didn't know many of the people her eyes found and studied. Many of them were old people like her Uncle Will. *They were slaves*, she thought to herself, and she studied them to see if they, like Uncle Will, looked both powerful and sad, but they just looked old, some of them older than Uncle Will. Then she spied her brothers, and she took off at a run.

"Hey, Girl," Si said when she reached them.

"'Bout time you got up," Tobias said. "Day's half gone," he added, sounding like their Pa, who thought the day was half gone any time the sun cracked the horizon. He looked off in the distance. "I'm s'pozed to be helpin' Pa gut and skin some deers to go on the spits, but I don't see him. Y'all see him?"

Ruthie and Little Si surveyed the crowd. "Yonder," Ruthie said, pointing like a hunting dog. Tobias nodded, patted his brother on the back and his sister on the head, and trotted off. "What're you gonna do?" she asked Si.

He made a face. "Gut all them dang fish Mr. Hiram brung from the river. Never seen so many dang fish in my whole life."

"I'll help you."

Si shook his head. "We need more wood. Pa said to tell you. Take the short axe and bring back as much as you can find and lay it out in the yard." Ruthie nodded and turned back toward the house. "And Ma said keep this side of that big pecan tree."

She stopped and turned back to face her brother. "What for, Si?"

He looked a little funny, like giving the answer caused a cramp in his guts. "Uncle Will says the dogs been actin' funny 'round that tree. He said somebody been climbin' up in it."

Ruthie knew exactly who that 'somebody' was. So did Si. Ruthie nodded that she'd obey her mother. "Whistle for me if Mr. First Freeman gets up before I get back," she said, and she trotted off to the tool shed to get the short-handled axe she needed to cut the felled tree limbs into smaller pieces and the big burlap bag she needed to carry the wood. She ran into the house and grabbed her book off the kitchen table—she didn't go anywhere anymore without a book tucked into her waistband—and within a couple of minutes, she was deep into the shady depths of the forest. The dim quiet wrapped around her, familiar as her mother's embrace. Ma was right: She was as at home in these woods as in their house.

Her eyes immediately adjusted to the filtered light, and she began to search for tree limbs the right size. She and Si already had gathered up the smaller branches and limbs, those they could break by hand. Now she needed to find ones slightly larger, ones she could chop into pieces with the hand axe and stuff into the burlap bag. She wondered only briefly at the need for more wood. Even though Pa and Uncle Will had said there was more than enough to cook for the Juneteenth Celebration, if they said more wood was needed, then more wood was needed.

Ruthie worked quickly, and in half an hour, the burlap bag was full. Despite the relative cool of the forest, she was hot and sweating. She also was hungry. She hesitated only briefly in her decision not to go home immediately. She took her book from the rope she tied around her waist to shorten her dress and sat on the cool ground with her back against an oak. As she always did, she ran her hands over the book's cover, then studied the front image. She knew one word on the cover and part of another. Then she opened the book to the first page and studied it, picking out all the words she knew. There weren't many. Ma said she'd taught them everything she knew; if they were to learn more, they'd have to go to Belle City as there wasn't, and most likely never would be, a school for Colored children in Carrie's Crossing. So, that meant it wasn't likely that they'd ever learn more than they already knew because every time anybody talked about moving to Belle City, Uncle Will got hopped-up mad. He didn't get mad at First Freeman anymore, and the Belle City man now visited at least twice a month, always bringing goods and gifts, but First Freeman didn't talk anymore about how much better things were for Colored people where he lived. At least not when Uncle Will could hear him.

Ruthie closed her eyes and leaned her head back against the rough bark of the tree and tried to imagine what Belle City was like—tried to imagine what it would be like to live in a city instead of on a farm, to go to school, to see Colored doctors and teachers and Colored schools and banks. She tried her best but no picture came to mind. No matter, she told herself. One day she'd go to Belle City and see all those things, then she wouldn't have to imagine. With a deep sigh, she closed the book and got to her feet. Then, in one swift, fluid movement, she grabbed the hand axe, whirled around and hurled it at the big, old pecan tree thirty feet away. Head over handle, the axe rotated as it flew through the air, making a whistling sound. The blade buried itself into the trunk of the pecan tree with a loud thunk.

"Hellfire and damnation!" Jonas screamed as he jumped away from tree trunk, waving his arms and jumping up and down. "You might coulda kilt me, Ruthie Thatcher."

"Why are you hidin' behind that tree, Jonas?"

"Why are you tryin' to kill me?"

"If I was wantin' to kill you, you'd be dead."

He looked at her standing there, tall and straight and clear-eyed, and he knew what she said was true. "What's that book you're read...you can read, Ruthie Thatcher? Can you?"

"Can you?"

He nodded, then shrugged. "Some little bit. Pa don't let me go to school much on account of he needs me in the fields, but yeah, I can read some. Can you?"

Ruthie shrugged too but didn't answer that question directly. "There ain't no school for Colored 'round here. But I 'spect you already know that."

Both her tone and her words gave Jonas pause. "There ain't no school for Colored nowhere," he said, making it more of a question than a statement.

"There's lots of 'em," Ruthie said, "over yonder in Belle City. Colleges, too. I'm goin' to one of 'em too."

Jonas gave her a hard, steady look, the kind of look that would root out and wither deceit or a lie. He got back the same hard, steady look, the kind of look that spoke truth to power. "What's that book you been readin'?"

Ruthie took the book from her waistband and handed it to him, watching him carefully, not letting on that she neither knew the name of the book or what it was about. His reaction both surprised and irritated her: He slapped the book against his thigh and gave her a wondering look.

"*Treasure Island* by Robert Louis Stevenson. It's just about the best book in the whole, wide world. Don't you think so, Ruthie? Ain't this just the best book in the whole wide world?"

Ruthie took the book from him, stuck it back in her waistband, and turned her attention to the task of freeing the axe blade from the trunk of the pecan tree. She had hurled it with all her might, and it was buried deep. "I don't know," she said to him, keeping her attention on the axe and the tree trunk.

"Why don't you read it to me so I can find out."

A stillness seemed to settle over the forest, as if all the living beings in it were waiting for the boy's response. "All right, Ruthie Thatcher. I'll do that," Jonas said. "When? We can meet right here at the pecan tree——"

"No, we cain't. Uncle Will knows somebody has been at this tree, climbing up in it. He's gon' leave the dogs down here. You got to stay away from this tree. You hear?"

"I hear," Jonas said. "Where can we read that your Uncle Will and your Pa and my Pa won't find out and skin us alive?"

Ruthie thought for a moment then said, "There's another big old pecan tree down by the wide part of the creek."

"I know the one you mean," Jonas said, grinning widely. "You were hiding up it that first day I met you."

Ruthie remembered and was about to say so when she heard a faint but sharp whistle. "I got to go." She gave the axe a final tug, freeing it from the tree, and slung the bulging burlap bag over her shoulder. "Bye, Jonas," she said, and she was moving through the dense woods so surely and so swiftly that Jonas would only watch in awed amazement.

Danged Injuns, he thought to himself as she disappeared from view without having made a single sound. Then he remembered and called out, "When?"

Silence. Then he heard, "That tree'll tell you when."

"What?" Jonas yelled at the forest. "Say what, Ruthie?" Jonas ran in the direction of Ruthie's disappearance. Then he stopped. There was nothing before or behind him but the dense forest. "Hellfire and damnation!" He kicked at the forest floor, scattering twigs and dead leaves. Then, aware that Ruthie probably was all the way back home now, he focused on his return to home and bent down to gather the twigs he had unearthed in his anger and frustration for, just as Ruthie never traveled without her book, Jonas no longer traveled without his burlap bag. Wishing that he, too, had a short-handled axe, Jonas knelt down and began searching beneath the leafy carpet that covered the ground for twigs and small tree limbs and branches. He had learned that going home with something useful kept his Pa's anger at bay. And for the first time ever, Jonas allowed himself to explore the reasons for his father's behavior based on what his ma had told him: Was he so angry all the time because he was no good as a farmer? And if he didn't farm, what would he do? What *could* he do?

Beyond that, though, Jonas wondered why it seemed that Si and Ruthie's

Pa wasn't ever mad at them, or why it seemed that their Ma never was sickly, and why there was a short-handled axe for Ruthie to bring into the forest to chop tree limbs, and why did Ruthie's and Si's clothes look new. And shoes. Why did they have shoes and he didn't? And why was Ruthie talking about going to college when Jonas's Pa had told him to "stop talkin' stupid" when Jonas said he wanted to go to Belle City to college? Jonas knew that he shouldn't but he couldn't help himself: Certain that Ruthie was long gone, and having forgotten what she'd said about the dogs, he hastily climbed the big pecan tree. He wouldn't stay long...

"Hellfire and damnation!" The combination of fear, shock and amazement at the sight before him was overwhelming. Jonas lost his grip, and he crashed to the ground.

Ruthie's breath caught in her throat when she emerged from the forest into the clearing that fronted her house, and it wasn't because she'd been running. She'd never seen anything like the sight before her: There were people everywhere, more than there had been when she left to go collect the firewood. Who were they? Where did they come from? She approached the open yard quickly but cautiously, eyes searching for someone familiar. The people she saw smiled and greeted her warmly, and she returned those greetings in kind, but she didn't know any of the people—had never seen them before, though they seemed to know who she was. Two of the women even stopped to help her lay her collected wood in the sun to dry, commenting on the wisdom of her action. "It's what my Ma and Pa told me to do," Ruthie said, unwilling to take credit.

"Nellie and Silas your Ma and Pa, ain't they?" one of the women asked, and when Ruthie nodded, both women smiled widely and one of them hugged her.

"If it ain't my friend Ruthie Thatcher." Ruthie pulled away from the woman stranger's embrace and jumped into First Freeman's arms. He whirled her around, then hurriedly returned her to earth with a grunt and a groan. "You done growed 'bout a foot and ten pounds since last time I seed you, Girl."

"And I had a birthday, too, Mr. First. I'm thirteen years old. I'm almost grown up." Ruthie danced around him. "And I made you a pie, Mr. First. With them bitter apples you like, and lots of brown sugar and pecans and some of them chokecherries. I made it all by myself. Ma didn't have to help me at all."

"And that's 'xactly why I drove that hoss and buggy all the way over here from Belle City, ridin' all night long, is to eat that pie."

"No, it's not," Ruthie said. "You came 'cause it's Juneteenth."

Freeman put his chin in his hand, deep in thought, then nodded. "You know, I had forgot all about Juneteenth, I was thinkin' so hard 'bout that pie." He looked all around, then at the two women strangers who had been enjoying the antics of the old man and the young girl. "What you Sisters, think: You come for the Juneteenth or for that pie?"

The women grinned, pleased to play along. "Well, sir, we come first for the Juneteenth, but then we heard about that pie," one of the women said.

"Yes, indeed." The other woman licked her lips. "That sounds like a mighty fine pie, Little Miss."

Ruthie was so pleased and embarrassed by all the attention she could barely speak. "I made it for Mr. First but y'all can have some if he says it's all right." All three adults laughed a good, loud laugh, and the two women strangers waved their colored scarves as they walked away and blended into the crowd. "Who all these people, Mr. First? And where they come from?"

"They come from 'round here, most of 'em," the old man said, looking around, touching the brim of his hat to women passersby and nodding greetings of recognition to almost all of the men. "Your Ma and Pa and Uncle Will'am know 'em."

"Then how come I don't know 'em?"

"Well, the men work in the fields together and the women tend to the houses and chil'ren together and cook together. What y'all need 'round here is a church. That way, people leastways could see one another on Sundays."

"I been to church. A preacher comes sometimes, and we have church in a place on the road goin' to Belle City."

Freeman nodded. "I know where 'bouts you mean, and I know the preacher you mean. He travels all 'round these parts—Stevensville and Belle City too— but that ain't the same as havin' regular church every Sunday and gettin' to know your neighbors." He surveyed the crowd, eyes squinting in the bright sun, nodding his head. "These good people. Some of 'em been 'round here long as your Uncle Will'am." Freeman removed his hat, wiped his face, head and neck with a big red kerchief, and set his hat back on his head and stuffed the kerchief back into his pocket. "I guess we better get to celebratin'," he said, heading toward the cooking area of firepits and roasting spits behind the house, Ruthie in his wake. The old man was tall and long-legged; so was the young girl, and she usually could keep up with him as they both were accustomed to her following him around. Today, however, First Freeman wasn't the most interesting thing in her orbit. All these people! She began counting them but quickly lost count; there were too many. Then she focused on the colors—bright, vibrant colors flying from sticks stuck in the ground, wrapped around heads as scarves and waists as skirts, sticking out the back pockets of overalls and work pants. This was a new thing for her.

"Mr. First!" She called his name and, running a bit to catch up, pulled on his arm. He hadn't heard her call his name because he too was intent on taking in the sights, sounds and feel of so many of his people gathered in one place for the single purpose of enjoyment.

He slowed his stride and turned to look down at her. "Yes, Missy?"

"All the colors. Red and yellow and orange and purple: What do they mean? I never seen so many colors at one time."

Freeman stopped walking and stood looking, squinting into the light despite the wide brim of his hat. Ruthie watched him, waiting for him to answer her question, for she never doubted that he had the answer. He stood frozen still, nothing moving but his eyes, and they darted from place to place—from color to color—as if he hadn't noticed them until Ruthie's question. Then his eyes stilled, and Ruthie knew that they were looking back, that First Freeman no longer was seeing the Juneteenth crowd that milled about in the yard surrounding Will Thatcher's house. She knew the look—the one that returned the old ones like Uncle Will to the remembrance of their painful past—and the feeling of stillness that settled over them, and the cloak of sadness that often accompanied it, and she regretted having asked about the colors. Then, as quickly as he'd gone, he was back. He looked down at her, his eyes seeing her, and said, "That's somethin' I hadn't thought on in quite a while." He was walking again, though slower, and Ruthie was able to keep up easily. "Back in the old days...you know when I mean, don't you, Missy?"

"Yessir, Mr. First, I know."

He nodded: Of course she did. Will and Big Si and Nellie taught their children the things that were important. "Back then, we couldn't have no clothes but what they give us, and they only give us homespun. Or worse: Cut up burlap sacks or flour sacks and we'd have to make pants or a dress from that. Ugly, they was, and we wasn't allowed to wear colors." He looked around him, at all the color, then took his big red kerchief from his pocket. He shook it out, then, holding both ends, twisted it into a scarf which he tied around his neck. Then he reached into another of the many pockets of his overalls and withdrew another kerchief, this one yellow, orange and green stripes, and he twisted it into a scarf too and tied it around Ruthie's neck. "Always wear pretty colors, Little Missy, just 'cause you can."

Jonas groaned, rolled over, groaned again. He tried to sit up and was discouraged—from the pain in his shoulder and the low growling in his ear. He inhaled and lay still, aware of the dampness seeping into his clothes that he usually welcomed because it was cooling in the hot, heavy heat of the day, but which now made him shiver. The growling continued until a sharp, low whistle silenced it.

"That's what you get for spyin' on folks. You shoulda broke your fool neck."

Willing himself not to show his pain or his fear, Jonas rolled over and jumped to his feet in a single, if not fluid, motion, and turned to find Si and Ruthie's big brother, Tobias, and two of their dogs, watching him. "I'm not spyin'."

"You think we don't know you climb up in that tree and watch us?"

Jonas didn't say anything. His arm and shoulder hurt from his fall. He wiggled his fingers to test for broken bones and the sharp pain that resulted suggested that, if not broken, his arm and shoulder would cause him misery for some time to come. "I won't do it no more."

"Why you care so much 'bout what we do, Jonas?"

He stopped himself from shrugging just in time: The pain would have pretty near killed him. He and Tobias, who was older, bigger and certainly stronger, stood staring at each other, separated by five or six feet of marshy forest land and a whole, wide world, one that Jonas struggled—and always failed— to understand. "I just—" There was no point in trying to explain himself to Tobias Thatcher, whom he knew disliked and distrusted him. Besides, if he couldn't explain himself to himself, how, then, could he put thoughts into words before a hostile boy and two equally hostile dogs?

"You just trespassin' is what, Jonas Thatcher. Bad enough you spyin', but trespassin', too? If we was trespassin' on your land, your Pa would shoot us dead."

Jonas knew he was right—or that he would be right if his Pa still owned a gun that would actually kill anything. Certainly he would make the effort. "You gonna shoot me?"

Tobias sucked in air through his teeth. "If that's what I was gonna do, you'd already be shot. Anyway, that's the kinda thing y'all do, not us."

Somewhere inside himself, Jonas knew he was right about that, too.

"Why things got to be like they is between us? Between Colored and white?"

Tobias looked at him long and hard, as if the answer might be written somewhere on the body of Jonas Thatcher, and when he spoke, it was without anger or hostility, but nor was it the voice of a boy; it was a man who said, "Why you askin' me? We ain't the ones made things the way they is." With a whistle for the dogs, he turned away and disappeared into the forest, still managing to have the last word. "Stay outta that tree, Jonas, and quit spyin' on us. Quit your trespassin'."

Jonas heard the words long after Tobias and the dogs vanished from sight. All of the words that Tobias Thatcher had spoken thrummed in his head like rain water beating on a tin roof, loud and steady and insistent: The words and the meanings held within them, meanings that Jonas felt rather than knew or understood. One thing he did know, though, was that if he obeyed Tobias—obeyed his own father—he no longer would be able to hunt with Si, exploring the woods and creatures and critters that lived in the marshes and trees. More crucially, though, he would not be able to read with Ruthie in the pecan tree down by the wide part of the creek. Then he had another thought that pushed all the others from his head: How would he explain the injury to his arm and shoulder? He couldn't admit to having fallen out of a tree while watching the Thatcher place, and he certainly couldn't tell Pa that they were having some kinda big celebration.

"Tobias, where you been?" Ruthie rushed to her brother, grabbed his hand, and began to pull him toward the sound of music. "You ever seen a real, live guitar, Toby? Or a fiddle? Or heard real, live music 'cept church singing?"

Ruthie was hopping from foot to foot, pointing at Henry Childs playing his guitar and Riley Huston playing his fiddle. She didn't know—no way she could know—that all the men who worked in the fields heard one or the other of the musicians play practically every day, that the music was their way of mitigating the backbreaking, never-ending work of tilling, growing and harvesting that was necessary to keep them all from starving to death. "Music is a very wonderful thing, ain't it, Toby?"

She was holding his arm out from his side like a streamer on a May pole, and twirling herself in circles beneath. "I 'spect you right about that, Little Sister," he said, but he wasn't looking at Ruthie or at the musicians. Instead, he was looking around, watching people enjoying themselves, and on the look-out for trouble, for there always seemed to be trouble whenever enough people gathered in the same place. His Ma had told everybody that there would be no spirits allowed and everybody had agreed that banning spirits was a good idea because usually it was the over-indulgence in them that caused the trouble, and Tobias had neither seen nor smelled any evidence that anybody was breaking the rules. Still...

"I'm hungry, Toby. When can we eat?"

Shading his eyes with the hand that Ruthie wasn't dancing with, he looked up at the sky, at where the sun was. "Soon, I 'spect. Let's go ask Ma."

The area between the barn and the house, between the house and the fields, and behind all three was the site of the gathering, where people had set up tents and lean-tos and various other shelter from the sun, as well as comfortable places to rest and eat. The cooking area was adjacent to the fields—farthest away from where people were resting. Here the men were overseeing the turning of the spits on which roasted rabbits, chickens and a deer, and the roasting pits in which potatoes, turnips and ears of corn, mixed with onions and garlic bulbs and covered with hot rocks, sizzled and grew tender. On open fires women fried fish in kettles of oil—so much fish that Si had told Uncle Will that maybe it was too much. "Ain't no such thing as too much food to people who just got used to eatin' at all," the old man had replied, putting a quick end to that kind of talk.

Uncle Will, years ago relieved of cooking duties, was content to enjoy the sight of all the food and all the people, and to have people know him, know that the land upon which they rested was his, and to know that they knew—that all these people whom he knew by name—also knew that as long as Will Thatcher had land to call his own, not one of them ever would be homeless. No matter what First Freeman and the folks who'd left the farms for the cities said, it was Will Thatcher's belief that a man who owned his own land was richer than any city folks with their banks and colleges and insurance companies and their painted houses.

Will stood looking at his own house—the largest in this corner of Carrie's Crossing—and thought to himself that it indeed would look mighty fine painted white, with red and yellow and purple flowers in pots on the porch and grass in the yard instead of hard-packed dirt that turned to mud when it rained. He also thought that the satisfaction of knowing that his house was larger, and indeed better, than that of the man he once called Master was better than a coat of paint, especially since painting the house would draw attention to him, and that he didn't want.

"Happy Juneteenth, Will." First Freeman was standing beside him, probably had been standing there for a while, as was his way: To be quiet and watchful. "You got ev'ry right to be proud of what you got here."

"Even if it ain't in Belle City?" The humor a passer-by would have heard in Will's voice would have resided only on the surface, which his old friend very well knew.

"Belle City ain't for ev'rybody. I know that, Will."

Will Thatcher nodded his head, but he didn't speak. First Freeman waited for him "And farmin' ain't for ev'rybody, either, I reckon," Will said, then added, before Freeman could form a response, "though I do b'lieve bein' able to grow food to eat makes right good sense, 'specially for folks ain't got two nickels to rub together."

Freeman chuckled. "You a stubborn man, Will'am Thatcher, but that's what makes you a man what can be counted on in the hard times, like these ones we havin' now."

Will looked hard at Freeman. "Y'all havin' hard times over yonder in Belle City?"

"Some folks is."

"Is you?"

"Naw, Will, thank you for askin', but I'm aw'right. Me and my mules and my wagons still make the rounds all over the city. Only diff'rence nowadays is that white folks ain't throwin' out as much as they used to, and what they do throw out is pretty well used up. I ain't seen a new pair of shoes or a suit or dress that wasn't wore shiny in quite a while now. Still," he said, managing another of his chuckles, "on the Colored side of town, ain't nobody throwin' nothin' away if it's any use at all. If it's on the curb on a Colored street, you can best b'lieve it's good for nothin' but the junk heap."

The gentle laughter that the two old men shared was the humor born of the need to laugh oneself through troubled times because crying served no purpose. "Just so you know, we, all of us, is mighty grateful for all the things you bring over here, 'specially the chil'ren."

Now First Freeman laughed out loud. "You mean Little Miss Ruth Thatcher." He shook his head, the laughter still rumbling deep inside him. "She is a stitch, she is."

"She's a right piece of work, and that's the truth," Will said, laughing with Freeman, but only briefly. "Her Ma's worried 'bout her."

Freeman's laugh caught in his throat. "How come?"

"Cain't keep her outta them woods. She got all Nellie's Injun blood in her and she roams them woods like she's inside the house. And ain't scared of nothin'—snakes, spiders, wild cats, thunder and lightnin'. The other night when it stormed so bad...did it rain like the end of the world over yonder in Belle City? Then you know how it was coming down: In buckets. Little Miss Ruth was out there in it. Between the dark and the water you couldn't see your hand in front of your face and she was out here in the yard singin' and dancin'." He shook his head in amazed, though confused, wonderment. "She done even made friend with one o' them big hooty owls. Give him a name and all."

"Made friends with a hooty owl and give him a name!" Freeman exclaimed. "I never heard of such a thing."

"That ain't the worst of it." Will took a deep breath, blew it out, took another one and used it to speak the distasteful words he'd wanted to be rid of. "Half the time Little Si's with her and they meet up with Zeb Thatcher's baby boy. Claim they friends."

"Good God! Friends? Cain't nobody Colored be friends with Zeb Thatcher nor anybody related to him." First Freeman thought about what he'd said, concluded that he was right and nodded. Then another thought intruded, a truly worrisome one. "Little Missy told me while ago that she just had herself a birthday. Says she's thirteen...?"

Will Thatcher answered the question that First Freeman hadn't asked: "She come on her womanhood two moons ago."

"Good God," Freeman said again, imagining the girl—young and pretty and wild— roaming the forest alone or singing and dancing at night in the rain, though he was deprived of the opportunity for further expression by Ruthie's arrival.

"Uncle Will! Mr. First!" She grabbed each man by the hand and pulled. "Y'all got to come on. We ready to eat."

"Y'all gon' eat up all the food 'fore we get there?" Freeman asked.

"No, sir," the girl responded, appalled at the thought. "Pa says we can't eat 'til y'all come so y'all got to come 'cause everybody's hungry."

"Then I guess we better come on, Freeman," Will said and led the way across the yard to the shady area where the tables were set up.

Ruthie had never seen so much food. Nobody present had ever seen so much food. Everybody had brought something to share and the two long tables that were set up under the tree near the cook pits were covered, every inch of them, with plates and bowls of food. Ruthie had believed that they'd be eating only what was cooked on the spits or in the pits, but the contents of all those bowls and plates contradicted that. To accompany the roasted meats and vegetables and fried fish were deviled eggs and cabbage slaw and bowls and bowls of greens and many platters of fried chicken. Then there were the cakes and pies and cobblers.

"Lord have mercy." Little Si's eyes were so big and his mouth was hanging wide open, Ruthie thought he looked like a hooked fish.

"You rather stand there watching the food, Si, or you want to eat it?" Ruthie said as she began choosing what she most wanted to eat: Roasted ears of corn, roasted yams and turnips, whole roasted fish—in fact, anything that was wrapped and buried in the hot coals to cook from the inside out was Ruthie's favorite food. She'd eat roasted cake and pie if such a thing existed.

Galvanized, her brother heaped food onto his wooden plate until there was no room left for more and Ruthie briefly misinterpreted the look of sadness on his face. Then, when finally she understood, she started to laugh, and she laughed so hard that she began to choke and the woman in the line behind her had to slap her back—hard—to bring the breath back. This is what Ruthie's Ma saw and which had her hurrying over.

"Ruthie?" her Ma said, bending down to look in her face.

"Oh, Ma," Ruthie said, the tears streaming down her face further confusing her mother. She had to speak, to explain. "Si thinks there ain't gonna be no food left if all these people eat."

Nellie gave her daughter an odd look, then switched her gaze to her son's over-filled plate and she didn't know which of the emotions and feelings that swept through her to give in to. In the end, she didn't have a choice for, like her daughter, she started to laugh. She turned to the woman behind her, whose concern was beginning to turn to annoyance, and said, "My boy fears not having enough food."

The old woman's dry cackle got the attention of everyone within in earshot. She reached out a gnarly hand and touched Little Si's face. "Boy," she said in a voice that sounded rusty, as if she hadn't used it a long time, "even if we was all still slaves and hadn't et in a week, wouldn't nobody go hungry today. There's food aplenty here, don't you worry 'bout that. Go 'long, now, you and Li'l Sis, 'fore I get some more hungry."

Nellie got the message and hurried her children out of the way so that the hungry line could move forward. With a hand on each of their heads, she guided them toward the lean-to where her family was gathered. It was an easily and hastily built structure—most families had built one—that kept the direct sun off them while providing a sense of togetherness for the familial units. There was no privacy as the structures were open on three sides, and anyway, privacy wasn't the issue—family was. Another of the arbitrary dictates of slavery, along with the prohibition against wearing bright colors, barred maintenance of the family unit. So, in the absence of blood relatives, slaves formed themselves into units based on proximity and need, and those units functioned like family, and it was that sense of family that always drew First Freeman back to Carrie's Crossing: To the former slaves who were his family.

Little Si stopped chewing and swallowing long enough to stare at his sister's plate. He frowned. "That's all you're gonna eat, is fish?" Her plate was piled as high as his own, but where he had piles of roasted meats, she had piles of fish—fried fish, roasted fish, grilled fish.

"I got corn and turnips and cucumbers and tomatoes too," Ruthie said."

"But what about chicken or rabbit or deer or..."

"Leave her alone, Si," Tobias said. He said it quietly, softly, almost, but Little Si gasped as if his big brother had yelled at him. Or worse, had hit him. Ruthie, too, was looking at him with something like fear in her eyes. He wished he could take back the words but he couldn't, any more than he could forget that his little sister no longer was a baby and that from now on—at least until she married and it was some other man's job—Pa had given him the task of watching over her, of keeping her safe. He wasn't sure how he would or could do that, especially since Ruthie had always been free to move about as she pleased, but Ma had just started keeping her out of the fields and kept her close to the house now, helping with the washing, ironing and cooking and planting seeds or pulling weeds in the garden the family kept for its own food, but she was just as likely to be down at the creek, catching, cleaning and gutting fish, or climbing up a tree to talk to a hooty owl, or sitting under it reading a book. And it was his job to know where she was at all times.

"Toby?" Ruthie called his name but both younger siblings were looking at him, their eyes large, round question marks: What had they done to upset him?

"I'm surprised you can still talk, Baby Sister, with those gills growing out the side of your face, all that fish you're eating. And you," he said, turning toward Little Si, "I expect you'll be walking on all fours by the time the sun sets. Or hopping like a bunny rabbit."

It took them several heavy seconds to realize that not only wasn't Tobias

angry with them, but he was playing with them, just like always. They started
to giggle, then to laugh out loud as they imagined themselves with gills and fins
and hopping like rabbits. They rolled themselves closer to their big brother and
leaned against him, assuring themselves of his continued love, and that it was
safe to return to the Celebration.

All of them—the more than one hundred Colored people gathered that
hot Georgia day in 1918—felt and behaved like family as they celebrated
Juneteenth on the land owned by Will Thatcher, proud of the fact that he, a
former slave, now owned property. A good many of them lived and worked on
Will's land, proud of that fact too; proud to call themselves farmers and not
sharecroppers, as were called those who worked the land owned by white men.
This sense of pride made their celebration all the sweeter—that and the fact
that they could, each and every one of them, eat as much food as they could
hold. For no matter their age or circumstance—former slave or child of former
slave—having enough to eat and drink remained a situation of catch-as-catch-
can. The prayers of thanks were deeply felt—for the freedom and for the food.

After the feasting came the fun—the music and dancing and games—
activities enjoyed almost exclusively by the younger people; the elders either
napped or wandered from family group to family group, exchanging greetings
and gossip. Everybody, young and old, sighed with relief as the sun began its
descent in the western sky. The day had been hot and while the night would not
necessarily be cool, the absence of the blazing sun would add to the evening's
enjoyment. Children and dogs chased each other and coming-of-age young
people got better acquainted with each other, while mothers kept a casually
vigilant watch over them all, and the men, not so casual in their vigilance,
patrolled the borders of the celebration area.

It was Little Si who first became aware of the danger coming their way,
but before he could find and alert Pa and Uncle Will, a woman who saw
what he saw when he saw it, alerted the entire gathering when she emitted
a high, keening wail. In an instant, silence invaded the grounds—even the
night creatures were shocked into a momentary ceasing of their chirping and
croaking—as they all sought the source and reason for the alarm; and when
they found it, their silence took on another meaning: Fear, as the white man
stumbled toward them muttering curses.

"Goddamniggers," those closest to him heard, and heard him say it over
and over, low and beneath his breath, as if some perverse form of prayer.
"Goddamniggers." He was bent over and breathing hard, as if he'd just tried

to outrun some wild, hungry animal. Then he stood up straight, and the effort clearly cost him because he coughed and he grabbed his chest, but he'd found his voice for he yelled, "Get offn my land, goddamniggers! Get offn my land!"

Nobody spoke because nobody was breathing. The children were paralyzed because the adults were paralyzed, and they all were watching the stumbling, mumbling, drunken white man who now had discovered the food-laden tables.

"Where y'all steal all this food?" He staggered toward the table, reached out and grabbed several pieces of fried fish. And that's when motion returned to those whose freedom celebration had been disturbed. It began with the dogs, three of them, medium-sized mongrels of no particular type or description: They silently bore down on the unaware white man, startling him so that he dropped the pieces of fish. Then the dogs stopped running but kept up their snarling and snapping, low on their haunches, ready to spring if ordered.

First Freeman held one hand low by his side—the hand that controlled his dogs—and the other raised toward the white man. "This ain't your land no more, Carney Thatcher. You knows that good as I do."

"*Carney Thatcher?*" The fearful, whispered query wove through the crowd on the thick night air. "*I thought he was long daid.*"

"*His pa's daid. This the son,*" another whisper replied.

"Goddamn niggers," Carney Thatcher yelled. "Get offn my land." The yelled words caught in his throat and he began to choke and cough.

"Back up, y'all." They all, including the dogs, obeyed Freeman's hissed order, several people ready to run if necessary.

"Stay on that road yonder and it'll take you on to your brother's place. To your land."

Carney Thatcher, swaying back and forth like a tree leaf in a breeze, squinted at First Freeman. "I know you, Boy. I know who you is."

"I 'spect you do," the old man said.

"You ain't one of them nigger Thatchers, though."

"No. I ain't."

Carney looked closer, squinting, as full darkness had descended and the only light in the velvet night was provided by the nearly full moon and the firmament of stars. "You one of Tom Fordham's niggers. I 'member you. You was good a fixin' things. Your name is Si…"

"My name First Freeman. Now get on 'way from here," First Freeman said in a low, cold voice, as his dogs resumed their low, cold snarling. "Go on home to your people. You stay on that road yonder, you'll see Zeb's place. It ain't moved since you was last 'round here."

Carney Thatcher first turned his head to look toward the road, then he turned his body and took a hesitant step, before turning back. "You say your name is *what?*"

Freeman turned his back on the strange visitor and waved his arm. "All the food on that table," he said, "bury it. Don't even let the dogs eat it. That man is bad, bad sick."

For a moment nobody moved, frozen in place by the emotional trauma brought by the unexpected visitor and struck dumb at the thought of throwing away food. Bury it? Surely not. But when Freeman upturned the table and Nellie Thatcher ran toward it with a shovel, it became clear that the food on that table would, indeed, be buried. As Nellie began digging, she sent one of her boys for a bucket of lime. He sprinted off and the crowd released its collective paralysis and several pairs of hands pitched in to assist as First Freeman exhorted them over and over, "Don't touch it! Don't y'all touch it!" Many of them would wonder later how the old man could know that such good food could be dangerous, but nobody questioned him at the time, and it was only a shriek from normally peaceful and quiet Nellie that shifted his focus from the task at hand.

Nellie looked up from her digging and burying and she wasn't certain, at first, that her eyes weren't playing tricks on her in the dark. She straightened up to get a better look and the horror on her face stilled and frightened those around her—especially her children. "Uncle Will! Where you goin'? You can't go out there. Come back here!"

Old Will Thatcher, already several steps out onto the road, stopped walking, but he didn't turn around. Many voices were calling to him now, urging— demanding—his return and he was grateful for the darkness that covered his fear, but he needed to go, to see, to be certain.

"Will'am! What is you doin'?" First Freeman grabbed his friend's arm and momentarily was startled by the resistance he found, though he shouldn't have been: Despite their ages, both were strong, powerful men; what else could they be after a lifetime of physical labor?

"I got to go see, Freeman. I got to know."

"See what? Ain't nothin' to see out here in the dark, 'specially if you get yourself kilt."

"Got to see did Carney tell Zeb 'bout Juneteenth, 'bout our celebration, that's what."

"Ain't nobody gon' pay Carney no mind, not even Zeb."

"Why, just 'cause he's drunk?"

"He ain't drunk, Will, he's sick, bad sick, and if he ain't already dead, he soon will be. Now, bring yourself off that road!"

Will allowed himself to be returned to his yard and his family and friends though he kept looking over his shoulder, peering into the darkness. "I'll go in the mornin', then."

All of First Freeman's pent up fear and anger exploded out of him then, but it was a quiet fury and so much more frightening than if he'd yelled and screamed. "Stop bein' so damn' bull headed, Will! Did you hear me tell you Carney Thatcher is sick to dyin'? You don't want to be no where near him 'cause what he got, anybody 'round him can catch. Why you think I had y'all bury that food what he touched?"

"'Cause you hate him."

His anger spent, First Freeman laughed a good laugh and clapped his old friend on the back. "I don't hate nobody bad enough to throw good food on the ground." He looked around at all the people crowded around him, still silent in their fear. "Y'all listen to me: Carney Thatcher ain't drunk, he's sick. They got some kinda sickness over yonder in Belle City—and everywhere else for that matter—that's takin' people 'way from here left and right. They call it 'fluenza and it's a catching sickness, so y'all got to stay 'way from him and anybody you see actin' like he was." He looked around at the faces looking back at him in the darkness, then he put his arm around Will Thatcher's shoulders. "Ain't nobody gon' believe nothin' come outta Carney Thatcher's mouth, Will, 'specially Zeb." Then he chuckled again. "You think Zeb Thatcher gon' believe that all you niggers is on his land, singin' and dancin' and eatin' just like you was rich white folks?"

All was still and silent for a moment, then a hoot of laughter cracked the dark silence, and everybody was laughing and somebody said, "Rich white folks: That's us, all right."

"I'm hungry," somebody else said. "Bein' scared is hard work."

And though there was no more music or dancing or running and chasing, the celebration resumed—after all the parents accounted for all their children and strict warnings were issued and reiterated about not venturing out onto the road at night and what to do if drunk-acting and crazy-talking people, white or Colored, were encountered. Uncle Will's family and his closest friends surrounded him and kept him close for the remainder of the evening, though only the most astute of the adults realized that in just a few moments, something very large had shifted and changed within the old man that night.

From the Diary of Jonas Farley Thatcher

June 1918. My Uncle Carney came home to die. Pa didn't know that. He just knowed that his big brother come to visit who he had not seen in many, manny years. He was awful bad sick that nite when he got to our house. I dint know who he was and he dint know who I was. He thot I was my brother. He called me Zeb. I tol him I was Jonas but he didt seem like he heard me. He didt see me nether. Not like you see peeple when you look at them. Uncle Carneys eyes was big and wide open but he didn seem like he culd see anything. Ma said he was burning up hot with a feever. He was sweting when he come to the door like it was the hotest part of the day. But it was the nite time and he was burning hot and wet. He told Pa he come home to get his land back. Pa said he was talking crazy out of his hed. Ma said he was deelerus. Pa sent me to fetch Doc Gray. I had to walk we don't have a hors no more. It was a long long walk I was hot and sweting like Uncle Carney when I got to docter Grays hous. but I was not deelerus. Docter gray say that meens the same as talking crazy and he sayd if Uncle Carney was like that he was to far gon. and he sayd we shuld al get out from the hous specialy Ma that Uncle carney had the flunza. Lot of foks in Belle City had it an they dyed. Docter gray sayd Uncle was dyed to. and he was dyed when I got walked back home. ma got scrad and she got mad we culd die from the fluenz she saed cause it is a catching sickness. She maid Pa dig a deep hol and put Uncle Crney it and cover him up with lim. then she washd evrthing in the hous with lie sop. Some thing I nevr tol my pa was Uncle carney was not talking crzy a tall. He kapt on saying about nigers singing and dancin and havein to much food and how he want his land back. Pa thot he was talk about Belle City but he was not. He was talk about ruthie Thatcher's farm and the party they was hav the nite Uncle Carney come home to die. I allso did not tell my pa I was glad uncle dyed becaus things got better when he dyed becaus of the mony. Evry thing for us was better except one.

From the Recorded Memories of Ruth Thatcher McGinnis

I know this will sound strange to you, Sissy, but when I was a young child, I didn't really know very much about white people and racism...really. It's true! There I was, living in a house built by ex-slaves who were my family, surrounded by former slaves and other people who had experienced unspeakable horrors, and I knew practically nothing of it. Oh, of course I knew that something called slavery had existed, but I didn't really understand, not then, what that meant. I was thirteen years old before I saw a grown-up white man up close.... what? Oh, yes, my brother Silas and I had a white playmate, a boy our age, but Jonas wasn't evil, and he was as terrified of his father as we'd been taught to be, though, no doubt, for different reasons. How could this be? Our parents shielded and protected us from as much of the ugliness that surrounded us as they could, just as I shielded and protected my children from it and just as your parents did. And you must keep in mind how we lived back then, especially out in the country. Not only were we separate, we were isolated. There was no radio, no newspaper. We shared land with a man who hated the sight of us—so he didn't see us and we didn't see him. But all that changed one night in June of 1918. We were celebrating Juneteenth—you know what Juneteenth is, don't you? Well, I have to ask, Sissy; so many of you young people don't know anything of your history. Anyway, nothing was ever again the same for us after that night, though it wasn't until many years later that I could pinpoint that night as the beginning of the changes that would impact our lives forever. Change for good or ill? Almost of it was ill—with one major exception: Your Grandpa.

Jonas had never in his life felt so miserable and so happy at the same time. In fact, if somebody had told him it was possible to feel such opposing emotions in the same moment, almost with the same breath, he'd have called that person a liar. Yet, here he was on a bright, hot September morning, dressing for the first day of school with the knowledge that he would, from now on, be going to school each and every day, and that knowledge rendered him practically speechless with joy. But his Ma, who had made Jonas's education possible by extracting the promise from his Pa—his Ma was dying. The promise was made and would be kept because it was a promise made to a dying wife. Jonas knew, though, that the promise would be kept only because his Pa no longer was burdened by having to try to be a farmer: He now was a business man, owning, as he did, two stores in the burgeoning town of Carrie's Crossing, situated at the crossroads of Belle City Road and Thatcher Farm Road, so called because Zeb's farm—former farm—bordered the road. Zeb bought the two buildings in the town with money that came to him when his brother, Carney, died, and it soon became apparent that Zeb was a much better businessman than he was a farmer.

Zeb recognized immediately the possibilities presented by the farming community of Carrie's Crossing shedding its overalls and brogans and becoming a town, and he didn't hesitate to spend practically every dime of Carney's money buying the two buildings. One became a general store, the other a bar, though his Ma liked referring to it as a pub, reminding her, she said, of Scotland. Of course Jonas had never seen a pub, but he imagined that they were elegant places where important men gathered to discuss important matters, in which case, the place his father owned couldn't have been less pub-like. It was long, narrow and dark even in the brightest sunlight, and always smoke-filled. It was called *ZEB'S* and Jonas disliked it and the people who frequented it. The store, on the other hand, called *THATCHER'S GENERAL STORE*, was bright and clean and orderly, due primarily to the fact that his mother had organized it before she became too ill to get out of bed. She had overseen the building of the shelves and the hanging of shutters and the white-washing of walls and the stocking of the place with things "that people always need: Flour, sugar, salt, jars for preserving food, needles, thread and cloth, dried beans, rice. You keep these things in the store, Zeb, and people will always come to buy."

Jonas tiptoed into his mother's bedroom, hoping that she was awake but being careful not to wake her in case she was sleeping. He wanted her to see him dressed for the first day of school, wanted to hear her tell him how tall he was getting and how handsome he looked, but she was asleep, as she almost always was these days, and it frightened Jonas because she looked dead. He stood beside the bed and looked down at her. She looked like a child, tiny and thin. Jonas felt that invisible strap tighten around his chest that he always felt when he thought how his freedom to attend school had come at the price of his mother's life. Yes, she'd always been sickly, that was true, but it was the flu sickness she'd caught from Uncle Carney that destroyed her lungs. Doc Gray swore that she'd already be dead if she weren't waiting for the younger Zeb to come home from the war.

"You look like a preacher," Pa said to him when he entered the kitchen.

Jonas looked down at himself, at his pants with the shirt tucked in that he'd begged and pleaded with his sister to iron for him, and his shined shoes. He didn't have on anything black; why did Pa think he looked like a preacher? Maybe because of the shirt buttoned all the way to the top? He undid the top button.

"You ridin' that hoss to the school?"

They now had two horses, one for each of them, and Jonas was so proud of his that he rode almost everywhere, even into the woods to meet Silas and Ruthie to practice their reading. "Yessir," he said.

"Reason I asked, I want you to come to the store after school and help me some more with them figures. I can't seem to make them numbers add up right for nothin'." He shook his head in disgust and began mumbling and muttering about the failure of the numbers to properly add themselves the same way he once railed at his pitiful cotton crop for failing to grow.

For his part, Jonas was pleased to be asked to help, though going to his father's store after school meant that he wouldn't be able to share the day's lessons with Ruthie as promised. Jonas and numbers were a natural fit despite his stated intention to be a be a famous writer like Mark Twain or Charles Dickens, but he understood that until his mother got well (and she would) he'd have to keep the books because his Pa could not read or write at all, and his figuring was as pitiful as his farming.

As he rode into the school yard, Jonas tried to remember when he'd last attended school and he could not. The best he could recall, it had been around Easter time, and he felt like a total stranger. He knew that a second room had been added to the one-room school building, and he knew that it had been painted and that there was a new teacher, but he wasn't prepared for the fact that the new part was a brick building, or that a foundation already was laid on the other side of the original structure for another new wing. The door of what had been the one-room school house had been painted a bright red and there was a hand-carved sign above it: *CARRIE'S CROSSING SCHOOL.*

Jonas got off his horse and looked for a hitch to tie it to and a water trough. When he could find neither, he finally took a good look around and felt not only like a stranger, but he felt strange as well: He, apparently, was the only one to have come to school on a horse, and he also was the only boy wearing long pants, a shirt with a collar, and shined shoes.

"You a preacher?" somebody asked him, while several others snickered.

"No, I ain't a preacher," he said, noticing, again with new eyes, that the boy who'd asked the question, and the other children—both boys and girls— were smaller and younger, and he had a moment of pure panic: Had he missed the opportunity to be educated? Was he too old?

A bell clanged and suddenly children were swarming—little ones and, thankfully, bigger ones as well. A woman whom Jonas did not recognize was standing in the schoolhouse doorway ringing the bell and smiling. The new teacher, he thought, as he hurriedly tied his horse to a pine tree, grateful that the changes that had come to the school in his six-month absence hadn't included chopping down all the trees. He'd figure out what to do about water at lunch time.

"Younger children in here," the new teacher said, "older children over to the new building."

Jonas followed directions and found himself in a room with eight other boys and girls of his approximate age, with desks for half a dozen more. He recognized one of the girls and one of the boys, though he couldn't remember their names until the girl smiled at him: Lucy Fordham and her brother, Tom. He hadn't seen her since the last time he was at school and... well...she surely didn't look like a little girl anymore.

"Take your seats, children. I'm Miss Carter," she said and turned to write her name on the blackboard that stretched across the front of the room. Jonas thought she looked too young to be a teacher, especially compared to Mrs. Moore, who was the only teacher in the school when it had but one room. It made sense, though: Two rooms, two teachers. "I just moved here from Spencerville."

"Spencerville. That's a long ways from here, ain't it?" This from a tall, skinny boy at the back of the room that Jonas hadn't seen before.

"*Isn't* it," Miss Carter said, "and it's just 'way,' not 'ways.' And I think grammar will be a good place to begin after we take the roll. So: I want each one of you to stand up and tell me your full name and date of birth and something about yourself."

"Something like what?" Lucy Fordham asked.

"Like what you want to be when you grow up, or what's your favorite book," the teacher said, and Jonas felt happier than at any other time in his life—somebody wanted to know that he wanted to be a writer—and it was a feeling he'd always be grateful for because by month's end, it had been submerged in a sea of grief, anger, pain and sadness.

It was just three weeks later that Jonas rode his horse to *THATCHER'S GENERAL STORE* after school, prepared to do the end-of-the-month bookkeeping. He was thinking about an ice cold Red Rock Cola when he opened the door to see not his father behind the counter, but his brother-in-law, Rachel's husband, Cory. "What're you doing here?"

"Your Pa said for you to hurry up home."

That's when Jonas knew something was wrong—knew that he should have known as soon as he saw Cory behind the counter. "Wha...Ma. Is it my Ma?"

Cory sighed deeply. "Just go on home, Jonas."

He should have galloped the horse, but he didn't. He took his time, let the horse follow his own way home through the woods. No point in hurrying now, Jonas thought. If Pa was at home at this time of the day, if Cory had been sent for to mind the store, that meant Rachel and Esther already were there and Ma already wasn't. Jonas sat astride the horse, not holding the reins, not looking where he was going, his entire being focused on trying to feel himself—his life—without his mother. "My Ma is dead," he said to himself, at first only in his mind, but then, out loud, so he could hear what it sounded like, feel what it felt like. What he felt was empty, hollow, as if he'd been gutted like a fish or a deer. Except he knew he hadn't been because his heart was thudding and pounding in his chest like it was trying to break out of his rib cage.

Coming out of the woods into the yard beside his house was still a little startling to Jonas; he'd not yet gotten accustomed to the freshly painted house with grass and flowers in the yard, or the brick walkway leading to the front door, nor had he accustomed himself to the vast, empty field where once there had been the uneven rows of cotton and the falling-down barn and the other rickety outbuildings that had given the place such a wretched look. Now there was a new horse barn behind the house with four stalls and a water trough in front. Jonas put his horse away, fed him, and walked slowly toward the front of the house. The sight of the motorcar was confirmation of his worse fear: Doc Gray was the only person they knew who had an automobile and if the doctor was here, surely his mother was dead.

"It ain't fair. It ain't right. It ain't fair. It ain't right." His Pa was sitting in the middle of the walkway in front of the house, crying and screaming, sometimes looking up at the sky, as if talking to God.

Jonas went into the house. Both his sisters were there, as was Esther's husband, Clem, and the doctor. "Ma's dead, ain't she?"

Rachel and Esther who clearly had been crying, began weeping again and Clem tried to get his arms around both of them. Doc Gray walked over and put a hand on his shoulder. "She is now, Jonas, yes. Your ma's gone."

Jonas looked at him. Something was odd about what he just said, but he didn't know what it was. "She stopped breathing like you said she would?"

The doctor shook his head. "She had a heart attack, Jonas, when she heard about Zeb."

Now Jonas was confused. "Zeb?"

"Your brother. He's not coming home, Jonas. He was killed. In the war. In France."

Jonas felt his heart thudding again but for a totally different reason: He had forgotten about Zeb. His own brother, fighting a war on the other side of the world and Jonas hadn't given him a single thought in...he didn't know how long. Probably not since last Christmas when they drove over to Belle City to the Army office to figure out how to send Zeb a Christmas package.

Since neither of the Zebs could read or write, nobody expected letters, so they didn't hear from Zeb, didn't know anything about him. And now he was dead. And so was his ma. He wanted to howl and cry like Pa: This wasn't right or fair. Instead he ran from the room, out of the house, and into the woods. He ran until he couldn't breathe, then he collapsed and lay face down in the leaves and cried so hard that he gave himself the hiccups.

When he finally sat up to blow his nose, he found Ruthie looking at him. She gave him her red, yellow and green scarf to wipe his face with and then she sat looking at him until he was able to speak. "My Ma is dead. So is my brother."

She was so still and quiet that she could have been dead, too. She sat cross-legged on the ground, her back against a tree, and she looked at him so hard he thought she probably could see how empty he was inside. "That's the worst news I ever heard, Jonas."

He nodded. "Me, too."

"Where 'bouts was your brother?"

"In France."

Now Ruthie's heart began to thud against her rib cage. "My brothers are in France too. In some forest. I don't remember the name."

Jonas stopped hurting long enough to process what he'd just heard. "You know where your brothers are? How you know, Ruthie?"

"From letters. Didn't your brother write letters, tell y'all how he was doing?"

"Zeb can't write. Read, neither."

"Beau and Eubie can't neither, but some of the educated soldiers write letters home for them who can't read and write, and then some of the people from the college read the letters to us, 'cause most of us can't read, neither."

Jonas was puzzled: What was she talking about, what people at what college. "Ruthie—?"

"Over in Belle City," she said, sounding like a ma or an auntie talking to a little child. "'Member I told you we had colleges in Belle City? Well, they read letters to us and the newspapers and explain all about the war."

"They tell you why we fightin' France?"

"We ain't fightin' France, we fightin' Germany, but—"

"My brother got killed in France."

"I know," she said, feeling almost as miserable he sounded. "The war is a mess. That's what the college professors told us, and I don't understand a lot of what they said 'cept that a lot of our boys is gettin' killed and dyin' in France and...and...I don't remember all them other places."

"You didn't tell me you been to Belle City."

Ruthie was shaking her head. She'd made a big mistake. "I wasn't s'posed to tell you."

"Why?"

"'Cause of your pa, him and all the other white folks. You know y'all hate us and don't want us doin' things like goin' to Belle City and learnin'."

"We ain't all like that, Ruthie Thatcher. Me and my Ma ain't like that... I forgot. Just that quick I forgot my Ma was dead. It ain't right. It ain't fair." He was crying again, but this time his tears were for himself, for how unfair things were.

Ruthie held her tears in check until she ran into the kitchen and into her mother's arms. Then she wailed, "Jonas's mother is dead and his brother too. He won't never see his Ma again. His brother won't never come home from the war."

Nellie had to work to keep her own tears from falling. This child of hers—the youngest, the only girl, the wildest and freest child she'd ever seen— was so much a part of herself that she literally shared the girl's pain and felt the fear that fueled it. As hard as she had to work to keep from crying, she had to work harder to find the right words to say, words that would be calming and comforting, and also that would be true. She had no time or space for anger over the girl's forbidden meeting with Jonas Thatcher; those would be wasted words anyway. How many times had she been warned to keep away from him? Nellie also knew better than to make promises relating to matters over which she had no control: Promising that she would live for a specific length of time or that Beau and Eubie would return from the war would be more wasted words. No mortal could know the time or circumstances of another's passing away.

"Didn't you tell me, Ruthie, that Jonas's mother was sickly?"

Ruthie nodded her head against her mother's shoulder. "She got that flu from his uncle who came home and died, and she didn't ever get well."

A shudder coursed through Nellie powerful enough that Ruthie felt it. She stepped away from her mother, but not out of her embrace. "You cold, Ma?"

"No." Nellie shook her head but could not dispel the anger that rose within her. "You got to start mindin' us, Ruthie. 'Spose you had got sick from that boy? 'Spose you had brought that sickness here to this house and Uncle Will had got sick and died? Or your Pa? Or me?"

Nellie watched realization birthed in her daughter's eyes, followed by remorse, and she pulled the girl close again with a sigh of thanksgiving: One lesson learned. "Anyway, Ruthie, you know I ain't sickly, don't you? You know I'm strong and full of life, don't you?"

"Yes, Ma."

"And we all read them last letters from Beau and Eubie..."

"And they was scared, Ma. They said the war was something awful."

"And they promised to be careful, didn't they? And to come home soon?" She felt Ruthie nod against her. "Then we just have trust them, don't we? And hope and pray they'll be safe."

"I don't want you to die, Ma, and I don't want my brothers to die in France."

"And I don't want you, Ruthie Girl, thinkin' and worryin' 'bout people dyin'."

"'Cause worryin' don't put no fish on the hook nor cornbread in the oven."

"You sound just like Uncle Will," Nellie said, laughing through the tears she'd tried so hard not to shed. "And that's just right..."

"'Cause worryin' a thing to death won't bring it back to life."

They shared a laugh, mother and daughter, both understanding the wisdom inherent in the sayings of the old man. Big Si called him pigheaded and mule-stubborn, but nobody ever called him wrong about anything. He refused to even think about going to Belle City for any reason, but it was he who insisted, ever since Beau and Eubie left, that they all go monthly to get news of the war—and of the world—and he took more pleasure than any of them in the notion of hospitals and banks and colleges and big, painted-white homes owned by "used-to-be slaves," and the newspapers and magazines they brought back. "Just look-a-here," he'd exclaim, turning pages and studying photographs of the men and women making names for themselves in the world. "Just look at all these fine Colored people. No wonder white folks miss slavery so hard. They don't want to be seein' no Colored folks look like these here."

The old man kept the newspapers and magazines beside him all the time, periodically opening them to look at the images, but sometimes just to hold them, caress them, and smile a secret smile of pride and satisfaction, even when he'd been told that the stories were not all about success and accomplishment—indeed most were not. A little more than fifty years since the end of slavery and most Colored people still lived meager, marginal lives, dictated by the whims of white people who resented their freedom. But it was that freedom that mattered to Uncle Will and First Freeman and all those like them: Freedom was all that mattered.

"Come Christmas-time, all the pictures in here gon' be Colored soldiers comin' home from that War," he said one evening in late October after a family trip to Belle City." They all looked at him, and nobody said a word, but five people were thinking the same thing: How do you know that? "'Cause Maisy Cooper told me," he said, answering the unasked question. "Y'all know Maisy's a conjure woman, right? She sees things, and she sees the war over by Christmas."

Everybody was smiling now, willing to accept the conjure woman's vision because they wanted it to be true. "She see my boys' pictures in them papers?" Nellie asked, her smile slowly fading as the old man closed and folded the papers and put them on the floor, leaving that question unanswered.

Maisy Cooper was right on both counts, but nobody remembered her predictions when the Armistice was signed on the eleventh hour of the eleventh day of the eleventh month, ending the War to End All Wars, and when, shortly thereafter, the soldiers began returning home, first in a trickle, and then wave after wave of them. Nobody was surprised that the white soldiers got to come home first because everybody was used to Colored being last, but it meant that Nellie would have to wait for her boys at home instead of in Belle City, which is what she wanted to do. "Don't nobody know when they comin,' Nellie, and you can't just be settin' 'round in Belle City waitin' on the gov'ment," Big Si told his wife, sounding grumpier than he intended; he was as anxious as she to have his sons back home and safe and would gladly have waited in Belle City as long as it took were it not for the fact of the farm needing his attention—and hers. "Don't worry, Nellie," he'd said, patting her gently on the back, "Mr. First gon' bring our boys to us soon as they get to Belle City—he promised."

"But...but..." Nellie sputtered in a rare display of confused uncertainty. "How they gon' find Freeman? How Freeman gon' find them?"

In his own rare—at least publicly—display, Silas Thatcher hugged his wife and kissed the top of her head. "We wrote 'em a letter and told 'em, Nellie. Leastways that professor did. Told 'em to run everything through the people at the college and First Freeman. 'Member?"

Nellie nodded; she remembered, though she didn't like having—needing— to route such a crucial aspect of her family's life through third parties. "I just hope it's soon. I want my boys back home where they belong. We won't have no Thanksgiving nor Christmas till they home."

"No Thanksgiving?" Little Si asked, thinking of feast that wouldn't happen.

"No Christmas?" Tobias asked, thinking of the new shotgun he was hoping could happen.

Nellie shook her head. "Not until Beau and Eubie come home. Then we'll have one big celebration, Thanksgiving and Christmas all together at one time."

– 1919 –

Children all over Georgia, whether they lived on a farm or not, knew not to complain about the rain because the farmers always needed rain. However, the rainfall in the waning days of January caused even the farmers to complain: It was, quite simply, too much of a good thing. It had rained for three days and nights. True, it was a slow, steady, soaking rain, the kind that would find and feed the deepest roots of the oldest and most noble trees, and therefore better than the hard, driving rain that would carry away the topsoil like some huge shovel. Still, enough was enough, especially when Carrie's Creek was lapping at her banks and starting to behave more like a river than a creek, running swiftly, with visible currents west, toward the big river that she fed. First thing in the morning, several times during the day, and last thing at night, the creek was checked, the water level monitored, and by the end of the third day, as night fell, anybody and everybody who knew Carrie's Creek, knew that unless the rain stopped that very minute, trouble was upon them. Since the second day of rain they'd been preparing themselves for the need to run to higher ground—stacking fire wood, furniture and clothes, and jars of food in attics and packing necessary items they'd take if—when—the time came to run.

"Get up, y'all! Get up!" Big Si was running and yelling—he had to yell to be heard over the pounding, driving rain. No longer slow and steady, it was coming down torrentially, fanned and fueled by a cold and furious wind blowing from the northwest. If it had been in the fall of the year instead of the winter, they'd have thought it was tail-end of one of the hurricanes that blew up the Atlantic coast every year, felling trees and dumping water by the bucketfull.

Nellie lit a lantern while all of them simultaneously pulled on clothes and shoes, nobody saying or asking anything. If Big Si told them to get up in the middle of the night, it could only be because it was time to run from the creek.

"Where's the water?" Uncle Will asked.

"Outside the door," Big Si answered, not attempting to hide the fear he felt. "Y'all grab what you gon' carry and let's go."

"What about the animals?" Nellie said.

"We'll take the mule and the wagon, but we'll have to carry things to it— can't bring 'em here to the house. The water's too high. The dogs'll follow us to high ground."

"The chickens," Nellie said, almost plaintively. "What about the chickens?"

Big Si looked as miserable as he felt and he shook his head. "We just have to hope and pray the water don't rise that high 'cause we can't carry no chickens."

"Lord have mercy," Uncle Will said, and he said it again, over and over. Nellie took his arm and then hugged him tight and close until he quieted. Then she told Tobias to help the old man gather his things, but Tobias did the gathering alone: Uncle Will was frozen in place at the front window, looking out into the storm, muttering under his breath.

The family worked fast and efficiently, and in just a few moments, burlap bags filled with as much food as they could carry and the best of the clothes and shoes they owned were loaded on their backs. "Come on, y'all, we got to go now." Big Si stood at the front door, ready to open it. "Tobias, you go first. Carry what you can and head straight for the barn, get the mule hitched up and ready."

"Yessir," Tobias said as Big Si opened the door.

"And y'all—watch out for snakes. The water's up and they looking for higher ground too." He was yelling and the wind and water were blowing in his face as he struggled to shut the door. "Nellie, you and Ruthie go next. Take the lights and candles with you, and try to keep the matches dry; we really gon' need 'em. Tobias oughta have the barn door open by the time y'all get there." He wrapped them in tight, brief embrace, helped them secure the bags and rolls they carried, opened the door, and steadied them as they descended the steps—steps that now were covered by water, ending all their unspoken hopes that their home might be spared.

"Pa..." Little Si saw the water rising even as they stood there.

"You go now, Son, and keep close on your ma and sister."

"Pa?"

"I'm comin', Son, don't worry. I'm gon' get Uncle Will, and we'll be right behind you. Go on now. Hurry up!" And he pushed his youngest boy out into the wild weather, not bothering this time to close the door—the water was already making its way in. He grabbed his uncle's arm and it felt like a twig. This big, strong man whom he called Uncle but who was the father to him that he'd never had—this man looked into the storm and wept like a little child.

"Lordhavemercylordhavemercylordhavemercylordhavemercy…"

"Come on, Uncle Will, we got to go. Come on." And when the old man didn't—or could not—move, Big Si got behind him and pushed, holding him tightly around the waist, until they descended the steps, and stayed behind him, pushing, as they sloshed through the dark, swift-moving water. Only the flicker of the kerosene lantern in the barn, blowing back and forth in the strong wind, was their guide to safety, for the rain was coming down in sheets, obscuring any landmark, and the ground was a raging river.

Hands and arms reached out to grab them as they reached the barn door, pulling them in for a brief moment's respite from the storm.

"He's shaking like a leaf." Nellie wrapped her arms around Uncle Will and murmured to him as if her were one of her children, and there was fear in the look that she shared with her husband: Would the old man survive this?

"Where we goin', Pa?" Ruthie asked.

"To the highest ground that's also safe ground."

"You think we got to worry 'bout white people *now*?"

"They got to get to high ground too, Little Sister," Tobias said, answering for his father, sounding like his father, "and they likely not to be none too happy to share it with us."

"Then where we goin'?" Little Si asked, looking down at the two inches of water he was standing in.

Big Si looked at his wife. "Maisy Cooper's place, I think," Nellie said.

Big Si nodded. Maisy Cooper's place would be perfect: She had a barn big enough for all of them—including the animals and the wagon—to take shelter in; but more importantly, she and her people were in touch with First Freeman and would let him know not to worry. She also would help them soothe and comfort Uncle Will. She was, like him, a former slave, and therefore would know what he was thinking and feeling. In fact, Big Si and Nellie had the simultaneous but independent thought that they should have consulted Maisy months ago about Uncle Will's behavior; he hadn't been himself since the night Carney Thatcher came back home and died.

"Si, you drive the wagon," Big Si said. "Me and Tobias gon' walk in front and guide it. Can't hardly see the road and Lord knows we don't need a mule with a broke leg. Nellie, you and Ruthie keep Uncle Will between you. Hold him tight. And put the dogs up there too. They can't keep their feet in this water and mud."

Closing the barn door felt as useless and foolish an effort as closing the door to the house had been: The water was coming and no door could stop it, and yet the act was necessary. This was their home and not one of them had spent a night away from it, either since being born in it or since moving into it or, in Uncle Will's case, since it was constructed, and Nellie knew that whatever trouble had taken hold of the old man in the last few months would be made worse by this night. As if to prove her correct, he began to moan and sway back and forth; Nellie and Ruthie held him tightly. Then he began a wordless moan that turned into a high wail and finally into a single-word keening:

"*Carrie! Carrie! CA-REEE! CA-REEE!*"

He was still rocking and wailing when they pulled into Maisy Cooper's yard more than an hour later—an hour that felt to all of them like a week or a month—a journey that should have taken less than half the time. There was a light on in Maisy's barn; she knew the rising water would send people to her and she was waiting, but it was the barking of her dogs that told her when to turn up the lanterns and open the barn door because she could hear no sound beyond the howling wind slamming rain against every surface in creation.

Not only was it dry in Maisy's barn, it was warm, too. She had laid several layers of burlap bags over piles of paper and rags just inside the door, and that's where she stopped the wagon and, after closing and locking the door, told them to drop their wet clothes where they stood, to unhitch the mule and "put 'im back yonder in that last stall, and y'all go stand 'round them buckets," for she'd filled a dozen metal receptacles of varying shapes and sizes with coal and wood chunks and set them ablaze and it was like having that many small cook stoves in the barn. Big Si, Little Si and Tobias obeyed immediately and gratefully. Maisy looked questioningly at Nellie and Ruthie, still sitting in the wagon, then she peered closely at Uncle Will.

"Oh, good God in heaven." And the old woman, as old as Will himself, clambered up into the wagon and cupped her friend's face in her hands. "Willie Thatcher. You hear me talkin' to you, Willie Thatcher? Look at me."

He opened his eyes and tried to focus them. "Carrie's out there and I got to go find her, Maize," he said, struggling now to free himself from the womens' embrace and climb down out of the wagon.

"Let him get down," Maisy said, then, calling out, "Silas! Y'all come here quick-like!"

Big Si and his sons grabbed Uncle Will before he could open the barn door and, with Maisy directing, they rid him of soaking wet clothes, got him dressed in dry clothes and covered in blankets and seated in a chair surrounded by buckets of warmth and sipping "some special tea, guaranteed to warm up your insides." Maisy had thought of and prepared for everything: There were roasted yams and biscuits to go with the tea and enough chunks of wood and coal to keep the mini-stoves going all night and more than enough straw-filled pallets for every body to sleep "up off the hard ground."

"We truly thank you, Miss Maisy," Nellie said, hugging the old woman, who waved off the thanks.

"We all fam'ly 'round here; leastways, that's how I feel," and she looked at Uncle Will who seemed to be looking at people and places only he could see. "Let's see if he'll eat a little bit more, then get him laid down to sleep."

"Carrie? Is that you, Carrie?"

"It's me, Maisy, Willie. Here's a biscuit with some molasses and butter on it."

He took the biscuit, ate it, and nodded thanks. "I got to go find Carrie," he said, suddenly standing up and seeming to regain all of his physical strength.

"We found her, Willie. We already found her," Maisy said. "You need to get some sleep now, so you'll be fit come the morning."

"You found Carrie?"

With the women speaking soothingly to him and the men all but wrestling him down and onto a pallet, Uncle Will finally settled, though the screaming of the wind and the rain pounding the barn on all sides didn't help matters. He was exhausted—spent emotionally as well as physically—and he slept almost immediately, to the immense relief of all of them.

"I didn't know he was took so bad," Maisy exclaimed.

"He ain't like this all the time," Big Si said in defense of his uncle. "It was all this rain, brought it on real bad, like you see him. He ain't like this all the time."

Maisy nodded her understanding, sympathy and sadness turning her deep-set, dark eyes into seemingly bottomless pools. "We hoped not to see rain like this again, hoped not to see the creek up this high again." She sighed deeply and, like Uncle Will and First Freeman, seemed to sink in on herself, seemed to disappear into another dimension. No longer straight and strong, the old ones seemed to wither and become ancient, to become slaves again. They all understood this transformation and the reason for it, but Ruthie, especially, disliked it.

"Miss Maisy," Nellie said, speaking as gently as she did to Uncle Will and Mr. First. "Miss Maisy," she said again, successfully returning the old woman to the present and to her conversation as if there'd been no break in her thought.

"Y'all know 'bout the last time the water got this high? Must be, oh, almost forty years ago, I reckon. That little, bitty creek ran like a river, knocking down and taking away everything got in its way: Crops, trees, barns...people." Maisy looked at Big Si. "Carrie. Willie's baby sister. Your Ma. You knowed all about that?"

Big Si nodded. "Yes, ma'am. Uncle Will told me."

"That's why he keeps on calling for Carrie—he's back there in his mind. Even after all these years, I don't think Willie ever got over losing Carrie. Not like she went."

"He's been...different...ever since Juneteenth," Nellie said and was startled by Maisy's reaction: The old woman began walking around in circles and muttering to herself. "Miss Maisy. What's wrong with you? What I say to upset you like that?"

"Juneteenth! You say Willie been troubled in his mind since back then? Now, here come all this rain. Carney Thatcher. That's what it is."

"What Carney Thatcher got to do with the rain?" Nellie and Big Si asked together.

"Poor Willie. No wonder his mind been took." She walked in circles for a while as they watched her, wondering and waiting. "Carrie got drowned down by the old Belle City Road. Y'all know where I mean? And two men was down there, scooping fish up out the creek with a net—that's how thick they was in the water—and then here come Carrie, riding along in the water with the fish. She was trying to grab hold of tree limbs, anything she could to save herself, and when she saw the men on the bank she screamed and hollered for them to save her."

"But they didn't," Ruthie said.

"They let her get drowned," Tobias said.

"Uncle Will and some men went looking for her," Little Si said.

Maisy nodded. "That's right, Chil'ren. My 'Zekiel was one of the men went with Willie. All night they was out, till they found Carrie...oh, Lord." She wiped her eyes. "One of them men on the bank, one of them men that day—one of 'em was Carney Thatcher."

For a long moment, the only sound was that of the wind and rain and Uncle Will snoring. Then Big Si said, "He ain't never told me that."

"Far as I know, he ain't never said Carney Thatcher's name from that day to this."

"Then he shows up Juneteenth," Nellie said, "and brings it all back to his mind."

"Well," Maisy said, and said no more. She went to the wood pile and gathered up several large chunks of wood, and without being told, the three children scurried to help her fill all the little stoves; they'd certainly be dry enough and warm enough overnight.

"I'll walk with you back to your house, Miss Maisy," Big Si said, but she waved him off and headed for the back wall of the barn and into one of the stalls where her mules were kept. "I had me a back door put in here," she said, "and laid a stone walkway, when 'Zekiel took so sick a while back. I can get up to the house right quick."

"Well, then, take these things with you," Big Si said, grabbing a burlap bag from the back of the wagon and extending it to Maisy, who accepted it with a questioning look. "Just some few things, Miss Maisy: Some flour and eggs and a couple of rabbits, already skinned and dressed."

She, in return, extended warm thanks, then looked around the barn. "Leave one of these lamps lit so if anybody else comes..."

"We'll take care of 'em good as you took care of us," Nellie said.

Maisy smiled then and her face lit up like a young girl's. "I know you will, Daughter. Now, y'all get some rest so we all can be ready for whatever the rest of this night and the day that's coming is gon' bring us."

The night brought five more seekers of high, dry ground, and, as promised, they were fed, warmed, dried and given a place to sleep. The following morning brought a bright and clear blue sky, close-to-freezing temperatures, and a William Thatcher returned to himself and wondering, loudly, "What we doin' in here? This 'Zekiel Cooper's barn. What we doin' in 'Zekiel's barn?"

It took Big Si several minutes to quiet, calm and soothe Uncle Will, who first refused to believe that he didn't remember why he'd awakened in a barn or the harrowing journey in the middle of the night that had brought him here. Then, as truth and reality set in, his agitation grew into anger. He ordered everybody up and out. "Y'all hurry up. We got to go!"

"We can't just leave, Uncle Will," Nellie said, trying to reason with him. "We got to thank Miss Maisy..."

"Maisy know I'm thankful to her. Now come on. We got to get on home. I don't want my house left. I don't want my house empty. I need to be in my house!"

The return journey was an improvement because it was day and because it wasn't raining in sheets, but the road was every bit as treacherous and dangerous as the previous night; now deep mud sucked at the wagon's wheels and the mule's feet, and debris made the road all but impassable. "I got to go home. I got to get to my house." Uncle Will grabbed Tobias by the arm. "You come with me. Me and him gon' walk. I got to go see 'bout my house."

From the Recorded Memories of Ruth Thatcher McGinnis

Uncle Will said it took more than five years to build their house because they could only work on it when they weren't working for Carney Thatcher, and because they couldn't do it alone, the two of them, Will and Carrie, and Uncle Will said old Carney didn't want to see them succeed at building a house or farming anyway. He only gave them the land so that they would stay and help him work his farm. See, after the end of the Civil War, many of the slaves, when they realized they were free, just took off. Didn't know where they were going, just that it would be away from wherever they had been enslaved. Quite a few others stayed where they were, figuring, as that old saying goes, that the devil they knew was preferable to the devil they didn't. Uncle Will didn't stay because he trusted Carney Thatcher or felt any loyalty to him but because he thought it would be too dangerous to be wandering around, especially for Carrie. Young Colored women, he said, were not safe, free or slave. He also said since they didn't know how to be free, they agreed that they should take some time to figure out what freedom really meant. They knew that Carney needed their help. His two oldest sons had been killed in the War and his other children—two girls and two boys—were too young to be much help. So they stayed, but Uncle Will said they knew Carney still thought of them as his property—as his slaves—and he didn't think he had to pay them. And, too, Carney Thatcher was almost as broke as they were. So, early one morning when they should have been headed to the field, they were headed up the road. Uncle Will said he timed it so that Carney would see them but they'd be far enough away that he couldn't shoot them. Instead, he came running after them, screaming and cursing, waving his arms, shaking his fists, calling them niggers. He caught up to them and wanted to know what they thought they were doing. "We ain't slaves no more," Uncle Will said he told him. "You have to pay us or we're free to go." He said Carney cursed at them for a while, then begged and pleaded with them not to leave. That's when Uncle Will made his offer: He and Carrie would stay in exchange for some land of their own. It took some doing, but Carney finally agreed to give them forty acres near the creek, land that was marshy and swampy because the creek flooded so often. But they took it because now they had something of their own.

Before they could build their house, though, they had to lay a solid foundation, one that wouldn't rot or float away. They dug a rectangular-shaped hole twelve inches deep by twenty feet long and fifteen feet wide and they filled it with rocks and stones, the largest they could find, from the creek bottom and from their land, which was rocky as well as swampy. It took almost a year, during which time they lived in a Union Army tent. Nobody knows where the tent came from but William and Carrie were grateful for it. And to answer your question, Sissy, it took so long because they didn't have any tools other than what they could fashion from sticks and stones and their own hands. Remember, these people had been slaves. They owned nothing, they had nothing. The only reason they didn't starve to death was because the forests and the creek were full of food, and because, as Uncle Will liked to say, things grew in earth touched by Carrie's hands.

After that, things got a bit better for William and Carrie because it got to be known that they were landowners. Many of the former slaves that had run at the first breath of freedom realized they didn't have any place to run to. They had no skills other than farming, no money, no jobs. William and Carrie welcomed former slaves on their land. All together, there were about thirty of them—men, women and a few children. Land was cleared for farming, shacks were built for living, and William and Carrie became the center of a community. Everybody helped Will cut and plane the trees to build his house and it was the neighbors who planted and grew the food on Will and Carrie's farm because they spent their days working for Carney Thatcher. It was years before he knew that a community of tenant farmers lived on his land but not to his benefit. Why didn't he know? Because like all white people of that time, it never occurred to him that Colored people could or would be doing anything of interest or value or concern to him. He only cared about William and Carrie's land because he hadn't wanted them to have it; and once they had it, he assumed that because he had judged it worthless, it would be worthless. And it would have been if not for the ingenuity and creativity of Will and Carrie's neighbors. It's very important for you to understand, Sissy, that these slaves had not lived and worked on large, prosperous plantations like you see in the movies. They had belonged to small farmers like Carney Thatcher, poor, uneducated people, some of them only able to own one or two slaves. But they still were slaves and they had to work harder, in a way, than those on a big plantation where there were thirty or forty or a hundred people to do the work. So, what I'm telling you—what Uncle Will told us—was that these people who now lived on his land were good at figuring out ways to get things done. At how to make a way out of no way. And what they figured out how to do was drain the water from one part of Will's land and send it to another part. What they did, Sissy, was to create an irrigation system. When it rained too much, the water drained off and didn't flood, and when it didn't rain enough, the drainage ditches funneled water to the crops.

But back to Will and Carrie's house: The stone foundation was finished in the summer of 1869. For more than a year, while all the people who lived and worked on their land felled trees to clear land for planting or to build their shelters, they also dedicated part of their time to planing the boards for William and Carrie's house, and they were ready to start the building. And out of nowhere—and I mean this literally because no one knew where he came from—came the biggest stroke of luck this community of Negroes had experienced in their few years of freedom: A carpenter with two bags of tools slung over his shoulders! He wouldn't tell them his name or anything about himself except to say that he was on the run. His former owner claimed that he'd stolen the tools but Carpenter, as everybody quickly came to call him, said the tools were his, that he'd been hired out and paid for his work, and that he'd bought his freedom, and his tools belonged to him. He was quickly absorbed into the community and just as quickly, he took charge of the building of William and Carrie's house. Uncle Will readily admitted that had it not been for Carpenter, the house likely would have collapsed within a year given how they had planned to construct it. The only thing they had done correctly, according to Carpenter, was to lay the stone foundation. He had the house elevated six inches above the foundation so that the ground moisture wouldn't penetrate the floorboards, and he put smudge pot hooks on the floorboards...what are smudge pots? You modern people could benefit from a healthy dose of old fashioned experience. Smudge pots, or smoke pots, burn substances that are smoky and offensive to critters: Spiders, snakes, mosquitoes. Having a crawl space beneath the house allowed air to circulate so the floorboards wouldn't mold or warp from the constant moisture, and hanging smudge pots in that space kept critters from living there. Anyway, Carpenter saw to it that the first room of William and Carrie's house— the kitchen—was completed before the bad weather set in. It was a beautiful room with a huge fireplace that also was the stove. When Carrie cooked, it was to feed most of the people in their community; that's how big this indoor pit was.

So, the house was started. It was only one room at first but that one room was solid. It was dry and warm and it was theirs, Carrie's and William's, and William loved that house more than anything or anybody—except maybe Carrie.

⸺⸺

Jonas was accepting of the fact that whenever he wasn't in school, he was to be at one his father's three businesses. "You got to be the one watchin' my money," Jonas's father had said to him, "'cause I don't trust nobody else since your Ma up and died." Jonas didn't bother to argue or complain because, in the first place, he knew it would do no good; beyond that, however, was the unspoken but nevertheless clear *quid pro quo* nature of the arrangement: Jonas could go to school every day, could even give thought and voice to the notion of going to college in Belle City, if he worked in the stores at all other times. He wasn't thrilled with the arrangement, but there was nothing he could do to change it.

The new business—*THATCHER'S DEPARTMENT STORE*—represented his Pa's decision to split the function and merchandise of the general store.

It now was a food market, and though the two establishments were across the street from each other, they were treated by Zeb, and thought of by him, as completely and totally different entities with no relationship to each other. In fact, he was a different man in each store, wearing an apron in the food market and a suit and tie in the department store; he was Zeb in the food market and Mr. Thatcher in the department store, as if furniture and clothing warranted more respect than food, and the only thing he enjoyed about either enterprise was the fact of his ownership of them and their growing profitability. But it was the pub that Zeb truly cared about because not only could he be himself there, freely and fully, he now lived there.

When Carrie's Creek flooded the previous month, Zeb's already run-down house was all but destroyed; the fresh coat of paint and the patches to the roof were too little, too late to save a structure that had been neglected for most of its existence. The flood did it—and Zeb—a favor: The house, full of mud and debris, was knocked down. So was the barn. The flooded fields were left to the land to reclaim. And Zeb, not only the proprietor of three prosperous establishments in the center of the burgeoning town of Carrie's Crossing, now owned one of the most valuable pieces of property in the area: One hundred vacant acres of developable land adjacent to the main road into and out of town.

Jonas was less pleased with his living arrangement. Shabby as the house had been, it was his home—where he was born and where his mother had lived and died—and no matter how dry and clean and nicely furnished his room above the department store was, it still was a room above a department store, necessitating a trip downstairs to use the bathroom, whether in the middle of a dark, cold night, or first thing in a dark, cold morning. Honesty, though, dictated that he acknowledge that the plusses of his new living arrangement outweighed the minuses, they being that he was but a short walk to school (walking being necessary since his horse had drowned in the flood), and he now could take all of his meals in the Crossing Café.

Jonas also enjoyed a front row seat from which he could witness all the changes that were coming to his hometown, changes that were happening so quickly that unless he wrote daily in his journal, he'd likely miss an important event: the paving of the streets and the laying of sidewalks, the erection of electrical poles and the wires that were strung between them to bring electricity to town, the arrival of the second automobile to be owned by the Baptist preacher (Doc Gray had the first), the groundbreaking for the new

Baptist Church, and the arrival of the big, noisy machines that would begin digging the two-lane road that would link Carrie's Crossing to Belle City and the rest of Georgia.

Jonas no longer had any brothers, but he did have two brothers-in-law—Cory, his sister Rachel's husband, and Clem, his sister Esther's husband, and both men now worked for Zeb, which made the old man both proud and wary. He truly was glad to be able to help his daughters, and while he'd never get over the loss of his son, he liked being able to tell his customers and friends how "his boys" were such a big help to him: Cory in charge at the food market, Clem in charge at the department store, and Jonas, "young as he is," Pa would brag to any who would listen, "watches my money better'n the bank." And it was true—Jonas was so good at balancing the books that the owner of the café wanted to hire him to keep his books too, but Pa surprised him by saying no. "He got to keep up with his schooling" was the reason he gave.

The entire experience was teaching Jonas some important things about himself. There was the fact of his natural proficiency with numbers and the understanding he shared with his father about the nature of business; but the other side of that was the fact of his natural preference for those numbers, for his schoolbooks, for his job of twice-daily washing the big front windows of both stores, for any activity that guaranteed his solitude and limited his interaction with the public. In fact, the only people that Jonas really liked, other than his family, were people that he now almost never had occasion to see: Little Si and Ruthie Thatcher, and he missed them so much that it hurt to think about them.

The day after the creek flooded and the water had receded, he'd snuck up the road to their house to see if they were all right. He'd had to take the road because water was still ankle deep in the woods. He was shocked to find their house empty, and it was only after he'd returned home that he realized that though all the land surrounding the house was a swampy, muddy mess, the house itself seemed to be bone-dry. There was a water line up to the third step of the house, but it went no further. There had been no time or opportunity to sneak away since that day; he'd been too busy dealing with the flood's aftermath in his own environment and, given what he'd seen of their farm, they'd be too busy, too. As far as he could tell, though, there wasn't much farm left.

The door to the market slammed open so hard that the bell didn't clang but once, loudly, instead of its usual, gentle tinkle, tinkle, snapping Jonas out of his reverie. "Y'all better come quick an' see 'bout Zeb 'fore he do somethin' crazy.

He's madder'n a stepped on snake." The man delivering this odd message was hopping from one foot to another. Jonas didn't know his name; he only knew that he was a regular at the pub. Clem hurried from behind the counter.

"What's wrong? Where's Pa at?"

"At the Bar, 'long with five or six of them Temp'rance ladies singing they songs 'bout the evils of drinkin' whiskey."

Jonas was off the ladder and out the front door like a shot. He saw the gathering crowd in front of *ZEB'S* at the same time that he heard his Pa cussing louder than the Christian Temperance ladies were singing.

"Get 'way from here! Get from in front of my place!" Zeb was shouting and jumping up and down and waving his arms, and he was so red in the face that it frightened Jonas. He pushed through the crowd and tried to grab his Pa, and got knocked to the ground; he'd come up on Zeb's blind side—not that it mattered in that moment; Zeb would have knocked down the Good Lord.

Several of Zeb's bar patrons had joined in the verbal assault on the women, then several of the onlookers joined in the song, and that's when the pushing and shoving and name-calling started. Realizing that perhaps things were about to get out of control, the women picked up their skirts and hurried away. Without a focus for their attention, the onlookers drifted away, too. Zeb was panting and sweating like he'd run a mile, and so red in the face that Jonas was on the verge of sending for the doctor.

"You got to calm down, Pa."

"I ain't got to do no such. Them people got to stay 'way from me and my bizness, that's what's got to happen. They got no right to tell me how to run my bizness."

"Pa, listen." Jonas grabbed him by the shoulders, startling him into calming down. "You know 'bout these Christian Temperance Union ladies. I read that newspaper article to you."

"That ain't got nothin' to do with me. That was way yonder in New York or Chicago."

"It's everywhere, Pa. The law's gonna be everywhere."

"What law, Boy? Ain't no Temp'rance lady law got nothin' to do with me." Zeb pulled away and was headed back to his bar when Jonas grabbed his arm.

"You got to listen, Pa. The law is for everybody. It starts next year in January, and it says you can't sell whiskey no more. Nobody can, in New York or Chicago or Georgia."

Zeb looked at his son like he'd turned purple, grown a tail, and was breathing fire. "What you mean I can't sell whiskey no more? What kinda law is that? Who made it?"

"The President and the Congress."

Zeb snorted, then spat. "Damn gov'ment. I got nothin' to do with them and they got less than nothin' to do with me. When they give me back my son, then they can talk to me 'bout what I do. Otherwise, I don't want to hear nothin' from 'em or 'bout 'em."

Every physical act from sun up until way after dark, in the days and weeks following the flood, involved clearing and cleaning the land in an effort to salvage some crop that might be edible. And every thought that was not related to how they would feed themselves in the immediate wake of the destruction of the crops, was of Beaudry and Eubie and when they would return. The war had been over for three months. They knew that the journey was a long one—an ocean voyage that took several weeks. But since they hadn't been to Belle City since the flood, they had no idea how long the wait would or should be. And, because they'd made no visit to the college and had no talks with the professors, they hadn't heard any of the stories about the returning soldiers and how some families secretly were thinking that the husbands, sons, fathers, and brothers who returned to them broken in body, mind and spirit, might have been better off had they perished in a muddy, bloody field somewhere in France or Germany or Belgium or Russia. Big Si and Nellie Thatcher certainly never would have thought they'd be better off without their Beau, even the spiritually wasted Beaudry Thatcher whom First Freeman returned home to his family late on an early March night.

Freeman had promised that he would come with Beau and Eubie as soon as they arrived home and there'd been a light burning in the front room since the announcement of the war's end. Big Si, who'd taken to sleeping in his clothes, was up and at the door at the sound of the first knock. "What?' he said, his face pressed against the door.

"It's me," First Freeman said, and everybody except Uncle Will was standing behind Big Si when he opened the door. Nobody paid heed to the gust of frigid air that blew in before either of the people entered. "Come on, Son, it's aw'right," the old man said as gently as if speaking to a young child, and he pushed a gaunt, hollow-eyed young man into the room.

Like all mothers everywhere, it was Nellie who first recognized her son in the stranger. She inhaled deeply, then breathed his name and reached for him, pulling him into a one-armed embrace, her other arm outstretched to enfold the other son, and she held it there until the truth dawned: There was only one son. Then she screamed and Beau blinked, realized where he was and with whom, and grabbed his mother and held on. Then everybody else grabbed Beau and held on. First Freeman closed and locked the door, then stirred the fire to life and added several logs and lit the lanterns.

Nellie was weeping so hard she couldn't speak a full sentence; she just kept repeating her sons' names over and over: "Beau, Eubie, Beau, Eubie."

Finally Beau spoke, a harsh croak of a voice, and everybody stilled to hear him. "Eubie ain't dead, Ma, Pa. He ain't dead, you hear?"

"Then where is he, Beau?"

Beau looked at his questioner as if at a stranger. Then he smiled, and the smile turned into a huge grin, and he became their Beau. "Ruthie. Is that *you*? Is that growed up lady my baby sister?" And he grabbed her and hugged her and swung her all around. She wrapped her arms around his neck and held on, unaware that she was crying. And when he finally put her down he grabbed his father and both men wept, the younger one sounding more like a little boy than a grown man. Then the big brother freed himself, wiped his eyes dry with the backs of his hands, and turned his attention to his little brothers—both now as tall as himself. He extended his arms and they rushed into his embrace. They didn't know what to say to each other so they just stood there, holding each other up, supporting each other. They stood like that until they heard Nellie say, "Eubie?" And it was not a name she spoke but a question.

Beaudry turned to his mother. "Eubie ain't dead, Ma, I swear. And he ain't hurt, neither."

"Then where is he, Beau?"

"He stayed there. In France."

"How, if the war is over?" Big Si demanded to know.

"Why?" his three younger siblings demanded in unison, the three of them looking and sounding so much alike that Beau felt as if he'd been away for twenty years instead of two.

"'Cause they treat Colored better over there than here. 'Cause he says he can be a man over there and he can't be here. They had parties for us, those French people did, and they treated us just like they treated the white soldiers, like we wasn't no different from them."

"Then why didn't you stay, Beau?" Tobias asked, and the look his pa gave him made him back up a step.

Beau looked at them, from one to the other. "'Cause of y'all...and 'cause all white people is the same to me, I don't care what language they talk. Fact is, it was a whole lot worse to me, not understandin' what they was sayin' while they was smilin' at me, than if they was cussin' and yellin' and callin me nigger."

"They don't do that, Beau? Cuss at us and call us niggers?" Little Si's eyes had widened at the thought though he couldn't really comprehend it. Then he thought about Jonas, who was his best friend and who wasn't anything like his pa. He wanted to talk more, to hear more about white people who didn't hate Colored people, but then Beau gave his head a forceful shake, as if trying to rid his brain of all the thoughts or memories residing there.

"Don't matter whether they do or not," he said, and suddenly he no longer looked like Beaudry Thatcher but again like the too-thin, bald, wild-eyed stranger Mr. First had brought into their home on a dark and cold March night.

Suddenly everybody was speaking at once: "Y'all need to eat," Big Si said, at the same time that Nellie said, "Beau, you hungry?" Tobias said, "Beau, we got a mule." Little Si said, "I can shoot the bow and arrow as good as any Injun." Ruthie said, "Guess what, Beau? I'm goin' to college." But it was First Freeman's growly baritone that overrode it all: "Where Will'am?" he said, and there was an almost accusatory tone to his voice.

Big Si looked toward the closed door that led up to the attic. "He sleeps like a dead man, Mr. First. Been that way ever since what happened on Juneteenth."

Beaudry was back to himself. "What's wrong with Uncle Will? What happened to him on Juneteenth?" He headed for the door. "I'm gon' go get him."

"Beau!" That much hadn't changed: His mother's quiet but powerful voice stopped him in his tracks and he turned to face her, a grown man who'd lived through a war, true, but first, his mother's son. "Sometimes when he first wakes up, he's...confused. You wake him up quick, this time of night—" She raised her hands, then brought them to her face and pressed, hard, as if she could contain or constrain the too many emotions inside her.

"Lord have mercy," Freeman said. "Y'all shoulda told me Will'am was took so bad."

"It ain't all the time," Big Si said defensively. "In fact, most times he's his usual self."

"What happened on Juneteenth?" Beaudry said again, and they told him. "You say he's dead? Good. That means I don't have to go kill him."

They could have been carved statues so still and silent were they, standing close together, almost in a circle, around the beloved son and brother who now was equally brooding—and quite possibly dangerous—and a stranger. He might have been able to kill white men in Germany or France, but he certainly could not kill a white man in Georgia.

"That kinda talk—that'll get you kilt," First Freeman said.

"I don't care," Beaudry said.

"It'll get your Ma, your Pa, your brothers and your sister and Will'am kilt, too."

Beaudry was silent and still for a moment. "It ain't right."

"No, it ain't right. Ain't never been right, won't never be right, Son, but ain't nothin' we can do 'bout any of it," Big Si said, his big hand wrapped almost all the way around the too thin arm of his son, holding him, holding on to him.

"They kilt a boy over in Sylvester not too long ago. Like you, he just come back from over yonder in the War, still had on his uniform. He said he wasn't payin' no more mind to no Jim Crow. They 'rested him and give him thirty days but a mob of white folks dragged him outta the jail and strung him up."

"That's why Eubie stayed in France," Beau said.

"But what will he *do*, Beau? What can he do in France?" Nellie asked.

"Farm, just like here. He already good as got him a farm—and a wife to go with it."

"No!" Nellie's one word cut like a hunting knife. "No. No. No. I ain't havin' that. No boy of mine is gon' marry with no white woman, 'specially no foreign white woman."

They all looked at her, no one of them willing—or able—to speak. Then all eyes shifted from Nellie to Big Si with the unspoken message: *Say something. Do something.*

Big Si cleared his throat. "Ain't nothin' we can do 'bout it, Nellie."

"Yes, I can."

"How? With him way over there and us over here?"

"I'm goin' to Belle City to talk to...what's that professor's name, Mr. First? The one who can read and talk that language?"

"You ain't goin' to no Belle City," Big Si said.

"I'm goin' to France if I have to. I want my boy back and I mean to have him back and nobody livin' can stop me."

Little Si, Ruthie and Jonas were so happy to see each other that they hugged and danced and whooped and hollered and laughed, all of them talking at once. They didn't have long to spend together this Friday night: Jonas knew he should be at the market helping Cory with the end-of-the-week shoppers and the money they spent, and Ruthie and Little Si were supposed to be hunting and fishing—finding something to put into the stew pot that would make the few onions and turnips they had stretch into a real meal. They weren't thinking about duty, though; they were, for the first time in a long time, just being children—doing what they wanted to do for a change instead of heeding parental dictates. Ruthie and Little Si also were getting a quickie of a spelling lesson.

"How does it feel to go to school every day, Jonas? I wish I could go to school every day. I'd be so happy." Ruthie grabbed the book that Jonas offered, staring so hard at the words and the images, imprinting them on her mind and memory.

"What part do you like the best?" Little Si asked. "I'd like reading the stories the best."

"I like writing the stories the best," Jonas said. "We get to write our own stories, anything we want to write about."

"You write about it raining and the creek flooding and killing all the crops?"

Jonas shook his head. "Nuh uh. My own stories, the ones I make up."

"Like what, then?" Little Si demanded to know.

Jonas was quiet for a moment. "Like me—not real me, make believe me, living in Belle City in a big house and having a motorcar and a radio and diff'rent shoes for every day."

What began as a giggle turned into a loud guffaw as Ruthie tried to imagine Jonas as a Belle City dandy. "And a hat, Jonas, you got to have hat," she said through her laughter, remembering photographs she'd seen in newspapers and magazines of fancy white men—and the real thing she'd seen in Belle City on the drive through town to get to the Black colleges.

"Yeah," Jonas said thoughtfully, "a hat, maybe a couple of hats."

"How you spell hat?" Little Si asked, grabbing the spelling book from Ruthie.

Jonas spelled 'hat' and both his friends repeated it several times. "Show us how to write it," Ruthie said, and Jonas did. Then they sat on the ground that had finally dried out from the flood, though being mid-April it wasn't as warm as it could be. The forest floor still was covered with muck and debris and though no longer soaked and soggy, it was messy and would probably take another five or six months to begin to degrade and blend into the naturally accumulated tree and plant matter. It was on that forest floor that they sat in a circle, the three of them, legs extended straight out to make a table. Ruthie and Little Si took turns writing the words that Jonas spoke: *Hat, man, woman, cow, horse, chicken.*

"Belle City," Ruthie called out. "Tell us how to write Belle City."

"B...e..." Jonas began, and was stopped by a loud, crashing noise that sounded like a boar coming toward them through the woods, and it was almost as dangerous: By the time the three of them leapt to their feet, Beau was upon them and he had grabbed Jonas before Ruthie and Little Si could stop him. He lifted Jonas and shook him like a rag doll. Jonas's eyes were huge and fear-filled, the fear rendering him speechless.

"Beau! Stop it!" It was Little Si who found his voice first.

"You keep away from my family." Beau had Jonas up in the air, level with his own face, and the two were nose to nose, eye to eye. "You keep away from my family," he said again.

"He's our friend, Beau," Ruthie said.

"He ain't your friend."

"Yes, he is, Beau," Little Si said, risking his own health and grabbing his brother's arm.

"He is our friend, Beau, honest," Ruthie said. "Please put him down, Beau, and don't hurt him. Please." Ruthie grabbed Beau's other arm, and the bigger boy released the smaller one, who fell to the ground and, on all fours, scuttled backwards.

"Uncle Will said cain' nobody be friends with Zeb Thatcher's kin."

"Jonas ain't like his Pa," Little Si said.

Beau looked hard at Jonas. "That right? You ain't like your Pa?" Jonas nodded his head. "How come you ain't? You don't care 'bout him?"

Jonas struggled with the thought and the dilemma it posed. "I do care 'bout him. He's my Pa. But sometimes..."

"Sometimes what? Sometimes like the other day when he ran me outta town, what about sometimes like that? I went lookin' for work and he ran me outta town, tol' me wouldn't nobody in Carrie's Crossing hire a nigger to do nothin'. What you think about that?"

Jonas shook his head, misery taking the place of the fear that had so recently filled him, and he didn't know which was worse—the fear or the misery—but neither allowed him to find his voice. He just shook his head again.

"Jonas is teaching us to read and write, Beau, 'cause we ain't got no school," Little Si said as he bent down to pick up the book. "See?"

Beau snatched the book from his brother and tossed it at Jonas. "Keep your book and your teachin' 'cause we don't need 'em."

"Yes, we do." Ruthie grabbed his arm and hung on to him. "I want to learn to read and write, Beau, and we ain't got no school. I want to go to college in Belle City. Ma said I can go, but I got to read and write first."

The forest air was soft and quiet and the three human beings did nothing to disturb it for a long moment. The three Colored Thatchers stood together facing the white Thatcher, no more than four feet separating them, the whole world between them.

"Will you tell me about the war?" Jonas asked in small voice.

"Naw, I ain't tellin' you nothin'."

"Please, Mr. Beau. Please."

Before his anger could take him again, Beau was startled into amazement: This young white boy had called him "mister," and judging by the look on his face and the tone of his voice, he meant it. "Why you wanna know 'bout the war?"

"'Cause my brother died over yonder. In France. And we don't know nothin' 'bout it."

"Where 'bouts in France? You know that much?"

Jonas nodded. "I can't say it, but I can spell it: Y-P-R-E-S."

Beau shuddered like it was the middle of winter and closed his eyes.

"That's what was on the paper the government sent us. Pa tore it up and threw it away but I wanted to know..." Jonas stopped talking because it seemed that Beau had stopped listening, but then he opened his eyes and it was clear to the three children that what Beau Thatcher saw was something, someplace other than the springtime woods of Carrie's Crossing, Georgia.

"Belgium," Beau said in a hoarse, dry whisper, as if once again choked by the gas that had permeated the battle fields of Europe.

The three children looked at Beau, then at each other; Jonas, finally, nudged Little Si and then Ruthie, the message being: He's your brother; you ask him.

"Say what, Beau?" Ruthie touched her brother's arm, and he came back. "Say what?"

"Ypres. It's in Belgium, not France."

"Where's Belgium? Is that a country?"

Beau nodded. "Next door to France and the people there, most of 'em, speak French. They speak some other thing too...I can't remember what it's called..." He shuddered again and his whole body convulsed.

"Was it cold over there, Beau?" Little Si asked.

"Good God yeah it was cold. And wet and muddy and...and..." He shuddered again. "And the stink. Good God the stink." He finally looked at them, at Jonas. "How old was your brother?"

"Twenty," Jonas said.

"Seemed like everybody who died was eighteen or nineteen or twenty," Beau said, again in that raspy, scratchy whisper. "Our boys or theirs, didn't matter."

"Was he a hero?" Jonas asked in a tiny voice. "You a hero, a war hero."

Beau gave him a hard look.

"Was my brother a hero like you?"

"He's lucky is what he is," Beau said.

Now Jonas was mad. "He's dead. Ain't nothin' lucky 'bout bein' dead."

Beau reached out and Jonas flinched, then relaxed as Beau put a hand on his shoulder. "One day, maybe, somebody'll write a book about what it was like over yonder and you can read it and know I'm tellin' the truth when I tell you if your brother was in Ypres, he's lucky to be dead 'cause them that ain't dead, wish they was—wish they really and truly was dead 'stead of just halfway dead."

"How can somebody be halfway dead, Beau?" Ruthie asked, grabbing his arm and forcing him to look at her, to come all the way back to them. "Dead is dead, ain't it?"

"A body can be walkin' 'round but can't sleep, can't eat, can't breathe, can't think. Like all them boys what came back from Ypres and the Somme and the Argonne Forest and the Russian front." He looked hard at Jonas again. "Y'all got newspapers. You don't have to wait for nobody to write a book. It was in the newspapers how it was."

"Yessir, I know it, and I did see some newspapers, but I can't read all of what it says—"

"What you mean you can't read it? You s'posed to be teachin' them how to read and write. Ain't that what y'all claim?" Beau was back to angry, glaring at Ruthie and Little Si.

"He is teachin' us, Beau."

"He just said he can't read."

"Not good enough to know all of what's in the newspaper," Jonas said, "but I can read some."

"He can read better'n us," Little Si said.

Beau grabbed his younger siblings by the shoulders, one each in each of his large hands as he turned away from Jonas and headed home. "You stay 'way from my family," he shouted over his shoulder. And to his brother and sister, "You stay 'way from that boy, you hear? He can't read his own self but he 'gon teach y'all somethin'? Don't make no kinda sense. We got to be the stupidest people in the world, take lessons from somebody don't know no more'n we do." Then he stopped and turned back to face Jonas. "And all them white people lynchin' Colored soldiers, mad 'cause they got on a uniform: You tell them I'm a hero, see what they say."

They crashed through the woods, the four of them, in opposite directions, their minds full of thoughts too complex for their understanding, their hearts full of emotions for which they had no words. Two of them, though, were in a hurry: Jonas Thatcher to reach the Crossing Café and to the box of leftover newspapers the owner kept in the storeroom and to find someone who could and would read the stories to him; Beaudry Thatcher to tell his parents of his intention to move to Belle City as soon as he could pack a bag. "I got to get 'way from here," he muttered as he strode through the woods. "I can't stay here no longer. I got to get 'way from here." He was practically running through the dense wood.

Ruthie and Little Si were moving at a pretty good clip too because their big brother was dragging them along and they had neither the strength nor, in that moment, the will to resist him. Both were thinking, though, and wondering— imagining—the impact that Beau's decision to leave would have on their family.

From the Recorded Memories of Ruth Thatcher McGinnis

Even after the passage of so much time, this is still difficult to talk about, the things that happened then. No...no...I want to. Perhaps it will help me to talk about it. After all, it's all dead and buried—except me. So—yes, Beau left us and moved to Belle City, and Toby went with him. He went, he said, to earn money, but Miss Isabelle Johnson's family had just moved to Belle City, and Mr. Tobias Thatcher was in love! Beau went, though, because he couldn't stand living in the country, in Carrie's Crossing. He could not tolerate rain or mud or bugs. I have, of course, read about the conditions on the Front during World War I, but back then, all we knew was that Beau had been deeply affected by his experience, and that he felt he had to leave. That was hard, especially on Ma. She'd changed after Beau came home without Eubie, but losing Toby, too... well... Anyway, there was a plus side to things: With both Beau and Toby working in Belle City, for the first time our family had money and the ability to go into a store and purchase things. We still grew the basics—greens and tomatoes, peppers, onions, corn—and we had the chickens and eggs and the fruit trees. But the farm never recovered after the flood, and it didn't much matter because so many people were leaving the country and moving to cities—and not just to Belle City but to Chicago and Detroit and New York—and without Beau and Toby and with Uncle Will finally showing his age, well, we didn't need such a large operation. And to tell the truth, it was a welcome change having the boys come over once a month bringing bags of flour and sugar and rice and coffee. So, as the calendar changed, the world entered a new era. Now we call it the Jazz Age, the Roaring Twenties, but then, especially for us out in the country, away from the trends, the politics, the excitement, it was just a new year and a new decade and the changes that came to us would have made the other things pale in comparison anyway...so it's just as well that we didn't know anything about them...what things? Radio. Women getting the right to vote. And I have to laugh at this because it's the one big thing we were *aware of: Prohibition.*

– 1920 –

Z eb was so mad he couldn't even cuss. He wasn't jumping up and down and waving his arms the way he usually did when he was red hot angry. Now he just seemed stunned. And wronged is what he felt. A terrible injustice was being done to him. "*Arrest* me? You gon' lock me up? Is that what you said?" He shook his head and his long, white beard waved, flag-like, from side to side. "If I'da knowed you'd do such a thing, Tom Fordham, I'da never put you up to be chief of police."

"It don't matter who the chief of police is, Zeb, if you gon' break the law and rub everybody's face in it. I been tellin' you for three months that you couldn't keep sellin' whiskey." Carrie's Crossing Police Chief Tom Fordham shook his own head and looked as sad as Zeb was mad. He'd known this man his whole life and, despite his often crude behavior and language, Tom liked him. "Now, either you come peaceable or the State boys'll come and get you."

"I closed up my place, Tom, like the law said."

"The law says no selling whiskey, Zeb. Period. And you didn't close your place; all you did was black out the windows and bar the front door. You still got people comin' in the back door and you still sellin' whiskey and you still breakin' the law. I been lettin' you get away with it since January, but people gettin' mad with me now, talkin' 'bout runnin' Sam Croft 'gainst me come next election." He put one hand on the badge on his chest and the other on his gun. "I'm sorry, Zeb, but you got to go."

"What about my bizness?"

"Your bizness in good hands. Your three boys can take care of things."

"How long I'm gon' be gone, Tom?"

Fordham looked at the ground, then up at the man who'd been one of his Pa's best friends for more than sixty years. "A year, Zeb, at least...maybe a bit longer."

The old man wept then, and Tom wondered, as he often did, why people let things get so far gone before they'd do right, and then want to blame somebody else, like Zeb getting mad at him when this was his own stubborn fault. He saw it time and again and put it down to human nature: If people thought they could get away with something, even with breaking the law they'd give it a try. And most times, he knew, they got away with it—like Zeb had gotten away with selling his whiskey day and night for the last three months, flying in the face of the Prohibition amendment. So no, he didn't feel sorry for Zeb, his tears notwithstanding. If ever he felt sorry for anybody, it was the good, honest people. They got caught every time.

Ruthie was so glad to have her mother "back" that she wanted to jump and shout with joy. As it was, she couldn't stop smiling, couldn't resist hugging her parents and Uncle Will every time she was near them. She'd have done the same to her brothers, too, but, "Stop it, Girl!" was their response after the second hug. She only hugged First Freeman once and the guest he brought with him not at all, though, she thought, she'd have liked to, but grown women did not hug strange men and she was, after all, a grown woman.

Mr. First introduced his guest as Mack McGinnis, "and I brung him here to teach y'all the readin' and writin' you want." He pointed at Ruthie and Little Si, then added, "Y'all and all the Colored chil'ren 'round here what wants to learn."

Ruthie was so excited that she forgot she was a grown woman. She hopped from foot to foot then grabbed Little Si and they danced around a bit. Then she hugged Mr. First and thanked him, she hugged Beau and thanked him because she knew he was responsible, and she was about to hug Mr. Mack McGinnis, but the look on his face stopped her: He was grinning like it was his birthday or Christmas and somebody had just given him the best present of all. He extended his hand to Ruthie at the same time he gave her a slight bow.

"Pleased to meet you, Miss Ruth," he said.

Ruthie had never shaken hands with anyone before so she didn't know what to say or do, but she followed his lead, offering him her right hand. "Pleased to meet you, too, Mr. Mack," but the excitement was too much. "Do you like Mr. Mark Twain?"

Still smiling, he said, "Yes, ma'am, I do, but I like Mr. Charles Dickens better, and I think you will too when you read his books."

Everybody was looking at them, waiting for more talk about books and reading, but Ruth didn't know what to say; thankfully, Beau did.

"Mack been to Chicago and St. Louis—on the train. He was tryin' out to be a pitcher on one of the Colored baseball teams." He held aloft two battered gloves and a ball fraying at the seams. "Let's go play some catch!"

The celebration that currently was underway, inside the house and out, was in honor of no particular occasion other than the presence, for the first time in many months, of the entire family, and no mention of the absence of Eubie. Beau, Tobias, Mr. First and Mack McGinnis had arrived the previous afternoon—Saturday—bringing so much food and other gifts there hadn't been a place to store it all. Nellie had been up and cooking since dawn Sunday—flapjacks with butter and maple syrup and bacon for breakfast, and now she was frying chicken and making pies and cobblers. Ruthie had snapped string beans and picked greens and shucked corn for what seemed like hours while the boys had swept the yard, repaired the lean-to and added a new awning of pine boughs, and cleaned what they called the outside kitchen—the plank table and tree stump seats they used for outside eating the half or more of the year when it was too hot to cook and eat inside. Better than all of that, though, was the fact of the return of Nellie's natural warmth and humor and kindness, all of which had been absent since Beau came home from the war without Eubie.

Uncle Will also was fully himself—not at all forgetful or looking and feeling like a frail old man. This fact so delighted Mr. First that he suggested that he and his old friend drive "up the road and fetch Maisy." This they did, returning with Maisy Cooper, her daughter, son-in-law, two grandchildren, two fried chickens, and a chocolate cake.

Big Si, too, was so grateful to have his Nellie back that he hovered in the kitchen, getting in her way, until she sent him on a mission. She'd pulled him down close so she could whisper in his ear, "Go talk to that young man Mr. First brought with him, see what he's like."

"What for?" Big Si said.

"Why you think he's here?" Nellie asked.

"To teach readin' and writin' to the chil'ren," her husband said. Nellie shook her head and gave her husband the look that told him he'd said or done the wrong thing. "What?"

"Mr. Mack McGinnis is here for Ruthie, Silas. Can't you see anything?"

It took several seconds but finally he did see, and then he couldn't catch his breath. A man was here *for his baby girl?* "No," he said. Then, "Not yet, Nellie. Not yet."

"It's time, Si."

"Not yet, Nellie."

"She's the same age I was when I married with you. She's a grown woman now."

Silas wanted to yell, *"She's* not *a grown woman, she's my baby girl."* but he knew he was wrong—on both counts—and it was the sudden memory of old Beaudry Eubanks, Nellie's Pa, that calmed and steadied him, for he'd had to prove himself in a hundred different ways before that old man would let him marry Nellie—who had, as she rightly reminded him, just turned fifteen herself. Now he knew and felt what old man Eubanks knew and felt: A man was proud of his sons, especially if those sons were good men, but what a man felt for his daughter, especially if he didn't have but one—Silas Thatcher wasn't much for words on any given day and he certainly didn't have the words to express this feeling. He gave his Nellie a kiss on top of her head and went out the back door. Good thing she was facing the stove, her back to him, or he'd have seen the river of tears streaming down her face and been more confused than ever.

That Mack McGinnis was a fine looking young man could not be disputed. He was tall—over six feet—and lean but muscular, leading Big Si to wonder what else he did besides teach. He also was the kind of man other men looked up to; he could see that from the way his own sons treated and reacted to him, including Beau, who probably was a year or two older, because on closer inspection, McGinnis wasn't as old as Silas had first thought. It was the man's bearing that gave him age, because he wasn't much older than nineteen or twenty. He was dark brown in color and had a head full of curly black hair and dark, deep-set eyes that never seemed still: No matter what he was doing, he was watching everything, but he paid particular attention to the road (Freeman no doubt had told him what happened on Juneteenth) and to Ruthie.

"Well bless my soul."

Big Si jumped, startled by the sound of his own voice; he'd not intended to speak his thought aloud, but he was so startled by what he'd just seen that he couldn't help himself: Ruthie was watching Mack McGinnis as closely as he was watching her and they caught each other at it; their eyes met and that's what Big Si witnessed, and that's when he knew that his precious daughter was a grown woman.

"What you think about him, Si?"

He didn't know how long First Freeman had been watching him watch McGinnis, but he knew Freeman was a watcher—maybe that's what drew the old man to the younger one. "I think it don't much matter what I think," he said, and both men chuckled. "But I reckon if I had any say in the matter..." Si hadn't taken his eyes off McGinnis, and he watched now as one of Maisy Cooper's grandchildren darted into the open area where the young men were playing catch. McGinnis saw the child and, with a laugh, bent to scoop up the little boy and swing him high into the air. "I'd say he's a good one, Mr. First, and I thank you. 'Course, I don't reckon a man can earn much of a living teaching poor, country Colored children how to read and write."

"He's a carpenter by trade, Silas, and one of the best I've ever seen." He looked toward the house. "His granddaddy the one helped Will'am put that house up."

"Well I'll be." Silas had heard the story of his home's construction many, many times over the years, the carpenter becoming almost mythical in the telling, the man's profession becoming his name: They all called him Carpenter and the man never corrected them. "Life is somethin', ain't it?"

"It surely is that," First Freeman said.

The meal they shared was as wonderful as a Juneteenth celebration—not as much food, and certainly not as many people, but the laughter and joy and fun—including lots of storytelling, embellished in the way only family and close friends can enhance the particulars of an event or occasion—elevated this Sunday dinner to celebration status. The presentation of the chocolate cake for dessert, however, stopped all conversation. Everyone looked toward Nellie, and she laughed and pointed toward Maisy, who gave a delighted whoop.

"Y'all think I got flour *and* butter *and* eggs *and* sugar? *And* some chocolate? That's me: The rich queen of England. Y'all bow down!"

First Freeman hopped to his feet and bowed to Maisy; Big Si, Ruthie and Little Si followed suit. When the laughter subsided, Maisy pointed to her daughter and said, "Sue baked it at work and brung it home for our Sunday supper."

Everybody looked at Sue, the youngest of Maisy's nine children. All of the grown-ups knew her, but she was a stranger to the younger people. She was a pretty-faced, brown, round woman who smiled easily and just as easily wore the warm thanks and admiration of her dinner companions, the way the well-loved baby of a family wears love and admiration. "Mr. Pace lets me cook whatever I want for myself," she said in a light, sweet voice—a voice that, if voices could be said to fit a person, fit Maisy's Sue to perfection. Her smile changed, though, when she saw the looks of confusion that met her explanation and, like the family's baby, she looked to her mother for assistance.

"Sue is the cook at the café," Maisy said proudly.

"The Crossing Café?" Beau asked, then, before anyone could reply, said, "Zeb Thatcher told me Colored couldn't work in town. He ran me out when I went to look for a job."

"Mr. Pace don't care what Zeb Thatcher says," Sue declared with a sniff.

"Zeb Thatcher's own kin don't care what he says." This from Sue's husband, Joe, who also was brown and round but who exuded strength to his wife's gentleness. And when confused eyes turned his way, he explained that he was the butcher in Thatcher's Market which was run by one of Zeb's daughters and her husband. "I butchered at a meat market in Belle City just like Sue cooked in a restaurant, and when we come here, they was happy to have us 'cause we know how things is done over yonder, and those folks in the Crossing want things done 'xactly the way things is done in Belle City."

"'Cept for Zeb Thatcher," Sue said.

"Zeb Thatcher's in jail, so it don't matter what he thinks," Joe said and was startled at the reaction his words drew. "Y'all didn't Zeb was locked up?" He laughed, then grew quiet and shook his head. "I'da felt sorry for him if he wasn't so mean and evil. And stupid." He looked from Uncle Will to First Freeman. "Y'all know him, right?" Both old men nodded. "How come he so bull-headed stupid? That man truly did believe that on his say so, he could just keep on sellin' whiskey no matter what the law said."

"Selling whiskey?"

"What law?"

"What jail? Ain't no jail in Carrie's Crossing."

"Who locked him up?"

The general hubbub created by the news of Zeb's arrest—along with the sense of relief at the fact of his absence—provided an opportunity for Mack McGinnis to speak without feeling so much like an outsider, for as kind and welcoming as Ruthie's people had been toward him, he was not a part of this community and he knew it and knew to tread lightly and carefully. "You mean the Prohibition," Mack said, a statement not a question.

Joe nodded. "That law means everybody, everywhere, but Zeb said it didn't mean him in Carrie's Crossing, Georgia."

"A lot of people everywhere, not just in Georgia, didn't think it would really happen," Mack said, looking around the table, meeting eyes—especially those of Nellie and Silas and Will Thatcher—and avoiding Ruthie's. "The U.S. Government passed the law and the president put his signature on it. Cain't nobody in the United States of America sell or drink whiskey."

There was a moment of stunned silence. Even though not a single person seated at the table under the trees in the late-day warmth had ever had a drop of whiskey, the magnitude of what they'd just heard overwhelmed them. As Mack was thinking—wondering—how best to do more than just teach reading and writing, but to introduce his newfound friends and family to the rest of the world, the man who would become his father-in-law put to rest the notion of the dumb country Colored person.

"I don't believe that makes a whole lotta sense," Big Silas Thatcher said. "Tellin' grown folks what they cain't do is just likely to make them do that thing."

The nodding of the grown heads in agreement reflected for Mack every argument against prohibition he had heard or read in the last two years. "The same people who didn't believe it would happen, don't believe it will last for that exact reason."

"If it don't last but a week, it'll be a good week 'cause it got Zeb Thatcher locked up," Beau said, and everybody laughed.

"Locked up where?" Nellie asked. "They got a jail in Carrie's Crossing now?"

"It's in Spencerville," Mack said, "and it belongs to the U.S. Government." And again he was stunned by the insightful reaction he information produced."

"I'm gettin' good and tired of the U.S. Gov'ment," Uncle Will said. "First they start a war, then they take our boys and send 'em over yonder and treat 'em worse than the people they was fightin' against, then they lynch 'em when they come home, and now that same gov'ment wants to tell me I cain't have a drink of whiskey if I want one?"

"Do you want one, Uncle Will?" Ruthie asked.

"I didn't 'till just now," the old man said, and joined in the great roar of laughter that his comment produced.

The entire chocolate cake, an apple pie and half a peach cobbler were devoured as talk of the developments and changes in Carrie's Crossing continued. Though that's where they all lived and called home, it was clearer than ever before that the differences between Colored and white were stark and the putting an end to slavery had not altered that fact. They now not only were isolated by color but by economics: Money was needed these days to survive. Cash money.

"I still can't get over anybody any kin to Zeb Thatcher hirin' you to work in his store," First Freeman said to Joe, "I don't care if he is in jail." Then he looked at Sue. "And that man who owns the café—when Zeb comes back, he's gonna give that man the devil of a time."

"Two of Zeb's chil'ren just like him, two just like their Mama," Maisy said, "one girl and one boy. The boy what got killed in the war and the girl what runs the furniture store—they just like Zeb: Mean and nasty and hate all Colored people, 'cludin' those ain't born yet. That other girl, the one what runs the meat market, and the baby boy—"

"Jonas," Ruthie said. "His name is Jonas. He's my friend and he ain't... isn't...anything like his pa." She looked directly at Mack McGinnis as she spoke, holding him in a direct, steady gaze, and if he'd had any doubt about his intentions regarding her, they vanished in that moment of naked honesty. She knew why he'd been brought to Carrie's Crossing, and teaching school was only part of it. She knew that her entire family wanted her kept away from Jonas Thatcher, and though they didn't think so, she knew why. Mack saw that in the look she gave him, the look that also told him she was smart enough to choose her own friends without apology. He gave her a brief nod of understanding, and she released his eyes, but the hold she had on his heart and mind tightened.

"That's right. Jonas," Maisy said. "He's a good boy and you right, Little Miss Ruth: He ain't nothin' like his pa; he is just like his ma. Him and his sister, Rachel her name is. And it's a funny thing now I think on it: Those girls married with men like they selves: Esther's husband is mean and nasty like Zeb and Rachel's husband is nice and easy like Miss Corrinne was, rest her soul."

"So, Mr. Joe, it was Jonas who said you could work at the store?" Little Si asked.

Joe nodded. "That boy made a lot of changes since his Pa been gone, and he ain't been gone that long."

"Changes like what?" Little Si wanted to know, adding, "He's my friend, too."

"One thing he did was say Colored could buy from the stores. We got go to the back door and ring a bell and wait for somebody to come help us, but it's more'n Zeb allowed, and it sure beats havin' to wait a week till somebody comes from Belle City to bring you a bag of flour or sugar or some sewing thread. 'Course they do charge us more than they charge white folks. Still and all, I guess you could say it's better."

All was quiet for a moment while each considered whether this was, in fact, better. "And somethin' else he did," Joe said, "and Sue don't even know 'bout this. Just happened Friday." He looked at his wife, then at everybody, one person at a time, up and down both sides of the table. "The man what Zeb bought his whiskey from, he didn't know Zeb had got locked up and his bar shut down, and he showed up to sell his whiskey and he got hoppin' mad when the boy, Jonas, told him what was what. *I ain't drivin' all the way back to Belle City carryin' that load of liquor. I'm liable to get locked up just like your pa.*' He was some kinda mad. But Jonas got him calmed down, then, know what he done? He bought the liquor. Paid him just what Zeb woulda paid him. Said he didn't want the man to get locked up."

"I don't blame the man," First Freeman said. "I know I wouldn't wanna get locked up for drivin' 'round with a load of moonshine."

Everybody laughed but Joe, whose raised a hand to put a stop to it. "It ain't moonshine," he said. "It's good whiskey with labels and seals and it come from up north somewhere."

"Now I done heard ever'thing," Uncle Will exclaimed. "Zeb Thatcher doin' bizness with folks from up North."

"No, sir, Mr. Will, the bootlegger ain't from up North, the whiskey is," Joe clarified.

"How long they gon' keep Zeb locked up?" Uncle Will asked in the middle of the discussion about the quality of the whiskey Zeb sold, saving Beau from having to ask the same question, though with less a understandable reason for wanting to know.

"His boy, Jonas, told Mr. Pace for 'bout a year, if not longer," Sue said.

"Then you know y'all gon' have to leave here in 'bout a year, 'cause it don't matter what his boy says or does, Zeb's the law 'round here," Will said to Sue and Joe, but he was looking at Maisy. "And you don't have to worry 'bout your Ma 'cause we'll take good care of her."

"I thank you, Will'am," Maisy said, "and I know what you say is true. So, I reckon I'll be goin' on to Belle City wit' them when they go back."

She was prepared for the surprise she saw on their faces: Her Sue and Joe because they'd begged her to move to Belle City with them and she'd refused, which is why they'd remained in Carrie's Crossing; Big Si and Nellie and Will Thatcher because they knew that she loved the land as much as they did; First Freeman because he didn't think she'd ever leave her birthplace.

"It's time to go, time to move on," she said.

"Maisy," Will said, and what she heard in his voice hurt her like physical pain.

"It's so, Will'am. Things ain't been the same since the flood."

That was true and they all knew it; they didn't have the words to explain or define exactly what was meant, but they knew it to be true, and the refusal of crops to grow and flourish as they once had and the absence of fish in the creek and fowl in the forest was only part of it. It was a large part, true: Being able to feed themselves literally was what kept them alive. But there was another something that had to do with the improvements that white people were making in their lives that seemed to be missing for Colored people, as if the end of slavery benefited the former masters more than it benefited the former slaves. "I want these grandchil'ren to be able to read and write and know their numbers." She looked at Mack McGinnis. "We surely 'preciate you comin' over here to teach these chil'ren." Then she looked at her old and dear friend. "But I want somethin' for myself, too, Will'am: I want to be 'round them educated Colored people, see 'em livin' in big, fine houses and drivin' motorcars and goin' to college. Even if it's too late for me, Will'am, to have those things, I want to *see* Colored people like that."

"Ever'body ain't got to go to college, Maisy. Ain't nothin' wrong wit' us what ain't been to college."

"That ain't what I'm sayin', Willie."

Sue started to speak then, and the gentle softness of her voice stilled the others so that she could be heard over them. "It's like this, Mr. Will: Me and Joe, we get paid for what we do. We get a envelope every week with money in it, but we can't read or do numbers, either one of us, so we don't know if we getting paid right or not. Now, I know I'm a good cook and Joe's just about the best butcher there is—don't neither one of us need to go to college, but we do need to know how to read and write—letters and numbers." She stopped talking and took a deep breath, then she looked at Mack. "We was gonna ask you, Mr. Mack, if you would look at our envelopes and tell us what's what."

Mack nodded but didn't speak; there was nothing more to be said—by him or anyone else—and as dusk was coming on, the time for talk was over anyway. Will stood up first and walked over to Maisy. He took both her hands in his and held them for a long moment. Both of them understood that when she moved to Belle City, they would not see each other again. "I'm gon' hitch up the mule," he said.

"I'll do it, Uncle Will, and I'll drive Miss Maisy and them back," Beau said, putting his arm across the old man's shoulders and feeling nothing there but bones where once muscles had rolled and rippled. His younger brothers followed him to the barn while the women cleaned up and put the food away, and his Pa locked the dogs on the porch to prevent them from following the wagon up the road. First Freeman, Maisy Cooper, and Uncle Will stood together in a tight circle, their heads almost touching, and it was impossible to tell whether they were talking or just being together for one of the last times. They had endured perhaps twenty years of slavery—no one knew for certain because none of them knew exactly when they were born—and so far, fifty-five years of freedom, and only those who had shared both experiences knew what that felt like, so none of those who observed those three, no matter how much they loved them, could know what they were feeling in that moment.

There was no sadness in the good-nights and the thank-yous that ended the evening, only promises to be together again soon, if not all of them at the same time, then Mack certainly with the children and with Sue and Joe; First Freeman, Beau, and Tobias would return the next month, as always; Big Si or Nellie would drive over to check on Maisy; and Sue and Joe would send from the restaurant, as often as possible, some item of food for the Thatcher family—a leftover piece of pie or cake or the butt end of a roast or some fried chicken.

As he left the lantern light of Maisy's house and turned into the pitch darkness of the road, Beau wished he had the dogs with him, both for company as well as protection. It wouldn't really be an issue if he were going immediately back home, but he wasn't; he was going into the town of Carrie's Crossing, specifically to the back door of what, until recently, was Zeb's bar, and which now was Jonas Thatcher's residence. He had listened carefully to every word that Sue and Joe Johnson had uttered, his war time experience coming in handy: He could close his eyes, hear a topographical or geographical description of a place once, and a map was imprinted on his memory. So, while he was certain that he could find his way in the dark, he wasn't prepared for street lighting. He pulled his wagon off the road and into the woods just at the edge of the town and proceeded on foot, keeping well-hidden, until he reached the rear of the bar, grateful that the town hadn't expanded to the extent that the woods no longer existed, though given what he was seeing, that wouldn't be long in coming.

When he was certain that he was alone, he darted across the road and up the two steps to the door and knocked, hard. In seconds, Jonas Thatcher opened the door and his eyes widened.

"You know who I am?" Beau asked.

"Yessir, Mr. Beau," Jonas said, and stepped back. "You want to come in?"

Beau hesitated only briefly. Whatever was on the other side of the door was safer than his standing outside—for both of them. "Thank you," he said as he entered, but he kept his back against the door in case escape was necessary. "I 'preciate it, and I won't take too long."

"Nobody here but me," Jonas said.

"Good," Beau said.

They stood looking at each other for a long moment: The Colored man older by three or four years, taller and bigger and thought a war hero by the younger man, who'd grown quite a bit since Beau had last seen him. He looked and sounded like a man. Beau inhaled and told Jonas what was on his mind. He talked for several minutes, saying out loud the thought, the idea that had been forming in his head. He repeated himself several times until he was clear and certain of his plan and his intentions. Then he stopped talking and waited. He'd watched Jonas's face as he talked, watched the boy's eyes widen in surprise, then narrow in calculated thought. He asked three questions, all of them good questions. Beau had answers for two of them. Regarding the third, he said, "I'll find a place and tell it to you next month when I come back to see my people. Is that all right?"

Jonas nodded. "That's fine, and so is your idea," and he extended his hand and Beau took it. "You want to take these two cases with you now? So you don't have to come back?"

Beau smiled. "You really ain't nothin' like your pa."

"Except when it comes to business," Jonas said and went into the storeroom to fetch the two cases of bootleg whiskey, with the labels and seals, that Beaudry Thatcher would take to Belle City to sell in the Colored establishments, the beginning of a business partnership that would make a small fortune for the two of them over the next thirteen years.

"You have to have a license to drive a automobile, Jonas," Police Chief Tom Fordham told him, "then, you got to have a automobile to drive." And he laughed at his own joke. Since Jonas had neither, the chief thought he could afford a little humor at the boy's expense, despite the fact that, in his father's absence, he was one of the wealthiest men in town.

"But I will have one, Chief, which is why I'm asking you what I need to do to drive it. I know how much you like for everybody to obey the law."

Chief Fordham gave him a hard look: Was this boy making fun of him? But Jonas looked like his usual serious self. "Where you gettin' a automobile from?"

"Doc Gray. He bought a new one and he's sellin' me his old one." Jonas couldn't contain his excitement. Doc Gray already had taught him how to drive it, practicing on the paved spaces in front of and behind the doctor's ever-expanding property.

"What you need with a automobile anyhow, Jonas? You got a gal you want to squire around town?"

Jonas flushed red, and the chief thought maybe he'd struck pay dirt. He didn't realize he'd made the boy angry. "Somebody's got to go over to Belle City for supplies. Rachel and Esther don't want to drive, and Cory and Clem have to run the stores. I'm the only one who can go."

Chief Fordham nodded. "I 'spect you right, boy." He turned to walk away, then turned back when he realized that Jonas hadn't moved. "Well, come on. You want that license or not?"

Jonas was confused. "You got the driving licenses?"

Chief Fordham laughed. "Who else you think got 'em if I don't?"

Right then Jonas understood why Beau Thatcher said they'd need to find a location on the outskirts of Belle City for Zeb's bootlegger to deliver the whiskey instead of bringing it all the way to Carrie's Crossing. Certainly it would be easier for the man, since he lived in Belle City, but now Jonas knew why Beaudry had said even if he had a motorcar to get back and forth between the two places, he'd never have a driving license: If Chief Fordham of Carrie's Crossing and all the police chiefs of Georgia handled the dispensing of driving licenses, very few Colored would be legal drivers; they'd be driving mule wagons forever.

Or riding horses, for that's how Tobias Thatcher and First Freeman traveled from Belle City to Carrie's Crossing three weeks after the big dinner. They weren't due or expected for another week, so when they pounded on the door that Friday night well after ten o'clock, they frightened everybody inside and terrified them when Big Si opened the door them.

"What's wrong?" he yelled. "What y'all doin' here?"

Nellie was so frightened she couldn't speak. Tobias grabbed her by the arms and shook her a little bit, kept calling her name over and over until she focused her eyes on him. "Toby," she said, calling him by Ruthie's nickname. "What y'all doin' here?"

He gave her an envelope. "It's from Eubie, Ma. Look! It's a letter from Eubie!"

Nellie took it, looked at it, turned it over and over in her hands but without a hint of recognition. Eubie couldn't write so she couldn't recognize his handwriting. She recognized the words, *Silas Thatcher* but not the. *Mr. and Mrs.* or the *c/o Dr. Renee Jordan* at the college. She held the envelope out toward Big Si but he backed up a step, as if the thing were dangerous. Finally, Ruthie took it from her mother.

"Mr. First. Toby. Where did this come from?" Ruthie asked.

"From France," Tobias said. "All the way from France and it's for us!"

Ruthie held the envelope in her two hands, as if trying to equally distribute its weight. "What does it say?"

The two men looked at her as if she'd said something incredibly ridiculous. "How we know what it says, Ruthie? We can't read. You the one learnin' to read, not me." Tobias really sounded angry. He looked angry, too.

"The college professor didn't read it to you?" Nellie asked.

First Freeman said, "We brought it right here to you. We thought Mack could read it."

Mack! Little Si was out the door in a flash. Mack McGinnis, carpenter by trade, had, in his three weeks of residency, constructed a one room school house on the rise behind the Thatcher house for the Colored children of Carrie's Crossing, where he also lived. He took his meals with the Thatcher family but since it was clear that he and Ruthie eventually would be more than tutor and pupil, he went to his own "home" at night, after dinner, as was appropriate.

In the brief time that it took for Little Si to return with Mack, Ruthie continued to stand holding the envelope containing Eubie's letter, and the others continued to stand watching her.

"See," Little Si said bursting into the room. "There it is."

Mack looked at Ruthie, then at the letter in her hands. She looked up at him, then gave him the envelope. He read: *To Mr. and Mrs. Silas Thatcher, c/o Dr. Renee Jordan, Department of French, Belle City College for Women, Belle City, Georgia.* "And it's got his name on the front too," Mack said. *E. Thatcher,* he read. "But I can't read the French place where it's from."

Nellie began to weep. Mack opened the envelope and removed two sheets of paper, both filled with writing in pencil. The letters were tall and strong.

Dear Mama, Papa, Uncle William, Brothers and Baby Sister:
I know you have worried about me but do not. I am fine and happy here.
I miss you all very much but I am happy here in France. I have a wife and soon to have my
child. As you can see, I have learned to read and to write a bit. And in English and French.
That is why I am here. In Carrie's Crossing, I could not learn to read and write not even in
one. I wish you all could come here. Every person you see would say Good Morning to you
and nobody would call you nigger. Nobody would hate you. I am a farmer here, like you are
farmers. I hope you can come here to live. All of you. I will teach you to talk like the people
here. They teach me to talk and to read and write. They give me papers from US and I cry
when I read what is happening to Colored people. I will not come back to US. Please come
here so we can be family.
    Yr. Son, E. Thatcher.

Nellie's tears had flowed throughout the reading of the letter and Big Si's face was a stone carving. Emotion traveled through Tobias, Little Si and Ruthie like wind blowing through the trees: They were happy to hear from their brother, happy to have proof that he was alive, and devastated by his statement that he would not be returning. Without speaking a word, Nellie returned to her bedroom, closing the door behind her. Nobody else moved until Ruthie reached for the letter. Mack gave it to her.

"Toby. Mr. First. Y'all must be hungry." She went to the kitchen.

Freeman roused himself. "Where Will'am?" But he knew. "He took bad again?"

Big Si nodded, then waved his arm toward the kitchen. "Y'all go on back."

"I got to put the horses up," Tobias said.

"I'll do it," his Pa said, and waved his arm toward the kitchen again. He started out the front door, then stopped. "Where Beaudry? How come he ain't with y'all?"

"He wasn't home when the lady brought the letter, Pa," Tobias said.

"Where is he?" Big Si demanded, looking at First Freeman.

"I don't know where he is, Silas, but ain't nothin' wrong with him," Freeman said. "He was fine this mornin' when left goin' to work."

Now Big Si had a target for his fear and his anger: "I thought he worked 'long with you, Freeman. Ain't that what you said when you took him 'way from us? That you was gon' look after him, give him a job."

"I do look after him. He drives one of my wagons cross town—diff'rent places from where me and Tobias go—Tobias rides with me. Beau drives by hisself, but he comes back ev'ry night."

"Why you let him ride 'round by hisself?"

"'Cause that's how he likes to be, Silas: By hisself. And he's just fine."

And Beaudry was just fine. He was parked behind the country club, just beyond the kitchen door, where nobody would give a second thought to a Colored man driving a mule wagon, talking to a white man driving an automobile, especially a Colored man holding his hat in his hands, his head down, his eyes looking at his feet. Jonas was counting the money Beaudry had given him from the sale of the whiskey, and Beau was hoping and praying that everything his people thought and said about this boy was correct, that he was honest and decent, because Beau, unable to read, could count only because Mr. First had taught him, but he counted slowly and he needed to be able to lay the money out on the table, like denominations together. And he hadn't known the value of whiskey. He knew only that the owners of the secret and illegal watering holes in the Colored sections of Belle City were so pleased to have real whiskey to sell that when the first man said, "I'll pay you six dollars a fifth and two-fifty a pint," Beau had accepted, and then demanded that same amount from all the others.

Jonas looked at his partner who was still looking at his feet. "Beau?"

Beau looked up. "What you think?"

Jonas smiled widely, then divided the money, giving Beau half. "I think you're one heck of a businessman, Beau Thatcher."

Beau looked at the money Jonas gave him, not knowing exactly how much it was, but knowing very clearly what to do with it. "I guess we need to buy some more whiskey from that fella," he said.

"A lot more," Jonas said. "I'll have him meet me right here. This is a good place you thought of, Beau."

Beau reached out to return the money, but Jonas shook his head. "Always save some of your money, and the more you have, the more you oughta save. That way, no matter what happens, you won't be broke."

Nodding, Beau studied the money in his hand, counting as quickly as he could, his effort further challenged by the fact that it was dark. Jonas had told him in almost the same exact words what Mr. First always said and he knew that they were right: Here was a boy younger than himself, who worked for a man who once was a slave, both of them probably with more money than the doctors and the preachers, and now that he knew why, he promised himself that one day he would be the man other men worked for. He separated the money, put some in his pocket and gave the rest to Jonas, who gave him a nod and a small smile. "I'm back here behind this country club every Friday evening," Beau said, climbing into his wagon which, Jonas noticed for the first time, was piled high with—he didn't know what because it was covered with tarps. Beau picked up the reins, gave a click, and the mule surged forward, as if in a hurry to be headed home.

"You didn't give him too much, did you?"

Jonas turned slowly, unwilling to display the shock he felt at having had someone sneak up on him. He was a child of the forest, used to the darkness and intimately aware of the motion and movement of the night's beings. The man standing so close to him in this darkness was something new— teaching him of the need to learn some new lessons: The lessons of the city. "I gave him what he earned," Jonas said.

The man laughed, blowing his whiskey breath on Jonas. "You mean you found one who'll work?"

Jonas tried but he couldn't make a laugh happen. "Man does nothin' but work."

"You wanna hire him out? I need me a good worker."

Now Jonas found his laugh at the thought of Beau Thatcher working for this man. He was a couple of inches taller than Jonas with very blond hair and very blue eyes and dressed the way he'd seen golfers dressed in newspaper and magazine photographs: In knickers and knee socks and wearing a checked cap. He stuck out his hand. "I'm Jonas Thatcher, and my pa would kill me dead if I gave away his best worker." He looked hard at the man. "Prob'ly kill you too."

The man laughed and clapped him on the back. "Horace Edwards at your service, Mr. Thatcher, and I congratulate your pa on havin' himself such wise man for a son." He now looked closely at Jonas. "You play golf, son?"

"No, sir...at least, not yet...I'm tryin' to learn." He recovered quickly; what would he be doing at a country club if he didn't play golf? Or tennis. Or drink whiskey. Or do any of the other things that people did at places like this. He couldn't tell this man why he was parked behind the country club but even as he formed and uttered the lie, he felt a little corner of truth being born, for he did think that perhaps he would learn to play golf. Or tennis. Because he knew, with the same sharp instinct that told him how to balance the books and increase the profits of his stores and form a partnership with Beau Thatcher, that a country club membership would be good for business. So would cultivating a relationship with Horace Edwards. "But you can't learn just by watching," he said, hoping that was an appropriate response.

"That's for sure, son. You got to swing the clubs." And Horace Edwards mimicked perfectly the fluid motion of the drive off the tee. Jonas didn't know whether or not he liked this man, but he did like the idea of swinging a golf club.

"I guess I'm gonna need some clubs to swing."

"I got a set I'll sell you, son."

"Why?" Jonas asked.

"'Cause," Horace Edwards smirked, "I just bought myself a brand new set. C'mere lemme show you something pretty." And he hurried toward the front of the parking lot, which was lit up like daytime, and toward a brand new automobile. He opened the door and Jonas saw two bags of golf clubs in the back of the car, one of them obviously as shiny and brand new as the car. Jonas gave an appreciative whistle; let Edwards think it was about the golf clubs. Jonas wondered how much longer he'd have to work to buy a car like this one. "Beautiful, ain't they?" Horace said, lifting a long, shiny metal stick from the bag, one of the ones with a shiny wooden head. He demonstrated the swing again, this time with the club.

"I'd sure like to be able to do that," Jonas said, and meant it. "How much you selling the old ones for?"

"Tell you what," Edwards said, and Jonas knew he wasn't going to like what was coming. "I'll trade you the clubs for a week of that Colored boy's time. Him and his mule wagon."

The internal battle raging between his good business sense and his sense of fair play was on the verge of spinning out of control. A split second decision was called for. "A couple of problems with that, Mr. Edwards," Jonas said. "First, he ain't mine to trade—the man works for himself. Then, there's the fact that he's on his way back to Carrie's Crossing to deliver that load of stuff to my store." The lie rolled smoothly from his mouth. "But biggest thing of all, Mr. Edwards, is this: What sense would it make for me to give away a man who helps me make money? That'd be like you giving me the new golf clubs 'stead of the old ones."

Horace Edwards looked long and hard at Jonas Thatcher. Horace was known to be a master manipulator, as well as an unpleasant character and an unworthy adversary. There were precious few grown men with nerves steady enough to put Horace in his place, but he'd been bested twice in just a few minutes by a boy probably the same age as his daughter. "You got a store over in Carrie's Crossing?"

"Three of 'em and one sittin' empty, thanks to prohibition." And as soon as he said the word, Jonas knew he could safely change the subject and put Edwards on the defensive, and he wondered what had taken him so long to realize it. "They sell whiskey in there, don't they?" he asked, nodding toward the country club, though he very well knew the answer: Of course they did. He'd been smelling it on Edwards the entirety of their conversation.

"Sellin' whiskey's illegal. So's buying it. So's drinking it, I guess, since you can't buy it or sell it," Edwards said, more snarling than talking. He slammed the door to his car. "And you way too young to own all them businesses."

"My pa owns 'em but I'm runnin' em 'cause—" He decided that with this man the truth would be better than any lie, "'cause Pa's in jail He wouldn't close down his bar and stop sellin' whiskey, so the chief locked him up."

Horace opened the driver's side door. "I think I might like your pa. I ain't so sure 'bout you, though." He got in the car, slammed the door, started the engine, and roared away.

"I don't like you either, but I surely would like to have an Oldsmobile car and bag of shiny new golf clubs," Jonas said to himself in the peace and quiet of the night, which he definitely preferred to talking to people at any time, but especially in the bright light of day when they seemed to have more to say and more energy with which to say it. As he walked back to his own car, he paid closer attention to where he was parked and to where Beau had parked his wagon. Then he looked back at where Horace's car had been parked. Where had Horace been and what had he been doing that he was able to sneak up on Jonas like he had? He peered into the darkness and saw nothing but woods.

He got in his car and looked at his watch: He wanted to time himself going back home. It would be a slower trip than normal because, like Beau's wagon, his car was loaded with various merchandise to take back to the stores— everything from needles and threads and straight pins to cast iron skillets to sheets and towels and socks and nylon stockings and long john underwear for the furniture store; flour, salt, sugar, baking powder, tea, coffee and three cured hams for the grocery store. He hadn't lied to the chief about needing the car for that purpose, but his greatest need was to know how long it would take him to get from home to the country club parking lot to meet the bootlegger for his twice-a-month delivery. And thinking again of Horace Edwards's silent appearance out of the darkness, he'd tell Beau to find a new place after the next delivery.

He exited the parking lot and could only turn toward home because he didn't know anywhere else to go, and as soon as the lights of the country club were behind him, the darkness was complete and all-enveloping. The headlights of the vehicle cast a dim yellowness on the road immediately in front of him, and he had to keep his eyes trained exactly there or he'd run off into a ditch. He found himself silently thanking Doc Gray for the constant reminder to "keep watch on the road, Jonas, 'specially when it's dark out." He wondered how Beau Thatcher found his way in the dark; there were no front lights on a mule wagon. But, then, Belle City had street lights practically everywhere, and Beau knew his way around. When he drove away from the country club, he probably had more than one option open to him, unlike Jonas who only knew how to work his way back to the road that connected the two cities, and he only knew that because Beau had told him how to get to Country Club Road from Belle Crossing Road, which was the official new name of the two-lane paved route between the two cities, for Jonas knew that his hometown now was a city in the making and that the Thatcher name was in large part responsible for it.

Jonas never ceased to marvel at that fact. True, he felt a pang of guilt at the feeling, but the facts could not be denied: No sane or rational person ever would have thought that old Zeb Thatcher would be *the* leading citizen of Carrie's Crossing. True, his brother Carney's untimely demise made it possible, but there remained the fact that Zeb, all on his own, made the decisions about what to do with the inheritance. And because Zeb was Citizen Number One, his only son Jonas was, by default, Citizen Number Two when Zeb was present and, while the old man was in jail, Jonas was The Boss. And he was equally surprised at himself at how easily and how well he made choices and decisions; at how he dealt with business men—with grown men—like Horace Edwards.

"He's one to watch," Jonas said out loud to himself. He didn't know why he thought that anymore than he knew why he'd accepted Beau Thatcher's offer or why he insisted that the Thatcher stores sell to Colored people or why he bought Doc Gray's car or why the idea just that moment occurred to him to buy a truck and to turn the defunct bar into a warehouse. "That'll save money in the long run" he said. And he thought: It'll be better to haul that whiskey in a truck with a bunch of other stuff instead of in the back seat of an automobile. "I bet Beau'll think it's a smart idea, too."

Nellie felt awful, and the struggle to conceal her illness from her family only made matters worse, but she couldn't let them know that she was sick. She had gone against her husband and Uncle Will in her insistence that she be able to travel to Belle City to meet with the professor at the college who knew how to write to Eubie, that she be able to leave with Mr. First and Beau and Tobias on Sunday evening. She wanted to send Eubie a letter telling him that it was time to come home, telling him that he could bring his French family if he wanted to, but the important thing was that he come home. Si had tried to reason with her, pointing out more than once, that Eubie had made it clear he had no intention of returning to Carrie's Crossing. Uncle Will, with considerably less patience, had pointed out that Eubie most definitely could *not* bring his French family with him: "They white folks, Nellie. He can't have no white wife here." She had been unwilling to yield, had made it clear that she would be going with Mr. First Freeman, Beau and Tobias on Sunday evening when they returned to Belle City, had made it clear that she was telling, not asking. Her intransigence on the matter had put a damper on the usually festive monthly visits of the three men. They'd brought the usual gifts and treats, but nobody got much enjoyment from the usually looked-forward-to ritual, even though Nellie and Ruthie were busy preparing the usual Saturday and Sunday feasts as if things were normal.

"Ma?"

Nellie forced herself to smile into her daughter's eyes. "You making the corn bread today?" she asked.

"You sick, Ma?" Ruthie asked.

"No, I ain't sick," Nellie said a bit too forcefully, then added, "It's hot in this kitchen."

Ruthie looked at her mother; it was always hot in the kitchen. "I'll make the corn bread. You go sit outside in the shade, and I'll bring you a glass of lemon tea."

Nellie wanted to protest, but the thought of sitting in the shade with a cool drink was more than a little appealing. She wiped her hands on her apron, then reached out for the table as the floor seemed to shift beneath her.

"Ma!" Ruthie screamed as she reached out to catch Nellie. Both women sank to the floor, Ruthie cushioning the dead weight of her unconscious mother.

Ruthie's scream had brought the men running. Pa burst into the kitchen, followed by her three brothers, Mack, Mr. First, and Uncle Will, all of them staring in shock and horror at the sight of Ruthie and Nellie on the kitchen floor, the girl gently tapping her mother's face in an attempt to restore consciousness.

Big Si dropped to his knees and took his wife's hands but not knowing what else to do and having no idea what to say.

"We got to get her up off the floor," Uncle Will yelled. "Y'all get her up from there."

Beau, Tobias, Little Si, and Mack, two on each side, slid their arms beneath Nellie, creating a stretcher, and lifted her. Ruthie scrambled to her feet and ran to the bedroom to turn down the bed covers.

"She's burning up," Little Si said.

Ruthie touched Nellie's forehead, then snatched her hand back. "Go get Miss Maisy. Tell her to please come quick."

Beau and Mack ran out together. "You hitch the mule," Beau called out as he headed for the road. "I'm gon' run on to her house and tell her we need her so she'll be ready to go when you get there."

Mack hitched the mule to the wagon as fast as he could. He thought it awfully smart of Beau to think to run ahead and give the old woman time to get ready. He also thought how much he had come to like Nellie Thatcher and how he hoped that the fainting spell didn't portend anything serious, for to lose her would devastate this family, especially Ruthie. He pushed from his mind the image of Ruth on the floor, cradling her mother, fear and anguish flooding her face. "Come on, mule," he said to the beast. "I got no time for your contrary ways today."

When he pulled into Maisy Cooper's yard twenty minutes later, she and Beau were waiting for him, the old woman hugging a large leather satchel to her chest. Without speaking a word, she let the two young men help her into the wagon. She settled herself and closed her eyes as Mack clicked the reins to get the mule moving as fast as it was willing to be prodded on the hard, rutted road. Mack willed himself not to look in the opposite direction, toward the white part of the Carrie's Crossing community where the road now was paved, but he still could see its smooth surface reflecting the sunlight, and he knew how much easier the trip would be—for the mule as well as for the people— on such a surface. But he also knew there was no point in thinking on things he couldn't change and concentrated instead on keeping the cart as steady as possible on the bumpy surface while Maisy concentrated on breathing— deeply in and slowly out, deeply in and slowly out—because she knew there was no point in speculating on the nature of Nellie Thatcher's illness: Whatever it was, she'd either be able to help or she wouldn't and she wouldn't know until she got there. Until then, all she could do was breathe and call to memory all that she'd ever known about healing with nature's medicinals.

And as soon as she walked in the door, even before she saw Nellie, she heard her, and knew that the first requirement was a sedative, for far from being passed out like Beau said she was, Nellie was awake and agitated. Ruthie was in bed with her, holding her from behind, while the two Silases, positioned on either side of the bed, each held an arm, and all the while Nellie was desperately trying to free herself. "Y'all turn me loose, I said. I got to go find my boy and bring him home," Nellie wailed. Tobias had an arm around Uncle Will's shoulders, whispering to him as tears streamed down his weathered face. Maisy touched the young man's arm.

"Son, bring me a pot of hot water, please, two cups, a spoon, and some clean towels."

"Yes, m'am," he said, but he didn't move. He looked from her to Uncle Will.

Maisy took Will's arm and led him to a chair. "I'm here, now, Willie, and we gon' make ev'rything all right. You hear me, Willie? We gon' take care of Nellie."

Uncle Will looked at her, saw her, and heard her. "I thank you, Maisy. I truly do."

Maisy went to the bed then and sat down close to Nellie. She touched the woman's face and her neck, her chest, both breasts and her stomach. She felt her arms and her legs and her feet and her hands, almost as if giving a massage. "Nellie," she finally said. "Nellie."

Nellie quieted and forced her eyes to focus in on the person shaking her and calling her name. "Miss Maisy," Nellie said, surprised to see her there.

"You got to get yourself calmed down."

"I got to go get my boy, Miss Maisy."

Tobias returned then and Maisy stood up. She looked at the Silases and at Ruthie, telling them in a glance to continue holding on to Nellie. Then she took up the tattered leather satchel she'd brought with her, unwound the straps that held it together, reached inside and brought out a small leather pouch and a large glass jar. She closed the bag and secured the straps and pushed the bag under the bed. From the leather pouch she took three pinches of a brownish-green powdery substance and put it into one of the cups and poured hot water over it, half filling the cup. She stirred the mixture, inhaled it, stirred it again, and took it the bed.

"I want you to drink this, Nellie. It's hot but that's how you need to take it." She sat on the bed beside Nellie. "Y'all lift her up straight." Ruthie pushed from behind and the Silases pulled, and Nellie was seated upright. Her hair was loose and wild and Maisy smoothed it down. Then she put the cup in front of her. "Nellie?"

Nellie looked at her. "Ma'am?"

"I need you to drink what's in this cup, drink it all."

Nellie looked at the cup and frowned. Then she looked at Maisy. "I know you a root woman, Miss Maisy, but I never had need of your doctorin' or nursin.' I ain't sick."

Maisy smoothed her hair again. "I know you ain't, Nellie, you just wore out tired."

Tears filled Nellie's eyes. "Yes'm, I surely am that. Wore out tired." She took the cup that Maisy offered and drank. She shuddered at the taste and blew on the brew to cool it, but she drank it all and seemed to calm almost immediately.

"Did you eat some breakfast today, or did you just cook?" Maisy asked, but Nellie didn't respond. "What about dinner last night?" Maisy asked, and again got no reply. She looked around the room. "When was the last time she took some food?"

Everybody looked at Ruthie. She was about to respond that of course her mother had eaten breakfast, had eaten dinner, had eaten whenever a meal was served, but when she thought about it, when she pictured the last few meal times, she realized that her mother, in fact, had not eaten. She had served food and passed bowls and platters, she was up and down from the table, back and forth from the table to the cook stove, but Nellie had not eaten in—

"Maybe two or three days," Ruthie said to a room of shocked expressions.

Maisy looked at Big Si. "How she sleepin'?"

He shook his head.

Maisy reached for the other cup and took up the jar. "Chicken fat," she said. "I stewed him last night and was getting' ready to make some dumplings for supper when Beaudry come runnin'." She poured some of the chicken fat into the cup and added hot water. Without being asked, Ruthie, her father and her brother raised Nellie to an upright position, a task now made easier by the fact that she had ceased her thrashing about. In fact, she was practically asleep. "Drink this, Nell," Maisy said, and Nellie drank. Her eyes were closed now, and she was breathing deeply, and she sighed when she finished drinking the broth.

"You men, y'all go on out now, and close the door."

"Is she—" four male voices inquired at the same time.

"Sleepin' and she gon' sleep for some little while," Maisy said, and closed the door behind the men. Then she turned to Ruthie. "Let's wash her up a little bit, and put her in a clean gown, comb and brush her hair, make her comfortable." The two women worked efficiently but silently and in just a few minutes, Nellie Thatcher was tucked in and softly snoring.

"What did you give Ma to drink, Miss Maisy?"

"That's one of my special mixes. Don't have a name, but it does its work."

Ruthie looked down at her mother, stroked her face, and began silently weeping. "How did you know she wasn't eating and sleeping and we didn't know?"

"I 'spect you got a few other things on your mind these days, Miss Ruth."

Ruthie's tears ran heavily down her face. "I'm sorry."

Maisy wrapped her arms around the girl. "Nothin' for you to be sorry 'bout. You a young girl feelin' her heart for the first time. It's natural that your mind—"

"This is my Ma, Miss Maisy. I shoulda been watching out for her."

Maisy patted the girl's back and calmed her. "Just tell me what your Ma's been doin' and maybe not doin.'"

"She just...ever since we got that letter from Eubie saying he wasn't coming home, she just...she cooks and she watches over the crops, does what she always does...except, I guess, for eating and sleeping." The tears started again. "I knew. Pa knew. Why didn't we help her, Miss Maisy? Why'd we let her get so sick?"

"You can't stop this kinda sickness."

Ruthie looked at her sleeping mother. "You stopped it."

"I just helped her go to sleep. Maybe if she sleeps deep enough, long enough, and maybe if we can get her to swallow some more of that nourishment, maybe she'll come back to herself a little bit. But it'll only be for a little while."

"So she'll have this...sickness...why, Miss Maisy? What kinda sickness is it?"

"Your ma is heartsick. Just like your heart is full of joy, hers is full of sadness. She's missing a child, and that's just about the worse thing that can happen to a woman."

"But Pa said he tried to make Ma feel better...he said it's not like Eubie was dead, and Ma got real mad and wouldn't talk to him. But Pa's right: Eubie's alive, and he just might come home some day."

Maisy shook her head. "It would be better for your ma if the boy was dead.

That way she could bury him and forget about ever holding him close to her heart again. This way, that's all she can think about, is holding him close, but she can't do that 'cause he's too far away." Now Maisy sounded mad. Looked mad, too. "They ain't had no biz'ness takin' our boys and sendin' 'em way over yonder. It was wrong." She smoothed the covers over Nellie, then leaned over to her. "They shouldn'ta took your boy if he couldn'ta come home a man." She collected her things and Ruthie gathered the dirty towels and clothes, and after a final check to be certain that Nellie was sleeping deeply and peacefully, they left her alone.

The men surrounded them when they opened the door, all wanting to peek in at Nellie, to see for themselves that she was, in fact, all right, that she was, in fact, just sleeping. Then they all wanted to hug Maisy, and to thank her, and to find out what they could do—what they should do—to help Nellie.

"Right now, let her sleep. In 'bout three, four hours, get her to drink some more of that chicken fat, but don't make it too hot. She's liable to burn herself."

"Will she wake up to drink it?" Ruthie asked, sounding as doubtful as she felt. Her mother didn't look as if she'd wake up for hours, and Maisy confirmed that.

"She won't wake up til way later on tonight, but now that she's had some nourishment, she'll be wantin' some more. Y'all sit her up like before, then put the cup under her nose, let her smell it. Then put some on her mouth, let her taste it. Then put the cup up—not too hot, now—and she'll nat'rally drink some."

Big Si took her hands. "Thank you, Miss Maisy."

"I got to go right now so I can finish fixin' dinner for Sue and Joe, but I'll be back later on tonight so I can give her some more sleeping powders."

"I'll come get you," Beau said.

"Me, too," Little Si, Tobias and Mack said in unison.

Maisy chuckled and waved them away. "Joe'll bring me over here."

"I can give her the powders, Miss Maisy," Ruthie said.

"No, you cain't. I got to do it myself."

"It's dangerous, right?" Mack asked.

"Yes, it is," she said, clutching her leather satchel even more tightly to her bosom. She accepted more hugs and thanks, and all of the men followed her outside, helped her into the wagon, and the three older men watched as the four younger ones rode away.

"I'll go finish dinner," Ruthie said.

"You need some help?"

"No, Pa, thank you, but all that's left to do is make the corn bread."

First Freeman ducked his head and looked at her over the top of the glasses he'd taken to wearing. "Can you make corn bread good as your ma?"

Ruthie gave him a sly grin. "You're so hungry you won't know if I can or if I can't."

He threw back his head and laughed a deep, full belly laugh, and she headed for the kitchen. "She's a stitch, she is."

Big Si grinned. "You right about that, and make no mistake."

"Young Mr. McGinnis gon' have his hands full, and that's a fact." And suddenly First was laughing by himself. "What?" he asked. "Y'all don't like him?"

"We like him just fine, Mr. First," Big Si said.

"What then?" he asked, and when neither man responded he looked at them closely, all but forcing their downcast eyes to lift to meet his. "Y'all ain't ready to let her go."

Uncle Will inhaled deeply. "I know she ain't no chile, but that's how I see her."

"Me, too," said her father. Then, with great effort, he managed a warm smile. "I couldn'ta found a better one myself, Mr. First, and I thank you. Me and her ma, we been talkin' 'bout it. We see what's what, and we see that he's a good man and we see that Ruth, that she..." Big Si had to stop. He couldn't say the words to his wife and he couldn't say them to these two men who were like fathers to him: Couldn't say that he had been watching his youngest child and his only daughter fall in love with Mack McGinnis. He had four sons and he'd had a lifetime with his Uncle Will and, just recently, time spent getting to know First Freeman, and he knew what made a good man and he knew that Mack McGinnis possessed all those things. He also knew that Tobias most likely was being scrutinized by Isabelle Johnson's father the same way he was scrutinizing Mack, and he hoped that Ed Johnson had reached a similar, positive conclusion about Toby.

As soon as the corn bread was in the stove Ruthie went to look in on her mother. Nellie was just as they'd left her: Motionless under the covers, arms at her sides, hair spread across the pillow, gently snoring. She wanted to speak, to say something, but she didn't know what to say. She picked up the hand closest to her, the right hand, the one that always stroked her face or her hair, and studied it. It was, Ruthie thought, a beautiful hand—long-fingered and strong.

Beautiful like her mother was beautiful. "I'm sorry, Ma," she said and hurried from the room.

Dinner was on the table when Beau, Tobias, Little Si, and Mack returned, and they all sat down to eat, Nellie's empty place at the table a magnet for their eyes and their thoughts. Not one of them was able to keep from looking toward the vacancy with every movement of fork from plate to mouth, with every swallow of tea. Only Mack looked at another of the diners—when his eyes weren't shifting from his plate to the vacant place, they were watching Ruthie, who had gone frighteningly still. Not in a physical sense—she was eating and passing bowls of food when asked—but she had retreated to a deep place inside herself, a place that he had not, in his relatively brief association with her, had occasion to witness or experience. It was the part of her that he had come to love best, the part where her sense of mischief and fun resided, where her amazing intelligence and creativity dwelled; it was that part that had gone still and silent. The spark that lit her eyes from within and produced her laugh quickly and easily had dimmed.

"You got to let her go, Pa," Beaudry said, the only one of them willing to voice what all the others were thinking.

"We'll keep watch over her," Tobias said. "We won't let nothin' happen to her."

"What could happen anyway?" Beau asked. "She'll go see the professor at the college and she'll come back home."

"She ain't goin' no place," Big Si said, and Mack thought he looked very much like the mule when it was refusing orders to work, with his head hanging low between his hunched shoulders. "Y'all heard what Miss Maisy said: She gon' give Nellie some more sleeping medicine tonight and she'll be sleep tomorrow. She cain't go to Belle City if she's sleep."

Ruthie roused herself. "No, Pa, she can't go tomorrow, but as soon as she's stronger, she should go. Maybe knowing that she's going will help her get her strength back."

Beau looked at his baby sister, who no longer was a baby. "I think you're right about that, Ruthie—in part," he said, and when she looked at him, he said, "If she has to wait for a whole month for us to come back to get her, though, she'll just get sick all over again."

"She can ride that trolley car," Tobias said.

"No she cain't," Big Si thundered. He was losing this battle and he knew it.

"Can I say something?" Mack asked.

He got surprised looks from everyone at the table, including Ruthie, but the reason for the looks surprised him when Uncle Will said, "You part of this family, son, you can say anything you want to say."

"Thank you, Uncle Will, and what I want to say is that I'd be happy to drive Ma Nellie over to Belle City whenever she's feeling strong enough to go, and I'll wait for her to do whatever she's got to do, and I'll bring her back. And I'll take real good care of her."

Everybody was nodding at his good idea except for Uncle Will. "You got to stay here at the school, son. All those chil'ren be waitin' for you ev'ry day, you can't just up and leave."

"You're right," Mack said, dejected.

"How 'bout that fella that come over here with Joe and Sue, helps Maisy out sometimes. What's his name? Somethin' Jenks? Y'all know who I mean?" First Freeman said, and they did. Tom Jenks was his name and he was from Belle City, but he was out of work and had no place to live and because he was kin to Sue's Joe, he lived with them and helped Maisy in exchange for a place to live.

It was agreed and a plan was hatched: Tom Jenks would be asked to drive Nellie to Belle City to the college, to take her to First Freeman's house after her business was finished, where she'd spend the night, and to return her to Carrie's Crossing the following morning.

"I'll pay him something for his time," Beau said.

"And I'll go too," Ruthie said

"I'll write a letter to the professor and tell her that Nellie's coming," Mack said.

"But we don't know when that's gon' be," Tobias said.

As it turned out, it was the following Thursday morning, and Nellie refused to have Ruth accompany her. "I need you to stay here and look after your Pa and Uncle Will," she said, but only her husband knew better: Silas knew that his wife wanted to go alone to Belle City not just to see the college professor but also to look at the Colored sections of the city with different eyes since the mother had decided that the daughter, when she married, would live not in the country but in the city where she could be educated and where she could educate her children. For his part, Tom Jenks was more than willing to run the errand; he missed Belle City, he didn't much care for country life, and what Beau would pay him would stake him in a poker game which, if good luck were on his side, would allow him to remain in Belle City, at least long enough to look for—and hopefully find—a decent job.

They left as soon as the sun was up on Thursday morning, and Tom's worries that the woman would want to talk all the way to Belle City proved groundless. Nellie Thatcher, after she bid him good morning, said no more, and he was grateful because, as it turned out, he needed all of his concentration to keep the mule and the cart on the road due to the greatly increased motorcar traffic. The road was paved all the way into Belle City, and streets were paved even in the Colored sections of town, so they traveled quickly and easily. Tom knew exactly where Mr. First Freeman lived and he drove directly there, as instructed, because the old man himself wanted to take Nellie to the college and wait for her.

"We'll see you back here at sunup t'morrow," Freeman said.

Tom nodded. "Yessir," he said, though he had no intention of returning if he did well at cards that evening. But no point in telling them that; they'd find out soon enough.

First Freeman had a small house on Ashby Street—Nellie had been there before—with a large yard behind it that extended back to the next street, and what he called a storage shed, that was larger than the house, where he stored and repaired the items that he picked up in his travels throughout the city. As was the case when she'd been there before, half the space was piled high with more goods than Nellie could have imagined existed, to say nothing of having been discarded. The other half was neat and clean and held three tables with benches. Tools hung on the wall behind two of the tables, and a woman worked at a sewing machine at the third. First Freeman introduced her as Mrs. Mason, a seamstress, who made the necessary mends and repairs to anything made of fabric—from shirts, pants and dresses to bed sheets, curtains and draperies, pillow cushions or bath towels—so that the items could be sold. Beau and Tobias, he said, worked at the other two benches repairing any and everything else and were making money "hand over fist. They can fix anything, those two."

Freeman's small house was neat, clean and beautifully furnished. He'd already told her that "everything in here is somethin' somebody didn't want, I didn't buy nothin' but the house," but it still amazed Nellie that people could and did discard useful things. Maybe, she thought, it's because she was from the country that she couldn't imagine a thing not being useful. Even so, she'd never want to be the kind of person able to discard a thing simply in order to have a new or another thing.

He took her to a room and put her bag on the bed. "You tired, Nellie? You need to rest?"

She shook her head. "I feel just fine, Mr. First, and what I want to do is see." She'd been to Belle City before, had seen the college for Colored women, had seen the Colored hospitals and banks and insurance companies, had seen the houses where well-to-do, educated Colored people lived; but she'd seen these things with the eyes of wonderment. She now wanted to see where her daughter might be able to live, to see the schools where her grandchildren might be able to learn to read and write, and to feel what it felt like to walk and ride the streets of Belle City, to know if it really was possible to live day-to-day without fear.

"The professor knows you're comin' and she's ready to write your letter."

Nellie reached into her skirt pocket and retrieved a piece of paper. "Mack already wrote the letter for me, but he didn't know what to write to make it go all the way to France." She unfolded the paper and held it out to First Freeman, who shook his head at it: He couldn't read, so no point in looking at it. Nellie refolded the letter and returned it to her pocket. "What time do we see the professor?"

He pulled a watch from his pocket and popped it open. "In 'bout a hour, but if we take the horse 'n buggy, it won't take long to get there."

"Can we walk? Seems like I recall it's not too far from here."

"Sure we can, it ain't far a'tall." He looked again at his watch. "We have to leave in a few minutes, though, if we gon' walk."

Nellie nodded. "I'm ready, Mr. First." Then she said, "I can't really tell time, you know? I mean, if I look at a time piece and the little hand is on a number and the big hand is straight up at the top, I know what time it is, but when the big hand is in the middle, I'm just confused."

First Freeman grinned at her. "That's somethin', ain't it?"

"What's that, Mr. First?"

"How some people is good with numbers and others is good with words. Like you: You can read, taught your chil'ren to read, but you can't tell time. And me, I'm good with numbers. I can count money, can tell time, but can't read a single word, not even my own name." He shook his head and laughed again. "If it wasn't for Mack McGinnis and his people, I wouldn't own this house, wouldn't have my name wrote on my wagons, nothin' like that."

"He's a good man, is Mack McGinnis. I already think on him like a son."

"I reckon I feel the same way. I think on him like I do Beaudry and Tobias...

like I do on my own boy..." He stopped talking and dropped his head and Nellie knew to change the subject and to do it quickly: She'd heard from Uncle Will that Freeman's son had just disappeared one day—he'd gone to work and had never come home.

"Has he said anything to you, Mr. First?"

"Mack ain't said nothin' to me 'bout his intentions concernin' Miss Ruthie, though I 'spect we all know what they are by now."

"Well...I truly hope so...but he hasn't said anything to Silas or Beau or Tobias. And he hasn't said anything to me...Ruthie! You think he's said somethin' to Ruthie?"

The old man threw his head back and cackled. "If he'd a said somethin' to Miss Ruthie we'd all know 'bout it by now. She'd a told ev'rybody."

Nellie had to smile, for the man spoke the truth: If Mack McGinnis had ever spoken to Ruthie about anything other than teaching and learning, she'd have told somebody or, as First Freeman said, everybody. "I guess we oughta be going then."

Freeman got his hat and opened the front door. Nellie paused to straighten her own hat and to smooth her skirt, to touch the pocket holding the letter to Eubie. She looked down at what she could see of herself and thought she looked like she belonged on Ashby Street in Belle City, for the dress she wore was one that Mr. First had brought to them in Carrie's Crossing, same for the hat and the shoes. *I don't look too country,* she thought to herself, though her confidence flagged as they drew closer to the big intersection of Hunter and Ashby Streets. She'd been here before, she reminded herself, she'd seen these sights. And yet. Colored women walking, holding parasols over their heads. Colored women riding in horse-drawn carriages—not mule carts. And Colored women riding in motorcars. She looked around at the paved streets and the stores and shops, behind her at the houses, and ahead of her toward what she knew were the colleges where only Colored children studied. She looked up and saw the lights that would brighten the streets once the darkness descended, and knew that inside the houses and the shops and the stores, a flick of a switch would deliver the same bright lights. *I want this for my children,* she thought. *I want this for myself.*

"It's kinda noisy and dusty, Miss Nellie."

"I think it's wonderful, Mr. First."

Freeman looked down at her, looking for some aspect of the sickly, feverish woman who had passed out on her kitchen floor just five days ago, and knew that the fears that her husband and his good friend had hesitated to express were, indeed, honest and worthy fears, for if made to swear, he'd have to speak the truth: Nellie Eubanks Thatcher had, for all intents and purposes, left the farm and moved to Belle City. "You get used to it," he said. "Tell the truth, much as I like bein' back home in Carrie's Crossing, at times it feels too quiet."

She nodded as if she understood exactly what he meant. And knowing Nellie, most likely she did. "There's all kinds of people here, Mr. First," she said. Her awe of the well-to-do, fine ladies had faded as she saw that more women were dressed as she was: Neatly and cleanly if not elegantly, and that most of the men were dressed like Mr. First. *I don't have to be rich and educated,* she thought to herself, *and my Ruthie don't have to be rich and educated to live here.* "You don't have to be rich and educated to live in Belle City."

He stopped walking. "I been livin' here so many years I cain't count 'em all and I ain't never been rich or educated. Is that what y'all think? That you got to be rich and educated to live here? Is that why Will'am and Silas won't bring y'all over here?"

"That ain't all of it, but that's a big part of it."

He grunted but didn't speak, and they continued their walk, having crossed the street at the intersection after waiting for the light to change. People walked briskly, as if in a big hurry to get somewhere. Or, Nellie thought, to get out of the way of the carriages and motorcars, for that certainly was the reason that Mr. First grabbed her arm and hurried her forward as a motorcar turned the corner too fast and too close behind them, and she giggled as she heard him mutter, "Damn fool."

Mr. First, understanding why Nellie wanted to watch and see, walked slowly and pointed out places of interest—people, too, when he saw them. "You see that lady right there?" His urgent whisper grabbed Nellie's attention, and, looking where he indicated, she saw a small, quiet looking woman, unlocking the door to a small, quiet-looking building. She wore a skirt, blouse and jacket but no hat, and she carried two purses—one in the crook of her arm, the other in her left hand—and as Nellie looked closer, she thought that bag too large to be a purse.

"That there's Dr. Dwelley. Dr. Anna Dwelley."

Nellie studied the woman. "She's a professor at the college?"

Freeman shook his head. "Not a professor kinda doctor, a doctorin' kind a doctor."

Nellie stopped in her tracks. The woman had the door open, and all the people Nellie had thought were just standing there followed her inside.

The door closed and Nellie saw the writing on the glass: *ANNA DWELLEY, M.D.* She inhaled deeply. "A Colored lady doctor! Oh, Mr. First. I heard tell of such things but I didn't know...I never thought...now I can tell Ruthie what a Colored lady doctor looks like. Why, Mr. First, she looks just like...a Colored lady."

The loud claxon of a motorcar horn right beside them froze his reply and, just as quickly, the angry look on his face softened into a surprised smile. "Beaudry! Boy, what you doin' in that motor vehicle?"

"Ma! Mr. First! I was lookin' for y'all."

Nellie, still recovering from one shock, received another: Her son at the wheel of a truck, smiling and waving for them to join him. Freeman wrestled the door open, lifted Nellie up and in, jumped in himself, and slammed the door. "Whose truck is this, Beau?"

"Ours, Mr. First."

"We ain't got no motor vehicle."

"Yeah, we do. Since first thing this morning. And here's the best part. I got a license to drive it, too." He waved a piece of paper with his right hand, then dropped it as he needed that hand to shift the gears. The groaning, screeching sound made Nellie cringe. "It's not a brand new truck," he said, having noticed his mother's response to the shifting of the gears, "but we sure can haul more stuff, Mr. First—haul more and haul it faster."

"Well I do declare," the old man said, wearing a 'now I've heard everything' look.

Beaudry quickly explained how it happened that between sunrise, when he left with the mule wagon for work, and now, a little past the noon hour, he came to own a truck: "I went by Mr. Allen's place, just like always, and back behind his house he's got two desks and two chairs, telling me to haul 'em off. I tell him I can't 'cause they're too heavy for my cart, and I just hate havin' to say that 'cause I promised Doc Dwelley I'd find her some office furniture and these are some really fine pieces of furniture. Wait til you see 'em, Mr. First."

"You got 'em here in the truck?"

"Yessir," Beaudry exclaimed.

"You gon' take this furniture to the Colored lady doctor?" Nellie asked.

"Yes, ma'am," Beaudry said, and his mother beamed at him.

"So...you tole the man the furniture was too heavy for your wagon..."

"And that's when he told me I needed a truck. I told him even if I could find somebody to sell me a truck, I couldn't get no license to drive it. And he looked at me—y'all shoulda seen how he looked at me. Like I was...I don't know what. *'What are you talkin' about, boy?'* he says to me, and he looks and sounds mean and mad. 'Mr. Allen,' I said, 'a Colored man can't buy a motorcar without a license to drive it, and the police won't give us the license 'less we a doctor or a professor or a preacher, somebody like that.' Well, he looked at me some more then told me to follow him, so I did, and goes back in his yard to this shed and opens and this here truck is in it. *'You think you can drive this?'* he says, and I told him I can drive anything with a motor. *'How's that?'* he wants to know, and when I told him I learned how to drive trucks and buses and tanks and everything else in Europe during the war, he looks at me some more, then he grabs my shoulder. *'You were over there?'* I told him I was, for two years. Then he looks at me some more and he says, *'Take that truck, son. It's yours if you want it. And I'm calling the chief and tellin' him to give you a license or he can find a new job.'* And that's what happened."

"Well I do declare," First Freeman said again, just as they turned into the front gate of the college campus.

"You want me to go with you, Ma?"

Nellie hesitated, then nodded. "I b'lieve I do, Beaudry."

"I'm gon' stay out here with this truck," Freeman said, walking around it and patting its rear as if it were an animal. "By the way, where's the mule and the cart?" he asked Beau.

"I gave it to Mr. Allen's yard man. He was pushin' a cart with wheels on it, his rakes and tools sticking up out of it. I figured since I moved up to a truck from a mule cart, he could move up from pushing his cart to ridin' in one."

His mother hugged him and Mr. First clapped him on the back, and for the first time since he came home from the war, Beaudry felt like he had a chance to be a man.

The feeling intensified at dinner that night. Nellie cooked, just as if they were at home in Carrie's Crossing, and Tobias brought Isabelle Johnson, so Nellie almost felt as if she had a daughter present along with her sons, especially when Isabelle was appropriately amazed, awed and impressed when Nellie recounted meeting Dr. Anna Dwelley. After dinner, Beau took turns giving everybody a ride in the truck, telling and re-telling the story of how he came by it, feeling more and more whole within himself with each telling.

Then Tobias had news to share: "Isabelle says she'll marry with me," he told them, and all the men clapped and laughed and shook his hand and hugged Isabelle—while Nellie wept and hugged Isabelle.

"But I'm not going to tell your Pa or your Uncle Will. That's for you to tell."

"I will," Tobias said, then added, "and by that time, I can tell something else: That me and Isabelle gon' have us a place of biz'ness of our own."

"What?" Nellie exclaimed.

Tobias grinned and looked from Isabelle to Mr. First to Beau, his grin growing wider. "A place on Fair Street. I'm gon' cut men's hair on one side and Isabelle's gon' press and curl ladies' hair on the other side and we gon' call it *TOBY AND BELLE'S*."

Nellie was speechless. It was enough to think that the first of her children was about to marry—and, she expected, a second wouldn't be far behind—but that a child of hers would own a business...it was too much to consider. Then the realization struck that her eldest child already was married and that she, perhaps, already was grandmother to a child she most likely would never see. Her eyes filled again. "I'm proud, Toby. And so is your Pa and Uncle Will and Little Si and Ruthie. And Eubie would be too..."

Beau and Tobias looked at each other, the message they telegraphed clear: Do something. "Beau's gon' help us buy the building," Tobias said, "and he's gon' live in it, upstairs."

"For as long as I can stand the smell," Beau said, holding his nose, and everyone laughed.

"Then me and Belle, we gon' buy a house down the block from Mr. First," Tobias said, "so we'll all be close together, just like in Carrie's Crossing."

"That's good," Nellie said, "real good. Y'all stay close like that, always."

"We will, Ma," Beau said and got ready to drive Isabelle home. "Come on, Toby, let's teach you how to drive the truck so you'll be ready when your time comes."

Nellie was up early the following morning making breakfast for the men after having not slept very much the previous night, but her restlessness was caused by too much happiness, not the opposite, as was the case in the previous weeks and months. Good fortune was coming to her children, and her letter was on its way to her son in France, and she had no doubt that once he read it, he would come to his senses and come home—with or without his wife and child—for his true home was with his true family in Georgia.

Beau and Tobias left for work, Beau driving the truck, Tobias a horse-pulled wagon that was larger than the mule carts. Nellie and Mr. First sat on the front porch to wait for Tom Jenks and "watch the world go by" as Freeman liked to say. He spoke to or waved at practically every person who walked, rode or drove past his house. The third time that he pulled his watch from his pocket to check the time, he said, "If that boy ain't here in a just a few minutes, I'm gon' be drivin' you over to Carrie's Crossing myself."

"Isn't that him?" Nellie asked, shading her eyes as she looked East into the rising sun.

Tom Jenks was walking toward them but it was more of a stumble than actual walking. His coat was slung over his shoulder, his hat was set at a crooked angle, and he seemed to be experiencing difficulty picking up his feet, one after the other. As he drew closer, Nellie thought he looked sick. Freeman thought he looked drunk, and he stood up and strode down the steps to his walkway to meet the young man, prepared to send him away if he smelled whiskey.

"You late, boy."

"Yessir. I'm sorry. I thought I'd get a ride, but I had to walk."

"From where?"

"Over by Auburn Avenue," Jenks said.

"Why didn't you ride the street car 'stead of walkin' all the way here from all the way over yonder on the East Side?" Freeman demanded to know.

Jenks shrugged; he was too tired for a discussion of any kind, especially one that focused on the fact that he'd lost every dime he had in a card game that had gone on all night long and had just ended with the dawn, leaving him literally penniless. He'd certainly rather have ridden the trolley car or the street car from the East Side of town here to the West Side, but that hadn't been an option. Neither had not keeping this appointment, for driving Nellie Thatcher back to Carrie's Crossing was the only way he'd be able to get back there, and he needed to return so that he'd have a place to sleep and food to eat. "I'll hitch up the mule," he said.

"The mule is already hitched and ready to go," Freeman told him, "but I ain't so sure 'bout you."

"I'm fine, Mr. First."

Freeman gave him another hard look, then stepped closer to him and sniffed. He smelled sweat and a dirty body, but no whiskey. "Then y'all better get goin' 'fore the sun gets too high. And I guess I better get you somethin' to eat and drink."

Tom sighed in gratitude, then spoke it; he hadn't eaten since the previous afternoon and had had nothing to drink but a root beer he'd stolen from the ice chest in the rooming house where the card game was held. He followed First Freeman around the house to the huge back yard where the mule and cart were standing ready to go. He noticed how neat and clean everything was, how close the grass was cut, how even the shed and barn were painted, how no weeds grew among the flowers. Freeman entered the back door of his house and emerged less than a minute later with at tin plate of fried chicken necks, grits, gravy and biscuits, and a gallon jug of water.

Jenks thanked him again and ate the food where he stood, returning the plate to Freeman. He then drank most of the water, wiped his mouth, and managed half a smile. "Thank you, sir. I'm ready to go now."

He walked the mule and cart out the back gate, down the alley, and around to the front of the house. Nellie was standing on the walk waiting for him. Her good-byes already said, she let Freeman lift her into the wagon seat. She bid Tom good morning, settled into the seat, opened her parasol, and prepared for the journey home, a trip as silent as yesterday's.

Tom thought long and hard about why he'd allowed himself to play cards with men he knew were better and smarter than himself, and no thought he had made any sense. Why hadn't he hired himself out to wash dishes or bus tables for the night? He'd have gotten a free meal, earned a few cents, and perhaps gotten a place to sleep for the night. *Now I got nothing,* he thought; *I got less than I had when I left Carrie's Crossing. I'm going back there with less than I left with.*

Nellie's thoughts were brighter, stronger, happier. She had good news to share with her family. She also was thinking that she owed her husband an apology for having been so hard to get along with. And now that she was certain that Eubie would be coming home, she also could be certain that she'd no longer succumb to the kind of sickness that frightened her family into calling Maisy Cooper, though she was grateful that they had.

The sun was high and hot, but they moved along at a good clip, not having to share the road with too many motorized vehicles this time of morning, though Nellie scrutinized every one that passed by, comparing its worthiness with that of Beau's truck and feeling a secret pleasure at knowing that her son could drive any vehicle on the road and do it better than most of those behind the wheels of the vehicles they saw. Then she saw a truck like Beau's and exclaimed, "My Beau's got a truck just like that one."

Startled from his thoughts, Tom said, "Ma'am?"

"That truck yonder. Beau's got one just like it."

"Beau's got a *truck?*"

Nellie nodded proudly. "He got it yesterday."

Beau Thatcher's got a truck, Tom thought, *and money enough to pay me to drive his ma up and down the road, and I got nothing. Maybe I oughta go to work for First Freeman.* It wasn't a pleasant thought; he didn't like the physical, back-breaking work of moving and hauling and loading and unloading. However, he liked even less having to walk from one side of town to the other for lack of a nickel to ride. If he could get a job working for Freeman, he could live again in Belle City and maybe, by driving around all day, he could luck up on a better kind of job.

"Hey! Hey, you, Boy!"

Tom snatched his mind back at the same time that Nellie Thatcher made a sound and put her hand on his arm, and he saw a white man standing in the middle of the road yelling and waving his arms. *If I'd been driving a truck, I'd have hit him,* Tom thought. As it was, a mule cart didn't run fast enough to hit a box turtle crossing the road. Tom pulled up on the reins, and the man walked to the side of the cart. He was red in the face and sweating profusely in the midday heat.

"I need to ride the rest of the way to Carrie's Crossing," the man said, even as he had a foot and a hand on the cart to climb in. Tom looked at Nellie, then toward the empty cart, but before he could say anything, the man said, "and I ain't ridin' in the back of some nigger mule wagon," and he pulled himself up next to Nellie.

"Get off my wagon," she said in such a cold, low tone that both Tom and the man were startled, then she shoved him and he tumbled on to the ground. "Drive, Tom," she said, hitting his arm. Tom drove, but a mule cart being slower than a box turtle, in a few moments the now angry, sweating white man was running beside them, and he had a gun.

"Stop!"

"Don't you stop, Tom Jenks. You best keeping driving."

Tom drove but it wasn't fast enough—almost but not quite. The white man, still running beside them and cussing a blue streak, reached out and grabbed Nellie's dress. The fabric ripped but the pull was sufficient to confuse the mule and it slowed, enough for the man to get a good hold on Nellie's arm. He pulled and as she tumbled from the cart, something flashed in her hand. Then the gun roared and the mule took off at something resembling a gallop. Tom wrestled with the reins to gain control of the cart and get it turned around. What he saw when he turned back hurt his eyes. "Oh no, oh no, oh no, OOOOH NOOOOO!"

The two bodies lay at the edge of the road, the white man with a knife in his chest and the Colored woman who had been Nellie Thatcher with a bullet hole in hers. "OH GOD NO!" Tom kicked the dead white man. "Look what you done, you dirty bastard! Look what you done!" He looked up and down the road as some measure of common sense returned to him; it wouldn't do for him to be found beside two dead bodies, one of them a white man. He half lifted Nellie and dragged her off the road and into the bush and arranged her ripped skirt neatly around her.

Then he ran back for the man and saw the mule headed toward home at a faster than normal pace, and he wasn't even angry; he didn't blame the mule; he wished he had a home to run to. He grabbed the white man by one foot and dragged him into the brush, taking no care how he landed as long as it was away from Nellie. The he saw the gun still in the man's hand and the gears in another part of his brain engaged: He could sell the gun in Belle City. He bent down and felt the man's pockets, retrieving a leather case which he could tell without opening it held money. The man's clothes were nothing special, and he'd been sweating and stinking like a pig, so Tom didn't want them; but his shoes. Tom looked at his own worn brogans and at the man's almost new ones and, after only a moment's hesitation, he dropped to the ground and exchanged the shoes.

Standing at the edge of the road, Tom considered his next move: Where should he go? Or more precisely, *when* should he head for Belle City? Now or wait until dark? His attention was drawn by heavy buzzing, and he looked toward a black cloud of flies on the road and realized that they'd discovered the pool of blood left by the bodies. He hurried over, unbuttoning his pants. A steady stream of urine not only discouraged the flies but washed away some of the blood. Not all of it, though. "I got to get away from here," Tom said to himself, and he stepped off the road into the woods and aimed himself back toward Belle City. He'd have the cover of the forest all the way to where the road forked at the country club. From there he could take the trolley car, and, thanks to a dead white man, he had the money to ride. That thought almost cooled him, for today was so hot that not even the tree canopy of the forest provided a respite from the blistering heat.

Jonas was thinking the exact same thought from his perch where he observed the doings of the Thatchers. His school was closed today, and he was hoping that Ruthie and Little Si would be free too. He hadn't seen them in so long that he almost forgot how they looked. He knew from Beau about the school and how "Ruthie's almost teaching the teacher," but he didn't know how much of that was fact and how much was a brother's pride in his sister, and there could be no doubt of the extent of the Thatcher siblings love for each other. It still made Jonas a bit envious. His sisters were marginally more tolerant of him, but he knew that was due to his position of prominence in his father's business, not to any intrinsic familial attachment to him. In fact, he sometimes felt closer to Beau Thatcher than to his sisters or brothers-in-law. His monthly meetings with Beau were the highlights of his very ordered life, for as much as he enjoyed being in the position—the much envied position in Carrie's Crossing—of running three businesses, of having money enough to buy a car, he preferred to listening to Beau talk about life in Belle City and, just recently and in very small bites, his European war experiences.

He was pulled from his reverie by a shout, and he saw Ruthie and Little Si's Uncle Will running toward the road waving his arms. Jonas stood up on the tree branch to get a better look. He saw a mule cart enter the yard—an empty mule cart, no one at the reins. Then he saw people running toward the cart: Big Si Thatcher, the two men who worked what was left of the farm, and then all the children from the school, and, finally, Little Si and Ruthie emerged, and Jonas's breath caught. She was even more beautiful than before...and...and... the man beside her...

Something was wrong. Jonas couldn't hear the words being shouted but he could hear the alarm in their voices. Then, suddenly, everybody was in motion. Big Si jumped into the cart and put it back out on the road as Little Si, Ruthie and the man with her took off running through the woods. The old man, Uncle Will, began walking up the road toward the Colored part of town. Then Jonas realized what was wrong. He didn't see their Ma. Something bad had happened to Miss Nellie, he could feel it. He hurriedly climbed down the tree and froze when he hit the ground. Now what? He walked a tight circle around the trunk of the tree, pausing now and then to peer futilely through the dense brush toward the house. He couldn't see anything from down here on the ground, which is why he'd been climbing the tree for so many years, so he stopped himself from pacing and peering and did what he did best: He thought. It was the return of the empty mule cart that got everybody all excited. Nellie Thatcher was nowhere to be seen, so maybe Nellie should have been the driver of the empty cart and if the cart returned without her, then that's what's wrong and no wonder they all were frantic. But where would Nellie Thatcher go in the wagon alone? He knew a lot about the family from watching them for so long and from his talks with Ruthie and Si, but he couldn't begin to answer that question. So, if he wanted to see what was happening at the Thatchers—and he did—he needed to be back up in the tree, so he climbed back up. Nobody was there. He told himself to wait and see what happened, to wait and see if they would need his help—would want his help—dealing with whatever the problem was, and he believed he knew what it was: Nellie Thatcher.

Uncle Will returned first, accompanied by a woman as old as himself, both of them moving faster than anybody their ages should have been able to move. The woman ran into the house, then back out again, as if she didn't believe Nellie wouldn't be in there. Uncle Will clearly was distraught and the woman worked hard to calm him, hugging and holding him, and once grabbing him by the shoulders and shaking him like a child. He sat on one of the tree stump stools at the table and put his head down and she bent over him, caressing his head and back. Jonas watched them and, as he had so many times, wondered about them, for in truth, he didn't really know them and knew nothing about them, but he did know that everything he heard said about Colored people was not and could not be true, not based on what he'd seen from his tree. And who was this woman? Something about her was vaguely familiar to Jonas, yet he didn't think that he knew her.

He grew drowsy in the damp heat and dozed for a bit, though it couldn't have for very long because he wasn't stiff or cramped and he hadn't lost circulation to a limb when he was aroused by sound—the turning of cart wheels on a rutted road, not a paved one. Why hadn't he noticed this before, the fact that the paved road stopped where the Colored town began? The wagon came into view, Big Silas Thatcher at the reins, Ruthie seated next to him, Little Si, the man he didn't know, and the two field hands walking behind. And laid out in the back, the body of Nellie Thatcher, and Jonas knew that she was dead, for even at this distance, he could see the huge red stain in the middle of her, and he knew very well what the drying blood of a dead animal looked like. Uncle Will and the woman with him heard the wagon and started toward it. Then they stopped at the sight of the funeral procession, for that's what it was. They stared in horror and disbelief at the back of the cart. The silent stillness was oppressive. Then Big Si Thatcher, like a wind-up toy top, spun into action. Jumped down from the cart and bore down on the old woman. At first she shrank away, then she reached for him, grabbed him, held on to him with two hands, tried to embrace him, but he pushed her away and, stumbling backwards, she fell, and that's when everybody else moved. Little Si and Uncle Will hurried to help her up while Ruthie and the man with her both grabbed Big Si, and they had to struggle to hold him.

"Where is he, Maisy? Tell me!" Jonas heard the man bellow. The old woman was shaking her head and sobbing and still reaching out to him.

Jonas couldn't watch anymore. For the first time he felt that he was, in fact, spying on them. He climbed down and, without looking back, headed toward town; there was nothing he could do here, no help he could offer, and certainly he'd not be welcome in their midst; this was a time for family...family! Beau and Tobias needed to know, and know quickly, that their mother was dead and that was something he could do.

He ran like a deer through the woods, emerging, as Beau did, across the road from the back door of the bar, where he kept the car parked. He'd started parking there as protection as well as convenience for Beau, but right now, in this moment, it offered the same service to him as he could be en route to Belle City without anyone knowing he'd left. And as he bounced up and down on the rutted, unpaved road, he vowed that he'd say something to...somebody...in complaint. He could make the point—the legitimate point—that it was faster to reach the Belle City Road from the Colored Town Road than from the Carrie's Crossing Road. That would get the notice of the decision-makers, for almost everybody complained about the time it took to get to Belle City these days.

He turned on to the BC Road and instead of putting on some speed, he drove slowly. He thought about how quickly her family had returned with Nellie's body. Whatever happened to her had to have happened near the intersection of the two roads. He was guessing that Miss Nellie had been coming back from Belle City. He crawled along on the wrong side of the road so that he could get a good, close look at...hellfire and damnation! He swerved to avoid what looked like a puddle of blood, and parking on the right side of the road, he jumped out of his car and ran to the other side. Yes, it was blood, and just a few steps into the underbrush confirmed that this was where Nellie Thatcher had died. And it didn't require too active an imagination to guess that the man with the knife in his chest was her killer. He bent to get a good look at the man's face, then hurried back up the slope to the road and across to his car, wondering how fast he could get to Belle City. Then he wondered, once he got there, how long it would take to reach First Freeman on Ashby Street. Beau had drawn him a map, a perfectly designed series of lines and squares to which Jonas had added the names of streets and landmarks—like the country club at the junction of Carrie's Crossing Road and Belle City Road and its junction with Hunter Road, which would lead him straight through Belle City, from the downtown shopping district into the Colored part of town. Beau had told him that Mr. First knew about their business arrangement and that if anything should happen to him, he should tell this man—"Not my Ma and Pa—Mr. First!"

When he got to the Colored part of town, Jonas had no difficulty understanding why Si and Ruthie and Beau wanted to live here; if he were Colored, he would, too. He wished that he had the time to stop and stare, to understand what he was seeing: A street wider than his street in Carrie's Crossing with businesses on both sides, and nothing but Colored people. They were dressed in every possible way, from the obviously destitute to the just as obviously well-to-do, and they walked, pushed two-wheel carts, rode mule or horse wagons and carts, and drove motorcars and trucks. He was looking at everything and everybody, but nobody seemed to notice him at all. *It wouldn't have happened turned the other way 'round,* he thought, and knew what would happen to a lone Colored man driving through the white section of town.

He saw Ashby Street and made his turn, then slowed almost immediately as he saw the number, then the house. It was small and painted white with green trim and a short, white picket fence surrounded the neat yard. He opened the gate and was following a brick walkway to the front door when he was stopped by shouted words.

"If you lookin' for Mr. First, you oughta know he ain't in the house."

Jonas looked toward the voice, but he didn't see anyone. "Where is he?"

A man stepped from behind a thick hedge in the next yard. He was old and bent. He wore a wide-brimmed straw hat and held a scythe. "He's in the back, where he oughta be."

"Thank you," Jonas said and changed direction, following the brick walkway around the side of the house to the back yard. He saw immediately why Mr. First "oughta be" there: Three men were unloading carts of items, carrying some into a huge shed, lining others up in the yard to be inspected by another old man wearing a wide-brimmed straw hat. The three workers stared at Jonas, stopping their work, and the old man turned, saw him, and headed his way.

"Mr. First?"

"Who're you?"

"Jonas That..."

"What's wrong?" The old man grabbed his arm. "What's wrong?"

"It's Miss Nellie."

"What's wrong with Nellie?" The vice-like grip on his arm tightened, tightened, and finally loosened as Jonas told him what was wrong, told him what he'd seen, told him what he knew. The hand dropped from his arm and Freeman sank down into a chair whose springs were sticking out through the fabric and cotton ticking. He buried his head in his hands and sobbed. The three workers stood awe-struck, not knowing what to do. They looked at Jonas with a mixture of emotional reactions: What could he have said to elicit such a reaction from this man, and *why* had he said it?

"I'm sorry, Mr. First."

The old man looked up at him and the three workers stared at him. None had ever heard a young white man call an old Colored man "mister." "Ruthie and Lil' Si always did say you was their friend."

"Yessir, I am. And they're my friends. Beau, too. That's why I came over here, to tell him and to take him home. Him and Tobias. So they don't have to drive the mule cart."

"Oh, Lord have mercy," Freeman moaned as if he'd just been delivered another, heavier load of bad news, and Jonas could do nothing but wait. Freeman looked up at him. "You don't know 'bout Beau's truck. Don't nobody know. Oh, Lord. Oh, Lord, ohLord, ohLord."

"No, sir, I didn't know Beau had a truck."

"Don't nobody know. Nobody but his ma. He just got it yesterday, and she was gon' tell 'em all when she got home today. Oh, Lord have mercy." He wept some more, then he pulled a wide square of orange and green material from his overalls pocket and wiped his face. Then he stood up, straightened his shoulders, returned his hat to his head and his scarf to his pocket and looked squarely at Jonas. "Where you say that dead white man was?"

Jonas was surprised by the question, but he answered it and every other question Freeman asked, and the more questions the old man asked, the more Jonas understood. The knife sticking out of the chest of the dead white man belonged to Nellie Thatcher. He might have killed her, but she didn't die alone. Whoever found the man, might be able to connect the knife to Nellie, and it wouldn't matter that she was dead—somebody Colored would pay.

"What should I do?" Jonas said.

"You sure you didn't know him?"

"I've never seen him before," Jonas said.

"Then go move him, and move him quick."

"And do what with him, Mr. First?"

"Take him to the river." Freeman, galvanized, moved quickly. *Another old person,* Jonas thought, *moving like a jack rabbit.* He ran into the shed and returned almost immediately with a pair of moth-eaten draperies, two pairs of rusted andirons, and some rope. "Wrap him up and weight him down: Arms, middle, legs. Drop him from the middle of the bridge, that low one, you know the one I mean?"

"You come to it right after the road makes that deep curve."

"That's it. Then, when you get back home, lissen to hear if anybody talks about missin' somebody." Freeman was walking him around the house, both of them carrying some part of the means for the watery burial of the dead stranger. "That man was goin' to see somebody in Carrie's Crossing. If it was kin and he don't show up, they gon' raise a stink. If it was biz'ness and he don't show up—" He shrugged his shoulders. "Might not be so bad, then."

"You want me to come tell you..."

"No!" They were in front of Freeman's house now, almost out to Jonas's car, and the old man's raised voice, especially toward the young white man, drew the attention of several people. Freeman put his arm around Jonas's shoulder and drew him close. "I truly thank you for what you did for us today, and I mean to make sure Beaudry and all of 'em know 'bout it. I mean to tell Ruthie and Little Si they was right—you are a friend. A good one. They lucky to have you." He stopped talking while they put the draperies and the andirons and the rope into the car. "But you make no mistake, Boy, you ain't like the rest of your people, and they find out you goin' behind 'em, bein' friends with Colored, they'll do you worse'n they do us. You got to stay 'way from Beaudry—at least in the Crossing—and you got to quit climbin' that tree. You hear me, Son? They'll hurt you bad if they catch you helpin' us."

Jonas nodded. He couldn't speak because he was fighting to prevent the tightness in his throat from springing a leak, leaving him crying like a baby right there on the street in front of First Freeman and his neighbors. "I'm going to the river, then I'm going straight to work."

First Freeman hugged him then, a tight, quick hug, then turned away, opened the gate to his yard, and walked back to his work. It was not a quick, jackrabbit walk. It was the walk of a man accustomed to carrying a heavy load, but who had just been given one ounce too much.

Jonas drove back the way he'd come. There was a little more traffic, but most of it was going back into Belle City; he had the road to Carrie's Crossing to himself, allowing time to think about how he was going to load a dead body into his car. He'd worry about wrapping it up and tying on the weights when he got to the river. Getting him into the car was the challenge. *A dead body is a dead body*, he heard in his head, and when he pulled up on the side of the road, he grabbed one of the lengths of rope and ran down the embankment. The sound and buzz of the flies that swarmed the body would have told him where the man lay if he hadn't already known. He kicked and threw leaves and tree limbs to disburse them, then quickly trussed the man like a deer, tying his arms and legs together tightly so that he looked like a V. Then he dragged him up to the road, ran back to the car for one of the drapery sheets, covered the body, then dragged it to the car. Hoisting it up and in was a challenge but he got it done. Then he drove like a bat out of hell to the river, partially because the man was beginning to stink, but also because, from the time he hit Carrie's Crossing and on to the river, he could encounter people he knew, and if he were driving slowly, they'd want him to stop and talk.

In the middle of the day, in the middle of the week, there weren't many people at the river. He parked off the road just beyond the deep curve in the road, dragged the body out of the car, used the remaining drapery to cover the body and the remaining rope to secure it, looping it through the andiron ends. The rope and the iron bars made dragging the body to the bridge easier, but he was worried about getting all the way to the middle of the bridge without being seen. He walked back to the road to see if anybody was approaching, then ran back to the bridge, got a good, tight grip on the ropes, and began dragging the body. He was dripping sweat and the heat of the midday sun was only partly to blame: He'd never been so scared in his life. In fact, he'd never really been frightened by anything, but he was truly and deeply scared now.

The low bridge hung directly above the water—and sat in the water during heavy rain when the river ran high. The sides of the bridge were low too, and the span was narrow. There was talk of tearing it down since there were so many motorcars now and people actually had driven them across. It was only a matter of time, everybody said, before some damn fool put a motorcar on the bridge and the whole thing dropped into the river. Better to tear it down first—a sentiment Jonas shared. They could tear it down *right now* he thought, as he heaved the body over. He watched it disappear almost immediately into the murky depths of the slow-moving water and knew that it would drop to wherever the bottom was—and stay there.

Jonas was dirty and he knew he stank, but he was so hungry his stomach hurt. Still, he knew he couldn't show up at the Crossing Café dirty and stinking, but he also couldn't yet face talking to anybody, especially his sisters or brothers-in-law. He remembered a secluded place on the river, almost a beach, where he and Silas swam, and he went there now and waded into the almost cool water wearing everything but his shoes—it was so hot he'd be dry in half an hour. He walked until he was covered, held his breath as long as he could, then, after floating on his back for a few minutes, he picked up his shoes and walked back to his car. He sat on the running board until he stopped dripping water, alternating between thinking about everything and making himself think about nothing, deciding that he liked it when his head was empty, free of thought or feeling, wishing that he could keep his head free and empty all the time.

He was practically dry when he got to the café, and hungrier than he remembered being since before his ma passed away. The bell tinkled when he opened the door, and he looked first toward the counter, expecting to see Sue's smiling face but then looked in the bucket beside the door for the discarded newspapers and magazines Mr. Pace put there, knowing that Sue would have heard the bell and would come to take his order by the time he was seated. In fact, if she'd taken a peek and seen him, she'd already have poured his lemonade and would be bringing it with her.

"Hey, Jonas."

Jonas looked up from the copy of yesterday's evening newspaper he was reading. "Hey, Mr. Pace," he said as he put his lemonade on the table, along with a napkin-wrapped set of cutlery. "Sue's got you working for her now," he said with a grin.

Pace smiled slightly then shook his head. "Sue ran outta here like a shot couple hours ago. Somebody came for her, said somebody kin to her died real sudden-like."

Jonas choked on the big gulp of lemonade he'd just taken, and Pace slapped him on the back. "I didn't know Sue had kin here," Jonas said, managing to cover his surprise. "I thought she was from Belle City."

Pace shook his head. "She was born right here. She didn't move over to BC 'til she got married. Her ma is Maisy Cooper. You prob'ly don't know her—she's one of the real old ones, used to be known 'round these parts for bein' what they called a root woman."

Of course, Jonas thought. That's who was with Uncle Will, and that's why she looked familiar to him; she used to bring medicine for his ma, something to help her sleep when she was in so much pain. Maisy Cooper. Uncle Will. Nellie Thatcher. Ruthie...

For the first time ever, Ruthie wasn't trying to fill her mother's shoes—she wasn't thinking or worrying about feeding or taking care of anybody. She wasn't doing anything, and that was of great concern to everybody: Her three brothers, Mack McGinnis, Uncle Will, First Freeman, Maisy Cooper, Sue and Joe Carter, and a dozen other people who were moving about in the house, and all of those people were alternating their focus between Ruthie and her father, who now was almost catatonic since it became clear that Tom Jenks wasn't available to be killed. His state was almost a welcome contrast to Ruthie's periodic hysteria. The only time she'd really calmed and quieted was when Beau, Tobias and Mr. First arrived—how had they known to come so quickly? And how had they managed to arrive so quickly? And when First Freeman told them how, Ruthie actually smiled, a told-you-so-smile that she shared with Little Si. Then she grabbed Beau's arm and hung on tightly.

"You got a motor vehicle, Beau? Show me." And they'd all trooped outside to see Beau's truck, to sit in it, Tobias to give Ruthie and Little Si a ride in it. Big Si and Uncle Will, with the same kind of a nod, acknowledged the thing's existence. Then the pall descended again. Ruthie began to cry and scream, and Big Si disappeared. Nobody knew where he was and everybody was frightened by the unspoken possibilities, so Tobias and Little Si took the dogs and went into the forest to look for him.

Maisy Cooper, greatly relieved to see Beau and Freeman—somebody who would take charge of things—told them that she'd managed to keep the circumstances of Nellie's death a secret from the community at large. "Don't nobody need to know a white man killed her 'cause if they know that, they'll want to know 'bout the white man, and we cain't tell 'em 'bout that."

"You right to keep the how and why 'bout Nellie secret," First said, "but don't worry 'bout the white man. That's all took care of." Maisy gave him a hard look but didn't question him; if he said it was taken care of, then it was, though she couldn't imagine how a Colored man 'took care of' the body of a dead white one.

"I know you know what you're doing," Maisy said.

"I'll tell you what I know, Maisy. I know Nellie Thatcher left my house alive and happy this mornin' with Tom Jenks and now she's dead, kilt by a white man with a gun, and ain't nobody seen Jenks from that time to this one. But what I'm gon' know before I leave here goin' back to Belle City is the name of ev'ry person and place known to Tom Jenks. You tell Joe Carter that, and make sure he understands."

"He already knows, First, and he feels bad as we do."

Freeman doubted that but he accepted it. "Then we best see 'bout gettin' Miss Nellie ready to be laid out."

Mack McGinnis was proving his worthiness as a carpenter with the casket he was building, with Joe Carter's assistance, and Maisy's creativity with wrapping and dressing the body ensured that no one who didn't already know the truth would guess that Nellie's death was due to anything but natural causes. By nightfall, all was ready for the wake, except that Nellie's husband and youngest child were not present. Her husband because he couldn't be found and her daughter because Maisy Cooper had drugged Ruthie and put her to bed "for her own good. She keep cryin' and screamin' like that, she'll be laid up yonder next to her Ma." And Beau, who, in Big Si's absence and Uncle Will's periodic absence from reality, was in charge of things, agreed with that decision, for Ruthie's hysteria was frightening to all of them.

Practically every Colored person still residing in Carrie's Crossing paid tribute to Nellie Thatcher that evening, a good number of them, both male and female with tears in their eyes, for Nellie was as well-loved as she was well-known. There was as much food as anyone would want to eat, and though people talked among themselves after they'd prayed and while they ate, there was little gayety or levity, either inside the house where Nellie lay in her casket surrounded and protected by the women, or outside in the yard where the men smoked their pipes and discussed the sorry state of farming. They talked about how tough times were, how hard it was to earn a living, and how tired they were of having all their hard work and their efforts count for nothing since white people could, would, and did prevent, by law, their participation in and enjoyment of practically every aspect of life. "We can't have the roads paved where we live 'less we pave 'em. We can't have electric lights where we live. We can't have indoor water where we live. We can't have a school for our children 'less we build it. I'm 'bout good sick and tired of white folks!"

As they listened—Maisy to the women and First Freeman to the men— both old people had the same thought: Maisy that she'd tell Sue and Joe she was ready to move to Belle City; Freeman how glad he was that he'd moved away from Carrie's Crossing back when he was a young man. It wouldn't have surprised them to know that their thoughts were so similar. In fact, they'd expect it, for not only had they known each other for practically all of their 75 or so years, they were, in many respects, closer than family as they had been slaves together on the same farm which created a bond deeper and stronger than family. That bond is what joined them on this night of tragedy, and it was their combined strength that was the glue holding everybody else together, for the loss of Nellie Thatcher was a crushing blow to the guts of the Colored community of Carrie's Crossing.

Nellie was not left alone that night. People took turns going home for a few hours rest and to change clothes so they'd be dressed for the funeral. Uncle Will and First Freeman had overseen the digging of the grave and Mack had carved the wooden marker. The twice-a-month preacher from Belle City had been sent for and arrived just at sunrise and just in time for the procession to the white-washed, clapboard church. Big Si had returned on his own in the wee hours of the morning, and Ruthie had awakened from her drug-induced sleep, had allowed herself to be washed and dressed by the women of the community, had promised Miss Maisy that she was fine and did not need to be sedated; she did not, after all, want to be absent from her mother's funeral.

Maisy and First had set the time of the funeral for sunrise. They'd told everybody it was so people wouldn't have to walk behind the casket in the heat of the day. The rapidly decaying condition of the body, though, was the real reason. All of Maisy's conjuring could not suppress the truth of what was happening to Nellie's body, and the sooner they got it in the ground, the better. The casket was loaded on the horse-drawn, black-draped wagon as the sun was coming up, and it was ready to go when the preacher arrived. Little Si and Tobias walked on either side of the horse, leading it. The preacher followed the wagon. Behind him were Uncle Will, Big Si, Beau and Ruthie, all in a row, and behind them, Mack, Maisy and First.

Jonas counted sixty-two people walking behind First Freeman, and he sorely wished that he could have been the sixty-third. He felt as if he'd known Nellie Thatcher. Certainly he had watched her work in the fields, hang up and take down the washing, sit on the porch and shuck corn and snap beans and pick greens, had watched her wring the necks of chickens. He had seen her embrace her husband and her children, had seen her play games with them in the yard. Nellie Thatcher had been a beautiful woman—alive and free and happy—and she had been loved. And now she was dead and for no good reason that he could tell. He'd kept his eyes and ears open as Mr. First had asked, and he'd heard no mention of a missing relative or friend, so whoever had killed Nellie, whoever he'd dumped in the river, remained a stranger as they buried Nellie.

Jonas watched as the procession wound its way up the road, deep into the Colored part of town, to where Beau and Little Si had told him the Colored cemetery was, then he climbed down from the tree and ventured, hesitantly, into the yard. He didn't think there'd be anybody left in the house to catch him, but because he knew he shouldn't be here, he proceeded cautiously. He stole all the way up to the front door and touched it, then he took off his hat and bowed his head. "Rest in peace, Miss Nellie," he whispered.

"Rock of Ages, cleft for me, let me find my strength in thee," the mourners sang, most of them through free-flowing tears and no small number of cries and wails, and ten men, five on each side, lowered the casket into the lime-lined hole. "Ashes to ashes and dust to dust," the preacher said, and the mourners took turns tossing fistfuls of dirt on top. Beau and Tobias held up their father, Little Si and Mack held up Ruthie, First and Maisy held up Uncle Will—literally, as all three were on the verge of collapsing. Then it was over, the funeral for Nellie Thatcher. Her family—Maisy and First included in that number—rode the horse-drawn wagon back home. About half of the mourners followed, the other half returning to their homes. Four men remained to cover the casket, completely filling in the hole, adding lime as a preserving agent as well as a scent-camouflaging and insect-repelling one. When they were finished, they anchored the carved plaque in the dirt:

NELLIE EUBANKS THATCHER

JAN. 17, 1878~JUNE 15, 1920

R.I.P.

From the Diary of Jonas Farley Thatcher

I don't know what I think or feel about anything anymore. I wish I could talk to Ruthie and Si about how they feel, but I don't see them at all these days. I'm better friends with Beau now than with Ruthie and Little Si, and I guess that's all right—but really, it's not. I do like Beau. I like him a lot, but he's different and we don't talk about the same things I talk about with Ruthie and Si. Beau and me talk about business and money but I want to talk about reading and writing and Beau is not interested in those things. Not for himself anyway. He cares about reading and writing for Ruthie and Si. He tells me about them going to school and about how much they are learning and about how they will be going to school in Belle City one day soon. I want to ask him is he sure but I know Beau does not say things that are not true. I tell him how much I am learning at my school and he says he can tell that I'm learning a lot because I sound to him like a grown man what's already been to college. That makes me feel good, but I wish that Ruthie and Si could hear me sound like a grown man.

From the Recorded Memories of Ruth Thatcher McGinnis

This was a very difficult time in my life, Sissy. Eighty-five years ago. That's how long it's been since my mother died. Was killed. A lot of what was happening around me is unclear. I suppose the truth is that I don't remember much. As a young adult, I'd look back on that time and realize that I'd come pretty close to what used to be called a nervous breakdown, and I don't think I exaggerate when I say that if I hadn't had Mack, I probably would have lost my mind. But having him love me and being able to love him in return—well, it gave me a place to put all the feeling I had for the mother who was gone. And there were my brothers, of course—my big brothers who loved and cared for and protected me, always. Pa and Uncle Will? Oh, yes, they loved me, too, but they were more distraught that I was. Pa would disappear into the woods for days, and Uncle Will would go for days without speaking. He'd just sit on the porch and stare. It was Beau who kept us together as a family during that time. For almost a year, because that's how long it took for the change to complete itself. What changed? Everything. Everything we knew and everything we were.

– 1921 –

They all, each and every one of them, had sworn and promised not to allow a single tear or moment of sadness spoil this day. It was, after all, New Year's Day—the first day of 1921—and a celebration was underway in First Freeman's house on Ashby Street in Belle City. But the day was special for another reason. It was the wedding day of Miss Isabelle Johnson and Mr. Tobias Thatcher, and so many people were packed into the little house that, despite the fact that it was freezing cold, both the front and back doors were open so some air could circulate, so they could cool off a bit—and they definitely needed to cool off, especially the young people. They'd been dancing and singing since last night, for goodness sake, though not there, at First Freeman's; they'd only been there since a little after one o'clock in the afternoon.

The young people all had been to a party for the soon-to-be-newlyweds at Beau's apartment above *TOBY AND BELLE'S BARBER AND BEAUTY SALON* the previous night, dancing until dawn to the music from the brand new radio that was Beau's gift to Isabelle and Tobias, and eating and laughing and talking and reveling in these rare moments of pure, free pleasure. Now at First Freeman's they were doing more of the same, in the company of their parents and elders, and with Toby and Belle who, as of one o'clock that afternoon, were officially Mr. and Mrs. Thatcher. It now was fully dark, though it wasn't really so late, given that it got dark early in the winter, and the night air was a welcome relief from the heat generated by the celebration.

For his part, First Freeman had done no dancing although, thanks to his radio, he now knew a few of the popular songs and he sang along now and then. His joy was in watching the people he loved enjoy themselves even though he knew their hearts were breaking. Will sat in the big armchair by the front door and always beside him, as if standing guard, was one of the children, Beau or Little Si or Ruthie. Only Tobias on this day was excused because on this day, his place now was at a different side—that of his wife. But his eyes were constantly in search of his family, and his father often was at his side, as if channeling the blessings of Nellie, about whom it was said more than once, was present in spirit if not in body. First wasn't certain that Will Thatcher really knew what was happening, but he did seem to be enjoying himself. They'd had to almost literally drag him to Belle City the night before after finally convincing him that no, Tobias was not going to get married in Carrie's Crossing and that if he wanted to see him wed, he'd have to go to Belle City to do it. And yes, he'd have to spend the night at First Freeman's house and they all had laughed when he'd asked why he couldn't stay with Toby and Belle. Will Thatcher, First thought, missed Nellie more than any of them because she'd always been Carrie in his mind. He'd never gotten over losing Carrie, and now he'd lost her a second time.

Ruthie and Mack danced, and when she wasn't at Mack's side, she was beside Beau or Uncle Will or Toby and Belle or Little Si or her father. She moved from one to the other and the old man could feel the girl's fear. Would another person she loved suddenly be snatched away from her? Not if she held on! First Freeman also noticed that Ruthie spent time with Clara and Mack McGinnis Sr., Mack's parents, and he saw how kindly they looked at the girl who most certainly would be their daughter-in-law. Nellie would like them, he thought.

"You sure do know how how to throw a party, Mr. First," Sue Carter said as she came to stand beside him.

"Well, it's a right special occasion," the old man said, with a proud look around. He'd have been no happier if he'd lived in one those big houses up on Hunter Road where the Colored doctors and undertakers lived.

"You and now Toby and Belle are the only Colored people I know who's got a radio," Sue said, adding, "It's a good thing I don't have one 'cause I wouldn't want to do anything but sit and listen to it."

Though he was loathe to admit it, from the moment Beau brought the thing in the door, Freeman hadn't wanted to do anything but listen to it, either. He'd initially resisted the purchase, but Beau had insisted, pointing out how Mr. First could learn all about what was happening in the world without having to know how to read. Then Freeman had argued that no white man would sell a Colored man a radio, and Beau had said that Mr. Allen would—the same Mr. Allen who had sold him a truck. So, he stopped resisting and gave Beau the money for the purchase, and the very next day Beau had come with the radio. Since then, First had taken in so much information that he thought his head would explode. "Where's your Ma?" he asked Sue.

Sue looked up at him with a wry grin. "In the kitchen, Mr. First. You know that's where she is. Takin' charge of the cookin' and servin' of the food."

"I thought you was gonna do that."

"I thought so, too," Sue replied as she turned away from him and headed toward the kitchen. "Maybe she'll let me back in the kitchen to help."

Everybody was ready to eat so when the kitchen door opened and Joe Carter backed out carrying a tray with the biggest turkey they'd ever seen, a great cheer went up. It increased in volume when Sue came out bearing a platter of hams, one smoked and one baked. Most of the women then flowed into the kitchen to help, and in short order the dining room table was laden with bowls and trays and platters of black eyed peas and rice and greens and yams and rolls. Then came the tray of glasses and another cheer split the air when Beau and Lil Si entered with a washtub filled with ice and bottles of champagne. Nobody asked how Beau had managed to find a case of champagne, though quite a few people wondered how he could afford it. Truthfully, though, nobody really cared. The corks popped, the champagne was poured, and the toasts to the new Mr. and Mrs. Tobias Thatcher flowed like the wine until First Freeman growled that he was getting hungry. Then the feasting began.

It was quieter as people ate, even the radio cooperated, playing a live concert of classical music by an orchestra in New York City. The young people grouped themselves together, most of them—except for the newlyweds—seated on the floor, and their elders in the chairs grouped around the table. The talk, though, among both groups, was the same: The inability to earn a living from the land anymore, the scarcity of any other kind of work and the pitiful money paid if a body could find a job, and the belief that if Colored people ever were to escape slavery's legacy, education would be the route, and every one of the young people found tangible hope and inspiration in the very fact of the five colleges and the one university in their community. Among them, only young Silas and Ruth Thatcher seriously entertained the notion of one day attending college, but the others knew that if not for them, then certainly for their children, a college education was the future, and some—like Beau Thatcher and Joe Carter—received immense pleasure and satisfaction just driving by the schools and watching the students. The older people, especially those for whom slavery was more than mere historical fact, took their gratification from up close and personal contact with Colored doctors, lawyers, bankers, preachers, teachers— the old ones literally would approach these professionals with the purpose of touching them, of looking into their eyes to see the proof that what they had endured had not been for naught.

As people finished eating, they took their plates and utensils into the kitchen where all the women—except for Maisy and Sue—were washing up and putting away and making space for the serving of the wedding cake. Several of the men stepped outside to light their cigars and their pipes. Big Si didn't smoke but he, too, was outside, in large part because he didn't think he could be polite and sociable for a single moment longer, and yet he didn't want to do or to say anything to spoil his son's special day. He felt a hand on his shoulder and turned to face Mack McGinnis Sr. He was exactly an older version of his son. Looking at this man, Silas knew how his son-in-law would look in twenty-five or thirty years, and he surprised himself with the thought.

He took McGinnis's proffered hand and the two men exchanged a powerful, silent grip. McGinnis spoke first.

"I'm so sorry 'bout your wife. I wish me and Clara could have known her. Mack Jr. liked her a whole lot."

"She liked him, too. A whole lot."

McGinnis sighed deeply. "I'm glad to know that. It means a lot to me and Clara." He cleared his throat. "We got us four boys, me and Clara, but no girls."

Silas surprised them both by smiling widely and sharing what he'd never told another soul: "We had us four boys, too, and had just about give up on gettin' a girl. Fact is, Nellie did give up. She said four chil'ren was enough to feed and if we was meant to have a girl, we'd have her by now. But it was me didn't want to give up. It was me wanted a baby girl!" The tears filled his eyes and began to fall then, and he didn't wipe them away. "She's just exactly like her Ma: Looks like her, acts like her, talks like her. And she's a handful."

McGinnis gave a dry chuckle. "So I hear tell."

"Her Ma said Ruthie could marry when she turned sixteen. That'll be on May fourth."

McGinnis nodded. "I'll tell Clara. And if it's all right with you, we'll handle things—"

"I can handle what needs to be handled."

"I mean 'bout a dress and...and all that kinda thing...women-folks things. That's all."

"Oh. Well, then, I 'spect that's all right." Silas gave McGinnis a sly look. "But your boy is gon' have to speak to my daughter and she is gon' have to say yes. Me and you standin' out here in the cold talkin' ain't gon' get nobody hitched."

Both men laughed, shook hands again, and returned to the warmth of the house, where, in the corner beside the kitchen First Freeman was talking quietly with Emma Johnson, the mother of the bride. She had thanked him at least half a dozen times—him and Beau—for making her eldest daughter's wedding day so memorable an event. She couldn't have done it on her own, as she was a woman alone raising three girls. Then she told the gentle old man something she had never told another soul: How her husband, her Ed, whom she'd trusted with her life, had simply vanished one day. They had a good marriage, she'd thought, and three baby girls, and Ed had been talking about trying one more time, for his son. Then, a month ago—he vanished. He'd just disappeared. She still hadn't gotten over the hurt, the confusion. She'd worked three jobs right up until the moment Isabelle had opened her beauty shop and brought Emma in to work with her. "She's such a good girl. All my girls are. I don't know how I got so lucky."

First Freeman gave her an awkward pat on the back, then leaned over to whisper in her ear, "And I 'spect your second girl's 'bout to get right lucky, too." He was looking across the room where Little Si, looking for all the world like a grown man, was smiling down at a pretty brown girl who clearly appreciated his attention.

"Oh," Emma Johnson said, her eyes widening. One hand flew to her heart, the other to her mouth. "That's my Catherine. And...and...Toby's little brother!"

It snowed on the third day of February, covering all of Tennessee and most of Georgia—all the way down to just south of Belle City—in a blanket of thick, heavy white. Few people were surprised; in .act, a few of the older citizens predicted it, knew in their bones that snow was coming. Though residents of the North and Midwest probably were not aware of the fact, snow, while not a regular occurrence in the South, happened often enough to be expected every few years. It also was expected that within twelve to twenty-four hours of the snowfall, the temperature would rise dramatically, melting the stuff so the Southerners could get on with their lives, for though they thought it was a pretty anomaly, they didn't know how to live with it—didn't have the tools to remove it or the clothes and shoes to wear in it. So when it snowed all day on the third of February, and then turned sharply colder that night, people were surprised, but they weren't worried, and school children, of course, were delighted because superintendents didn't even try to open schools when it snowed. When dawn broke on February 4th, it brought a frigid, howling wind from the north that blew the snow into deep drifts, obscuring or burying low-slung walls and fences, and guaranteed a second day without school for the children but not even they ventured outside. It simply was too cold.

It was warm inside the Thatcher's home. Curtains now hung at all the windows and rugs covered all the floors, though when it was this cold, the wind always managed to find points of entry, and Little Si and Mack, on that Wednesday morning, roamed the house looking for—and finding—those entry points and stuffed them with rags. Uncle Will and Big Si dozed in front of the fire, thankful for the two days of rest; farming now was more a thankless chore than a labor of love and neither man reaped pleasure from the backbreaking work. Mack read to Ruthie and Little Si—first from Charles Dickens's *A Tale of Two Cities*, then from Louisa May Alcott's *Little Women*. Then Ruthie and Si took the books from Mack and read to themselves, an ability that brought them more joy than they could express.

On the fifth day of February, it was cloudy and a bit warmer, and the wind had become little more than a breeze. "'Bout time the weather got itself back to normal," Big Si said from his vantage point on the front porch, though nothing in his field of vision was "normal" for Georgia. He tilted his head back and sniffed the air—it was cold and clean—then he scanned the sky, satisfied with what he saw, until he turned all the way around and looked due north. He frowned into the distance, opened the door, and called out, "Uncle Will!"

The old man came to the porch. So did everybody else. "What's wrong, Pa?" Little Si asked, stepping out into the cold to stand beside his father.

Big Si pointed north. "Look there," he said. Everybody looked, but only Uncle Will saw the huge bank of dark, rolling clouds for what they were. "What do you think?"

Uncle Will shivered and wrapped his arms around himself. "Same thing you think," he said, and went back inside the house.

Mack look at clouds that moved as he watched—moved toward them, seemingly in a hurry, if clouds could hurry. "More snow coming?"

Big Si nodded. "Soon, too," he said and followed Uncle Will back inside the house.

Mack, Ruthie and Little Si watched the clouds rush across the sky toward them. Ruthie, standing between the two men, put an arm around the waist of each man, big brother and soon-to-be husband, and drew them in close, as much for warmth as out of love. "I don't think I've ever seen clouds move like that."

"Me either," Little Si said."

"I wonder how far away they are," Ruthie mused. "As far as Tennessee? More?"

"Fast as they're moving, doesn't matter," Mack answered, and they all shivered and, as a unit, turned to go back inside.

The snow began just as they finished the meal—which nobody ate because, not having worked for three days, nobody was hungry. It was a light snowfall, tiny flakes floating toward the ground in no particular hurry to get there, unlike the clouds that brought them. Supper that evening was the midday meal that nobody had eaten, followed by baked apples with raisins. Ruthie was washing dishes when Mack ran into the kitchen. The look on his face frightened her. "What is it, Mack?"

He grabbed her hand, pulling her toward the front of the house. "Come look at this."

Uncle Will, her Pa and Little Si were standing in the front window, curtain pulled back, peering into the darkness. They were stark still, their only movement was in the expressions on their faces: Confusion, awe, worry, and something like fear. Ruthie stood between the two older men and looked out. The snow was up to the window and the wind was whipping it back and forth, and then up against the house, and it was coming down so hard and fast it looked like a solid sheet instead of individual flakes. "I never seen nothin' like this," Uncle Will said in a whisper. "Never in my life. Never woulda thought it could snow like this in Georgia."

"Me, neither," Big Si said, sounding almost relieved that the older man was as awestruck and mystified as himself.

"What should we do, Pa?" Little Si asked, hoping he didn't sound as fearful as he felt.

"Nothin' we can do," his father said.

"Go to bed," Uncle Will said, "and pray that it's finished by morning."

The snow was finished by morning, but so was their store of food—the last of the bacon and eggs and grits cooked for breakfast, the last of the meat and beans and corn bread eaten the day before. Now, for the first time since the storm began, people were worried, and not just the five people in this one house in Carrie's Crossing, Georgia, but all the people who were buried under three feet of snow that would not be melting any time soon due to temperatures that would not rise above twenty-five degrees for the next two days. "What are we going to do?" Ruthie asked Mack and Little Si. "We can't eat fruit preserves and pickled okra and cucumbers and tomatoes, and that's all we've got—the cans and jars in the pantry." She didn't need to say that the stored fruit and vegetables would be fine if there was meat, too, but without meat—and there would be no hunting or fishing for the foreseeable future—they wouldn't survive. They would be warm—there was no danger of their freezing—firewood was stacked to the ceiling on the back porch, as was always the case in winter. And they could drink the melted snow after boiling it. Food was their problem. Were it not for the snow, Beau and Mr. First would have arrived today with the monthly store of provisions, but not even Beau's truck could plow through the field of snow and ice that surrounded them.

Mack and Little Si tried not to look as worried and frightened as Ruthie though neither of them were doing a very good job until suddenly Little Si's eyes widened and grabbed Ruthie's arms, and he lifted her into a big hug before handing her off to Mack, who kept her lifted and hugged as Si hopped from one foot to the other. "We got money, y'all. We got money! We can go to the store and buy us some food!"

It took a moment for the meaning of his words to register fully, but when they did, Ruthie pounded Mack's shoulders. "Put me down, Mack."

He did and she scurried across the kitchen to the pantry, disappeared, then reappeared, a tin can held aloft. They watched as she upended the can on the kitchen table, and they all gasped at the amount of money that tumbled out. "Good God," Little Si yelled, which brought his father and uncle running into the kitchen.

"What's wrong?" the two older men exclaimed in unison. They saw the money at the same moment and had the same reaction. Stunned silence. Big Si recovered first.

"I forgot all about Nellie's money."

"Whose money?" Uncle Will said. Then, "Nellie's money? Where Nellie get money?"

"From Beau," Big Si said. "Beau was always givin' her money and she'd just put it in this can. Said she didn't need money what with him and First always bringing things. And he's kept right on with bringing money and I just put it in the can where Nellie put it, didn't think no more about it."

"Well I do declare," Uncle Will said, reaching out a hesitant hand to the wad of bills. "I don't b'lieve I ever saw so much money. How much is it?"

Everybody looked at Mack, then backed away from the table a step so that he could step forward and count. He did it quickly, then did it again. He looked up at them, a big grin replacing the amazement on his face. "Five hundred and sixteen dollars and forty-seven cents."

The quiet in the room was as deep as the drifting snow outside—and as rare. Not one of them spoke for a few long moments, and each of them was wishing that Nellie were there so that she not only could share the wonder, but if anyone could think of something to say, it would be Nellie. It was Little Si who finally found words.

"That's enough money to buy a motorcar," he said, eyes watching the piles of bills and coins on the kitchen table as if he expected the money to come alive.

"Then I guess it's enough to buy some groceries at Thatcher's Market," Ruthie said.

"And it'll be the first, last and only time anybody from this fam'ly stands at the back door of that store to buy anything," Uncle Will said. "Y'all know how I feel about that."

"Yes, sir," everybody—including Big Si—said. And they did: He had forbidden any of them to buy anything from any of the Zeb Thatcher-owned establishments, no matter that Zeb himself still was in jail. Today, however, they had no choice—because they had no food.

Uncle Will pointed at Little Si and Mack. "Y'all two go to the store—"

"I'm going too," Ruthie said, interrupting the old man.

"No, you are not." All the men in the room glared at her. She had not been able to travel on any of the nearby roads since Nellie was killed except in Beau's truck and surrounded by all the men in her family. She knew and understood what they felt, but their protective curtain felt more stifling every day.

"What could happen in all this snow? We'll prob'ly be the only ones out in it," Ruthie said, working hard to keep her voice from conveying the anger, frustration and pain she felt.

Mack put his arm around her. "We'll go and come back as fast as we can," putting an end to her insistence that she accompany them.

Big Si rushed from the room and returned almost immediately, unwrapping something in a burlap bag. "Y'all take this with you," he said, holding a long-barreled pistol. "It's loaded up and ready to shoot."

Mack and Little Si looked at each other, then Si reached for the weapon.

He was, after all, a child of the forest, and weapons were familiar tools to him—as familiar as a plow or a hoe. However, he'd never held a pistol, a weapon designed solely for the purpose of shooting another man. He was used to shooting—with a shotgun—deer or squirrel or rabbit or fowl for food, used to shooting snakes or bobcats in self-defense. He'd never shot or shot at a man, but he would, just as he'd shoot that snake or that cat, to protect himself and his family. Then he wondered how and when his Pa had come to own a pistol, and the answer came to his mind as quickly as had the query: From First Freeman after Nellie's murder. Nobody knew—probably never would know—who had killed her, but nobody doubted that it had been a white man because, until very recently, only white men owned pistols.

He and Mack wrapped themselves in practically every article of clothing they owned though they both realized it for the exercise in futility that it was: The layers of clothes would help them stay warm only if they could stay dry, and that they could not do. They'd be waist-deep in snow as soon as they opened the door and stepped out on the porch, and by the time they found their way to the road, the snow would have penetrated all their layers of clothing. They'd be both cold and wet before they were out of sight.

"How long do you think it'll take you to get there?" Ruthie asked, her irritation at not being able to accompany them replaced by concern for their well-being.

Mack shook his head and said, "No way to know." *Probably way too long* was what he thought as he hugged her.

"Y'all take these things with you," Uncle Will said, coming into the living room carrying one of the eight foot long poles used to support the fruits and vegetables that grew upward on vines and two burlap bags. When they all looked askance at him, he explained, as if to very young children, that if they tied the bags of groceries to either end of the pole, then placed the pole across their shoulders, they could balance the weight of the food and also give themselves some support on the trek back through the snow.

"That's a real good idea, Uncle Will," Big Si exclaimed.

The snort the old man emitted said he knew what a good idea it was and didn't need anybody to tell him, either. Ruthie laughed and hugged him, and they all followed Little Si and Mack to the front door and huddled together as the razor-sharp cold air rushed in.

"Y'all be careful," Uncle Will called out, not hearing the answer as the door slammed shut against the weather.

The three remaining Thatchers hurriedly stuffed the rags back into the cracks around the door, then Ruthie hurried to the window to watch the two men disappear into the bright whiteness that surrounded them. "You ever seen so much snow, Uncle Will?" she asked.

"I don't b'lieve I ever did."

"You ever felt this much cold?"

He nodded, then stopped himself. "I was 'bout to say back in the old times it got pretty cold, then I 'membered the places where we lived—they didn't have no doors or windows—and we didn't hardly have no clothes, so we was always hot or cold or wet or being et by bugs." He looked around the room, at the huge fire casting its warmth, at the curtains covering the windows, at the rugs on the floor, even at the rags stuffed into the cracks, and he shivered, not because he was cold—he wasn't, and he knew that many people, both Colored and white, were much colder this day than he was—but he shivered at the force of the dredged up memory of his life as a slave. No matter how many years of freedom he had enjoyed, the horror of that time still had the power to weaken him and lessen him.

Ruthie left the window, dropping the curtain back into place, and hurried to the fire to warm herself. "Anybody hungry?" she asked, though she knew that nobody would eat or sleep or do anything but watch and worry until Little Si and Mack returned.

"This is the only time I've ever been glad white folks take such good care of their own selves," Little Si said, breathless from the exertion but grateful that they'd finally left the deeply rutted and frozen solid dirt road in the Colored section and now were walking on the smoothly paved part of the road that led into the Carrie's Crossing shopping district. "We're lucky we didn't break a foot or a leg back there."

Mack looked behind them. "If nobody comes along behind us, we can go back in our same tracks, where we know it's safe to step."

Little Si nodded, unable and unwilling to speak: Whenever he opened his mouth, the cold air burned his throat and lungs like fire, sucking out what little breath he had.

"We're almost there," Mack said, his own breath labored, and hugged his almost-brother a little closer. They'd walked with their arms around each other, as much for warmth as for support, Mack using the long pole to probe beneath the snow looking for a safe place to walk. They were soaked to the bone and shivering, and they whispered prayers of thanks in unison as the buildings of Carrie's Crossing came into view.

They helped each other up the wooden steps to the back door of the market, steps that had been swept clear of snow, letting them know that they weren't the only Colored people in town who had run out of food during the past few days of bad weather. Si pulled the bell over the door, and they still were holding each other up and breathing hard when the door opened.

Jonas's shock was total. He gaped at them, then grinned and pushed the door open wider and stood back, waving them forward. They stood where they were, Mack working to unwrap the shirt that Ruthie had wrapped around his hand for warmth, so that he could give Jonas their grocery list.

"Hey, Silas," Jonas finally managed. "How're you doing? I almost forgot what you looked like, been so long since I saw you. How's Ruthie? Why didn't she come with you?"

"Ruthie's just fine," Mack said, "and she didn't come 'cause she's not allowed out on this road since her Ma got killed." He took the grocery list from his pocket.

Jonas felt like he'd been slapped, felt like Mack McGinnis might as well have slapped his face. Jonas had come to suspect that McGinnis was more than just the teacher. Now he knew for certain: The way he spoke for Ruthie, the way Si was looking at him—looking up to him the way he looked up to Beau. "Y'all come in," Jonas finally said, "where it's warm."

"Who else is here?" Little Si asked, remembering all the warnings he'd heard about the brother-in-law who was just like Jonas's pa.

Jonas's face fell, then changed into an expression Little Si had never seen before as he read the list that Mack had given him. Mack, however, knew exactly how to read what was written on Jonas's face—on the business face of the man who once was the boyhood friend of Little Silas Thatcher. Jonas looked from the list to the two men who stood before him. Without a word, he took a pencil from his pocket and wrote a number beside each item on the list, then looked again at his customers. Mack withdrew money from his pocket— obviously more money than was needed to purchase the items on the list.

As Jonas turned to go into the store, they heard a bell ring from inside. Jonas turned back to his back door customers. "Y'all step in and close the door. He'll be busy up front for a while," he said, referring to his brother-in-law. Then he hustled away to fill their order.

"He thought we didn't have money?" Little Si looked at his almost brother-

160

in-law. "He thought we came here expecting him to *give* us something?" He pulled open the door with such force that Mack had to grab it keep it from slamming against the wall. "I'd rather stand out here in the cold," he said. Mack joined him, and they stood huddled together on the narrow porch, stamping their feet to keep them from freezing.

Jonas returned quickly enough that they knew he'd rushed to fill their order. He opened the door holding a large box. "I told y'all you didn't have to stand out here—" He let the words trail off when he saw Little Si's face. "I put everything in a box for you."

"We don't need a box, Jonas. We got these sacks," Little Si said, and he began filling the burlap bags from the box Jonas held.

Mack grabbed a bag of dried lima beans. "This wasn't on our list," he said, holding the bag toward Jonas, who waved it off.

"We always give our good customers a free gift. Keeps them coming back," he said with a smile.

"We're not some of your good customers," Little Si said. "This is our first time here and unless it keeps snowing like this, it'll be our last time."

"I know Beau and Tobias bring y'all things from Belle City," Jonas said, trying to boost his morale after the shoot-down from Mack McGinnis. "They been doing that for quite a while."

"That's right," Mack said. "They buy from a store where they can walk in the front door any time they want." Then he tied the tops of the burlap bags with a thick rope, looped the bags over the end of a long pole and started down the steps. "I'll tell Ruthie you said hello, Jonas," he said and started down the steps, holding one end of the pole.

Little Si picked up the other end of the pole. "You thought we didn't have any money, didn't you, Jonas? You thought we'd come here to beg."

"I didn't know what to think, Si, since y'all never been here before."

"Suppose we had come here with no money. What then?"

Jonas gave Si the look that was foreign to him, the look of the businessman. "Then I'd give you what you asked for and have you sign a IOU slip, which I'd then give to Beau."

"Give it to Beau? Why, if we're the ones who did the buying?"

"'Cause Beau's the one with the money."

That made sense, Little Si thought, if the idea was to get money, but the thought, the idea that had been drummed into their heads all their lives was pounding its beat: Get education first, and everything else would follow. But they were Colored, and things were different for them. No point in thinking about money if you couldn't count it. Even Mr. First could count, though he couldn't read a word. Still...

"Ruthie read a whole book by Miss Louisa May Alcott all by herself, and I read one by Mr. Charles Dickens. We like them better than Mr. Mark Twain."

Jonas looked at Si for a long moment. "Tell Ruthie..."

"Ruthie's gettin' married in three months and maybe even movin' to Belle City," Little Si said, hoisting the long pole up to his shoulder, willing himself not to watch Jonas to see the impact of his words. He and Mack shifted the bags and pole several times until the weight was as evenly distributed as possible, given that Mack was a couple of inches taller. Then they started off home, looking down at the ground and taking care to place their feet in their own footprints, Mack thinking how right the older men had been regarding Jonas Thatcher's feelings toward Ruthie. He had just witnessed it firsthand: Jonas loved Ruthie. It was ridiculous, but it was true.

Jonas, standing in the doorway, oblivious to the cold, watched their careful progress, thinking he'd walk twice as far in twice as much snow and ice, carrying twice as much weight, if Ruth Thatcher were waiting for him. And both Little Si and Jonas were thinking, wondering, if their friendship was completely over.

The first time Ruthie spent an entire weekend in Belle City she knew that she wanted to live there because that's what she wanted for herself and not because it's what her mother had wanted for her. Her weekend visits began at the end of March so that she could attend Friendship Baptist Church on Easter Sunday, March 27th, and the plan was that she'd spend every weekend thereafter in Belle City until her wedding day at the end of May. And then what? She didn't like to think about that. She found that she didn't like to think about her home, about Carrie's Crossing, at all because it made her sad. Certainly contributing to the sadness was the ever-present memory of her mother, but it was more than that: It was how small the place seemed in comparison to Belle City, and she didn't mean "small" in the weights and measurements sense, but in the way that Carrie's Crossing diminished life for Colored people.

Her weekend visits had begun at the suggestion of Maisy Cooper, Emma Johnson, Tobias's mother-in-law, and Clara McGinnis, Mack's mother, who were planning her wedding. In addition to the shopping that was necessary for a bride-to-be, it was even more necessary, according to her surrogate mothers, that she establish a presence in the Friendship Baptist Church, where she would be married. Ruthie remembered Mr. First telling her, years ago, that Colored in Carrie's Crossing needed a church, a permanent one, not a once-a-month traveling preacher. Now she understood his meaning, for Friendship Baptist was about more than religious or spiritual development; it was about connections and relationships—friendships—strength in numbers, for on Sunday mornings, inside the churches where Colored people gathered, the perpetual threat to their existence that was white people was obliterated for an hour or two. That wasn't just true in Friendship Baptist, but also within the Wheat Street Baptist Church, where Maisy Cooper was a member. Ruthie visited there only once because it was across town, in the Fourth Ward. It was a structure of similar size and beauty to Friendship, and filled with similar Colored people—that is, people of all ages and descriptions, men, women and children, educated and not, the obviously well-to-do and the just as obviously down-and-out. She was no expert at church-going, but it seemed—and felt—to Ruthie that the people all attended church on Sunday for the same reason: To be a part of each other's lives.

She was made to feel welcome at Friendship immediately, partially because she was to be married to Mack McGinnis, whose family had belonged since the beginning, but in large part, she soon realized, because she was connected to First Freeman, and he was revered in the church. He also was revered in her heart, for the more time she spent with the old man, the more she found to love. He was kind and generous and nurturing—she already knew that about him. What she hadn't known was that he was funny, that he loved telling stories—tall tales they were—and when Ruthie would look askance and ask, "Is that the truth, Mr. First?" he would slap his thigh and giggle like a boy—and that he could cook! Her joy in him, however, always was tempered by a sadness there was no hiding from, the sadness that was what awaited her at home: Pa and Uncle Will, as lonely and dispirited as First Freeman was lively and connected to his surroundings. She also was sad for Little Si, who had to stay home and take care of Uncle Will and Pa, not one of whom could cook on a stove. All three were expert hunters, though, and they never tired of roasting on a spit over a fire whatever game they caught. Good thing they also liked coal-roasted potatoes, corn and turnips because that's all they ate when Ruthie was gone.

Ruthie also took great pleasure in the time spent alone with Beau. He picked her up on Friday night and drove her home on Sunday night, just the two of them in Beau's truck, and they talked almost the entire time. She hadn't known her older brothers well before they went to the War, and since Eubie didn't come home, she most likely never would get to know him. She knew Beau, though, and the more she learned about him, the more he surprised her. He naturally was a quiet man, made more so by the things he'd witnessed and experienced in Europe, things he couldn't bring himself to describe or explain. "It was too...too...ugly, Baby Sister. That's the only word I can think of. You and Little Silas and Mack, y'all read books and prob'ly have better words than that, but that's the best I can do. It was ugly and it stank."

"What do you mean, Beau? Stank how? Like the outhouse?"

"No, Baby Sister, not like that. Like...rot. Like...death. Like...blood. Like... everything evil and hateful and...and...ugly. That's all I can say. Except that it won't leave me alone. I close my eyes and I hear it and I see it. Bombs and mud and rotting bodies. And I always smell it."

"Is that why you won't eat meat? And why you don't like when it rains?"

"That's why."

"I'm going to learn French, Beau: How to speak it and read it and write it. And then I'm going to go find Eubie and bring him home."

"You think Mack's gon' let you go way 'cross that ocean to look for Eubie?"

"I already told him I was going."

"Then those Europeans better watch out. Ruth Thatcher McGinnis is comin' to town!"

"I never heard my name said like that."

"I hope you like how it sounds 'cause in two weeks, it'll be yours to keep."

Jonas didn't recognize his Pa when he walked into the grocery store in the middle of a muggy May afternoon. It had been raining off and on since breakfast, the humidity level rising with every cloudburst. It was as hot and muggy inside the store as out, and Jonas and his sister, who was working with him that day, decided to leave the front door open, so there was no tinkle of the above-the-door bell to alert them when a customer entered the store. So, Jonas looked up from his position behind the cash register every few seconds, and he saw the old man enter. And at first, that's all he saw: An old man walk in then pause and look all around. It was this looking around that identified his father to Jonas, for it wasn't the kind of looking a customer would do in search of a particular item; it was an assessing kind of look, determining whether things were in the right place, whether he liked what he saw.

Jonas came from behind the counter at full bore. He ran to the old man and grabbed him.

"Boy. You done growed quite a bit."

"Hey, Pa. Why didn't you call me to come get you?" He wrapped the old man in a bear hug and quickly released him, afraid of doing harm to what was little more than skin and bone.

"I tol' you I didn't want you nowhere near that prison."

Jonas nodded. After his first and only visit, he'd been ordered to stay away. He sent a box every week with pipe tobacco and the old man's favorite bologna, hard cheese and crackers, but he hadn't seen his father in more than a year, and as glad as he was that Pa was home, in truth, he had not missed him. "I'm glad you're back, Pa. Hey, Rachel. Come see who's here!"

Rachel looked their way then ran toward them, arms outstretched. "Oh, Pa. You're back. Thank God for that!"

"God ain't had nothin' to do with it."

Rachel was about to remonstrate but a look from Jonas stilled her, and the simultaneous arrival of several customers shifted her focus. She kissed her father's cheek and hurried away to tend to the customers, her business sense being almost as keen as her baby brother's.

"Things look real good 'round here, Boy. I been hearin' 'bout what a fine job you been doin' and it looks like that was nothin' but the truth."

Jonas was taken aback and more than a little angry. "Who told you that, Pa? You let other people come see you but not me?"

His Pa grabbed his arm with more strength than would have been expected from such a frail body. "You don't belong in a place that, you hear me? Not even to visit."

"You didn't belong there either, Pa."

"Maybe not for the reason they sent me, but I ain't so different from them who was in there with me. You—you surely are different, Boy. You and your Ma—y'all the same kinda people and I'm truly glad she never had to see me sent to a place like that. You understand me?"

"Yes, sir," Jonas said. "You hungry, Pa? Tired?"

The old man's shoulders drooped, and he sagged against Jonas. "I reckon I am, Boy."

"Let's go to the Crossing Café and get you fed. What do you feel like? Fried chicken and mashed potatoes or smothered pork chops? Some greens and yams?"

"All that, Boy. All that and some peach cobbler."

Jonas sought out Rachel and caught her eye. She nodded at him, letting him know that it was all right for him to leave, and, holding his Pa's arm, he led him out of the store. A fine mist was falling, warm like bath water. Zeb was taking in the scenery as if he'd been away for a dozen years instead of just slightly more than one. It was true that many changes had come to Carrie's Crossing in the last year. It also was true that the two most prominent commercial structures in the town bore the Thatcher name. Zeb noticed and a small smile lifted the corners of his mouth.

The bell above the door announced their arrival, but instead of Mr. Pace, Jonas and Zeb were welcomed by the new cook whose name Jonas had forgotten. She replaced Sue and was just as Colored and Jonas had forgotten about her. Or, more accurately, had given no particular thought to her. Zeb stopped in his tracks, and Jonas bumped into the back of him. He stared at the woman who was smiling a greeting at him.

"Good day to you, sir. And to you, Jonas. Y'all take a seat."

"What the hell?" Zeb roared, and all movement in the restaurant stopped. Quite a few of the diners didn't know or didn't recognize Zeb, but those who did readied themselves for whatever was coming next, which, as it happened, was the emergence of Charlie Pace from the kitchen, frowning and ready to pounce on whoever was making so much noise in his place. The frown turned into a scowl when he saw who it was.

"Zeb. I didn't know you were home."

"What the hell do you think you're doin' hirin' Colored? You know better'n that."

"I don't tell you how to run your stores, Zeb, you don't tell me how to run my café. Now, if you and Jonas are gonna eat, take a seat. Otherwise, close the door behind you."

Zeb glared at the Colored cook, who turned away and resumed her post at the grill. "I don't want her servin' me," he said, taking a table in the far corner of the room, his back to the cook. "Why didn't you tell me 'bout her, Boy?"

Jonas shrugged and shook his head. "Tell you what, Pa?" he said, hoping that he'd been successful at hiding the irritation he felt. Not back in town fifteen minutes—

"Tell me that Pace had hired a Colored. I don't want her cookin' my food, either."

"Then you'll be hungry, Pa, because there's no place else to eat and she's the cook." Jonas put his napkin in his lap as Zeb got to his feet.

"Come on, Boy. Let's go."

"The food is really good, Pa."

"Don't tell me you eat here."

"Every day, breakfast and dinner," Jonas said. Then he looked directly into his father's eyes. "We don't have a house anymore, and even if we did, there wouldn't be anybody in it to cook for us. But you know what, Pa? I'd eat here anyway. I like eating here."

Zeb gave Jonas a hard look, then dropped back into his chair. He sat in silence as Jonas ordered food for them, as Charlie Pace brought napkins, cutlery, glasses of iced tea and a bowl of rolls. "I'm gon' get my land back is what I'm gon' do," he finally said, grabbing a roll and eating it whole, barely chewing before he swallowed.

"Get what land back, Pa?"

"You know what land," Zeb said in a tone of voice previously unknown to his son.

Jonas looked at his father, really looked at him. He looked different. Somebody who hadn't known him well before he went away most likely wouldn't recognize him now, without the long, prophet-like beard he'd always worn and with his hair cut close to the scalp instead of flowing around his head like some kind of hairy flower. Zeb's long, lean face now was clearly visible, as if he'd stopped trying to hide himself. His deep-set eyes were fiercely and brightly blue, the only part of him that didn't look old, because the rest of him clearly was. He was thin, too thin, and he seemed unable to straighten his back. His clothes, the same clothes that he'd worn when he was arrested over a year ago, hung on his skinny frame like the clothes that hung on wire hangers in their department store. The veins stood up in the backs of his hands like cords of wood stacked on a back porch, and Jonas noticed one thing that hadn't changed—his nails still were long and claw-like, still were dirty. He needed a bath and some clean clothes, and Jonas needed somebody to talk to, somebody he could tell how he felt about his pa who wouldn't think he was a bad son, somebody like Ruthie or Little Si.

Jonas had not allowed himself to think about his friends since that snowy day when Si told him that Ruthie was getting married, since that day when he came face-to-face with Mr. Mack McGinnis, the man who might already be married to Ruthie. Si had said in three months. That was in February. It now was May. Was Ruthie already married? Jonas hadn't visited his tree since Nellie

Thatcher's death, since Mr. First Freeman told him to stay away. But he'd have to go there now. He needed to know...what? If Ruthie was married or if he still had any friends?

"Why do you hate Colored like you do, Pa?"

The question startled them both. Zeb stopped chewing and looked at Jonas as if the boy had told him there was poison in the food. "What kinda damfool question is that?"

Jonas shrugged, truly sorry that he'd spoken, for he knew there was no answer, and even if Pa did have some reason in his mind, he'd never share it with Jonas, or if he did, it probably wouldn't be the truth. "No kind, Pa. It don't...doesn't matter."

The old man gave a hoot, but Jonas didn't mistake it for laughter; it was anything but. "Sure it matters. Somebody as educated and right-talking like yourself—your kind don't say things if they don't matter," he said, the words both a challenge and a demand for an answer. The arrival of their food provided a temporary reprieve, but Jonas knew it was only temporary, for he could see the anger emanating from his father like heat waves off the blacktop road in the summer. They ate in silence, Jonas enjoying and appreciating the food as always. His Pa ate hunched over his plate, his arms encircling it protectively, and Jonas couldn't tell whether he was enjoying the food or whether he merely was all but half starved. Whatever the reason, he ate enough for two men twice his size, without apparent concern about who had cooked the food. It occurred to Jonas that the prison cooks probably were Colored and he had to will himself not to make the comment. *Best to leave well enough alone.* He heard his mother's voice in his head as clearly as if she was seated next to him, and he relaxed.

"Y'all doin' all right?" Charlie Pace asked as he gathered their empty places.

"Yessir, Mr. Pace. Doing just fine, thank you," Jonas answered. "If I ate any more, I'd pop a gut," he said, rubbing his belly.

"How 'bout some dessert? Pie, cake, cobbler?"

"We don't want no dessert," Zeb snarled, pushing is chair back. "We got to go."

Jonas got to his feet, reaching into his pocket for money. Pace waved the money away. "On the house," he said. "A welcome home to Zeb."

"Pay the man, Boy," he snapped at Jonas. "We don't take charity." He huffed his way to the front door.

"I'm sorry, Mr. Pace," Jonas said as he paid for their meal.

"No need for you to be sorry," Pace said, emphasizing the *you*.

It didn't take much for Jonas to catch up with Zeb, who walked slowly and hunched over. Like an old man, Jonas thought, not like a jack rabbit. Not like First Freeman and Maisy Cooper. "It's not just Colored you hate, is it? You hate everybody. Why, Pa? Why?"

Zeb didn't say anything for a moment. He just kept walking. It was raining now, not just misting, and because he walked so slowly, Zeb was getting soaked, though he seemed not to notice. Or to care. He stopped outside *THATCHER'S MARKET* and studied the store. Jonas knew he couldn't read, but he also knew his Pa had a keen eye and a keener intuition. "You been sellin' to niggers in my store?"

"Not inside the store, out the back door. To those who'll buy out the back door."

Zeb now turned his piercing gaze on his son. "What's that mean, those who'll buy out the back door? If they cain't come inside, where else they gon' buy?"

"Belle City," Jonas answered, "where they *can* go inside."

"Then let 'em all go to Belle City. We won't do no more sellin' to niggers."

"You're throwing away a lot of money," Jonas said. "I keep a separate ledger for the Back Door Sales, and it's a good bit of money."

Zeb opened the door to the market and the bell tinkled. "Don't matter," he said, "I don't need no nigger money."

Jonas didn't follow him inside. Instead, he walked around to the rear of the building and, as he expected, there were several people at the back door, huddled under the eaves, waiting to be served. "Y'all can't buy here anymore. My Pa is back and any of you who know him, you know how he is."

"Yeah, we know," said a man whom Jonas did not know. "Come on, y'all," he said and led the people away from the back door of *THATCHER'S MARKET* out into the rain.

"Tell everybody," Jonas called out as he watched them disappear into what had become a downpour, though he hadn't needed to say that; everybody would know soon enough that Zeb Thatcher was out of jail and back home. Everybody white and Colored, and at that thought, that realization, a swell of feelings and emotions so powerful rose in him that he literally staggered and fell back against the wall. Had he only pretended to be saddened by his father's imprisonment, pretended to miss him? That must be the case, he thought, because what he felt so overwhelmingly at the moment was a disgust that bordered on dislike, and he knew that if Zeb weren't his Pa, he'd have nothing to do with the man.

The door swung open with unnecessary force, slamming Jonas in the back. He moved quickly aside to find Pa glaring at him.

"I thought you'd be out here. Where your niggers?"

"Gone."

"Gone where? Ain't nowhere for 'em to go," he said, peering into the rain.

"Why do you care where they went? You don't want 'em here so I told em to go."

He shook his head. "You might shouldn'ta done that, Boy. I just got a look at how much money we made through the back door already today—and that's with it rainin' cats and dogs." He looked at the rain again, as if reading it. "That was right smart thinkin' on your part, keepin' the money separated like that, so we can know what's what." He turned to go back inside. "Don't matter. They'll be back t'morrow."

"Who'll be back tomorrow?" Jonas asked.

"The niggers."

"No, they won't. I told them to tell everybody that you were back and to stay away."

Zeb gave him a hard look, then he grinned. "Guess they know I mean bizness."

"Guess they hate you same as you hate them," Jonas said, and stepped into the rain. Before he could take more than two steps, Zeb had grabbed his arm and swung him around.

"They tell you that? They tell you they hate me?"

"They don't have to tell me, not in words."

"How you tell a body a thing if not with words?"

Jonas remembered First Freeman talking about Zeb. "I saw their eyes when I said they couldn't buy from here anymore, and why."

Zeb was quiet for a moment. "Let's get in outta the rain," he finally said. "Let's go to the pub." And he did a quick-step toward the building next door, to what Jonas called the storeroom. He unlocked the door and turned on the light. Zeb gasped. "What—" He looked around. "What is all this stuff? Who does it belong to?"

"It's ours, Pa. I buy things wholesale so we always have what we need, so we don't run out of things, especially things people buy all the time."

Zeb grabbed him in a tight hug. "Boy, I wish your Ma was here to see you. Ev'rything she said about you is the truth. You got to be the smartest man I ever met."

Jonas was rendered speechless. All the animosity and dislike his father had fostered in him in the last hour was on the verge of evaporating. "You left me in charge, Pa. I didn't want to let you down."

"If it hadn'ta been for you, I'd be broke right now."

"No, Pa. That's not true," Jonas said, and he started to tell Zeb how hard his sisters and brothers-in-law had worked during the last year. Zeb listened and nodded his head as he walked around looking at and touching the various items of merchandise piled about.

"They just did what you told 'em to do," he said, then asked, "How much money we got?"

Jonas told him because he knew, almost to the penny. "You want to see it?"

Zeb hopped from one foot to the other like a young child expecting a visit from St. Nick, and he followed Jonas as he weaved through the boxes and crates of goods until he was behind what used to be the bar of Zeb's Pub. He lifted a floorboard in the corner and began to remove metal boxes— six in all. Zeb's eyes were huge. "That's money? In all them boxes? That's all my money?" He danced a little jig, around and around in a circle. "Show it to me, Boy. Show it to me. I wanna see it. I wanna count it."

Jonas opened the boxes and displayed the cash, and he was almost as overcome as Zeb, despite the fact that he knew how much money there was— after all, he'd put it there—but he'd never looked at all of it at one time, in all six boxes.

"I need me a drink of whiskey. Let's celebrate. Where's the whiskey?"

Jonas looked at his Pa as if he'd spoken in tongues. "There's no whiskey here."

"Where is it, then? What happened to it? You didn't sell it all, did you?"

"Pa, what are you talking about?"

"I'm talkin' 'about the whiskey that fella from Belle City brings over here," Zeb snarled. "What whiskey you think I'm talkin' 'bout?"

Jonas knew now to be very, very careful. He wouldn't lie to Zeb, but neither would he leave himself vulnerable to the man's abuse. "You want me to tell what that man said when he got here to deliver his whiskey and found out you were in jail? If you want I'll tell you what he called me, what he called Rachel."

"I don't care what he called you. What did you do with the whiskey?"

"What do you think I did with it, Pa, seeing as how it had gotten you locked up? Since I wasn't locked up with you, what do you think I did with the whiskey?" Jonas was angry and he didn't care if Zeb knew it. One thing for sure: The old man couldn't beat on him anymore and, Jonas realized, he no longer was afraid of him. He saw Zeb reach that same conclusion at the moment he felt it, and he reveled in the power he felt. That's how you tell a body a thing without using words, Jonas thought.

"Then who sells whiskey 'round here? Somebody got to sell it." Jonas shook his head and left it to Zeb to interpret the action: Either Jonas didn't know or he was prepared to write his father off as a hopeless case. "That's all right, I don't need you. I'll find out for myself what I need to know." He grabbed some bills from one of the boxes and stuffed it into his pants pocket. "Hide this money back where cain't nobody find it," he said and stomped away and out.

Jonas stood where he was for a long moment, thinking too many thoughts at once. He had to will his brain to slow down, and when that happened, the first thing he did was banish all angry thoughts of Zeb. He would waste no more time or energy on the man. His mother had told him once, in her gentle way, not to judge him too harshly. *"Your pa is who he is, Jonas, and that's all he can be. It's all any of us can be, is who we are. He's not a bad man, he's just who he is."* Well, Jonas thought to himself: You be who you are, and I'll be who I am. And who Jonas was in that moment was a man determined to protect what he'd earned so that he could live the life of his choosing. He looked around for a new hiding place for the six metal boxes that he had shown Zeb—and for the two metal boxes that he had not displayed, for that money was his and his alone. That was the money he had earned working with Beau Thatcher buying and selling illegal whiskey, and he had no intention of sharing if with Zeb— or anyone else.

He knew every inch of this place. He'd chosen to hide the profits from the stores behind the bar because he'd easily discovered the loose floorboards. He returned two of the boxes to this place, knowing—expecting—that Zeb would look for it. Then he went in search of another place, a place that Zeb couldn't find. His own money he kept hidden in a crawlspace in the ceiling, but he didn't want the two sources of money in the same location; he needed to find a new place to hide the profits from the stores. He was walking around in circles before he realized what he was doing and stopped himself. He had, not five minutes ago, sworn not to give his Pa anymore power over him, and what was he doing? He shook his head, disgusted with his own self. He stalked over to the bar and glared at the boxes of money as if they'd done something to offend him. He returned them to their place beneath the floorboard, along with the other two. If Zeb wanted to come take all the money and spend it on cheap whiskey, so be it. Of course, Jonas thought to himself with a wicked grin as he locked the door, he'd have to break in first.

⌒

Beau had the gate open and was waiting for him at the alley entrance to First Freeman's backyard. Jonas liked the alleys in Belle City and wished there were more of them, but as the city grew and prospered, the alleys became driveways and backyards because those responsible for the growth and prosperity thought alleys were common and country.

"Hey, Jonas."

"Hey, Beau."

And that was all they said to each other until the whiskey was transferred from Jonas's car to Beau's car and they'd taken care of the monetary matters, which was so satisfactory that they had seriously considered quitting because they'd made so much money. However, First Freeman put a stop to that thought in hurry with his pronouncement that "there's no such thing as enough money" along with his suggestion that they actually increase their sales—most of Beau's clients were out of whiskey before the end of the month and Jonas only made one delivery each month—on the last Thursday—so his customers would be ready for the weekend.

Jonas looked forward to the monthly visits with Beau and Mr. First, and he looked all around for the old man. "Where's Mr. First?" he asked Beau.

"He's over at the church. He thinks they can't get everything ready without him," Beau said and pulled out his pocket watch and pressed the button that flipped it open. Beau was, Jonas thought, more proud of having learned how to tell time than he was of all the money he'd made.

Jonas gave him a wide smile. "Y'all got yourselves a new kinda church, one you go to on Thursdays?"

In return, Beau gave him an odd look. "You know Ruthie's gettin' herself married, don't you? To Mack McGinnis?"

The grin fled from Jonas's face. He nodded. "Si told me."

"It's on Saturday, and it's—" Beau didn't finish his sentence because the look on Jonas's face stopped the words in his throat: The boy looked like a giant mosquito had sucked all the blood out of him in one gulp, and Beau knew that

Mack had been one hundred percent right in saying that Jonas loved Ruthie—they all had been right. It had been only Little Si and Beau himself who'd doubted such a possibility. He studied Jonas's face. All the blood had returned in a rush, and he now looked like he was burning with fever. Beau didn't know what to say to him—how to tell him to stop being such a fool, how to tell him that every male related to Ruthie would kill him if ever he acted on his feelings. As far as Beau knew, that had never happened, and given what he knew of Jonas, he really didn't think it ever would. Yet and still...

"Tell Ruthie for me...and Mack...I said congratulations and many happy returns," Jonas said, backing away from Beau and toward his car.

"I'll do that, Jonas, and I'll see you next month—if not before," and at the confused look on the boy's face, he explained that Ruthie and Mack would be living in Carrie's Crossing after they married. "We can't get Pa and Uncle Will to move over here, and we can't leave 'em by their selves, 'specially with your Pa talking crazy like he's doing."

"What do you mean, Beau, about my Pa talking crazy?"

Beau had to laugh at the mix of confusion, shock and surprise that played across Jonas's face. Uncle Will and Mr. First often said that white people treated Colored people as if they were blind, deaf and dumb—as if they neither saw, heard nor understood what whites were saying or doing, and Beau had seen the point proved more than once...and now, again. "He tells it to just about anybody who'll listen, Jonas, how he's taking back his land, taking back what belongs to him, and what he'll do to anybody gets in his way."

"Oh, Lord," Jonas groaned. Zeb had made that claim to him, but he didn't know the old man was saying it to other people. He shook Beau's hand and got in his car. Beau opened the gate and Jonas backed out into the alley. None of the several Colored people who had moved out of the way gave him any particular notice, but Jonas noticed them, noticed them pay him little heed, and not for the first time; he marveled at how different things would be if one of them were alone in an alley in the white section of town. It's why he and Beau conducted their business in First Freeman's backyard instead of on the side of the road or in darkened parking lots—no matter where they'd met, a white person would notice Beau and demand that Jonas explain what the nigger was doing. Why, then, didn't they remark on his presence in their environment? What did they think he was doing there? Did Beau ever worry about his safety the way he worried about Beau's?

It would have pained Jonas to know that Beau gave him not another thought, for even as he was closing and locking the gate with Jonas not yet out of sight, he was out of mind. Beau's only thought was of his baby sister's wedding and what a special occasion it would be and how proud he was of her and how so many people that she hadn't even known a few short months ago were now doing everything they could to make Saturday a day she would never forget.

If someone had asked her to give words to her feelings, Ruthie would first have had to stop her head from spinning. She didn't know, from moment to moment, what she was thinking or feeling beyond the excitement that was, at times, so intense she felt she would faint. She was a farm girl who'd spent her life in the company only of her family—and all of them men and boys, the only woman regularly part of her life was her mother. Now she was surrounded by women—old ones and young ones—all of them infused with the same purpose. And the boys and men whom she loved now more than ever, her Pa and her brothers and Uncle Will and Mr. First, the way they looked at her—she knew they were seeing Nellie, missing Nellie, and putting all their love for the absent Nellie on the shoulders of the one remaining woman in their lives.

Of the women now caring for Ruthie, only Maisy Cooper had known Nellie Thatcher, but all the others—her soon to be mother-in-law, Tobias's mother-in-law, Tobias's wife and her sisters, the women of Friendship Baptist Church—they all told Ruthie how proud Nellie would be of her, and how happy she would be for her, and Ruthie believed them. Individually, these women knew more about life and living than Ruthie ever had. Collectively, they knew all there was to know, and Ruthie was and forever would be grateful to them for sharing that knowledge.

Her wedding day was a blur. She remembered waking that Saturday morning only because in that first instant of awareness, she'd forgotten what day it was. As soon as she remembered, her head began spinning, and the spinning continued unabated until that evening. She did remember arriving at the church and having a moment of panic when there was no one there. "Everybody's inside already," Little Si told her, and she looked at him as if her were a stranger. He had on a suit with a tie. She'd never seen him in a suit—didn't know he owned one. Her next memory was of being inside the church, and indeed, everybody was inside already, so many people her eyes couldn't see them all at one time. Holding the arms of Pa and Uncle Will, the three of them walked down the aisle. That's when she saw Mack standing there, his Pa and brothers beside him. Pa and Uncle Will, holding her arms, holding her up, were all but carrying her until her feet found themselves. She didn't remember Pa and Uncle Will saying they gave the bride to her groom, and she didn't really remember promising to love, honor and obey her husband though standing beside Mack, holding his hand, turning from the minister to face the congregation is clear in her mind. Her head finally stopped spinning at the reception at Mack's parents house where all the people she loved and who loved her laughed and cried and hugged her and told her how beautiful she was, how much like Nellie she was. But she wasn't Nellie. She was Ruth Thatcher McGinnis.

How different things were—and yet how much the same. She already knew how small her hometown looked from her weekend visits back and forth to Belle City, but she hadn't expected that her house would seem so small. Pa and Uncle Will now slept in the cabin Mack had built and called home, and Little Si slept up in the attic, giving Ruthie and Mack most of the house to call their own. It was Ruthie's house now, as it once had been Nellie's house.

Ruthie still did all the cooking and cleaning, but now the men deferred to her: What vegetables did she want planted, what game did she want hunted, did she want fish or fowl, and would she please make corn bread for dinner or biscuits for breakfast?

Almost all of the few Colored still remaining in the town came to visit her and Mack, and to wish them well. They all brought gifts—usually a pie or a cake—but Louise Cooper, who was Maisy's husband's sister, brought two very pretty plates, cups and saucers, and Essie Mae Miller, the cook at the café, brought flowers to plant in the yard. Ruthie hugged her tightly, then pulled her out into the yard to discuss where they'd look best. Pa, Little Si, and Mack were painting the house, the decision having been made that they no longer would abide by the unspoken law that prohibited Colored people from painting their houses and planting flowers in their yards. Their boldness worried Uncle Will, but it pleased him, too.

It took Ruthie a while to realize it, but her visitors and well-wishers came to bear witness to the truth of what the Thatchers were up to, as well as to extend their congratulations. Yes, it was true: The house gleamed white in the bright sun and the flowers of many colors raised their faces to that same brightness to be nourished, and though only the front was painted so far, in addition to being impressed, the visitors were giddy with pride that there were Colored people sufficiently bold and well-off to indulge such a luxury. And though the Thatchers basked in the warmth of all the well-wishing, they also instinctively understood that some things were best left undisplayed and unsaid. That's why Ruthie told no one about the house Mack's father and brothers were building for them in Belle City, and why the automobile that was their wedding present always was parked in the barn. Still, their efforts to beautify their surroundings did not go unnoticed. On the day that Ruthie and Mack were celebrating their two-month anniversary, Police Chief Tom Fordham paid them a visit.

Big Si, who'd been up since before daybreak weeding and hoeing, was napping on the porch on a long, low bench that Mack had made for him. It had pillows and a head rest and Big Si said it was more comfortable than his bed. In fact, he'd slept there on the last three nights because it was so hot. Ruthie was sitting on the porch steps shelling the peas and shucking the corn that she had picked that morning. Little Si, who'd been hunting and fishing, was in the barn cleaning his catch. Mack, who had been in the schoolhouse preparing the next day's lesson after hauling water from the creek, was headed back to the house when he saw the police car. He ran to the house and up the porch steps without a word, alerting Ruthie and Big Si to potential trouble. They knew how much trouble when the wireless suddenly went silent. Mack was on the porch, standing in front of Ruthie, when the police car roared into the yard, kicking up dust and gravel.

Little Si, hearing the unusual sound of a motor vehicle moving too fast, looked out the barn door. He saw the police car and hurried out of the back door of the barn, into the back door of the house, carrying both his shot gun and his rifle. He gave only a fleeting thought to the consequences of shooting a white man, especially the chief of police, because he would shoot him to protect his family.

Tom Fordham took his time getting out of his car, took his time walking up the path of river rocks and stones to the front of the house, took his time looking all around, all the while making certain that none of his thoughts were readable on his face, for what he was thinking was that it was no wonder people like Zeb Thatcher and his cronies were resentful of how these Coloreds were living because it indeed was better than how the poor whites of Carrie's Crossing were living. The chief could have pointed out that hard work was the key, because everything he saw screamed out that back-breaking hard labor is what made the place look like it looked: The river stones had to be carried from the river—hundreds of them; the path had be dug and the stones arranged so they would fit. It must have taken months, if not years. Same thing was true for the rocks that bordered the flower beds—and these were big rocks, not stones. It would take mules and men to move them up here to the house. And this yard was swept every day, probably twice a day. The weeding and hoeing had to be done daily, and the chicken coop looked as if it had been built yesterday. Just like Zeb, the chief thought, to be mad 'cause niggers had a nice place to live, without giving a single thought to how much work they'd had to do to have such a place.

"How y'all?" the chief said when he finally made his way to the front of the house. Squinting, because he was looking directly into the sun, he saw a man on the steps behind the young woman who was sitting there, and a man in front of her, and he saw somebody standing behind the screen door, and he put his hand on his gun belt.

"We fine, Chief Fordham, how you doin'?" Big Si nodded and lifted his hat. Then he wiped his brow and head with his kerchief before returning the hat, as if that's why he'd removed it in the first place.

Fordham noticed, and his eyes narrowed into an even tighter squint. "Y'all know better'n to go paintin' the house and plantin' these flowers, ain't that right?" And when nobody spoke, he looked at the door. You, inside. Come on out here.

Little Si pushed open the screen and stepped out, walking over to stand beside his father. The chief studied the people grouped before him and realized that he didn't know a single one of them, not firsthand. He knew who they were but he'd never seen one of them in town, and he'd certainly never seen one of the men in his jail. But he had seen and did know Old Will Thatcher.

"Where's Will'am?"

"Inside," Big Si said. "He's 'sleep."

"What he doin' sleep this time of day?"

"He's old and he's sick."

"Go get him!"

For a frozen moment, nobody moved and Fordham thought he was going to have to shoot somebody. Then the boy turned and headed back into the house. The chief bent down and began unearthing the brightly colored plants blooming so neatly in the garden that abutted the house's stone foundation. He pulled them up and tossed them into the yard, roots and all. Under the broiling sun, they'd be dead in an hour. He aimed a kick at the stones in the foundation and shock waves traveled up his leg. This house was old and better built than those of all but the richest white people. The chief began to feel uneasy though he wasn't sure why. He knew better than to get worked up over anything Zeb Thatcher said or did, and the only reason he was here was because Zeb was, after all, one of the richest men in town. The chief liked his job and he wanted to keep it; therefore, he occasionally had to treat Zeb like the important citizen that he, in fact, was. It wasn't Zeb's irritation with high-living Colored folks, though, that caused Fordham's uneasiness. He looked again at the three people before him. Not one of them had moved since the boy went inside to get Old Will, and not one pair of eyes had looked directly at him, though he knew they knew every move he made. He thought he'd heard the girl's breath catch when he pulled up the flowers, but he could have been mistaken. And he thought the one standing in front of her had leaned slightly toward her at the same time, but he could have been wrong about that, too.

"What's your name, boy?" he asked him.

"Mack McGinnis Jr."

"I thought y'all was Thatchers over here," the chief said, casting around his mind for memory of McGinnises. Then it came to him. "You the one from over in Belle City, the one just now got married with this Thatcher girl." He looked at Ruthie. "Your Ma's the one who passed away a while back."

Ruthie nodded. "A year ago June."

He tried to recall what he'd heard, that there was something not quite right about it. "What carried her off?" he asked, but before she could answer, the boy came back out with Old William Thatcher, and if he hadn't been standing in the man's front yard, he never would have known who he was. The chief knew Thatcher was old—he was one of the few left from the slavery—but this man looked to be a hundred. The Will Thatcher he remembered had been tall and strong, built like a pecan tree.

Little Si, one arm around Uncle Will's waist and one of the old man's arms across his shoulders, all but carried him out. He hadn't wanted to wake up, and he still was groggy. The sun hurt his eyes and he had to work to get them focused, and when he did, he drew back. "I didn't do nothin'. I didn't do nothin'. I didn't do nothin'."

It was a high wail of terror that galvanized his family. Ruthie ran to him and helped her brother carry him back inside—and they literally carried him, for the old man was dead weight between them. At the same time, Big Si stepped off the porch, coming to stand beside Mack, so that the two of them faced the chief, and it was then that the chief knew what it was about these people that made him uneasy: They did not fear him. He'd given no permission for anybody to take the old man back inside the house, yet that's what they had done, without a single glance at him. And that girl, the look she gave him when he asked what it was that had carried her Ma off so quick and sudden: Nobody had ever looked at him like that so he didn't know what it meant. He knew only that it wasn't the kind of eyes that some young Colored girl ought to be turning on him. And these two standing in front of him, looking at him eye-to-eye, not a bit of fear in either one of them. If he shot them both dead right now, which he could do, the other ones still would not show him fear…but hate! That's what it was. If looks could kill, he'd be the one dead in the dirt. For once in his miserable life, Zeb Thatcher was right: These niggers had to be gotten rid of.

Jonas was exhausted, and if he'd had some place to sleep, he'd have spent the night in Belle City instead of driving back home to Carrie's Crossing. A couple of times he'd caught himself falling asleep at the wheel, only to jerk awake and then find himself unable to keep his eyes open for longer than a minute or two. He tried reciting poetry out loud—Walt Whitman and Edgar Allan Poe—but he couldn't remember the words. He sang for a while, loudly and so off-key that he achieved the objective of keeping himself awake for the last mile of the trip home. He'd already decided that he wouldn't bother to unload the car, and he was so looking forward to falling into bed that the light from inside the warehouse building didn't register until he was out of the car and almost to the door. Then all of his senses went on full alert: There was light coming from inside, and he heard voices and smelled smoke. "Dadburnit," he muttered to himself. Zeb was here with his moonshine drinking cronies, probably playing cards. It would go on for hours, which meant he'd have to go to one of his sisters' houses to sleep or sleep in the car. "Dadburnit all to hell." He'd known that giving Zeb a key was a mistake, but he couldn't get around it—after all, the building did belong to the old man.

He looked around. He could sleep here on the porch but the mosquitoes would eat him alive, and he'd sweat to death inside the car. Besides, he was so loaded down with merchandise there barely was room for him to drive it, to say nothing of trying to stretch out to sleep. Maybe he could sneak inside without being heard and curl up in the space behind the bar. He was good at entering the back door late at night without being seen or heard, and so once inside, he pulled the door closed and stood still and silent to adjust his eyes and his breathing. He listened and at first did not recognize any of the voices he heard; these men were not Zeb's drinking cronies though they were drinking. He could smell the whiskey. He inched forward for a look and a closer listen and what he saw and heard caused his heart to hammer so hard in chest he was certain it could be heard. He was spying on a meeting of the Ku Klux Klan, and they were discussing their plan to seize William Thatcher's farm—tonight!— because he'd missed today's tax filing deadline. Jonas couldn't recognize faces because of the sheets, but he recognized voices: Zeb's, his brother-in-law Clem's, and Chief Fordham.

Jonas now was wide awake. He began slowly backing up. He hadn't wanted to be heard entering, and he most certainly did not want do be heard leaving. If he could open the door and get out—if he could get in the car and get it started. Instead, he ran, full out and as fast as he could, running on the hard, rutted road instead of cutting through the woods as he once would have done back when he was a child and afraid of being seen anywhere near the Thatcher's place. He no longer was a child, and he didn't care who saw him this night, though it was doubtful that anyone would. At almost midnight, nobody would be out on the road, and there were no streetlights in the Colored section for the same reason that the road was unpaved.

When he got to the Thatcher's he took a deep breath before climbing the steps to the porch. He'd only been to the front door of this house once—when Nellie died and he knew there was nobody inside. Tonight, there were people inside though the house was in total darkness. He took another breath and knocked. In seconds he heard footsteps approach the door and stop. "It's me, Jonas Thatcher," he whispered, and after a brief pause, the door opened.

"What is it you want here, Jonas?" Mack McGinnis stood in the doorway.

"I got something to say to Ruthie, Mack."

"My wife's not coming out in the dark to talk to you. And anyway, you got no business having anything to say to her."

"It's important."

"Then tell it to me."

They could have been twins, standing there staring at each other with their flat, unblinking gazes: They were the same height and they were built the same rangy, lean way; they wore the same denim pants, flannel work shirts and heavy brogans; they wore their hair cut close to the scalp, as much to deny lice a home as in defiance of any sartorial dictate. Because Mack had not lit a lantern when he opened the front door, and because the stingy half moon was hidden behind thick cloud banks, there was no light to reveal that one of the men was white and the other Colored, though the two of them knew that fact as well as they knew their own names.

"Y'all got to leave here tonight, Mack, you and Ruthie and her Pa and Old William. Pack what you can and get out, quick as you can."

"What in hell are you are talking about, Jonas? Pack and get out? Why—" Mack didn't finish the question because he knew the answer. There was only one reason that Colored people packed up and fled in the middle of night. "Why, Jonas? Dammit, *why?*" Confusion, anger, resentment or some combination of the three raised Mack's voice from its usual low rumble to a thunder clap so that Ruth heard it at the back of the house, and it frightened her because Mack did not raise his voice. She came running.

"What is it, Mack? Who's here?" She peered around her husband despite his attempt to prevent it. "Jonas! What are you doing here this time of night?" She pushed open the screen door to look at him.

"He came to tell us to run."

"Run? Why?"

Mack put an around Ruth and drew her in close to him, noticed Jonas's reaction, and held her tighter. "Yeah. Why?"

"'Cause they're comin' to burn you out, that's why." He spit the words from his mouth and looked over his shoulder, as if "they" were imminent.

Mack and Ruthie looked at him, and Jonas watched their expressions change as they grasped the meaning of his words. Impossibly, they drew even closer together, each feeding off the other's anger and growing stronger. Jonas saw it happen, saw them strengthen. What he did not see—what he expected to see— was fear. If they were frightened, he realized that they'd never show him that feeling, and that made him sad, made him know for sure that he existed outside the reality of their world.

"I guess you know this 'cause it'll be your Pa and his sheet-wearin' friends who'll be coming to do the burning," Mack said.

"Why, Jonas?" Ruthie asked. "Why are you doing this?" The question was real.

"I'm not doing it. I'm the one risking life and limb to come over here and tell you about it, to give you a chance to get away."

"You want us to thank you?" Mack's anger frightened both Jonas and Ruthie, and both inched a little away from him.

"Why, Jonas?" Ruth asked again.

Jonas looked over his shoulder again, then back at Mack and Ruth. He blew a big burst of air from between his lips, then shook his head. "They know you missed the tax filing deadline today."

"Which means your no-count daddy can steal my land with the law on his side." Mack spit into the dirt, missing Jonas's feet by inches. "I'm not running from your daddy or anybody else, and you can ride on back over there and tell him I'll be waiting for him if he shows up on my land."

"No, Mack." Now Jonas saw a flicker of fear in Ruth. "We better go."

"I have not ever in my life run in fear from no crackers, Ruth. This land belongs to you—to your people. You can't just run off and leave it."

Tears filled up and spilled out of Ruth's eyes. She lifted her shoulders, first the right one, then the left, wiping her face on the shoulders of her dress; she kept her hands wrapped around her husband's arms. "We can't fight them and win. If we stay here, they'll kill us and take the land anyway. What good are we dead?" She released Mack's arms and put both hands on her belly.

Jonas noticed and knew immediately what the gesture meant. He wanted to say something but didn't know what, and even if he could have thought of something, they wouldn't want to hear it. Not now, tonight.

"We didn't *miss* the filing deadline today, Jonas," she said in the still, quiet way she had. Her hands still rested on her belly but her eyes held Jonas's, saw his confusion, and, with the slightest shake of her head, the kind of shake that people use to convey a feeling that words can't, she said, "The tax office closed early today. You didn't know that? When we got there after lunch time, when it was supposed to open back up, the place was locked up tight. A sign on the door said it was closed 'cause of an emergency. You didn't know that, Jonas?" But she could tell, even in the dark, that he hadn't known, and when he understood what had happened, he couldn't hide the shame and sorrow he felt. He also couldn't prevent the inevitable.

"They'll be coming about four-thirty, and they plan to come up through the woods 'stead of up the road. Y'all got plenty of time." Jonas turned away to leave.

Ruth's voice stopped him. "Jonas."

He turned back. "What, Ruth?"

"I don't blame you, and I thank you, once again, for being a friend."

Her words surprised him almost as much as the gentleness in her voice. She knew that it mattered to him that she held him blameless for this most recent transgression. But he knew that she couldn't forget that he was white any more than he could stop being what he was, any more than he could prevent things from being as they were. The state and county government offices were open in the morning for whites and in the afternoon for Colored—except if a white person decided to conduct business in the afternoon. Then the Colored would be required to leave. And if the office was closed early, without reason or notice—that's just how it was, how it always had been, how it most likely always would be. Nothing any of them could do about it. He nodded his head in thanks and walked slowly down the steps into the deep darkness, realizing suddenly that no dogs barked.

The Thatchers had always had dogs. Just as they'd always had mules to plow the acres of food they grew, though even in the dark he could see that the fields were barren. So much had changed. Everything had changed, and now there would be no more Ruthie and Little Si, no more Thatchers in Carrie's Crossing. No more Colored Thatchers. Then he pulled up short. There would be no more Colored in Carrie's Crossing at all. The plan he'd heard involved the Klan members splitting into groups with each one targeting one of the four remaining Colored farms in Carrie's Crossing, Zeb keeping this one for himself: Getting back his land, just like he said he would.

Jonas stepped onto the rutted road and almost fell as his foot sank into a deep rut. As he regained his balance, he had the thought that this road would be paved by next month this time. The sound of an automobile engine made him stop in his tracks. He stilled and listened. It was coming from behind that Thatcher house. He quickly switched directions and hurried up the road as it ran behind the house, and what he saw stunned him: A brand new motorcar backing out of the barn. He had, he realized, been listening for the clattery sound of a mule and cart. Ruthie and Mack had an automobile! Beau had told him that Mack's family was well-off, but he hadn't given much thought to what that meant. Now he knew. He crept closer to the side of the house. He couldn't see very much, but neither would he be seen, and he could hear some of what was said. What he heard first was Mack telling Ruth to wake up her Pa and Little Si, and he heard her footsteps as she scurried away. There was no light; the Thatchers, like Jonas himself, were as relaxed and comfortable in the darkness as in the daylight. He heard Ruthie knock and open a door. It wasn't house but the school building. Beau had told him that Mack had built and lived in the one-room school for Colored children, and he guessed that since their marriage, Mack and Ruthie lived in the main house and the Silases slept in the school house.

"I'll shoot dead the first one of 'em I see," an angry voice yelled, and Jonas knew that was Little Si, and his yell was followed by the sound of both barrels of his shotgun being loaded. As good a shot as his friend was, though, he was no match for half a dozen whiskey-fueled white men in sheets, and fear coursed through Jonas. He strained to hear more, willing the creatures of the night to hush the constant cacophony that defined their existence so that he could pick up a word or two. He heard feet running, heard the front door of the house open and slam shut. He moved around the side of the house to stand beneath a window.

"How we gon' get all our things in one car?" Big Si asked, looking all around the room.

"We don't need to take much," Mack said. "Everything we need is waiting for us in Belle City."

After a moment of silence, Ruthie said, "That's true. Our house is almost finished. Pa, you and Si will live with us, and Uncle Will will live with Mr. First, and both houses have furniture and everything else."

"And you don't need to take clothes," Mack said. "These clothes we wear out here in the country, we won't need them in town."

It was quiet again. Then Little Si said, "Can we take all our books?"

"We can take the books," Mack said, "and get your wedding presents, Ruth. Then let's get Uncle Will up and get out of here."

Getting the old man up required all their effort and the better part of an hour. Ruthie finally made coffee, and when Uncle Will smelled it, he asked why she was cooking breakfast in the dark. Little Si lit a candle and Uncle Will gladly accepted a cup of his favorite brew. After the second cup, he was much less querulous and much more rational. His eyes narrowed to slits when they told him what was happening, and he shocked and surprised them all by slapping his thigh and cackling. "Ignorant old coot. He always said he'd get this land back. It took him a while, but he did what he said." Then Uncle Will said, "Y'all better get yourselves out the door 'fore Zeb and his sheets get here."

"You're coming with us," Ruthie said, beginning to weep at the stubborn look on the old man's face. "You have to, Uncle Will. We can't leave you here."

"This is my home, Little Miss Ruth."

He hadn't called her that in many years, and his words and the love they held caused her to choke on her tears in a way she hadn't since her Ma was killed. "Please, Uncle Will. Please come with us. We can't have a home without you." She dropped to her knees and put her head in his lap and wept.

He stroked her head as he'd done when she was a child. Her husband, her father and her brother all watched, unable to do or say anything that would lessen her grief, and unwilling to say what they all knew must be said: It was time to leave this place.

"There's some things I need to tell y'all, then there's something I need y'all to do for me."

"We'll do anything you want, Uncle Will," Big Si said, "if you let me stay here with you."

Ruthie jumped to her feet. "No, Pa, no!"

"Lissen, y'all!" Uncle Will actually raised his voice. "Lissen!" He raised his hands and silence descended in the flickering darkness, the candle close to burning itself out. "Y'all know how we got this land, Carrie and me? Old Carney Thatcher, Zeb's Pa, gave it to us 'cause he needed somebody to farm his land 'cause everybody else, soon as they heard about The 'Mancipation, they took off. Well, that's only part of the story. The rest of it is this: Old Carney, he was our Pa, too, me and Carrie. Zeb's our brother, and that's why he hates me so, and why he wants this land back. See, Old Carney always claimed us, me and Carrie, like he was proud of what he'd done. Zeb would scream and holler that no niggers was any kin to him, but that was a lie and everybody knew it."

Nobody said anything because nobody knew what to say, though everybody was working to find words that would express their feelings. None of them was surprised at the fact of white ancestry—it was as common among Colored as Indian blood. They were just surprised that not only was it a fact for them, but at how close that connection was. Finally Ruthie said, "I wonder if Jonas knows."

"Lord, no," Uncle Will said. "Zeb never woulda told anybody that. Only people what know are those who lived back in those times, and ain't nobody left to know but me and Zeb." He cackled again, then quieted and sobered. "One more thing I got to tell you, and it's why, Silas, you got to go tonight with the chil'ren…"

"I cain't leave you, Uncle Will. I just cain't. I won't."

"Lissen to me, Silas. Just lissen." He inhaled deeply. "I know you think on me like your Pa and I raised you like you was my son. You were Carrie's boy and that made you mine. But you got a Pa, Silas. First Freeman is your Pa, and he's these chil'ren's Grandpa."

Big Si made a noise. He was trying to speak but he ended up choking.

Mack and Little Si slapped him on the back until he was breathing properly, though still unable to form the words that he sought. Uncle Will answered the unasked questions.

"Don't blame First. It was my fault. He wanted Carrie, wanted to take her with him to Belle City, but I didn't want her to go. Just like I didn't want Nellie to go and take y'all. If it hadn't been for me, Carrie might still be living, and Nellie surely would. First Freeman is a good man. Always has been. He wanted to do right by you and Carrie, but I got in the way."

Only Mack's brain was capable of clear thinking in that moment, and he wondered how many more secrets this old man had buried inside himself, wondered how he'd managed to live so long with all that knowledge and not tell it. He touched Ruth's arm—a signal that they needed to go. Then he put a hand on Little Si's shoulder and squeezed, sending the same message. Then he said, "What is it you wanted us to help you do, Uncle Will?"

"I want y'all to put everything you ain't takin' with you in the barn—furniture, clothes, pots and pans, food—everything."

"Why, Uncle Will?" Little Si asked.

"'Cause I'm gon set fire to it. Them sheet wearers like fire and burnin' things, so I'm gon' give 'em a fire. I'm not gon' let 'em burn me out. I'm gon' be the one doin' the burnin' here."

"You're going to burn down the barn?" Ruthie finally retrieved her voice, if not her ability to think clearly. "Why?"

"To let Zeb know he's still not in charge over me, that's why. I ain't no slave no more. It's my barn and I can burn it down if I want to. He might get my house, but I don't want him sittin' on my chairs or eatin' at my table off my plates."

"Uncle Will." Big Si spoke, but just barely. "After you set the fire, then what?"

Uncle Will sighed deeply. "I'm sick, y'all, ain't got much time left…"

This was too much for them. As one, their voices raised in shock, sadness, even a touch of anger: Why had he not told them? They loved him! How could he keep such secrets from them?

"Lissen to me! Lissen! I got some tea Maisy give me to drink to help me sleep, and to take when the pain gets too bad. That's why I sleep so hard at night, and why y'all cain't wake me up."

They all remembered how well Miss Maisy's brew worked for Nellie, how she refused to allow any of them to prepare the tea because the slightest error in preparation would have resulted in a permanent sleep. Uncle Will had a supply of this tea, had had it for—how long?

"So, I'm gon' light my fire, drink my tea, and lay down. Now, y'all get everything put in the barn. Go 'long, now, and do like I ask you."

They did, and when they were finished, Uncle Will already was drowsy. He'd lit a kerosene lantern and was weaving his way to the barn with it. Ruthie and Little Si hurried to him. Ruthie took the lantern and Si wrapped his arms around the old man to help him walk. He could have picked him up and carried him, so little did he weigh. How did they not realize that he must have been ill to have wasted away so? They sat him on the parlor couch, which now resided in a corner of the barn, but he wouldn't let them make him comfortable. He could not, he said, go to sleep just yet. They had to leave first. He insisted. So, after tears and hugs and declarations of love, the man William Thatcher had raised as his son, that man's daughter, son and son-in-law got into their automobile and drove away from Carrie's Crossing for the last time. They drove in silence, their thoughts and feelings too big and too heavy to share, even with each other. Each of them first tried to picture Uncle Will in his final act of defiance, but the image was too painful, so they replayed in their memories his final words to them: "Y'all go over yonder to Belle City and live like free Colored people who ain't never been slaves. Get educated and educate your chil'ren. And, please, tell First Freeman I said thank you. And tell Maisy—tell her I said I'm sorry."

Jonas watched the car disappear into the darkness that was deepest just before the dawn. He knew that the rising sun would light the final few miles of their journey, and he pictured the early morning streets as they'd come to life in the Colored section of Belle City where Mr. First lived. He would, he thought, never again see his friends, and the thought hurt him like a mule kick to the chest, but it was nothing compared to the pounding in his head brought on by what he'd heard as he crouched beneath the window of the Thatcher's house. He chastised himself for spying on them again, and promised that it would be the last time. *Of course it would, you ninny!* his brain said to him—they were gone. But if he hadn't been spying, he wouldn't know that his Pa and Ruthie and Si's Uncle Will were brothers. More than being just friends with them, he was kin to them: Cousins! Beau was his cousin too! *No wonder we all like each other so much*, he thought. And he understood, in a small way, why his Pa hated the Colored Thatchers so much: Not only were they related to him, they were, in a way, better than him, even though they were Colored. He wanted to talk to

Pa about all this, but he knew he could not, not ever. He could never tell anyone what he knew. It would be his secret, and he was good at keeping secrets. *Just like Uncle Will!* he thought.

At that moment, he remembered where Uncle Will was, and why, and the first whiff of smoke blew his way, and he hurried toward the barn. He could see the flames inside, curling and rising—and growing. He considered what he should do. Pa and his Klan friends would be arriving in less than an hour. He could wait for them, tell them what he'd heard and what he knew, but that would just make Pa madder than he already was going to be at the sight of the burning barn. Uncle Will couldn't have known it, but Pa had plans for that barn: It was going to be the storeroom so that he could re-claim his bar. It was true that they needed a larger storage space, but Pa surely did not need to open another bar. Did he really think that just because Chief Fordham wore a sheet he'd let somebody—Zeb Thatcher—sell whiskey in his town? Zeb might have property and money but it was Doc Gray and the preachers and lawyers that pulled the chief's strings, the people who had education to go with their money.

Jonas watched as the first flames burst through the roof of the barn, making a noise like both thunder and lightning. Pa was going to be hopping mad, and Jonas decided he wanted to see that, so he found another place from which to spy. His first thought was to take refuge in the tree from which he'd watched the Thatchers when he was a kid, which he'd still climbed until last year when Mr. First Freeman made him promise to stop. That promise, though, is not what stopped him this night; rather, it was the realization that in the dark, he couldn't see what snakes and other dangers the huge tree might be harboring. With his brain still whirling and reeling from what he'd overheard, he was unable to think clearly about what to do, or where.

He wandered around the yard, to the front of the house, where the front door was wide open, around the side nearest the woods, and toward the back, where he could feel the heat now from the burning barn. He had refused to allow himself to think of the burning barn as a funeral pyre, had refused to picture Ruthie and Si's beloved Uncle Will becoming ash, for surely, given how hot and hard the fire was burning, that's what was happening to him. Then, he thought—remembered—*My Uncle Will, too.*

Sound snatched him back to the place where he again was wary, his senses on alert. He stood still and listened, straining to hear the sound that had overridden, for an instant, the roar and crackle of the burning barn. He heard it again and knew what it was. He sprinted for the little building that was the

Colored school house, rushed in, and dropped to the floor. The light from the fire threw huge, frightening shadows against the empty space. Everything that had been in here now was in the barn, burning. He crawled to the door and looked out and what he saw was terrifying: Half a dozen men in white hoods and sheets carrying burning torches were running toward the barn. He could hear their voices raised in angry curses. He remembered what Uncle Will said about the Klan liking to burn things. He also remembered what one of the sheeted men at the table had said about how the very sight of them in their robes, carrying their torches, frightened the Colored. And now, angry because there was nobody to frighten here, angry because the Colored had escaped, but not before setting their own barn alight, they set off up the road, toward the next destination. They left, all but Zeb.

When they were gone, Jonas emerged from the school building and walked slowly toward his Pa, who didn't hear him approach over the roar of the fire. "Why, Pa?"

Zeb whirled around, his eyes glittering with rage. "I shoulda knowed. Ev'rybody wanted to know how them niggers knew to run, how they knew we was comin' and I didn't want to know, but I shoulda knowed."

"Why, Pa?" Jonas asked again.

Zeb reached into the top pocket of his overalls and withdrew a piece of paper. "This is why."

"What is that?"

"The deed to my land, that's what it is. The deed to all this, includin' that burnt up piece of barn. It's mine now, like it always shoulda been."

"You've got the deed already?"

"Got it when I paid the taxes that were due. The taxes the niggers didn't pay. It's my land now, just like the law says."

"You stole this land."

Zeb slapped him. "You shame me. My only son left and he got to be a nigger lover. You wanted to go over younder to Belle City to go to some dam' fool college? Then go on. Get outta here 'cause you ain't no kin to me."

Jonas wanted to hit him back, to knock him down, but there was a better way to hurt him, and more than anything, Jonas wanted to hurt his Pa. "If you could steal from your own brother, I guess it's easy for you to send me away."

Zeb's eyes emptied and his face went slack. "Say what, Boy?"

"The people who lived in this house were your kin. Your brother and sister, your nephew..."

Zeb raised up his shotgun and slid in a load of buckshot, but Jonas grabbed it away before the old man could fire, and the look in his eyes told Jonas that had he not taken the gun, he'd be dead now. "That's a lie!"

"It's the truth and you know it. These were good people you ran from their home tonight."

"If I'da had my way, it woulda been sooner, but that fella from up yonder in Spencerville just never showed up. Shoulda knowed he wouldn't 'cause he was ginger haired, and your Ma taught me never to trust a man with red hair, just like I shoulda knowed you'd betray your own."

"What are you talking about?" Jonas knew what his Pa was talking about but he didn't want it to be the truth. "What fella with red hair?"

"We had us a fella last year was s'posed to come over here and help us get our Klaven fixed up right, but he just never showed up."

The man who killed Nellie Thatcher. The man Nellie Thatcher killed. Jonas looked at the barn, burned now nearly to the ground, Uncle Will burned with it. "Why did you have to do this, Pa?" Jonas raised the shotgun, leveled it at his Pa, and emptied both barrels. Almost without thinking about it, Jonas grabbed his Pa's arms and began dragging the dead body of his father toward the burning barn. There wasn't much of the structure remaining, but there still was plenty of fire, and Jonas began rolling the body into the flames. He stopped suddenly, cursing himself for a fool. He reached into Zeb's top overall pocket and withdrew the land deed. By the time the sun was fully up, nothing would remain of the barn but a huge pile of smoldering ashes, and Jonas doubted that anybody would be interested enough to look for two sets of bones.

Mack drove as fast as the car would go on the road to Belle City, not worried about being stopped: No police officer or sheriff would expect Colored people to be driving a new motorcar in the middle of the night. He slowed and drove with caution, though, upon entering the Belle City limits. Colored people with motorcars were all too familiar a sight here, one that white people neither liked nor appreciated, and until they reached the Colored section of town, they were in danger. They exhaled as one as they turned on to Auburn Avenue in the Fourth Ward, the East Side Colored section of Belle City.

Though the sun was barely up, Auburn Avenue was already awake and bustling with street cars, horse and mule-drawn carts, motorcars, and with people who had worked all night and were now heading home and those on their way to work. The places that sold meals were doing a brisk business, whether café or restaurant with tables and chairs, or the slot in the back door of someone's kitchen. It was busy and it was noisy and every person in the slow-moving vehicle that had just out-run horror in their hometown reveled in the sights and sounds because all were generated by Colored people and as long as that was the case, they were relatively safe.

Mack drove slowly through the Fourth Ward, mentally plotting the route he would take to get them to the West Side and home. The most direct route was not the safest route. There was no way to avoid traversing a white section, but it was imperative that he steer clear of the poor white trash part of town. Going through downtown was dangerous too but only if they crossed paths with a policeman. Nobody in the car spoke so as not to distract Mack—they knew what he was thinking. Ruthie squeezed his arm in a gesture of support and their exhaled breath became a cheer when they crossed Northside Drive. They officially were in the Colored section of Belle City on the West Side, though any white person or any policeman could stop them for any reason. It just was not as likely to happen here.

"We should go to Beau's before we go to Mr. F…" Ruthie stopped herself from calling him what they'd always called him; nobody had said out loud the truth as they now knew it: He was Little Si and Ruthie's Grandpa; he was Big Si's Pa.

"That's right, we should go tell Beau first," Big Si said.

When they turned the corner on to the street where *TOBY AND BELLE'S BARBER AND BEAUTY SALON* was housed, and where Beau lived, a cheer of joy and relief went up, and Ruthie couldn't stifle the sob that had been lodged in her throat since they left Carrie's Crossing. Mack parked beside Beau's truck and Little Si jumped from the car. Instead of going around the corner to access the alleyway that ran behind Toby and Belle's place, Little Si squeezed into the space between the two wooden buildings and then ran up the stairs that led to Beau's top floor apartment. His knock was answered immediately and when Beau saw who was at his door, the mix of emotions that crossed his face would have been comical if the final one hadn't been fear. Beau grabbed his arms so hard it hurt. "What, Si? What?"

Si told him quickly, just the major points. Beau, who already was dressed for work, grabbed his cap, pulled his door shut, grabbed his baby brother by the arm, and propelled them so fast down the stairs that they were running when they hit the ground, and kept running until Beau was beside Mack's car, leaning in, looking in, looking for some sign that his brother had been wrong about the absence of Uncle Will on this journey. Beau squeezed his father's arm and touched his baby sister's cheek and patted his brother-in-law on the shoulder, all the while gazing inside the car, front to back, back to front, looking for the one who wasn't there. "Y'all follow me," he finally said, turning from the escape vehicle to his own. Little Si went with his brother and the two-car caravan slowly made its way through the West Side Colored section of Belle City, to tell First Freeman—everything.

Because he was expecting Beau, the old man had the back gate open and was waiting for him, but when he saw the second car, recognized its passengers, the breath caught in his chest in a painful spasm. Everybody saw the fear in his face and they all rushed to him, embracing him, as they told the story. They waited for him to express a feeling—sadness, pain, anger—but when he gave a small smile and nodded his head, they all were confused. Until he said, "Good for him. Good for Will'am. He left outta here the way he wanted to go. He didn't come to this life a free man, but he left here that way." He smiled again, and nodded again. "Good for Will'am."

They stood together quiet and solemn for a few moments, if not praying the same prayer then certainly having similar, if not the same, thoughts: That life as they'd known it was over. A new life began for each of them this day.

Big Si cleared his throat, then touched his daughter's face. "You and Mack go on over to your house. That's your home now. First, though, go see Big Mack and Clara, tell 'em what's happened, tell 'em how things…" He couldn't finish; Ruthie finished for him.

"We'll tell them what's happened and that we're here to stay."

"Good," Big Si said, turning to his sons. "Beau, I 'spect you 'bout ready to get to work."

"Yessir, Pa. And Si can go with me if he wants to. He can live with me, too."

Little Si, who first felt gratitude, followed by an overwhelming sadness, couldn't speak. Beau grabbed him and hugged him close.

"And you can live here, Silas," First Freeman said. "If you want to," he added.

"Thank you…Pa. I 'preciate it."

The old man's face went from stunned amazement to a grin so wide it seemed to split his face. "Will'am told y'all. He told you!" He clapped his hands together, then rubbed them back and forth, the calloused palms making a sound like rustling leaves. Then he scrutinized the faces arrayed before him to see if his joy was shared. It was, though there was a shyness attached to it, as if they, the Thatchers, were greeting a stranger instead a man they'd known all their lives.

"Uncle Will said to tell you thank you," Big Si said, remembering. "And he said to tell Miss Maisy he was sorry."

"Oh, Lord. Maisy. I'll have to go tell her."

"We can do it, Mr. Fir…Grandpa," Ruthie said, amazed at the emotion on the man's face at the sound of that one word.

He shook his head. "She needs to hear it from me, but I'll tell it just like you told me."

"What is Uncle Will sorry for?" Ruthie said.

For the second time in less than twelve hours, they heard a story about lives that had played out long before they were born. This one involved another pair of young lovers—Maisy and William. They loved each other fiercely and deeply, but William also was connected to his baby sister just as fiercely and deeply, and she, too, loved a man who wanted to take her away to make a life in a big city. William didn't want to lose his sister so he had to make a choice. Maisy married Ezekiel Cooper and for the rest of his life, William loved her from a distance, though he didn't regret his choice until his sister was swept away by flood waters. William had many years to ponder his decisions and his choices—until that very morning when what he decided to do for himself would finally free those he loved from his love.

"He was the best man I ever knew, was Will'am," First Freeman said. Then, as if some internal switch were thrown, he seemed to realize how early in the morning it was, seemed to realize that these former residents of Carrie's Crossing would have have had no sleep and nothing to eat. So he turned all of his attention to feeding these people he'd known all their lives—people he now could claim publicly as his family. And when they'd eaten and cleaned the kitchen, when those who were leaving had taken their leave, father and son were left with each other.

"Do you want to get some sleep, Silas?"

"Yessir, Pa, I do, 'cause I truly am tired."

"You know where your room is," and Silas did—it was the same room he'd slept in when last he was here, for Ruthie's wedding. "And you know where to find anything you need."

Silas nodded and pushed himself to his feet. He suddenly was wearier than he'd ever been in his life, and though most of it was brain and heart weariness, it was his legs that seemed not to have the strength to walk him into the next room. First watched him leave, this man who was his son, and saw the very strong resemblance to himself. Maisy always marveled that no one ever remarked on their similarity.

He walked out into his backyard and toward the work shed, but he didn't go in. He was not yet ready to interact with other people, and his four workers would be busy converting the items that Beau salvaged into useable and saleable goods and, as always, they'd want his advice or opinion about their performance. For now, he wanted only to think—and to feel—and perhaps to remember his other life, when he and Carrie and William and Maisy were young…

As deep in thought as he was, he heard the car that turned too fast into the alley at the end of his street. He heard it stop too suddenly at his back fence, heard the door open and slam shut. He opened the gate and was rendered speechless to find Jonas Thatcher standing there. The boy looked like hell had run over him and left him lying in the road. "What is it, Jonas?"

Jonas told him—everything. Then he said, "I can't give Miss Nellie back, but I can give this back," and he held out a piece of paper.

"What is that?" First Freeman asked, looking at the paper but not accepting it. Even if he could read, he wasn't inclined to accept anything from this boy at this moment, for, in truth, the first time in his life, First Freeman had been totally and completely startled. Surprised and struck dumb. Even after all he'd learned this day, including the fact that he was recognized by his son and grandchildren, what Jonas told him left him unsteady.

"The deed to Uncle Will's property. Pa had it. He went and and got it right away. He knew what was going to happen and he was ready." The disgust in the boy's voice bordered on hatred and that was even more unsettling to the man who, until this very moment, would have sworn his own hatred of Zeb Thatcher.

"You hungry, Son?"

"Yessir, Mr. First."

"Come on, then," First said, turning toward the house.

"What about my car?"

"It'll be awright. Anybody needs to get by, they'll let me know."

Jonas followed the brick path through the perfectly cut grass to the back door of the white house, both house and green trim looking newly painted. He, too, wiped his feet on the straw mat and entered the house. It was dark and almost cool inside, and quiet and still. Jonas dropped into a seat at the kitchen table, suddenly feeling more exhausted than hungry. He closed his eyes and opened them when he felt a hand on his shoulder to see a plate of bacon, eggs, grits and buttered toast. "Thank you, Mr. First," he said, and began to eat. He drank both the coffee and the milk he was given, and ate two additional pieces of toast, these with apple butter on them. He'd never eaten apple butter and when Mr. First saw how much Jonas liked it, the old man pulled two jars from the pantry and put them on the table.

"I love it too, and Maisy Cooper makes good and sure I have plenty of it."

Jonas picked up one of the jars and studied it closely. "I could sell this in my store, Mr. First. Charge a lot of money for it, too. If Miss Maisy wants to make some extra money—"

First Freeman gave a loud back of laughter. "Beau sure was right about you. You just a money-makin' machine." He laughed again. "I'm gon' be seein' Maisy this evenin' and I'll ask her. She might like the idea of havin' some money of her own." In fact, he was certain Maisy would like the idea, especially since Zeb was dead and gone. But not buried. He pointed to the land deed Jonas had placed beside his plate. "That land is yours now, Son, fair and square."

"Nothing fair about it." Jonas slapped the table and his dishes jumped. "My Pa stole this land from Uncle Will and you know it."

"Don't matter how he got it, the deed says the land is his. And if he's dead, then the law says the land is yours. That means ALL the land: Them stores and that house." First stood up and grabbed Jonas by the shoulder. "You go 'long on home, Jonas. That house is *your* home now. Ruthie got a home with Mack. Little Si got a home with Beau, and Big Si got a home with me. Go on back to the Crossing, go to your store and get you some furniture, and live in your house." The old man was walking him out of the back door and down the brick path to the back gate. "And if you would, ev'ry now and then, think about Carrie and Nellie and Ruthie—the women who made that house a home—they'll help you make it your home. One more thing you got to do, though, when you get back: When them ashes cool off, you got to get rid of them bones."

From the Dairy of Jonas Farley Thatcher Fall, 1921

My whole life, my whole world changed in a few minutes over the summer. Which few minutes? The ones around the first of July when I was hiding and listening to my pa and the klan planning to steal all the land from the colored people and run them out of town?

The few minutes when I was hiding under the window of the Thatchers house listening to Uncle will tell everybody he and my pa was brothers and how it felt when I knew I was some kin to Ruthie and Si and Beau? The few minutes when I knew that my pa would shoot and kill me? The few minutes when I shot and killed him? The few minutes when Mr. First told me everything my pa owned was mine? When I got back to CC that morning—it was still morning. I couldn't hardly believe it. It felt like it should be night and time to go to bed, I was so tired. Course I had not been to bed the night before but my mind was more tired than my body. Still I did what Mr. First told me, just like always. When mr. First tells you a thing, you do it. So I went to the store and got me a bed, a table and some chairs, and some soap and some sheets and towels. I made Clem help me put everything in the car and take it home. He liked that, thought it was for Pa. He kept asking where was pa and after we got all the furntures in the house, I showed him where pa was and he got reel scred and then he got mad when I told him it was his fault pa was dead. Then I went to find chief Fordham and I showed him pa and told him the same thing I told clem. It was there fault pa was dead for wearing sheets. I told them pa got burnt up trying to put the fire out because he was mad that they were burning down his barn and they beleved me because they know how pa acts sometimes. then I went in my house and went to sleep and I slept for a long, long time, until the next day. Then I got up early and went to my stores. I fired clem and esther. It was my store and I could do that I told them I didn't want sheet warers working for me. then I went and told doc gray and Rev Wilson about chief Fordham and they got hopping mad like I knew they woud. They like to think that CC is high class and that peple who live here are high class and they think klan peple are low class. I told them I alreddy fired clem and they got all the high class rich peple in town together for a meetng—I was there, too, and we fired chief Fordham! But it didn't matter bcaus all the colored peple were gone now. Rev Wilson told me I was the richest man in CC now and I would have to go to church now. I don't like it but I go to set an example. That's what he and doc gray said I have to do. And they said I have to fix my house. Make it bigger. I don't want to do that because I don't know if miss carrie and miss Nellie and Ruthie would like that, but I can't tell nobody why I don't want to make the hous bigger so I will do this. Doc gray says one day I will have a wife and children and I will need a big hous. but I don't want a wife since I can't marry with Ruthie so I will live in my big house myself.

From the Recorded Memories of Ruth Thatcher McGinnis

My life changed completely and totally in the time it took us to drive from Carrie's Crossing to Belle City that night. Or morning, I should say. I think it was about two or two-thirty when we left. The burning barn lit up the night sky for miles. We later learned that more than our barn burned that night, but I think Uncle Will was the only one to set fire to his own property. We also weren't the only ones on the road that night. Every other Black family in Carrie's Crossing fled that night. The whites got their wish—there were no Colored left in town—and I've never been back there. Miss it? What's to miss? Everything I cared about was either dead or with me in Belle City. I did miss Jonas. He was a good friend and, at the time, I thought I'd never see him again. Mack stayed furious with him for a while, still believing that Jonas knew what Zeb and the klan had planned for us, but he finally came around, especially after Mr. First—Grandpa—told us about the visit. I have to laugh when I think how difficult it was for us to call him Grandpa, and how easy it was for Pa to call him Pa. I also have to laugh when I remember how we all, at the same time one night, looked at the two of them standing side-by-side, and realized they look almost exactly alike. Of course Pa was his son. How we could not have known? But we didn't. At least we children didn't. I think Ma knew. I remember how she'd look at Mr. First sometimes when she thought nobody was watching her. Stare at him like she was trying to read the writing on his bones. But if anybody else noticed, nobody said a word, and by the time we all got to Belle City early that August morning, it didn't matter. We were home and we knew it. Mack and me only stayed a week or so with his parents—our house was so close to being finished that we moved in. What we hadn't planned on was having to get a baby's room ready so soon, but we had so much help. But what I remember most clearly about those first few months was that Si and I got to go to school every day. What a joy! Beau needed him on the truck but he said that learning was the most important thing, so Si went to school every day, then worked with Beau evenings and on Saturdays. Of course nobody worked on Sundays. We all went to church, and we rotated the location of Sunday dinner: Mack's parents' house, then our house, then Toby and Belle's, then Belle's ma's, then Mr. First's, then we'd all go over to the East Side to Miss Maisy's. Of course it wasn't long before I had to prepare myself for being a mother. I had to stop going to school when I began to show. Why? Because back then, unlike now, girls didn't go to school pregnant, Sissy. That's why. It didn't matter that I was married. The schools back then thought it was important to set an example and a pregnant girl in class, married or not, was not the kind of example they wanted to set. Anyway, I used those three months to immerse myself in the study of French—I still harbored the notion that I was going to France to rescue Eubie—and to read each and every newspaper I could get my hands on. So much about the world we didn't know living in Carrie's Crossing. Then we got radio and oh, my goodness.

From the Diary of Jonas Farley Thatcher

March 1923. Beau got me a birthday present. A set of golf clubs! Brand new except for 1 missing club which the owner threw in the water. Seems like Beau remembered better than I did how much I wanted to learn to play golf. He also knows me well and knows I would not spend money to buy golf clubs. I spent money on my house and on my business and on land.

I buy up land whenever I can. Beau does too but he won't talk about it so much like I do. Beau doesn't like talking about money. He also doesn't like talking about his family to me and that's what I want to know about—how are Ruthie and Si doing. It was Mr. First who told me Ruthie and Mack had their baby. A boy named Mack McGinnis the third and he was born on the 19th day of march.

From the Recorded Memories of Ruth Thatcher McGinnis

Time moved so fast in Belle City. One thing after another after another. Mackie was born then Si got married then Toby and Belle had Little Belle and we all were so happy for them. She had lost one baby and we were fearful for her health. Then I had Thatcher. It seemed like it happened overnight, but Mackie was two already. Si and I graduated from Booker T. Washington High School and started college. We were so proud of ourselves—and so proud of Mack for being a good enough teacher to prepare us to hold our own among students who'd always gone to school every day. And we never forgot for a single moment where and how it all began—with Ma at the kitchen table, late at night, teaching us the alphabet and numbers. I often thought, though I never expressed it, how unfair it was that Ma never got a chance to live in Belle City with us. That was her dream for us, but it also was her dream for herself.

From the Diary of Jonas Farley Thatcher

New Year's Day 1926. This is the year I'm going to college. I promised myself—and my Ma—that I would go to college. I'll be 21 years this year and if I don't go to college soon it will be too late. We have so many new teachers in CC now and we have a high school that I have graduated from and all the teachers say I could go to college. They say I'm lucky because I have the money and so many others do not. Yes I have the money but I do not have the time. I do not have anybody to take care of my business. I wish things were different because the one man I would trust to take care of my businss is Beau Thatcher. Good thing all the high class people in CC can't read this but it is true. In fact, I would trust two men. First Freeman is the other one. Two colored men I would trust with anything but I cant because theyre colored. That preacher we got is always preaching to us to be good and decent and honest men and that's what Mr. First and Beau are but they are colored and I don't understand that. It makes me not want to like white people who wear sheets at night and go to church on Sunday. Good, decent and honest men?

From the Recorded Memories of Ruth Thatcher McGinnis

Talking about these things is very painful, Sissy, but also very good for me, for a number of reasons. First, it lets me know that dementia hasn't yet set in despite my advanced age. Who's being ridiculous? I'm a hundred years old! Of course it occurs to me that my mind might go, though I don't suppose I'd know if it did, would I? But a major reason this recollection is good for me is it requires that I say out loud some things I've refused to think about for many years, and one of them is how easily we convinced ourselves that we outran slavery the night we ran away from Carrie's Crossing. What I mean, Sissy, is that even though people I loved with all my strength—Uncle Will and First Freeman and Maisy Cooper—had been released from slavery in 1865, some 60 years later the laws in Georgia, indeed throughout most of the country, guaranteed that we still lived in bondage. Those of us fortunate enough to live in places like Belle City—and there weren't many places like it for our people—most of the time we lived like we truly were free, and so came to think we were. Of course, reality always was just a Jim Crow law away. I'd also let myself forget that bad news arrived in clusters. I should have known 1926 would be a bad year because Maisy Cooper died in January. We were stunned, though I don't know why. She was 81 years old and had been a slave. The miracle was that she'd lived as long as she had. But because we couldn't imagine life without her, we gave no thought to the possibility of her death. Sue said it was peaceful. She went to sleep and never woke up. It was a month before any of us had a peaceful night's sleep because we were so afraid that Mr. First—Grandpa—would go to sleep and not wake up. They all were born in the same year—1845. Doesn't that sound....I don't know how to describe it, to talk about knowing people who were born in 1845. How could you possibly understand, Sissy? Oh. Yes, I see. After all, I was born in 1905 and it's now 2005. Well. 1926. Si was ready to give up on his dream of being a school teacher. Georgia would rather hire a criminal than a Colored man to teach school. And I had to give up on my dream of going to France because Colored people couldn't get permission to leave town, to say nothing of being able to leave the country.

From the Diary of Jonas Farley Thatcher

November 1927. I left the state of Georgia for the first time in my life. I didn't go far—just to South Carolina—but it was exciting anyway, and very pretty where I was. It was a golf resort on the coast and the golf course looked like something out of a magazine. I felt country and out of place except when I was on the golf course. Then I was the one everybody looked up to. I won all my rounds. When I'm with people like that, I don't feel like a rich man, though that's what I am. And they all had wifes. I wouldn't want a wife like those women. I don't know exactly why. I just know I don't, even though I don't know much about wifes. My Ma was sick most of the time and my sisters, well, they're just my sisters. So, I'll think about golf not a wife.

From the Recorded Memories of Ruth Thatcher McGinnis

We thought we had seen hard times, thought we knew hard times. What was to come was child's play in comparison. It's a good thing that nobody knew what was coming or that we weren't warned because nobody would have believed it. I think back on it and still can't believe it—not only how bad it was but how long it took some of us to really understand how bad it was, and I put myself in that category. Remember I told you how spoiled we were living in Belle City? Well, I didn't understand then that there can be a negative side to good fortune, and that is if you're fortunate, you don't think about what it is to be unfortunate. That's the hard lesson I learned when the Roaring Twenties came to a screaming close.

PART TWO

Carrie's Crossing and Belle City, Georgia

-and-

The Mountains of North Carolina

1934-1945

– Carrie's Crossing –
Jonas

J onas swung the golf club like the pro he often imagined himself to be. He was on the driving range at the Belle City Country Club, but he imagined himself on the newly-opened course designed by the great Bobby Jones. He already had a set of Bobby Jones golf clubs, and he'd imitated the Bobby Jones swing so long and so often that he had all but perfected it. He watched the ball smoothly lift and soar for what seemed like forever before it began its descent. It was a thing of beauty, golf was, and Jonas easily could spend the rest of his life in pursuit of perfecting it. He certainly could afford it, but he was almost thirty years old. Bobby Jones had quit the game before his thirtieth birthday.

Jonas sighed deeply and as he bent to place another ball on the tee, he felt, rather than saw, someone approaching from the rear, and it annoyed him. All this space out here and somebody wanted to practice next to him. When he turned to face the interloper his annoyance increased, tinged with surprise.

"Young Jonas Thatcher, all grown up."

"Mr. Edwards," Jonas said sourly, noting that the man still wore plaid knickers with striped knee socks.

"Mark of every good business man that he remembers the names of the men he does business with," Horace Edwards said, sticking out his hand.

Jonas shook it. "We haven't done any business together, Mr. Edwards," he said.

"Not yet, Jonas, but I'm hoping that we will." Edwards looked all around. They were alone on the golf course. "Practically every businessman in America is wringing his hands—those who haven't already jumped out the window— and I hear you spend several days a week practicing your swing, sometimes even playing a round. When there's somebody to play with." He gave Jonas an appraising look. "And a mighty fine swing it is, too. You look like Bobby Jones from a distance."

"Practice makes perfect," Jonas said, wishing the man would go away. He didn't like Horace Edwards—hadn't liked him when he'd met him all those years ago, in the parking lot of this very club, and he didn't like him now, though if pressed he wouldn't have been able to say exactly why. Something to do with the man's arrogance. And his insistence, all those years ago, that Jonas "rent out" Beau Thatcher to him.

"I'd like to know what else you were practicing that's let you survive this great depression perfecting your golf swing." Horace faked a drive and gave Jonas a hard look. "If you don't mind me asking."

"Not being greedy," Jonas said, getting the kind of reaction he knew Edwards would have: Anger. With Horace Edwards and men like him, the anger was always just beneath the surface.

"You wanna explain that?"

"What I want is to get back to practicing my off-the-tee shot."

"Your drive is perfect, Jonas, and you know it. What I want to know is what you meant by that being greedy remark. What I hear is that you didn't lose any money when the market crashed because you didn't have any money in the market. Or in the bank."

"Since you already know that, what is it you want me tell you?"

"How, dammit, did you know the market was gonna crash?"

"I didn't. I just don't believe, number one, in giving my hard-earned money to another man, no matter that he calls himself a banker or a stockbroker. He's a man just like me, and I can't think of a single reason I should give him my money on his promise to give me back more than I gave him. And that's where the greed comes in: This notion of getting something for nothing. I give a man—a banker, a stockbroker—a hundred or a thousand or ten thousand dollars, and in a year or two he gives me back a hundred twenty or twelve hundred or twelve thousand dollars, and I'm supposed to be so excited that I'll then give him all my money. And what happens if he's a thief, or worse, a fool? All my money is gone is what."

Edwards gave Jonas a long appraising look then said, "I'd like to make you a business proposition, Mr. Thatcher."

"Why me, Mr. Edwards? You don't like me and I don't like you."

"That's true, Son, but you're the only man I know who's still got any money."

Jonas had to laugh. He wasn't interested in any proposition Horace Edwards had to offer but he'd listen; that much arrogance deserved to be heard. Jonas believed that you had to ask for what you wanted, that you didn't get anything or anywhere waiting for something or somebody to come to you. There were only two possible responses to a request, which meant a fifty percent chance of getting what you wanted. "What is it, Mr. Edwards?"

Horace nodded his head, as if he'd already gotten the answer he wanted. "I've bought up a lot of land in and around Carrie's Crossing. Stupid name, by the way, needs changing. Anyway, I can't make the notes on the loans for the land. I don't want to forfeit because that land is valuable, and it's going to be even more valuable when the economy gets itself right again."

"What land in and around the Crossing?" Jonas asked, and when Horace Edwards told him, Jonas knew the man was right: The land alone was worth a fortune. Anything built on it would be worth two fortunes, whether residential or commercial. "I won't give you a loan, Horace, but I will partner with you."

Edwards gave a nasty bark of laughter. "I don't want a partner, boy. I am the H.L. Edwards Real Estate Company all by myself, and I intend to keep it that way."

"Until the bank forecloses on you and puts your land up for auction. And with me being the only man around with cash money, I'd end up with it all anyway."

"You little bastard." Edwards opened and closed his fists at his sides. He wanted to punch Jonas, that was clear, but Jonas, still holding a golf club, was younger, taller and stronger, not to mention richer.

They stood looking at each other for a long moment, each man standing his ground, but only one of them from a position of strength, and they both knew which one. Then, almost simultaneously, they shifted their gaze to the green lawn of the practice range, an expanse that no longer was nearly as lush as it should have been, and the fact that it was mid-October had nothing to do with it. Jonas hadn't noticed before now; all his attention had been focused on his ball and its flight. Looking at the country club's lawn, he saw the Depression. He looked at his watch. "I need to go," he said, returning his club to the bag.

"I'll be at your store first thing in the morning with the partnership papers for you to sign," Edwards said, his expression speaking the self-disgust his words did not convey. "Or should I look for you out here?"

"I'll be in the store," Jonas said. "I open at seven o'clock sharp."

Seven is when he opened, but Jonas had been there since six. He finished washing the front window, a task he'd enjoyed ever since his father first opened the store more than ten years ago. He always used a mixture of vinegar and water, and he scrubbed the glass with newspaper until it squeaked. He'd once wondered why he liked washing the store's window until he realized that standing on the ladder, looking out at the street, gave him a bird's eye view of all that happening on the town's main street among the town's principal merchants and their customers, drawn from the most prosperous and or socially elite segment of the town's population. That was back when he was a child and intimidated by people and commerce. Now, at ripe old age of twenty-nine, he was one of the town's leading merchants , and while he no longer was intimidated by people, he'd still rather observe them than interact with them. And he could do all his observing without seeming to be observing because he was, after all, merely washing the window. However, Jonas also liked— had always liked—order and cleanliness and the sparkling front window screamed order and cleanliness. These days, of course, there wasn't much to see from the front window. Yes, those merchants lucky enough to still be in business were, as he was, preparing to open for the day, but unlike in times past, there were no car-loads of customers jockeying for parking spaces on the street, just a cluster of fallen leaves scurrying past, pushed by a brisk, fall breeze.

He climbed down from the ladder and put it in the storeroom and got out the mop and broom. These tasks he took less pleasure from, but since the onset of hard times that people were calling The Great Depression, he couldn't afford to pay anybody to clean up, even if there had been someone willing to do the job—and for the last few months, there hadn't been anyone. The poorest of Carrie's Crossing's citizens had all left, though Jonas wasn't sure where they'd gone. Doc Gray said they'd gone to Belle City, where it was possible to get a bowl of weak soup and crust of day-old bread, even if it no longer was possible to find work—in Belle City or anywhere else.

"The Great Depression," Jonas muttered to himself as he pushed the mop back and forth across the tile floor, emphasizing the word great. "Like everybody being broke is a wonderful thing. Like they called the war The Great War. Nothing great about it," he said of the war that had left his older brother dead in the French mud in 1919 at the hands of Germans.

Jonas knew he was more fortunate than most of the other merchants in town simply because, like Horace Edwards said, he still had his money. So much money that he literally could not count it all, the large majority of it the proceeds of the bootleg whiskey business he'd run with Beau Thatcher for the thirteen-year duration of Prohibition. The thought of Beau and their business brought a quick smile. While they both were relieved when the law finally was repealed last year, they had, for a while, enjoyed flouting it— and not just the law that forbade the selling or drinking of whiskey, but also, and perhaps more importantly, the one that made it illegal for a Colored man and a white man to do business together.

Jonas finished mopping and sweeping, wondering if it was wasted activity, wondering if any paying customers would cross the threshold of THATCHER'S MARKET this day. It had been three days since anybody had bought anything, though he'd given away quite a bit, his reasoning being that having somebody eat it was better than having to throw away spoiled food. He'd closed the furniture store until further notice. His only employees were his sister Rachel and her husband, Cory, and he'd asked them to come in an hour later than usual today. He didn't want them to be affected if things got ugly with Edwards. He didn't expect that, but matters pertaining to money these days often led to unexpected places. People were broke and desperate and therefore were unpredictable. It was a testament to the sorry times they lived in that there were people who'd do more work for less money, just in order to have some money at all, even if there was precious little to buy with it. The price of everything was sky high, and people were buying only what they truly needed. That's why he'd closed the furniture store: Nobody really *needed* a table or a chair or even a bed, if the choice was between the furniture and food.

One of those Jonas felt most sorry for was old Doc Gray, who had lost every penny of his savings between the failed banks and the crashed stock market. Jonas, who'd never been sick a day in his life, had taken to visiting the doctor every week, each time with a newly imagined ailment. Mrs. Gray was acting as his nurse again—a job she'd relinquished two dozen years earlier—and she'd greet Jonas the same as always: "And what brings you to see us this fine day?" He'd feign embarrassment, say it was something he needed to discuss with the doctor, and she'd usher him into the examining room where the doctor would listen to his heart and lungs, look down his throat and into his eyes and ears, thump his back, take his pulse, and then ask Jonas to describe in more detail his new ailment. Then the old doctor would take out his pad and write some instructions for Jonas to follow: *Eat more vegetables. Get more rest. Soak tired muscles in hot water. Drink warm milk with honey before bed.* Jonas would thank him, get dressed, and go out to the front. Doc Gray would follow him and give Mrs. Gray the chart and Jonas would give her an envelope of cash. Neither of the old people would look at the envelope. They looked at Jonas, directly into his eyes, told him to take better care of himself, smiled at him, and kept the smiles in place until he'd left. Of course, Jonas wasn't the only one showing kindness to the Grays; he was just the only one able to give them money.

Any number of others brought them food—cooked dishes as well as chickens, eggs, freshly caught fish and freshly killed rabbit or deer—because it was well and widely known that Doc Gray had never turned away a patient who couldn't pay in good times. He certainly wouldn't in hard times. The grass was cut, the hedges trimmed, the gutters cleaned, the trim painted, and it was the patients who took care of the doctor and his home because he no longer could pay his hired help, either.

Jonas shook his head, as he often did, at the truly sorry state of affairs, and wondered, as he often did, how much longer it could last. He wondered what ultimately would happen to those who, like Doc Gray, had lost so much, and he wondered what would happen to those like himself who were holding on by sheer force of will. He returned the ladder and cleaning supplies to the storeroom, removed his smock and replaced it with a dress shirt, tie, and suit jacket. Business men wore suits to business meetings, even if the meeting was in a grocery store. He checked his reflected image in the sparkling clean glass, straightening his tie, before he unlocked the front door and turned the CLOSED sign around to OPEN. He took his place behind the counter. He was open and ready for business if a hundred people came today—or if nobody but Horace Edwards came. He reached down to the low shelf and turned on the radio, which had become a constant source of companionship and comfort to him, as well as his primary source of entertainment. He still relied on the newspaper for news and information, though the radio people were getting pretty good at that, too. Classical music was playing now. He didn't know what, just that it probably was coming from New York or Chicago or Detroit and that he liked it. He also liked that jazz music but people were trying to make the radio station in Belle City stop playing it because it was nigger music. As if music had a color.

The bell over the door tinkled, and Jonas looked up. Horace Edwards walked in the door, briefcase in hand. His hat looked newly blocked, his brown suit was freshly pressed, his white shirt crisply starched, his shoes highly polished. He gave the store a top-to-bottom and front-to-back scrutinizing. Then Jonas got the same treatment when he stepped from behind the counter and Horace's eyes widened as he saw how Jonas was dressed: Exactly as he himself was except Jonas's suit was navy blue. "Nice place, Jonas," he said, covering his surprise. "Top of the line. Especially the black and white tile floor. Saw one like it in a market in New York City but never one down here." He stopped studying the store and turned his appraising gaze to Jonas. "You been up North?"

Jonas shook his head. "I saw it in a magazine and liked it."

"Where'd you come by the tiles?" He bent over and rubbed the smooth floor. "Not from around here."

"North Carolina," Jonas said.

"That suit didn't come from North Carolina," he said. "Those shoes, either."

Jonas smiled. "No, they sure didn't. Might not have cost so much, though, if they had." He'd custom-ordered both from New York, but he suspected Horace knew that.

Horace smiled, too, then nodded, more, it seemed, at the thoughts in his own head than at anything Jonas had said. He touched the place on his face where he'd cut himself shaving. "You're a natural, Jonas. You were born to be a business man. You could not have been anything else."

Jonas looked down at the floor, looked at the pattern of the tiles. He did like his floor. He also liked people's reaction to it—to its uniqueness. He looked up at Horace. "I wanted to be a writer, but we didn't have money for me to go to school. Then when we did have money, I was needed in the store. Then my pa died and, well, there didn't seem to be much point after a while. School is for young people. I missed my chance." He paused a moment, seemingly as surprised as his audience that so many words had poured from him at one time, then added, "Besides, I think you're right: Best to do what comes naturally and, to tell the truth, writing was hard work. Reading's easier."

"You read a lot, Jonas?"

"Whenever I'm not working, Mr. Edwards."

"I think, Jonas, under the circumstances, you can call me Horace." He stuck out his hand and gave a lopsided grin that gave him an almost boyish look. He'd removed his hat and his light brown, almost blond, hair fell forward. No money, then, for a haircut and a shave. "So, what do you like to read? Probably the same stuff as my daughter."

Jonas shrugged. He'd revealed enough information about himself for one day. Now he wanted Horace to talk—about the land he owned in Carrie's Crossing and about his plans for it—and this Horace was happy to do, for unlike Jonas, Horace very much liked talking about himself. It followed, of course, that he also liked hearing himself talk, and Jonas noticed that he sounded not quite as uncouth and ignorant as he had when they'd met last. He was, however, every bit as annoying. He also clearly was a canny and astute businessman who had carefully, methodically—and brilliantly—watched and invested as Carrie's Crossing grew from a small country town a few miles down the road from the big city into its own city, a thriving, prosperous place populated almost entirely by wealthy white people. Wealthy, that is, until the stock market crashed and the banks failed. All the property that Edwards owned in Belle City and in Carrie's Crossing was, for all intents and purposes, worthless and would remain so until the financial tide turned. But when it did, Horace Edwards would become one of the wealthiest men in the entire state. So would Jonas.

Horace put his briefcase on the counter and opened it. He inhaled deeply, then withdrew a stack of papers. Papers that would make Jonas a full partner in the H.L. Edwards Real Estate Company. He gave the papers to Jonas to read and sign. "Even though I'm not happy about having to do this, Jonas, I do appreciate it."

"Believe it or not, I wish you didn't have to do this either. I know I wouldn't like it if I had to turn over half my business to another man, but I also don't think you'll be losing anything in this deal." Jonas looked directly at the older man as he spoke.

Horace inhaled again. "You're wrong about that, but I won't argue with you." Then, at the look on Jonas's face, he took another breath and said, "My pride." He tapped the sheaf of papers. "This represents a great loss of pride to me, and not only because I need your money…how old are you?"

"Twenty-nine."

Horace gave a bark of laughter. "Five years older than my daughter. Who, by the way, had to leave school because I couldn't keep up with the tuition. She rides around with me, calling herself my secretary, but I know my wife put her up to it, to keep an eye on me because she—my wife, that is—is worried that I'll drink too much and run my car into a tree or a ditch." He made that noise again, but it was more sob than laugh. "I've got two kids saving my hide and you think I haven't lost anything?"

"I'm sorry you feel this way."

Horace waved him off. "Nothing for you to be sorry about. I'm just glad you've got so much money, Son, because this is gonna cost you a lot of your secret money." The arrogant, brash Horace Edwards, the one Jonas didn't like but whom he was beginning to understand, was back. "And I don't mind telling you I'd feel lot better about all this if I knew where you got all that money, boy, and why you wouldn't put it in the bank."

"If I'd put it in the bank, I wouldn't be able to bail you out, would I?"

"You would if you'd put it in the First National Bank of Belle City. Only bank in the entire state that's still in business."

"Is that where you bank?" Jonas asked, and when Horace nodded Jonas said, "Then how is it you don't have any money?"

"Because I haven't been able to make any money," he snapped. "I didn't lose any, but everything I had saved I had to spend to keep my business going, until I didn't have anything left. Answer your question, Jonas?"

Jonas turned away from Horace and began to read the documents before him. His future partner stood still as a rock, watching and waiting, and Jonas knew what he was waiting for. He smiled inside himself and kept reading. Only two people in the world knew that on those days he drove over to Belle City to play golf, his real reason for the journey was that he was taking business classes at the state college. Horace didn't expect that he'd understand what he was reading. Jonas understood every word of it and was thinking that Horace Edwards had himself one heck of a good lawyer when the bell over the door tinkled.

He looked up from his reading, briefly alternating between being annoyed that he would have to stop reading the contracts and hopeful that a paying customer was at hand, and was struck speechless. The young woman who entered could have stepped directly from the pages of one of those New York fashion magazines. She was tall and lean and had clear blue eyes that sparkled all the way across the room. She wore a cloche hat and two-toned shoes and a dress that hugged her like somebody's arms. She looked around in delighted amazement.

"Papa! This looks just like that market on Broadway. Why didn't you tell me that Mr. Thatcher was so *au courant*? Where is he? I want to meet him." She danced forward and grabbed Horace's arm. He melted like an ice cube on the sidewalk in August.

"Jonas, this is my daughter, Audrey."

"*You're* Jonas Thatcher?"

Jonas stepped from behind the counter and extended his hand. "Miss Edwards. Pleased to meet you, sorry to disappoint you."

She laughed as she took his hand. "I'm not disappointed. Not at all. It's just that I was expecting an old man. Or at least one as old as my papa."

"Your papa's not old," Horace growled, trying to sound menacing, though his daughter knew better, knew him better.

Audrey backed a step away from Jonas and gave him a frank, appraising look, one that made him flush. "But you're not as young as Jonas Thatcher," she said.

Horace looked closely at his daughter and her reaction to Jonas. Then he looked at Jonas's reaction to his daughter: The boy was grinning like a circus clown, his cheeks and nose red, his eyes wide and staring. The sight put Horace at war with himself. The man who was the father of this girl was witnessing the reaction of a woman to a man, and he wasn't ready for that. She was his only daughter and his baby. The man who lived and breathed business, however, saw a deal in the making. His two sons were useless as tits on a boar hog—stupid as well as lazy. Audrey, on the other hand, was smart as a whip and was learning as much about his business as he was willing to teach her. He'd thought, more than once, that it would be his daughter who inherited his business—and if his daughter should marry Jonas Thatcher?

"How'd you like to take a ride with us, Jonas, and see what's what?"

Jonas looked at his watch. "I'd like that a lot, Horace. My sister and brother-in-law should be here any minute—"

At that moment, the bell tinkled over the door, and Rachel and Cory entered the store. Jonas introduced them all to each other, hands were shaken all around, and Rachel assured her brother that everything would be well taken care of. He nodded and kissed her cheek, causing her to blush deeply. They had not grown up with such displays of love and affection, and while they both felt awkward about it, they also both wanted very much to be part of a family that had such strong feelings for each other and expressed it. They knew families who greeted each other with hugs and kisses every time they saw each other, which often was daily. But even though they did it—hugged and kissed each other—it was neither easy nor natural for them. Ever since he was a child Jonas had wished that he and his siblings loved each other the way Ruthie and her brothers loved each other. Now that he was grown, he understood that children learned how to love from their parents, and while he was certain that his mother had loved her children, she had not given out hugs and kisses with frequency, and the only time his father touched his sons was to smack them. As far as Jonas knew, his father had never touched his daughters.

And as that thought crossed his brain, Horace Edwards put his arm across his daughter's shoulders and guided her out the door. Once outside, Audrey put her arm around her father's waist and they strolled toward their automobile—a two-year old, four door Packard. They stopped and waited for

Jonas to catch up.

"Audrey'll chauffeur while you and me sightsee, Jonas." He opened the driver's side door for his daughter then walked around to the other side of the car. Jonas got into the back seat, Horace took his place up front, and Audrey started the car. The next hour left Jonas reeling. He'd thought of himself as a businessman, and a pretty good one—maybe even a better one than Horace Edwards, since the older man was borrowing his money. How wrong he was. Looking at the land that Horace had bought, and listening to his plans for developing it, Jonas realized that the man was purely brilliant. Some day soon—as soon as the depression was over—Carrie's Crossing would be as important as Belle City. It certainly would be richer, for Horace's plans didn't include making any provisions for anybody who couldn't afford his prices. No wonder he'd been furious at having to accept Jonas as a partner.

"My hat's off to you, Horace. I've lived here all my life and I never would have seen what you've seen, to say nothing of having what it takes to bring a dream to life."

"You've done all right for yourself, Jonas. Better than all right, especially for such a young man." Horace looked out at the empty field at the back end of Carrie's Crossing, his eyes seeing much more than the waist-high weeds and wild flowers and stands of pine, all lush and green thanks to the narrow trickle of Carrie's Creek that ran through it. He tapped the rolled up blueprint against the palm of his hand, the drawings that would transform the field into an exclusive residential enclave. "In fact, you've got something that I don't have, something that I need."

"What's that?"

"You can hold on to a dollar and I can't for the life of me. I make a lot of money, but I spend it soon as it comes in the door. But you—I'll bet you've got the first dollar you ever made. Am I right?"

Jonas wasn't certain that he wasn't being made fun of. It was Audrey's smile that let him know that wasn't the case. "Pretty much," he answered.

"That's because we're opposite sides of the same coin, you and me."

"How's that?"

"We both came from nothing. Oh, don't get your back up, boy. I asked around about you and learned all about your pa, and if you asked about me up around Mountain View way, you'd know that my pa was worse than yours by miles. At least I hear good things about your ma. Mine wasn't much better than the old man. And at least yours left you something, gave you a start.

Everything I have, I got on my own, usually with somebody standing in my way, trying to stop me."

"I thought you were from Belle City."

Horace gave a nasty bark of laughter, reminding Jonas who lived inside the man. "Naw, I'm a backwoods, country boy. I didn't even have a pair of shoes until I was just about a grown man, and I stole them. I couldn't run away all the way to Belle City on my bare feet." He laughed again, but there was no humor in it. He looked at his watch. "Come on. Got something else to show you."

They climbed back into the car. Horace didn't speak. Remembering his past, it seemed, brought on a dark moodiness. Audrey, who seemed to know her father very well, kept the conversation going, asking Jonas about himself, telling him about herself, all the while handling the vehicle smoothly and surely.

"How long have you been driving?"

"Since I was nine. Pa was teaching H.J. and Gil—that's my brothers— and I threw a fit until he taught me too."

"And she's the best driver of all," Horace said, literally shaking himself out of his dark place. "She's the smartest one in the family."

"No, I'm not," Audrey said. "Mama is."

Horace turned around and looked at Jonas. "She's right about that. Her ma—my wife—she's the first thing I ever fought for and won. And she's the reason I've fought for everything else I have 'cause her pa sure didn't want her to marry me. He said I came from nothing and would amount to nothing, and I have spent my life proving him wrong."

"Papa," Audrey said, drawing his attention back to the road as she drove into the lot of Carrie's Crossing High School. She parked beside a new Cadillac, and Horace was out of the car before she turned off the engine.

A tall, thin, slightly stooped man got out of the Cadillac, and Horace hurried over to him and shook his hand. It took a moment but Jonas recognized the man and he, too, hurried over, hand extended.

"Mr. Allen."

"Why if it isn't Jonas Thatcher." His eyes narrowed as he looked from Horace to Jonas and back again. "I think I know who your new partner is, Horace, and I approve."

Horace looked from his banker to his new partner, uncertain how to feel about the obvious warmth between the two men. "How is it you two know each other?"

Grady Allen ignored the question and pointed to the land adjacent to the school's parking lot. "Did Horace tell you what we're doing here, Jonas? Tell him, Horace."

Horace Edwards swallowed and did as he was told, the pecking order between the two men clearly established: Grady Allen was the founder and principal shareholder of the First National Bank of Belle City, the only financial establishment in that town not to fail, primarily because Allen's personal wealth was sufficient to prop up his bank's stock and guarantee the safety of the deposits. When his customers realized that he'd put up his money to protect their money, not only did they leave their money in place, but people from as far away as North Carolina brought money to deposit with Grady Allen. It is said that he'd open an account for a person with as little as a dollar. Grady Allen's new bank, the First National Bank of Carrie's Crossing, was to be built next door to the elementary and high schools on land owned by Horace Edwards.

"We're going to have a bank?" Jonas was asking a question though it didn't sound like it. He was flabbergasted. "Your bank?"

"As I recall, you told me eight or ten years ago that I should put a bank here. Have you changed your mind?"

Jonas shook his head. "No, sir. I just…I didn't think…" He shut his mouth, annoyed with himself for being so tongue-tied. He sounded like an ignorant kid, and Horace noticed. Grady Allen seemed not to.

"I knew you were right. I just didn't know it would take me so long to get around to doing it."

"But the Depression," Jonas said.

"I think maybe we've turned Hoover's corner—"

"I *know* we have!" In his exuberance, Horace failed to notice the old banker's displeasure at being interrupted.

"Thanks to Mr. Roosevelt," Allen said and waited for the response he obviously knew was coming.

"It's got nothing to do with Roosevelt," Horace all but shouted.

"It's got everything to do with Roosevelt," Allen said quietly. "If Hoover were still the president we'd all be in the poorhouse by now, me included. Hoover was dead wrong about the government not being responsible for fixing the mess we're in. Only the government could fix it, and with Roosevelt putting people back to work, we'll soon get back on track."

Horace looked sour, but he didn't say anything.

"How does that help us, Mr. Allen? Mr. Roosevelt's public works projects,

I mean," Jonas said. "Us here in Carrie's Crossing, I mean." He wanted to kick himself for sounding so childish, but Grady Allen gave no hint that he was talking to a child.

"I understand that a major road construction project is due to start up right around the first of the year out at the end of the county, out Stevensville way, run around to the old Colored Town Road, and connect up to the Belle City Road."

"That's a big project," Horace exclaimed, his pique forgotten. "A lot of workers. And they'll have to spend their money somewhere." He looked at Jonas. "Good thing you kept the food market open, and you might have to open up the furniture store."

"And we'll have the only bank—only *open* bank—for miles around."

Jonas listened and nodded his agreement to all that was said. "They're going to need somewhere to live, all those workers, aren't they?"

There was a moment of stunned silence. Then Grady Allen gave a hoot of a laugh and clapped him on the back, but addressed Horace. "I like the site, Horace: Next to the schools. People drop their children off, make a deposit, go on to work. Yessir, I like it a lot. I like your new partner, too. Yessir, I like a man with ideas. We can do the paperwork tomorrow at my office if that's all right with you boys."

"But I thought you needed to have the money today," Horace said.

"If it was anybody but Jonas Thatcher I would need it today. But if he says he'll be in my office first thing in the morning with the money, then that's all right with me. We can get the contracts signed and notarized and get you back in business, Horace. Besides," and he gave Jonas a sly grin, "I don't have time to wait around while he digs up all that money." He laughed and clapped Jonas on the back again.

Horace was back to being deeply morose by the time they settled into a booth in the Crossing Café, but Jonas was too hungry to focus on anything but eating. Besides, he had a pretty good idea what was stuck in Horace's craw and it wasn't meat loaf, mashed potatoes and string beans. Horace Edwards could pout all he wanted, but Jonas had not the slightest intention of telling him that Beau Thatcher, a Colored man, had introduced him to the richest man in Belle City more than ten years ago. Instead, he and Audrey focused their attention on each other. He liked talking to and listening to her. She was smart and funny and she had traveled—to Philadelphia and New York and Boston and to Europe. She'd been to Paris and London!

"I've only traveled in my mind. Through books and magazines. You're lucky," Jonas said.

"I know, believe me. Especially now, with everything so…so…I'm just glad I had a chance to see some of the world when I did, in case…in case…"

"You'll go again, Audrey. This depression won't last forever."

"It's already been five years. It feels like forever."

"I know. But men like Mr. Allen and your father wouldn't be building a new bank if they thought otherwise. And don't forget that road construction project. I don't think a man like Mr. Roosevelt would be spending so much money—"

Horace cut him off with a snarled, "Taxpayers' money."

"People are getting back to work," Jonas continued. "That's what matters."

She wrinkled her forehead in thought. "You're right, I suppose. Of course you're right, Jonas. Nobody would build a new bank if they thought it would fail."

"Besides," Jonas said as he was pondering whether he'd have apple pie à la mode or bread pudding for dessert, "with a bank right here in town, especially one owned by Mr. Allen, I might even make a deposit or two myself."

That roused Horace. "Since you and Grady Allen are such good friends and all, any reason why you don't already have your money in his bank?"

"His bank is in Belle City. Like I just said, when his bank opens here, where I live and work, I'll give some thought to depositing some of my money in it." Jonas didn't want to be rude to Horace in front of his daughter, but he was tired of the man's moody and childish behavior. "What do you all want for dessert?"

"What are you having?" Audrey asked.

"Bread pudding, I think."

"Oooh. Me too."

"Any reason you can't tell us how it is you happen to know the man?" Edwards all but spat the words, shocking his daughter who'd probably never seen this side of him.

"It's none of your business," Jonas said calmly, politely even, shocking Audrey even more. Her breath caught and she looked from one man to the other, confused and a little bit frightened, which aroused a strange sympathy within Jonas. He looked at her, and when he spoke, it was to her that he said, "A mutual friend introduced us, a man who had survived The Great War and thought that we could, I don't know, comfort each other since he had a son and I had a brother who had not survived it. And he was right: We did and probably still do provide an odd kind of comfort for each other, even though we no longer need to talk about it."

"Oh, Jonas, I'm so sorry." Audrey looked truly sorry, as if the death of his brother had just happened. "How old was your brother?"

"Nineteen," Jonas said, as he tried—and failed—to conjure up an image of his long dead older brother. He barely remembered his name. He looked at his watch and stood up. "I'm sorry but I don't really have time for dessert. I need to get home to change clothes and get back to the store." He put some money on the table. "You all stay as long as like, have tea or coffee or dessert—whatever you like—no need for you to rush." He finally looked at his new partner. "I'll see you in the morning, Horace." Then he looked at Audrey and smiled. "It was a real pleasure meeting you, Miss Edwards. I hope to see you again. Soon."

Horace stood up quickly. Audrey did too, still looking distressed. "We'll give you a ride home, Jonas," Horace said.

"Why do you have to change clothes?" Audrey asked, then blushed at the look her father gave her.

Jonas laughed. "I don't wear a suit and tie every day like Mr. Allen and your papa because I work in a grocery store, not a bank or a real estate office."

"Speaking of which," Horace said as they headed for the exit, "we're gonna need us an office here in Carrie's Crossing so we can figure out where all those road workers are gonna live."

"I think I can help with that," Jonas said, leading them out of the restaurant and toward the three buildings he owned on the street. They passed the furniture store and the grocery store and stopped in front of the defunct pub. He unlocked and opened the door and switched on the light, then stood back for Audrey and Horace to enter. Audrey stood beside him. Horace walked all around, front to back, even pushing his way through all the boxes of canned goods, to see every corner of the space. "What do you think?" Jonas asked when Horace finally completed his inspection.

"I remember you told me about this place the first time we met. You remember that?" When Jonas nodded, Horace said, "I think you better get used to wearing a suit and tie every day" and clapped him on the back, as if there hadn't been a moment of tension or hostility between them. "This is perfect. And right in the heart of downtown."

"I'll find new warehouse space and get this place cleaned out," Jonas said.

"And I guess I'd better buy some new suits."

"Come on, we'll take you home," Horace said, and Jonas stopped himself from refusing the offer. He knew that Horace wanted to see where he lived, and he could avoid that for only so long. After all, the man now was his partner. He'd have to invite him and his wife to dinner…or whatever it was that high class business people did. He'd need to learn the rules.

The drive from his stores to his home was a brief one. Horace was driving now—too fast—and he skidded to stop just past the driveway, requiring him to back up and then turn in. He drove all the way up beside the house, threw the car into gear, and got out. Then he walked all the way around the house, the way he'd walked all the way through the warehouse just a few moments ago. The house sat atop a small rise and there were no other houses visible, though one of Horace Edwards's developments would, one day in the not to distant future, rise on the other side of the woods.

"This is a very nice house, Jonas," Horace finally said.

"It's a very beautiful house, Jonas," Audrey said. "A bit unusual, but beautiful."

Jonas didn't say anything because what he wanted to say would do nothing but cause upset and trouble, and there was no point to that. And anyway, his house was none of their business. "If you take a right turn out of the yard here, Horace, the road will run you right into the Belle City Road. You won't have to go back through town unless you just want to."

Horace gave him a look he was learning to understand all to well. It was the look of a balking mule: Stubborn, recalcitrant, rebellious, hostile. Horace wanted to ask about the house, but he was learning a bit about Jonas too: To ask about what was none of his business likely would earn him the kind of stinging rebuke his ego was loathe to accept. "I didn't know there was a shortcut to the Belle City Road."

Jonas gave him a conciliatory smile. "Nobody but us old-timers knows about it. It wasn't even paved for a long time, nothing but wheel ruts and mud."

"This is the road Grady Allen was talking about, isn't it? Colored Town Road, isn't that what he called it?" Horace stared at the road behind Jonas's house. "Colored folks lived 'round here? This close to your house?"

"That's right," Jonas said, spoiling for the fight he'd been avoiding all day. Horace looked beyond the road and pointed toward the empty fields and the acres of wild growth beyond it. "Who owns all that land yonder?"

"I do," Jonas said.

"All of it?" Horace asked.

"All of it," Jonas answered.

"Well," Horace said and lifted his hat and scratched his head. "Well, now," he said, and let his eyes scan the horizon. Then he turned away, walked to his car, got in and started the motor. If his daughter hadn't run to open the door and fling herself into the passenger seat, Jonas thought the man would have left her. He watched them disappear down the road, his thoughts a jumble of contradictions. He was flat-out glad to see the back of Horace Edwards and was not looking forward to the following day when he'd have to see him again. On the other hand, he'd have liked to spend more time with Audrey, and he hoped that she would accompany her father to the bank in the morning.

He walked to the road and looked beyond the emptiness into the past. He could see Maisy Cooper's house and barn, and the houses and farms of the other Colored families who had lived there. He allowed himself a momentary delight as he realized that Horace thought that he had lived on Colored Town Road across the street from Colored people. The thought took hold and, as he recalled the look on the man's face, he laughed out loud. Then, as always happened when he looked across the road and remembered, the shade of sadness dropped down. He had bought up all the houses and land stolen from the Colored people the night that his own pa had stolen Will Thatcher's land, and the KKK thieves were happy to sell it, especially those like the police chief who were, themselves, being run out of town. He'd driven over to Belle City, to First Freeman's house, with the five property deeds in his pocket, proud to be able to return the land to the rightful owners. He would never, if he lived to be a hundred, forget the look on the old man's face: Stunned amazement that quickly turned into disbelief that just as quickly was replaced by something that felt to Jonas like pity. *"They don't want that land, Jonas. They don't want no parts of the Crossing, not no more and not ever again. They call Belle City home now. They forgot all about a place called Carrie's Crossing, like it never was."*

Jonas shook himself back to the present. He needed to go get his car and to begin cleaning out the warehouse so that it could become a real estate office and he could become—what?

He shook hands with Grady Allen and Horace Edwards after all the contracts were signed. Both men clapped him on the back. "How does it feel to be a real estate developer, Jonas?" Allen asked him.

"Is that what I am? A developer?"

The two older men chuckled in a worldly, all knowing kind of way. "What do you think we should call you?" Horace asked in a challenging kind of way.

"How about builder?"

"You plan on building something, Jonas?" Allen asked.

"Yep," Jonas said, looking at Horace. "Me and my real estate partner are gonna build some places for those road construction workers to live. On some of that land I own on the old Colored Town Road. And we truly do need to give it a new name."

They looked at him, each in a different way. Allen's look was speculative. He was imagining the housing. Horace's look was belligerent and defiant, and he was shaking his head back and forth. "One thing we don't want in Belle City, not now, not ever, is low class people, and you build some place for construction workers to live and it starts out as low class and goes down from there. You might as well keep the Colored Town name."

Jonas studied him for a moment, then turned to look at Grady Allen, who was studying him. Jonas let him and waited for him to speak.

"What's your thinking, Son?"

"We're going to need to run water and electricity through there anyway. You know there isn't any because we didn't put it in for the Colored." Allen flushed a bit at those words, but nodded for Jonas to continue. "We can build some dormitory-like places for the workers—nothing but men anyway, right? But they'll have hot and cold running water and toilets and kitchens and heat. We can put those up cheap and when the road is finished, we can pull 'em down and put up something better, something nicer. Something more high class, Horace. And they'll be paying rent, the road workers, which should off-set the cost of building the places and tearing them down."

Allen was nodding. "Can probably get the government to pay to level the land and cut the road through."

"Maybe run the water and electricity, too?" Jonas asked.

"Then we better get started," Horace said. "Weather is holding pretty good for it being almost winter, but it won't last. Nobody but that damfool Roosevelt would start to build a road in the winter time."

From the Diary of Jonas Farley Thatcher

Christmas 1934. I wish I had a friend, somebody I could talk to about things, about what I think and feel. About whether I should marry Audrey Edwards. I do truly like her a lot, more than I ever liked a girl, and people keep telling me it's time to get married and start a family.

Until I met Audrey I didn't agree with that but now I do. Except I don't know if she loves me more or loves her pa more and I don't think a man should have a wife he cannot trust. I also donnot like her mother. Alice is her name and she calls colored people niggers and coons all the time. She did it so many times at dinner tonite at Mr. Allen's house that Mrs. Allen had to ask her to stop that kind of talk at the dinner table. She was talking to Mrs. Allen's help, calling them things right when they were in the room serving the food. Mr. Allen said he didn't like that kind of talk either, like his wife. Then I said I didn't like it either and Audrey looked at me, then she looked at her pa. I never heard her talk like that so I don't know if she thinks that way but I will have to find out. I think I will have to ask my sister what I should do because I donot have any friends. I wish Beau thought I was his friend but he does not. Si either. I wish Mr. First was still here but he is gone now--him and Miss Maisy Cooper both. I tell myself I should be more happy. I am rich. I have maybe more business than a man needs. The men are ready to start building Mr. Roosevelt's road. The CCC it is called and it will be one place in Georgia where The Great Depression will be over. No matter what Horace Edwards says or thinks, Mr. Roosevelt is a good president. He is doing good things for everybody.

– Belle City –
Ruthie

I t might be a new deal for some people, but it's the same old deal for us."
Little Si paced back and forth, fists tight balls at his sides. "No Colored
men will be hired to help build that road from Carrie's Crossing to Belle City.
What *exactly* do we have to do to get a fair deal?"

Big Si held up several newspapers—the *Chicago Defender*, the *Amsterdam
Daily News*, the *Pittsburg Courier*—newspapers that he could not read but which
his two children who could read would read to him in their entirety almost
every day. "But I thought it said that Colored were getting work in that CCC
and WPA." He looked over at Little Si, who was still pacing, and at Ruth, who
was sitting beside her husband, head on his shoulder, almost asleep. "Isn't that
what y'all read in these newspapers? And didn't I hear that same thing on the
radio? Isn't that what you read to me, Ruth?"

Ruthie roused herself. "Yes, Pa—" she began, but Beau cut her off.

"Roosevelt's paying for it, Pa, but he's letting the local governments do the
hiring, by their own rules, and no government down here is gon' hire Colored.
So Si is right: It's the same ol' deal for us."

"So it's only the Colored people up North who're gettin' the New Deal?"
Big Si asked.

They all nodded, and Beau added, "We won't see the end of this Depression
'til all the white folks in America is back to work. Maybe the white folks in Italy
and France and Germany, too. Then maybe we can find ourselves a job."

"I hope it's soon." Mack, Ruth's husband, stood and began to pace,
but had to stop because the living room wasn't large enough for both him
and Little Si. "I can't build houses if people don't have money to buy 'em."

"You should've been hired to help build that road, or those new school
houses," Little Si said. "They're closing schools for Colored children 'cause
they say they can't pay the teachers, but they're building new schools for white
children. It's wrong, Pa. It's just plain wrong, and I'm sick and tired of it."

"But the law," Big Si said, still brandishing the newspapers. "Don't the law
say they got to let Colored get some of this gov'ment money?"

"They make laws to fit their wants and needs, not ours," Little Si said bitterly.

"I wish that wasn't the truth," Mack said, "but the truth is: It is."

Big Si looked up at them. "Why don't y'all sit down," he said in his steady, calm voice, but it was not a request, and both men sat, Mack beside his wife and Si beside his wife, and for a brief moment there was no sound but the crackle and pop of the fire that roared in the grate. Though it was just a little past three in the afternoon, wintertime dusk was falling outside, so the fire did double duty: Heat and light.

This after-church Sunday dinner was rare in its peace and quiet because all the children were elsewhere—with grandparents or aunts and uncles. Rare also because it was just Big Si's children and their spouses at Big Si's house—the house that had belonged to First Freeman until his death four years earlier. Big Si had added a second sofa to the living room and had Mack build a dining table long enough to seat twenty adults, and there still wasn't enough room when the whole family gathered. Only Mack's parents had a house that large, and they had hosted the New Year's celebration five days ago, though there wasn't much joy or merriment. The only good thing about the arrival of 1935, they all agreed, was it brought an end to 1934. The Depression, however, was still going strong.

"Are you ready to eat, Pa?" Ruth asked, getting so slowly to her feet that Mack had to help her. She was exhausted; it was her natural state these days and Mack stood beside her, supporting her. Despite the fact that she loved her children to distraction, she was glad to have them parceled out today: Nellie at Mack's parents' and the boys at Tobias and Little Si's mother-in-law's. As much as Big Si appreciated the huge extended family that his offspring's marriages had produced, he got real pleasure from having them to himself on occasion. It meant he got to see how they were doing, and Ruth looked about to fall over. He stood up at the same time that Tobias's wife, Belle, pushed herself to her feet, one hand to her lower back, the other cradling her eight months of pregnancy. That got Toby to his feet and they all headed for the kitchen. Big Si turned to see if Little Si and Catherine followed and what he saw hurt him more deeply than he had words to express: They sat side by side, not looking at each other, not talking to each other, not touching each other. Two granite statues.

"Pa, do you know what's troubling Little Si and Cathy?" Ruthie was at his side, leaning into him, as she placed bowls of food on the table to join those that he'd already placed there. There would be a lot of food. Whoever served food these days made extra for the visitors to take home. Whoever had food these days shared, as a matter of course, and Big Si Thatcher had more than most: His entire backyard was a garden. All his years of experience as a farmer had been recalled, thanks to the depression.

"I was thinkin' maybe you knew," he said sadly. "Whatever it is, it's bad."

"Belle's baby?" Ruth whispered the query. That Little Si and Catherine remained childless was a pain borne not just by them but by the entire family. Belle's baby would make three for her and Tobias. Ruthie and Mack had four. Only the unmarried Beau and Belle and Cathy's unmarried baby sister, Helen, had no children. Both said, with obvious and heartfelt relief, that they were content to be auntie and uncle.

"Her Ma said she wasn't upset by that anymore."

"Then I don't know, Pa," Ruthie said. "I can ask Mack to ask Si—"

Big Si was shaking his head. "Don't do that. Just leave it be."

"But if something's wrong—?"

"If they want us to know, they'll tell us," he said and called them to the table. "Silas, Catherine. Y'all come on so the food don't get cold."

Everybody's spirits picked up with the eating of good food. Ruthie's exhaustion abated as Beau regaled them with tales of his illegal whiskey dealing during the thirteen years of Prohibition. Nobody but Pa had known while it was happening, and it still would be a secret had Beau not inadvertently let it slip while talking about something else, but he had, and then was forced to tell all. They never tired of hearing about the risks and the near misses—events that Beau could laugh about now but which, when they happened, frightened him to his core.

"I do wish I coulda seen the look on Zeb Thatcher's face when he got outta jail and got home to find all his whiskey gone," Pa said, laughing his deep belly laugh. "Y'all didn't know Zeb, hadn't seen him cut the fool the way he could. I give that youngest boy of his, Jonas, real credit. He had to be scared half to death of that man."

"But it was his own pa, wasn't it?" Catherine asked.

"Didn't matter none at all. Zeb Thatcher was one mean, evil white man. He hated whatever lived and breathed, his own kin included. If my pa was still with us, he'd tell you 'bout Zeb. That boy, Jonas, used to come over here and talk to 'Mr. First,' he called him. Told him all kinds of things." He looked from Ruth to Little Si. "Y'all always said that boy was y'all's friend. We didn't believe it at first, but it was true."

"It was," Ruthie said. "He was my friend, but he was more Silas's friend."

They looked to Silas to speak of his friendship with the white boy, but when Silas spoke, he said, "I'm going north. To Chicago." He spoke in a quiet, determined way, and it took several seconds for all the minds at the table to shift from evil Zeb Thatcher and his not-evil son to what Si had just said. Then there were more full, heavy seconds of stunned disbelief. Then everybody was talking at once. Everybody but Catherine, who was sitting again like a stone statue, her head lowered as if praying. She didn't look at anyone, and especially not at her husband, not even when he stood up.

"I know what you all think and feel. I've been doing nothing but thinking and feeling for weeks, and I'm convinced that I'm doing the best thing." He looked at his sister. "They made you the school principal and they fired me, Ruthie. I'm happy for you but I'm angry too. I'm the one with the Ph.D."

"They shut your school down, Si." Beau was on his feet now, too, glowering at his brother. "You can't blame Ruthie for that."

"I'm not blaming Ruthie for anything."

"That's what it sounds like, Si. They made Ruthie a principal 'stead of you, so you gon' run off to Chicago 'cause you're mad."

"That's not why I'm going. You think just because you made so much money on your illegal whiskey that you know so much, but you don't. You don't know anything. You can't even read."

Beau was stung, but he shot back, "Readin' ain't everything."

"It's the only thing that is truly important, Beau."

"You wrong 'bout that, Si. Havin' something to call your own is more important. Something nobody can take from you. Not even white people."

"Knowledge, Beau. That's exactly what I'm talking about: Nobody can take what I've got in my head, in my brain," Si said.

"But they can take your job, little brother, 'cause it wasn't yours to start with. It was their job in their school, and they took it from you and all your book learnin' couldn't stop 'em."

"And what do you have that's yours, Mr. Know-It-All Beau Thatcher?"

Ruthie jumped up and put a hand out to Beau. He was so protective of her that it sometimes was frightening. He even thought that her own brother—their own brother—was a threat to her. He'd been this way ever since their Ma was murdered. It was as if he meant to keep all harm from her. She reached out to both men, to both of her brothers, but did not speak. She didn't know what to say, but she did know that if she spoke to either brother by name, the other would feel insulted, hurt. She looked at Tobias. Older by two years, he usually managed to have a calming effect on Little Si, but Tobias was watching the food on his plate, his brow wrinkled in a deep frown. *What was wrong with him?* For the first time in her life, Ruthie resented her big brothers, all of them, including Eubanks whom nobody had heard from in more than ten years. She wanted to yell at them, to chastise them in the name of their mother, but that, she knew, would only make matters worse. Big Si solved the problem.

"Beaudry. Silas." That was all he said, but the tone of his voice is what took all the air out them. Yes, he was angry, but there also was hurt and sadness and confusion. The bewildered look on his face was as unnerving as the tone of his voice. His boys. This behavior from his sons, talking against each other. How was that possible? He'd never witnessed any dispute among them that called for voices raised in anger, not even when they were children. He sighed deeply, and the sound he made in his throat was something they'd never heard, not even when his beloved Nellie was snatched from him so horribly.

Ruthie was at his side in a second, the fatigue that had wracked her body, mind and spirit for days, forgotten. "Pa!" She wrapped her arms around him, and he bent his head into her neck and let her hold him, just for a few seconds. Then he patted her back and eased himself up straighter in his chair. He looked at Silas.

"Didn't they put you in charge of the school over at the church?"

"That's not a school, Pa. That's some tables and chairs in a church basement."

"You're teaching and chil'ren is learning. It's a school." Pa was fully mad now. No trace of sadness or confusion remained. "Everybody over there calls you Professor Thatcher or Dr. Thatcher, just like they ought to. You always complained that the white folks down at the Board of Education always called you Silas. Never would give you the credit for your education. But now you got that, and it ain't enough? It ain't enough that your people give you what you said you wanted: To be in charge of a school and have the people call you by your right name?" Pa waited for an answer and when none came, he asked, "You think the white folks at the Board of Education in Chicago is gon' call you Dr. Thatcher? Is that why you goin' to Chicago? To hear some white folks call you by a certain name? Is it gon' sound better when they say it?"

Little Si shook his head. "I'm going to Chicago, Pa, because I think things are better for us in the North. There are more opportunities..."

"More opportunities to starve to death," Beau said. He pointed to the platters and bowls heaped with food. "You think folks in Chicago can grow food like this in the backyard?"

"I didn't go to school all those years to be a farmer again."

"Nothin' wrong with bein' a farmer," Big Si said, challenge hard in his voice, "'specially when you own the land that's growin' your food."

"I didn't say there was, Pa—not for anybody who wants to farm. But it's not what I want."

"What do you want, then?" Big Si asked, and waited for his son to answer.

"I want to teach, maybe to write. I want to use my mind, my brain, and I believe I can do that in Chicago better than here."

"Chicago! Just full of opportunity, ain't it?" Beau snarled.

"Yeah, Beau, it is," Little Si shot back. "Plenty of opportunity."

"To freeze to death while you're starving."

"Is that what you think too, Catherine?" Pa asked quickly before Si could rejoin. "That things are better for us in the North?"

Catherine, who hadn't spoken all evening, raised her eyes and met the glance of every pair of eyes at the table, except those of her husband. "I'm not going to Chicago with Silas," she said.

The stunned silence that met those words could have been considered humorous by someone seeing only six wide-eyed people, their mouths gaping, staring at the prim and proper young woman who had lowered her head again to stare at the trembling hands folded in her lap.

Tobias's wife, Belle, grabbed her pregnant belly and cried out to her younger sister, cried out to ask why, what was wrong? Then she grabbed Catherine and held her close, the two sisters holding each other and whispering and crying. Belle looked over her sister's shoulder at her husband, pleading with her eyes for him to do something.

"Si—" Tobias tried, failed, to find some words. He gave his wife a helpless look.

"Why not, Catherine?" Mack asked, his arm tight around Ruth.

Catherine raised her eyes and looked at him, giving him a small smile. She and Belle and Mack shared an undiscussed bond: They had married into the closely-knit Thatcher clan, and while they knew they were loved and respected within the family, they also felt that they were, in some sense, outsiders. "Why what, Mack? Why I'm not going to Chicago, or why I don't think things are better for Colored up there?"

Mack nodded his head. "Both things."

She inhaled and looked at her husband. The look was almost defiant but her words were not. They were sad. "I don't have as much education as Silas, but I can read, and I've read about how Colored are treated up north: Same way we're treated down here, and I don't think I want to go so far from home just to be a nigger when I get there. And they got all manner of foreign people up north—people who can't even speak English, but they can call us nigger. That's one reason I don't want to go to Chicago." She turned in her chair and looked directly at her husband. He met her gaze. "And Silas, you can't tell me for sure that we can have a house in Chicago. We have a house here with a garden in the backyard. And I know we don't have family in Chicago. We have family here—" She stopped suddenly and put her hands to her mouth. She looked around the table. "Oh my Lord. If I don't go with Silas, will y'all still be my family?"

A great sound erupted from the gathering, voices raised, chairs scraping the floor as people jumped to their feet and swarmed her. Arms grabbed and hugged her, voices joining the assurances that she was a Thatcher "for good and always." She sought Mack and Belle, and the look they shared said that maybe they weren't outsiders after all.

"Why can't you all feel that for me?" Little Si said. All the pain and anger and resentment Little Si had been holding inside for months escaped in a sorrowful wail. "I tell you I'm going to do something big and important and I get criticism. Catherine tells you she's going to do the exact opposite and you can't show her enough support." If he'd been younger he would have wept.

"That's not how it is, Silas," Pa said.

"That's exactly how it is. That's exactly how you all are. Catherine's too afraid of being called a nigger to try to make a better life, and that's fine with you all. Beau runs up and down the road with some cracker selling illegal whiskey and that's fine with you all. Tobias runs a gambling parlor and writes the numbers *and* sells illegal whiskey and that's all right with you—"

"Tobias does *what?*" Beau jumped up so fast he knocked his chair back into the wall, leaving a mark in the paint. "What are you talking about, Si?"

"Ask Tobias what I'm talking about."

All turned to Tobias who looked angry enough to chew rocks. Belle grabbed his hand but he shook her off. "You feel better now, Si? I guess I don't have to worry 'bout tellin' you nothin' else 'cause you won't be here to talk to, and right now I'm thinkin' that'll be a good thing."

"Is that true, Toby, what Si said?" Ruthie asked. "A gambling parlor?"

"That ain't none of your business," he snapped.

"It is my business," Pa said.

"No, Pa, it ain't. I'm a grown man."

"You're my son and if you're breakin' the law, it's my business."

"What law, Pa? Something some crackers made up? Every time one of us takes a breath, some cracker makes a law tellin' us we can't take so many breaths. If they got 'em a law says I got sit by and watch my wife and chil'ren starve to death, I'll be happy to tell 'em what they can do their law."

"But Toby—"

"But nothin', Ruthie. Mack ain't makin' no money buildin' houses, but I 'spect that's all right 'cause you makin' money bein' the school principal and teachin' French to college students on the side. But I ain't makin' no money cuttin' hair, and Belle ain't making no money curlin' hair, and the reason we ain't makin' no money is Colored folks ain't got no money to buy houses *or* worry 'bout how their hair looks."

"But they got money to play the numbers and gamble," Beau snarled.

"Yeah, Beau, they do. Just like they had money to buy your illegal whiskey. No matter how hard times get, a drink of whiskey and believin' you got a chance to win a few cents or a few dollars—those are things that can keep people from givin' up hope."

"Me and Beau ain't gon' let you and Belle and the chil'ren go without, Tobias. You know that."

"I'm a grown man, Pa. I ain't gon' be asking you or my brother *or* my sister to take care of me and my family. Now, y'all just go on about your business and leave my business alone. Just forget Si ever opened his big mouth."

"We can't just forget it, Tobias."

"Then don't think about it, Pa. Don't talk about it. Don't worry about it. Me and Belle and the chil'ren are gon' be just fine." He touched his wife's shoulder. "And the new one is gon' be just fine, too."

"Just don't you have my wife involved in your illegal activities," Little Si said, meaning to have the last word but instead igniting another firestorm over the fact that Belle actually worked alongside Toby in the gambling room, which occupied the flat above their barber shop/beauty salon where Beau had lived before he moved in with Pa.

"Number one, Si, keep your mouth off my wife. And number two: If you care so much about what *your* wife is doing, stay here and look after her 'stead of running off to Chicago." And that was the last word.

Ruthie was never so glad to be going home. She'd always enjoyed spending time with her family. Today was an exception. She'd been exhausted when she arrived, and if the situation with Catherine and Little Si drained the last energy from her, the news of Si and Belle's newest enterprise pierced her with what felt like thousands of pain darts. It was the first time that they'd all taken leave of each other without declarations of their love.

They barely looked at each other as they cleared the table and fixed bowls and plates of food to take home, and they all but ran to the front door in an exit that was more escape than leave-taking, and the knife-sharp cold air that met them told how the temperature had dropped during the afternoon. As Ruthie and Mack hurried to their car, she looked to see if Catherine and Little Si would travel home together. She saw Pa grab Little Si's arm, saw Little Si pull away and run down the front porch steps, saw Catherine get in the car with Belle and Tobias. That's when the tears started. Mack looked over at her but he didn't speak. He didn't know that there was anything he could say that wouldn't make an already awful situation worse. She fumbled in her purse for a handkerchief and wiped her eyes and blew her nose, but she still stared straight ahead without speaking. Their drive home was a short one and tonight, a direct one as it already had been decided that that the children would stay the night with their relatives.

The house was dark and teeth-chattering cold. They hadn't been home since leaving for church that morning and all the brightness and warmth of playing children—of family—had long since seeped out. Mack hurried to light the fire in the living room, a small one, just to knock the chill off, and then he rushed upstairs to light the one in their bedroom—a bigger one of both wood and coal chunks that would burn hot and bright for a while, before slowing to a simmer that would warm them through the night. Ruthie lit a similar one in the big potbelly stove in the kitchen and put the kettle on. Mack had been so upset by the goings-on at the table at Pa's house that he hadn't eaten any dessert or had an after-dinner cup of coffee. He'd want both now. So would Ruthie, for that matter. He'd also want to talk to her and hear what she had to say about what they'd learned about her brothers, for Mack knew only what she said to him when they were seated at the kitchen table, warmed by the heat from the stove and the coffee and the apple pie. "I want to see it," Ruthie had said. "Whatever it is that Tobias and Belle are doing, I want to go there and see it with my own eyes."

Mack knew he should have expected this. Ruthie would not pass judgment on any person, and especially not on a member of her family, without firsthand knowledge of the situation. When Beau's rum-running activities came to light, while everybody else was expressing fearful shock, her first question to him had been, "How'd you happen upon that enterprise, Beau?" She understood perfectly the forces that had driven her brother and sister-in-law into illegal activity. What she'd want to know is why they chose that one, and how were they making it work. That it was risky—dangerous, even—was a given, for being Colored was risky and dangerous.

"I want to see it for myself, Mack."

He nodded his understanding. "I know you do, but you also know if Colored are doing anything illegal—and making money at it—white folks know about it, or they soon will. You know that."

"Yes, I surely do. Quite a few Colored people earn all of what little money they have telling white people what we're up to."

"So, if they haven't been raided or arrested yet, either they're paying some cops to look the other way, or it's just a matter of time before the raid happens, and I don't want you to be one of the ones arrested."

She gave him a long, speculative look, then took his hand and kissed it. "Then I guess neither one of us will know what a gambling parlor looks like." She stood up and began clearing the table. Her back to him, she said, "I must say, Mack McGinnis, that you have gotten right clever in the wife-managing department."

"I wouldn't call it that," he said.

"That's why you're so successful with it," she said.

They both enjoyed the warmth of the moment, then Mack said, "You're not mad about what Tobias and Belle are doing, are you?"

"No, I'm not mad. They're right: They have to do whatever is necessary to take care of their family. But I am...maybe not frightened, but...worried. You?"

Mack nodded. "Yeah, me too. Worried. But here's what I think, Ruthie: I think maybe the police already know and Tobias is paying them to look the other way. This Depression has made poor folks out of everybody."

"We were already poor, and they just keep finding ways to steal another penny or drop of water from us."

Her bitterness and anger startled him. She never gave in to those feelings and never let anybody else do it, either. *"That's how they act,"* she'd always say. *"We start acting mean and nasty, and we'll be just like them."* He put his arms around her and pulled her in close. She held herself rigid for a moment, then relaxed into him. "They'll be just fine. And so will Si."

She pulled away from him. "I don't want to talk about Si."

She might not have been mad about Tobias and Belle's gambling parlor, but she surely was mad about Si's plan to go north. He could tell, though, that she was a long way from being ready to talk about it. So was he, for that matter. Bad enough Si wanted go away, but being willing to leave Catherine behind? There was no understanding that.

Emma Johnson, Belle and Catherine's mother, returned the four McGinnis boys to their parents at six o'clock the following morning, fed, dressed and ready for school. Though it had been less than twenty-four hours, Ruthie and Mack greeted their sons as if they hadn't seen them in weeks, and the boys regaled them with their exploits as if they'd been away for weeks. It always surprised and amazed Ruthie that Emma never tired of the boys; she insisted that as the mother of three daughters, she delighted in the wild and rambunctious nature of the boys in the same way that Mack's parents, after having raised four sons, never tired of time spent with Nellie and thought that every breath she took was a miracle of creation. Of course she and Mack felt the same way, after waiting so long for their girl.

"What are they cooking for our lunch today, Ma?" Jack asked.

"Didn't you just eat breakfast?" Mack asked his youngest son. "I know for sure Miss Emma fed y'all."

"She did, Pa," Jack said, hopping around like a cricket, "but I'm hungry again."

"You're always hungry," Mack Jr. said, suddenly grabbing his baby brother and holding him upside down. "Maybe if I shake the food from your big feet, your belly will recollect all them grits and eggs you ate."

"Pick me up, Mackie. Do me too, Mackie!" Thatcher, a year older, was hopping from foot to foot and yelling while Jack, upside down, laughed hysterically.

Wilton, next to Mack Jr. in age, attempted to accommodate Thatcher but wasn't yet tall enough or strong enough, and both boys ended up in a pile on the floor, causing them to shriek with laughter.

Ruthie looked at Mack, and and he made to calm and quiet them before they got all dirty. "Go get your books and things and get in the car." He would take Mack Jr. to the school in the basement of their church, the school run by Dr. Silas Thatcher Jr., and then pick up his baby daughter from his parents.

The youngest boys would go with their mother to the school where she was principal, and she didn't know what the children would be fed for lunch. Since the city no longer provided food for the Colored schools, it had fallen to her and a handful of parents to scrounge and scavenge for lunch provisions, and she didn't know what was left in the kitchen pantry. More than likely it would be beans and rice, and for too many of the children, it would be the only food they would have that day. She cursed the meanness of white people, cursed it because she'd given up trying to understand it.

Despite the neglect of the school board, Ashdale Elementary School was, Ruthie thought, a beautiful sight. It was a small single-story brick building, its white wood trim and red door shiny with new paint, its small patch of front yard grass bright green in spring and summer and closely cropped all year—all thanks to the generosity of parents whose children attended the school and of local merchants and residents who took pride in every aspect of their neighborhood. The playground behind the building was recently paved, thanks to the McGinnis Construction Company which, unable these days to build houses, had both the time and the resources to grade and pave the schoolyard.

The front door of the school building opened as Ruthie opened her car door. She knew from the smoke billowing from the chimney that caretaker George Tennison had arrived. He saw it as his duty, if not his job, to have the building heated when the first pupils arrived, which usually was as soon as the parents knew that heat was spreading through the building, for just as the food they ate at school was their only meal, this was the only heat many of the children experienced.

The boys scrambled out of the car and raced down the walkway to the school, their shouts of "good morning, Mr. Tennison" ringing in the frigid morning air. Ruthie gathered her belongings and followed her sons, adding her greeting to theirs.

"Good morning to you, too, Miz. McGinnis." He touched his hat and held the door open for her. "How's Mack?"

"Like you, Mr. Tennison: Bored to tears and ready to get back to work,"

she told him and was surprised not to receive the response she expected. She looked more closely at him. "Is something wrong, Mr. Tennison?"

"Three little children," he said. "When I got here they were sittin' there on the steps, shakin' with cold and hunger. Nothin' but babies, two of 'em. It was an awful sight to see first thing in the mornin' and that's the truth."

"Where are they now?"

"I put 'em in the kitchen so they could get warm. I don't know how long they'd been sittin' on them steps, but they weren't hardly dressed, wrapped in the thinnest old blanket you ever saw. And…and…I fed 'em, Miz McGinnis. I'm sorry but…"

"You did the right thing, Mr. Tennison." She paused at her office to deposit her bags and coat and then followed him down the hallway to the cafeteria and kitchen, not once taking her usual pride and pleasure in the highly polished wood floors, the gleaming white walls, or the artwork of the children that hung on one side of the hall facing the art and portraits of notable Colored Americans that hung on the opposite side. She'd known George Tennison for as long as she'd been married to Mack, and while he was not an unkind or a cold man, he also was not an emotional one, so whatever circumstance had occurred this morning to so thoroughly alter his behavior was worthy of her total focus.

They entered the cafeteria to a chorus of "good morning Mrs. McGinnis" at full voice by the two dozen or so students, including her own children, clustered around Mrs. Roberta Samuels who volunteered to read to them every morning. Ruthie returned their greeting with love and warmth but continued on to the kitchen where it was indeed warm.

And curled up in a corner of the battered sofa were three children, deeply asleep under a thick blanket that Ruth herself had brought to the school. The older child she recognized, a third grader named Hazel Hill. Under each of Hazel's arms was tucked a smaller child, a girl and a boy, and Hazel held them tightly, as protective as if she were their mother, and as she watched them, a feeling was churning in Ruth's stomach, one that warned that something was very wrong and that she should have known about it. "What did you give them to eat, Mr. Tennison?"

"I heated up some of the powdered milk and put some of that blackstrap molasses in it, and some of that hard, old bread, and they ate it like it was meat and potatoes."

At that moment the back door flew open admitting Gertrude Butler, the cook. Her noisy, bustling arrival awoke Hazel and her siblings—startled them, really—and the little ones began to howl in fear. Hazel's wide eyes proclaimed her own fear, but she didn't cry. "Miz McGinnis. Is I'm in trouble?"

"Am I in trouble, and no, Hazel, you're not in trouble. Not at all," Ruth said. "It's really all right to be here, all of you," she said, and to the relief of the other two adults, the little ones ceased their wailing. "Your sister and brother?"

"Yes'm," Hazel said, sliding off the couch to her feet. "This here is Dor'thy and this is Will'am. She three and he four. Stand up, y'all," Hazel ordered, and Dorothy and William struggled to their feet and nobody could say a thing. Not only were the three of them filthy, not only were their clothes barely more than rags, they were little more than skin and bone. Ruth had known that Hazel wore the same two or three outfits to school every day, but so did most of the children, and the clothes were patched hand-me-downs if the children were fortunate, tied-together rags if they weren't. But what Ruth witnessed on the skeletal frames of Hazel, William and Dorothy Hill was worse than anything she'd ever seen, and she didn't know what to say. Had she become inured to others' misery?

"I have a daughter your age," she finally managed to say, forcing a smile at Dorothy. Then she looked at William. "And my Uncle Will taught me how to hunt and fish and ride a mule." The children gave her the kind of wide-eyed stare that suggested that they had not understood anything she'd said, which really left her at a loss for words until Mrs. Butler took over.

Just as George Tennison was so much more than a janitor and maintenance man—he was, in reality, the construction foreman for the McGinnis Construction Company—Mrs. Gertrude Butler was much more than a cook: She was the dietician at one of the Colored hospitals until it was forced to shut it doors, another casualty of the Depression. Ruth had hired them both, embarrassed to offer the pitiful salary the school board paid its Colored employees, but both had accepted the jobs, grateful to be earning any money at all. Mrs. Butler also collected old clothes and shoes, most of it barely more than rags, but often enough better than what many of the school children had. She was a large woman with a large voice, and she always proved a calming, soothing presence. This moment was not an exception. She put one hand on Dorothy's head, the other on William's. "Y'all look cold and hungry," she boomed.

They looked up at her and nodded, saying "yes'm" in unison.

Ruth managed a smile of thanks. "Hazel, will it be all right if the children stay with Mrs. Butler for a few minutes while you and I go talk in my office?"

"But I'm cold and hungry too, Miz McGinnis," Hazel wailed, all her big sister strength and resolve ebbing away.

Ruth looked at the big-faced clock on the wall. Everything was behind schedule. She looked at Gertrude. "I'll take the three of them with me while you get the oatmeal ready, then we'll come back in time to eat. How's that?" By now there probably were at least fifty students waiting for breakfast before the bell rang for the start of classes. She had far too many thoughts and feelings vying for her attention at the same time. First things first: Let Mrs. Butler get breakfast ready and the children fed; let Mr. Tennison get the classrooms open and ready for the teachers; and she would find out why Hazel and her siblings were here. "Mr. Tennison, please make sure my boys lend a hand," Ruth said, another way of saying make sure they didn't eat food meant for children who hadn't had any breakfast. Wilton and Thatcher knew better, but Jack wouldn't hesitate.

She started toward the door that would lead them through the cafeteria and halted. She couldn't parade Hazel and the children through that room full of students.

"Let's take the secret passage to your office," George Tennison said.

"Secret passage!" They had Hazel's full attention. "We got us a secret passage in this school, Mr. Tennison?"

"Sure do," he said, unlocking the storage room and turning on the light. He led them through the cavernous space—empty, aside from the few clothes Gertrude had collected and surplus bits and pieces of wood and cans of paint Mack donated, because the Ashdale Elementary School had nothing to store. A door at the far end of the room led to the back of the library which was unused in the winter because they couldn't afford to heat it, and they all but ran through it, it was so cold. George unlocked the door and stepped into the warmth of the center hallway, two doors from the Principal's Office.

Hazel was impressed. Ruth was, too, having forgotten that the various rooms and areas of the building connected to each other. "When breakfast is over, ask Miss Gert if she'll bring some clothes for the children." He nodded and left them. Ruth got Dorothy and William comfortable on the couch and Hazel in the chair adjacent to her desk, and she took her place behind the desk. She looked at the girl. "Where's you mother, Hazel?"

Tears filled the girl's eyes. "They won't let her come home."

"Who won't let her come home?"

"The white folks what she does for. They ain't got no money to pay her. They ain't paid her in a month, and they say she can't leave 'cause she won't come back, and she won't go back. Ain't hardly nobody got they Colored help 'cause the white folks ain't got no money, and Ma said it don't make no sense to work for no money. She said they used to call that slav'ry back in the old times." Hazel took a deep breath, giving Ruth an opportunity to ask a question.

"How long has it been since you've seen your mother?"

The girl's eyes filled. "It's been two weeks since they started lockin' her up in her room at night."

"You've had responsibility for William and Dorothy for two weeks? All by yourself?" Ruth didn't know whether to be more appalled at the notion of an eight-year old having total responsibility for two younger siblings or the reason why it was necessary.

"I don't need no help takin' care of Will'am and Dor'thy. I know what to do. I wouldn'ta had to come to the school if we hadn'ta run outta food. And there wasn't no more wood or coal for the stove. We was cold. And hungry."

"I'm not blaming you, Hazel. In fact, I'm very proud of you—for taking such good care of William and Dorothy *and* for knowing when it was time to get help."

Hazel accepted the praise with a nod of her head, the grown-up response halted abruptly by a wide and unstifled yawn. Add sleepy to cold and hungry, Ruth thought, at the same time relieved to know that the child was no longer frightened and neither were the little ones; they were both fast asleep, huddled together in the chair in a ball, like kittens.

"Do you know the names of the people your mother works for, Hazel? Or their telephone number?"

Hazel rattled off the name and number so fast Ruth had to ask her to repeat it as she wrote. Then she picked up the telephone and dialed, not certain what she would say until she heard Sadie Hill's voice.

"Woodbridge residence."

"This is Ruth McGinnis at Ashdale Elementary School," she began and heard the ragged intake of breath, a choked-bad sob. "Your children are fine, Mrs. Hill. They're sitting here with me in my office. All three of them: Hazel, Dorothy and William, and they're fine, I promise."

"They can't answer the phone right now. Can I give 'em a message?"

"When can I call you back? When can you talk?"

"If you want to leave a number, I'll ask Miz Woodbridge to call you."

Ruth gave the office number and as the call disconnected, she wondered if she should have given her home number; there was no telling when the woman would have the time or the opportunity to make a telephone call. As if reading her mind, Hazel said her mother would call after the Woodbridges finished their breakfast and the kitchen was cleaned up. They read in the library until lunch while Sadie cleaned the upstairs rooms. "They got a telephone upstairs too, and Ma can use it if she talks real quiet."

Hazel, it was clear, was no ordinary eight-year old, wise as she was in the ways of the adult world and in the ways Colored people were called upon to navigate that world. Sadie Hill most likely had no other person in whom to confide the intricacies of the world that was her home-away-from-home and especially not under the existing set of circumstances. The ringing of the bell meant that she would not, for the next several minutes, think anymore about the Hill family. Just as Ruth stood, the office door opened to admit Gertrude Butler and George Tennison carrying food and clothing for the Hill children. Ruth smiled her gratitude and, knowing that everything would be taken care of, made her presence known in the hallway as the children flowed, on best behavior, to their respective classrooms, their teachers, ever observant, monitoring their progress.

She heard a chorus of "good morning Mrs. McGinnis" and she touched several heads and shoulders and hands as the children filed past her. They knew her love for them—she never concealed or withheld it, just as she never concealed or withheld it from the five who were her own. Children were children and every one of them needed not only to be loved but to be shown that they were. And as far as she was concerned, it was extra important for Colored children to know love.

When all the children were in their rooms, she checked to make certain the front doors were locked, then visited each classroom, as was her habit. Because the school board also had eliminated all paid clerical staff from the Colored schools, often she would wait until all the rolls had been called and take the tally sheets with her, but not this morning; she didn't want to miss Sadie Hill's call. She made eye contact with each of her teachers, got the nod that told her all was well, and hurried back to her office.

"We had oatmeal with 'lasses and raisins, Miz McGinnis," Hazel proclaimed with excited joy. "I ain't never had that before."

"Haven't, Hazel, please."

"Yes'm," Hazel said, her excitement undiminished by the correction. "I haven't never had that before and I likes it a lot."

Hazel certainly didn't need to miss anymore school, but unless, somehow, they could get her mother back...Ruth couldn't complete the thought. Of course Sadie Hill would return home. She had to because there was nobody to take care of her children—not every day. The Depression had drained and leeched out every ounce of surplus or extra anything that anybody had, including goodness and kindness. Everyone she knew, including family, neighbors, church members, former classmates—everybody—was in a day-to-day frame of mind: If I can just make it through today. So, Sadie Hill needed to come home *today*. Surely there had to be a law against what the Woodbridges were doing to her. *"They make laws to fit their wants and needs, not ours."* Little Si's angry words rang in her memory, and she knew them to be true. How many times had her Uncle Will and her grandpa, First Freeman, said, *"They can do any damn thing they want with us or to us and nothing we can do about it."*

She shook off the thoughts and returned to the present to find five pairs of eyes on her, the children's frightened, the adults' worried. "Hazel, will you help Mrs. Butler take these bowls back to the kitchen? And maybe help her fix our lunch?"

Hazel nodded proudly. "Yes'm. My Ma says I helps real good in the kitchen."

"Thank you," Ruth said. Then, turning her attention to Dorothy and William, she asked if they'd like to keep their sister and Mrs. Butler company in the kitchen. They would and exited the office as if launched. When they'd gone, Ruth turned to George Tennison, but he spoke before she did.

"I'm gon' go stoke all the stoves and make sure it's plenty warm in the rooms and make sure Miss Gert got enough wood stacked where she can get to it. Then I'll be back here in case you need me."

She nodded her thanks and tried for a smile that failed. She felt totally exhausted and the day had barely begun. She dropped down into the chair behind her desk and tried to order her thoughts. Suppose Sadie Hill didn't—or couldn't—call? What would she do with the three Hill children? This shouldn't be her problem. She didn't want it to be her problem. Yet it was because there was no one else to give it to. No one else who would take it. She looked up at the wall clock and marveled that the school board hadn't ordered them removed. Probably forgot we had them, she thought. In just a few moments students would begin arriving from the various classrooms with the roll call tally sheets since she hadn't gone to get them. She got up and went to stand in the hall to receive each of the messengers, calling each by name, inquiring about his or her family, and thanking each with a hug.

She returned to her desk and checked the sheets, noting who was absent—in her class, *Hazel Hill* was marked *ABSENT*, with a note from her teacher asking what Ruth could do if the school received no answer to its "Request for Student Information" letter sent a week ago to Hazel's home. Ruth froze momentarily, then pushed her chair back so she could reach the file cabinet behind her. Each week, all of the roll call tallies were compiled and sent to the school board, with special note being made of any abnormalities and, if necessary, requesting that the central office send a letter to the home of the student in question requesting information and, in this case, concerning the student's protracted absence from school. Hazel Hill hadn't been to school for a week prior to her appearance this morning. She'd been absent every day last week. Ruth buried her face in her hands. Even if the central office had sent the notice to Sadie Hill—which she knew was doubtful—she hadn't been home to receive it.

The despair that she struggled daily to keep at bay descended like a sudden fog on the leading edge of bad weather. Mack had so often pleaded with her to give up teaching, to stay home. She should have done as he asked. Of course, if she had, perhaps they'd be running a gambling, parlor, too…

The phone rang, and she snatched it up, grateful in that moment that there was no clerk fielding calls. "Ashdale Elementary School, Principal McGinnis speaking."

"This Sadie Hill. My chil'ren all right, Miz McGinnis?"

"They're fine, Mrs. Hill, but I need to know if what Hazel said is true: Are you being held in that home against your will?"

"Yes'm, Miz McGinnis. They say I can't leave 'cause Miz Woodbridge, she ain't never in her life cooked nor cleaned nothin' and they ain't never lived in a house without no help. Everybody else left when we didn't get paid but I didn't 'cause I believed Mr. Woodbridge when he said he had some money comin' and would pay me." She took a deep, ragged breath. "They locks me in my room ev'ry night after dinner."

"What time is dinner?"

"Seven o'clock sharp, ev'ry night 'cept if they have company, which they don't no more 'cause they ain't got no money for them big dinners, all that food and whiskey."

"Tonight, Sadie, when you put the food on the table, run! I'm coming to get you. Can you get out of the house without being seen?"

"Yes'm. But…"

"I'll be parked in front of the house. You just run. You hear? Just run."

Mack and Beau sat across from the desk staring at her as if she were some strange and alien life form they'd never seen before. She sat there, waiting for one of them to say something. They'd both come immediately when she'd called and had listened intently as she told them about the situation with the Hill family and what she'd done. They'd listened and watched her until she finished talking. That was approximately three very long minutes ago, and not one of them had spoken. Until Beau did.

"You can't go. Mack and me'll go get her but you can't go."

"I have to. She doesn't know you. She knows me."

"You can't go, Ruthie," Mack said. "And since I don't imagine there will be a lot of automobiles with Colored people in them in front of the Woodbridge house tonight, I doubt she'll be confused."

"But why can't I go?"

"Because, Ruthie," Beau said, his voice hard and flat the way it got when he was well and truly angry, "if something bad happens, we don't need two sets of chil'ren with no Ma to look after 'em."

She gave them the address. Beau knew exactly where the street was and the house from his years of hauling with Mr. First Freeman. "Those people used to throw out a lot of stuff—clothing and furniture—that nothing was wrong with. They'd just get all new and throw out what they had. No wonder they're broke. They oughta be."

Mack and Beau made Ruth promise that after school, she'd take the Hill children home and wait until they brought their mother. Nobody asked what would happen if they failed because there was no acceptable answer. After they left, she told Gert Butler and George Tennison everything. After they first agreed that Beau and Mack had been right not to let her go, they then both agreed to join her at the Hill home after school. Without Ruth having to suggest it, they packed a box with rice and beans and powdered milk and oatmeal and Blackstrap molasses and raisins, firewood, coal and clothes, and at the end of the day, after all the children had gone and the doors and windows were locked and the ashes cleaned out of the stoves, the three Hill children left Ashdale School with Mrs. Butler in her automobile. Mr. Tennison followed in his truck. Ruthie knew that Mack had taken Nellie to his parent's and Mack Jr. to Big Si's, where she dropped the three younger boys—she'd already called Pa to ask if she could bring them and told him why—then followed his directions to the street where the Hills lived. He'd wanted to drive her, but neither of them wanted to tell the boys what she was doing, and he needed to be home when Little Si dropped off Mackie. Pa whispered, "You be careful, Ruthie-girl" and his tight hug stayed with her for the duration of the trip.

She was appalled by what she saw in the neighborhood called Pig Town. She knew that there was desperate poverty in Belle City, but she'd never seen it and could not have imagined what she saw. She knew that the name originated at the turn of the 20th century when the area was all farmland, when pigs, goats, chickens and cows roamed freely. There still were many plots of what in spring and summer would be carefully tended vegetables but now were overgrown, winter-burned ugliness. The streets were unpaved, there were no streetlights, and, from what she tell, very little electricity. The houses were little more than shacks, unpainted and weather-beaten, piled on top of brick columns that served to keep them off the ground which would be thick, gooey mud at least half the year.

She found the Hill house easily: It was the only one with two vehicles parked in front of it. Ruthie added her own and was halfway up rickety steps when the front door opened and Hazel dashed out, grabbed her arm, and pulled her up the last two steps and inside. The house was surprisingly well furnished, and, recalling what Beau said about the Woodbridge's propensity for throwing things away, she imagined that Sadie had been able to take full advantage of her employers' wastefulness. The place also was spotless, but it was icy cold. George Tennison had gotten fires going in the fireplace and in the stove in the kitchen, but the place obviously had been without heat for many days.

William and Dorothy looked wide-eyed at the unusual goings-on in their home, their gazes shifting from George Tennison's fire-building to Gertrude Butler's cooking beans and rice and corn bread to Ruth's whispered conversation with their big sister. Ruthie was trying to stop short of promising the girl that her mother would be home for dinner, but Hazel was a believer. Ruthie was still at the prayer stage.

Neither Mack nor Beau was big on praying. They trusted in what they could do and what they could see. Because it was winter and night fell early, they drove over to the North Side of town and parked off the road, in a woods less than a quarter mile from the Woodbridge home. Beau, driving because he was familiar with the area, told his brother-in-law what he knew of the Woodbridge's street and the adjacent ones. Because it was dark and cold, he didn't expect much activity. Most people, like the Woodbridges, would be having their dinner.

Those lucky enough to still have gainful employment would be making their way home, but one vehicle at a time, not in a stream. At exactly seven, Beau backed out of the woods and drove carefully to the Woodbridge's street, turned in, and, lights off, in neutral, coasted toward the house and to a stop. Almost immediately they saw a figure in the darkness moving toward them, rapidly.

"I don't believe I ever saw a woman run that fast," Beau said.

"I didn't know a woman *could* run that fast," Mack said, as he jumped out of the car and held the door open. "Miz Hill," he said and after the barest hesitation, she got in. Mack closed the door and got into the back, the door not closed when Beau eased into gear and slid away from the Woodbridge house. "I'm Mack McGinnis and that's Beau Thatcher, Ruth's brother. We're taking you home."

With a great cry, Sadie Hill released all the emotion she'd pent up for the past two weeks. She wept so fiercely that Beau stopped the car, which stopped her tears. "Don't stop. Please, don't stop. Keep goin', Mr. Beau. Keep goin'." So he kept going—slow enough not to arouse suspicion, not so fast as to attract attention, and Mack stretched out in the back until they reached the Colored part of town because too many Colored people in a vehicle automatically drew white suspicion.

Sadie wept again, when in front of her house she saw three vehicles parked and from the chimney a thick plume of smoke and from the windows, lights. She jumped from the car and ran up the steps and flung open the door. It was a good thing that Beau and Mack were behind her because when all three children flung themselves at her, she was knocked backwards. She recovered her balance and immediately quieted the children who, though they needed her command to be quiet, refused to release their grip on her.

"I don't know how to thank y'all."

"You don't need to," Ruth said.

"Yes, I do," Sadie Hill said, sounding almost angry. "Ain't nobody ever done me a good deed in my life, and what you people done for me this day made up for a whole lifetime of hard luck, and I won't forget it. Not never. And I will, somehow, someway, do a good deed for each one of you. I mean that."

She shook each of the men's hands and hugged Gertrude and Ruth. "These three chil'ren is all I got left in this world. I don't know what happened to my...to Mr. Hill. He left goin' to work one day and just...I guess...kep' goin'. But I live for these chil'ren and I'm gon' do my best by 'em." She looked at Ruth. "Hazel gon' be at school on time ev'ry day from now on. And soon as

I find me a job…" Emotion took over again and she wept, her children trying to comfort her. "I know that sounds crazy, don't it? Ain't no jobs in this world for Colored people, I know that. But I got to try. And I'll tell you this: I won't never work for no white folks again. Not never."

Mack and Beau exchanged a look that initially confused Ruth. Then she got it.

"Would you stop by my office in the morning when you drop Hazel off?"

Sadie said she would, and she thanked them all again, this time hugging everybody, the men included, and when they stepped out into the frigid night, they realized how warm it finally had gotten in Sadie's house.

Gert and George said good night and hurried to their vehicles. Mack opened the door for Ruth, put her in the car, and then turned to have a whispered conversation with Beau.

"I know what you're up to," Ruth yelled through the closed car door. Mack opened it and stuck his head in.

"You think it's a good idea?"

"It's a wonderful idea," she said, and added, "I want to go too." When both Beau and Mack shook their heads, she said, "I thank you, too, for what you did tonight."

"You did right to help her," Beau said, heading for his car. "I'll call y'all when I get home."

Mack got in the car and started it but didn't put it into gear. He sat looking at the house—the shack, really—that Sadie Hill called home. It looked like every other home on the block and on the adjacent ones. "What you did for those little children tonight, Ruth—you saved their lives is what you did. It was good and it was right, like Beau said. I don't know what made you tell that woman you'd go get her, but I'm glad you did."

"Hazel hadn't been to school in a week, and I hadn't noticed. She was skin and bone and wearing rags and I hadn't noticed. I'm not good, Mack."

"How many don't show up every day? And you feed them out of your own pocket and Miss Gert brings clothes and George brings firewood and coal because y'all know they're hungry and cold and raggedy. What else can you do—especially when the school board is doing nothing? Those crackers ought to be shot!"

Ruth sighed, rubbed her eyes. "Hazel is one of the brightest children in that school, but it doesn't matter because we both know that she'll have to go to work as soon as her Ma can find two jobs—one for herself and one for Hazel—" She stopped mid-sentence and turned toward her husband. "That child cannot work in a gambling parlor!"

Mack chuckled, patted his wife's arm, put the car in gear and eased away, taking extra care on the deeply rutted, unpaved road. "We don't know for sure that Sadie's even going to have a job there, so don't you start worrying before time."

"I think Tobias will forget he's mad at Beau and give him a big ol' hug. He can't be happy about Belle being...doing...working...what does she do, exactly?"

"I don't have any idea, but I think you're right: Whatever it is, no man in his right mind would want his wife working there, especially in Belle's condition. She looks 'bout ready to have that baby any minute now."

They rode in silence for a while, knowing that they were having the same feelings and thinking the same thoughts, especially about being in a hurry to retrieve their own children and take them home. But the thought of her own children returned Ruthie to thoughts of those she was responsible for every day at the Ashdale Elementary School—Colored children abandoned by the education authorities who didn't care whether they learned or not, didn't care whether their school buildings had heat and lights, didn't care if there was food to feed their bodies or books to feed their minds. Didn't care if there were enough teachers to fill the classrooms and didn't think it necessary to pay the few teachers who remained even half what the white teachers were paid.

"I did what I did tonight because I'm tired of white people and their meanness. Their *evil!* When I told Sadie Hill I'd come get her, I wasn't thinking about those children, I was thinking about how that woman was *stolen* from her family, just like those people were stolen from Africa and brought here to be slaves. That woman was a slave in that house and neither she nor us could do anything about it. We don't have not one law that helps us or protects us. All their laws, every one they make, tells us what we *can't* do, where we *can't* go, and I'm sick of it, Mack." She was crying as hard as Sadie Hill had cried earlier, and maybe for the same reasons. But just as there had been nothing he or Beau could have done or said to ease Sadie, there was nothing he could do or say to soothe his wife.

They agreed to pick up Nellie first, from his parents, then gather the boys from her father's. All had been fed dinner and were practically asleep, but the arrival of their parents spurred them into wakefulness, and the boys were especially pleased to see their baby sister and she them. She giggled with delight as she was passed from brother to brother for a hug and a kiss, then finally to her grandfather who swung her high over his head and held her there for a moment gazing at her, before lowering her into a tight hug and gently whispered, "My Nellie."

"My GaPa," she whispered back to him in his ear, rubbing his back the way he rubbed hers. Their bond was special, and it was as heartbreaking to witness as it was heartwarming: She, the girl finally born to her parents after three sons, as Ruth finally came to her parents after four sons—and named Nellie after the grandmother she'd never know. Nellie, the name of the wife GaPa mourned and missed every day of his life. "I got my Nellie back," he'd whisper to the child. "My Nellie."

With Nellie nestled in one arm, Big Si Thatcher enveloped his four grandsons in the other, pulling them in tight and close and planting a kiss on top of each of their heads and threatening, as always, to sprinkle them with Stop Growing So Tall Powder. Truth be told, he wouldn't be able to kiss the tops of their heads much longer and the old man, as he often did, marveled at the miracle of creation that was playing out before him for the second time in his life: Boys growing into men in the blink of an eye, a girl into a woman. He loved his grandchildren with the same passion and pride he'd visited upon his children and took every opportunity to tell them so.

Ruthie kissed his cheek and would have relieved him of Nellie but he wouldn't let her go. "Everything went all right, then," he said, a statement, not a question.

"Fine, Pa," Ruth answered.

"Better than fine," Mack said. "Like a miracle, really."

"Speaking of which," Big Si said, disentangling himself momentarily from the four boys still snuggling under his arm and reaching for an envelope on the table. "What do you make of this?"

Mack took the envelope and his eyes widened as he read the front of it. He passed it to Ruth and her surprise was greater than his. "Open it!"

Mack read the front of the envelope again: *TO Mack McGinnis Construction Company, Ashby St. Alley, Belle City, Georgia.* But it was the return address that grabbed their attention: *EDWARDS/THATCHER REAL ESTATE DEVELOPMENT CO., Carries Crossing, GA.* He opened the envelope and removed a single sheet of paper. Ruth watched his face, his eyes, as he read. Her father and her children watched Ruth as she waited for Mack's response to whatever the miracle envelope contained. With apparent effort, Mack tore his eyes from the paper and held it out to his wife. "Did you know that Jonas had a real estate company?"

"No, I didn't," Ruth said, taking the paper but keeping her eyes on her husband. "What does that have to do with you?"

"This is an invitation to bid on a construction project in the Crossing. On *Jonas's* construction project."

– Carrie's Crossing –
Jonas

When the telephone jangled at seven minutes before eight o'clock, Audrey didn't even look up from the *Saturday Evening Post* she was reading. Nobody would call her that early in the morning; the phone would be for Jonas. Still holding the piece of bacon he'd just bitten, he got up and went to the phone in the hallway and swallowed before he answered. Good thing he had because he almost choked when he heard Beau Thatcher's voice.

"How are you, Jonas?"

"I'm real fine, Beau, yourself?"

"I'm good, and everybody over here is good so I don't want you worryin' 'bout why I'm ringing your telephone so early in the morning."

Jonas laughed softly. "I guess you know me pretty well."

"I guess I ought to," Beau replied, the tiniest hint of times past in his voice. "I'm sorry to call so early, 'specially since what I want to say might rub you the wrong way and I truly don't mean to do that, to say something you might take offense to."

Jonas, taken completely and totally off guard, didn't, for a long moment, know how to respond, and he knew that Beau would know that, allowing time for Jonas to recover.

Then Beau said, "I know you got that bid opening at eight o'clock. Mack is probably parked outside your office right now, waiting for the clock to tell him it's all right to go inside..."

"It *is* all right, Beau. I wouldn't have sent him the invitation to bid if it wasn't."

"That's not what I mean." Beau inhaled so deeply that Jonas heard it down the telephone line. "And Mack's got nothin' to do with my thinkin' so if it makes you mad, don't take it out on him."

"What in the world?" Jonas let his exasperation fully express itself. "What are you going on about? What could you say that would make me that mad?"

"I keep thinkin' and rememberin' how we lost our house. How the tax office closed up that day and we didn't know 'bout it."

It took a full five seconds for Jonas to understand what Beau was talking about and one second for him to respond. "Why you saying something like that to me, Beau?"

"'Cause I know Horace Edwards, know the kinda man he is."

Jonas did too, and the sudden memory of his partner's insistence that Jonas didn't need to arrive early for the bid opening caused his stomach to jump. "I'm going to the office right now, Beau, and I promise you if Mack's there, his bid will get the exact same attention as anybody else's."

"Can't ask for any more'n that. Thank you, Jonas."

He pressed the bar to disconnect Beau's call and quickly dialed the office, fully expecting Horace to answer. Instead, the line rang and rang. Horace should be there. He slammed down the receiver and ran up the stairs. Good thing he'd already bathed and shaved and that Audrey had laid out his clothes. He stripped off his pajamas and threw on his pants, shirt and shoes and, carrying his suit jacket and tie, rushed back down the stairs and into the kitchen, startling his wife. His kiss landed somewhere to the left of her mouth. "I gotta go. I'll call you later."

"Jonas!" she cried out, but he didn't hear her. He was out the door, down the steps and halfway to the car.

Taking the back way to the office naturally would have been quicker, but that road—the old Colored Town Road—was being paved and, despite his protestations, was being re-named Thatcher Road. It was a few minutes after eight when he pulled up in front the *Edwards/Thatcher Real Estate Development* office and saw Mack McGinnis getting into a pickup truck that had *McGINNIS CONSTRUCTION* painted on the side. He tapped his horn as he slowed to a stop. He leaned over and rolled down the passenger side window. "Mack," he said, and he could tell by the look the other man gave him that Beau's suspicions were correct.

"You left your bid, didn't you?"

"No, Jonas, I didn't because nobody was there to leave it with." Mack gave him a long look. "But somebody's inside your office. I saw a white fella go in as I was parking. I know him. Jasper and Sons Construction. I was on here on time, Jonas."

"Your bid will get the same consideration as the others, Mack."

The other man's response was overridden by a blaring horn. They were blocking several parked cars, and somebody wanted to move one of them. Jonas signaled that he'd move his car. They didn't speak as Jonas waited for the other car to leave and took its parking space. They didn't speak as they walked back to the Jonas's office. At the front door, they met Grady Allen who, because he was driven by his chauffeur that morning, hadn't had the problem of looking for a parking space.

"'Morning, Jonas," he said extending his hand, and, turning to Mack, "Do I know you, young man?"

"This is Mack McGinnis, Grady. Beau Thatcher's brother-in-law," Jonas said.

"Of course. I've heard all about you," the banker said, extending his hand. "I understand you're quite a fine builder of homes, Mr. McGinnis."

Mack, taken aback, didn't know what to say and was saved from having to figure something out by the opening of the office door. Horace Edwards's grin froze in its place when he saw who was with his son-in-law partner and his banker. Jonas pushed him back out of the way, gestured for the older man to enter, then Mack. He closed the door behind him and swung around to face Horace so fast that the man, backing up out of the way, stumbled and only kept himself from falling by grabbing the edge of a desk.

"Dammit, Jonas. What's wrong with you?"

"Who are these people?" Jonas said, pointing to three men standing at the rear of the office. Then, addressing them directly, "Who are you?"

"I'm Alvin Jasper, this is my brother—"

Horace asserted himself and stepped between Jonas and the other men. "These are the fellas who got their bids in on time."

Jonas walked over to them. "What time did you get here?" He turned quickly to Horace and raised a hand to stop him from speaking and turned back to the men. "Well?"

"We all were here at seven-thirty, just like Mr. Edwards told us to be," Jasper said and looked to Horace for confirmation.

"The letter we sent—the invitation to bid—that letter said eight o'clock."

"Yeah," Jasper said, "but then Horace—Mr. Edwards—he called and said to be here at seven-thirty."

"I see. Well, thank you. We'll consider all the proposals and notify you by mail of our decision." Jonas walked to front door and opened it.

"What about him?" Jasper said, pointing at Mack.

"What about him?" Jonas said, the challenge in his voice cold and cutting. "His bid is late."

"His bid is none of your business."

Jasper and the other men looked to Horace for help. Horace was looking to Grady Allen for help. Grady Allen was looking at his watch as if it could explain the reason for the time discrepancies. The men finally left with a last questioning look at Horace. Jonas closed and locked the door then looked from Horace to Mack to Grady as if deciding whom to address first. The banker relieved him of the decision. "If you didn't have Jonas for a partner, I'd never do a dollar's worth of business with you again," he said. "I don't believe I've ever heard of anything so underhanded. I don't do business that way, Horace, and I don't do business with people who do."

"And I don't do business with niggers," Horace said. "I told you that, Jonas."

Ignoring Horace, he walked back to the desk and picked up the two bids. He read through them quickly, each three pages, then turned to Mack. "Can I see your bid?"

Mack handed over a thick envelope which Jonas opened. He spread out a sheaf of papers, read intently for several seconds, then whistled. "Will you look at this."

They did. "Where did you get this, boy?" Horace snarled. He whirled around to face Mack when there was no response. "I asked you a question."

"What do you mean, where did I get it? It's my proposal. I wrote it out and my wife typed it up for me."

"What about the blueprints?" Horace snarled.

"I'm a draughtsman," Mack replied.

"Let me see the others," Grady Allen said, then, "You only sent out three?"

"We sent out five," Jonas said. "What happened to the other two, Horace?"

"I know these boys, the Jaspers and Billy Mike O'Connor. I've worked with them before. They're good—"

"What happened to the other two, Horace?"

"I told 'em I didn't need 'em this time, that I'd have work for 'em later on. This time around, I'm gonna let Billy Mike build the housing for the road crews and Jasper and his sons can build the bank, Grady."

"The McGinnis proposal is far superior to the others—"

"I told you I ain't havin' no nigger building nothin' for me."

"You don't tell me who will build my bank."

"*Your* bank is on *my* land."

Grady Allen looked at Mack. Then he gathered up the pages of Mack's proposal, returned them to the envelope and returned the envelope to Mack. "You put a lot of work into this, but it wasn't a total waste, Mr. McGinnis.

I'd like you to build my bank." Then he looked at Jonas. "I believe you own some land in that area? Is it enough for the bank?"

"No, Grady," Horace exploded. "You can't do that!"

"With my money, Horace, I can do anything I want. What do you say, Mack? Want to build a bank? The First National Bank of Carrie's Crossing?"

Mack's heart was beating so hard and fast he thought it would explode through his chest. "I'd be pleased to build your bank, Mr. Allen."

"Then what say we go look at the site right now? I can tell you what I'm thinking and seeing and you come up with some sketches and plans—"

"Grady. Please don't do this."

Allen gave him a long look, the kind that sought to see beneath whatever was on the surface, right into the core. "Why not, Horace?"

"Because it's not right."

"What's not right," said Jonas, his voice sounding rusty, scratchy, as if he'd been silent for much longer than the last few minutes, "is what you did here this morning. You seem not to understand the nature of a partnership. You are not in business by yourself, Horace. I am your partner and Grady Allen is our banker. You don't make decisions alone—especially ones that involve my money and Grady's money. And you don't do dishonest business in my name. And if you ever do again, I will take every one of my dollars out of this company."

"You can't. Audrey won't stand for it."

Jonas gave him another hard look, then everything about him changed and he laughed out loud. "Mack," he said, "when you've finished looking at Grady's bank site, would you come by my house? My wife and I've been talking about putting on an addition or doing a renovation—I don't know what she wants to do—but whatever it is, I think you're just the man to do it."

Mack looked at Jonas and realized what he'd been asked, and remembered: Ruthie's house, Ruthie's home! Jonas and his wife wanted him to remodel Ruth's house. "I'd be honored to do work on your home, Mr. Thatcher," he said, and with those few words, all the years of distrust and dislike they harbored for each other dissipated. He looked from one man to the other. "Bank first? Then the house?" Both men nodded. "You'll have to direct me," Mack said, with a pointed look at Jonas, who got the message: Mack would be, as far as anybody was concerned, a stranger in Carrie's Crossing. He didn't think there was anybody still around who'd recognize him. He hadn't grown up here and none of the white residents would have known or cared who Ruth Thatcher married, wouldn't have known him to be in-laws to the Colored Thatchers.

"You can ride with me, Mack," Grady Allen said, and then he added, as if he'd been privy to Mack's thoughts, "You might know my driver. He used to live here. Or he had people who lived here—I'm not sure which. Fella by the name of Tom Jenks?"

Mack's head swam for a second before he got control of himself. "I'm not from these parts, Mr. Allen—Belle City is my home—though I do know quite a few people who are from around here, my wife included. I don't remember any Jenks family, though."

"If y'all don't mind," Horace said nastily, "can we get back to the business at hand, namely building the housing for the road construction crew? We're supposed to decide on a contractor today so we can get started."

"You already decided, Horace. Hire whoever you want. Just make sure I see the contract and that we *both* sign it. Otherwise it won't be worth a Confederate dollar."

Horace shot Jonas such a look of pure hatred that Mack wondered if it didn't hurt him somehow, didn't bruise or burn his skin. He held the door open for Allen and Jonas and followed them out, closing the door behind him. A Colored man in a black suit and cap jumped out of a shiny black Cadillac sedan and stood waiting. Tom Jenks, Mack thought. He'd never met the man. The only two of their family who had, Nellie Thatcher and First Freeman, were dead, but they all knew who he was: The man who let Nellie be murdered. Mack was moving like a man in a dream. All the joy and excitement he'd felt about telling Ruthie their Great Depression was over faded in the face of having to tell her, all of them, that their search for Tom Jenks was over. Then, he thought, he could not possibly ride in the same vehicle with the man. He'd strangle him!

Mack felt a hand on his arm: Jonas, one hand on him and the other reaching out for Grady Allen, already halfway to the door the chauffeur was holding open for him. "I've got an idea, Grady. If it's not too cold for Mack, I'm thinking we could walk to the bank site so I can show him a bit of the town, some of the development we've got planned, and he can see what's near where the bank will be, get a feel for things."

"Too cold for me, Jonas, but if you young men don't mind, I think that's a right good idea."

"Then we'll see you in a little while, Grady," Jonas said and waited for the older man to get into his car. Then he turned to Mack. "I'm sorry about this morning, Mack. Truly I am," and he was startled when Mack threw back his head and laughed.

"I'm not sorry. I'm gonna build a bank and work on a house that means as much to me as my own." He suddenly grew serious. "I am surprised, though, that a man like that is your partner. You don't seem to have much in common with him."

Jonas didn't know how to reply, so he didn't. He started walking, and Mack fell in beside him, looking all around as if he really were a stranger in town. He had given no thought to Carrie's Crossing since the night thirteen years before when they made their middle-of-the-night escape from the KKK, led by Jonas's father. Big Si, Ruthie, Beau, Tobias, Little Si, none of them ever spoke of Carrie's Crossing, and, like First Freeman, didn't call it or consider it home. Belle City was home for them. When they spoke of Nellie and Uncle Will, it was with love, not longing for a past time or place. So, Mack could look at the city of Carrie's Crossing with new eyes and if a memory of a person or a place surfaced, he'd file it away to tell Ruthie about...unless he felt he could ask Jonas about it. But nothing like that would happen in this part of town. When he searched his memory, he thought he'd been in the white section of Carrie's Crossing only once, and that was in a blizzard at the back door of Jonas's food market.

Jonas didn't talk much as they walked, except to speak to people who spoke to him and that was almost everyone they encountered. If any one of them wondered or took offense at the richest man in town walking about with a Colored man, Mack never heard, felt or saw evidence of it, which made Horace Edwards's behavior all the more odd. Why had Jonas ever partnered with such a man? He couldn't wait to talk to Ruthie about it. Also to tell her how good the town looked, almost "big city."

"The Depression doesn't seem to be hurting you all too bad over here. You opened up a new real estate business—congratulations, by the way— and Mr. Allen's building himself a new bank." Mack gave a wry chuckle. "Maybe Hoover was talkin' about you all over here in Carrie's Crossing when he kept claiming prosperity was just around the corner."

Jonas gave him a wry, crooked grin. "Oh, we're hurting plenty bad, Mack, it's just that most folks try to keep the evidence behind closed doors. Or rather in the backyard. Everybody—and I do mean *everybody*— is growing greens and cabbage and peas and corn out behind their houses, and half of 'em got chicken coops." Then he pointed to the stores they walked past, the *OPEN* signs prominent in the windows. "Most of these people come to work every day to have something to do, not because they're doing any real business. I do the same thing: I go to the grocery store every day, put my apron on and get behind the counter, whether anybody comes to buy or not."

"You don't go to the real estate office?" Mack asked, giving a hard look to Jonas in his suit, causing him to explain in the driest terms how he stumbled into the real estate business, how relieved he was to have his warehouse building being used despite his misgivings about the business itself, and how he still thought of himself as a grocer. Though, he added, he didn't mind if Roosevelt's New Deal was going to spell prosperity for Carrie's Crossing.

"Ah," Mack said, "the New Deal."

"You don't think Mr. Roosevelt is going to bring an end to this Depression?"

"I think some people will get a new deal and some people won't."

They walked in silence for a few steps, Mack trying to decide whether to tell Jonas about Sadie Hill, Jonas trying to think of something to say that wouldn't sound too stupid; of course people with little money to start with—white and Colored both—would be feeling the pain of the Depression like a Max Baer punch to the gut. Mack spoke first and when he finished telling Sadie Hill's story, he told Jonas about Silas's plan to move to Chicago and the reason for it. Jonas was speechless for a long moment. Then his face lit up in wide, happy grin. "Ruthie's a school principal! And when I see Si I'm gonna have to call him Doctor! I'm real proud of the both of them, Mack. Will you tell 'em that for me, please? Will you tell 'em both that I'm real proud?" He said nothing about Sadie Hill, most probably, Mack thought, either because there was nothing to be said or he was thinking about people he knew, people like Horace Edwards, who'd treat the Sadie Hills of the world the same way without a single moment's hesitation. But he did speak to the issue of the poor treatment of Colored schools by the board of education...in a way: He told Mack that he knew of four school buildings scheduled for complete renovations, courtesy of the WPA, three of them in Belle City and the one in Carrie's Crossing. None of the contractors would be Colored. Neither would the renovated schools. "You're right. Same old deal." But Mack couldn't tell whether Jonas thought there was anything wrong with that; his tone of voice gave no indication.

Grady Allen stepped out of his Cadillac as they approached, excitement

lighting up his face. It faltered and faded when he saw the grim expressions of the two younger men. "What's wrong? What happened?"

"Mack here was just telling me how there's not so much of a New Deal in his part of Belle City."

"No," the banker said, "I imagine that's true."

Knowing that he had to change the mood, and quickly, Mack straightened himself and gave his head a patrician tilt. "I think I'll start calling myself Mack Roosevelt since I'll be starting my own new deal," he said, imitating the President's distinctive drawl. "Between building your bank, Mr. Allen, and renovating your house, Mr. Thatcher, I'll be putting enough men back to work to make a difference to a whole lot of families."

They looked at him, at first not certain what he was talking about and then, their faces and manner still very serious despite his attempt to inject a bit of lightness and humor, they both nodded.

"I hadn't thought about it that way, but you're right," Grady Allen exclaimed. "You can't build a bank by yourself or renovate a house by yourself. You have to hire men to work for you." He kept nodding his head. "Good. Good." Then he walked a few steps away from them and pointed toward the empty field adjacent to the school. "That's where I was going to put the bank. But down the road, what, Jonas? A quarter mile? Turn right and that's where Jonas owns a few parcels. Bigger than this one, actually, when you put 'em together." The old man seemed to be talking to himself, thinking through ideas and plans only he knew about.

Mack began walking up the road. Jonas followed for a few steps, then halted as Mack turned around and came back to them. "That's where the new WPA road is coming from, isn't it? And where it'll connect to the old Colored Town Road?" And when he got confirmation of what he already knew to be true, Mack suggested that would be a better place for the bank. "When that road is built, all kinds of cars will be coming through, some coming here to the Crossing, others going on through to BC, but all of 'em riding right past your bank. Right here, next to the school, nobody will see it but the people who already live here." Mack stopped talking. He knew what he said made sense, but the decision wasn't his and it didn't matter to him where the man wanted to build his bank. What suddenly and overwhelmingly mattered to Mack was whether he could, actually, really and truly, build it. He knew he could build a house—any kind of house. But a bank. What had he gotten himself into? Why had he said he could build a bank when he'd never done such a thing? Suppose he couldn't?

"Next Monday morning, nine o'clock, Mr. McGinnis," Grady Allen said, "will you come to my office at the Belle City bank? And bring your drafting pad?"

"Yes, sir, Mr. Allen," Mack said, knowing it was too late to say anything else.

"Good, because we're going to design ourselves a bank. And Jonas? I'll need something from you saying I've got permission to build a bank on your land and what you intend to charge me for the privilege."

The man shook their hands, got into the backseat of his car and appeared to think no more about them as he immediately began reading a newspaper. Chauffeur Tom Jenks tipped his hat in their direction, got behind the wheel, and drove slowly away. Mack let out a breath he hadn't been aware he was holding. "Do you have a surveyor's map of that land, Jonas?"

He nodded. "It's at home. You have time to go look at my house now?"

Mack nodded and they walked back to where their vehicles were parked. Mack got in his truck, Jonas got in his Packard, and they drove to the house that had been home to them both and to give Audrey Edwards Thatcher the shock of her life.

"I didn't think he was paying any attention to me at all, Mr. McGinnis, when I'd talk to him about what I wanted to do. I thought he was ignoring me." Audrey was more excited than Jonas had ever seen her, which made him almost sorry that he hadn't thought to call Mack months ago. Jonas followed behind the two of them as they walked around the house, back to front, front to back, twice, three times. Mack readily agreed that yes, it was possible to add an enclosed porch to the back of the house from top to bottom, that it would pose no difficulty to open the back of the house to receive the addition. It was when Mack suggested adding wings to either side of the house and creating a formal entry hall at the front that Audrey all but swooned. She jumped up and down like a little girl, happiness pouring from her like water from a spigot. She could discuss her plans for the house for the next hour. Jonas could not.

"I've got to get back to the office and to the store, Audrey. You and Mack can make your plans and fill me in later."

Mack was so startled he couldn't speak for a moment. He quickly gathered his wits and addressed Audrey. "Let me make some drawings, Mrs. Thatcher, which I'll send to you for your approval. You'll be able to write on them, tell me what you like, what you don't like, until we come up with a final plan." He looked at Jonas. "Is that acceptable?"

"Of course," Jonas said, not hiding his annoyance with Mack.

"It was a pleasure meeting you, Mrs. Thatcher."

"I'm thrilled, Mr. McGinnis. When can you get started?"

"As soon as you all approve the plans and give me the OK." He shook her hand and followed Jonas down the front steps and around the house to the back where their vehicles were parked and then released his anger. "Don't you know you can't leave me in your house with your wife, Jonas? What were you thinking?"

Jonas was totally confused. "What's wrong with you, Mack?"

Mack was furious. And frightened. "I'm a Colored man. She's a white woman—and your wife. That's what's wrong with me."

As it dawned on Jonas what Mack meant, his steps faltered and he tripped, almost falling. Mack caught him, steadied him, and they looked at each other, each man seeing the other as they had that night long ago, Mack the man on the inside of the house with a wife to protect, Jonas the interloper standing outside.

"I didn't think...nobody would," Jonas said. "Audrey's... she's not that kind of person, Mack, to say...things."

Mack had heard from Ruthie and her family for years how Jonas was not like other white men, had heard it and even had seen evidence to prove the point. However, he couldn't believe that even if the man didn't behave like his brethren, he didn't know where the perils and pitfalls lay. "Don't forget the kind of man your father-in-law is," Mack said and hurried to get into his truck and be on his way before Jonas left.

Jonas was too shocked to move, not even when Audrey came running down the front steps, hurling herself at him. This time, he was stone to her bubbling excitement.

"What's the matter, Jonas? And why did Mr. McGinnis leave like that?"

He told her and was surprised when she understood immediately. "I didn't even think about that. Poor man. Whoever would do such a thing? Make up a lie just to get somebody in trouble?"

"The lies don't just get 'em in trouble, Audrey, they get 'em lynched. As for the who: Your ma and your pa would do such a thing. Your brothers."

"No, Jonas, they wouldn't. I don't believe it."

He told her what Horace had done that very morning and then left her standing there in the chilly morning air while he went to confront the man who was her father, the man she loved more than she loved her husband, and he wished that she had come with him when Horace's first words were, "Did you

261

leave that nigger in the house with my daughter?"

Jonas hit him then, punched him right in the nose, and was glad that Audrey was not with him. Blood spurted and Horace fell to his knees, cursing and crying. Jonas wanted to hit him again, but he wanted more not to have to be in the man's presence any longer. "Get up, Horace, and wash your face so we can talk about who's going to build the dormitories for the construction workers. But I tell you, I've got a mind not to do it. Just not to be bothered."

"That's too much money to let go, Jonas. The rent, the groceries, the furniture." Even gushing blood, Horace Edwards didn't lose sight of money-making opportunities.

"And if I do lose it, it'll be your fault. The McGinnis proposal was the best one and you know it. These?" He snatched up the two remaining bids and waved them at Horace. "They're not worth a depression nickel." He threw the papers on the desk and they flew into the air and toward the floor. "What materials they gonna use? What's the start date? The completion date? What are the payment dates? Penalties? None of that stuff is in here, Horace."

"Is it in the...other one?" Horace asked, struggling to get to his feet.

"Yeah, it is. All that and more, including a couple of different drawings of what the buildings could look like, letting us make the choice."

"Then get him to give it to you. My man can build it from his plans."

Jonas grabbed Horace by his shirt front and hauled him to his feet and pulled him in close, not caring about the dripping blood. "You get two proper bids in here by tomorrow this time. We got to have that housing built by the end of March." Jonas released the older man and pushed him away then Jonas turned and headed for the door. "I'm going to the store."

"Why'd you do it, Jonas?"

"Do what?"

"Ask him to bid. Why?"

Without turning or answering, Jonas walked out, closing the door hard, and trying to find an answer. The right answer. Why *had* he invited Mack McGinnis to bid? Most likely because he remembered Beau and First Freeman talking about what a master builder the man was. If he were honest with himself, he'd have to admit that it certainly was not because he had any idea of the man's professional proficiency. Maybe it was about Ruth: She still haunted his memory and his thoughts. But no, it wasn't that. It was, he realized, that he thought he could get the job done more cheaply; that McGinnis, being Colored, would be so happy to be working that he'd do the job for less. He envisioned the dollar amounts of the three bids. Mack's was the lowest. He went back inside the office. Horace, wet towel to his face, was dialing the telephone.

"When you talk to Jasper and O'Connor, tell 'em to knock fifteen percent off their bids," Jonas said. "And tell 'em it's your fault they're not making a killing on this job."

"You're a bastard, Jonas."

"Takes one to know one, Horace."

From the Recorded Memories of Ruth Thatcher McGinnis

What should have been a wonderful couple of years suddenly became nightmarish. Those two years—1936 and 1937—were the heart of the Depression for almost every Colored person in America, but for a precious few of us in Belle City, Georgia, those years began a period of prosperity, and if I'm honest, I have to thank Jonas Thatcher. When Mack was hired to build Carrie's Crossing's first bank and renovate Jonas's house, he was able to put to work, almost overnight, about twenty men. And the way we were looking out for each other back then, that meant forty families lifted out of poverty. Mack had to hire a subcontractor to help with the bank because he had no idea how to put a steel vault inside a building. The fella he hired was white and a much bigger contractor than Mack, but he was so grateful to have work that from that day forward, every job he got, he offered Mack work. Then, when people saw what he'd done to Jonas and Audrey's house, everybody wanted him to build or renovate their homes. He was so busy that he was away from home more than he was present, which gave me the opportunity to leave the school system on a positive note instead of an angry one, because I truly was angry at how we had been treated. I was able to resign, I told the superintendent, because I was needed at home, and I was. My Pa and Mack's parents were getting too old to keep up with young children. For that matter, there were days when I felt too old to keep up with them. By the end of 1937, we were financially set for life, Mack and me and the children. I should've know better than to expect it to last...no, it's not cynical, it's realistic. I'd experienced it—overwhelming good fortune, followed by excruciating pain and disappointment. Sorrow follows joy as night follows day. What? Lose our money? Oh, no. We didn't lose our money. That we could have withstood. Money could have been replaced. No, we lost...Sissy, please turn off the recorder now. I can't...that's enough for now, please.

– Belle City –
Ruthie

It was times like this that Ruthie sorely regretted having left the structured and mandated order of Ashdale Elementary School for the absolutely unpredictable life of full-time wife, mother, and student. The wife and mother part were manageable, though she knew women who marveled at her ability to keep all six of those balls—five children and one husband—safely in the air. She had an excellent role model: Her mother, who'd managed a home of five children, a husband, and an uncle; a twenty-plus acre farm that usually employed a dozen workers; and was central to a community. No, the family and the home didn't pose a challenge for Ruthie. Completing a dissertation, however, was proving to be more than a mere challenge; it was a mountain that grew taller every day. She no longer knew why she'd ever thought she needed a Ph.D. And in French! She'd more than made good on her promise to learn the language—she was fluent—and she knew as much about the history and geography of the country as it was possible to learn from a book. However, since she'd had no contact with her brother for more than five years now and since it became less likely with every passing year that she'd be able to journey across the Atlantic Ocean to look for him, the pursuit of things French seemed an absurd one. But what else would she do with her time? All five of the children went to school every day, none more enthusiastically than Nellie, and Mack worked, ate, and slept.

She was so relieved when the telephone rang that she sprung up from the desk and all but ran down the hallway to answer it.

"McGinnis residence."

"Good day, Miz McGinnis, and I'm sorry to bother you. This is Grady Allen."

"Good day to you, Mr. Allen, and you're not bothering me at all, and I'm sure you want Mack, but he's not here."

"No, m'am, it's you I want..."

Ruthie sat down hard in the chair beside the telephone stand. The man's words and tone of his voice—Beau! "Mr. Allen! Beau? Is it about Beau?"

"Yes, ma'am, it is. He's...I think you'd better come and get him. He's here at my house. And he's...not well, Miz McGinnis. He's sick."

She wrote down the address Grady Allen gave her, along with his telephone number. Then she sat holding the handset until she heard the operator asking her to please hang up. She did, and still she sat. Her brain had ceased to function in a logical and linear fashion. *Beau was sick.* She had to go get him. She couldn't. What to do? Beau is who they all turned to when there was a problem—Beau and Mack. And now it was Beau who needed help and Mack was—she didn't know where he was.

She forced herself to her feet and found herself in the kitchen. She turned around and went back to the phone. Pa would know what to do. She dialed his number but then quickly put the phone down. Pa was sick, too—something with his heart. He wasn't to get upset, the doctor said, and Beau being so sick that they had to go get him would surely upset him. Silas was in Chicago. Tobias! She would ask Tobias to go with her. She donned coat, hat and gloves, grabbed her purse and keys, and ran out of the house, then ran back in to get Grady Allen's address and was back out and in the car faster than she would have thought she could move. It reminded her of what Beau and Mack said about Sadie Hill the night they rescued her.

"Beau. Beau. Oh, please be all right, Beau."

The curtains were drawn at Toby and Belle's house, and a small stream of smoke drifted lazily from the chimney. It hadn't occurred to her to call first, but surely they'd be home; where else would they be? The barber and beauty businesses had been closed for years now, and, as she understood it, they didn't go to the gambling parlor until night. So, Toby would be home. She prayed that he would be home.

Sadie Hill opened the door to her knock and each woman showed her surprise at the sight of the other. "Miz McGinnis. What you doin' here? What's wrong? Somebody is sick? Your Pa? Mr. Thatcher?"

"Calm down, Sadie, please. Pa is fine. It's Beau—"

"Mr. Beau! What's wrong with Mr. Beau?"

"He's sick, and I need Toby to go with me to get him."

Sadie stiffened and her expressive face, which had, in the last few seconds, registered shock, joy, pain and sorrow, shuttered like a window in a storm. "Oh, I don't know 'bout that, Miz McGinnis."

"There's nothing for you to know, Sadie. Tobias is my brother and I need him to help me bring Beau home. Now, go get him, please."

Now her face re-opened and anguish is what was there, and shame. "You don't know 'bout how things is with your brother these days, Miz McGinnis."

Ruthie snapped. "I don't know what you're talking about Sadie, and I don't have time to listen to it. Tell Tobias I need him right now. I don't care if he just got home from his gambling two minutes ago."

At that moment Belle appeared behind Sadie, covering a yawn with one hand and holding a red silk robe together with the other, the nails of both hands and her lips the same siren red as the robe. "It's me just got home from the club, Ruthie, and what Sadie is tryin' so hard not to tell you is that whatever it is you want with Tobias, you can't have it because he's on the drugs."

Ruth didn't understand and said as much. Belle yawned again, told Sadie that it was fine to explain it, excused herself, and left them standing there. Sadie hung her head and mumbled something, then lifted her head and repeated it: "He's a heroin addict, Miz McGinnis. Like them jazz musicians what you read about in the magazines."

"That's absurd. Where is he? Where's Toby?" Ruth pushed past Sadie into the dark and heavily curtained living room. Jazz played on the radio and smoke rose in a spiral from an ashtray on the floor next to a big, overstuffed easy chair, in which Toby sprawled. Ruthie knew that it was Toby because it must be. What other man would be sprawled in the easy chair in Toby's living room? A room that looked and smelled like a...like a...gambling parlor.

"Miz McGinnis." Sadie pulled on Ruth's sleeve, tried to prevent her from getting any closer to Tobias. She shook off her hand and walked up to him.

"Toby, Toby. Wake up!" She reached out, grabbed his arm, shook him. "Toby! Wake up! Beau's sick and we have to go get him."

Tobias shifted in the chair and his eyes opened to narrow slits. He mumbled a bit, things that didn't sound like words, and he smiled lazily. Then his eyes closed again, the lazy smile still in place. For a long moment, Ruth did nothing, thought nothing. She stood like a statue, immobile, emotionless, staring at what once had been her brother, her friend. At the thought of yet another brother lost, anger rose in her like the cigarette smoke in the ashtray and she grabbed Toby's shirt front with more strength than she'd have thought she possessed and pulled him almost straight up. "Wake up!" she yelled at him. "Do you hear me, Tobias Thatcher? Wake up!"

"No, he probably can't hear you," Belle said from behind her. Startled, Ruthie released Toby and he flopped back into the chair like a rag doll. "And if he does hear you, he doesn't understand you, doesn't understand what you want or why you want it." Belle bent down and picked up the cigarette that was burning in the ashtray, put it to her mouth and inhaled, then stubbed it out.

She angled her head up and blew smoke from the corner of her mouth, away from Ruth, then lowered her head and met her eyes. "But the really bad, really hard thing to take, Ruth, is that he doesn't care. *If* he heard what you said, *if* he understood what you said, what you wanted—he wouldn't care. That's what hurts."

"How did you let him get like this, Belle?"

"I didn't let him. Nobody lets a person start using that stuff, and nobody can stop 'em once they start. He'd have to want to stop." She looked down at her husband, then turned away from him, took Ruth's arm and led her toward the front door. "This is how Tobias decided to deal with the Depression and with white folks. He escaped. For him, the Depression is over and white folks don't exist."

"But that's crazy."

"'Course it is, but Tobias don't know that."

Ruth kept the front door closed; she wasn't yet ready to leave. She had to understand. "What about the children?"

"What about 'em, Ruthie? Do they know their pa is...sick? Yeah, they do. Do they understand what it is and why? 'Bout like I do. But I know what it is you're really asking: Suppose that happens to one of them? And you want the honest truth? I would rather one of 'em be on the dope than locked up by some crazy white people or bein' called nigger every day of their lives, workin' theirselves into bad health for four or five dollars a week. I know you don't think what I do is respectable, Ruth, but don't nobody call me nigger and I make more money than most folks, Colored or white, and if this is what my chil'ren do 'stead of cleanin' up after white folks—well, all right with me."

"But suppose they want to be doctors or lawyers or teachers?"

Belle gave her a slow, lazy smile; not the kind of lazy one Toby had given, but lazy like a cat stretching after a nap. "Well, that'd be all right—the doctor or lawyer part—but not the school teacher part. You and Silas showed us 'bout how much that's worth."

Ruthie stumbled down the walkway to her car, the only clear thought in her mind was the need to get Beau and bring him home because he was her last brother. Eubie was lost somewhere in France. Si may not have been lost but wherever he was in Chicago, he was of no use or value to her now. And Tobias—he certainly was lost. Where was Mack working? She should know... Big Mack. That's who would go with her. She needed to turn around and go the other way, but she found that she couldn't see to back up. She was crying.

She had to stop. She had to get control of herself. Beau needed her.

Family and friends always used the kitchen door at Big Mack and Clara's but Ruth went to the front door and rang the bell—as much to guarantee that Big Mack would be the one to open the door as to save time. But when her father-in-law opened the door, expecting a stranger, she fell into his arms, weeping so hard she frightened him. His panicked call for Clara brought her at a dead run, and Ruthie realized too late that they thought something had happened to Mack or one of the children.

"Oh, I'm so sorry. I wasn't thinking," she said, but she couldn't stop crying.

"You're going to make yourself sick," Clara said, shushing and soothing her, and after a few minutes, she calmed down enough to tell them everything. Big Mack had his hat and coat on in seconds. Clara said she'd pick the children up from school, take them home and wait there for Mack. "Where will you take Beau? Do you want to bring him here?"

Ruthie thought about that. It was a good idea, but she knew that Pa would want him at home if he were sick. She enjoyed a moment's refuge in her mother-in-law's strong embrace. "I'm so sorry that I frightened you."

"The fright leaves with the fear. Mack and the children are all right. That means we have the strength to take care of Beau." She looked at her husband. "And Tobias."

Big Mack snorted a response that was less than agreeable, took Ruthie's arm, and led her out of the front door and down the walkway. She gave him the keys and when they got in the car, she read him Grady Allen's address. "I know where that is," he said and headed north. "I know Beau's been acquainted with Mr. Allen for some while, but I don't know how that came about. And I know Beau's been chauffeuring them for 'bout a year now, but I don't know how that came about, either. Can you tell me, Ruthie, before we get there so I know what's what?"

It was, she thought, not only a reasonable request but an excellent way to get her calm and quiet before they got there, so she began talking. She knew very well how Beau and Mr. Allen became acquainted, and the memories invoked in the telling did what Big Mack wanted: They calmed and steadied her. She found a deep joy in the memory of her mother and of First Freeman, of Beau's first motor vehicle and of their first visits to Belle City, of Beau's eventual healing from the brutality of his experiences in The Great War.

"I know Mack thinks a lot of him, and I must say he sounds like a good man, Mr. Grady Allen does," Big Mack said.

Ruthie nodded. "I think that's true. I know he thinks highly of Beau." What she didn't know, though, was how or why Beau became the Allen's chauffeur. "I know that Beau likes automobiles—likes driving them, fixing them, polishing them. But I also know that he does *not* like the idea of working for white people, Grady Allen included, and I don't know what changed his mind about that."

"Well, we're 'bout to find out. This is the street," Big Mack said, turning on to a wide boulevard with houses the size of hotels looming on both sides and set so far back from the road they'd be invisible in the spring and summer when leaves were on the trees. "And this is the number," he said, turning into the long drive leading to the house.

"Good Lord," Ruthie exclaimed when Grady Allen's house became visible.

"How many people live here?" Big Mack asked.

Ruthie shook her head; she didn't know. She'd heard Beau and Mack speak of Mr. and Mrs. Allen but never of children or grandchildren. And given their descriptions of the Allens, they were elderly, so any children would be grown and gone. "All of our houses would fit inside this one—yours, mine, Pa's, Catherine's—with rooms left over."

Big Mack automatically drove around to the back of the house where its size was even more evident. And there was a swimming pool, just like in some Hollywood movie magazine. He parked the car adjacent to the Service Delivery Entrance and they got out, and all of Ruthie's fear and trepidation returned in a rush. She grabbed Big Mack's arm and they approached the door. It opened before they could ring the bell. The man who opened it could only be Grady Allen. He was tall and thin with just the slightest hint of a stoop, but he had a full head of white hair, and the crinkles around his eyes were proof of a man who looked at the world with a sense of enjoyment.

"You are Miz McGinnis, and I can't tell you how pleased I am to make your acquaintance, though I do wish it had occurred under different circumstances." He held her hand tightly for a moment, then released it, ushered her inside, and turned his gaze on Big Mack. "And this must be your...why, no. Not your pa, Mack's. The resemblance is quite strong. That's a fine, fine boy, you have Mr. McGinnis, though I'm sure you both know that."

He ushered them through a storage area and into an industrial-sized kitchen that was warm and aromatic: Several things were cooking, the overwhelming smells being of roast beef and pastry. He led them to a table set with a coffee pot and three cups and a covered cake dish with a knife and three forks and plates. Ruthie wanted to scream. This was not a social visit. Where was Beau?

She wanted Beau.

"I know you want your brother, but I'd appreciate it if you'd sit for a moment, have some coffee and cake, and let me explain. It's my fault, you see—"

"Please, Mr. Allen. Just tell us," Ruthie said.

He sighed deeply and dropped down into one of the chairs. Ruthie and Big Mack could only join him at the table. "Beau was arrested—"

Ruthie gasped. "But you said he was here."

"He is, he is. I made them bring him here to me when I found out—" He inhaled deeply and released the breath in a whoosh. "Beau drove us, my wife and me, to a New Year's Day celebration at our daughter's house over in Stevensville. We got there around eleven in the morning because it was our granddaughter's Sweet Sixteen birthday and we wanted to be there to open presents with her. But it's also New Year's Day, so there were people in and out all day, and food and drink and even a live band for dancing. It was a wonderful party and we had a wonderful time, but by seven, or a little after, Laurel—my wife—was ready to leave. She tires easily. But we'd brought our cook, so after he drove us home, Beau was to go back and get her, take her home, and then just take the car home with him. Only he never made it. She thought we had forgotten about her so she called her husband to pick her up. We didn't know anything was wrong until Monday. You see, the bank was closed the day after New Year's—Sunday—so I wasn't expecting Beau until Monday...this is all my fault. I should have known he wouldn't just accept it—"

"What happened, Mr. Allen? Please," Ruthie said.

He nodded, took a sip of coffee, wiped his mouth. "The police called here early Monday morning, said they had my car, where did I want it? I asked where my driver was and they said in jail. To make a long story short, I called the Chief of Police and told him to find out what had happened and where Beau was." He inhaled deeply again and swallowed. "They had put him on a chain gang—"

Ruthie fainted and would have fallen to the floor had not both men jumped up and reached for her at the same time. Big Mack put her in the chair while Grady Allen filled a glass with ice and water and got a cold towel. Her father-in-law bathed her face, and, as she began to come around, he got her to drink some cold water. Her eyes focused and she looked directly at Grady Allen. "Dirt and filth and mud. For almost forty-eight hours. Is that where he was? In dirt and filth and mud?" And when the old man nodded, she asked, "He's

like he was when he came back from France, isn't he? A walking dead man."
She swayed and Big Mack held on to her until she steadied. She struggled to
her feet. "Where is he? Where is my brother?"

Big Mack held up his hand. "What did you mean, sir, when you said you
knew it was your fault because somebody wouldn't accept something?"

"I hired Beau even though Horace Edwards wanted me to hire one of his
sons. I know both of Horace's boys, and they're both useless and worthless.
I would never trust one of them with my wife or with my car. The one who
arrested Beau is a city policeman named Gilbert Edwards. The one who
wanted the job is Horace, named after his pa, and he's just a bum. But it gripes
Horace that I'd hire a Colored man over his son."

"You had a driver before Beau, Mr. Allen. My son met him one time,
over in the Crossing, the day you asked him to build your bank."

"I remember," Allen said, nodding. "Tom Jenks. He got himself killed last
year in a gambling parlor, of all places. He was some kin to Sue. My cook."

This time it was Ruthie who took the deep breath. "Sue Thomas is your
cook," she said, making it a statement, not a question. "I know Sue. I knew her
mother very well. She lived up the road from us in Carrie's Crossing. And Tom
Jenks was her cousin."

Grady Allen was nodding. "That's right. She recommended him for the
job, and I hired him on her say so. And I will say that I found him completely
satisfactory, never had a single reason for complaint. If he chose to frequent a
gambling parlor on his off time, well, that's none of my business, is it?"

Ruthie had stopped listening; she was thinking, figuring: Sue had known
where Tom Jenks was but hadn't told them. Beau had found out somehow.
From Tobias? They all had known that gambling was Tom's weakness—he'd
been gambling the night before Nellie was killed and was late meeting her.
If he'd been on time...and finally Beau had found him, and Ruthie knew with
absolute certainty, he had killed him. And that's why he'd taken a job working
for a white man—because he'd killed Grady Allen's chauffeur.

"Thank you, Mr. Allen, for saving Beau," she said. "We never could have
gotten him out of that place on our own. In fact, we never would have known
where he was, so we owe you a great debt of gratitude."

"You owe me nothing, Miz McGinnis. Like I said, this whole thing is my
fault." He turned toward a passageway. "Beau's in here," he said and led them
into a labyrinth of small, narrow rooms off a small, narrow corridor. The
servants' quarters. He opened a door but did not turn on a light. Beau hated

bright light, especially sudden bright light. But he hated mud and dirt and filth worse than anything.

"Beau," she said softly. "It's me. I'm here. We're going to take you home."

"Ma? Ma, is that you?" he said and followed it with a deep, dark wail. "They won't let me out, Ma. They won't let me go home."

Ruthie rushed into the room and grabbed her big brother and held him tight, wrapping her arms all the way around him. He'd become skeletally thin so quickly. "I'm taking you home, Beau, and I don't care what they say. Come on. We're going home." She tried to pull him up to stand but could not budge his dead weight. Big Mack moved her aside and lifted Beau as if he were a child.

"Pa? Is that you, Pa?"

"Yeah, Son. It's me and we're gonna take you home, but you got to walk 'cause you too big for me to carry. That's right, come on now."

They led, dragged, pushed, and carried Beau out to the car and laid him in the backseat. They thanked Grady Allen again and drove as fast as they thought they safely could back to the Colored part of town. Big Mack hesitated only briefly where he would have turned going to his own house. He knew as well as Ruthie did that Big Si would want his son at home. He parked in front of the house, and Ruthie went in to explain the situation to her Pa. He was out the front door and down the walk before she finished talking.

"Beau, boy. I'm gon' take care of you just like I did before, when you come back from that filthy war. 'Member how we looked after you? Helped you get better? We gon' do it again, don't you worry none."

It required a great effort to get him from the car into the house and into bed, more than before because now Beau wasn't walking at all, wasn't speaking, wasn't moving. He was an inanimate object, a dead weight. They all were winded, but Big Si's breath came in great, loud gasps.

"Sit down, Pa."

"I'm fine."

"No, you're not. Now please sit down." She knew she'd spoken too sharply, but she was on the edge. She reached out a hand to him in apology. He took her hand, then sat down and asked them to tell him everything again, from the beginning.

"You believe Beau killed Tom Jenks," he said to Ruth. When she didn't say anything, he asked, "You think anybody else knows? Sue? Tobias? That's got to be the gambling parlor he was talking about."

Ruthie hadn't told him about Tobias and now wasn't the time. "I think Sue knew where Tom Jenks was all along and didn't tell us."

"Prob'ly 'cause she knew what would happen. He is her kin, after all."

Ruth nodded her acceptance of this fact. "I just care that she doesn't tell, and I think if she had told, Beau already would have been arrested."

Big Mack agreed. "Anyway, they don't care 'bout us killing each other. As far as they're concerned, Jenks is just another dead Colored man, killed by one of his own. It's the kind of thing we do," he said dryly. "Only reason they asked any questions at all is 'cause of who he worked for."

They agreed to that truth. "So," Big Si said. "Beau is safe?"

"I think so," Ruth said.

"Me, too," Big Mack said."

"Then," Big Si said, pulling himself up to standing, "let's try to get him well, and hope we can do it twice."

– Carrie's Crossing –
Jonas

The antics of two-year old Jonas Farley Thatcher Jr. were the only reason that Grady Allen was still seated in the same room, at the same table, with Horace Edwards, and Jonas thought that Grady was doing a pretty good job of being polite to Horace, though Horace, of course, didn't see it that way. Typically, he'd made himself the injured party: He professed not to understand why Grady would hold him responsible for what his son had done. For more than six months, Grady had flatly refused to meet with or talk to Horace because of police officer Gilbert Edwards's illegal arrest of Beau Thatcher. Jonas had played intermediary only because his partnership agreements with Horace were too complex for easy extrication. At the moment, though, what was more galling to Horace was the fact that JJ preferred Uncle Grady to him—his own grandfather! The little boy toddled back and forth on the highly polished conference room table between his Papa and his Uncle Grady, ignoring all attempts by his grandfather to capture him—or even his attention. To add insult to injury, their meeting, called at Horace's request, was being held in the First National Bank of Carrie's Crossing boardroom because Grady refused to step foot in the offices of the Edwards-Thatcher Real Estate Company as long as *Edwards* remained a name on the stationery.

"Uncle Grady Allen! Catch me!" the little boy sang out and launched himself at the old banker, who caught him on the fly. Jonas initially had tried to restrain JJ. A two-year-old's exuberance was sometimes too much even for him, and Grady Allen was, he guessed, at least seventy—even the man's grandchildren were grown. But the old man loved the interaction with the little boy and never seemed to worry about what was happening to his crisp white shirt or his silk tie or the gold watch chain across his vest.

"You're not his uncle," Horace snarled, "and I *am* his grandpa!" As if those facts were in doubt. "And we're supposed to be having a meeting, in case y'all forgot."

Jonas reached for his son. "Come here, JJ, and give your papa a big hug."

The boy flung himself at his father and buried his face in his neck. Jonas held him tightly, amazed, as always, at the intensity of his feeling and wondering, as always, if his own father had ever loved him as much since he'd never displayed his love.

"What is it you want to discuss, Horace?" Grady snapped open his pocket watch, and the message was clear: I've got plenty of time to play with a little boy but not much to listen to you.

"The situation in Europe is what I want to talk about. War, to be exact."

"Why do you want to talk about the war in Europe? That's got nothing to do with us, and I hope we keep it that way," Jonas said.

"That's where you're wrong, Jonas," Horace said. "Everything they do over there is tied to us, and everything we do over here is tied to them. It's almost like that Atlantic Ocean's not even there. If some of those boys are spoiling for a fight, you can bet a dollar or two that some of our boys will be right in the middle of it."

"I still don't see what that has to do with us, especially since I haven't read or heard about anybody in our government backing such a notion. Just the opposite, in fact," Jonas said, shifting in his chair so that he could better hold a yawning JJ; the boy would be asleep in just a few moments. "All those neutrality acts the Congress has passed over the last few years—they mean we're not going to war."

"Don't you believe it. Roosevelt's not gonna sit still and watch them Germans and Italians take over all those countries like they been doing."

"Nothing Roosevelt can do about it. It's none of his business," Jonas said.

"And anyway," Grady said, finally joining the conversation, "it's illegal for any American business to sell guns or any kind of war weapon to European countries. Not that we have any weapons to sell. So how is it you think you can make a dollar?"

Horace grinned widely. "The other part of that law says those countries have to pay cash for anything they buy."

"So what? You want us to sell the German government Doc Gray's house and farm?" Grady laughed.

Horace scowled. "We should buy up as many pairs of underwear and socks and shoes as we can. We should buy up cans of soup and beans and... and...bags of rice and sugar and flour—stuff people are gonna need. And we'll be the ones who'll have it and who they'll have to buy it from."

Jonas had to admit there was a certain logic in the idea. "But why would they come to us? Why not a businessman in their own country?"

"'Cause they're gonna be at war—they're already at war—and war uses up lots of things real fast. That's the good thing about war: It's a big, greedy machine that just—"

Grady pushed back from the table so fast and stood up so quickly that his chair tipped over, and he rushed from the room without a backward glance, slamming the door.

Jonas sighed. "You can't seem to not make him mad, Horace."

"Now what's wrong?"

"He lost a son in The Great War, and I lost a brother. We don't think there's too much good about war at all."

Horace hung his head in momentary shame; he'd forgotten about Grady's son and Jonas's brother. "I guess First Bank of CC won't be giving us a loan for our goods in stock business. That's what I think we oughta call it, by the way: Goods In Stock. Whatever people need, we've got it in stock. And we don't need Grady Allen. That fella at State Bank has been after me for a while. We can get a loan from him."

"You don't get it, do you Horace? We are *partners*. That means we discuss plans, especially for a new business. You don't go off on your own."

"I don't need to discuss my ideas and plans with you. That's a good idea and you know it, Jonas, whether or not you think war is good for the economy. There's gonna be a war, and people are gonna need basic supplies, and somebody is gonna sell those supplies, and it might as well be us."

"It is a good idea, and there's nothing stopping you from pursuing it." Jonas hoisted JJ up on his shoulder. The boy weighed a ton. Audrey could barely lift him.

"Then why don't you want to be in on it?"

"Because it involves too many things that I know nothing about, and they're things I don't care to learn anything about, including the laws on international trade. We'd have to hire a bunch of lawyers and accountants who do understand those things, just to make it possible to do business with people I don't think I want to do business with." He headed for the door, Horace close on his heels. "And anyway, I really don't believe there's going to be another war," he said, once they were outside. "At least not one involving us."

Horace gave him a look, a mixture of disdain, disgust and disappointment. "And my daughter thinks you're so smart. You think the whole world is just gonna let Hitler and that crazy Italian take over all those countries? And I'll bet Hitler's good and mad now." He gave a wild cackle. "First that Jesse Owens wins all those gold medals, then the other day Joe Louis whipped that Schmeling.

Ol' Hitler's prob'ly tryin' to figure out how he can take over America."

Jonas lay JJ down on the backseat of the car and turned to Horace. "You're glad that Jesse Owens and Joe Louis whipped the Germans?"

"That's what they do. They run and they fight. That's what they're good at, so no, I don't mind that they won. Besides, I made a lot of money on that fight."

"I've got to go."

"You going home? I'll go with you, make sure my daughter's all right, see if she needs anything."

"My wife is fine, you don't need to check on her, and anything she needs, I'll get for her." JJ stirred and whimpered. "I've got to go."

"Audrey told me the new baby, if it's a boy, she's gonna name it after me."

"If he's a boy, he'll be a he and not an it, and we haven't decided on a name yet," Jonas said, not telling the whole truth. Audrey did want to name their next boy after her father, but Jonas, if he had a baseball team of boys, wouldn't name one of them Horace. He'd name one Edward, but that's as far as he was willing to go. Besides, he wanted a girl next—a boy and girl— that would be perfection.

Horace looked at his watch. "You really don't want any part of stockpiling goods in advance of the war, huh? Well, your loss. But you do make a good point about lawyers and such who know about international law. I'm gonna go to the office right now and start makin' some calls."

"I'll be there later. I'll take him home, then go check on Rachel at the store."

They got into their respective cars, doors slamming almost simultaneously. The older man started his engine first, backed too fast out of his parking space, and screeched off. Jonas sat for a moment, thinking too much about his father-in-law, then forcing all thoughts away and clearing his mind because thoughts of Horace upset him. He started the car, slowly backed up, and just as slowly headed toward home, constantly reaching into the backseat to make certain his son was in no danger of rolling off. What Horace didn't know—what he and Audrey didn't want either of her parents to know—was that she had been having a very difficult time with this pregnancy. That's why Jonas took JJ with him as often as possible—that and because he enjoyed the boy's company. Audrey simply could not keep up with him, and they'd had no household help in months. Nobody in The Crossing had any help because, since the Beau Thatcher incident, Colored domestic staff from Belle City had refused to make the journey to Carrie's Crossing, either by car or bus no matter how much they needed the money—and they all needed the money. What Jonas had not known was that for years, Colored men had been vanishing from Belle City— all kinds of men. They'd leave going to work or to the barber shop or to a baseball game and just never come home. What happened to Beau Thatcher was the straw that broke the camel's back. Add to that the Sadie Hill story— and that was a story everybody, Colored and white knew—and Colored people literally feared for their lives every time they left the safety of their homes.

JJ woke when Jonas picked him up, and he was glad he didn't have to carry the boy into the house. "You've got to stop growing, boy," he said.

"I like growing, Papa."

"You do? And why is that?"

"I get big like you."

"In that case, I guess you'd better keep growing. But maybe we should ask your Mama, see what she thinks."

"Yaaaa! Go ask Mama! Go ask Mama!" he yelled when Jonas opened the door. Then he had to run to catch him before he took a flying leap at Audrey.

She'd been lying down on the couch in the solarium and was barely in a sitting position when they entered the room. She's too pale, Jonas thought as he swooped JJ up into a flying bird, catching him just before he launched himself at his mother. "Tell your Ma why you're not going to stop growing," he said, settling him on the couch beside her.

"I grow big like Papa."

She put her arms around him and kissed him. "Yes, you will, my boy," she said. Then to Jonas, "How was your meeting?" Meaning, *What did my father want and did you argue with him?* Jonas knew that his dislike of her parents— and he actively disliked them both—was hard for her to accept, and he truly did try to limit his negative responses, especially verbal ones, and especially in JJ's presence. He told her about the meeting, omitting what Horace had said that upset Grady. He told her only his reaction and the reason for it. "It does sound like it would be an awful lot of work," she said.

"I've got an idea about something else," he said, an idea had sprung into his head that very moment. "What if I called Mack and asked for his help organizing a…a…I don't know exactly what to call it—a transportation group. Some way to safely get help back and forth between here and BC. At first, we'd have to do all the driving—white folks, I mean. We could probably get Grady to talk to the police chief and tell him what we're doing and to leave people alone. Then, after a while, the Colored could do all the driving or ride the street cars. I bet most people would even pay a few cents a week to help out. I know I would."

"It's a wonderful idea, Jonas. Really wonderful. Thank you."

He lifted JJ into his lap and sat next to Audrey. "Here's another thought: Suppose we turn that little building out there into a maid's room or servant's quarters. We'd have to run some water out to it and some electricity, but it would be private. Nobody working in this house would ever have to fear being locked in."

She leaned into his embrace and wept. He held her, not really alarmed, because he knew enough by now to understand that her pregnancies caused wide and wild swings of emotion. He'd witnessed it in his mother and his sisters but hadn't understood it. Now he did.

"Those poor people, Jonas. They shouldn't have to live like that, in fear all the time."

Jonas agreed with that thought but said nothing for fear that it would lead to a discussion of her parents' beliefs, and that he didn't want. "I'll call Mack tonight. I'm sure he's at work this time of day."

"Maybe not tonight," Audrey said. "Wouldn't it be better if we could say for certain that people would be willing participate? I could make some calls then you could say how many people were willing to drive, even say how many jobs were waiting."

And so two weeks later, Jonas made his call. Mack was often at work until nine o'clock at night during the summer months when it was light that late, so it was Ruthie that Jonas talked to when he called that evening. They hadn't talked to each other since that night in 1921 when the Colored Thatchers left Carrie's Crossing for the last time, and their initial conversation now was hesitant and stilted. Ruth congratulated him on the birth of his son and Audrey's new pregnancy. Jonas said he already felt overwhelmed at the thought of two children and asked how she managed five. She laughed and said, "Don't think about it." He laughed and the ice was broken, and Jonas told her the reason for his call. She listened intently, as was her way, then she thought about what he'd said before she spoke, and though he couldn't see her, he remembered how her eyes focused and seemed to darken when she was deep in thought, and he felt a pang of loss so intense it caused a pain in his chest. Finally she spoke.

"That is a very good idea, Jonas, and I certainly will help. People here need to go to work and not be afraid. I also like the idea of using the old schoolhouse as a private residence for your housekeeper. Maybe others will do the same thing for their live-ins, at least until people have had time to forget what happened to Sadie."

They spent another half-hour talking, working out the details. Ruth promised to get a list of people willing to participate—maids, cooks, gardeners, chauffeurs—and to call when she had the necessary commitments. Jonas had thirty job offers, and Ruth expected no difficulty in filling them. Jonas hung up the telephone with a sense of satisfaction. Not only had he performed a useful and necessary service to and for his neighbors, but he had bridged the gulf of distance between Ruthie and himself.

– Belle City –
Beau

Beau knew more people than he could begin to count, and more different kinds of people. For such a solitary man, for such a private and internal man, he was a people magnet. All those years of driving a mule cart and later a horse cart and finally a truck all over town picking up salvage, and later, all those years of delivering cases of illegal whiskey back and forth across Belle City, put him in the path of good people and some not-so-good people and some truly bad people. Beau treated them all the same. He spoke to everybody he encountered: Good morning, good afternoon, good evening. He tipped his hat to every woman he encountered: Grandmothers, mothers, aunties, sisters, teachers, cheap women, for sale women. He had been known to give a dime or a dollar when asked, and to give much more than that when not asked—when he saw the need. So when Beau Thatcher asked for a favor, he didn't have to ask but once, and the request wafted over the Colored neighborhoods of Belle City like the scent of fresh baked peach cobbler on a summer afternoon. What Beau wanted was the name of the white police officer who had put him in the work camp. He knew that Grady Allen knew the man's name but he would not ask, partly because he didn't trust white people, not even the "good" ones like Grady Allen, but also because he didn't want anybody close to him knowing that he was looking, and that would have included his sister and brother-in-law had he known that they knew the white policeman's name. And perhaps if he'd known that, he'd not have had the thoughts he was having, that plagued him: He needed to kill this man just as he had needed to kill Tom Jenks. He wanted the man's name and anything else anybody could find out about him. Nobody asked why Beau Thatcher wanted this information because anybody who knew him knew why. They also knew to forget that Beau had ever asked and, if it came to that, to forget they'd ever known Beau.

The information came quickly and in greater detail than he could have wished for. The white policeman's name was Gilbert Edwards, and he had an unreasonable hatred of Colored people. Beau had encountered more than a few white people like that—people whose hatred of Colored people was a raw, festering ugly thing that contorted their features and sometimes their very bodies. Mr. First used to say that hating Colored made them feel better about themselves since the only thing that separated poor white people from poor Colored people was skin color, but Beau thought it was more than that, though he really didn't care why he was hated. He knew it to be unreasonable and ridiculous since the rigidity of the laws of segregation made it impossible for Colored people ever to have gotten close enough to white people to do anything to warrant such hatred, so he didn't waste time trying to understand it. He merely avoided them. The only white people he'd ever had regular contact with were Jonas Thatcher and Grady Allen. Jonas he hadn't seen since the end of Prohibition, and prior to his brief stint as the man's chauffeur, the only time he saw Mr. Allen was when one of his relatives needed a new motor vehicle. In addition to all the other things he owned, Grady Allen also owned the local Ford and Packard motorcar stores, and he would sell a car to a Colored person for the same price he sold them to white people. He was the only white man Beau knew of who didn't charge Colored more for the same things, whether for food, clothing, or an automobile. This did not mean, however, that he liked them or considered them friends. Business was business. Mr. First had taught him that and both Jonas and Mr. Allen reinforced it. That they didn't seem to hate him, that they didn't appear enraged by the very fact of his existence, is what had made it possible for Beau to conduct business, and both men had profited from their business relationship with him.

What Beau did not understand at all were those white people who violently hated Colored people but still sought them out. Gilbert Edwards, he learned, was such a man. He spent considerable time in the most disreputable Colored establishments of the Fourth Ward. He drank, he got drunk, and he beat people, men and women—the women after he'd forced himself on them and then refused to pay. Friday and Saturday nights, Beau was told, he could almost always find Gilbert Edwards parked in one of two unpaved alleys well off the main thoroughfare and in so broken and ragged an area that even longtime Fourth Ward residents wouldn't know they existed.

Beau wore his oldest clothes and shoes and rode the trolley car across town. Even though he was well-acquainted with the East Side of Belle City, and had been given explicit directions, he still got lost. This was as ugly and desolate a neighborhood as he'd ever seen. He kept his head down and his hands in his pockets, one of them cradling a knife, the other a lead pipe. He had only enough money to ride the trolley car back to the West Side and hoped that nobody would jump him and take it; he didn't want to have to walk around here any longer than absolutely necessary.

Loud shouts and the sound of breaking glass caused Beau to stop in his tracks and lift his head. He was practically at the mouth of an alley he'd not have seen otherwise, for the darkness down that alley was complete and total. He took a hesitant step forward, arms outstretched, like a blind person in an unfamiliar room. He brought to mind the sketch he'd drawn of the area. The alleyway really was a driveway behind the buildings on parallel streets, residential on one street, commercial on the other, but both so poor that little light would spill out from the buildings because there was no electricity here. If the inhabitants were lucky, there'd be a kerosene lantern. If not, wax candles would light their way. Six steps into the alley and Beau could make out structures on either side, but no light was visible in any of them, not necessarily surprising on the residential side: It was after midnight, and people who didn't earn a living working the work that the night offered were asleep. Beau turned his attention to the right side of the alley, creeping forward slowly, step by step, arms moving from side to side. Suddenly he saw dim light ahead, and heard the tinny sound of radio music. And saw the *Belle City Police Department* car parked in the mud beside a grime-covered Packard roadster that he knew belonged to a hoodlum named Ollie Smith and which hadn't been driven in months because Ollie, his reputation as a high roller notwithstanding, couldn't afford to put gasoline in it.

Beau stood still, his breathing shallow, while thoughts bounced around in his head until they formed a plan. With the knife in one hand and the lead pipe in the other, he hastily circled the police car, slashing all four tires. Then he slashed Ollie's tires, as he saw his plan gain clarity. He planned to kill Gilbert Edwards as soon as he showed his face, but he had experienced a moment of trepidation when he tried to imagine the firestorm that would erupt when a white man—a white policeman—was found murdered in a Colored neighborhood. The thought of Ollie Smith being the Colored man called on to explain the situation almost made Beau smile, but the levity was momentary as angry shouts ruptured the still darkness. It was him—Gilbert Edwards. He was drunk enough that his words were slurred, but the vile hatred that he'd spewed at Beau now was directed to a woman whom he was dragging into the alley by her hair. He cursed her. He threw her to the ground and kicked her. She tried to stand, but he knocked her down, and as she tried to crawl away, he kicked her again. The he turned away from her and, drinking from a bottle, he staggered toward his car.

"Somethin's wrong," he muttered as he approached the car. "Wha's wrong?" He got to the car and leaned heavily on it. He bent over to look at the tires and fell into the mud and mire. "Goddammit!" he roared. "Goddamn niggers! I'll kill you. I'll kill every one of you ugly..."

Beau was behind Edwards and whispered in his ear, "You won't kill nobody, and you won't hurt nobody, not ever again."

Edwards whipped around and when he did, Beau hit him with the lead pipe, and as he dropped to his knees, he looked up, surprise and recognition in his face giving way to snarling hatred. Before he could speak, Beau kicked him in the gut, just as Edwards had kicked the woman, except Beau kept kicking him, and then he no longer was in a filthy alley in East Belle City but back in the prison work camp being forced to wallow in mud and slop for the amusement and entertainment of the prison guards who wanted to see the Colored pigs "do what comes nat'rally." Beau kicked and kicked. Then he bent forward and grabbed Edwards by his shirt front and pulled him into a sitting position. His head rolled from side to side as he struggled to open his eyes. Beau hit him in the face and blood gushed out of his nose. Beau hit him again, and kept hitting him, neither man any longer feeling pain—one because his body was dead, the other because his spirit was.

"Hey! Hey! Who you? Get on 'way from here 'fore Mr. Gilbert find you up next to his police car. He won't like that none atall. Go on, now. Git!"

Beau dropped to his knees, as much from exhaustion as to disappear from sight. A weak lantern light had illuminated a tiny circle around the man who'd called out, but there wasn't enough light for him to have seen anything more than the shape of a man. On his hands and knees in the mud, Beau wretched as he felt around for his knife. He didn't care about the pipe—anybody could have a lead pipe—but the knife was distinctive. Beau had taken it from a German soldier who had tried to kill him. The two soldiers had rolled around in the stinking mud, grunting and growling, their hands too slippery to grip or to hold anything—a man or a knife—and the German had dropped it when Beau gave him a head butt. Beau had grabbed it and shoved it into the German's gut, lay beneath him while he died, then rolled away, snatching the knife as he did. This mud this night was not as deep and not nearly as putrid as that French mud those long years ago, and this night Beau was not afraid. He found his knife, struggled to his feet and lurched toward the mouth of the alley. He did not look back.

He could see the glow of the streetlights ahead of him and knew that he could not walk there in his condition. He'd passed a horse barn and his nose led him to it. There'd be a trough inside, and buckets. The owner would wonder in the morning at his horse's sudden great thirst, Beau thought, as he scooped out water and poured it over himself. He made sure to get the mud out of his hair and off his face and hands. He couldn't see himself, but he could feel when he was free of the thick, cloying goo. Because it was July, it was as hot at night as during the day, so his hair and clothes dried a bit as he made his way out of the alleys and dead ends back to the main street and a trolley stop.

He kept his head down as he walked, waiting for a feeling of some kind to present itself as it had—quite suddenly—after he had made Tom Jenks pay for what he'd done to Nellie. He hadn't expected to feel anything. He knew where the man would be and when. He watched and waited and attacked when the opportunity presented itself. He made sure Jenks saw him and knew who he was so he'd know why he was about to die. Afterward, he felt an enormous relief, as if some huge weight had been lifted. But he felt nothing as he walked away from the dead Gilbert Edwards, not relief or excitement or satisfaction.

– Belle City –
Ruthie and Jonas

Neither Audrey nor Grady wanted Jonas to go to Belle City to talk personally to the Colored workers who'd be making the weekly journey under the auspices of the newly formed Belle City-Carrie's Crossing Transportation Committee, quickly dubbed by Ruth the BCCCTC. It was, they said, too dangerous. Jonas argued that if it was dangerous for him, it certainly would be dangerous for the Colored people they were trying to convince it was safe. "We can't have it both ways," he said, deliberately ignoring the real source of their fear, the reason neither would say out loud: Jonas would be meeting with Mack and Ruthie and some thirty-five maids, butlers, chauffeurs, and gardeners at the Baptist church most of them attended. What Audrey and Grady didn't know was that Jonas was no stranger to Belle City's Colored communities, that he'd been driving in and out of them for close on fifteen years.

Jonas wanted to tell them that he, a white man, was safer in their parts of town than they ever would be in his, but then he'd have to explain how he knew this and that he could not do. The only thing bothering Jonas was the fact that he did not like churches—any of them. He belonged to the First Baptist Church of Carrie's Crossing at his wife's insistence. He went under duress, the Sunday morning service merely the beginning of his least favorite day of the week, since after church they made the obligatory journey to her parents' house for Sunday dinner. It was bad enough he had to endure her parents, but to also endure her two brothers, their wives and children was too much though, thankfully, Horace Jr. rarely attended because he usually had to work on Sunday. But to make bad matters even worse, now Jonas had to shelter JJ from the stupidity of his mother's relatives.

He pulled into the parking lot behind the Friendship Baptist Church eleven minutes early. He knew where the church was because he knew this was where Ruthie had gotten married, though he'd never acknowledged that fact to any one. He parked his Packard sedan next to an identical one and, after his surprise abated, he surmised that it probably belonged to the pastor, until he saw that the parking spot labeled *PASTOR* was empty. His question was answered when the church door opened and Mack stepped out. It was Mack's car. They walked to meet each other and Jonas got another surprise. He'd only ever seen Mark dressed in his work clothes—either the overalls, flannel shirts and well-worn boots he wore while on a construction site, or the khaki pants, jacket and shirt he wore to meetings or bid openings. Today he was dressed like the pillar of the community he obviously was in a suit, shirt, tie and shoes the excellence of which rivaled Jonas's own. New York haberdashers were doing great mail-order business in Belle City.

"Thank you for coming, Jonas," Mack said, extending his hand.

"Thank you for making it possible, Mack, you and Ruthie. I don't doubt for one minute that the people inside are here because y'all told 'em it was all right to be here and that it would be all right—and safe—for them to come to the Crossing to work, and I do appreciate it." He gave a sideways grin. "So does my wife, even more than me."

Mack held the door open and Jonas stepped into a long, cool hallway. He could hear the low murmur of voices coming from one of the meeting rooms near the fellowship hall, knew because this church—all Baptist churches, he thought—was laid out like the one he attended. The front door was for church service; the side door was for meetings, social gatherings, fellowship, though he doubted that any pastor, Colored or white, would call what was about to happen here "fellowship." He wasn't sure what exactly it was, but he knew the information about this evening's meeting, in the wrong hands, would spell trouble for all the participants, which probably is why the *PASTOR* space in the lot was empty. It did speak well of the man, though, that he allowed the meeting to take place in his church, and it made clear how highly Mack and Ruth McGinnis were regarded.

Jonas thought that since he'd spoken to Ruth, since they'd had a relaxed and warm conversation, that he'd have no particular reaction to seeing her. He was wrong. At the sight of her, the breath caught in his chest just as it had done all those years ago when he first saw her. She was more beautiful now—still tall and lean and bronze but now with the poise and elegance of a grown woman. Her hair was gathered at the base of her neck in a bun. She wore a suit that only could have been handmade. Audrey had told him that men could order designer suits from New York and have them fit. A woman, she said, could not. Clothes had to be tried on, and even then, adjustments had to be made. Or—and this was Audrey's preference—start from scratch with a good pattern and a talented seamstress. Judging by the suit Ruthie wore, the seamstress was extremely talented. Nobody looking at her would imagine that she'd borne five children, the oldest of whom was sixteen years old.

The circle of people that was surrounding her shifted, and she looked up and saw him. She smiled warmly and walked toward him, hands outstretched. "Jonas. How wonderful to see you. Thank you for coming."

He took her hands in his. "I'll tell you the same thing I told Mack: I'm the one should be doing the thanking since you're the ones doing the favor."

"We should get started" Jonas heard Mack say; he'd forgotten the man was there.

"Yes," Ruth said, "if we want to be finished before it gets dark." And they did, all of them, want to be finished and gone before night fell. A young man approached them and both Ruthie and Mack smiled at him. "Jonas, this is our oldest son, Mack McGinnis the third. Mackie, this is Jonas Thatcher from Carrie's Crossing."

"Pleased to meet you, Mr. Thatcher," Mackie said, extending his hand.

Jonas took it, momentarily speechless as he looked directly across at the boy, he was that tall, and very good-looking; he looked more like Ruth's side of the family—looked a lot like Beau as a matter of fact. "I'm pleased to meet you, too, Mackie. I've got a son—he's still just a little fella—but when he grows up, I surely do hope he's as fine a young man as you are."

Mackie gave a slight smile and ducked his head. "Thank you, sir," he said and, like a much younger child, he grabbed his mother's hand and pulled her along with him to the meeting room. She hadn't wanted him to be here, but Mack had thought it important that he see what she was calling an historic moment. The BCCCTC was an unprecedented organization, and if they could get it off the ground without anybody being killed, surely it would be an unprecedented and historic event.

Some fifty people sat quietly in the meeting room though Jonas knew they probably felt anything but quiet inside themselves, expected that their insides were roiling too, just like his. He was standing on a slightly raised platform behind a podium. He gripped it with both hands so the audience wouldn't see them shaking. Public speaking was not his strong suit. In fact, he'd never done it before. "Good evening, ladies and gentlemen," he said and was startled when a lively chorus of "good evening" came back to him. "My name is Jonas Thatcher, and I live in Carrie's Crossing."

"You any kin to Silas and Beau and Ruth Thatcher McGinnis?" somebody called out.

"We grew up on the same land," Jonas said, knowing that the older members of the group would understand his meaning. "Little Si—you know him as Dr. Silas Thatcher—and Ruth and I played together as children. Their folks didn't like that, and my folks didn't like it, but we were friends, and we spent time together whenever we could. We fished and hunted, picked berries and climbed trees and talked about what we were going to do when we grew up." He looked out at the faces turned toward him. "Sometimes friends can be closer to you than family, and when I was growing up, Ruth and Little Si felt closer to me than my own brother and sisters."

"Y'all still friends?" somebody else called out.

"Of course we don't see each other like we did, but when I called Mack and Ruth to ask for their help, they agreed right away. And when they told me I needed to come over here and talk to y'all in person, I agreed right away. I'd say that's how friends treat each other."

Murmurs of assent floated through the crowd, and several people asked Mack and Ruth directly if Jonas was telling the truth about the friendship; when they responded in the affirmative, the crowd settled and returned their attention to Jonas. He explained the proposal and how it would work. He answered questions, and he asked a few. Finally he said, "I know it's not a perfect plan, but if it works, we can add to it. Right now, it's only for the live-in help because the pick-ups are on Monday morning at six o'clock and the return is Friday evening at six o'clock, in the parking lot of the Episcopal Church on Ashby Street. And here's something for you to think about while you're thinking about what happened to Sadie Hill: We've got a list of everybody who's participating. I have a copy and Mack and Ruth have a copy. We know who's working where. I also have the word of every person on that list that nobody will ever do what was done to Sadie Hill." He looked at the list in his hand and called out three names: "Miz Ernestine Smith, Miz Ruby Johnson and Mr. Samuel Johnson. If I could make your acquaintance, please?" He went out into the audience to meet them and shook their hands. "I'm pleased to have y'all working for me and my wife, and I'm also pleased to tell you, Samuel and Ruby, that you will have your own, private quarters in a separate structure on my property."

When the clapping stopped, Mack read the list of drivers who would make the first trip on the following Monday morning, and the names of those who'd ride with each driver. "We know that many people want to do day work, want to be able to ride the street car or drive to work in the morning and come home in the evening, and we are still talking to the police chief about how we can make your journey safe, and how we can make sure that what happened to Beau Thatcher doesn't happen to anyone else—"

"You won't have to worry 'bout that," a man called out. "He won't be doin' that to nobody else." And at Mack's confusion and lack of response, the man added, "That's 'cause he dead. The one put Beau on the chain gang—he dead."

More applause, this time louder than before, and Mack had to work harder to restore order, a task made more difficult by the look on Jonas's and Ruthie's faces. "How do you know that?" Mack said. "Is that just some gossip? What's your name, sir?"

"I'm Leroy Patrick and no, indeed, that ain't no gossip. My brother is the janitor at the police station and he told me. They found the man's body early this morning over in the Fourth Ward. Beat to death."

The energy in the room shifted so suddenly that Mack had to yell to be heard. "Monday morning at six o'clock in the Episcopal Church parking lot. If you're gonna work in the Crossing, be there on time." Excitement carried the crowd out of the room. Mack hurried over to Leroy Patrick, took his arm, and pulled him aside. "Can you tell me everything you know about what happened to that police officer?"

"Yessir, Mr. McGinnis, and I swear it ain't no gossip. They say he got kilt some time last night, but they didn't find him 'til early this mornin' on account of where he was: In a alley over on the East Side, a place so rough the rats and roaches is scared to go there. It's a place for gamblers and 'hos and cutthroats, a place where that Officer Edwards used to go pract'ly every night."

Mack was astounded. "The police chief knew Edwards went to a place like that?"

Patrick nodded his head. "My brother said they don't bother him too much 'cause his pappy is a rich man. Only reason they got after him for what he did to Beau Thatcher is 'cause the man Beau worked for is even richer."

"Do they know who did this thing? Did your brother say?"

"Yeah. Pimp by the name of Ollie Smith. And one other thing: They can't find where he lives, that policeman. The place where he told 'em he lived, the woman there said she ain't his wife and he don't live there."

Mack thanked the man and hurried over to Ruthie and Jonas. Mackie was there with his arm around his mother. Mack didn't want him to hear what he had to say but at this point, it couldn't be helped. He told them what he'd learned, and Ruthie began breathing again at the news that perhaps Ollie Smith had killed Horace Edwards, Jr., but Jonas still was ghost-white.

"I have to go," Jonas said. "Maybe I can get home before somebody calls Audrey."

They shook hands all around. Mack urged Jonas to be careful and to drive carefully and he hurried away.

"I want to see Beau," Ruth said.

"It was Ollie Smith," Mack said.

"I want to see Beau."

Mack and his son straightened the chairs in the meeting room, made sure no trash was left behind, turned out the lights and locked the doors. Ruth was in the car waiting for them. "Why don't you call him tomorrow, Ruthie, instead of upsetting your Pa by going over there now."

She didn't respond, and he knew he had little choice but to take her to her father's house. He again wished that Mackie wouldn't hear the discussion or the reason for it, but again, it was too late to do anything about that.

Big Si opened the door almost immediately, as if he'd been expecting them, and his first words hinted at some uneasiness within him. "What's done happened?"

"Where's Beau, Pa?"

"Upstairs 'sleep. What's done happened?"

"Was he home last night?"

"Oh Lord have mercy! I knew somethin' wasn't right." Ruth put her arm around his waist and led him to the sofa in the living room, sat him down, and waited for him to continue. "He went out and when he got back it was late and he was soaking wet and it didn't rain last night. I asked him how come he was wet and you know what he said? 'Cause he was hungry. I told him I'd fix him some food but he had to take off them wet clothes first. So, you know what he did? He stood in the middle of the kitchen and took off ev'ry stitch he had on, socks and shoes, too, rolled it up in a ball, and took it outside to the firepit. You hear me? He was butt nekkid, it was the middle of the night, and he took them things out to the firepit. Then he come back in here and set at the table, ready to eat. I told him to go put some clothes on and I'd get the food ready. He ate six eggs, a whole pot of grits, and half a loaf of bread. The boy hadn't ate that much food all together since he been back from that work camp." Pa took a deep breath; so many words all at once had exhausted him. He leaned heavily against Ruth. "What's done happened?" he asked again.

"That police officer, the one who arrested Beau, he's dead. Somebody killed him."

"They think it was Beau?"

"They think it was a man named Ollie Smith."

"Why you think it ain't Ollie Smith?" Pa asked, barbed wire in his voice.

Ruth stood up and began to pace. Her father, her husband and her eldest son watched her every step. They knew her so well—too well—she sometimes thought. "Something the man told you, Mack, doesn't make sense, and for now, it doesn't matter. White people very often don't make sense and that can work to our benefit: A white man is dead, they have a Colored man— Ollie Smith—to blame for it. But here's what doesn't make sense: Why would Smith cut the tires on his own car if he'd just killed a white man?"

Mack began to pace with his wife. "Maybe all the police are as stupid as Edwards and nobody will think what you just thought, Ruth."

"Will they even care?" Mackie asked. "Will it even matter to them that they've got the wrong Colored man as long they have a Colored man to blame?"

Nobody who loved Mackie wanted to know that he'd already come to such a horrible realization, yet they all were relieved that he had. The sooner the better. It was this kind of knowledge and awareness that would keep him alive.

"Pa," Ruth said, "I think we need to find another place for Beau to live."

Big Si nodded. "I been thinkin' that same thing for a while now. Some place where there ain't so many people. 'Specially white ones. But where?"

"I have an idea," Ruth said. "I need to look into it some more. I'll let you know."

– Carrie's Crossing –
Jonas

Y ou can't call your pa, Audrey," Jonas said.

"But if Junior is dead, pa needs to know."

"I still don't understand why he doesn't know. Seems to me telling his wife would be the last thing they'd want to do—under the circumstances." Jonas knew well how men's minds worked, knew it would be easier for one man to tell another some version of a sordid truth than to tell a woman any aspect of it, especially if that woman was the man's wife.

"That's exactly why they wouldn't tell him first. You know how he acts— yelling and screaming and cussing."

"I also don't understand why you didn't tell me that he didn't live with his wife."

"I told you, Jonas. I was ashamed. My brother goes with whores and then brings diseases home to his wife. I didn't want to tell you anything like that. You already don't like my family, and I didn't want to give you another reason."

He tightened his hold on her. "You are not your family, Audrey."

"How is that? Why is that? Do you know? Do you understand?"

He shook his head. It was a question he couldn't answer, despite the fact that he'd asked it of himself a million times: Why wasn't he like Zeb? How had he escaped being like Zeb? And it wasn't just his pa's hatred of Colored people that Jonas was relieved to have not inherited; it also was the man's inherent laziness, his fondness for alcohol, and the petty, vindictive streak that had earned him the general dislike of most of his peers. "I don't guess it matters. What matters is that you're you and I'm me."

"Suppose JJ is like them? Or the new baby?" She started to cry again, and he soothed and quieted her, then held her as she tried to stand. "I should call pa. I *should*."

"Then you'll have to tell him how you know which means you'll have to tell him how I know—tell him where I was and what I was doing there."

Still sniffling, she slumped against him…and the phone rang. He ran to answer it.

"Thatcher residence," he said, though he knew who was calling.

"Let me talk to my daughter."

"She's resting, Horace. Can I give her a message?"

"You can get her to the damn telephone is what you can do."

"And you can talk to me like you've got some sense or I'm hanging up."

Audrey was standing beside him now, reaching for the telephone.

"I need to talk to my daughter, Jonas. Her brother is dead."

Jonas gave her the telephone and left the room, went upstairs to look in on JJ, and as he watched the little boy sleep, he pictured Ernestine Smith, the woman who, in less than a week from now, would have bathed this little boy and put his night clothes on him and brought him down to his mama and his papa for a story and good night hugs and kisses. He had said that Audrey was the one looking forward to having household help again but in truth, he was the one. He heard Audrey behind him.

"You know we have to go over there."

"What did he say?"

"That some niggers had killed his son. I asked what happened, where it happened, who did the police think did it. He wouldn't answer; he said it didn't matter. All that mattered, he said, was that Junior was dead and that somebody would pay."

"You think he knows the truth? You think they told him what really happened?"

Audrey was quiet for a long moment, whether thinking about his question or the answer she'd give, Jonas didn't know. She seemed to be looking at something in the distance, then she turned her gaze directly on him. "I think he knows who his son was and what he was and how he was. I think if pa can keep his focus on somebody else, on some Colored man, then that poor man better make his peace with his Maker because Horace Edwards will see him sent to the electric chair."

– The Mountains of North Carolina –
Ruthie

The sun sliding down behind the peaks of the Appalachian Mountains leaving snail trails of gold and pink and orange was one of the most beautiful things Ruthie had ever seen. Or maybe those were the Great Smokey Mountains. She didn't care and it didn't matter. It was beautiful and peaceful and, for Beau, safe. It also was cold. Back home in Belle City, in the last week of October, nights were chilly. Leaves were beginning to turn on the trees. Up here the transformation was complete, and when the chill breeze blew, the leaves fell, covering the forest floor with a carpet of red, orange and gold. The forest floor would drift white with snow in the winter, the prints of various critters left as proof of their existence.

"You like this place all right then, Beau?" she asked him as he appeared out of the shadows and dropped down beside her.

"That's the third time you asked me that, Baby Sister, and my answer is the same: This is a good place, a very good place, and I'm glad you found it for me."

"Good because I don't want you to feel..."

"I know you're just takin' care of me, Ruthie. You just like Ma that way— she always would know what was good for somebody before they knew it for their selves."

The tears rose and fell before she could stop them. Beau put his arms around her and pulled her close, and they sat like that for a while. She told him how much she would miss him, told him much she had always relied and depended on him, how he'd never let her or any member of their family down.

"Yeah, I did. I let ev'rybody down when I...did what I did. I thought I was doin' the right thing. I still think so, but I see, though, how what I did could cause y'all trouble, so I'm glad to be livin' up here in these mountains, outta the way."

She wept again. "Oh, Beau. That's not why we wanted you away from Belle City."

"Why then?" he asked, surprised.

"Because...here's what I believe: Killing Tom Jenks and that policeman killed a part of you, too, because what you did made you like them, and that's not who you are. You're nothing like those men. You're the kind of man who gets mad at evil and at people who hurt other people, and you want to make it right. But Beau: There's always going to be people hurting Colored people and you can't make it right. Seems like not even God can make them different, so you'll surely kill yourself trying, and I don't want you to be dead on the inside. That War almost killed your spirit and your mind. Ma and Pa brought you back to us. Then, that chain gang took you away again, and Pa brought you back again. Next time—"

"Won't be a next time, Baby Sister, 'cause I live up here on a mountain." He picked her up as he'd done when she was a girl and swung her around as he'd done then, and they both laughed like children, which brought Pa and Mack to see what was going on.

"I see you already made yourself at home," Pa said, overwhelmed at the sight of his eldest and youngest engaged in a moment of pure joy.

"This is a good place y'all found, Pa. Good people up here, too. Fellas'll be 'round in the mornin' to help me and Mack dig and pour the foundation, and we think to be able to get it framed in and the roof on before the real bad weather sets in."

"I can help too," Pa said, and Beau and Mack both agreed that he certainly could, though neither voiced the thought that it would be over their dead bodies. Ruthie had extracted that promise from them as a condition for her agreeing to Pa moving up here with Beau—as if she could have prevented it. *He* was *her* parent, not the other way around, and Beau was her big brother and Mack was her husband. That the three of them conspired to have her believe that she was having her way with them both infuriated and enchanted her. She adored the three of them and had almost perfected the smile she now pasted on when she said how excited and happy she was for Beau and how glad she was that Pa would be living with him. It was breaking her heart. Pa was almost sixty-five years old and had a bad heart. There was no doctor up here…

"I'm getting hungry," Mack said, then to Ruthie, "Do you still remember how to cook outside?"

"Of course I do. You don't forget the things you love."

They laughed, the three of them, making various comments about how far removed Ruthie now was from the life she was born into. "That's why, after we cook and eat, you're gonna ride down the mountain and spend the night with the professor and his wife in their house, 'stead of out here under the stars,"

Beau said.

She laughed with them, acknowledging the truth of their words, though for reasons vastly different from what they were imagining. She had no more fear of the forest now than she did as a girl. What she needed from Professor Burgess was more reassurance that Pa and Beau would be safe, though she was secretly pleased that she wouldn't have to make do without indoor toilet facilities and electric lights.

"That's Indian land," Arthur Burgess told her when they first met. That was almost two months ago in Belle City. She and Mack accepted his invitation to visit the following weekend. She loved the land, but many of the Indians she'd met looked enough like white people to cause her to question the professor, himself a white native North Carolinian but a student of the history of the Indians of the state. He'd taken one look at Beau and proclaimed he'd have no trouble being accepted in Hendersonville, and Pa would be accepted because he was with Beau. "For that matter, you could live up here too, without any difficulty. Don't worry."

He had helped them find the land, and when it became clear that Beau could afford to buy and build anything he wanted, the locals became downright expansive. He could hire as many men as he could afford to pay, and these were men who knew how to build houses for mountain living. He would have as much seasoned wood as his soon-to-be-built shed could hold. Two dozen men were waiting for them when their two trucks pulled into the clearing an hour earlier. They inspected the wood, the nails, the window sashes, the door, the roof shingles, the cement, and the tools—hammers, chisels, trowels, saws, mitre boxes—and found everything acceptable. They would, they said, return at dawn, ready to work.

Mack had, a month ago, made sketches of the mountain house, and Beau had given his approval—with one request: That Mack make it bigger. He didn't want a house just large enough for Pa and himself. He wanted a house large enough to accommodate his entire family, he said, for he wanted and expected that they would be regular visitors. He had looked pointedly from Mack to Ruthie and said, "'Specially you and the chil'ren. I'm gon' have me a measurement wall and I'm gon' mark off how they grow, so you can't keep 'em away from me for too long." So, instead of a cabin in the mountains of North Carolina, Beau would have a house.

In the remaining daylight, Mack and Beau began staking the ground while Ruthie and Pa began digging the firepit and lining it with rocks, then piling in the kindling and the wood chunks that would burn hot, fully cooking the chickens and potatoes that would be their supper tonight and breakfast in the morning.

From the Recorded Memories of Ruth Thatcher McGinnis

We celebrated Christmas that year in North Carolina. Everybody went—Big Mack and Clara and their other sons and their families; Belle and her children and her Ma and Catherine, Mack and me and the children. It was one of the best times of my life. We had all brought something for the house—pots and pans, dishes, knives and forks, bedsheets and towels and blankets—everybody brought blankets and we needed every one of them. We brought rugs for the floors and curtains for the windows, and kerosene lanterns—they had gotten hot and cold water, but they didn't have electricity yet—and of course, we brought food. From the moment we arrived until we left, somebody was cooking and somebody was eating. Pa kept wishing he had a radio; he missed his music, but I was glad because I didn't want Beau hearing the news about the war in Europe. That was the frightening, ugly side to that wonderful Christmas holiday that nobody would talk about but which was on everybody's mind: Nobody believed that the U.S. could stay out of the war. It was a strange and difficult time. The decade of the 1930s had begun in a terrible depression, and was ending on the brink of war. But for that one week, we refused to allow ourselves to think horrible thoughts, and war wasn't the only horrible thought or the only secret we were harboring. Tobias was dead from a drug overdose. He died just after Thanksgiving. That was the last time any of us saw him—he came to dinner at Big Mack and Clara's and passed out in the bathroom with a needle in his arm. Nobody said anything to or about him after that, but we still couldn't tell Pa that he was dead. Beau either, for that matter. They thought he hadn't come because of what happened Thanksgiving, and they read Belle's strangeness as that—but that was only a part of what was on Belle's mind. With Toby's death, she became the biggest numbers writer in Belle City and we all were worried, but she said she paid the police enough protection money that they'd leave her alone. Plus, she said, the cops didn't bother her as much since that Edwards was killed over in Fourth Ward: Seems the chief of police was keeping a closer eye on his officers. But that was only part of the reason for our worry—we feared for the children, which seemed not to concern Belle at all. It bothered Sadie, though, so much that she wouldn't work for Belle anymore, so she went to work in our house, and from that time until she died, she rented Pa's house. She didn't want her children exposed to gambling and drugs and what she called "loose folks." A truly funny sight, one I'll never forget, was Pa's face when he heard relatives of his referred to as "loose folks."

From the Journal of Jonas Farley Thatcher Mar. 18, 1940

Only one thing could make me stop thinking and worrying about war coming and that was Alice Corrinne Thatcher. My baby daughter, born on my 35th birthday. Poor Audrey is so worn out I don't think she even heard the doctor tell her it was a girl. She was in labor for the better part of a whole day. She had a real rough time and as sorry as I am about that, I'm glad that my baby girl shares a birthday with me. I'm also glad I'm not a woman. Whoever in the world ever thought they are the weaker sex? I couldn't take 22 seconds of labor, never mind 22 hrs. And to think women have been doing this since the beginning of time, and will do so until the end of time. And do it more than once. They say that women love their children more than men and maybe that is why, because of what they have to suffer to bear a child into this world. And I know I didn't suffer, but I don't believe anybody can love this little girl more than I do. Or love JJ any more than I do. He is so happy and excited. He's about to drive Ernestine and Ruby crazy, jumping up and down and calling her name. Alice Corrinne! He hollers as loud as he can. She's named after her two grandmas, Audrey's ma, Alice, and my ma, Corrinne. When I called Horace to tell him, he wanted to know why we hadn't named the baby after HIS ma. Lord I wish I didn't ever have to talk to that man again. It's only that it would make Audrey unhappy that I don't cut all ties with him. But Audrey or no Audrey, I'll throttle him if he asks me one more time to invest in his war business. He truly does not understand when I tell him money is not the most important thing to me. He keeps telling me how much he's going to make—how much money I can make if I invest with him. In the first place, I don't think he stands to make that much, but even if I'm wrong, I don't want to make any more money if it means being at work more and at home less. I will be so happy when Alice and Audrey can come home. JJ will too. We've got a little crib set up for her in our room. Ernestine and Ruby decorated Alice's room so it will be ready for her when she's old enough to sleep in her own room. It's next door to JJ's room and he has said that he will guard her. Ernestine and Ruby are a blessing. I don't know how we got on without them. Yes, they are good cooks and housekeepers and they look after JJ like he was a son to them, but they are also very, very nice people. They eat dinner at the table with us—Ruby's Samuel too—and they tell us about their family. Their children are all grown up and that's why they don't mind being live-in help. I'm glad we have them. And Audrey made me promise not to tell anybody that we eat supper with the help.

– The Mountains of North Carolina –
Ruthie

Happy birthday to you, happy birthday to you! Happy birthday dear Ruthie, happy birthday to you!" The clapping and cheering was loud and raucous, and it was a good thing they were out of doors; an inside room, even a huge one like the living room of Beau's house, couldn't have contained so much sound. Somebody started *For She's a Jolly Good Fellow* and it quickly became an even louder proclamation of their love for her. She began to feel a bit emotional, but Nellie's insistence that she hurry up and blow out the candles so the cake could be cut quashed that. She inhaled deeply, held her breath long enough to make a wish, and blew. And blew again. And again, this time getting an assist from Mackie, until they all were extinguished.

"Let's cut the cake, let's cut the cake," Nellie sang, hopping from foot to foot. "I want cake."

Mack Jr. scooped her up. "Pa has to toast first, Nell, you know that."

"I forgot," she said, then beckoned to her father. "C'mon, Papa. Toast!"

Mack faced his wife and raised his glass to her. Two dozen other glasses were raised in her direction. Mack, smiling, began to recite: *May you live a long time and your heart remain mine. May your body be strong, may your Spirit be free, and may all your good deeds be seen as the seeds that grow to fullness in your eternity. Since I love you, all that's left is for God to bless you.* Ruthie touched her glass to Mack's, then lifted it to the crowd. After the clapping and cheering died down, she cut the first piece of cake, then passed the knife to Nellie and Mack Jr. so they could finish. Everybody stood quietly, watching, waiting, plates at the ready, for their piece.

"Is thirty-five old, Ma?" Wilton asked into the silence, starting the laughter and hoots and catcalls all over again.

"Depends on who's doing the counting," Ruthie answered through her own laugh, and kissed him. "If it's you doing the counting, then, yes, I expect thirty-five is rather old. If, on the other hand—" and she surveyed the crowd, eyes stopping on Beau, "it's my BIG BROTHER Beau doing the counting, well, then, no, thirty-five isn't all that old."

Beau bent over at the waist and began hobbling around like an old, decrepit man, to everyone's delight. He looked happier than Ruth had ever seen him.

Of course he was thrilled that his baby sister had wanted to have her thirty-fifth birthday party at his home, and he was justifiably proud of the home he had created for himself and his family in the North Carolina mountains.

The central feature of the towering A-frame house was the stone fireplace that occupied an entire wall and which, in the winter, heated the entire structure. It was in front of the fireplace that everyone gathered—to listen to and tell stories, to listen to the radio, and to eat, sleep and just be. At night, the children would climb into the loft and look down on the grownups below, listening and learning before falling asleep. The three bedrooms on the ground floor always were occupied by Big Si, who lived there and kept his own room even when company came, by Big Mack and Clara, who slept in the guest room when they visited, and by Ruthie and Mack Jr., who slept in Beau's room while he, happily, climbed the ladder to the sleep-loft and joined the children. And that, she realized, was what was different about Beau, what made him look and feel happy: He now was an integral part of the family. No longer just the one who was summoned when there was trouble or a problem; Uncle Beau now was the one children wanted to visit, to play with, to talk to. He was the one who could repair a broken toy or fairly mitigate a dispute. He no longer was the brooding, silent, angry avenger. He had emerged as a man quick to laugh and to want to make others laugh.

The land behind the house had been cleared, and it appeared that Pa and Beau had planted every vegetable that would grow in dirt, along with several varieties of fruit trees. Along the front and one side of the house bloomed flowers of every color, and Ruthie's eyes misted as she imagined the joy her mother would have taken in the riot of blossoms. She knew, without a doubt, that her father was responsible and that her mother was the reason. She knew also that the chicken coop outside the back door was her father's—he loved fried chicken more than anything in the world, could eat it every meal of every day, and he kept the coop close to the house so he could prevent the foxes and mountain cats from eating the chickens before he did. He told her that Beau, now and then, would even eat a piece of fried chicken or fish if he hadn't witnessed its killing and gutting.

Looking at the land and the people, remembering her mother, reminded her of home, a long time ago, and the big June 'Teenth Celebration. It had been like this—their yard teeming with people, the scent of cooking food and the sound of happy voices carried on the breeze...a breeze that in Carrie's Crossing, Georgia, had been warmer than this one in the North Carolina mountains. Even in May, the nights could be chilly.

"What are you thinkin' 'bout, Baby Sister?"

He still could do that—appear beside or behind her, silent as an animal hunting its dinner, which always made her grateful that she was friend and not foe. "About, you, Big Brother, and how much I like your home. If they had schools up this mountain, I'd think about living here myself." She looked out at the merrymaking in the yard. "Schools and a few more Colored people," and they laughed dryly at what wasn't funny: No matter the oasis created, no matter where it was, being Colored was still a perilous proposition, even in this part of North Carolina, where there were a good number of Indians who definitely did not consider themselves Colored but who definitely were in the eyes of white people. "You all ever get lonely, you and Pa?"

He shook his head. "We work too hard for that. And in the evening, after supper, we listen to the radio and then go to bed so we can get up with the chickens." He paused and surveyed his surroundings. "Sometimes in the winter, though..."

He trailed off and even though she could imagine what he was going to say, she waited for him to tell her about the snow, and he did, how it snowed and snowed and how the wind blew it and how it drifted. How beautiful and quiet it was, and how frightening at the same time. She was reminded of the freak blizzard that paralyzed their world the winter after she and Mack first were married and still living in the Crossing. Even though they had each other and even though they knew that friends and neighbors were a stone's throw away—that they were not isolated and alone—it still unnerved and frightened them. She could remember the feeling still. But up here, where they truly were isolated and alone? She shivered, and Beau put is arm around her.

"Nothin' for you to be worried 'bout."

"Did they say when you'll be getting your phone?"

Now he did laugh. "You mean you're not happy 'bout the 'lectricity they finally strung in? Now you want telephone poles?"

She did, indeed, want telephone poles, and the sooner the better—preferably sometime in the next six months before winter set in again. "I wouldn't mind," she said in an offhanded way and poked him in the ribs.

"Then I'll just go right on down to the Bell telephone company office and tell 'em my baby sister said they better have me a telephone in my house before the next snow."

"And it had better not be a party line."

Between guffaws he asked, "You think they'll shoot me the deadest for bein' Colored or for bein' crazy?"

"There's a difference?"

They were holding their sides and laughing so hard their eyes were running, and it felt good. Ruthie tried to remember the last time she'd laughed until she cried and could not. Had there ever been a time she'd laughed so hard and so freely? Certainly not with Beau or because of Beau.

Mack and his parents were walking toward them, and Ruthie and Beau tried to compose themselves, but when Clara asked, "What's so funny?" and when they tried to answer, they only laughed harder, and soon the other three were laughing too. They all put their arms around each other and, still laughing, returned to the crowd, most of whom were busy with plates of ice cream and cake.

Nellie and Wilton ran to meet her. "Ma, Mackie cranked this ice cream all by his self," Nellie said, ice cream traces all around her mouth, "and it is deeelicious."

"Himself, Nell, please. You know better."

The girl grinned up at her mother; of course she knew better, and to prove it, she repeated the statement in grammatically correct French.

"C'est bon, *ma cherie*," Ruth said, as Big Mack and Clara applauded. It never ceased to amaze them that their grandchildren spoke French. Truth be told, the children's father never ceased to be amazed, either, not to mention proud.

"Wil said I was the baby of this family. I'm not, am I? Angel's younger than I am which makes *her* the baby of the family. Will you tell him, please?"

Angel was Belle's new daughter and to quote Pa, "The less said about that, the better." And while Angel certainly was younger than Nellie, answering the question Nell posed was problematic, at best. Thankfully, the child's attention was easily captured by one of the half-dozen other activities and conversations swirling around her, and she ran off to join whatever game was in progress, oblivious to the fact that they shared Wilton's view of her status in the family, not to mention their ambivalence about Angel.

– Carrie's Crossing –
Jonas

It was their first big entertainment, and Jonas found himself as excited and nervous as Audrey. They thought the timing was perfect: All of the improvements, renovations, additions and enhancements to the house and property finally were finished. Mack and his crew put the final coat of white paint on the stable and the fences the previous day and drove away for the final time. Everybody stood in the drive and waved good-bye. Then they all spent the better part of an hour just walking around and looking at everything. Even Mack said he wouldn't have recognized the house had he not been the one to make all the changes, and Audrey was so happy she couldn't form complete sentences. For Jonas, the *pièce de résistance* was the stable. He'd always loved horses, loved to ride, and Audrey did too. The few times they took the children riding convinced them of the need to have their own horses, and they certainly had enough land for them.

Jonas's second favorite addition was the barbecue pit and smoker. It had been Mack's idea and his design—based, he said, on the one that his own father had built in their backyard. "You can grill, roast, smoke, cook any kind of meat you like on this pit," he had said, and when Charlie Pace from the *Crossing Café* came to take a look, he, like Audrey, was rendered speechless.

"You gotta let me cook on this thing, Jonas. I'll pay you to let me cook on this thing. I'll even buy the meat!"

That's when they decided that the Fourth of July would be a perfect time to invite all their family and friends for a backyard barbecue. Horace and Alice had insisted on coming over the night before because Alice wanted to "help," which had given Audrey so severe a headache that she threatened to cancel the whole event. And if Jonas hadn't intervened, the event would have had to be cancelled because there would have been nobody to cook the food. Ernestine and Ruby, who had had the dubious pleasure of meeting Alice and Horace once before, went from sullen to openly hostile and threatened to quit on the spot if Jonas and Audrey didn't get her out of "their" kitchen.

"What are we going to do, Jonas?" Audrey moaned.

"Get her drunk," Jonas said.

"You can't."

"It's either that or try to call thirty people on the telephone tonight and cancel the party," he said. "And look at it this way: We get her good and drunk tonight, she'll be so hung over tomorrow, she could be almost polite."

Audrey didn't like it, but she agreed; she even helped. She settled Alice in chaise lounge under an umbrella on the back patio and told her that Jonas needed her to try out a new drink he wanted to serve at the party, and because neither of them drank, he needed to be certain that it would be acceptable to serve their guests. Alice was only too happy to help. The drink was something Audrey had seen in a magazine—a gin fizz—but Jonas didn't bother with the precise measurements. He made it sweet, with plenty of lemon juice, fizzy water and ice, and he served it in a tall glass. She slept through dinner. Infuriated, Horace threatened to pack her up and go back home, but when the threat was met with little resistance, he backed off.

Audrey wanted Ernestine to feed the children in the kitchen, but Horace wanted them at the table so he could talk to them. Without Alice, Jonas thought, it would be all right. And it was—for a while. Audrey told him all about the party and the food and how Mr. Pace would begin cooking the meat that night; it already was marinating in his big refrigerator at the Café. Ernestine and Ruby would shuck several dozen ears of corn after dinner and peel and cut ten pounds of potatoes to cook for the potato salad that Rachel would come over later to make.

"His sister makes the best potato salad I've ever eaten," Audrey enthused.

"Your ma makes the best potato salad, Audrey, and you know that."

Jonas should have kept his mouth shut and he knew it. But he didn't. "If you want to go wake her up, Horace, and get her to make the potato salad, I'll call Rachel and tell her to stay home."

"Oh, Jonas," Audrey whispered. She was holding Alice, wiping the baby's hands and face, and Jonas barely heard her, but he heard her tone, and its sadness cut him. He had promised to try to be more understanding and tolerant of Horace; after all, she'd once reminded him, suppose Zeb were alive? Suppose there were two of them?

"Horace, I'm sorry. I shouldn't have said that. Alice needs her rest—we all know that. Tomorrow is a big day—"

The baby heard her name and began to laugh and gurgle and clap her hands.

"Yes, you, Alice. You need your rest too because tomorrow is a big day."

He scooped her up and swung her over his head, eliciting more gurgles and a stream of drool on to his shirt front. "You also are a very messy girl," he said, giving her back to Audrey.

"Am I messy too, Papa?" JJ asked.

Jonas lifted him from his seat—he and Audrey were very conscious of giving the same time and attention to both children—"Not anymore, and do you know why?"

"Because I'm a big boy."

"That's right, you are, and the best big boy there ever was." He gave the boy a big kiss, and the child kissed him back and wrapped his arms tightly around his neck.

"You shouldn't be kissin' a boy like that. And lettin' him kiss you. You'll make a sissy out of him."

Before Jonas and Audrey could intervene, JJ asked, "What's a sissy, Papa?"

Jonas turned to Horace. "I don't ever want to hear that word out of your mouth in my house in front of my children again." To JJ he said, "It's a bad word to call a person, and we don't call people bad names, do we?"

"No, Papa."

"And since tomorrow is such a big day, it's time for you little ones to get bathed and ready for bed." He walked over to the wall and pressed a button. "Let's call Miss Ernestine and ask her to come get you and your baby sister—"

"*Miss* Ernestine." Horace gave a nasty bark of laughter. "Y'all got these chil'ren callin' the niggers 'miss'? No wonder they're the way they are."

Audrey jumped to her feet and startled Jonas by yelling at her father. "What do you mean the way they are? What way are they, Pa? Are you saying something is wrong with my children?" His daughter's fury surprised, frightened and chastened the man, and he tried back-pedaling, stuttering out a kind of apology, but she wasn't listening to him. Her raised voice—something none of them had ever heard—terrified the children, and their screams snatched Audrey back to herself, and she sought to soothe them.

The call bell, along with the raised voices and screaming children, had brought Ernestine and Ruby on the run. They stood in the doorway, waiting for Audrey to tell them what to do. Horace saw them and turned purple.

"What you niggers want? Get outta here!"

"Those people work for me. *You* don't tell them what to do," Jonas said, one arm around Audrey and the screeching Alice, the other holding a weeping JJ. He looked up at Ernestine and Ruby. "Y'all come on in and take the children, please."

Both women, studiously ignoring Horace, came in and each took a child and as they whispered soothing words, the children quieted almost immediately. Before they could leave, however, Sam appeared, a wide grin on his face.

"'Scuse me, Miz Thatcher, Mr. Jonas, you wanted me to come tell you—"

Horace jumped to his feet. "Y'all got to stop this! You can't have niggers in an' out whenever they choose. And you can't be sayin' 'please' to 'em. You got to be the voice of authority, you got to be in charge. You! Boy!" he said, pointing at Sam, "You get on outta here. Go on!"

Sam looked at Jonas, who shook his head, then said, "This is the last time I'll say this to you, Horace: You will not use that kind of language in my house, and you will not tell the people that I pay what to do. They do what Audrey asks and what I ask. They do not take orders from you or from Alice." He looked at Ernestine and Ruby: "Y'all get them ready for bed. Audrey'll be on up to read their stories and sing their lullabies."

"Yes, sir, Mr. Jonas," they said in unison and hurried out, hugging the children to them as if to protect them from some awful thing.

"Sam," Jonas said, "did you want to say something?"

"Yes, sir. You told me to come tell you when Mr. Pace got here."

"Thank you, Sam. I'll change my clothes—put on my cookin' uniform—and I'll be right out. Don't y'all start without me!"

Sam touched his hat, threw a slit-lid glance at Horace, said "good evenin', m'am" to Audrey, and left the room. A deep silence reigned for several long seconds, broken only by the sound of Jonas's footsteps as he crossed the room to stand beside his wife. He put his arm around her and pulled her close.

"The only reason I continue to do business with you, Horace, is because of your daughter. The only reason I invite you into my home is because of Audrey. But I will not tolerate your disrespect not one more minute. I don't care what you say in your home, but in mine, you will respect my wishes. You will not speak to my help, and you will not use foul, ignorant language in front of my children. Do you hear me, Horace?"

"What I hear is a whole lot of 'my': *My* house, *my* children, *my* help. Your wife have any say-so in *your* house?"

Audrey stepped away from Jonas, out of his embrace and toward her father. "Yes, Pa, I do. I have all the say-so I want or need, whenever I want it or need it. I have more than Ma ever had in *your* house, and I don't need to beg for it."

Horace looked at her as if at a stranger who'd said something awful to him. "You turned my own daughter against me. With all your highfalutin airs, actin' and talkin' like you're better'n everybody else. Callin' me ignorant 'cause I don't sound like you. Well let me tell you somethin', Mr. Jonas Thatcher: You're a country cracker just like me and everybody knows it. Audrey knows it too."

"I am a country cracker, Horace, but I'm nothing like you, and I've never tried to be anything but what I was. Yes, I wanted to get educated but not because I wanted to be or to try to be somebody else. I like knowing things. And that's one of the things I first loved about Audrey: She knows things. More things than I do. But I do know this one thing, Horace, and it's something my own pa never learned: You can't treat people badly and think they'll do for you. They won't. My pa used to jump up and down, cussin' at the farm hands, callin' 'em niggers—and worse—and then try to shortchange their wages and wonder why they wouldn't work for him. You ever stop to wonder why you and Alice can't keep any help? And don't tell me it's because Colored people are lazy. Do y'all even know why you hate those people so much you have to make up lies about 'em?"

Horace looked at him with eyes bulging with hate. Jonas stood there and held his gaze, waiting for him to speak. When he didn't, Jonas suggested that he go to bed so that Ruby could clear the table and wash the dishes. Audrey, he said, was going to put the children to bed and he was going to join Sam and Charlie Pace in the yard to start cooking the meat for the following day's July Fourth celebration. "Leave Audrey alone, Horace. Don't say anything to her. Not one word."

"She's my daughter. I can talk to her if I want to."

"She's my wife, and this is my house. You will leave her alone." To Audrey he said, "When you get the children down, you might want to come out and see that…what did Charlie call it? Monument to meat?" He laughed gently, kissed her, and left the room.

Audrey crossed to Horace and kissed his cheek. "Good night, Pa. See you in the morning." She turned to leave the room.

"Audrey!"

She stopped in the doorway but did not turn to face him.

"He hit me once. Did you know that? He hit me."

She nodded her head, acknowledging that she heard him or knew that Jonas had hit him—he didn't know which—but still she did not turn or speak, and when he didn't say anything else, she crossed the hallway and went up the stairs to her children. For her part, Ruby waited until she heard Horace Edwards slowly and heavily climb the stairs before she entered the dining room.

———

– Belle City –
Ruthie

Why do I have to take French if I already know it?" Jack demanded. "The teacher already said she was impressed with my fluency."

"Easily impressed, is she?" Ruthie said, as she drew a red line under a sentence Nellie had written without a single mark of punctuation. Mackie snickered and Jack, who hadn't understood the sarcasm in his mother's remark, now realized that there was more to the words than the words themselves.

"Why are you at the homework table anyway?" he demanded of Mackie.

"Where should I be?"

"You're in college. You don't have to do homework."

Mackie laughed. "They give you more homework in college than ever. It's so much that sometimes I don't even go to sleep. I just read and study all night long."

All of the other children stopped what they were doing and looked at him. Then they looked at their mother. "Is that true?" Nellie asked, face wrinkled in consternation, "'Cause if it is, I'm not going to college."

"You haven't even gotten to high school yet," Thatcher said, head down, eyes, as always, focused on what he was doing or thinking. "It's too soon for you to be worrying about college. Anyway, you have to go. We all do."

Ruthie gave him a surprised, quizzical look, which he didn't see because his eyes were on his book. He was her dreamy child, the one always reading or thinking, the one always wondering why or what if, and he rarely interjected himself into the arguments and disputes of the other four, so she hadn't realized he was attuned to the discussion at the table. Mack thought it was because he was the middle child—he was younger than Mackie and Wilton, older than Jack and Nellie—and therefore unable or unwilling to take sides. Ruth didn't think that was the case.

She'd witnessed all four of the others, at one time or another, defer to Thatcher and defend him, as if they intuited the specialness about him that Ruthie believed was there, a thing that she could neither name nor define but which bothered her a bit. If it was an aspect of herself that he shared, a preference for solitude over people, for thought over talk, but which he could sublimate in order to share himself with family and loved ones—that was all right, she thought. But along with those inclinations, she knew, was a tendency toward darkness, to harbor deep, dark thoughts. The key for her was not to linger in that place. Not only did she not wish to, there was no opportunity and there never had been—except the one time: When Nellie was killed.

The slammed back door and Mack's rushed entrance halted all discussion and captured all attention. That he hadn't stopped to remove his work boots before crossing through the kitchen into the dining room told them something was wrong, but it was the look on his face that confused the children and frightened Ruth. She stood quickly and rushed to him. "What is it?"

"On the radio. Y'all didn't hear it?" He looked around, realized what they'd been doing instead of listening to the radio. "Oh, yeah: Homework Table. Anyhow, President Roosevelt just announced it. The first ever peacetime draft."

Ruth and Mackie understood immediately but neither of them spoke. The other children set off a clamor, demanding to know what a peacetime draft was, and even after Mack explained it, only Wilton fully understood its implications.

"When?" Ruth asked. "What ages?"

"Starting next month. Men twenty-one to thirty-five are supposed to report to their local draft boards to register."

Mackie let out the breath he was holding. He was just twenty.

"What else?" Ruthie asked, and Mack's hesitation caused her stomach to clench.

"If war is declared, all men eighteen to thirty-six will be required to register."

Ruth walked away. Two of her sons—Mackie and Wilton—would be required to register, and to register would mean going to war, and there would be a war to go to. Mr. Roosevelt had just made that very clear. And depending on when the war began and how long it lasted, it could claim her third son as well. There was no point in hoping for what could not happen: That Europe would awaken to peace tomorrow morning. Practically the entire continent had been at war for the last three years...or more precisely, that Hitler had been waging war on the continent for the last three years with nobody much waging back at him. It was almost the end of 1940. The first registrations were required next month, October. Did Roosevelt plan to go to war at the end of the year? Early next year?

She was, she realized, outside, walking, going she didn't know where. Between thoughts, she'd been trying to define what she was feeling and recognizing the irony of what she'd so recently concluded about her middle son. Her own thoughts at this moment were deeply dark. But there was something else, the thing that had so tightened in her stomach that doubled her over. She was angry, more so than she'd ever been, even when Nellie was killed or their home in Carrie's Crossing was stolen by the KKK. She had not imagined anger could be more fierce than that. Yet, in this moment, it was. But anger stood her up straight, prepared her to fight. What she wanted to do now was gather her sons and run...Fear! She felt fear, deep and wrenching, and she hadn't recognized it because she had never in her life been afraid—of anyone or anything.

She should go home. Where was she? She looked around and got her bearings: Four blocks from her house, and it still was daylight; she could see people in their houses and their yards. She knew all of them, and she nodded and waved greetings and wondered how many of them she had ignored just a little while earlier, when her thoughts had owned her. She knew that there were men of draft age in many of these houses. Had they heard the news? Were they angry or fearful? Was it only the women who would be afraid, or would the men, too, feel fear? Did young men feel fear? The men who'd gone to that first war, The Great War, certainly would, for they would know what was in store for them. She remembered Beau saying to Jonas, all those years ago, that he was lucky that his brother had died in France because being dead in body was better than being dead in mind and spirit while still physically alive. Surely if Beau thought he'd have to go to war again he'd be afraid. But Beau now was too old for war. So was her husband. It was just her sons who would be called on to go to a far off foreign place to fight—again—for a country that still hated them, and perhaps always would, just because they were who they were.

Now the anger shoved the fear aside. She wanted to kill them, the ones who made war, all of them. How dare they do this again? Then the anger waned as quickly as it had arisen because she realized that even if it were possible to kill them all, their thoughts and ideas wouldn't die with them; they kept records of their cruelty and some future one of them would read the record and consider it worthy, and she would have damned her soul for naught.

– Carrie's Crossing –
Jonas

Jonas Farley Thatcher, you come down off that ladder right now!"

"But I'm helping, Audrey. Aren't I, Sam?"

Sam looked from one to the other, a sly grin spreading across his face. "Well, now, Miss Audrey," he said slowly, "he does have his uses, Mr. Jonas does."

Audrey gave them both the same disgusted look. "Men. You all stick together, don't you?" She stalked away to sound of their giggling, glad they couldn't see her own laughter. Jonas was as excited as the children, stringing white lights around the roof of the stables and in the trees and on the house. They'd decorate the inside tree tonight. It would be a family affair: Rachel and Cory and their children would join Audrey and Jonas and their children. They'd sit in front of the fireplace and drink hot cider and sing carols. That their family wasn't as large as some others weighed like a boulder on both of them, but, they told each other, some family was better than none, and they both were grateful for sweet, gentle Rachel. Audrey said that Jonas and Rachel were as they were because of his mother, while she was, as she put it, the only sane one in her family because both of her parents were crazy. Jonas had had no contact with Esther and her husband, Caleb, since he fired them the night of Zeb's death. He knew they lived somewhere near Stevensville, but he didn't know exactly where, and if Rachel hadn't asked about Esther, he'd not have thought about her. His entire focus was on the holiday season and the Christmas Eve party they were having. Already, Jonas and Audrey's July Fourth and upcoming Christmas Eve functions had taken on tradition status: There'd been but one July Fourth party and this would be the first Christmas Eve gathering, but an invitation was a sought-after commodity, and the assumption was that the success of the parties would be the *raison d'être* for their continuance.

Audrey was not so secretly pleased that, without having tried, she'd succeeded in becoming an important social arbiter in Carrie's Crossing and was becoming known in Belle City though over there, birthright and family both were as necessary as money for social standing, and, as Jonas forthrightly would acknowledge to any who asked, he and his wife were just a couple of country crackers who'd made good. But they were well-matched in their dislike of pretension and had no desire to traverse the Belle City social circuit. They took great delight and joy in their children, and Jonas in his work. His success as a developer was well-known, and he owned and developed property in three states. That was the only negative to Jonas's way of thinking: That his business more and more often required him to travel. He took Audrey and the children with him when he could—to Nashville and Memphis and Charleston—but as often as not, the land he purchased for development was undeveloped or rural; he'd slept in his car more than once.

Baby Alice did not yet understand Christmas, but she felt the excitement in the house and reacted to it. JJ understood full well what was happening and was so enthused at the prospect of decorating the fifteen foot fir in the living room that he threw up his lunch, refused to take his nap, and by supper time was so cranky that Jonas had to carry him around like a baby, whispering and singing to him, until he finally dropped off to sleep, where they'd leave him until Rachel and Cory and their children arrived.

Jonas was every bit as excited as JJ. He didn't throw up his lunch and he was anything but cranky, but he refused to sit down, even for a moment. He had never had a Christmas like this. During his growing up, his ma was so often sick that skipping special days was the rule rather than the exception. Then there was the question of money: There wasn't any for the buying of presents, even if Zeb had been inclined to treat his children to the myth of St. Nick or Father Christmas or, as Zeb called him, Sandy Claws, as in, "There ain't no such person as Sandy Claws bringin' presents to nobody." Jonas vowed that for as long as his children were inclined to receive the myth, he'd be inclined to foster it. Audrey felt the same way, though she had, throughout her childhood, enjoyed a whole season of merrymaking: "From Thanksgiving straight through to the New Year!" Her parents believed in celebrating and in providing elaborate gifts for their children. Jonas had to give Alice and Horace credit where credit was due, and the truth was that the three Edwards children knew that they were loved. No child could ask for more, and no child could ever get over the feeling of not being loved if he never knew that feeling.

Jonas burst into the house, grabbed Audrey by the hand, and pulled her toward the kitchen door. He beckoned to Ernestine and Ruby. "Y'all come see the lights. It looks like paradise."

From the Dairy of Jonas Farley Thatcher December 9, 1941

My thoughts alternate between what happened at the Pearl Harbor navy base the other day, and my memories of last Christmas—it was the best one of my life. We could not know that it would be the last good Christmas for a while. We'll put the lights up this year— Audrey says we should for the children's sake because they don't understand war but they do understand Christmas and we shouldn't ruin it for them. I suppose she's right, but I can't summon the feeling. All that death and destruction. And of course we are a country at war now. Hitler and Tojo wanted a fight. Well, now they've got one, and I think they'll be sorry. I know nobody can predict the future, but I think this war is going to change everything— for us in America and for everybody around the world.

From the Recorded Memories of Ruth Thatcher McGinnis

Pa and Beau showed up early on the morning of December 9th. They had driven all night. Beau said he figured the police had more to worry about than the two of them, and he was right. All the police in all the coastal states were on alert, charged with guarding the coastline in case of a second attack. Nobody was asleep when they arrived because none of us had been to bed. We had spent the entire day listening to the radio, absorbing every bit of news that was broadcast. They walked in the door, and I started to cry. I had never shed tears in front of my children, but this time I couldn't help myself. I wept for Beau who should never have had to think about war again, and even though he wouldn't have to go, two, perhaps three, of his nephews would, and that was all but destroying him. He wept with me, and so did Pa. We were so distraught that Mackie and Wilton begged us to stop. They said we were frightening them, and they didn't want to be any more scared than they already were. As I remember that day, and I recall it in vivid detail, I'm aware that I have to work at not sounding platitudinous…oh, Sissy, you know how you all are always chiding me for being able to put a positive spin on every event? Well, there was a positive aspect to Mackie and Wil being called up—no, really there was. See, they both were in college, and there weren't very many Black men in college in 1941, and they both were fluent in French. The army hadn't been integrated yet, but there were some divisions of Black soldiers being trained for more than menial and manual labor. And of course when the real fighting started, the French army was only too pleased to have Black soldiers fighting with them. But—before that, the army had established the first flight school for Black pilots at the base in Tuskegee. That's right, you now know them as the Tuskegee Airmen, but in 1941, it was an experiment that the army fully expected to fail. They did it because the NAACP and the National Urban League had threatened to bring a hundred thousand Black people to Washington to protest the situation in the army and in the defense contracts. It was just like World War I all over again and people weren't going to stand for it. So, to start out, Mackie and Wilton went to Tuskegee and taught French. They also taught our soldiers how to recognize other European languages—German and Italian—how to tell the difference between our Allies and our enemies.

From the Diary of Jonas Farley Thatcher

July 2, 1942. Here is something I never would have thought could happen, but it did: Horace is now more of a pain in the neck than he was before. He can't stop telling everybody who'll listen—and a few who have tried to ignore him—how smart he was to see early on that war was coming and how to capitalize on it. He stands to make quite a lot of money, and he is very happy that he doesn't have to share it with me. He keeps saying over and over how he wanted me to partner with him and how I wouldn't do it, and how I'm missing out on a big payday. Audrey threatened not to invite him to the July 4th celebration if he didn't stop talking about his money. We discussed not having a party this year, but people wanted us to do it. They said it was more important now than ever to celebrate the U.S. of A, and I suppose that's true. One thing for sure: We won't have as much food as we did last year. Everything is hard to come by now—Horace will tell you that. There's talk of rationing, which has been happening in Europe for years now. But what is important is not how much food we have but the fellowship, and there will be plenty of that. And, best of all, Charlie Pace and me get to spend the night cooking on the Monument to Meat. Well, not all night like before because we don't have that much meat this year, mostly just chickens and half a pig that Charlie butchered up real good. We do have a lot of whiskey, though, most of it left over from Christmas, and Sam got us some fireworks, so I expect we'll make a good time of it. Happy Birthday USA!

– Belle City –
Ruthie

Ruth walked every day for hours, with no particular destination or reason. After she took the younger children, Jack and Nellie, to school—Thatcher walked by himself to Booker T. Washington High School—she walked because it was better than sitting at home and thinking. Of course she thought as she walked, but as there were things to see and people to talk to, sometimes even activities to engage in (she occasionally taught French to young girls at the Phyllis Wheatley YWCA and watched the tennis matches at Washington Park, and on Friday evenings she was in the Episcopal Church parking lot when the BCCCTC cars returned), she could free her mind of the dark thoughts, of wondering exactly where Mackie and Wilton were, whether they were injured or frightened, whether they were too cold or too hot, wet or hungry or dirty, whether they were still in France. That's the thought that was most destructive to her equilibrium: That her boys would not only be fighting a war, often surrounded by people who should be companions but who hated them as if they were the enemy, but could be in a place where they could not understand what was being said. At least in France, she told herself, if they met soldiers not wearing the uniform of the U.S. Army, they'd understand what was being said.

Mack had stopped telling her that it didn't matter what language somebody aiming a gun at you was speaking, and he brushed aside her argument that French soldiers would not be aiming guns at American soldiers. He stopped short of calling her hysterical and made her look directly at him when he made her promise to restrict her marathon walks to the Colored side of town. "I mean it, Ruth. You got to pay enough attention to where you're going that you don't end up in trouble. Promise me."

She promised, and she meant it. It would do no good for her to get into trouble, and she didn't want to worry him. Just as she walked, he worked, usually beginning before the sun rose and working until exhaustion sent him home. Had George Tennison not been at his side, she'd have worried, but she knew that George would keep a close eye on him. She also knew that Mack had enlisted any number of their friends and neighbors to keep an eye on her. She'd even seen Big Mack following her one day, and she'd slowed down so he wouldn't get winded trying to keep up; he was too old to be playing detective.

Most days Pa walked for a while with her. A little exercise was good for him, but too much was dangerous. Because people instinctively were drawn to him, walks with Pa always were punctuated by conversations with people they passed, and more often than not, Ruthie would leave him sitting on someone's porch, sipping something or sampling fresh-baked something, and talking about everything under the sun. She had urged Pa to return to North Carolina so that Beau wouldn't be alone, but he was torn: He wanted to be with Ruthie in case news came about one of his grandsons, but he also needed to be with the son who'd already survived one war and who felt the horror of what was happening in Europe more than any one of them. Ruthie and Mack had each other and three of their children to see them through this war. Beau had no one, and that wasn't right, which is why, they said to Big Si, he should be with Beau.

"Ruthie!"

She stopped, startled, at the sound of her name yelled almost in anger. Then she saw why: Belle was running to catch up and had probably called her name several times. Ruth saw immediately that her sister-in-law had gained weight, and she was breathless when she got close enough to say, "Are you all right? Didn't you hear me calling you?"

"I'm sorry, Belle. No, I didn't hear you. I was just..." Just what? She shrugged another apology. "What are you doing over here this time of day? Is everything all right?" Now it was her turn for concern.

Belle nodded and took her arm. "Are you goin' home? Can I walk with you?"

Ruth took stock of where she was, and she was, indeed, headed home, and she thought that having Belle for company would be a nice change. Big Mack and Clara, she remembered, would have the children for tonight and would take them to church the next day. Mack wouldn't be home until who knew what time. Yes, she thought, Belle would be good and welcome company. For Pa, too.

The old man's warm embrace of his daughter-in-law proved Ruthie correct, and Belle's tears were additional proof to all of them that they had indeed missed each other. It wasn't necessary to say that it was Belle who had removed herself from them, any more than it was necessary for them to admit that their judgment of Belle's activities was likely the cause of her distancing. Their togetherness in that moment was as perfect as ever. She asked for news

318

of Mackie and Wilton, and she accepted, as they all had, that having heard nothing to the contrary of what they had said in their last letter—"they were as well as can be expected in the circumstances and a lot better off than a lot of the other men"— was good news. She asked for news of Beau and expressed her concern about him being "up there on that mountain all alone. Beau might seem to like being by hisself all the time, but he likes it as long as some one of his people is close at hand."

Pa looked at Belle as if the words she'd spoken were hanging in the air outside her mouth, able to be read. Then he nodded. "You right, Belle. Ruthie and Mack been tellin' me for months to go on back to North Car'lina to look after Beau, but 'till you said what you just said 'bout Beau likin' his loneliness just so long as he can reach out and touch me or Ruth or one of his brothers— that's the truth." He remembered what First Freeman said all those years ago about Beau preferring to make his rounds of the city alone, what Toby had told him when Beau first bought the building they shared—they'd only see Beau once a day: First thing in the morning he'd rush downstairs and into the shop and look at them, as if to make certain they were there. He thought of what he knew first hand from sharing a living space with his eldest son: As long as Beau knew that Pa would be home at the end of the day, Beau often would be away from before sunup until well after dark. He looked at Ruthie. "Will y'all drive me back up there? I been away from that boy too long."

Ruthie hugged Pa, then hugged Belle. "I wish I'd thought to say what you just said, and I am so glad you said it. Yes, Pa. We'll go tomorrow. Do you and the children want to go, Belle?"

"No, thank you." Belle inhaled deeply, and it was clear that she wanted to speak, so they waited for her. "I'm goin' back to work at the beauty salon. Ma and Helen and Catherine are gonna help me get it ready to open, and I got a barber ready to take over on...on the barbering side."

Ruth and Pa looked at her but didn't speak. They didn't need to; Belle read their expressions. Surprise, joy, confusion, and finally the question: What brought this on after so many years away? Belle tried to explain, tried to answer all of their questions but found that she didn't really have the words because so much of what was happening inside her was feeling, and she'd never been good at putting her feelings into words. Ruth rescued her.

"Even with the War on, Belle, people are ready and able to get back to taking care of how they look."

Belle nodded. "Most people seem to be back to doing some kinda work.

'Course we still can't get the good-paying jobs in the factories and plants, still can't do nothin' but clean up or cook, but some kinda job is better'n no job, and while people can't buy new clothes or a new car, they *can* buy groceries now, and they *can* look nice, get their hair cut or curled, men can get a barber's shave now and again." She gave a small smile. "You know how we like to look good even if we're doin' bad. That's why people gamble, play the numbers: If they don't have but a dime, they know that's not enough to buy a haircut and a shave or a press and curl, but if they can turn that dime into two bits or a dollar, why, then——"

Suddenly an overwhelming sadness replaced the smile, tears filled her eyes, and she no longer was at Ruth and Mack's kitchen table but in some other place that was not warm and familiar. She wrapped her arms around herself and shivered. "It was that Depression that almost killed us. That did kill Tobias. That was a terrible, terrible time. We couldn't tell y'all everything that was going on. Tobias wouldn't let me tell you. He was proud and 'shamed, both. He wanted y'all to see that he could stand up on his own two feet and take care of his own fam'ly, but he didn't want you to see what the cost was to us." She sobbed and shook, and Ruth and Pa left their chairs to embrace and enfold this woman who had returned to them. Like the prodigal, it didn't matter why she'd left, only that she had returned. But she told them why, and they wished she hadn't.

Throughout the Depression, Belle said, new and increasingly exorbitant taxes were imposed on Colored businesses. Silas told them, before he left for Chicago, that the new taxes were illegal and that collection of them could not be enforced. Toby found out that indeed individual tax collectors were illegally collecting money from Colored store and shop owners and threatening to foreclose on their properties if they didn't pay. Some of the more prosperous businesses could and did pay. Many more were forced to sign over their deeds or leases to people chosen by the tax collectors—people who then would pay the extra "tax." She and Toby paid for as long as they could, Belle said, and when they literally ran out of money, the collector for their area said there was another way they could make payment. "That's when I became a prostitute."

Ruth now wept with Belle, and Pa, in an uncharacteristic and unprecedented display of fury, threw his coffee cup across the room. The sharp sound of the shattering china startled the women. So did the rare profane invective that flew from his mouth.

"Y'all shoulda said something!" Big Si yelled. "Why didn't y'all tell somebody?"

"We couldn't," Belle said, wiping her face, blowing her nose. "Beau already had given us that building. *Gave* it to us. How could we turn around and ask for anything else? And we couldn't lose it. We couldn't do anything else." She sank back down into her chair, deflated. She bent over, head down between her knees, breathing deeply. Then she straightened and faced them. "Besides, if we hadda told Beau what was happening he woulda killed that tax collector. Y'all know that. And we couldn't let that happen either."

After Belle became their regular payment to the tax collector, Tobias changed. He treated her like it was her fault, Belle said, even as she was helping him implement their plan to close the barber and beauty businesses that fronted on the sidewalk and open the gambling parlor upstairs at the back of the building. They'd been open less than a week when the first cop showed up demanding payment. Toby had agreed to pay him weekly if he got rid of the tax collector, which he did. "I didn't have to be a 'ho anymore, but by that time I'd lost my husband. He already was drinking a lot—I think he's the only one of you Thatchers to ever take a drink of whiskey—but then somebody introduced him to the dope and that was that. I had to learn the gambling business and—" she smiled broadly, "I was good at it. I got a real head for numbers. And after what happened with that tax man, I swore no man would ever take advantage of me again, so I ran a *tight* ship. Lots of people thought that with Toby the way he was, they could run over me. They found out different. All but one of 'em, and he didn't run over me as much as I laid down."

As long as Tobias was alive, Belle convinced herself that she was not alone, that she had a husband and her children had a father, and she needed this belief to hold on to because by this time, she believed that she had no family. She saw her mother and sisters only if she sought them out because, like the Thatchers, they were disappointed if not disgusted by how she was earning a living. Angered by that response, Belle convinced herself that she didn't care what anyone thought, that she didn't need anyone but herself to take care of herself. Into this mind-set strolled Freddie Lee Durham, the man who is Angel's father. Belle said she fell hard but got up quickly when she realized that Freddie expected her to spend money on him, to take care of him, expected that he would live in her house and eat her food. This in the house where her children lived. She ran home to her mother who, Belle said, called Catherine and Helen and the three women appeared at Belle's door early on a Sunday morning. They awakened Mr. Durham, helped him into his clothes, helped him pack, helped him to the front door and out to the street, where "Ma told him she'd shoot him if her ever came back, and she pulled a pistol out of her purse and fired it. I didn't know Ma even had a gun. I bet ol' Freddie is still runnin'."

"Your Ma is not one to take a lot of foolishness," Pa said appreciatively.

"My Ma is my savior, and I don't know why it took me so long to see that."

"You see it now," Pa said, "and that's what counts."

"She cried when I told her I wanted to stop the gambling stuff and open up my shop again. She's been helping me every day, her and Cat and Helen."

"What can we do to help, Belle?" Ruth asked.

"You know we'll do anything we can," Pa said.

Belle raised her hands. "I don't need no money, if that's what you're askin'. That's one thing I got a lot of, no thanks to Freddie Durham who thought I was gonna spend it all on him. But if I could borrow Miz Hill, I sure would appreciate it, and I'll pay her whatever y'all pay her."

Ruth nodded. The trip to North Carolina and back would take several days. "I'll ask her, but if it's all right with her, it's fine with me."

"One more thing," Belle said. "And if y'all don't like it, I understand, but I'd like to make Angel's name Thatcher. I want her to be a part of this family like the other children. I want her to call you auntie and you grandpa. But mostly I don't want her to know that her ma was such a big fool. I don't regret that child, but I do regret how I got her. I don't want the child to feel like a bastard. She don't deserve that."

Big Si's response was immediate. "No, she don't, and just like we'll always think on you as a Thatcher, we'll think on that child the same way: Angel Thatcher."

"Her name's not really Angel," Belle said. "That's just what I called her before I knew what a devil her pa was. Her name is Emma, after my Ma."

Pa and Ruthie smiled widely. They liked the name Emma much better.

The Grand re-opening of *BELLE'S BEAUTY AND BARBER SALON* took place the week before Thanksgiving in order to, Belle said, "put the idea of bein' thankful for lookin' good in people's heads." It was a strategy that worked. The event took place on a Monday evening, normally the day the shop would be closed. Belle hung balloons out front and inside; she'd hung colored streamers and more balloons. She also served tea and cookies, which earned her enough good will, it seemed, that those who knew about her stint running a gambling house were willing to forget it.

As Ruth surveyed the crowd, she noticed that the appearance of abject poverty that marked the Depression had been replaced by a more genteel poverty, the kind that was commonplace before the hard times set in. She didn't see a single pair of pants held up with rope or string, not a single pair of shoe flaps held together with tape or rope, not a single dress or skirt hemmed with straight pins or purse straps held with safety pins. Most of the trouser legs and suit jackets and dresses and skirts were shiny from use and wear, and certainly no one wore the fashion of the day, but all were clean and pressed. With one exception: Belle's new barber. The man looked like a picture from a magazine—like Duke Ellington or Count Basie. She watched the response of the women to him, and, in that moment, she caught Belle's eye and gave her a wide smile: Hiring this man was a stroke of genius. Women could not sit in his chair, but they'd come to the shop, sit in Belle's chair, and watch him. Perhaps a few of the single women might warrant a dinner invitation. She leaned in and whispered her thoughts to Mack, who threw his head back and laughed out loud.

"What?"

Mack took her arm and walked her away from the crowd and into a corner. She was, he said, exactly right about the barber's attractiveness to women, and he probably would be a draw but only if Belle could keep him under control. "The women may come in the shop to see him, but it's the men he'll be interested in."

It took a moment for her to understand his meaning, and when she did, she hissed at him, "Mack McGinnis. You should be ashamed of yourself. You can't know a thing like that simply by looking at a person."

"Yes, you can, Ruthie. Not all the time, but often enough. In fact, it's one of the few things that you *can* tell about a person just by looking at him."

Ruthie looked again at the young barber, and the only thing she saw that made him different from the other men in the room was that his suit, shirt, tie and shoes looked new. They were not as elegant as Mack's, and Mack never would have worn those colors—they were too flashy, too attention-getting—but there was nothing else to set him apart. "Where did Belle find him?"

"He worked for her in the other place."

"Is he any good as a barber?"

As if he'd heard the question, Ruthie saw him beckon to a man who obviously had not had a professional haircut or shave in a while. The man shyly but quickly got into the barber's chair, a look of pure joy on his face. He leaned back and was covered, foot to neck, with a striped cloth that the barber tied in the back. Then, as if by magic, the young man withdrew steaming towels from a shelf and wrapped them around the man's face. So quiet was the crowd that the man's pleasurable sigh was audible. The barber worked his straight razor back and forth along the leather strop, then touched the razor with his thumb. He nodded his satisfaction, then began whipping the shaving cream with the brush. Ruthie knew what he was doing because she'd watched Mack do the same thing a million times, but there was something mesmerizing about watching a stranger being shaved by another stranger. Especially with a straight razor.

The young barber worked swiftly and surely, giving the chosen-at-random man a close, smooth shave, followed by a close, neat haircut. He patted lotion on the man's face and brushed his neck with talcum powder, whipped off the draped cover, and took a bow to the applause that filled the room. The women hovered while the men shook his hand and slapped him on the back. He received the praise graciously and gratefully. No matter his proclivities, this young man, Ruthie thought, would be a fine partner for Belle.

Ruthie and Mack and Belle's mother, sisters and children—and the new barber—were the last to leave. Belle introduced him: James Jackson was his name, and he smiled broadly when Mack announced that he'd be in once a week—at least—for a shave. "No reason for me to shave myself when you're right in the neighborhood."

"I hope everybody that was in here today feels that way," Belle said.

"I don't think you'll be hurting for business," Mack said, hugging Belle.

"How's Pa?" she asked. "And Beau? Y'all heard from 'em?"

Ruthie nodded. "And from Mackie and Wilton." Everyone followed an unspoken and unwritten rule: They didn't ask about the boys, but Ruthie and Mack told everybody when a letter arrived, took the letter and showed it and shared it.

"Oh, let me see," Emma Johnson exclaimed, and she took the letter and held it to her breast before she opened it. She read slowly, one word at a time, touching her finger to the paper, as if touching the words could bring Mackie and Wil closer to her. She truly did love the Thatcher boys like sons. "I'm so glad they're together," she whispered like a prayer, returning the letter to Ruth.

They all were glad they were together. It was the one aspect of their being in the Army that was positive: They were together. They could take care of each other, protect each other. They both wrote, so the letters were long and chatty and by reading between the lines, Ruthie could tell how they really were, aside from the hungry, cold, hungry, dirty, and hungry they always were.

"I expect it'll be busy in here right on through to Thanksgiving," Mack said, his arm around Emma Johnson. "But we'll be looking for all of you at my ma and pa's for dinner," he said as he and Ruthie took their leave. Then he turned and looked directly at James Jackson. "And you're welcome too, Mr. Jackson, if you don't have a place to be."

– Carrie's Crossing –
Jonas

Alice Corrinne seemed to know the exact second when all the adults were looking the other way. That's when she shimmied out of her highchair and on to the dining room table where her birthday cake held the center spot. She crawled over to it, sat down, and plunged both hands in. When her mother turned to see what she was doing—one of those moments when parents realize that the silence is unnatural—the little girl looked like a chocolate-covered bunny. Audrey shrieked, which caused Jonas to drop the camera he'd been loading film into. JJ hurried over to Baby Alice and the cake and grabbed his own hand full and stuffed it into his mouth before his parents could stop him. Ernestine, just coming into the room carrying a cylinder of fresh-churned ice cream, began to laugh so hard she gave herself hiccups and ran out of the room, which caused Ruby to hurry in to see what the trouble was. By this time, everyone was laughing hysterically, and it was into this scene that Alice and Horace Edwards arrived with birthday presents for little Alice Corrine.

Audrey, gradually bringing herself under control, went to greet her parents, while Jonas, who'd finally gotten the camera loaded, began to take picture after picture of the two children with chocolate all over themselves, eating cake with their hands. JJ started to sing happy birthday and everyone joined in.

"Allie! You're three years old," her mother exclaimed.

Alice held up two chocolately fingers. Audrey held up three fingers. Allie looked at Audrey's hand, then at her own, and added a third finger. "Three. I'm three."

JJ gave her a big kiss, then turned and started to run from the room.

Jonas grabbed him. "Where you goin', Buddy?"

"To tell Ernestine to bring the ice cream. You got to have ice cream with cake."

"Don't touch anything, and ask her to bring a bunch of wet towels."

"Yes, Papa!" he yelled and jetted out of the room.

"Aren't you gonna say hello to your grandma and grandpa, Alice?" Horace asked as he approached the little girl and her cake.

"Want some cake, Gran'pa?" She grabbed a handful and offered it to him, and Horace backed away.

"No, Alice, I don't think I want any cake."

"Papa want cake?"

Jonas, still snapping pictures, leaned in and let her shove cake into his mouth. "Ummm, good cake, Allie."

"Ruby did it."

"Ruby's a very good cake baker."

Ruby and Ernestine came in then with ice cream, bowls and spoons. They both spoke to Horace and Alice, who ignored them, though they didn't react, by now being used to the rudeness. Besides, Ernestine had opined, "them not speaking was better than what came out of their mouths when they did speak."

They all sang happy birthday to Alice again, and, cleaned up now, she opened her presents—with JJ's assistance and supervision—and, after thanking and hugging parents and grandparents, she took her presents and her brother and went with Ernestine to play in the solarium; it was too cold and blustery this March day to be outside.

Ruby had made a second cake—a coconut one—for Jonas's birthday and the four adults took coffee and cake to the living room where Sam had laid and lit a fire. It had caught and was roaring like some large beast. Jonas and Audrey sat together on the couch facing the fire, Alice and Horace took the easy chairs flanking them, and they ate cake and drank coffee and watched the fire. The peace and quiet was an unusual and welcome interlude, one that didn't last long because Horace abhorred silence.

"Jonas, you remember I told you about those three lots of wool socks I got a line on? In a warehouse some place in New Jersey? You remember me telling you 'bout it?"

"I remember."

"I bought 'em and turned around a sold 'em at a two hundred and twenty percent mark up. Now I got a line of long underwear that I'm gon' put out to bid. Every army's gonna want 'em, and now's the right time to offer 'em, just before it gets warm. They'll want to be prepared for next winter."

"Suppose the war ends over the summer? Then what?"

"War ain't gonna end over the summer."

"Doesn't it bother you to be taking advantage of other people's misery?"

"Take a good listen, Alice, to the sound of sour grapes," Horace chortled.

"What are you talking about, sour grapes?"

"You're mad now, Jonas, 'cause you didn't get in on the ground floor.

I'm makin' money hand over fist and you're left in the dust—"

Audrey jumped to her feet. "Pa, stop it. Always talking about money, how much you have, how much you made. Can you talk about anything else?"

"You always take his side. Seems to me you'd be worried about all the money he's losin' 'cause he wouldn't go in with me on this idea. But don't matter to me. I'm happy to keep it all to myself."

"If you only knew how ridiculous you sounded."

"Audrey Edwards!" Alice sat up straight, glaring at her daughter. "That's about enough of talking to your pa like that. It's disrespectful."

"That's all right, Alice, she'll see the error of her ways one of these days soon."

"Listen to this, Pa, and listen carefully: Last week, Jonas sold—"

Jonas reached toward his wife. "Audrey—"

"I'm going to tell him, Jonas. He needs to hear it."

"Hear what? What did you sell, Jonas?"

"Some beach front property in Florida. Miami Beach, Florida."

"We don't own no property in Miami Beach. Not down there with all them Jews."

"Not *we*, Horace, me. I bought the land with my own money—with our money, Audrey's and mine—two years ago."

"And we just sold it for one and a half million dollars. That's what we put in the bank. So don't ever say again that Jonas needs you or your money or your deal."

Horace and Alice sat with their mouths hanging open, Alice in amazement, her husband furious. "I better not find out that was a Edwards/Thatcher deal, or that you used any company money for that."

"Shut up, Horace," Jonas said wearily.

Ignoring the admonition, he looked at his daughter. "You keep sayin' *our* money. If some of it's yours, what do you get to do with *your* money?"

"I'm starting my own business," Audrey said and enjoyed a couple of minutes of complete and total silence.

"What kind of business?" Alice asked.

"Interior decorating," Audrey answered. "It seems that I'm good at it."

"Who told you that?" Horace spat.

"I did," Jonas said. "Mack McGinnis did—"

"You think you're some kinda interior decorator 'cause some nig— some jig said so? Where's your common sense, girl?"

"Too bad you can't find it in yourself to be proud of your daughter, Horace, but for the record, she's decorated seven homes and right now is consulting on three others." And in case there was doubt, Jonas named names and invited his in-laws to call Audrey's clients to check if they didn't believe him.

More silence followed during which Ruby came in with the coffee pot and plate of cake. Jonas held his cup to be refilled and his plate for more cake. Audrey punched him in the belly and suggested that he'd better start watching his weight. Ruby chuckled and said if she wanted to see what too much cake looked like around the middle, take a close look at Sam next time he was in the house.

"Who's Sam?" Alice asked.

In that instant Ruby realized her error, and Audrey and Jonas thought of how to mitigate it; there was a heavy thud from above, quickly followed by a loud wail. Audrey was on her feet and out the door in a flash, Ruby fast on her heels after shooting Jonas an apologetic glance. Jonas was up too, listening. JJ had added his cries to Allie's, but the volume was decreasing, and Audrey's footsteps had her almost at the top of the stairs. Between her and Ernestine, they'd have the children quiet and playing again in a few seconds. He returned to his place on the sofa, unaware that he was smiling.

"What are you grinning like that for?" Horace asked.

Jonas tried to straighten his face and didn't quite make it. "That Allie has a fully working set of lungs on her." His face broke into a wide grin again. "She's already got her big brother wrapped around her little finger. Did you hear him start up right after Allie started? He cries if she cries."

"I told you you're making a sissy out of him."

Jonas, immediately angry, started to reply, but stopped himself, reaching instead for his cake. He watched Alice and Horace watch him in surprise; both fully expected his defense of himself and his son, and when it didn't come, they were thrown off balance. Audrey taught him that. He wished he'd learned sooner.

Horace recovered and shifted gears. "Why don't you go upstairs and see 'bout Audrey and the children?" he said to his wife: An order, not a suggestion.

Silence reigned upstairs, and they all heard it. Alice looked questioningly at Horace, which he ignored. She, in turn, grabbed a handful of magazines from the basket beside her chair and, ignoring him, began to page through them. He glared at her, which she didn't noticed, engrossed as she was in the *Saturday Evening Post.* "I've never seen this magazine before," Alice said.

"Does Audrey read it often?"

"We both do," Jonas said.

"I've got some business to discuss with Jonas, Alice, so if you don't mind——"

"I've discussed enough business for the day, Horace," Jonas said.

"No such thing as enough business."

"There is for me."

"Why didn't you talk to me about that Florida beach property?"

Jonas gave him a disgusted look. "You mean the beach property down there with all the Jews? *That* beach property? Why would I talk to you about that?"

He gave a Jonas a pained look, then glared again at his wife. "You know I don't discuss business in front of my wife."

"Maybe you should. Audrey's the one who suggested I buy the Florida property. She said it would be a good investment, and she was right."

"All my wife knows about money is how to spend it."

Alice didn't seem to have heard him, but Jonas knew better. "You're probably wrong about that, Horace, as you are about so many things," he said, and the twitching of Alice's lips proved his point.

"Horace wants to borrow some money, Jonas, to buy that lot of long underwear. Most of what he made selling the socks he owed out, and the rest he put down on that underwear. But he'll lose that if he can't pay the balance when it comes due." Alice had said all that without ever raising her eyes from the magazine, so she didn't see the look Horace gave her—a mixture of awe and anger. An unusual feat, Jonas thought.

Horace sputtered a bit before he could form words. "How do you know all that?"

Alice looked at him. "Just because you treat me like I'm stupid doesn't mean that I am. If you treated me like Jonas treats Audrey, I could be some help to you, keep you from making a fool of yourself some times. Like now, for an instance: Jonas is *not* going to lend you any money, and Audrey won't, either."

"What won't Audrey do?" she said coming into the room, resuming her place on the sofa beside Jonas.

"Lend your pa eleven thousand dollars," Alice said.

Audrey froze in the motion of leaning forward to retrieve her coffee cup. The look she gave her mother was priceless. "How do you know Pa wants to borrow money? And from me?"

Jonas got up. "I told you I was done discussing business for today, Horace, and I meant that. I'm celebrating my birthday and my daughter's birthday. No more talk about money today."

"Then I won't talk to you, I'll talk to my daughter, if that's all right with you."

"I don't care what you do, Horace."

"Do you care what she does with *her* money?"

"She can do what she wants to do," Jonas said and left the room.

"Well, now," Horace said, face creasing into a wide grin. He clapped his hands, then rubbed them together, then leaned forward and placed his hands on his knees. "It'll just be for five, six months, then I'll pay you back with interest—that is if you charge your pa interest."

"All these years and you still don't listen to your wife." She leaned toward her mother. "What are you reading, Ma?"

"This *Harper's Bazaar* magazine. You surely do have some interesting ones."

"What does that mean, Audrey? You *are* going to lend me the money."

"No, Pa, I'm not."

"You have to, Audrey. I'm in some real trouble here."

"I'm sorry, Pa. I really am. Maybe you should learn to save instead of spend."

"I don't need advice from you," he snapped, and she wished again, for at least the millionth time, that her husband would end the partnership with her father. She knew he continued it for her sake, but she'd gladly release him from that sense of obligation

The opportunity presented itself the following morning. Jonas and Rachel were doing a brisk business at the store when the phone rang. Jonas answered to hear Grady Allen's secretary ask if he'd be kind enough to come to the bank right away. Whipping off his apron and donning his hat and coat, he whispered to Rachel that he'd return as soon as possible and hurried out the front door, not bothering to get his car that was parked in the back. He half walked, half ran to the bank, unable to imagine why Grady would want to see him in a hurry. Not bothering with the bank's front entrance, he knocked at the back door—Grady's private entrance—and it was opened almost immediately by a man Jonas had seen before but did not know. The man didn't speak but beckoned Jonas to follow him into Grady's office, where he was surprised to find the old banker seated on the sofa while the man sat behind Grady's desk.

"Hello, Jonas," Grady said, and Jonas risked rudeness to stare, which netted a wry smile and the wave of a bony hand. "Look like hell, don't I?"

He looked like death, Jonas thought, then realized how right he was: Grady Allen was as near death as it was possible to be and not be tethered to a hospital bed. "Grady… I don't know what to say. I'm so sorry."

He waved his hand again. "Nothing to be sorry about, Jonas. I've lived a full life and am as ready as any man to go meet his Maker. But while I'm still able, I wanted to introduce you to Randall Woodbridge, the new president of the Carrie's Crossing Branch. Randy, this is Jonas Thatcher, one of this bank's most important clients, and an old and dear friend. I've known him since he was a boy."

Jonas shook hands with the new bank president and wondered how closely he was related to *those* Woodbridges. He'd have to ask Audrey or, better, Alice. "Welcome to Carrie's Crossing, Mr. Woodbridge, and congratulations."

"Thank you, Mr. Thatcher. I look forward to doing business with you." He looked at Grady, who nodded, and continued. "I'll be doing things a little differently, and I just wanted to say that to you in person."

"How different? Different enough that I'll have to withdraw all my money from your bank?"

Woodbridge paled. "Good heavens, no." And Grady Allen, deathly sick as he was, managed a dry chuckle.

"Horace was in here this morning trying to get some money out of you all's business account. You know how he does."

"That account requires two signatures, Mr. Thatcher, and I'll enforce that rule. That's what I meant about doing things differently. In the past, I know Grady would call you to get the OK to release the funds, but I won't be doing that."

Jonas nodded. "That's fine with me, Mr. Woodbridge."

"He also tried to withdraw funds from you wife's account—"

"He what?"

"Of course I wouldn't let him do that, Jonas," Grady said, "but Randy was going to have him arrested for fraud, theft, and a few other things." Grady had clearly enjoyed the spectacle that must have been.

Randall Woodbridge touched a stack of files on the desk in front of him. "I've been carefully reviewing your accounts, Mr. Thatcher, and if you don't mind an impartial observation—?" When Jonas nodded, he went on, "I don't know why you're in business with Mr. Edwards. I see why he needed you— still needs you—but why you need him I don't know."

Jonas looked at Grady who explained the how and the why of the improbable and unlikely Thatcher/Edwards partnership. He also detailed its volatility. Then he gave Jonas a look unweakened by illness and recommended in a strong, clear voice that Jonas buy out Horace and terminate the partnership. "It'll cost you roughly three hundred thousand, but it'll be worth it, both long and short term. And given his love of cash, I think he'll jump at the chance."

Grady Allen didn't live to see it; he died just after Thanksgiving, but Jonas took and followed his advice and by Christmas, the Edwards/Thatcher partnership no longer existed. It cost him and Audrey almost four hundred thousand dollars, and it was worth it. They hung lights on the house and the stable and the trees in the yard; they decorated the huge tree in the living room and had their big holiday party. But what they most enjoyed about that Christmas was planning the January 1944 Grand Opening of the *Audrey Thatcher Interior Decorating Company*. They would write the name in gold lettering on the front window of the no-longer-in-existence real estate development company. Jonas would move his office to the rear of the building—he didn't need a lot of space anyway, he said—and the big front room would be taken up with fabric books and swatches, paint color wheels, and sketches that Mack would draw of potential bathrooms, kitchens and solariums. She would hang draperies in several colors and styles from the walls, and blinds and shutters, too. Audrey was so excited she was vibrating. She was so excited that her father's Christmas present to her—a 1941 Cadillac Darrin—was met with only a mild reaction, which infuriated Horace. "A car like this is hard to come by," he fumed, "and 'specially with Cadillac and all the car companies makin' tanks and fighter planes these days. Only way I came by it is the fella who owned it got killed over there and his folks wanted to get rid of his things. I got it a real bargain price."

"You thought I'd like to have a dead man's car," Audrey said.

"And you found a new way to make a buck off the casualties of war," Jonas said.

Instead of increasing his fury, though, Jonas's remark provided Horace with the entrée he needed to talk about the several new business ventures he had in the works and all the money he would make. As an afterthought, he mentioned his Christmas present to his wife, something neither Audrey nor Jonas had noticed when Alice arrived, and for which they felt an enormous guilt: It was a full-length mink coat, and despite the fact of its total impracticality, it was gorgeous, and Alice was as excited about it as Audrey was about her new business. That they hadn't noticed her wearing it hurt her deeply.

"Don't let yourself become too much like your pa," Alice had said as they were talking in the kitchen after dinner. "Paying attention only to what matters to you."

"I won't, Ma."

"Don't become too much like Jonas, either," Alice said.

"What do you mean?"

"You worry too much about niggers, and I *will* call 'em that 'cause that's what they are. And that's what I mean about lettin' Jonas rub off on you too much: You heard 'em called that all your life and it never bothered you."

"It did bother me. I just didn't know it bothered anybody else."

"They're not like us, and they never will be, no matter how nice you treat 'em. They lie, they cheat, they steal, and they won't do a full day's work unless you're standin' right over 'em with a stick."

Audrey walked away from her mother then, feeling a deadening inside more than anger. She knew that what her mother and father believed was wrong—she had firsthand knowledge and proof that they were wrong— but how was it that more people believed as they did than shared her and Jonas's view?

"Don't think anymore sad thoughts." Audrey hadn't heard Jonas approach. "It's the Christmas holiday. It's almost the New Year, and I've got a resolution for us: From now on, we won't let anybody make us sad or angry. How does that sound?"

"People you love can always hurt you or make you sad," Audrey said. "How do you stop loving your parents? That's the question."

"I don't have the answer to that. I wish I did."

"I have made a decision about one thing, though: I'm giving Pa that car back."

"It *is* a beautiful automobile, Audrey."

"Then you drive it. I don't like it. I feel like I'm in a magazine advertisement and I should be smiling and waving. But the reason that he gave it to me is the reason I won't keep it."

"He gave it to you because he's your father and he loves you."

"Oh, stop it, Jonas. You hate him, and he hates you. You know as well as I do that he gave me the car to spite you, to be better than you, to give me a gift bigger than the gift you gave me, and what he doesn't understand—oh never mind. I'm going to take it back tomorrow and get my old car. I'll say I'm coming to have a New Year's lunch with them, just me and Allie. We'll be back before dark."

Jonas had just convinced JJ to lie down on the sofa and take a nap while he finished the job of undecorating the Christmas tree when the phone rang. JJ's eyes snapped open, and he was wide awake and off the sofa quick as a lightning strike. "I can answer it, Papa," he yelled, running towards the hall. As he was halfway up a ladder, there was no way Jonas could stop him, so he took his time getting to the phone which JJ gave to him. "Grandpa said where is Mama."

"Horace?"

"Where's my daughter?"

"What do you mean, where is she? She's at your house."

"If she was at my house I wouldn't be askin' you where she was."

Jonas's heart was in his stomach, and his stomach had dropped below his knees. "She left here at twelve o'clock, said y'all were serving dinner at one."

"We been waitin' on her," Horace said, bluster gone, replaced by worry.

Jonas couldn't think. She had to be there. Where else could she be? He'd go look for her...but where? Think. Think. "I'm going to look for her," he said and hung up.

"Where's Mama?" JJ asked.

"I'm going to go get her, Buddy, but I can't take you." And just as he thought to ring for Ernestine, he remembered that the three of them were at their own homes and wouldn't return until tomorrow night. He picked up the telephone and dialed Rachel, told her what he could without alarming JJ and found that it was sufficient to alarm his sister. "Your Aunt Ra is gonna watch you while I go get your Mama and Allie," he said.

"Ok, Papa," the boy said, some wise thing within him knowing this was not the time to resist.

Jonas got himself and his son dressed and out the door in record time. There was little traffic; it was two o'clock on Saturday afternoon, the second of January, and still part of the long holiday weekend. Many people wouldn't return home from their New Year's celebrations until Sunday. Rachel and Cory lived halfway between Carrie's Crossing and Stevensville, where Horace and Alice lived, so dropping JJ off was convenient. Rachel met Jonas in the yard, hugged him tightly, told him not to worry about JJ. Then she hugged him again, even more tightly, and the fear inside him turned to terror.

His was the only car on the road, and he took advantage of the opportunity to drive much too fast, thinking and hoping that he'd get to Stevensville and find Audrey seated at the dining room table, eating her lunch. He was paying so little attention to his driving that when the curve in the road straightened, he almost stripped his gears downshifting to stop the car. The road ahead was blocked by two police cars, a truck with a winch, and a hearse from the funeral home in Stevensville. Jonas stopped his car in the middle of the road and jumped out, but then he had to jump back in because he hadn't set the brake. He was just running, not thinking, just running, past all the people standing in the roadway and all the vehicles. Many pairs of hands tried to stop him, and voices called out to him—they even called him by name. He ran until he could run no farther, until he could see clearly what they all saw: The crumpled Cadillac roadster on its side in the ditch, improbably wedged between two pine trees. He didn't remember seeing or hearing or feeling anything else for several days.

– Belle City –
Ruthie

I'm not afraid, Ma," Thatcher said. He was holding both her hands in his, and she studied them, his man-hands, and wondered when they had become such. He was her third child and still a child to her, and yet they wanted him to register for the draft because, as of three days ago, he now was eighteen years old. Her two eldest children—no matter that they were twenty and twenty-two years old, they were and always would be her children—had been two years in the United States Army, and now that Army wanted Thatcher.

"I know you're not, Thatch, but I am. I'm terrified."

"Mackie and Wil are fine, Ma, and I will be, too. Besides, if I don't go register, they'll come arrest me and send me to jail." That was the fate of two of Thatch's friends who'd refused to register, declaring themselves Conscientious Objectors. Apparently that wasn't a designation available to Colored men, for both presently were housed in the Federal Penitentiary.

Bastards! Ruth thought she'd only thought the word, but the look on the faces of her three youngest children and her husband told her she had spoken it aloud. Mack had been dozing beside the fireplace, the book he'd been pretending to read open on his lap. He got up and came to her on the sofa. So did Jack and Nellie, who'd been sprawled on the floor in front of the fire playing Monopoly.

"I'm sorry. I shouldn't have said that. All the preaching I do about not using bad language, and I say something like that. I hope you'll forgive me," she said, looking at each pair of eyes in turn, "and I truly do hope that none of you will follow my example."

"Miss Sadie says that word all the time when she's talking about white people," Jack said. "Dirty bastards, she calls them, all the time."

If anybody had reason for calling white people dirty bastards, both Ruthie and Mack were thinking, it would be Sadie Hill. Still…

"I've heard her muttering to herself," Thatch said, "especially after I've read something to her from one of the newspapers, but I'm surprised she lets you all hear her."

"What does it mean, Ma? That word?" Nellie said.

Ruthie looked at Nellie. The girl's mind never shut down, never even slowed to a walk. There was always something she wanted to know. "It means a despicable, horrible and disgusting person, the kind of person you'd never invite into your home," Ruth said. "And before you ask, it's *always* a bad word no matter who uses it." She looked directly at Thatcher. "Especially your mother, and I apologize for it. I'm sorry and it won't—"

"I think you already apologized enough," Mack said. He looked pointedly at the children. "Don't y'all think your Ma has apologized enough for her mistake?"

"Yes, Pa." This time there were three voices in unison, and Ruthie relaxed.

"I'm going with you tomorrow, Thatch," Mack said. "I went with your brothers, and I'll go with you."

Thatcher smiled his thanks, bravado and bravery on the back burner for the moment. Mack and Ruth already had pulled every string at their disposal to ensure that Thatcher, when he was called up (nobody thought "if" was a possibility) would go directly to Tuskegee. He was a college student fluent in French. The top Colored Army officers would want him close at hand. For what purpose though? To train other recruits or to be used as "eyes and ears on the ground," as Mackie and Wilton were.

"I think I'd like a piece of fruitcake and some eggnog," Mack said, and the children were in the kitchen before he finished his sentence. He gave his wife a tight hug. He didn't speak—no point in telling her not to worry or that everything would be all right. She *would* worry, just as he did, and not a single person, Franklin Roosevelt or Winston Churchill included, could tell them, or any parent, that their sons would be all right.

The following day, the third day of January, 1944, Ruthie took Jack and Nellie to school, then visited Belle, her mother and sisters. The beauty salon was closed Mondays and the women were at home. They knew what the day meant for Thatcher and didn't need to ask her how Ruthie felt; they knew, especially Emma who loved the boys as if they were her own sons. Instead, they talked about their customers—they gossiped about their customers— and shared laughter that more than once grew loud and raucous before turning to behind-the-hand fits of giggling. Then Catherine had shared her good news: She was reuniting with Little Si and moving to Chicago! He'd gotten them a house, she said, next door to a family from Treutland County, Georgia, and in the summer, they kept a garden and promised Catherine all the homegrown fruits and vegetables she could eat. When Ruthie left them, she didn't need to tell them how much she appreciated their taking her mind off her boys for a couple of hours. She didn't know if Mack and Thatcher would have returned home; she thought probably not, so she just walked. The day was cold and even walking briskly, she shivered. Her growing discomfort presented the perfect opportunity to visit the Episcopal Church, something she'd been wanting to do.

The building was stone and not nearly as large as the Friendship or Wheat Street Baptist Churches. The stained glass windows were beautiful depictions of people she did not recognize, Jesus being the one exception. She opened the heavy door and stepped into a warm, aromatic dimness. A deep red carpet covered the floor. A wide center aisle led to an altar. There were rows of pews on both sides of the center aisle, and aisles on the other side of these pews, with smaller rows of pews off those aisles, and adjacent to the walls hung tapestries and art featuring more people unfamiliar to her. She walked slowly up the aisle to the front, to the railing that separated the pews from steps leading up to the altar. She sat in the front row, the deep silence and sweetly pungent scent enveloping her and, she realized, calming her. She was so relaxed that she jumped when she heard her name called.

"I'm sorry I startled you, Mrs. McGinnis."

Ruthie stood up as she recognized the pastor of the church. She had seen him several times, had spoken to him, but she didn't recall his name. He was tall, thin and dark brown, and the oval eyeglasses that he wore made him appear both inquisitive and knowledgeable. His black suit and waistcoat with its stiff white collar gave him an air of authority which he wore with ease but did not seem to require.

"Good day to you, Reverend. I hope it's all right for me to be here."

"This is the House of God, and you are a child of God and always welcome here." He gestured that she should resume her seat and he sat beside her. "Is this the first time you've been inside?"

She nodded. "Yes, it is, though it shouldn't be. It's very beautiful. And very peaceful. And it smells wonderful. What is that scent?"

"Incense. We use it in our services."

Ruthie nodded again but said nothing. Her silence didn't seem to bother the priest; he sat silently beside her, eyes on the crucified Christ above the altar. Ruthie studied the tableau before her, too, though seeking to understand what she was seeing rather than meditating upon it. "What do you think of dancing, Reverend?"

"It's an activity I'd probably think more positively of if I weren't cursed with two left feet. My parishioners enjoy watching me make a spectacle of myself even as they're offering their sympathies to my wife."

Ruthie was shocked. "Your church—the Episcopal Church—doesn't ban dancing or music? You *allow* it?"

He started to nod his head, stopped, and considered. "*To everything there is a season and a time to every purpose under heaven.* There's dancing and there's dancing, there's music and there's music," he said, adding, "though some may call that judgmental."

"I'm speaking of me dancing with my husband, my husband and my sons dancing with our daughter or the boys dancing with their aunts."

"There's nothing wrong with a family and friends gathered before the radio on a Saturday night, listening to Duke Ellington or Count Basie, dancing the night away, just as there's nothing wrong with hosting monthly gatherings here at our Parish Hall. You and your husband are welcome to join us some time. And bring the children."

"What do you think about turning the other cheek?"

He reached into his pocket and brought out a small black book in beautiful, soft leather and gilt edges, opened it, turned a few pages, and gave the book to Ruth. She read as he recited, "*To everything there is a season, and a time to every purpose under heaven. A time to be born, and a time to die; a time to plant, and a time to pluck up that which is planted; A time to kill, and a time to heal; a time to break down, and a time to build up; A time to weep, and a time to laugh; a time to mourn, and a time to dance; A time to cast away stones, and a time to gather stones together.*"

He stopped reciting, but she continued to read to the end: *A time to love, a time to hate; a time of war and a time of peace.* "Today, my husband took our third-born son to register for the draft. Our two oldest boys already are over there. How much is enough, Reverend?"

"It would be easier to take, would it not, Mrs. McGinnis, if we were full citizens in this nation? If by fighting and dying our men were securing our full participation in the democracy they're fighting and dying to preserve? No mother wants to lose a son—or two or three—but she wants even less for those sons to return home alive only to be lynched in their hometowns for daring to wear the uniform of their service branch." He turned the little black book over and over in his hands. "That was my eldest brother's fate upon his return from The Great War. My mother went to her grave wishing he'd died in France."

"Yet you still believe in their God." She could not conceal her bitterness.

"I believe in *my* God, Mrs. McGinnis," he said and smiled gently at the look on her face. "They're not the only ones free to interpret scripture to suit their needs. We only have two cheeks, and after they've both been slapped— *a time to keep silence and a time to speak*—so says the Bible. And my interpretation is that we are duty-bound, obligated even, to speak out against injustice. We can use the Bible against them just as they use it against us. And nowhere in there does it say we have to keep turning the same two cheeks to be slapped over and over again. I don't know exactly how much is enough, but I do know there is such a thing as enough."

She got to her feet. She was warm now and strangely relaxed, comforted. "How long has this church been here?"

"In this location since 1933, but the congregation was born in 1880." He walked with her to the front door. "You'd be most welcome to visit us, either on Sunday morning or at one of our Saturday night socials." In the vestibule, just before he opened the door, he reached into a basket and withdrew a brochure. "Our Church Bulletin for the month."

She folded it, put it in her pocket, then extended her hand. "I feel better leaving than I did when I came in. It's something I'd been intending to do ever since you gave the BCCCTC permission to use your parking lot. I'm sorry it's taken me so long."

He took her hand but transferred it to his left hand. With his right hand he made the sign of the cross over her: "May the blessing of God the Father, God the Son and God the Holy Ghost be upon you now and forever. Amen."

Ruth thanked him for the blessing and hurried down the walkway, not to get away from him but to get home as quickly as possible, for she found that she very much wished to be there with Mack and Thatcher and Jack and Nellie. She listened carefully to what Mack and Thatch said about their experience at the draft board and understood that her son would be called up in the very near future, and that he almost certainly would be sent to do his basic training in Tuskegee, then on to Michigan for more training before being sent to the Front. She learned that basic training could last as long as four months and as little as three, depending on the need for additional troops, and that men who trained together most likely would serve together, just as Mackie and Wilton had remained in the same unit. She hugged her son, kissed him and told him how much she loved him.

"I'll be fine, Ma. Honest I will. I will take care of myself. I'll be careful."

"I know you will, Son," she said, holding him tightly, then releasing him.

"I'm kinda hungry," he said.

"Sadie made soup and baked some bread."

They watched him head for the kitchen, and when he was out of sight and earshot, Ruthie leaned into her husband and wept. He held her tightly with one arm while he dug in his pocket for his handkerchief with the other. She wiped her eyes and blew her nose and told him about her two visits that day. He wanted to call Pa and Beau right away to tell them about Si and Catherine. They'd already decided not to tell Pa about registering Thatch for the draft. Nobody wanted to say it out loud, but Big Silas Thatcher was not in the best health. Just shy of seventy, he didn't hear or see well, and his heart was fragile. Any major news could prove disastrous—good or bad. But they agreed that they had to tell Beau about Thatch. He'd worry but he was the only one of them who could hear a radio broadcast or read a newspaper account of what was happening on the Front and know what it meant. He was the only one of them who could manage not to let his fear show.

Then Ruthie told Mack about her conversation with the Episcopal priest—Bowers was his name; she finally remembered it—Richard Bowers. "Sounds like an interesting man," Mack said when she finished. "And a smart one."

"I want to go to that church on Sunday," she said and froze at the look of horror on his face. Surely he didn't—couldn't, wouldn't—object to her attending service at another church...then she got it: His great-grandparents had been founding members of Friendship Baptist Church, and his family had belonged consistently since then. He probably was gauging the impact her decision would have on his parents. "I'll talk to Ma, Mack. I'm not defecting." At least not yet, she thought.

Clara McGinnis not only understood why Ruthie believed it was a good idea for her to attended a service at St. Paul's Episcopal—out of respect and gratitude for that church's participation in the transportation committee effort, Ruthie had said—but Clara said that perhaps she and some of the Ladies Auxiliary might attend some Sunday too. She drew the line, however, at Mack and the children attending, so Ruthie went alone, a situation she much preferred under the circumstances: She very much wanted to explore and learn more about the Episcopal Church and its teachings, and she'd do that better on her own, not having to talk or explain or justify or share.

The day was cold and clear, and after the service Richard Bowers stood in the door of the church greeting his parishioners. His eyes lit up when he saw Ruth, but before either of them could speak, however, Ruthie heard her name called.

"Dr. McGinnis. What a pleasant surprise to see you here."

The greeting came from a woman who'd already descended the church steps to the walkway but who now returned to the steps. Ruth recognized her as a faculty member in the Fine Arts Department but didn't really know her except to say hello. Not being a full-time faculty member, Ruth only knew most of the faculty casually; those in Foreign Languages she knew better.

"*Doctor* McGinnis?" Reverend Bowers said, taken aback. "And here I've been calling you *Mrs.* McGinnis. I do apologize."

"No need for it. I *am* Mrs. McGinnis and have been since I was sixteen."

"You two are acquainted, Dr. Foster, you and Dr. McGinnis?"

"Dr. McGinnis is part-time on the French faculty, though we have tried— so far unsuccessfully—to convince her to join us on a full-time basis," Frances Foster said; that was her name, Ruthie remembered, and she taught English literature.

"I may finally be ready to be convinced," Ruthie said, surprising herself as she expressed verbally what she'd not even allowed herself to fully think. "My children are all practically grown up—even my babies. I don't think I'll be missed at home if I go to work full-time now."

Given the fact that Episcopal Church services were shorter than Baptist ones, she was home well ahead of Mack and the children, and she reveled in the quiet time alone. Dinner was ready and waiting, so she had nothing to do but think—about the service and about her verbalized admission that she was considering teaching full-time. She lit the fire that Mack had laid before they left, then went upstairs to change her clothes; they wouldn't be going out again today, not even to have dinner at Big Mack and Clara's as they usually did on Sunday. Jack and Nellie returned to school the following day after the Christmas holiday, Mack was half-expected in Carrie's Crossing to help Audrey Thatcher open her decorating business, and Ruthie wanted to be on hand in case Thatcher needed her. He'd already decided there was no point in his registering for Winter semester classes, and Ruthie knew he'd be at loose ends, not certain what to do with himself while waiting for the Army to send for him.

The fire was roaring when she got back downstairs, and she happily settled herself on the sofa beside the pile of books, newspapers and magazines waiting to be read, but as she lifted her feet onto the hassock, she knew she wouldn't read. Her eyes closed and almost immediately she fell asleep. It was a wonderful, deep, peaceful sleep that she didn't awaken from until the slamming of the kitchen door and Jack's running feet announced the return of her family. They all were ready to eat, and by the time they were changed, she had the food on the table, and while they ate, she answered their questions about the service she'd attended, and then told them, when they asked, why she went.

"He said that, the Reverend?" Thatcher exclaimed when Ruth repeated what Richard Bowers said about speaking out against injustice and using the Bible as a tool. The children were awed, especially when they elicited agreement with the sentiment of both parents.

"I wonder if he ever gets scared," Nellie said in a quiet voice. As it hadn't been a question, nobody tried to answer, though both of her parents wished for some appropriate response. The telephone rang, and Thatcher ran for it; every sound now meant the Army was sending for him. They heard him answer, heard him say, 'yes, sir' and saw by his face when he returned that he still was safe—for a while.

"Mr. Atkinson wants you, Pa," he said.

Mack had been expecting Jonas Thatcher and frowned slightly as he went to the telephone. Charlie Atkinson was the large general contractor he'd brought on to help him build Grady Allen's Carrie's Crossing bank. "Happy New Year, Charlie," he said, and listened for just a few seconds when he exclaimed, "You'd better believe it. Just tell me when and where." He took the pad and pencil from the telephone table drawer, wrote an address and directions, said thank you, and all but ran back into the living room. "Charlie's hiring me as his principal sub-contractor on a job big enough for me to put all my guys to work for the next ten to twelve weeks. Looks like 1944 is getting off to a pretty good start."

They were less enthusiastic about President Roosevelt's take on things in his State of the Union speech delivered the following day in the form of one of his Fireside Chats. He had not gone to Capitol Hill to deliver the speech to Congress as usual because he had the flu. So did both of Mack's parents, and all three of them sounded weak and tired. The President called for a continuation of National Service—the employment of civilian war workers. *"It is argued that we have passed the stage in the war where national service is necessary. But our soldiers and sailors know that this is not true... The national war program calls for the employment of more people in 1944 than in 1943."* He also called for what he termed "a new Bill of Rights," the details of which lent themselves to much heated discussion, though there was almost universal agreement that none of the factory and munitions plant jobs would be available to Negroes. "No matter what they call a thing," Big Mack McGinnis said, "if it's got something good to it, we'll never see it, feel it, taste it, or know it."

"But he's keeping them in line, too," his wife argued. She was a bigger fan of the President than her husband. "You heard what he said about putting a stop to those people trying to make a dollar off the war. He called 'em selfish."

"I heard what he said, Clara," Big Mack snapped. "I also know *exactly* who'll get a job at those war factories and who won't. I also know that no Colored people are makin' a dime off this war, so I don't care 'bout his Bill of Rights, old or new."

The words of the President that resonated for Ruth had to do with his suggestion that the end was near: *"We are going forward on a long, rough road—and in all journeys, the last miles are the hardest. And it is for that final effort—for the total defeat of our enemies—that we must mobilize our total resources."* To Ruth's ears, Roosevelt was saying the war was almost over. To Mack's ears, the President was wishing, hoping and praying that the war was almost over, like every other sane person in the world.

"If it lasts more than another year—"

"You don't have to say it, Ruthie; I know it just like you do."

What they both knew—and feared—was that if the war still raged in July of 1945, they'd have to register their youngest son for the draft. Most immediately, however, was the notice that Thatcher received ordering him to report to his induction center on the last day of February. The entire family gathered the night before to embrace the young man and to wish him well, a gathering diminished by the absence of Beau and Big Si—they still hadn't told the old man that his third grandson was heading off to war—but a gathering enhanced by the presence of Little Si, who'd come from Chicago to collect his wife. There was true joy at seeing him, and for the two of them. Catherine would be deeply missed, but all agreed that she belonged in Chicago with her husband.

Ruthie and Si had a few moments together, just the two of them, and for most of that time they simply held each other. Words were not necessary. They were, they knew, thinking and feeling the same things: Past memories, joyful and sad, and funny. Both remembered when their elder brothers, Beau and Eubie, were readying to go off to that other World War and the discussion they'd had with Jonas Thatcher, whose older brother also was heading off to war: Jonas's family having a celebration dinner; Ruth and Si's family not considering it a celebration. More than twenty-five years later, they still didn't.

"How sick is Pa, Ruthie? Please tell me the truth," Little Si said.

"It's not that he's so terribly sick, Si, but where he lives, there's no doctor up that mountain, and no Negro doctor at all for miles. His heart is weak, no arguing that fact, but if we can keep him from experiencing too much emotion, well, then, all the better."

"When I called him to tell him about Catherine and me, he cried, and that really scared me."

It scared Ruth, too, just thinking about it, so she banished the thought, something she got more proficient at every day, being able to not think about a person or a situation, especially painful or disturbing ones. Like where Mackie and Wilton were at any given moment. Like where Thatcher would be in three months after his basic training.

"Do you really like Chicago, Si? Really and truly?"

"I really and truly do. Even the winters. Remember that blizzard—"

"In the Crossing, the first year Mack and I were married."

"We walked to Jonas's Pa's store, Mack and me. Well, that's what winter is like in Chicago all the time. But when you've got the right clothes and shoes— and you've only got to walk a block or two—it's really not so bad. And I've met some wonderful people, people you'd enjoy, people who've been to Europe and Africa. Some of them, of course, are a bit arrogant, and when they find out I'm from Georgia, well, let's just say I've had to shatter a few pre-conceived notions about me and my family. I love telling them about my baby sister with the Ph.D. in French and five children who're fluent in French."

"You don't tell people that," Ruthie exclaimed in mock horror.

"Indeed I do, Baby Sister," Si said.

Everybody went to the train station the following day to see Thatcher off to basic training in Alabama (and the platform was packed with young Negro men—boys, really—with the same destination) and, on an adjacent platform, to see Catherine and Si off to Chicago. Cat wept so hard she got the hiccups. Tears of joy, she kept saying, and her mother and sisters shared them with her. They hugged Si so hard he said he thought he heard a rib crack, and Miss Emma, Cat's ma, said she'd show him a cracked rib, and punched him in the belly. Cat promised to write everybody and to send lots of photographs. Thatch made a similar promise with the caveat that he couldn't start, however, before the end of March.

Ruthie spent that next month struggling to occupy her mind during all those hours of the day she was alone, and on some evenings, after she'd done homework with Nellie and Jack and put them to bed, she was still alone; Mack often left at dawn and didn't return until nightfall. The daily walks helped less and less. The only times she was fully occupied was when she was talking with Father Bowers at St. Paul's and when she was teaching French at the YWCA, and she did neither thing every day, and she needed to. That's when she decided that as soon as there was a staff position available, she'd join the college faculty full-time, if they'd still have her.

That's what she was thinking, wondering on the Friday as she was awaiting the BCCCTC cars from Carrie's Crossing in the St. Paul's parking lot. Suppose she'd waited too long to reach a decision? Maybe she could go back to Ashdale Elementary School where nobody would care about her Ph.D.

"Miz McGinnis, Miz McGinnis. Oh, I'm so glad to see you."

Ruthie brought her attention back to the parking lot and to the three people literally surrounding her, as if to prevent her escape. They were familiar, but she didn't really know them: Two women and a man. The man spoke.

"I'm Sam Johnson. That's my wife, Ruby, and that there's Ernestine Smith. We work for Mr. Jonas Thatcher. I b'lieve he's a friend of yours and Mr. McGinnis?"

"Yes, he is," Ruthie said, suddenly on guard. Something about how these three people were holding themselves—rigidly, tightly, as they were afraid they'd shatter.

"He's in a bad way, Miz McGinnis. Real bad."

"So bad he don't hardly talk to that sweet little boy a'tall, which just makes him cry and cry and cry, poor baby," Ernestine Smith said, weeping uncontrollably.

Ruthie was thoroughly confused. "You're saying Jonas doesn't talk to his son?"

"She don't know, y'all," Ruby Johnson said. "You don't know, do you, Miz McGinnis? 'Bout what happened to Miss Audrey and Baby Alice?"

Ruth's stomach dropped, and she felt dizzy. She shook her head. "I don't know anything about Audrey and the baby. What about them?"

"They dead," Ernestine Smith said, wailing. "They got kilt on the second day of the New Year. The car turned over and run off the road and killed 'em."

"Mr. Jonas, he won't do nothin', won't go nowhere, won't talk to nobody. We keep goin' over there and we clean and cook, just like always, but now one of us takes JJ to school and picks him up. We feed him and bathe him—we always did that—but his ma read him stories and sang little songs to him at night and Mr. Jonas, he don't do none of that. Every time he looks at that little boy, he starts cryin'. Mr. Jonas, I mean, and little JJ don't know what to do. Miss Rachel, Jonas's sister, she come 'round and tries to talk to him, and he'll listen to her—she's the only one he'll listen to—but he don't do nothin' but sit up in that room in the back holdin' a picture of Miss Audrey."

"I'm just glad he ain't a drinkin' man," Ruby said, "'cause if he was, he'd a drunk hisself to death by now."

Ruthie couldn't find words. Sam, Ruby and Ernestine, still in their tight circle around her, watched her, waiting, expecting. Something. "We didn't know." Mack would be devastated. He liked Audrey Thatcher very much. He liked Jonas, too. "I'll go tell my husband right away and we'll..." What? "If you still have the information sheet we gave you at the first BCCCTC meeting, my telephone number is on it. Please call me before you go back on Sunday." She shook each of their hands, thanked them for telling her about Jonas, and hurried home, very much aware of experiencing a complete opposite set of feelings than when she began her walk: Instead of numb emptiness inside, she was too full of feeling and emotion—pain, sadness, loss. A man's wife and one of his children had been killed. Her sons were merely endangered—not dead—and terror was her constant companion. One of them dead? As much as she feared that, she could not imagine it. And Mack: How would he be if she were suddenly killed? Her father had not, in more than twenty years, recovered from or reconciled the murder of his wife. Jonas! Poor Jonas. She ran the last block home as she remembered that Mack now came home early on Friday. He paid his men and let them go just after lunch in exchange for their working half an hour longer Monday through Thursday.

Mack's initial disbelief turned so quickly to so deep a sorrow that Ruthie initially was frightened. She had never seen him display this kind or level of emotion. He dropped on to the couch—literally dropped down, for he didn't seat himself—and put his head in his hands. Sadie had Jack and Nellie in the kitchen and Ruth went to make certain she'd keep them there, then she hurried back to sit beside Mack. Again she found herself speechless, so she waited for him to speak to her.

"I think a lot of Jonas, you know that, but I don't think I know him well. I don't think anybody knows him well—nobody but Audrey. She's the only person he ever let get close enough to know him." He broke off and looked at her. "I would be a lost man if I didn't have you, Ruthie, but I have a lot of people who would try to...I don't know what to call it...try to make me see I still had a reason to live, even if I wouldn't think so. Like we tried to help your pa, remember?"

"I do remember, Mack. I also know he misses her every minute he's alive."

Mack nodded. "But he let y'all help him, his children and his pa, and me and my ma and pa—he let us touch him and hold him—" Mack jumped to his feet. "Beau! He'll let Beau help him. He'll listen to Beau," he exclaimed, running for the telephone.

Beau immediately agreed to come and arrived just after dawn on Sunday, having driven all night. He slept for several hours and awoke with a plan: He would go get Jonas and JJ and bring them back to North Carolina.

"That's a fine idea, Beau," Mack enthused.

"It is a terrible idea." Ruthie fumed, shocking both men.

"Why?" they asked, almost in unison.

"Because of Pa," Ruthie said, her tone of voice indicating that she shouldn't have had to make the point. "It would be too much for him."

"It would be perfect for him," Beau said. "Exactly what he needs. And listen to me before you say anything, Ruthie. Yeah, I know Pa's slowin' down, but I also know he's been feelin' not so useful. When we first moved up the mountain, you know how I was. I needed Pa, no doubt about it. I was a sick man. I'm not sick now, and as much as I love that old man and his good company, I don't need him to take care of me. Now, if he could still farm that land, he'd be all right, but all he can do now is be the overseer, and you know how he'd rather do a thing than tell somebody else how to do it."

Ruthie knew that was true, but what did Jonas and his son have to do with any of that, she demanded to know; how would their presence create a perfect situation for Pa instead of just more for him to worry about? "We try really hard, Beau, to see to it that he has nothing to worry about."

"And he don't like it one bit," Beau said. "He knows you mean well, but he don't like it. Havin' Jonas and his boy there will give him somebody to take care of. He misses that. And you know how he loves children. Yours all just about all grown up—Miss Nell thinks she's the Queen of England—and Jonas's boy is what, five or six? Pa will love it."

Ruthie struggled to curb her anger, and as she did, she was forced to acknowledge the truth of Beau's words, which meant acknowledging the fallacy of her own viewpoint. Forced to take an impartial view of Big Si Thatcher, what Beau said about him was the exact truth: The man did love children, and he was very good at taking care of people, no matter their age."

"But will Jonas go?" Mack asked the relevant question, and both he and Beau looked to Ruth for the answer. Why did they think she'd know? She'd seen him once in twenty-three years. She thought about the boy she'd known all those years ago, and the man she'd seen and talked to just last year. Were the two people different, and who was she to judge?

She looked at Beau. "I think that until Jonas got to know Mack these past couple of years, you and First Freeman were the only two people he had ever trusted and the only people whose opinion he respected. I still think that's true, and I think that even in his grief, if you showed up at his house—perhaps especially in his grief—he'd gladly let you spirit him off to the mountains of North Carolina." Still looking steadily at her big brother, Ruthie said, "Jonas thinks of us as his kin. He thinks of you as the big brother he never had."

"He had a big brother, Ruthie, the one killed in the war."

"But it was you who treated him the way he wanted a brother to treat him."

– Carrie's Crossing –
Jonas

R uby, Sam and Ernestine were standing at the kitchen door waiting for them early Monday morning when Mack and Beau arrived, in separate vehicles, at Jonas's house. As promised, they hadn't told him guests were expected. They also hadn't told JJ, so when the sleepy-looking, pajama-footed boy saw Mack, his face lit up, and he launched himself out of his chair at the kitchen table into Mack's arms, wrapping his pajamaed feet and legs around Mack's waist and his arms around Mack's neck.

"Mr. Mack McGinnis!" he shouted before dissolving into tears. "My mama's dead and my grandpa killed her, and my papa is so sad."

Mack held the little boy as tightly as the child held him, patting his back, rubbing his head, whispering soothingly in his ear. Beau, standing off to the side, explained to the three servants what his plan was. He knew that he could be placing them in a difficult if not dangerous situation. They knew it, too. All of them also knew that the danger, if it came, would not come from Jonas or from his sister. His in-laws, though, were another matter. Jonas had forbidden them from ever entering his home, but that had not prevented them from trying. They had a right, they said, to see their grandson. The only time Jonas roused himself was to refute them. Sam explained all of this to Beau, as well as why JJ said his grandpa had killed his mother.

"If Jonas leaves here with me, some one of y'all is gon' have to stay here to make sure they don't get in this house," Beau said. "Either that or have his sister move in here if Jonas is trusting of her."

Sam, Ruby and Ernestine communicated with their eyes, then Sam said as he was leaving them to go upstairs to fetch Jonas, "Maybe both things. Maybe we stay *and* Miss Rachel and Mr. Cory come stay, too."

In less time than any of them would have expected, Jonas was down the stairs and in the kitchen. He was unshaven, and he needed a haircut, and his clothes hung on him as if on a peg, but the clothes were clean and pressed, and he was clear-eyed. He stared at his guests, looking from one to the other of them.

"It really is you, Beau. I thought Sam had made a mistake."

"I'm so very sorry 'bout your wife, Jonas. Mack has told me what kind of woman she was, and it sounds like you were a very lucky man."

"Luckier than I ever expected or deserved to be," Jonas said.

"We didn't know what had happened—not me nor Mack nor Ruthie—not until Friday night when Sam and Ruby and Ernestine told us. They're real worried 'bout you, Jonas."

Tears began to trickle down his face, and he nodded. He looked at the three of them and saw the concern—and the care—etched in their faces and cursed himself for a fool for not having seen it before. Then he looked at Mack, still holding his son, and the tears flowed. He sat down and buried his face in his hands.

"Miss Ruby, Miss Ernestine," Beau said, seating himself at the table beside Jonas. "I'm right hungry, and I know Mack is, too, and I imagine my friend, Jonas, could do with a little something to eat. If it's not too much trouble—"

The women sprang into action, grateful not only to have a mission, but to have someone to direct it. JJ still clung to Mack, who joined Jonas and Beau at the table. Beau gave Jonas the handkerchief from his pocket, gave him time to wipe his face and blow his nose, then told him what he had planned. "I'll drive you and the boy up there and bring you back when you're ready. Ruby, Sam and Ernestine said they'd stay here in the house while you're gone, look after things. Maybe your sister and her husband'll stay, too."

Jonas nodded, then got up. "I'll go call Rachel and Cory, ask 'em to come." He left the room, and they heard him pick up the telephone in the hall. The five adults in the room exchanged looks of amazed disbelief. JJ must have sensed the exchange because he lifted his face from where it had been buried in Mack's neck and looked around the room.

"Where's my papa?"

"He's on the telephone calling your Aunt Rachel," Ernestine said, reaching for him. "You wanna let me put some clothes on you while Ruby finishes fixin' breakfast?"

The child considered, looking from Beau to Mack, and into the eyes of the three people who'd been his safe harbor since the death of his mother. "Mr. Mack McGinnis, are you going to stay here and eat breakfast?"

"Yes, Mr. JJ Thatcher, I am," Mack replied, releasing him to Ernestine. He first insisted on kissing Ruby and Sam before he left, and waved solemnly at the two guests as they left. Ruby wiped her face on her apron, and Sam cleared his throat several times.

"I don't know how y'all handled this for three months," Mack said.

"We don't, either," Sam said.

"'Cept we didn't have no choice," Ruby said. "We couldn't leave that baby here all by hisself...well, not by hisself, but with Mr. Jonas like he was."

"Y'all are good people," Beau said. "Real good people."

Jonas returned then, pencil and paper in hand. "Beau, if it's all right, can I have your telephone number? I'm telling everybody that I'm going away for a while, to rest." He gave a sad smile. "Funny how everybody thinks that's a good idea and wished I'd had done it sooner." He squeezed his eyes shut and inhaled deeply; he was trying so hard not to cry again. "It's for the lawyer and the bank, to guarantee that Horace Edwards, if he gets wind that I'm gone, doesn't try any funny business."

Beau gave him the number and Jonas left again, back to the telephone in the hallway, as Ruby placed cups, saucers, bowls of cream and sugar, and a fresh pot of coffee on the table. Mack and Beau were finishing their first cup when Jonas returned, and Ruby poured him a cup and refreshed the other two. She gave Beau and Mack a pointed look before turning back to the stove, a look they didn't understand until they watched Jonas staring at the table without seeing the steaming coffee before him.

"How do you take your coffee, Jonas?" Mack asked. Jonas focused on the cup before him but seemed either not to have understood the question or not to know the answer. "Cream and sugar?" Mack asked.

"Yes," Jonas said. "Yes. Cream and sugar but sweeter rather than lighter. Audrey used to say that: Lighter rather than sweeter for hers, sweeter rather than lighter for mine."

"This is a beautiful house, Jonas," Beau said. "Mack had told me what a fine job your Audrey did designing it, but seeing it in person—it's really something."

"Mack had as much to do with it as Audrey did," Jonas said. "That's the truth and you know it, Mack. She had some fine ideas, it's true, but so did you. It's when y'all put'em together that we got this house the way it is."

"It's one of the finest in Carrie's Crossing," Mack said, "and I'll always be proud that I could have a hand in it."

Ernestine and JJ returned then, the little boy fully dressed, his hair combed, eyes sparkling. "'Morning, Papa," he said shyly, standing beside his father's chair.

Jonas scooped him up and hugged him tightly. "'Morning, my favorite JJ."

The boy giggled. "I'm your *only* JJ."

Jonas looked surprised. "Why, I do believe you're right about that." It clearly was a game they'd played often, father and son, though just as clearly, not for a while, and both savored the moment.

Ruby put a plate of sausage, eggs and grits before each of the men at the table, and Ernestine took JJ and sat him on a pile of books in a chair and pushed it up to the table; Ruby placed a plate before him, too. They bowed their heads, Sam said grace, and Mack, Beau and JJ began to eat. Jonas stared at his plate as he had at his coffee, which he'd finally had several sips of.

"You want some more butter in your grits, Jonas?" Beau asked. Jonas looked at the table, surprised to find the plate in front of him. He put a forkful of grits in his mouth but didn't chew for a few seconds. Then he did, swallowed, looked again at the plate. He forked up some eggs. Ruby put a bowl of biscuits on the table and everybody took one, including Jonas. "What kind of jelly you want on that biscuit, Jonas?" Beau said. "We got jelly, right, Miss Ruby?"

"Yessir. We got every kinda jelly you can name. But Mr. Jonas, he likes apple butter 'stead of jelly."

"Me, too," JJ yelled.

"Me, too," Beau added, and, taking the jar of apple butter from Ruby, spread a generous amount on biscuits for everybody. "Is that enough apple butter, Jonas?"

Jonas bit the biscuit, remembered to chew, then bit it again. Ruby's not-quite-so-whispered, "Thank you, Jesus!" was a sentiment shared by everybody in the room.

Jonas's near catatonia returned after breakfast, however, and Mack had to help Ernestine and Ruby pack for him and JJ. Fortunately, no dress-up clothes would be required, and by the time the bags were packed, Rachel and Cory had arrived. Jonas initially seemed surprised to see them but eventually remembered why they were there. He didn't know when he'd return, he said, but thought in a couple of weeks. Rachel told him to take as long as he needed. She thanked Mack and Beau for their "friendship for my brother," kissed him and JJ, and walked with them to Beau's truck.

Beau already had given Sam and Ruby his telephone number and he added Mack and Clara McGinniss's. "If there's a problem, don't call my sister; she's got enough on her mind." That upset all three of them, and they demanded to know what was troubling Miz McGinnis. "Three sons in the army," Beau said. Ernestine and Ruby gasped and grabbed their chests, and Sam muttered darkly under his breath, but Beau heard enough to grasp the intent of his words. He did not intend to wish blessings on the U.S. Army or the Nazis.

Mack followed Beau's truck out of Carrie's Crossing to the junction of the road that led into Belle City and the one that skirted the city to the north and which would ultimately lead out of Georgia and into South Carolina. They honked their horns and waved to each other as they both headed for home.

From the Diary of Jonas Farley Thatcher

Summer 1944. This is the first time I have written in this book since Audrey left this earth and I would not be doing it if Beau Thatcher and Mack McGinnis had not come to my house just before Easter and got me and taken me up to North Carolina. I stayed a whole month. I don't recall much about the first week but I do know that I will forever be truly and deeply grateful for Beau and his Pa, for the two of them took care of me like I was the child, and they looked after JJ like he was their own. Big Silas Thatcher was so much like First Freeman I would sometimes forget that he wasn't, but the one thing he could help me with that no other man I knew could help me with was how to go on living. He didn't know that I had seen him get the news of Miss Nellie's death, and I didn't tell him. What he told me, though, when it was just the two of us talking—him talking and me listening—was what I imagine it would be like listening to God. So much kindness and goodness and wisdom, right alongside the all the pain and sadness that had never left him. One thing he told me that I'll never forget was to be grateful that I'd had Audrey in my life. Instead of being sad and mad, he said, be thankful that we'd had those few years together. Imagine your life without her at all. It was those words that helped me find the way to put my son back in my heart, and I'm glad I had Big Si to help me, and my little boy couldn't have done better than to have Beau, a man who didn't have any children of his own but who knew how a good Pa loved his children, do that same thing for my little boy. I'll also never forget how Mack McGinnis was holding him that morning they came to my house—holding him like a man would hold his own son, like I used to hold mine before I lost his Mama—like I do hold him right now, today. They can say what they want, think what they want, but those people are my kin, my family and there's nothing I wouldn't do for any of them. We're going back up to N.C. next week to spend Labor Day and this time, Ruthie and Mack and their children and Mack's ma and pa will be there. JJ is so happy. He wants to live there.

From the Recorded Memories of Ruth Thatcher McGinnis

My biggest challenge during that time—the war years—was learning to occupy my mind in a constructive way. As I spent more time with Father Bowers, I got to know his wife, Eleanor, and she became a real lifeline for me. She was the first person to tell me to stop trying not to worry about Mackie, Wil and Thatch. She said that would be unnatural for a mother to not worry about her children, especially if those children were in a perilous situation—and war certainly is perilous. She asked if she could make a suggestion, and of course I said I'd welcome it. Think about them, she said—think about which one is the funny one, the serious one, the cutup. Think of special moments I'd shared with them, she suggested. In other words, she said, rather than worry or fear, let happy memories guide my thoughts. It was advice I gladly took, so instead of picturing fiery bombs and spurting blood and shattered limbs— which is what I'd been seeing in my mind—I saw my boys not as fodder for the Nazis but as my wonderful sons. I saw them as alive, as living, rather than dead. Taking that approach helped me more than I can tell you, and it also helped my relationship with Mack and with the children I still had at home. I wasn't fully aware of how my fear for the three who were away was affecting my love for the two who were at home. With Mack's blessing, I began teaching full-time at the College and with that, stopped seeing myself as useless. Oh indeed, that is how I felt, Sissy. My three eldest children were at war and my two youngest were teenagers in high school. My husband, thankfully, was so successful that he worked non-stop. And what did I do? I walked. I was studying theology a bit—just a bit, mind you—but only for my own edification, not to benefit anybody else. Periodically I would recall the surprise with which Father Bowers called me Dr. McGinnis, and the ease with which I shrugged off his apology and claimed my Mrs. status, as if having earned a Ph.D. was of no importance. My brother left his home and his family because people hadn't respected that achievement. And speaking of Si. One of the things my newly-formulated self did was accept his invitation to visit him and Cat for Thanksgiving. Mack, Jack, Nellie and me took the train to Chicago.

I had a few very rough moments during the trip, though. It often happened that the passenger trains would slow down and change tracks to give the right of way to the troop trains. I'll never forget the sight: Train cars packed with boys—and that's what they were, Sissy—boys, children, looking like they were playing dress-up in their uniforms, on their way to war. People waved at the trains and saluted them. And many people wept. All of the boys on the trains we saw were white, and I wondered whether, when the trains carrying my sons passed through towns, anybody waved at them or saluted them or wept at the sight of them. It required every ounce of resolve within me not to allow those thoughts to ruin that trip for Mack and the children—especially them.

From the Diary of Jonas Farley Thatcher

Christmas 1944. I'm having to really force myself to have any kind of Christmas at all, and I'm only doing it for JJ. I can't bring myself to string all those lights everywhere even though Sam said he would do it. It would remind me too much of Audrey. I also can't have the big party, either. I will get a small tree for the living room. I told JJ we'd go into the woods and cut a pine. I'll let him pick it out and we'll decorate it and I'll put all the presents under it—his and the ones he got for Ernestine, Sam and Ruby. I spend all the time I have alone trying to make myself remember the wonderful Christmases I had with Audrey instead of missing her so much this Christmas. And I don't know how I'm going to get through New Year's. Beau said I could go up to N.Carolina if I wanted to. We would be by ourselves, me and JJ for a few days. Beau and Big Si are in Belle City for the holidays which makes me wish all over again that I was part of a big family like that. That's what me and Audrey were building, a big, loving family. But that's all gone now. I don't think I would mind being at Beau's place by myself but I don't think JJ would like it much. He loves following Big Si around, talking to him about what all the fruits and vegetables are and going into the woods with Beau to hunt and fish. I had all but forgot how to do those things but I am remembering. Maybe I could take my son hunting and fishing. I'll ask him if he wants to go. And I will stop feeling sorry for myself long enough to call Mack and Ruthie to say merry Christmas. I still feel bad that I didn't know their boys were in the War. Just like they still feel bad they didn't know about Audrey and Allie. We promised to stay in better touch.

– Belle City –
Ruthie

Christmas dinner at Big Mack and Clara's brought a full house. Not as full as in the past but full enough that there were two adult tables and two children's tables and every seat was taken; full enough that Clara beamed her satisfaction as two turkeys and two hams and four dozen yeast rolls were devoured, in addition to the too-many-to-count platters and bowls of greens and green beans, squash soufflé, mashed potatoes, candied yams, beets and turnips and carrots. Big Si and Beau were there and brought with them deer meat cooked over a spit, and it too was devoured. Then there was dessert. Belle's barber, James Jackson, had become a regular at family gatherings, along with his companion, Aaron Stevenson, who was a pastry chef at one of the big downtown hotels and who was as relaxed and casual as James was formal and elegant. Today, he wore one of his trademark three-piece suits with vest, tie perfectly knotted, black shoes shined and, of course, hair perfectly cut. Aaron's hair was well-cut too, and his shave was smooth and close, but he still wore the white apron and chef's hat from the morning spent at the hotel baking the desserts for the dinners that would be served that day, and it did not and would not occur to him to change his clothes.

He'd arrived carrying two cakes, followed by James carrying two more, and had asked somebody—somebody who wasn't clumsy, he'd said—to go out to the car and get the pies. Beau had raced the younger children to the front door—Belle's three, Nellie and Jack, and Sadie's Dorothy and William— teasing that whoever got there first would get a whole pie to eat without having to share. Aaron was laughing and giggling louder than the children when the front door slammed.

They were a fine addition to the family gatherings, James and Aaron. Both had families that didn't want anything to do with them—Mack had correctly assessed their lack of interest in women—and they welcomed the opportunity to be part of a family. James always insisted on buying the food. All of it. He didn't cook but he did eat, he said, and thought it only fair that he pay for the food. After all, he said, it was the cooks who did the real work in preparing a meal for twenty or twenty-five people. Then he'd give his shy, quiet smile and offer that anyway, he ate enough for three people. There was nothing shy or quiet about Aaron. Older than James by eight or nine years—in fact, he and Beau were the same age—he was funny and gregarious and at least half the life of any party. He was generous to a fault and now considered everybody connected to either the Thatcher or McGinnis families as "my own kin" and treated them as such. He had taken a particular liking to Sadie Hill, getting her a job at the hotel where he worked to help her supplement her income. Though Mack and Ruth continued to pay her full salary, with the three oldest boys gone, there wasn't much work for her to do, and Sadie's pride would not allow her to accept money she hadn't earned. She had worked overnight at the hotel and now was at home sleeping. William and Dorothy had spent Christmas Eve with Mack and Ruthie, opening their presents on Christmas morning with Jack and Nellie. She would, she said, be at Big Mack and Clara's by five o'clock—just in time for Aaron's desserts.

Big Si, Big Mack and Aaron were each cutting a cake—chocolate, coconut and pound—when the telephone rang. "I'll get it," Mack said. "It's probably Si and Cat. They said they'd call before it got too late."

Emma Johnson got to her feet, ready to run for the phone and talk to her daughter, when she stopped in her tracks at the sound of Mack's voice: Whoever it was, it wasn't Si and Catherine. Mack's voice was raised, and he was telling whoever was on the other end to quiet down and calm down and start from the beginning. "We'll be right there" they heard him say, and everybody was standing up when he hurried back into the room.

"That was Sadie. She says there's a man at the front door who says his name is Henry Fordham, and he's First Freeman's son!"

"Good God Almighty," Big Si exclaimed, startling them all. "He did have a son by that name. That was his name before he changed it—Fordham—Silas Fordham, and he had a son he said just disappeared one day. Went out and never came back. But Good God. That was…that was…way long time ago." He rushed for the front door. "Come on, y'all. Beau, Mack. Ruthie, you better come too."

They rushed out of the front door then had to run around to the back of the house to get Mack's car. As there was practically no traffic on the street on Christmas Day, they got to Sadie's house—that had been Pa and Beau's house and before that, First Freeman's house—in just a few minutes. They all saw the man on the front porch: Thin, stooped, white-haired. He had a blanket around his shoulders and was drinking a cup of something hot; they could see the steam rising. Sadie had given him a blanket and a beverage but had drawn the line at letting him in her house, and they didn't blame her. Mack pulled into the driveway and parked. Big Si and Beau were out of the car before the hand brake was set, Ruthie hard on their heels. The stranger had heard their arrival and turned to face them, and when they got close enough to see him clearly, Pa stopped in his tracks and said Great God Almighty again. There could be no doubt that this man was related to First Freeman—and to Silas Thatcher.

He looked at them and they looked at him and Sadie Hill watched all of them through the window. "It's cold out here," Ruth said. "Let's see if Sadie thinks it's all right for us to come in."

She excused herself as she passed the strange man on the porch and rang the bell. Sadie opened the door immediately. Ruth entered and pulled Sadie to the side. Her father, brother and husband stood aside and allowed the stranger to enter first. They followed and closed the door behind him. He walked to the center of the room and looked all around. Then he looked at each of the people in the room, studied their faces, for several seconds, and finally pointed to Big Si.

"You. You some kin to me." It wasn't a question.

Pa nodded. "He was my pa, too. I was raised in Carrie's Crossing. He told me 'bout you. It was the biggest sadness in his life that he didn't know what happened to you or why you left him like you did."

The man began to shake and shiver. Ruth took the cup from him before he dropped it, and Mack and Beau led him closer to the fireplace. He stood directly in front of it until he stopped shaking. "I didn't leave," he said. "I got took."

Then Henry Fordham told them the story of the past twenty-six years of his life: He'd been standing in front of a pool hall on Simpson Road on a Friday night. He had just gotten off work and gotten a haircut and was considering shooting a couple of games of pool, but he was hungry and didn't want to eat the pool hall offerings; he wanted a real meal. As he was pondering his next move, a truck pulled up and two men jumped out—two Colored men. Both were talking loudly and at the same time, so he couldn't make out what they were saying. Then they were beside him and he was between them and they had his arms and they threw him into the back of the truck, jumped in behind him, and the truck sped away. There were six other men in the truck, in addition to the kidnappers, and they were bound and gagged. So was he, in a matter of moments. They drove almost all night. It was still dark when they stopped. They were pulled from the truck and forced to walk into some woods where there were huts and cabins, barely visible in the just-breaking dawn. Henry said he was vaguely aware of a noise, a deep rumbling, maybe even roaring noise, that was constant. Then, as he eyes adjusted to the light, he saw men emerging from the huts and cabins and other men walking toward them. It was, he was soon to learn, the shift change: The men who had worked all night were returning to the structures to sleep, while the other men were off to work their twelve-hour shift. They worked twelve hours a day, seven days a week, every week of every year, Henry said, and they got paid not one dime. Not ever. Not in twenty-six years was he ever paid for his labor. And it was labor, he said: In plants and factories in Georgia and in Alabama. They moved the men around so they'd never know exactly where they were. Men would escape, and they wouldn't care because there was no place to escape to—the factories or plants were always far away from a city and always in or near woods. The men who returned spoke of snakes and wild boars and the occasional bobcat in the woods. There were others who never returned. They were fed a bowl of beans and rice three times a day, and it never was enough. They always were hungry and thirsty. There were buckets of water placed around the factory floor, but a man had to secure permission to get a drink, and it was rarely given. So they fainted from dehydration, they soiled themselves since the same permission was required to go to the toilet and they learned not to notice or care.

Henry Fordham stopped talking and stood still as a statue, Sadie's blanket still hanging on him. He watched them watch him, but there was nothing in his eyes to suggest that he wanted or needed or expected any one of them to say anything. He knew that there was nothing to be said. He knew what had happened to him, and he knew that there was no explaining it. He knew that being held as a slave sixty years after slavery's end was not the basis for a rational conversation. Even an uneducated, broken-spirited new kind of slave knew that much. So he didn't say anything. He just looked at them, and that he found interesting; he'd never seen Colored people like these. The tall man in the most beautiful suit of clothes he could imagine—during those low, deeply dark times when he fantasized about being set free, he imagined having rich-man things—and the tall, beautiful woman, who held his arm so tightly that it must be painful, could have stepped out of a magazine. She looked like a lot of the men enslaved with him—like an Indian—like the other man with them, the only one not wearing a suit. He looked more like an Indian than the woman, with his hair in a long braid down his back and the deerskin shoes on his feet. The old man, the man who was his brother, Silas, had on a suit too, but not a fancy one, and he didn't wear a tie, and he wore brogans, not fancy city shoes. True, they were new brogans, and they were shined—but nothing fancy about them.

The first one to speak was the lady who now lived in his pa's house. Her name was Sadie, she'd told him. She was crying and beating her hands against her chest. "I knew he hadn't just run off and left me and the chil'ren. I knew Willie wouldn't do a thing like that. That's what happened to him, y'all. What happened to Mr. Fordham here is what happened to my Willie, and I'll bet to Miss Emma's man, too." She was shrieking, and Ruth let go of Mack so that she could hold Sadie. Ruth was the next to speak.

"How many men, Mr. Fordham, in these factories and plants? How many men?"

"Too many. Way too many. And I only seen the ones where I worked, and they was always movin' us around, always at night so we couldn't see nothin' but the dark."

For years there had been wonderment about men who just disappeared without any provocation—good husbands and fathers, the women left behind all claimed. Now they understood. Now they knew. "How did you get here, Mr. Fordham?" Ruthie asked.

For the first time some hint of life showed in his eyes. "I wouldn't die so they brung me back," he answered, and when it was clear that they hadn't understood his meaning, he explained that he'd gotten too old and too sick to work. "They got this one shack for mens like that where they put 'em to die. Don't feed 'em much, don't give 'em much water, and they just die. But I didn't. I wasn't no use to 'em no more, so they brung me back here. They lookin' for some more, but all the young mens is gone to that war, and old mens, like y'all, is got jobs and workin' and ain't hardly nobody on the streets at night no more. 'Least that's what I heared the boss mens say."

Pa looked at Beau. "I guess we better take Henry with us." Then he looked at the man. "I'm Silas Thatcher, and this here is my son, Beaudry. That's my daughter, Ruth, and that's her husband, Mack. And that there is Miz Sadie Hill. She lives in this house now with her chil'ren. Me and Beau live in North Car'lina, and we'd be pleased to have you with us if you care to go."

Henry Fordham nodded his head and said a whispered thank you.

"Willie Hill," Sadie said. "Did you ever know Willie Hill from Belle

City? He had a shoe shine bizness. Had a big box that he rolled all around—downtown in front of the hotels, out in front of the train station, in front of the banks. He was real good at shinin' shoes. Did you ever see him, Mr. Fordham, Willie Hill?" Sadie was shrieking again and sobbing. Ruth held her, wiped her face with the handkerchief Mack gave her.

They all felt Sadie's grief for a moment, Henry Fordham included. Then Big Si said they needed to get back to Big Mack and Clara's so folks wouldn't worry about them anymore than they probably already were worried. "We were havin' Christmas dinner at my in-laws house, and it was some kinda good food. Would you like to come eat?"

Henry looked at them, and then down at himself, at his thread-bare work clothes and patched brogans, and shook his head. "I ain't dressed no kinda way to go into folks' house for dinner."

"It's a family dinner, Henry, and you're my brother. Won't nobody care what you got on."

He was right; nobody cared what Henry Fordham was wearing, so struck were they by his story, as told by Pa, Mack, Beau and Ruth. Emma Johnson fainted dead away when she fully understood what happened to Henry and when they revived her, she, like Sadie, asked over and over whether Henry had know her Ed. Then, finally grasping the horrible enormity of the situation, she, too, wept helplessly and hopelessly. They all felt the same way: Helpless and hopeless. There was nobody to tell what they'd learned, and nobody to halt it. Even now, according to Henry, the hunt was on for new slaves. The only thing they could do, they agreed, was tell all the ministers at all the churches, who then would sound the alarm: No able-bodied Negro male should be out alone after dark. It was cold comfort certainly, but now the ministers could tell families where at least some of their missing men were, and confirming for them that they'd been right all along: The men hadn't just up and left one day for no reason.

Pa and Beau cut their visit short and left with Henry Fordham the following day. In whispered conversations, both had expressed the opinion that Henry did not have long to live; however, they said they'd make him feel as at home as possible, would tell him all the First Freeman stories they could think of, would feed him good food and give him a comfortable place to sleep—in short, guarantee that he'd have everything he'd lacked during the previous twenty-six years.

The rest of them, in groups large and small, talked about nothing but

Henry for the rest of the week, until the New Year dawned and brought them another topic: The possible end of the war. German troops were trounced and routed on New Year's Day 1945, and almost every day brought news that American and British forces were gaining the upper hand against the Germans. Dare they hope the war would end soon? According to Si and Cat, people in Chicago thought so. According to Pa and Beau, people in the North Carolina mountains thought so. According to Jonas, people in Carrie's Crossing thought so. Ruthie and Mack allowed themselves to think and hope so, and by March, the hope turned to belief as the Army had the Japanese on the run in the Pacific. At the beginning of April, they did something the swore they'd never do: They went downtown to the Fox Theater, climbed the stairs on the outside of the building to the Crow's Nest, the top tier of seats in the massive auditorium where Colored were relegated, and watched the News Reels. They'd sworn, all of them, that they'd never in their lives pay a penny of their hard-earned money to crackers to sit in a filthy corner of any place for any reason. They had heard that the Crow's Nest was filthy because the theater management never cleaned it. The rumors were true. Ruthie held tightly to Mack's arm so she wouldn't have to touch the stair railings outside or inside, and she wished she hadn't had to sit on the hard seats, though for once she was grateful for the meanness of white people: How much worse would the seats in the Crow's Nest be if they were cushioned and upholstered? The awful surroundings receded when the lights dimmed. The News Reel footage was dramatic and impressive. The total defeat of Japan was imminent. Yes, it was too soon to start planning the Homecoming Celebration for the boys, but they certainly could begin thinking about it: Thanksgiving? Christmas?

As often happened when there was good news, when all the attention was focused in that direction, bad news blew in the back door, blindsiding everybody. Ruthie knew this to be true from firsthand experience, but she wasn't the only person taken totally and completely off guard by the news on April 12th that FDR had died. The whole world, it seemed, reeled. Quickly, though, the shock was replaced by worry and concern: A new president taking over in the middle of a war? But the war wasn't at midpoint. The end of it was in sight, and Truman had Eisenhower. That's what people said. Ruthie didn't think that was true, but before she could give the matter really serious thought, they had to shift focus again. Henry Fordham died the day after Roosevelt. Beau called with the news that evening, and it almost was anti-climatic since they'd already buried him.

"But Beau. You can't just bury people."

He laughed. "Baby Sister. You are a treat." Then he explained that he and Pa had discussed their options at length, and concluded that since nobody had heard anything of Henry or anything about Henry in twenty-six years, since nobody knew where he'd been or that he'd returned, since nobody was looking for him and since nobody missed him, the logical thing to do was to bury him. He'd died in his sleep. "He just didn't wake up this morning," Beau said, and since they couldn't leave a dead body in the house, they had dug a deep pit, lined it with rocks and lime, said a prayer (Pa had said the prayer), wrapped Henry in a sheet, and laid him to rest. "It was the right thing to do, Ruthie," he said.

She sat thinking. Was Beau right? Had he and Pa done the right thing? If so, then she was wrong. She'd been wrong a lot lately. "How's Pa taking it?"

"He was kinda upset at first, but not broken-hearted 'bout it. After all, he didn't know the man, even if it was his brother. But he said the whole thing made him sad—that the man died and didn't but two people in the whole world know or care. Then he started talking about how when he died, how many people would care, and I had to move him off that subject," Beau paused. "He talks about dyin' a lot, Ruthie."

"How is he, Beau? Really?"

"Old. Weak. Tired."

"Do we need to move him back down here?"

Beau sighed deeply, sounding as if he had something caught in his throat. "Maybe when it gets a little warmer. June, July."

She hung up the phone thinking that this summer, her pa would be coming home to die, just as his brother had done. She was still sitting there when the phone rang again. It was Jonas. They had kept their promise to keep in touch, and he was calling to share thoughts with her about FDR's death. When she ruefully admitted that at the moment the dead president was the furthest thing from her mind, he asked why, and she told him. All of it. He was very quiet for a long time. Only the ubiquitous hum on the telephone line let her know he was still there. When he finally spoke, it was almost in a whisper, as if he didn't want to be heard. And when she heard what he said, she imagined that he did not want Ernestine or Sam or Ruby to overhear.

"I think I've heard about those places, Ruthie. I don't recall the names of them, but I've been asked to invest in plants and factories in Georgia and Alabama that make unheard of profits. At first, I didn't believe it;

nobody makes that kind of profit. But if it's from slave labor, if workers aren't being paid—well, then, yeah, they'd be makin' a huge profit. And all I can think right now is how glad I am I didn't invest. I know that sounds self-serving, but to think I could have been a part of something like that."

"You couldn't be blamed if you didn't know."

"How often do people hide behind ignorance as an excuse? Besides, somebody, a lot of somebodies, do know what's going on and are doing nothing."

"Can you find out about them? Where they are, what they're called? We know two women whose husbands just disappeared one day, and it's possible that they're in one of these places."

"I'll try to learn more. But Ruthie—?"

"What is it, Jonas? What's wrong?"

"If men are being stolen off the street, driven to a different state and not paid for their work, then it's possible that those places don't know their names, that there are no records of who they are or where they're from."

She hung up the phone thinking that what happened to Henry Fordham and, in all likelihood, to Willie Hill and Ed Johnson, was worse than slavery. At least the slaves had names and people who worked them without pay knew their names. Even if, at some point, they changed them. Silas Fordham became First Freeman, but everyone who knew him, knew that. Then she had a horrible thought: Suppose, when Pa moved away to be with Beau, they had rented or sold the house to a stranger. When Henry appeared, nobody would have known about First Freeman. Henry would have been sent away. He'd have been penniless and alone and about to die. Beau was right: They had done the right thing.

– Carrie's Crossing –
Jonas

They had slowed from a canter to a walk, and JJ slowed his horse first. Jonas was glad because the boy had turned a deaf ear to any attempt by his father to discuss selling the horses. JJ wasn't going to sell his horse, and no argument his father could offer could change his mind, and the argument was a good one: Carrie's Crossing was becoming so urban and developed that there almost was no place to ride a horse anymore. What had been open fields and meadows now were parts of estates, fenced-off private property, no horses allowed. They couldn't even ride on their own land anymore because the road and the traffic came so close it frightened the horses. "It's not fair to them, Son," Jonas had argued, "to have them spooked and scared all the time."

"What's the point of having a horse if you have to walk him?" JJ complained to his father. "Horses were made to run."

"I guess we just have to face the truth: We don't live in a little country town anymore; we live in a big city."

"Belle City is a big city, Papa, not us."

"That used to be true, Son, but not anymore. It's called progress. One day we'll have just as many people living here as live over there."

"I don't like progress," JJ growled.

Jonas wasn't terribly fond of it either, but what he said to his son was that, like everything else, progress had its place; like everything else, there was some good with it and some not-so-good. The key, he always told his son, was to find the good and enjoy it, and not to let the bad destroy you—that's if you couldn't change it. And a way for them to keep progress from destroying them was to sell the horses to a farmer in South Georgia who had a lot of land—open land where the horses could run. That way, he told his son, the horses would be happy, and they would, too, knowing the horses wouldn't be scared and spooked all the time.

If not contradicting everything he said meant that JJ finally was ready to accept the sale of the horses, then he'd shout like Ruby, thank you Jesus! The last thing he'd wanted was to have to force him to accept getting rid of the horse he loved.

When they heard the clanging of the bell, the horses turned and headed for home without having to be told. Jonas had found an old ship's bell and hung it from the side of the barn to be rung any time he was too far away from the house to hear himself being called. A couple of clangs was all it took, and he'd head back. Continuous clanging meant hurry back. A brisk canter was the best they could do, and when they trotted into the yard the urgency was obvious: Horace's car was parked in the driveway and he was on the front steps, and Jonas could see from a distance that he was hopping mad. Indeed, he was hopping from foot to foot, and Jonas could guess the reason: He wanted in and Ernestine wouldn't open the door.

Sam met them at the barn door and took the reins of Jonas's horse as he dismounted. Sam didn't say a word as he helped JJ down and solicited the boy's help grooming the animals, a request he only needed to make once.

As Jonas made his way to the front of the house, he could hear Horace yelling to Ernestine to open the damn door. "You know she's not going to do that, Horace, so why are you making all that noise?"

"Why can't I go in the house?"

"You know very well why you can't go in my house. Now, what do you want?"

Horace stood looking down at him. He looked worn and tired. "Can we go in and sit down and talk like grownups?"

"We have nothing to talk about."

"Jonas, please." The desperation in his voice could mean only one thing.

"You broke again?"

"I'm about to lose everything. Even my house. I can't do that to Alice. You got to help me."

"No, I don't. Whatever mess you're in this time, it's your own fault, just like all the other times—spend, spend, spend. You never met a dollar you didn't want to spend."

"It's not like that this time. Three businesses I got money invested in, they all been shut down by the government. Feds just waltzed in, seized the merchandise, and shut 'em down."

"These the places you told me about? The ones returning the huge profits?"

Horace's head was bobbing up and down like apples in a barrel. "And I wasn't spending. I plowed back everything I made, and I'd made a ton. I put it all back in these places. They were the best investments I'd ever made. Then here come the Feds."

"Roosevelt warned against profiteering over a year ago," Jonas said.

"Damn Roosevelt!" Horace shouted. "I wish he hadda died years ago. He had no right interfering in business like that. This is a free-market society. We're capitalists in this country, not socialists or communists."

Jonas laughed out loud. "Who've you been listening to? You got yourself an economics professor on the payroll?"

"This ain't funny. Every dime I had was invested in those three plants, and now I can't get it back. None of it, and that ain't right. It ain't fair."

"That's probably what the people who worked there thought: That it wasn't right or fair that they worked twelve-hour shifts, seven days a week, for absolutely no pay, so you could make huge profits on your investments."

He came down off the top step now and stood face to face with Jonas. "What do you know 'bout how them places was run?" All the country cracker in him surfaced when he was mad. "Who you been talkin' to? You been talkin' to the Feds, boy? I'll kill you I find out you been talkin' to the Feds."

"You don't have the courage or the strength to kill me. Now, get off my property and don't come back, Horace. I mean that. Tell me who holds your mortgage, and I'll pay the note only because of Audrey. Because of her memory. That's why I didn't knock you down just then when you threatened to kill me. But if you step foot back on my property again, I will kill you, and believe me, it'll be easier the second time."

Horace was about to ask what he meant when the front door swung open at the same time that Sam came running around the side of the house.

"Hitler's dead!" Ernestine shouted from the doorway. "Hitler's dead!"

"He killed hisself!" Sam yelled. "Before we could get to him, he killed hisself. All along, nothin' but a big ol' coward."

"The War got to be over soon, now, ain't that right, Mr. Jonas?" Ruby demanded to know. "Ain't it? And our boys can come home where they belong."

It was a lot to take in. Hitler dead, by his own hand. Yes, certainly this part of the War was over—the European part. At least the part waged by Hitler. What about Japan, and, according to Charlie Pace, Russia? Even though they're supposed to be our allies, Charlie said they couldn't be trusted as far you could throw Adolph Hitler. "I don't know how soon we should start looking for troops to come home," he said, thinking of Ruthie and Mack's boys, knowing they were wondering the exact same thing. "Just because ol' Adolph is dead doesn't mean his Army is dead. We'll have to wait and see."

"What did you mean by what you said, Jonas?"

"You're still here? I thought you'd left."

"I was talkin' to you before we got interrupted," he spat out, looking pointedly at Ruby, Sam and Ernestine. "What did you mean about killin' me bein' easier the second time? Who've you killed? You killed somebody, didn't you? Ha! I knew it. You ain't nothin' but trash. I tried to tell Audrey, but she wouldn't listen."

– Belle City –
Ruthie

Four days after Ruthie's fortieth birthday, Germany surrendered. They'd had a big party that weekend—music, dancing, barbecue, and three of Aaron's cakes. Beau and Pa came but nobody but Ruthie and Beau knew that Pa wouldn't be returning, though a close look at him told his truth: He was not well. He would not live for very much longer.

Ruthie's party started Friday night and ended when it was time to go to church on Sunday morning. It resumed on Tuesday evening when they got news of the German army's unconditional surrender. It won't be long now, they told themselves. It has to be over soon. And, as if to punctuate that sentiment, five letters arrived from Mackie, Wil and Thatch over the next six weeks.

Every time a letter came was cause for celebration, and so they continued their merrymaking, especially as, in the letters, the boys reported themselves to be well and healthy, if dirty, tired and hungry most of the time. They could not, of course, say where they were or what they were doing, but the fact that they were still alive and still healthy was sufficient. Mackie and Wil were still together and they had not seen Thatch, though they did get one letter from him and he was not close. Thatcher's letters, though, sounded like Mackie and Wil's letters—and none indicated any reason for worry. The one letter that was different was from Mackie and Wil and it arrived the first week of June. As always, they first described themselves as well and healthy so nobody would worry. Then they wrote, "sit down, everybody, and catch your breath. Are you ready for this? We found Eubanks Thatcher!"

Mack was reading the letter out loud and had to stop when Ruthie screamed. She grabbed the letter from him and read it to herself, all the way to the end. Then she held it, looked at it, shaking her head back and forth. Beau got up, took the letter from her, and gave it back to Mack and asked him to please continue reading. He was breathing hard, and he was shaking, and he stood beside Mack as he read, as if by being so near he could hear the words as they left Mack's mouth an instant before everyone else.

"Uncle Eubanks lives in a small village near Sainte-Menehould. He has a wife and four children. His two sons are in the army. When we knocked on his door and he opened it,

he stared at us, then he started to cry. He reached out and grabbed us and held us. We hadn't said anything, hadn't told him who we were, but I guess we look enough like the family that he knew. His wife and daughters embraced us too, all of them crying, and pretty soon we were crying too. It was a very, very emotional moment. When we finally told him who we were— that we were his sister's sons—he started dancing all around the room and singing, Ruthie, Ruthie Ruthie! Then he asked our names and how old we were then he just started asking questions one after the other, fast, like machine gun fire. His wife—her name is Berthe—had to tell him to stop, to let us sit down. She made coffee and gave us cake and we told him everything we could think of IN FRENCH. He was amazed, especially when we told him why we were fluent French speakers. We couldn't stay too long and he understood why. We told him we would try to come back to see him but we couldn't promise anything. He understood. Of course he did. He'd been in a war, too. He cried again when he talked about his mother, and he wanted us to tell him again and again about Grandpa and Uncle Beau. Here is his address. Write to him soon in case we are not able to get back to see him."

"When did they write that?" Beau asked. "Before Hitler died, before Germany surrendered?" Mack looked at the date and nodded. "So, they could be on their way back home by now. Ruthie! We got to write Eubie a letter—"

They were startled by a sound from Pa. They all turned in time to see him grab his left arm with his right hand, then slide out of his chair on to the floor. The two Macks got to him before his head hit the floor, and with James and Aaron's help, they lifted him on to the sofa. Beau knelt beside the sofa and rested his head on his father's chest and wept like a little child.

Silas Thatcher's funeral was held on his seventieth birthday. Every inch of every pew in the Friendship Baptist Church was occupied. Dr. Silas Thatcher from Chicago delivered his father's eulogy and wept when he said his one regret was that Big Si—that's what he called him—would never know the grandchild that his wife, Catherine, was carrying. And to honor him, Little Si said, they would remain in Belle City until the child was born, and if it happened to be a boy, his name would be Silas Thatcher the Third. There were more tears and lots of laughter before the service was over as people shared their remembrances, which Big Si would have applauded and approved. But it was the tears shed by the tall, thin white man sitting in the front row with the family that the congregation found most wrenching, for when the choir sang, *Rock of Ages cleft for me, let me find my strength in thee,* Jonas broke and wept for every person he'd ever loved. JJ tried to comfort his father, but there was no comforting Jonas Farley Thatcher that day. And as Beau and Mack had supported Big Si on the day of his wife's funeral as the choir sang Rock of Ages, they supported their friend, Jonas, on that day, and Ruth Thatcher McGinnis's two youngest children, Jack and Nellie, held the hands of young Jonas Farley Thatcher Jr. as they left the church.

From the Recorded Memories of Ruth Thatcher McGinnis

There was a schedule for servicemen returning home after the war. A hierarchy: Those who'd been in the army longest and in combat longest came home first, especially those with children. The war didn't end and everybody came home—it wasn't that simple, so I stopped trying to calculate the likely date that Mackie and Wil would come home. I just waited and knew that Thatch would follow eventually. We had hoped otherwise, but even though the war was over, Jack still was deployed after he registered, and we still had to worry because there were those who didn't trust the Russians. Turned out they were right. But it just meant that our days and nights of worrying weren't completely over. Mackie and Wil were home for Christmas and two skinnier things you've never seen. We hadn't told them about Pa, and they cried like little babies. We also didn't tell them how he died; that would have made them feel even worse, if they thought that telling us they'd found Eubie led to Pa's death. What odd and difficult feelings. The joy of finding Eubie, of having our sons returned to us whole and healthy, opposite the pain of losing Pa. There was a huge hole in all of our hearts and minds, and nobody expected that it would or could be filled any time soon. Having Pa present was like taking a breath—it was a necessary thing. Not having him present was like choking, suffocating. Trying to catch a breath and being unable. You'd think that his being in North Carolina would have prepared us, but it didn't. And to make matters worse, both Big Mack and Clara were ailing, and losing Pa sank them both into a deep depression. Not only had they lost a friend as close as a brother, they'd witnessed their own mortality. They never recovered.

From the Diary of Jonas Farley Thatcher

New Year's Day 1946. My Audrey has been gone from me for two years. It feels like 20 sometimes, and then it feels like just yesterday she and Allie were here and my house and my life were full of love and life. But I am alive and my son is alive and for the first time in my life I have friends and family—real family. It would hurt Rachel to read that. She is my family and she is a good sister and I love her very much and she loves me. But no matter how much we both try, we cannot change the part of ourselves that was raised by Zeb, and those parts do not know how to love people or let people love you. Mack and Ruthie and Beau let me and JJ celebrate with them—the boys coming home from the war, finding their long-lost Eubie— and they let me be sad with them. But it seems that whatever happens to them, they draw closer together. Maybe that's what life is all about; it's how you are no matter what things happen, good things or bad things. This is something I would never say to them, but when I am with them I forget that they are Colored or that I am White. I forget that we are different and I still don't understand or like why that is. Si still won't have much to do with me. He does not have any white friends in Chicago and he does not like white people. He is polite to me but that is all. Funny thing is, I understand. But I do wonder if this will ever change or if my pa was right: It's how things are and how they will always be. I hope he's wrong about that like he was wrong about everything he said and did.

PART THREE

Belle City and Carrie's Crossing

2005

– 1 –

It was raining sideways, the kind of change-of-season storm as peculiar to the Deep South as a drawl. The water came down in sheets instead of individual droplets, as if it were being sloshed from a million mighty washtubs. As if Grandma were sloshing out the water, Sissy thought, lending a helping hand to the forces of nature.

Until, at age seventy-five, she succumbed to familial pressure and began using the long-ignored washing machine inside the pantry, Grandma washed her own clothes by hand in a twenty-gallon galvanized steel tub, using a huge cake of Octagon soap and a ribbed metal washboard, and nobody could convince her that her clothes weren't the cleanest in town. From April through November she washed on the screened-in back porch; in the winter months she worked in a corner of the kitchen between the stove and the pantry. Always she sat on a low, three-legged stool and hummed low-down-dirty blues tunes as she scrubbed the garments against the washboard, her foot and the tune she was humming and the scratch of the fabric against the metal-sided board joining in melodic syncopation. When she was finished, she would scoop up the huge tub as easily as if it were one of her grandchildren and heave the dirty soapy water over the porch railing, and the water would gush out in a wide, flat wall and hit the brick walkway with a smack. That's how the rain was coming down now, and the wind accentuated that impression, for it was blowing hard and cold like it thought it was in big, wild Montana or Wyoming, instead of in little, peaceful Georgia.

Pretty soon, Grandma would be in the ground, the hard-driving rainwater seeping at her through the dirt. How far down could it go? All the way down to Grandma and into her state-of-the-art, guaranteed waterproof box? Sissy enjoyed the thought and impatiently wiped away the tears sliding down her cheeks. Hard rain was Grandma's favorite weather. She'd like the idea of getting wet much better than she'd like the idea of the ten thousand dollar casket designed to keep her dry for eternity. But Sissy's mother—Grandma's youngest child and only daughter—also owned the biggest Black mortuary chain in three states, so she naturally had the last word on the matter of the casket.

Quickly, and with a low howl, the wind shifted direction, and before Sissy could save herself, she was bathed by the water rushing in through the screen door. It was such a shock, and it was so cold, that she opened her mouth in a great intake of breath, but no sound came from her for several seconds. Then she laughed out loud. It was too late to do anything else. She already was wet, so it made no sense to close the door. So she did what Grandma would have done: She walked out into the storm and let herself cry for her grandmother, her hot tears mingling with the cold rain, her wail harmonizing with the windstorm's song.

She was her grandmother's favorite and she knew it, had always known it, but she'd merely enjoyed the knowledge, had never taken advantage of it, so her brothers and cousins had never felt slighted or cheated. It was Sissy the old woman had sent for when she'd known her time was coming to an end. They all were there when Ruth Thatcher McGinnis inhaled for the final time—three of her five surviving children, twenty grandchildren, a half-dozen great-grandchildren, three great-great-grands, more nieces, nephews, cousins and other kin than anybody but Grandma could keep track of—but Sissy had been there for eleven days, holding the old woman's hand and listening to her memory travel back almost one hundred years with almost frightening detail, receiving the burden and the blessing of long-held secrets. Ruthie McGinnis was three months shy of her one hundred and first birthday when she died, and though her body had failed, her mind and memory remained lithe and agile and dependable.

"That camera recorder thing. Go get it. You won't remember all I say. I'll be gone and so will these words if you don't get a machine to keep them," Grandma said. Sissy had given the old woman a cockeyed glance that had produced a surprisingly hearty chuckle. "Machines have their uses," she'd said, adding the reminder that she had, eventually, used the washing machine— and the telephone answering machine and the VCR, though she'd drawn the line at the cell phone—and had conceded their usefulness. So, Sissy had recorded her grandmother's memories of a life and a way of living foreign to Sissy, though somehow strangely comforting despite the layers of pain, humiliation, degradation, and angst that draped Colored life in the time and place of Ruthie's coming of age. And then there were the secrets. Sissy was a lawyer and knew about secrets—and she knew what to do with them. Grandma's recorded secrets were in a safety deposit box at a bank on the other side of town. The knowledge of them rattled around inside Sissy, along with the sorrow of loss, like small stones in a tin can, alternating with each other for a place of prominence within her emptiness.

Sissy knew she should go inside and change and dress and get over to her mother's house, but this was the last chance for her and Grandma to share their love of rain in all its many forms. And who but her Grandma had ever defined kinds of rain? Hurried, downpour rain; gentle, sweet rain; steady, driving, crop-growing rain; and, like now, sideways rain, the kind that gets started and seems like it'll keep going until there's no more wind and water left. The kind of rain blues singers write songs about. As Brook Benton sang, "When it's raining in Georgia, it seems like it's raining all over the world."

Sissy turned and sloshed up the walkway to the porch and into the kitchen, puddling with every step. She stripped where she stood and tossed the drenched garments back out onto the porch. She'd wash them later—tomorrow, perhaps, or the next day, or after the funeral. Wash them in the good-as-new Montgomery Ward machine in the pantry. Now, she needed to hurry to her mother's house where the pre-funeral celebration would be in full swing, but she'd had to come here, to Grandma's house first. Somebody had to come here, on this first day that Ruth Thatcher McGinnis herself would not come home to the house built, more than half a century earlier, by her husband's hands. Now Sissy could go to her mother's and enjoy the party. Grandma never believed in crying for the dead and had elicited promises that her friends and family would celebrate her life rather than mourn her death. And a hell of a party it would be.

– 2 –

JayFar shifted his butt around on the Naugahyde chair, trying for something close to comfort. Only his oversized leather club chair and matching ottoman at home could provide true comfort, but he wasn't at home; he was in a private room in County Baptist Hospital, keeping vigil over the comatose form of his grandfather. Not that Grandpa knew, and certainly he wouldn't care if, by some miracle of creation, he should awaken and see JayFar there. Grandpa, JayFar thought, had never liked him, and JayFar was terrified of his grandfather. But it was his duty to be here. He could not, in good conscience, let the old man die alone, even though the old man would have preferred it. He'd always preferred being alone. His memories kept him company, he liked to say.

"I spoiled your daddy until he was worse than rotten. Smart as a whip—three graduate degrees—but never held a steady job. But it was my fault and I know that, and truth be told, I didn't begrudge him his life. JJ brought me a lot of joy, and so did your mama. I loved her like she was my own blood. Then your fool daddy kills her trying to fly an airplane. Kills her and your sister. Second time that happened to me. But that was my fault too 'cause I'm the one who bought him the airplane."

JayFar shivered. He'd heard the old man's raspy baritone as clearly as if the words had been spoken for the first time instead of remembered. He was a hundred years old and had the voice of a young fire-and-brimstone Baptist preacher. The voice didn't leave him until consciousness did. One moment he was sitting on his wide-planked front porch drinking iced tea and reading the poetry of Walt Whitman out loud. The next moment, he was on the floor, still and silent, his starched white shirt and creased navy gabardine pants stained by spilled tea and released pee. And still and silent he had been for the past three weeks.

JayFar gave up trying to get comfortable in the ugly chair and stood up. He looked down at his grandfather, at the sunken chest beneath the dark blue Brooks Brother's pajama top rising and falling with weak but steady motion, assuring himself that death hadn't snuck in and snatched the old man away.

The heart monitor still beeped softly—the doctor said it would scream like a banshee if something went wrong—but JayFar checked his chest anyway. Then he went to the window.

The wind howled and slammed the rain against the glass like it was mad about something, pounded the glass like it wanted to get in. This was the second full day of rain, and it could rain just as hard for another two or three days. He'd heard on the news that there was a blizzard raging out west somewhere; out there, that's how winter held on, refusing to give in to spring. In Georgia, it rained like a sumbitch; and in Carrie's Crossing, where Grandpa lived, Carrie's Creek soon would overflow its banks and, if the rain didn't stop, would flood the basements and ruin the expensive landscaping of the expensive homes in the neighborhood.

JayFar checked his watch, then returned to the hard chair, took up the remote control, and switched on the television. He'd watch *Antiques Roadshow* and then whatever was on the Travel or Food Channel until visiting hours were over and he could leave.

"You can leave now, boy. I don't need you. Don't need anybody."

JayFar shivered again. Why was this happening? Why was he hearing his grandfather? The old man was as good as dead; the doctor said so, though JayFar didn't put a lot of stock in the good doctor's opinion. The doctor had no idea what to do with a hundred-year-old stroke victim still breathing on his own with good vital signs. He'd never seen such a thing, he told JayFar. He was certain only that the stroke was deep and irreversible. Jonas Farley Thatcher could lie in this bed, deeply comatose, for years, and there was nothing that Jonas Farley Thatcher the Third could do but sit in the hard, awful chair and wait. And wait he would. He was the sole heir to the Thatcher estate and fortune, but what he wanted was Grandpa's house. Or, more accurately, the land on which the hundred-year-old house sat. Land that had been in the Thatcher family for close to a hundred and fifty years. Land that was worth untold millions to JayFar and his real estate development and investment group.

He punched the remote control searching through the endless channels for the public television station. How could there be so much nothing on TV? And the news was the worst of the nothing, but that's all there was for the next few moments. He looked at his watch again, sighed deeply, and raised the volume. The camera was tight on the face of the perky blond female news reader wearing a sincere smile.

"And finally this evening, what perhaps would be a sad story for any other family, is a joyous one for the family of Ruth Thatcher McGinnis, who died yesterday at the age of one hundred, several months shy of her one hundred and first birthday. Her large, extended family was at her side when she died, and they are ready to keep the promise they made to her on her one hundredth birthday."

JayFar craned his neck to look at the wall-mounted screen. He saw a tiny, pecan-brown woman blowing out the candles on a huge cake. She blew and blew, then laughed, then blew some more. Finally, several people helped her, and finally all the candles were extinguished. "If I live to be a hundred and one," she said, "we'll start all over with just one candle. But if I don't make it, I want you all to have a party anyway, not a funeral. Celebrate my life, don't mourn my death."

The happy-faced television lady was back, smiling her happiness, but JayFar didn't hear what she said this time. The uncomfortable Naugahyde chair was upended, and he was standing across the room, staring at his grandfather, who was sitting upright in bed, his eyes wide open.

"Ruthie is that you? Yeah, I'm ready. Here I come. Wait for me!"

The old man flopped back on his pillows. The heart monitor screamed like a banshee. JayFar ran into the bathroom and threw up his steak, baked potato and five-year-old Merlot supper.

– 3 –

S issy's mother was surprisingly calm and wonderfully, though uncharacteristically, gracious and magnanimous to the unending stream of distant relatives, acquaintances, and flat-out unknowns who continued to stream through her house a full day and a half after her mother's funeral. Ruth Thatcher McGinnis had been known, loved and revered by many hundreds of people of all ages and classes and races and persuasions. She was an equal-opportunity human being long before that catch phrase possessed any cultural or colloquial relevance. Ruthie's last-born child and only daughter, Nellie McGinnis Nelson, did not share her mother's view of the world and those who populated it, human or beast. "You mother's a snob," Sissy's father would announce to his children whenever he felt his wife's behavior needed defining or explaining, and since he never smiled when he said it, and since his wife never denied the accusation, it was accepted within the family as truth. Outside the family, too. But this was the final celebration of her mother's life and Nellie, dutiful daughter to the end, would do her duty.

Nellie was a magnificent woman. She'd been pretty as a girl and glamorous as a young woman, and she'd matured into an elegant and stunning grown woman. Now, approaching seventy, she was nothing short of magnificent. She'd inherited height from her father and a lithe, lean quality from her mother. Her mahogany skin was as flawless as a baby's, and her hair was silver and so perfectly cut as to appear designed rather than styled. She sat effortlessly straight in the high-backed Empire chair, her legs crossed at the knee, ankles together, her black crepe suit haute couture, her diamonds real, and her smile fading. Nellie had been polite long enough, duty notwithstanding.

Sissy studied her mother from across the wide expanse of the drawing room. Only someone as close to Nellie as her only daughter would be able to discern the grief beneath the highly polished veneer of Nellie Nelson's public persona, and Nellie was grieving. She had adored her mother, and had been adored by her. The youngest of five children and the only girl, beautiful and smart and talented and chock-full of personality, Nellie McGinnis was born to be adored. By her doting parents, by her rambunctious brothers, by her husband, and, finally, by three of her four children. Sissy was among the adorers even if she sometimes found her mother hard to like. This was not one of those times. Right now, she liked her mother very much.

Nellie and Sissy exchanged glances across the room, and Nellie's smile regained its luster. As her mother had adored her, Nellie worshiped her only daughter. Sissy crossed to her mother and waited while she finished making small-talk with two white women who looked to be as old as Grandma, though with white people it was hard to tell, so easily and early did their skin wrinkle and sag, especially those who lived with and on the land.

"Thank you for coming," Nellie said, the words rote by now. "Mama would have appreciated your kindness."

When the two women turned to depart, Sissy saw tears in their eyes and sadness etched into the deep folds of their skin. Their grief, too, was genuine. "Who are they?" she asked, bending down into her mother's embrace.

"I don't know." Nellie's fatigue was becoming exasperation. "They mentioned anti-lynching work in the 1920's."

"The Ida Wells Barnett Anti-Lynching Society?" Sissy exclaimed, her excitement lost on her mother. Grandma had talked to Sissy and the video recorder about the daring organization made up of Colored and white people, mostly women, at a time when such fraternizing was outlawed, especially since they were trying to put a stop to the widespread and random stringing up of Negro men.

"Certainly not. I'd have paid careful attention to any reference to Ida Wells Barnett, as you very well know." Nellie's exasperation was becoming irritability, but before it could become full-blown, Dorothy, the housekeeper, approached.

"'Scuse me, m'am, Sissy. There's about thirty people still in the house, but no more comin', and Douglass said to lock the front door. You want me to?"

"As quickly as you can, Dorothy," Nellie said, and Sissy had to laugh. Nellie and her eldest son were so much alike: They'd both had more than enough egalitarianism for one week, and the sooner it came to an end, the better, though Dorothy couldn't do much of anything quickly these days. She was almost as old as Nellie, her body weakened by half a century of domestic servitude and a propensity for "eating anything that didn't bite back," Sissy's father always said. Still, she made it across the room and out into the foyer at a pretty good clip, and Sissy could only imagine the woman's own gratitude at bringing an end to the week-long celebration of Ruthie McGinnis's life. Even though hired staff had done all the cooking, serving and cleaning, it was Dorothy's house and therefore her responsibility, and she took it seriously, had always taken seriously the job of caring for her friend and savior, Ruthie McGinnis' only daughter and that daughter's home and family.

The hired caterer's servers still passed back and forth with trays of hors d'oeuvres and white wine, and the serving table in the dining room would be replenished until Nellie put a stop to it, but whoever was left could help themselves to as much food as they wanted and could entertain themselves, too, as far as Nellie was concerned. She and her family were now officially done with the public display of reverence for the memory of her mother and would, from now on, mourn privately.

Douglass and DuBois came in, drawing the doors closed behind them, and Nellie stood up, stretched, and re-seated herself in the corner of the sofa. She sighed deeply, closed her eyes, and raised her legs, just as Douglass slid an ottoman beneath them. She kicked off her shoes and allowed herself to fully relax. Sissy and her brothers removed their jackets and Sissy her shoes, and they all sat near their mother—Sissy on the floor next to the ottoman, Douglass on the sofa next to Nellie, and DuBois in an adjacent wing chair. They enjoyed several seconds of silence that was broken by the distant peal of the doorbell. Nellie sat up.

"Relax, Mama," DuBois said, "Monty and Gabe have everything under control."

Nellie nodded and leaned back. One thing she and her boys knew how to do was attend to death. When she married Theodore Nelson fifty-two years earlier, his family owned one of the more prosperous Negro funeral homes in town. Since then, it had become a massive enterprise, operating in South Carolina and Tennessee as well as Georgia, burying as many well-heeled whites as Blacks, testament to the elevated level of service provided. True, it cost a small fortune to be laid to one's final earthly rest by the Nelson Mortuary, but it was worth every penny. Nellie had spent the better part of her life seeing to that; and after the death of her husband two years earlier, her two sons and two of her nephews—Montgomery and Gabriel, the sons of her husband's sisters—had assumed the responsibility for management of the enterprise. Nellie now merely provided presence, and some thought that, in and of itself, was worth the price of a Nelson Mortuary funeral.

"Where's Teddy?" she asked, her eyes still closed, preventing her from witnessing the look that passed between Doug and DuBois.

"Where Teddy always is," Douglass said. "Following the wine and the women and occasionally breaking into song."

"Off key," DuBois added.

"Grandma wanted us to enjoy ourselves," Sissy said.

"You always defend him," Doug said.

Sissy knew that irritated him, but she also knew how excruciating it had been for Teddy to follow the path laid by Douglass and Dubois, not to mention impossible. So, as family babies often did, Teddy had carved his own path, and walked it on his own terms, often unsteadily.

"He's a grown man," Doug said, "and it's time he started acting like one. And it's time you and Mama stopped defending him."

"He's grieving, Doug."

"We're all grieving, but he's the only one who's drunk and acting like a jackass. You think that's what Grandma wanted?" DuBois gave Sissy a long, steady look, over the tops of his glasses and down his nose at the same time.

She wanted to tell him that he was the one behaving like a jackass but stopped herself, as she usually did, in order to keep the peace. Her mother didn't like dissension and as the only girl among the boys, it usually fell to Sissy to ensure Nellie's comfort level. In truth, Sissy didn't mind. It was better for everyone when Nellie was calm and composed, though Sissy wasn't always sure that what was better was necessarily the best.

She'd like nothing better than to tell DuBois that he, not Teddy, was the jackass, but she knew it would be wasted breath because he'd never understand why she thought so, to say nothing of ever agreeing with any negative assessment of himself. Sissy had done her family dynamics homework and knew that DuBois personified the cursed middle child, if being the third of four could be considered the middle. Doug was the first born and therefore special. She was the only girl and therefore special. Teddy was the baby and therefore the most special. That left DuBois the middle child, and he lived up—or down—to every expectation. The fact that he was the only one of the boys not to achieve six foot status didn't help matters.

"Well, do you?" DuBois demanded with a practiced sneer.

"Do I what?" She'd left the genesis of the conversation and was deep into her analysis of her brother—and her mother's foot massage—and had no idea why he was sneering at her.

"You're as bad as Teddy. You can't focus on anything that doesn't relate to you." Now he really was pissed, and Sissy felt something close to a guilt pang.

"I'm sorry, Du. I guess my mind was wandering."

"Like I said, Big Sister and Baby Brother, patches of the same quilt."

"Enough," Nellie said, lifting a hand in admonition. It had the same effect as always. Nobody said anything else, and the relief was palpable when the door opened and Dorothy entered, carrying a bottle of Veuve Clicquot in one hand and four flutes in the other, and followed by one of the caterers pushing a food-laden cart. Nellie opened her eyes and sat up at the sound, her smile warm and genuine. "Bless you, Dorothy."

"It's time you ate something, Miz Nelson, and a taste of champagne ain't never hurt nobody."

"I'll second that!" Teddy bounded into the room, hoisting his own bottle of champagne, electrifying the room with his presence if not with the pattern of his tie. "You guys are missing a hell of a party out there," he said, dropping down on the sofa between Nellie and Doug. "Grandma knew some interesting people."

"Did you meet the two little old ladies from the anti-lynching society?" Sissy asked.

"Yeah. Sarah Jane Somebody and Martha Ann The Same Somebody. They're sisters, as if you couldn't tell, and I honest to God think they're older than Grandma."

"Kind of them to travel so far," Nellie murmured.

"Carrie's Crossing isn't that far," Teddy said. "And it's where that old white dude lived, too," Teddy refilled his flute and downed it in one noisy gulp.

"What old white dude?" Sissy asked.

"The one who died the same day as Grandma. It was in the newspaper. He was a hundred, too, and his name was Thatcher, which made me wonder..."

"Wonder what?" DuBois snapped.

"What do you think, Du? Him and Grandma had the same name and came from the same place—the same place as Miss Martha Ann and Miss Sarah Jane, for that matter. Does your pea brain have any cells that it uses for imagination?"

"That will be enough," Nellie said, and this time there was flint in the voice.

Doug pushed up from the sofa with a grunt and walked wide-legged toward the food cart, trying discreetly to unwedge his pants from his butt crack. Doug these days was, to put it kindly, portly, and he didn't buy suits as often as he bought groceries. Some men wore the increased bulk of their middle age handsomely. Doug did not. He'd always had a big butt, but years earlier, when it had topped off long legs in a pair of tight Levis, it had been a sight worthy of appreciation by Sissy's friends, male and female. Today, with butt and gut protruding in opposite directions, appreciation wasn't the first reaction.

"You better start coming to the gym with me, Doug," DuBois said, giving voice to Sissy's thoughts.

"Or to the construction site with me," Teddy chimed in. "Nothing like manual labor to keep a man fit," he said, slapping his solid abdomen with the palm of his hand.

Douglass perused the food cart as if he'd heard neither of them, and perhaps he hadn't; he was mesmerized by the food, as he'd always been, and cared nothing for anyone else's opinion of what he did, as he never had. "Fix you a plate, Mother?"

"Please, Doug. And don't skimp. I didn't realize how hungry I was until Dorothy reminded me I hadn't eaten today." None of them tried to conceal their grins, and Nellie enjoyed the joke at her expense. Her appetite was legendary. Nellie could outeat anybody, male or female, at any meal, and she weighed exactly eleven pounds more today than she had on her wedding day. She always claimed it was in the genes. Her husband claimed that Nellie's metabolism was in overdrive, even when she slept. Teddy, on the other hand, said Nellie ate to feed her voracious mean streak, though he never said it out loud.

"Where's JoAnne?" Sissy asked, suddenly aware that she hadn't seen Doug's wife in the last hour.

"Upstairs looking after Uncle Mack and Auntie Eula," he answered.

Nellie sat up quickly. "Looking after Mack and Eula? Why?" Nellie's children quickly waved off her concern, calming her, and DuBois answered her.

"Because she weighs too much and he smokes and drinks too much, they both have blood pressure readings off the chart, and they're both pushing eighty. We'll be lucky if they don't stroke out and die on us before the week is over," Du said dryly. Teddy laughed and Nellie gave him a look.

JoAnne was a physician, and she took care of the entire family, not because she'd married into it, but because she was good and kind and gentle—and a damn good doctor. Sissy had been aware that her Uncle Mack, the oldest of her mother's four brothers, was distraught and grieving, and that his wife could go to pieces at the drop of a hat. It had not occurred to her that their ages, coupled with their general ill health, would require medical attention. Leave it to Jo to recognize what needed doing and to do it.

"How long are they planning to stay?" Teddy asked as he refilled his champagne flute.

"Why?" his mother asked, giving him another look.

"They're very needy, and I don't want to have to sit around talking to them all day and half the night."

"He's my brother, and he can stay as long as he likes," Nellie said, "and you don't have to sit and talk to them at all." And the look she gave Teddy this time caused him to change the topic of discussion.

"These shrimp are scrumptious. New caterer, Ma?"

"Umhum," Nellie murmured, accepting an overflowing plate from Doug and scrutinizing the food. "Mr. Flowers was already booked, but I'm glad. I like this woman. Gertrude Something-or-Other. Her people are quite professional. And this food looks and smells wonderful."

"It's marvelous," Doug said, talking with his mouth full. His plate was piled higher than Nellie's. He sat in one of the wing chairs and spread a napkin across his lap. "You think we should use her for the anniversary party?"

"What anniversary party?" Teddy asked, piling turkey, ham, roast beef and shrimp on a plate.

"Don't eat all the shrimp," Doug said.

"Dorothy'll bring more, and what anniversary party?"

"Doug and JoAnne celebrate their twenty-fifth in June," Nellie said.

"No better reason to join me at the gym, Doug. What man wouldn't want to look like his groom self on his twenty-fifth?" Easy for DuBois to say, Sissy thought. He looked better. He'd compensated for his lack of height with physical prowess. His five feet seven inches frame was lithe and muscular, honed and shaped by years of weight lifting and quasi-competitive boxing in the bantam weight category. DuBois could go ten rounds with any man half his age in his boxing club. "Whaddaya say, Doug?"

"I say mind your own business," Doug snapped.

DuBois shrugged. "Suit yourself. If your wife doesn't care that you look like the Goodyear blimp, I certainly don't."

"At least my wife spends enough time with me to know what I look like. Do you even know where your wife is?"

The silence was long and uncomfortable. Nobody said a word because there was nothing to say. DuBois had brought the bear to his own door. He was mired in an unfortunate marriage with an unpleasant woman who wasted not an ounce of effort trying to disguise her antipathy for DuBois and his family. She would, however, remain married to him as long he belonged to one of the wealthiest Black families in Georgia. And he would remain married to her– Carolyn was her name–because, God help him, he loved her.

So they all ate their way through the silence, and Sissy was surprised to find herself with an empty plate. She was contemplating seconds when Nellie stood and cleared her throat.

"Shall we toast now?"

They stood, filled and raised their flutes, and waited for the familiar words: *May you live a long time, and your heart remain mine. May your body be strong, may your Spirit be free, and may all your good deeds be seen as the seeds that grow to fullness in your eternity. Since I love you, all that's left is for God to bless you.*

Nellie's tears flowed as she drank the toast to her mother. Sissy held hers in check, Doug cleared his throat a few times too many, and DuBois sniffled. Teddy refilled his glass and drank it empty.

"What year did Grandpa write that? I always forget," he said, saving the moment from turning maudlin and completing the move away from thoughts of DuBois and his marriage.

Nellie forced a smile through her tears. "Papa recited that toast for the first time on their first wedding anniversary in 1922, and on her birthday and anniversary thereafter, until he died in 1986."

"Which is when Uncle Mack took over," Teddy said.

Nellie shook her head. "Si did it first, then Thatch, and then Mack. And I've got to go check on Thatch before it gets too late. Maybe Mack'll feel like going with me."

"You don't really have to do that today, Mama. You can go tomorrow. He'll never know the difference."

"But I'll know, Doug. He's my brother, and his mother is dead and buried, and somebody needs to be with him. Besides, he has moments."

"Uncle Thatch hasn't had a "moment" in over a year, Mama."

Doug's words were wasted. Nellie's shoes were on her feet, and she was headed for the door. Teddy caught up with her.

"Can I get the keys to Grandma's before you go?"

Nellie turned to face him, and some shift in her gaze, some tightening in her body, alerted Sissy, and she stood up and crossed to her mother as Nellie asked, "The keys to Mama's? Why?"

"I'm going to stay there."

Nellie didn't move or speak, but Teddy backed up half a step and the others, unwittingly, eased closer to their mother. Sissy wasn't the only to sense a shift in the climate.

"Since it's going to be my house..."

"Since *what?*" Doug bore down on Teddy faster than his girth should have allowed.

Teddy ignored him and kept his focus on Nellie. "Grandma's leaving me the house. I want to start living in it."

Nellie, without speaking, stepped around him, opened the door, and left them standing there. Her uncharacteristic dismissal of her favorite child stilled them all. They watched her back until she was out of sight, then the three eldest turned their gazes on their youngest sibling who, had he been sober and focused, would have mocked their incredulity.

"You're an idiot." Du's sneer bore no trace of his earlier embarrassment. "You can't seriously think that Grandma would leave *you* the house her husband built for her with his own hands. That's ridiculous even for you, Teddy."

"I've been staying at Grandma's, Ted. You can stay there with me," Sissy said.

"Staying there since when?" Teddy's voice was tight with anger, which was rendered virtually ineffectual by the slurring effects of the alcohol.

"Since she got here three weeks ago, which you'd have known if you hadn't been too focused on drinking and fucking to realize that your grandmother was dying, you little jerk." Du squared his shoulders and clenched his fists at his sides. With Nellie gone he was free to flaunt his disdain for his brother.

"I came to the hospital when Mama called me."

"She shouldn't have had to call you, Teddy. She didn't have to call anybody else."

"Du..."

"Shut up, Sissy. For once, just once, would you take a look at your precious baby brother and see him for what he is?"

"Du..."

"He's right, Sis," Doug said.

"We'll see who's right when the will's read," Teddy said. "Which will be when, by the way?"

"In due time," Doug said. "There's no rush."

"Yeah, Doug, there is a rush," Teddy said. "I want it read right now. Immediately. So I can move into my house. And so you can move out, Big Sis.

Who's Grandma's executor?"

"I am," Sissy said.

Teddy gave her that look again, and Sissy realized that her baby brother didn't like her. That he didn't like any of them and perhaps never had.

"Why you?"

"Because she's a lawyer, asswipe," Du snarled. "One who specializes in estate and probate law."

"So you know she left me the house."

"I don't know what's in her will, Teddy; I didn't draw it up. I'm just the estate executor."

"Then set a time and place for reading the will, Big Sister-in-Charge-of-Everything. You *can* do that, can't you?"

"All the legatees have to be notified..."

"All the what?"

"Everybody to whom Grandma bequeathed anything. They have to be notified so they can attend the reading of the will," Sissy began to explain, but Teddy cut her off.

"What's the big fucking deal? Just call everybody and tell 'em when and where."

"There are a hundred thirteen of them, and they must be notified by registered mail," Sissy said, sounding like the highly paid lawyer she was.

Teddy's eyes and mouth opened wide in surprise, and Doug laughed at him. "What a jerk you are," he said, and stalked out.

"You're really surprised, aren't you?" Du asked, not expecting an answer. "Did you think only our family would be in Grandma's will? She's got twenty-three grandchildren, Teddy, for Jesus Christ's sake. And why would she leave the house to you and not one of the others? Or to one of the greats? Or to one of her own children? Or to any one of the hundreds of people she knew and loved?"

Teddy lost the struggle to coordinate thought and speech as the alcohol took over and replaced the anger with something a lot less energetic. "It's gonna be my house."

"Yeah, right," Du said.

"You can stay with me at Grandma's if you want, Teddy," Sissy said.

"Fuck you," Teddy said, too drunk to sidestep Du's fist aimed at his gut, and Teddy doubled over, heaved, and dropped to the floor. Sissy and Du left him there for Dorothy to clean up.

– 4 –

When he was a little boy, JayFar had fervently believed that the stork delivered him to the wrong place. He was convinced that he never should have been born in the South. He had never liked things southern, especially the food and the annoying preoccupation with family. Overcoming the food bias was easy—he just didn't eat anything fried, smothered, glazed or stewed. The family thing was not so easy to overcome. Perhaps if he'd been born into a different family, he thought, he could have liked its members better and therefore not minded the constant references to "kin."

The fawning and pawing that had been going on since Grandpa died was driving him crazy, especially since he'd seen none of those long-lost relations the whole time the old man was hospitalized. Then, at will-reading time, here they came, his dead father's relations: Aunt ~~Alice and the~~ drunk she'd been married to for fifty years and their four worthless offspring who called JayFar "cuz"; Uncle Gill, who fancied himself a playboy, his third wife, and a collection of his progeny, half of them born out-of-wedlock and none of whom ever showed up at any family event that didn't feature free food and booze; and a bunch of his great-aunt and uncle's descendants, relatives of Grandpa's long-dead siblings. Here they all came, wearing their mourning faces, offering their condolences to JayFar and nattering on about "what a wonderful old man" Grandpa had been, and hoping for a handout.

Then there were his mother's relatives, whom JayFar didn't dislike but whom he hadn't seen five times in twenty years. They weren't related to the old man, not really, so why come all the way from North Carolina for his funeral? Then there were the perfect strangers, most of them old enough to be JayFar's parents if not his grandparents. These were the people who had filled Downtown First Baptist for the funeral, who had patted him and hugged him and expressed their sorrow "for his loss." Since Grandpa had never liked or been liked by many people, JayFar didn't understand why they all were there.

"It's not always about like and dislike," his law partner Richard Gayle had said. "In your grandpa's case, it's respect. He was important in this town."

"Do you know how much their 'respect' cost me?" JayFar was still reeling from the caterer's bill for the after-funeral reception.

"It's also a generation thing," Richard had said, paying no attention to his friend's grumbling. Stinginess was a trait among certain kinds of rich people.

"What's that mean?" JayFar had asked.

"Not many of his generation left, and when they're all gone, we won't have any connection to the past," Richard had said, sounding sad. "That's why I went to his funeral."

"I thought you went because you're my law partner." JayFar had tried not to sound as irritated as he felt. But that was then, right after the funeral. Now, a week later, he didn't mind displaying his irritation with Richard, especially since Richard was steadfastly justifying the actions of his late grandfather's lawyer, Willie Cummings.

"Why are you defending that old fool?" he fumed, running his hands through his hair, barely disturbing the expensive coif, before smoothing the thick mane back into place.

"Because he's right, Jay, and you know he's right."

JayFar paced the length of his living room, his right hand now stuffed into his pocket jiggling the change there. Richard sat way back and comfortable in one of the leather club chairs, long legs crossed at the knee, head tilted back, blowing cigar smoke rings at the ceiling and sipping aged sour mash whiskey. Jay stopped pacing and stood in front of Richard.

"What I know is that he's treating me like a...like a stranger. Or worse, like an interloper, and it's not right."

"Willie Cummings was your grandpa's lawyer for fifty years, and he can't stop acting like a lawyer just 'cause his client's dead. He's also damn near eighty years old, and you keep harassing him, he's liable to have a heart attack and die on you. You know how long it'd take to get a will out of probate if the executor dies?"

"I just want to get the damn will read, Richard. Is that too much to ask?"

"It gets read day after tomorrow, Jay, nine a.m. sharp. Now, sit down and relax, have a drink, and leave your hair alone. You're making me nervous pacing up and down like that and playing with your hair like one of those effete English actors."

JayFar sighed loudly and dropped down into the adjacent club chair. He was glad to be back in his own home, a stately center-hall town house built the year of his grandfather's birth. He'd spent the days between the old man's death and his funeral out in Carrie's Crossing, in the "family home" as the family called it. Grandpa's house, JayFar called it, soon to be his. It was a relatively modest structure, two stories with a gabled roof and a wraparound porch, sitting atop a gentle slope of a hill and surrounded by all that was left of what had been a five hundred acre farm and what now was twenty-five acres of prime real estate in the middle of one of the most expensive and exclusive enclaves in America. The preservationists had already been to see him about the house; it was almost a hundred and fifty years old, and the Carrie's Crossing Historical Society wanted him to do some damn fool thing that he had no intention of doing.

"Do you hear me talking to you, Jay?"

JayFar looked over at Richard. "What did you say?"

"What were you thinking about?"

"Those hysterical society people."

"The *what* people?"

JayFar laughed. "The Historical Society people. They came to pay their respects after the funeral, or so they said. You should've seen 'em swarming through the house, admiring the joists and the molding and floorboards and the banisters. I'm surprised Margaret wasn't with them."

"Margaret knows that house as well as she knows her own. What'd you tell 'em?"

JayFar fixed his face into an imitation of the mourning mask he'd worn for the past couple of weeks. "I told 'em that I couldn't possibly think about business at a time like this."

Richard laughed, drained his glass, stood up, and walked over to the drinks cabinet. "It really is a pretty house. Margaret says it's a treasure."

"It's a relic."

"Your grandpa was a relic, an important one too. The last of a dying generation."

"Don't start with the dying generation song again."

"I can't believe you're so insensitive. I wish I had a relative that old."

"You would've if they hadn't drunk themselves into early graves."

Richard returned to his chair carrying his glass with its three fingers of whiskey and the half-full crystal decanter. He sat and tilted his glass toward JayFar in a toast. "My old granddaddy might be dead and long gone, but he was right about one thing: There is something to be said for aged sour mash." He sipped deeply. "Lord, that's good."

They were the same age, JayFar and Richard, but Richard looked a decade older—all that Southern food settled on his waist and thighs, all that whiskey settled in his face.

"That's hereditary, you know."

"So they say. So's a long life span, they also say, but we know that's bullshit, don't we?"

"How do we know that?" JayFar asked.

"Nobody in your family but your grandpa lived to be a hundred."

"Nobody in anybody's family lives to be a hundred."

"That old Black lady did. Boy, I'd have loved to talk to her like I used to talk to your grandpa."

JayFar sat up straight. "You used to talk to Grandpa?"

"Sure did," Richard said sounding wistful. "I'm really gonna miss that crotchety old bastard."

"When? About what?"

"All the time," Richard said, the whiskey sheltering him from the change in JayFar. "Talked about everything. I used to drive over and take him books and Red Rock Cola. You 'member that stuff? My daddy used to drink it 'cause he said it kicked like moonshine. I don't know but one place around here where you can still get it."

"Everything like what?" JayFar was perched on the edge of his chair, body turned so that he faced Richard. "What did you and Grandpa talk about?"

"The old days. Stuff you're not interested in and don't care about." The whiskey now was talking for Richard. "He knew you didn't care about kin and connections, and he did care about that stuff. He used to talk till he fell asleep some times. He'd nod off, then wake up and start talking, pick up a story right where he'd left off. He said your mother was the only other person who used to listen to his stories. He said she was like his own daughter instead of a daughter-in-law. He used to show me pictures of her. She was really pretty."

"Do you know how long my mother's been dead?"

Richard nodded. "July 12th, 1962. You were six."

"I know how old I was."

Richard looked at his watch. "I better go. Margaret'll be calling in a minute, asking where I am." He took his cell phone from his pocket, checked that it was on, and put it back.

"That's one reason I don't have a wife," JayFar said.

"It's nice having somebody miss you."

"That's not missing; it's meddling."

Richard stood up and grinned down at JayFar. "The old man sure had you pegged just right."

JayFar got up quickly. Not only didn't he like anybody standing over him, he still was smarting from the knowledge that Richard had shared time with his grandfather. "Pegged how?"

"Like what you just said about Margaret. Your grandpa understood that's how people love each other, but you think it's meddling. He thought that was a strange way of thinking, and he worried about you."

"He worried about *me*?" JayFar now was worried, too. He didn't like the direction this conversation was taking, and he wasn't sure why. "Why was he worried about me, and why would he tell you?"

"Because," Richard said, pulling on his jacket and zipping it up, "he knew I was the closest thing you have to a real friend."

"That's bullshit."

"Name me another one," Richard said, then drained his glass and splashed in another good snort. He gave JayFar another couple of seconds to formulate a response then continued, "See, that's what your grandpa knew about you that you don't even know about yourself. You must know a thousand people, and you keep all of 'em at arm's length."

"So did he."

"Yeah, but not because he was afraid to let anybody in close. He just didn't have a lot in common with that many people anymore."

"He told you that?" JayFar's eyes glittered mad, and Richard realized he might have said too much. He really would have to stop drinking to excess, at least in public.

"Yeah, he told me that. He said he felt lonesome not having anybody to talk to, family or friends. Except one old guy in a nursing home somewhere he used to call. But the old fella's mind is gone. Didn't know who he was talking to, but your grandpa called him anyway. He thought if he kept talking to him, something familiar would click in."

"Maybe *you* should've been his grandson, Richard, since he liked you a lot better than he liked me." JayFar followed Richard out of the library and down the hallway to the front door. The sun shone brightly, and a warm spring breeze drifted in off the front porch when the door opened, carrying the scent of freshly mowed grass. "Tell Margaret I said hey."

"I'll tell her. Thanks for the libation."

"We'll have a real celebration after the will reading."

"Hell, I might even stay sober that day, since I'll officially be a rich son of a bitch like you," Richard said, and he skipped down the steps like a kid, showing no effects of the alcohol.

JayFar watched him hurry down the brick walkway to his Cadillac convertible, heard the cell phone ring, watched him answer the phone, heard his "Hey, Darlin', I'm on my way" before he got in his car and shut the door. JayFar watched his friend drive away, aware that he still felt wounded by the revelation of Richard's relationship with Grandpa, and he couldn't shake the strange feeling of knowing that the old man had worried about him.

He noticed that something was blooming along the walkway and focused his attention on the blossoms to get his mind off his grandfather. He didn't know what the blooming things were and didn't really care—that's why he paid a gardener. What he cared about was how his house looked, and how the beauty and symmetry of the place made him feel. Then, unbidden, he thought that his grandfather, and most other southerners, would know the names of the flowers, and that thought unnerved him. He turned and hurried up the steps to the porch. That's as far as he'd got when he heard his name called. He turned back toward the street.

Halfway down the block, two women were getting out of a light-colored sedan. They both waved at him, then slammed their car doors. The sound carried on the breeze, sharp and clear. Then he recognized the women— his mother's sisters, his aunts. He'd seen them at the funeral and at the reception afterwards, Faye and Evie and their husbands. Prior to that, he hadn't seen them in probably ten years, but that hadn't dimmed their pleasure in seeing him and now, here they were again, smiling broadly as they approached, and at a faster clip than would be expected for women their age, so he knew nothing was wrong. But still.

"We're so glad you're home," Aunt Evie said as they reached his walkway.

"Dropping in unannounced is so rude," Aunt Faye said, "and we truly do apologize, JayFar."

They called him JayFar, as if he were still a little boy. They called him that because his mother had been delighted with the moniker, bestowed by his sister, and she had called him JayFar. "That's all right," he said, hurrying down to hug them and offer his arms for them to hold as they ascended the steep steps. "I thought y'all had gone back to North Carolina."

He ushered them in and down the hallway to the living room, worried that the library still smelled like cigar smoke and sour mash whiskey. "We had,"

Aunt Fay said, settling herself into one corner of the sofa. She rubbed the fabric. "You have such lovely taste, JayFar. Your mother would be very pleased." She was the youngest of the sisters, JayFar knew, probably just barely seventy, but her face was smooth, her hair mid-length and the color of champagne.

"Don't digress, Faye," Aunt Evie said, commandeering the other end of the sofa and giving JayFar a look that halted his downward progress on to the love seat that matched the sofa. She was the eldest of the sisters, tall, thin, and regal, with sparkling silver hair cut short and styled to perfection.

"Is something wrong?" he asked, looking from one aunt to the other, wondering if this is how his mother would have looked had she had the chance to live this long—beautiful and elegant and commanding.

"We came back for the reading of the will," Evie said, and they both watched JayFar, waiting for his reaction. It was slow coming because it took several seconds for him to understand that they meant the reading of his grandfather's will, then to further understand that they were beneficiaries.

"We're as surprised as you are," Faye said.

"More so," Evie said. "We certainly had no expectation of being included in your grandfather's will. After all, we're no relation to him."

"But we did like him," Faye said. "We liked him very much. And he liked us because he thought we were like Catherine."

"I guess it was his way of holding on to her," Evie said. "He really and truly loved your mother, and he missed her terribly, and he appreciated that we kept in touch with him over the years."

"You kept in touch with him?"

"Oh, yes," Evie and Faye spoke in unison and looked at JayFar like he was something in a specimen dish, the same way that Richard had eyed him earlier.

He learned that his grandfather and his mother's sisters had exchanged birthday and Christmas cards and phone calls every year since his mother's death, that his grandfather never forgot to send them mother's day cards and that they never forgot to send him father's day cards, and that every couple of years, until they all got too old for it, the aunts and their husbands and Grandpa had met at a hunting and fishing lodge in the North Carolina mountains where they spent a month laughing, talking, drinking, eating and "catching up on family." JayFar tried to remember his grandfather being away from home for a month at a time and could not. Yet he had, every couple of years for— how long? Twenty years? Thirty? Forty?

"I'm sorry, what did you say?" He realized that Aunt Faye had asked him something.

"Mack and Eulalee McGinnis. Do you know them? Or their sons, Jack and Beaudry?"

JayFar shook his head. "Who are they?"

"Good friends of Jonas's. They used to join us up in the woods sometimes, and you should have heard the whooping and hollering when they did. Jonas had known them all his life, had grown up with Mack's people, back when Carrie's Crossing was still just the country, and the tales they used to tell on each other." Faye's eyes filled up, and she produced an embroidered lace handkerchief like a magician, catching the tears before they spilled.

"He wouldn't know the McGinnis people anyway," Evie said and gave Faye a look that JayFar couldn't read but which her sister obviously understood very clearly, because she quickly and neatly changed the subject.

"Anyway, JayFar, we just came to tell you that whatever Jonas put in his will, we make no claim to it," Aunt Faye said, getting to her feet.

"That's right," Aunt Evie said. "That's what we came to tell you." She stood, too.

JayFar jumped to his feet. "Don't go. I didn't offer you anything. I'm sorry, my manners." His heart was thudding, and his brain couldn't process all the thoughts running through it quickly enough. One thing he knew about being Southern, though, was that good manners covered a multitude of sins, including bad manners. "Please, let me get you something. Are you hungry? You know I've got more food than I'll eat in a month. All that food from after the funeral." He'd given away a refrigerator full and still had a refrigerator full of food left.

This made his aunts very happy—the thought of eating and the knowledge that they were needed to organize the feeding, for they had unnerved their nephew and they knew it, and they wanted to make things right with him, Catherine's only remaining child. They couldn't stand to see him upset. They followed JayFar into the kitchen and, after they oohed and aahed over its gleaming stainless steel-ness, they made themselves at home. Seventy-something year old Southern women could make themselves at home in any kind of kitchen, he thought, recalling those who had so deftly taken charge of Grandpa's kitchen as the food came rolling in within hours of the old man's demise.

"Uncle Pete and Uncle Terrell didn't come with you?" JayFar asked, just to get the conversation going again.

Faye was slicing roast beef, and Evie was scooping green bean casserole and corn soufflé into pans for warming, and both shook their heads at the question. It was Evie who answered. "We had barely gotten home from the funeral when we got that registered letter telling us to come for the will reading. Terrell had too much work piling up, and Petey just plain hates traveling, so he wasn't about to get on another plane."

Evie's husband, Terrell, was a Dean Emeritus at the University of North Carolina, a man so erudite that he spoke an academic brand of English difficult even for the educated to understand. When he was younger, JayFar had thought him silly and pretentious. He was wrong. True, Terrell operated on a higher plane than Everyman, but he descended often enough and long enough to father five children and to receive regular doses of Evie's doting, which he clearly enjoyed. Faye's Petey, a good ol' boy made good, didn't enjoy any occasion that required a tie, dress shoes, and shaving, especially if he had to travel to get there. So the sisters had flown into Belle City, rented a car at the airport, and come directly to JayFar's to tell him that they didn't want anything that was rightfully his.

"I really don't know what to say," JayFar said.

"No need to say anything," Evie said.

"That's right," Faye added. "Except we're mighty grateful for this delicious repast. I don't care what anybody says, hotel food just doesn't measure up."

There also was enough Southern left in JayFar for him to be appalled. "Hotel?"

"The Ritz Carlton."

"Oh, no. Certainly not. You'll stay right here. I've got plenty of room."

"We couldn't put you out," Faye said.

"It's just for two nights," Evie said.

JayFar held out his hand. "Give me the car keys. I'll get your things. Unless—" he looked from one to the other of them as the thought took hold. "Unless you'd rather stay at Grandpa's?" And the delight on the old women's faces actually made him blush.

"Oh, yes," Evie enthused.

"I love that old house," Faye said. "We had such good times there." Her eyes misted again, and for the first time, JayFar recalled huge family gatherings at his grandfather's place, back when there still were stables and horses, when they ate what they raised and grew—chickens and hogs and fruits and vegetables—before Carrie's Crossing land became too valuable for that kind of simple use. There were July 4th celebrations with fireworks that lit the night sky, and Christmas celebrations with lights and adornments that made the house and outbuilding look like something out of a fairy tale. The last such fete had been the week before his parents and sister died.

"You want to eat in the dining room or in here?"

JayFar drifted back to the present to find himself holding a plate with slices of rare roast beef, buttery scalloped potatoes, and a crisp green salad. He was about to opt for eating in the kitchen but a glance at the high stools at the counter changed his mind. That and Faye's "Is that all right? We know you don't like Southern food."

"The dining room," he said. "I'll open a bottle of wine. Red or white?"

"Red," his aunts said in unison and surprised him again by knowing the Cabernet he opened. Then they surprised him with their appetites—both had plates piled high with roast beef, fried chicken, corn soufflé, green bean casserole, yams, and yeast rolls—and they ate with gusto. They clearly enjoyed good food and good wine, and he realized, as he looked more closely at them, they enjoyed the good life in general. Their clothes were tasteful and expensive, as was their jewelry. They looked healthy. They looked interesting, and JayFar wished that he knew more about them. He ran his hands through his hair a couple of times, a habit so practiced he wasn't aware of it.

"Your mother used to do that," Evie said.

"Do what?" JayFar asked.

"You've got hair like her," Fay said. "Thick and dark and heavy."

"We miss her, too," Evie said. "We've never stopped missing her."

"How did you know?" JayFar asked, then hurried to explain when he saw the puzzled looks on his aunts' faces. "What to put on my plate. That I don't like Southern food. How did you know?"

Evie threw back her head and laughed. It was a sweet, tinkly sound, delicate like wind chimes. "Everybody in the family knows that. From when you were a little boy, you never liked anything Southern. Just like your Grandma in that respect."

"My Grandma?"

"Audrey, your father's mother, not Clemmie, our mother. She was Southern through and through. Fought the Union Army until the day she died." The sisters chuckled and shook their heads at the memory of their Confederate-loyal mother while JayFar struggled for some memory of his grandmother. Either of them. All he could come up with were photographic images, and those blurred in his memory. Which was Audrey and which was Clemmie?

Four

And if he was so like one of them, why didn't he know that?

The aunts cleared the table, put the plates, glasses and utensils in the dishwasher, freshened themselves in "the powder room," and met JayFar at the front door, insisting that he really didn't need to escort them; they knew "by heart the way to Jonas's." But he didn't mind. He wanted to go. He wanted to look again at the photographs of Audrey Thatcher, Jonas's wife. His grandmother. The one he was like.

"The forsythia are beautiful," Faye said, standing on the sidewalk and looking back at the house. "And that crepe myrtle is a lovely touch."

JayFar looked back at the house, too. The gardener was worth every cent.

– 5 –

Ruth Thatcher McGinnis's lawyer, an elderly, sweet-faced woman improbably named Jag Badenhoff and possessor of the kind of Southern accent that marked her a native despite the name, stood behind the lectern in her firm's conference room, looked out at the one hundred and thirteen people seated before her, cleared her throat, and told a bawdy, hilarious story about her late client. Ice broken, she then got down to the business at hand: The reading of Ruthie's will.

All eyes were on the lawyer, especially those of the cousins who really hadn't believed that Sissy Nelson wasn't in charge of the will reading. Sissy sat at a table off to the right of the lectern, slightly behind Jag. She had a copy of the will but hadn't read it. She considered that the time she'd spent with Grandma before her death, and the fourteen hours of recorded memory, were more than sufficient legacy.

The will dispensed with the bequests to charities first, and there were some surprises: A battered women's shelter, a drug treatment center, a private music and arts academy, and a South African orphanage, none of which any of the family had ever heard of, got the most money, and the United Negro College Fund and the National Council of Negro Women, the least. The room was quiet as Jag read the bequests of personal items: Dozens of pieces of jewelry, hundreds of books, a collection of old record albums, several hand-stitched quilts dating back to the Emancipation, thousands of photographs, a hundred year old family Bible, a 1952 Buick Roadster, dozens of pieces of crystal, sterling silver table settings, china and glassware, and the baptismal gowns of dozens of grandchildren, nieces and nephews. The reading of this section was followed by considerable sniffling and nose-blowing, and Sissy wondered how long it had taken her grandmother to craft the detailed and very personal list. Certainly she had known and understood and appreciated her progeny.

Jag told another story about Grandma to get everybody settled down again so she could read off the money bequests. The gasps and shouts grew with the recitation of the dollar amounts, and when it was over, Ruthie McGinnis had left her offspring more than half a million dollars in cash. Not only didn't anybody know she'd had that kind of money, all were amazed at the evenhanded dispensation of it. Those who needed the most money, got the most money. Those who didn't need any, including Sissy, her mother, and two of her brothers, didn't get any. Teddy got twenty thousand dollars, and his facial expression wavered between glee and expectation: He welcomed the money and waited for the house. Sissy found that she couldn't look at him, so she looked at the lawyer, whose strands of silver-streaked hair gradually were freeing themselves from the tight bun at the nape of her neck: They'd been restrained too long.

She adjusted her glasses, sipped from a glass of water, and read a letter from Ruth to her family that started the sniffling again. Nellie was so moved that Doug and Du became flustered, and Sissy had to hurry to her mother and calm her. Then it was she who needed calming as she heard herself named as the recipient of her grandmother's home "and all other real property, wholly owned or in part with others." Sissy was too stunned to be aware of Teddy's reaction. She vaguely registered the conditions of the bequest: That her home never be sold as long as a blood relative lived; that if Sissy didn't live in the house, she should choose among the relatives the one most likely to care for the house properly; and that she study carefully a private memo regarding her rental properties.

"What rental properties?" floated in the air around the room as relatives looked from one to the other in amazement. Truly, Ruth Thatcher McGinnis had been a more complex and layered woman than any of her relatives realized. And she wasn't finished with them yet. Her surviving children— Nellie, Thatcher, Mack Jr. and Wilton, whom nobody had seen or heard from in a quarter century—were to share the contents of one safety deposit box. The contents of another safety deposit box were bequeathed to Jonas Farley Thatcher of Carrie's Crossing, Georgia. There was no quieting the room after that, though the more astute of those gathered did finally understand the presence of the tiny, old and distinguished looking white gentleman sitting all the way in the back of the room.

"Who the hell is Ruth Thatcher McGinnis?" JayFar jumped up from the chair with such power and speed that he knocked it over, earning him a look and a sound of reproach from Willie Cummings. "I asked you a question," JayFar bellowed.

Willie Cummings snatched his glasses off his nose, squared his shoulders, and glowered across the podium that almost totally concealed him. "Your behavior is totally unacceptable, Mr. Thatcher, and I'll not read another word of this will until you change it."

Somebody grabbed one of JayFar's arms, and he swung wildly to loosen the grip, only to discover that he'd practically knocked Aunt Faye to the floor. He lunged toward her, caught her, and steadied them both. Then he released her and turned back to face the lawyer, who was ready for him. "I'm almost finished. If you'd sit down, I will finish, and I'll present you with your copy of the will."

Jay sat, and it was just as well. He felt nauseous and dizzy and terribly confused. His grandfather had left the house to somebody JayFar had never heard of, Ruth Somebody. True, he'd left Jay almost ten million dollars in cash and securities, considerably more than the twenty-five thousand dollars each of the nieces and nephews received. But the house and its acreage! Worth close to ten million dollars as the centerpiece of his and Richard's real estate development plan. More if they decided to retain any of the units.

"Are you all right?" Aunt Faye asked him.

He shook himself, literally, like a wet animal. Aunt Faye and Aunt Evie were leaning over him. His other aunts and uncles and cousins were standing around him. Only Faye and Evie looked happy.

"You can challenge it, you know," his Uncle Gill said. "He was old. You could argue that he was mentally incompetent."

"He most certainly cannot." Willie Cummings pushed his way through the small knot of people and stood in front of JayFar who immediately stood up. "In the first place, young man, you know as well as I do that your grandfather never had an incompetent moment in his waking life. And in the second place, that will was written over twenty years ago." He thrust a copy of the will at JayFar. "There's also the matter of Mrs. McGinnis's bequeath to your grandfather. Call me at your convenience to make an appointment to discuss it," he said and turned on his heel and began to push back through the crowd that had closed around him.

"Mrs. *Who?*" JayFar said, thinking that another surprise surely would kill him. "Why would she leave anything to Grandpa? Who is she?" JayFar yelled.

"Read the newspapers," Cummings yelled back without turning around, and he hurried from his law firm's conference room, his hand on the elbow of a woman of gentle middle age who had attended the reading of the will but whom none of the Thatcher family knew.

"She's an old Colored woman," his Aunt Georgia said, and her mouth turned down so sharply that the corners of her lips seemed to touch her chin. "She died the same day as Paw Paw Jonas."

"They went on and on about her on the TV and in that stupid ass newspaper. More than they talked about Paw Paw," Gill said. "Just 'cause she had a bunch of relatives."

Jonas Farley Thatcher's relatives, the thirteen of them summoned to the reading of his will, were silent for a moment. They stood in a tight circle around Jonas Farley Thatcher III, whom they had known would be the principal beneficiary of his grandfather. Faye Jenkins McCullough and Evelyn Jenkins Langley, who had inherited a collection of first edition books, old maps, artwork, and diaries and memoirs of a dozen unnamed Southerners from the deceased, had been pushed to the outside edge of the circle, despite the fact that the dollar value of their bequest exceeded everybody's but JayFar's. Emotionally and sentimentally, the gifts were priceless. They wanted to be close to their nephew to comfort him, to tell him that he could keep Jonas's things if he wanted them, and to tell him who Ruth Thatcher McGinnis was. But JayFar thought he was beginning to figure it out, and it felt like the heart monitor was screeching like a banshee in his head.

Richard Gayle had known JayFar for over forty years—they'd met in nursery school—and not only was he certain that he knew his friend better than any other living person, he would have bet money that he'd seen JayFar express every emotion that he possessed. Until this moment. Pacing, cursing, muttering unintelligibly, and finally weeping, JayFar appeared more despondent than Richard would have imagined possible, and it unnerved him. He certainly never would have imagined JayFar shedding tears. JayFar, Richard would have said, didn't care enough about anything to shed tears over it—no, not even money. Yet, as Richard watched him and listened to him, it certainly seemed that the loss of his grandfather's property had opened in JayFar a wellspring of untapped emotion. Richard had never seen him really come unglued before, had never seen him this...angry. JayFar's tears were pure anger. Irrational, uncontrollable anger. A tantrum. JayFar was having a tantrum.

"What the hell are you laughing at, Richard? If you can't take this seriously, go home. Just get the hell out of here and leave me alone."

"I'm sorry, 'ol buddy," Richard said, recovering his own equilibrium as he found himself able to understand the source of his friend's imbalance. And as if to prove that he had, indeed, recovered, he strolled over to the drinks cabinet to pour himself a much-needed libation. "I guess I'm living that old saying, laugh to keep from crying. And speaking of old sayings, I'm reminded of another one: 'You can't miss what you never had.' But I swear I'm feeling the loss of my multimillionaire status. I do believe I'd actually started to think of myself as rich." And Richard laughed again as he realized the truth of his statement: He had assumed JayFar's excitement at the thought of inheriting old Jonas's land and the notion of what that would mean to their real estate development company.

"How could he do this to me? I'm his family."

"So's Ruth McGinnis."

"Goddammit, she is not, Richard, and don't you say that to me again."

"Anyway, Jay, you can't stand kin and connections and all that sort of thing, and the old man knew you didn't care, so he probably thought—"

"Thought what? That I didn't care whether or not I inherited one of the most valuable pieces of land in the state of Georgia? In the entire southeastern United States? Since you knew him so well, tell me: Is that what he thought? And what does Miss Nelson think? That I'll just meet her at old Willie's office, shake her hand, tell her it's nice to meet her, and then hand over the keys to Grandpa's? 'Cause if that's what she thinks, she's got another think coming, and I don't give a damn about her being a New York lawyer."

Richard had never seen JayFar so intensely angry, and it frightened him: Not the anger itself but what it could lead to, for Richard was a descendant from a long line of intensely angry people, and he knew firsthand what unchecked or, worse, misdirected rage could unleash, and not only was JayFar angry, he had taken to raging against Barnett Nelson, Ruth Thatcher McGinnis's granddaughter, the executor of her will, and, as fate and chance would have it, the heir to the property that Jonas Thatcher willed to Ruth Thatcher McGinnis. Surely Jay couldn't be thinking that he didn't have to honor the bequest. "Maybe she'll take pity on you and deed the land over to you. After all, she's richer than you are."

"What are you talking about? Who's richer than me?"

"Barnett Nelson. That's who we were discussing, isn't it? Old Mrs. McGinnis's granddaughter." Richard swallowed hugely from the heavy crystal highball glass. Being sober when JayFar was angry took way too much effort.

"You looked her up, didn't you?"

JayFar stopped pacing and looked hard at Richard, a sign that he was cooling off a bit. "No, I didn't look her up. Why would I do that?"

"Because you'd know that she's more than just a 'New York City lawyer,' that she's one of the best probate and estate lawyers up there—and in that town, 'best' means best paid. She's a partner in one their top-drawer firms, and she's earned more than a million dollars a year for a few years running. On top of that, she belongs to one of the richest Black families in Georgia. And on top of *that*, your grandfather left her property worth..."

"I know what it's worth. To us. Question is: What's it worth to her?"

"Might not be about money, Jay."

"It's always about money, Richard. Who has it, who doesn't, how to get it, how to keep it. You say Miss Nelson's already got money. I say she'd like to have more. It costs a lot of money to live in New York, right?"

Richard didn't attempt to soften his anger. "What is the matter with you? No wonder your grandpa didn't leave you the damn land. You just flat-out don't deserve it."

JayFar looked as if he'd been hit. Felt as if he had. Richard had never spoken this way to him. He'd never have thought it possible. He was, literally, shocked speechless. So, too, was Richard, who couldn't think of a way to mitigate that rare and difficult moment, so he allowed it to pass in silence— a silence that JayFar broke first.

"You really were more like him than I saw or knew," JayFar said, his voice without expression or emotion. He went behind his desk and picked up a cardboard box—the writing on it said that it once had held shelled pecans from a farm that hadn't existed for a least twenty-five years. JayFar extended the box to Richard, and he took it without asking what was in it, though he knew it wasn't shelled pecans. "These are his diaries. There's twenty-five or thirty of them; I lost count. I didn't even know he kept a diary, though you probably did, huh?"

Richard put the box down so he could open it. He was mesmerized by the thought of the old man's journals; he wanted to see them, to touch them, even as he realized that he could never take them, and he said that to JayFar. "I take it you haven't read them." It was a statement, not a question. "You should, you know."

"That's why I'm giving them to you, Richard: Because you think they should be read and because you'll read them, first page to last. Probably stay up late nights too."

Richard lifted a stack of the books from the box. They were old and worn, some of them worm-and-moth-eaten. He could see that books at the bottom of the box had covers of fine leather, while those he held definitely were cheaper—begun, no doubt, when the writer was young and without the funds to spend good money for a book of empty pages. "I wish I had something from my ancestors—something of what they thought and believed, what they saw, what they did, what they wanted to do."

"You can read these and find out what my ancestor thought and did."

"Maybe if you read them you'd find out why the old man left his land to…"

"Don't say her name in this room again."

"At least admit that it's a possibility before you give away these books."

Jay reached out and snatched the diary that Richard held and the old book tore in half. Ignoring the destruction, he flipped it open. "Some possibility. The first entry is dated, *'Summer 1917*,' and it looks like an illiterate wrote it."

"My God, Jay, he'd have been just a boy then." Richard leaned into the box and lifted out one of the leather volumes. It felt as smooth as his favorite driving gloves. The initials *JFT* were embossed in gold on the cover and beneath them, also in the same gold, *1985*. He opened the book at midpoint. "Look at the difference between the writing of a boy and that of a man," he said, taking the torn book—tablet, really, the kind used by school children of the day—from JayFar and giving him the leather-bound volume. "You can see how important his diaries were to him. I wonder when he started buying these fancy ones?"

"Who knows? Who cares?"

Richard's anger was rising again. "I care. It's a life, told in a man's own words as he was living it. Why can't you understand how valuable that is?"

"Land is valuable. Land that should have been mine. Land that would be worth millions if it were mine. Instead, it belongs to a big-city lady lawyer—what's her name again? You seem to have a knack for remembering the names of people who inherited my inheritance right out from under me."

"Barnett Nelson," Richard said, his eyes squinting with the effort of reading the penciled script of a twelve-year old boy on lined paper in an almost seventy-year old journal. "And Jay? You really should get to know her 'cause your granddaddy sure as hell knew her grandma. Listen to this: *I want to marry Ruthie but I know I can't. She is the most beautiful girl I ever saw.* He wrote that in 1917, Jay. My God, wait 'til Margaret sees this stuff!"

"I can't see why it's taking you so long to make up your mind, Sissy. Either you're gonna keep the Carrie's Crossing property or you're not. Either you're gonna keep Grandma's house or you're not. Just decide for Chrissakes."

Sissy watched her baby brother watch her. He'd made his pronouncement and issued his order and now it was her turn, and he really and truly expected that she would respond and when she didn't, his anger rose swiftly, as it seemed to do with greater and greater regularity since their grandmother died. Sissy knew that death—and more specifically, the process of sorting out and disposing of the various components of a life—brought out the worst in the best of people: Her work as a probate attorney had shown her more than she ever cared to know about people's desire for dollars and things to which they felt themselves entitled.

Before Grandma's death, if asked, Sissy would have described her youngest brother as sweet and funny and fun and fun-loving. He was none of those things, she realized. He was spoiled and quite possibly lazy and almost certainly an opportunist. Of course, the fact that she only saw Teddy a couple of times a year could be used as a excuse for her failure to see him as he really was, but she knew that the real reason was that she hadn't wanted to accept her older brothers' assessment of the family baby. They both were so smug and self-righteous and...and...correct. They always did everything just right—the exception being, in Doug's case, his marriage—and even then, Carolyn certainly looked the part—she was poised and elegant—even if she had relinquished the role in the middle of the second act.

"I haven't decided what I'm going to do, Teddy, but I'm certainly not going to be rushed or pushed into any decision, so do me a favor and don't ask me again."

"You are so fucking selfish," he screamed at her.

"How does that make me selfish?" she asked, really wanting to know.

"You've already got a house. Or a condo or whatever it is in New York, And now you've got Grandma's house and that old dude's house in Carrie's Crossing. You can't live in but one place at a time. How does it hurt you to give me something? That's how it makes you selfish: If you just keep all of it to yourself. You could give me the Carrie's Crossing house."

"I thought you were head over heels to have Grandma's house," Sissy said.

"I don't want to live in the ghetto if I don't have to," he said, crossing to the window to look out at the world he'd just reduced to a stereotype.

"Is that what you think this is? A ghetto? Your mother was raised in this house. Your grandfather built this house with his own hands."

"Save your breath, Sis, I already know the ancient history lesson. And maybe it wasn't a ghetto back then, but it is now. I mean, just look out the window."

Once again, Teddy expected his sister to follow his command, but Sissy didn't move. She didn't need to look out of the window to see the street outside, any more than she needed to survey the wide living room in which she stood with its gleaming oak floors, wood cut and laid by Mack McGinnis. The fireplace, open on two sides—living room and dining room—was an inspired act in the days before central heat, expensive firewood and atmospheric concerns. The built-in, floor-to-ceiling bookshelves that flanked the fireplace in the living room were testament to a mind that loved learning until Ruthie McGinnis breathed her last. The other downstairs rooms—the parlor, a bedroom with its own bathroom, a kitchen which ran the length of the back of the house, a pantry and a laundry room—displayed the same gleaming hardwood floors and sparkling white walls. There were photographs everywhere and vases that would have held fresh flowers if Ruthie were still alive. Sissy had finally thrown away the dead ones that had filled the vases, but she hadn't been able to force herself to buy replacements. All she'd done since Grandma died was walk around, from room to room downstairs, then up the wide staircase to the second floor and down the hallway, pausing at each doorway and looking into each of the three bedrooms and the large, square, white-tiled bathroom, until she reached the bedroom at the end of the hall. Grandma's room, its door still closed. Sissy hadn't opened the door. Not yet.

"I'm probably going to live in this house, Teddy. At least for a while. And I'm probably going to rent out my condo in New York. At least for a while. And I don't know what I'm going to do with the house in Carrie's Crossing. Not yet. But what I won't be doing is giving it to you, so please stop asking."

Sissy stood in front of the bookcase that held Grandma's collection of first edition books by Black American authors: Contemporary works by Toni Morrison and June Jordan and Octavia Butler and Samuel Delaney and earlier works by Langston Hughes and James Baldwin and Dorothy West and Zora Neale Hurston. How had Ruthie McGinnis known that these books one day would be priceless? But, of course, she hadn't known that; she wouldn't have bought or kept them for that reason. Sissy touched the books, ran her fingers over their spines and envisioned the empty spaces that she would have to fill when her cousin the literature professor came to collect her inheritance. Sissy would, she decided, replace the first editions with copies of the same works, then begin reading them again, one by one, until she'd read them all.

"You're doing this just to spite me, aren't you?" Teddy's fury was a presence in the room—a poltergeist or a decaying rodent trapped behind the wall—ubiquitous and unpleasant and unwelcome.

Sissy left the living room, crossed the dining room, and went to stand in the kitchen. She looked out into the backyard for a moment, seeing not a ghetto but the memory of Grandma tending her garden—pulling weeds or checking leaves for the presence of aphids or cutting flowers to bring inside to fill the many vases—on her hands and knees more often than not. The memory brought tears, and Sissy hurried to the sink, turned on the water and splashed her face, as much to clear the tears as to prevent her eyes from becoming red and puffy; she had an appointment with Jonas Thatcher and his lawyer to see the Carrie's Crossing property, and she didn't want to arrive looking grief-stricken, since she'd most likely leave looking that way. Besides, she was more than just a legatee—she was a New York lawyer. She had practiced law in New York for more than fifteen years and had never been called that. Since the funeral and the will readings, she'd been nothing but—on both sides of the Thatcher family. So, she thought she'd look and act the part. Whatever that was. She wasn't entirely certain, but it no doubt did not include red, puffy eyes.

Sissy pulled paper towels from the roll above the sink and dried her face, then she turned from the sink to the pantry and opened the door. She ignored the shelves of food and, instead, stepped all the way in. She didn't open the secret door all the way in the left side corner, the door that was invisible unless one squeezed into the pantry, which is something nobody would do—unless opening the secret door was the objective, and as badly as Sissy wanted to get away from Teddy, she didn't want to share this secret with him. This door inside the pantry would remain Grandma's for a while longer...maybe even forever. Because, after all, secrets have power.

– 6 –

O ne good thing about the absurd traffic that Sissy confronted on her drive
across town to Carrie's Crossing was that it took her mind off the reason
for the journey. She'd often heard her mother complain that traffic in Belle
City rivaled that of Los Angeles, but she'd thought that was just her mother
being her usual dramatic self. Sissy knew that her hometown had grown,
that it even thought of itself as an international city, but the density of the
traffic congestion that mirrored the density of the residential and commercial
development lining both sides of the wide boulevard suggested that Belle City's
bragging rights were well earned: Not only was there a lot of development,
it was bright and shiny and prosperous looking. Sissy thought that buying a
condo in one of the dozens of buildings she passed would likely cost as much
as the two million she'd spent on her own Chelsea loft. She also thought she'd
likely get a lot more for her money here in the glass and steel canyons of
Carrie's Crossing.

She slowed to a crawl as the computerized navigational voice alerted her
to the approaching right turn which she couldn't have missed if she'd wanted
to—not by driving too fast anyway. How or why anybody would drive every
day in traffic like this was a mystery to her, whether in Los Angeles or New York
or Belle City. True, few cities had the kind of public transportation networks
enjoyed by New York and Chicago and London and Paris, but, Sissy thought,
next time she came to Carrie's Crossing she'd take a taxi. Then she scanned the
traffic surrounding her: Not a taxi in sight. Maybe she wouldn't be returning to
her roots after all.

Willie Cummings had an office on the top floor of an older but more
elegant building in an older and more elegant section of Carrie's Crossing that
Sissy actually had some memory of. She didn't know why, exactly, but she was
certain she'd been on this street at some time. Or perhaps she was creating a
memory based on those long hours of listening to her grandmother reminisce?
No, Sissy told herself, that couldn't be true. Her grandmother had left Carrie's
Crossing almost eighty years ago and she'd never returned, had never even
mentioned the place of her birth. In fact, for most of her own life, Sissy had

thought that her grandmother's birthplace was Belle City. Only in recent years did knowledge of Carrie's Crossing surface, and that only because of proposals to change the town's name.

Sissy stopped at the parking garage entrance, got a ticket, drove into the underground lot, and followed directions to a parking space with her name on a placard directly adjacent to the elevator. Jag Badenhoff had told her that Cummings was "a gentleman of the old school," but she hadn't expected a reserved parking space. She definitely wasn't in New York anymore. She checked her face in the mirror: Eyes bright and clear, not a hint of puffiness or redness. She gathered her purse and briefcase, exited and locked the car, and was on the elevator, riding up to the top floor one minute ahead of her scheduled appointment.

Cummings didn't just have an office on the top floor, his office *was* the top floor, a warm, welcoming mix of Old South meets English gentleman's club. As might be expected, the only people immediately visible when Sissy stepped off the elevator and sank into the plush crimson carpet were women. But unlike the brash, polished twenty-to-thirty-something blonds preferred by law firms on the East Coast, the women here were elegantly attired and coiffed fifty-somethings who probably knew as much law as the people in the offices on the other side of the massive double doors. There were four of these women, each seated at a desk skillfully concealed behind a brass and wood-fitted partition. Phones buzzed politely, barely audible beneath the classical concerto that wafted down from the discreet ceiling speakers. Sissy chuckled to herself as she recalled that Willie Cummings had referred to himself in their several telephone calls as "just an old country lawyer."

One of the women—dare she think of them as receptionists?—rose and met her at the elevator door. "Good day, Miss Nelson. Mr. Cummings is expecting you. Will you follow me, please?"

Sissy followed her across the expanse of crimson, through the double doors, and into a bright hallway of offices that resembled every big-dollar law firm she'd ever seen. They turned right and stopped at an open door. Willie Cummings jumped up from his desk and bounded across the room to greet her, looking even more like a leprechaun than she remembered from their first meeting at the reading of Grandma's will.

"Mr. Cummings," she said, extending her hand.

"Miss Nelson. It is good to see you again." He took her hand in both of his, held it for a moment, then released it and took her elbow as he led her away from the desk and toward a cozy grouping of leather club chairs in front of a fireplace. "We'll have a cup of tea, shall we? It's something exotic—what's it called, Mrs. Pfeiffer?"

This is definitely not New York, Sissy thought: He calls his secretary 'Mrs.'

"It's called Yogi tea, and it really is quite good. It's the cardamom that does it."

"It sounds delicious. Thank you," Sissy said, and Mrs. Pfeiffer left them, leaving the door open, which Sissy was thinking was a bit odd until a figure immediately filled the doorway.

"Jay. Come on in," Cummings said, waving his arm. "You two haven't met."

Sissy stood. So this was Jonas Thatcher the Third, the man who had expected to inherit his grandfather's house in Carrie's Crossing. Sissy watched him enter and cross the room, watched him assessing her with each step he took. He was tall and trim—obviously an athlete of some sort, or at least he was regularly physically active. His thick dark hair had a few strands of silver that perfectly complimented the pearl gray suit he wore, and his black shoes gleamed. They could have been twins, so similarly were they dressed. Sissy's mother-of-pearl earrings and necklace and the absence of any silver in her hair, due to her mother's insistence that she get her hair done, was the primary difference. That and his white maleness as opposed to her Black femaleness.

"I'm very pleased to meet you, Mr. Thatcher, though I do regret the circumstances that probably mean you're not terribly pleased to meet me."

Jonas couldn't help the near smile, the raised left corner of his mouth. "I'm very sorry for your loss, Miss Nelson. And for mine," he said as he shook her hand.

"I do regret that the circumstance causes you additional pain, Mr. Thatcher. The loss of your grandfather is more than enough to bear, I imagine," Sissy said.

"I must honestly admit that his not being here has hit me harder than I thought it would," Jonas said. He dipped his head in Willie Cummings's direction. "You were right. I did experience a kind of delayed reaction. I keep picking up the phone to call to check on him then I remember that he's gone." He gave a rueful half-grin that was more grimace and shook his head. "Part of you tries for the logical approach: He was a hundred years old. It was time for him to die, you tell yourself. Why are you surprised? But another part of yourself has come to believe that since he's lived for so long, he'll just keep on living. Why stop now?"

Willie Cummings started to say something but Sissy beat him to it, surprising herself with her outburst. "That's it. That expresses exactly what I've been thinking and feeling but hadn't found the words for. I'd been with Grandma for two weeks. I knew she was dying. She told me she was dying. Yet, when it happened, I was still surprised."

Mrs. Pfeiffer arrived with the tea, saving them from having to think of a clever something to say. She put the tray on the table, and Sissy was surprised and pleased to see that there were big, thick mugs, not delicate little cups, along with a pot of honey and one of steamed milk. Then the scent wafted up— cardamom, for sure, and cinnamon and some other spices that earned the tea the right to call itself yogi.

"This is good stuff," Cummings said. "You're going to like it."

"If it tastes half as good as it smells, I already do," Sissy said, bringing her cup to her face to inhale the aroma.

"Couldn't get your grandpa to even taste it," Cummings said.

"If you'd disguised it as Red Rock Cola you could have," Jay said dryly, and the little old lawyer giggled like a school boy. "You ever heard of Red Rock Cola?" Jay asked Sissy.

"Grandma loved it," she said. "There's still half a case left in her pantry. I had to drive way out to...I don't even remember where I had to go to get the stuff."

"Stevensville," Willie Cummings, Jay Far and Mrs. Pfeiffer said in unison, and they all laughed, the four of them, Sissy working hard to keep the tears at bay. If the others noticed, they were too polite to let on. Ah, Southern manners. No, she wasn't in New York.

"If you'd like, Miss Nelson, I'd be happy to take you out to Grandpa's... ah...to..."

"Thank you, Mr. Thatcher, but I have a car here. And given what I've seen of the traffic, I wouldn't ask my best friend or worst enemy to make an unnecessary trip in it."

"I hear that New York City's traffic is pretty bad too," Cummings said, succeeding in not sounding too defensive.

"It's awful," Sissy conceded, "but if you're in the backseat of a taxi, it's somebody else's problem. You can read over a brief or dictate notes or check your messages—do anything but count the number of traffic lights you've sat through."

"You don't get home very often, then?" Jonas asked, ulterior motive barely veiled.

Sissy drained the last of her tea and wiped her mouth on a napkin. "Two or three times a year and usually for no more than four or five days at a time, and I usually stick pretty close to home—to my parents' or to Grandma's. I never come to this part of town, so I'm really anxious to see more of the area, and especially to see—why don't we keep calling it your grandfather's house since I'm not sure I'm ready to call it my house?"

JayFar thought his lifting spirits must be visible to everybody in the room, so relieved did he feel. Surely her words conveyed at least the thought, if not the actual intention, that perhaps she'd relinquish her claim to the Carrie's Crossing land. "How's this, then," Jay said: "I'll lead the way. I know some pretty good shortcuts through the traffic."

"With appreciation," Sissy said, getting to her feet. "Mr. Cummings, is there anything else I need to know? Anything I need to do?"

Cummings swallowed the last of his tea and jumped to his feet. He hurried over to his desk and grabbed an envelope that he held to his chest a moment before extending it to Sissy. "The keys to the house," he said. "And the deed." There were tears in his eyes.

"You were his lawyer for a long time," Sissy said.

"More than fifty years. I inherited the account from my father."

"Then I'd be pleased and honored, Mr. Cummings, if Jag and I can call on you to assist in any matters that might pertain to this property. You know Jag, of course."

He was overcome with emotion. He grabbed her hands. "Of course I know Jag. We're good friends. And I thank you, Miss Nelson, for that kindness. It means a lot to me. More than a client, Jonas was my friend, and I spent many a happy time at that house."

Sissy took the envelope Cummings gave her, gathered up her briefcase and her purse, and turned to Jonas Thatcher, and she knew that she would spend a lot of her time trying to decipher the expression on his face. She'd seen the barely disguised hopeful look when she said she wasn't ready to call the house her own, and the relief when she accepted his offer to lead her to the house. But what the hell was the expression she'd just witnessed?

She couldn't think about it now. Willie Cummings was saying something, and Jonas was shifting into a different gear, one that felt like he was taking charge. It made her wish she hadn't said she'd follow him to...dammit.

She had to call it something. She wouldn't call it his grandfather's house and she couldn't call it her house. It was Carrie's house. And Uncle Will's. And Grandma's. Carrie's house: That sounded right, felt right. "Shall we go?" she said. "To Carrie's house."

Once back out in the dense traffic, Sissy was glad she'd agreed to follow JayFar because she doubted that she'd have been able to find the place on her own, even with Willie Cummings's written directions or the car's computerized navigator leading her. All of a sudden, right in the middle of an active pocket of sprawl on the edge of Carrie's Crossing with sleek high rises and even sleeker shopping malls sprouting on both sides of the road, the scenery turned pastoral, bucolic. The growth and sprawl gave way to grass and trees, and a two-lane blacktop road without sidewalks replaced the four lanes of bumper-to-bumper traffic that had led them for several miles deep into the heart of Carrie's Crossing. Sissy felt something inside of her shift.

JayFar's left turn signal blinked, and Sissy followed his car into what was little more than a lane. But it must be more than that because it widened and then it split so that there was a grassy median strip and a road on either side. They kept to the right and the road seemed to rise a bit, then level off. The next view was of a construction site. Two of them, actually, one on either side of the road, which continued for another quarter mile, when it ended at a circular gravel drive. And there was Carrie's house. Sissy wasn't certain what she had expected, but it wasn't this. It was beautiful, yes, but it wasn't grand or impressive—those of her mother and her two oldest brothers were larger, grander than this. This was a two-story structure on a foundation of stones with a porch that wrapped around three sides. It had four chimneys, two at either end of the house. It was painted a pale, pale yellow. There was a swing on the south end of the front porch and big planters full of multicolored flowers on either side of the front door. Sissy closed her eyes and tried to imagine what the house had looked like when Grandma had lived in it.

She jumped at the tap on the window and opened her eyes to see Jonas Farley Thatcher standing there. Jonas Farley Thatcher the Third who thought the house was his grandfather's. Sissy opened the car door and got out, then leaned back in to get the envelope with the keys.

"That's your construction project down the road?" Sissy said.

He nodded and turned to look down the road, as if to make sure it was still there. Then he looked back at the house. "It's all neat and clean inside. My aunts were here for the reading of the will, and they stayed here. They love this place. They used to come here when they were young, and they've got these memories. They didn't know...we didn't know..."

"Of course you didn't; nobody did. And it's good that somebody who loved it was in it, taking care of it in your grandfather's absence. That's why I'm living at Grandma's. Houses that were homes shouldn't be empty." Sissy walked around the side of the house, touching it as she walked, touching the stones of the foundation and the boards of the house. "I think I can feel them," she said, more to herself than to JayFar.

"Feel who?" he asked.

"My grandma. My great-grandma. Uncle Will."

He looked confused, and he looked at her as if she were confused. "Why would you think you could feel them here?"

"Why wouldn't I? After all, it was their house. They built it. My grandma was born in this house and my great uncle died in this house." Well...in the burning barn behind the house."

"What?"

"You didn't know that?" Anger rose in Sissy, strongly and quickly. "How could you not know? I don't believe you."

"I didn't. I swear to God I didn't. I thought Grandpa had always lived here."

"Did he say that? Did he tell you that?" Sissy demanded.

"I don't know that he ever said those words, said he'd always lived here. I just assumed—"

"Well don't," Sissy snapped. "This is Carrie's house. The Carrie of Carrie's Creek. The Carrie of Carrie's Crossing. She and William, her brother, built this house. They carried these huge rocks from the creek, and they cut down the trees for the wood."

"When?" JayFar asked. "When?"

"After they were freed," Sissy answered.

"Freed?" he asked, confused again.

"They were slaves on Carney Thatcher's farm." Sissy turned in circles trying to get her bearings, tried to remember all the things Grandma had told her about growing up here, about the woods and trails through the woods leading to Jonas's house and to the creek and to the other farms. "That way," Sissy pointed toward the construction site. "Down that way is where Carney Thatcher's farm was, where your grandfather was born and grew up."

"My grandfather's father was named Zeb. Who's Carney Thatcher?"

"Zeb's father," Sissy said, "and Carrie and William's father." She turned away from JayFar and walked up the stone steps to the front porch. She had the key in her hand and it trembled slightly when she put it in the lock. It turned smoothly, the door opened and Sissy stepped inside.

JayFar's hand trembled, too, as he put the car key into the ignition, but he didn't turn it. He sat in the car looking at the house that he'd known all his life—the house that he'd thought of as his family home, as his ancestral home. That he'd never revered things familial or ancestral didn't mean that he couldn't think of his grandfather's house in those terms, but it certainly could explain why he hadn't known that the house hadn't always been in his family: Nobody had told him because everybody had known that he didn't care, wouldn't care now if the house and the land it occupied weren't part of his plan for developing the land.

At that moment, several thoughts bombarded JayFar at once: Grandfather had known that Jay would level the house if it became his, which is why he left it to the one person most likely to preserve it, and if old Ruthie Thatcher wasn't likely to destroy the house, neither would her granddaughter be inclined to do so, all of which meant that JayFar's brilliant and lucrative development plan was, for all intents and purposes, dead in the water. He closed his eyes and watched his dreams die behind his eyelids. Then he opened them and looked again at the house and wondered whether the letter that was part of his grandfather's will had explained why he hadn't left the house to his grandson.

The letter that JayFar had, in his anger and disappointment, crumpled into a ball and thrown across the room without bothering to read. Where was it now? Where had he been at the time? He could see Richard and Willie Cummings...yes. It was in Willie's office and, knowing the two of them, that letter would have been smoothed out and saved because that's the kind of thing that Richard and Willie did. Because that's the kind of thing they cared about: How Jonas Farley Thatcher's house had been built and owned by freed slaves, slaves once owned by Jonas's great-grandfather, a man he'd never heard of until just a few moments ago: Carney Thatcher, his own grandfather's grandfather. And something else Sissy Nelson said—that Carney was the father of Carrie and William, the two slaves who'd built the house.

JayFar steadied his hands, punched a button on his cell phone, then started the car. Jonas Thatcher's journals, he asked Richard: Where were they?

Sissy watched from an upstairs window as JayFar drove slowly away. She had marveled at his lack of knowledge. How could he know so little of his own history? If it weren't so stupid she'd have felt sorry for him. But it was stupid not to know one's past, especially when not only written records existed but the people who could remember were still alive. Sissy didn't know much about Jonas's living family, but she did know that Willie Cummings knew things and that, she thought, is what she'd seen on Jonas's face back at the office: He hadn't known that the lawyer and his grandpa had been friends. "You should be ashamed of yourself," she said, as JayFar reached the end of the drive. She was surprised that he turned right, heading deeper into Carrie's Crossing, rather than left and back to Belle City, but she'd have been even more surprised to hear his thoughts at that moment, which so perfectly matched her own.

Sissy resumed her exploration of Carrie and William's house. This second floor hadn't existed in 1922 when the Black Thatchers made their midnight run from the Klan, only a dormer space where the brothers slept. Jonas, then, had added this second floor. Like the first floor, it had a long, wide center hallway with rooms left and right. There were two bathrooms and, at the back of the house, upstairs and down, there were sunrooms: Glass on three sides that provided a view of what would have been the stables and the land that still was farmed and, Sissy realized, the little building that once had been Mack McGinnis's one room school house. She tried—as she had so many, many times in her life—to put herself in her grandmother's time and place, but could not.

Sissy knew the truth of the history that Ruthie Thatcher and her parents and siblings had lived—right here in this very spot—but she could not imagine it as her own, and for that she was grateful. How horrible an existence that had been. At least it seemed so to her, and yet, until she was on her deathbed and recording her memories, Sissy had never heard her grandmother speak of the pain and horror of that time. Perhaps it was better to, if not forget it, at least move forward without speaking of it? "No," Sissy spoke out loud. "The truth is better told, out loud and in full; otherwise, it creates space for lies to take hold and grow."

Downstairs, she thought again, what a beautiful house it was. Beautiful in the same way her grandmother's house was beautiful: In its elegant simplicity. Both homes were beautifully furnished; money clearly had been spent. But there was no hint of ostentation, not even in the Persian and Turkish rugs that graced the highly polished, gleaming, wide-planked wood floors. In fact, the only difference that Sissy could see between the two homes, her Grandmother's and Jonas Thatcher's, was the evidence of regular and frequent visitors to Ruthie McGinnis's home and the absence of the same here. She could tell where Jonas Thatcher sat and read, where he ate and where he slept, but there was no evidence that he entertained. If Willie Cummings or anyone else visited, they left behind no trace. Or Jonas had removed all such traces.

The refrigerator and the cabinets were fully stocked. So was the temperature controlled wine bar in a corner of the dining room that was, Sissy thought, at least one indication that the old man entertained, but the entire bottom shelf of the refrigerator was filled with Red Rock Cola, as was a shelf in the pantry. Sissy opened a bottle, toasted both the old people, then took a long pull from the bottle, choking and coughing as she knew she would. The stuff had a kick as powerful as whiskey. She knew that Ruthie had never consumed alcohol. Had Jonas? They were so much alike!

Sissy opened a very respectable bottle of a California Cabernet, got a wine glass from the cabinet, and took wine and Red Rock Cola out to the solarium. She didn't sit in Jonas's chair but the adjacent one, the one that would have been for company, and as she sat, she wondered why she was sitting here drinking wine instead of heading back to Belle City and her mother's house. Staring out at the peaceful green view, she understood why Jonas Thatcher didn't bequeath this house to his grandson, and she understood equally as clearly why, as her grandmother's legatee, she could not permit the house's destruction. But what would she do with it?

She got up and walked through the house again, in and out of rooms where her ancestors had lived and where they had been happy—happy because they had each other. Had Jonas been happy here? She touched things as she passed through—a chair, a chest, a drapery panel—and she thought yes, Jonas had been happy here, because she was comfortable. A bit egotistical, she told herself, but it was true: If the old man had been miserable and unhappy here, this place would have spoken of that. Then, with a start, Sissy realized one thing it did not speak of: Where was the evidence of Jonas's wife? Had she died long ago, leaving Jonas to stamp his own mark? Had she left him, and in so doing, left him to his own devices?

She hurried back upstairs and to the room that was the office. She thought she'd seen photographs here...and yes, there they were, grouped on a shelf, two different families, related but separate: One from the distant past, another from the more recent past. There was a boy who could have been the Jonas she just met, with, she thought, his parents and sister, and there were several photos of old Jonas Thatcher as a young man with a woman who likely was his wife. Sissy scrutinized the photos, looking for a hint of a date, but all she could determine was that they were old.

She returned to the solarium, saw the phone, called her mother and told her where she was and what she was doing. "It's a beautiful house, Mom, and so peaceful and relaxing." She'd expected resistance, or denial. She got neither. Instead Nellie asked what she'd said to Teddy to upset him so, and when she relayed that conversation, her mother's only response was that she was glad Sissy had decided to stay for a while. "I also might stay the night out here. I need to give some very serious thought about what to do with this house, Mom, but one thing I cannot do is allow it to be torn down."

When she hung up, Sissy felt even more relaxed. She realized that she had expected resistance from her mother, and not getting it was a relief. She also had surprised herself with the idea of spending the night here, and with how comfortable that felt, and she said a silent prayer of gratitude that she'd made Teddy leave Grandma's house when she left, otherwise she'd have had to return to Belle City. No way she'd have left her baby brother there alone. And speaking of him, her mother not jumping to Teddy's defense was a first. Was she the last to see the truth of who Teddy really was? Or perhaps she merely was the last one to whom he had revealed his true self. Suddenly a memory surfaced: A fight between Teddy and her father. Teddy had dropped out of school and spent his days in bed, hung over, watching television and listening to music, and his nights hanging out, working on the next day's hangover. Dad had issued an ultimatum: Teddy would re-enroll in school, get a job, or he would get out. He had thirty days, at the end of which, still an unemployed drop-out, Dad evicted him.

"Theodore. You can't be serious."

"I've never been more serious, Nellie. Teddy, give me those car keys, and put down that suitcase."

"That's my car, Dad. And my clothes."

Why she could recall the scene so vividly and clearly Sissy didn't know, but what she now saw so clearly was that Teddy was so drunk or high he was barely conscious.

"I bought and paid for the car and the clothes—and the suitcase, too, for that matter. You should be thankful that I don't make you strip and…"

"Theodore! No! Don't, please!" Nellie grabbed her husband's arm with one hand and her son with the other. The son shoved her, and she'd have fallen if her husband hadn't caught her. It was the proverbial last straw. Theodore Nelson, still attired in the three-piece hand tailored suit he wore every day, picked up his youngest son as if he still were a child and not an almost-grown man of nineteen, and brought him in close, nose to nose.

"If you ever raise your hand or your voice to my wife again, I will kill you," the father said to the son, and put him down. "Now, get out of my house."

Teddy had gone to his grandparents' home that night and they, of course, had taken him in—and put him to work the following day on one of Grandpa's construction sites.

The force of the memory left Sissy breathless. She put her feet on the ottoman and held the envelope Willie Cummings had given her just a couple of hours ago, and when her breathing returned to normal, she opened it: The deed to the house, a surveyor's report which, even though Sissy knew what it would show, nevertheless was startling, and a letter, in a bold hand, addressed to Mrs. Ruth Thatcher McGinnis. She opened it.

March 1985

My Dear Ruthie:

If you're reading this then I am gone on to the Other Side, and it's about time. I pen this on my 80th birthday and know that you will reach this milestone in another two months. Did we ever imagine that we would live so long? Perhaps you did seeing as how long life spans were your heritage and how none of your relatives ever seemed ready to go. I, on the other hand, am more than ready, though I must confess I'm healthy as a horse. Still, I can't live forever and when I'm gone, these things must be set right. The first, of course, is to return to you the land my father stole from your family in 1922. I don't know if Mr. First ever told you all but I came to see him that same day—later that morning—and brought him the deed to your house and land that my father had claimed. Mr. First wouldn't take it. He said the land was mine now according to the law, since my father was dead. Did Mr. First tell you any of this? If not, then prepare for a shock: I killed my father that morning when I found out what he and the KKK had done, and if the land was mine, then I wanted to return it to the rightful owner. But I knew Mr. First was right (he always was!). BC was your place where you all were happy and CC is the place where I have had some happiness but also much sadness. I have one grandchild left, a man who carries my name: Jonas Farley Thatcher III. My family seems very small compared to yours, but I know that it is not good to compare ourselves to others, so I will cease and desist. The other thing to make right with you is this: Here is the deed to my cabin in the North Carolina mountains. The land it is on was—still is—owned by your brother Beau. You know that when Beau moved, when he left BC, it was to the Cherokee Reservation. No white man could own land up there but Beau could, him being both Black and Indian. Beau bought a lot of land up there, just like he did in BC, and he let me build my cabin on his land. I haven't been up there but twice since Beau died and don't expect to go again. No point now. Beaudry Thatcher was the best man I ever knew, along with First Freeman and your father, Big Silas Thatcher. If every man in the world was like them, well, what a world we'd have! One more thing I must tell you, Ruthie, a thing you may not want to know but which I think you should know: Beau killed the man Tom Jenks who was with Miss Nellie when she got killed that day. That's why Beau moved away from BC and up to the mountains. He never got over what they did to him on that chain gang and he didn't want to get caught for killing Tom Jenks even though nobody knew but me and I surely wasn't going to tell.

So, Ruthie, that's what I have to tell you. And this: Having you and your brothers be my friends has been the greatest joy of my life. I wish I could explain to my grandson how important you all are to me but while he is a very good man, and a very smart one, he does not like a lot of talk about kin and connections. So nobody who is related to me on the white side of the family knows how I feel about all of you on the Black side. When I was younger I used to wish that you all were white. I don't wish that anymore. I wish I could have been Black. And if wishes were horses, beggars would ride. God bless you, Ruthie, and your family.

Sissy was weeping when she finished reading the letter from Jonas Farley Thatcher to her grandmother. Much of what he'd written she already knew. Grandma had talked about her lengthy friendship with Jonas Thatcher, specifically how pleased they were when, at some point in the 1970s, they could stop hiding it. Grandma said they'd had dinner together at a fancy restaurant downtown and nobody had given them a second glance. But reading Jonas's words, especially his admission to having killed his own father, had a more powerful impact than she could ever have imagined.

She jumped up, restless now, and more than that—edgy—and she wasn't certain why. She grabbed her car keys and ran out the front door. Her gym bag was in the trunk of the car—grandma's car. She'd go for a run, clear her head, exhaust whatever willies were bedeviling her and making her feel off balance. But first: The last thing her mother had said as they ended their phone conversation was, "Don't forget to take the video." She wanted to see the house, but she didn't want to visit it. Because Ruthie McGinnis had sworn never to set foot in Carrie's Crossing again, her only daughter carried out that promise. But they all wanted to see the house that had been the family's home since the days of slavery; they needed some visual confirmation of its existence.

Upstairs in what she assumed to be the guest bathroom, she changed into workout pants and a tee shirt, pulled her hair into a pony tail, put a cap on, laced up her shoes, and skipped down the stairs. She snapped on her waist pouch, grabbed keys, ID and the camcorder, and was out the door. She spent half an hour shooting the exterior of the house and the grounds from every angle, from a distance and up-close. She'd shoot the interior later, she thought, taking the camera inside and returning to the porch to do some quick stretches.

She ran down the road the way she'd come to the house, ran through Jonas's construction site, ran through an older part of Carrie's Crossing that was close enough to the new part that she could hear constant din of the traffic—hear it but not see it; the foliage was too thick. She ran back toward Carrie's house and stopped when she got to the creek. Carrie's Creek. And she was weeping again. Had some part of her believed that the creek was an invention, some kind of make-believe? It seemed little more than a stream. The water was shallow but clear, and it moved quickly and steadily. She closed her eyes and inhaled deeply. Yes, there was the taste of vehicular emissions at the back of her throat, but it was overridden by the scent of grass, trees and dirt, and the tiny trickle and babble of the little stream overrode the muted traffic noise. She could almost imagine what it had been like when Grandma and great-uncles Si and Tobias and Beau had roamed the woods and played with Jonas Thatcher... that was it!

That's what had put her on edge, had her feeling unbalanced and out of sorts: Jonas Thatcher writing that he wished he were Black. Had any white man anywhere ever said such a thing—and meant it? And how was one to take those words? That he had proven himself a friend in the face of the virulent racism of the time could not be disputed. So, given that he knew what life was like for Black people, why would he wish to have been born Black? She found the idea discomfiting, perhaps even a bit insulting. Who was this man to make light of the burden of having been born Colored in America at the turn of the Twentieth Century? Or...perhaps that's not at all what he was doing. Perhaps he was asking to be able to share the weight?

Picking up the pace, she followed the construction road all the way to a paved road that she thought must be the one that ran behind Carrie's house. Houses faced the road on one side, trees on the other, but the bucolic nature of the setting was spoiled by the constant flow of traffic in both directions. Obviously the road was a shortcut for motorists few of whom, it seemed, were inclined to share the road with a jogger, there being no sidewalks.

She was dripping sweat and at least an hour past hungry when she got back to Carrie's house. Despite the lack of central air conditioning, the house was relatively cool. She opened and drank down a bottle of water, then a bottle of Red Rock Cola, though it wasn't possible to guzzle the stuff like water. She burped and choked her way through it, enjoying every swallow. It was icy cold and every bit as thirst quenching as those expensive electrolyte replacement beverages she bought by the case back home in New York. And as she thought the words "home" and "New York," she realized that she had given absolutely no thought to her job and her life there, and even as she had the thought, she felt no panic or regret or sense of loss. Though she'd been born and raised in Belle City, had not left the place until law school at Harvard, and though she'd never been to Carrie's Crossing, what she'd felt here in this hot, humid Southern city over the past month felt very much like a homecoming to her.

She opened another Red Rock and took it out to the porch where she sat on the steps and looked out at the world. As peaceful and beautiful as it was, she could not, she knew, ever live in a place like this. She needed a city around—and beneath—her, and therefore, she could never live permanently in her grandmother's house, either. But could she live again in Belle City? Was it enough of a city? And if she did decide to live in Belle City, what would she do with herself, with her time, her energy? It would not pain her to leave New York. That's something she'd been considering for a while, though with no clear plan in mind and no clear decision made. She just knew that her perpetual restlessness of mind and spirit meant that it was time to move on. She'd proven herself to herself and to everyone else. She had a sterling reputation, lots of money, and no desire to work fourteen-hour days any longer. But if not New York, where? London? Paris?

She yawned and stretched, and her stomach growled. She was tired as well as hungry. She had, she realized, built up a load of tension around visiting her grandmother's birthplace for the first time and now, having released it, she was ready to relax. There was, she knew, plenty of food in the refrigerator and plenty of wine and Red Rock Cola. She'd seen a television, and, she realized with surprise, she'd seen a discretely placed satellite dish at the rear of the house while shooting the video. The library, she was certain, was worth exploring. So...should she shower first or cook and eat first? The thought of food caused her stomach to rumble again, answering the question.

As she stood, she saw a car turn into the road leading to the house and she soon recognized Jonas Thatcher's silver Jaguar XK150 sedan gliding none too slowly toward her, and she took the time now to admire its classic lines as she hadn't earlier when she'd followed him here. She didn't wonder why he now was returning; she merely awaited his arrival. He exited the driver's door, still dressed as he'd been earlier, opened the back door, withdrew a box and a large bag, closed both doors with his hip and came around the car to the steps. She opened the front door for him and stood aside as he entered.

"Did you have a good run?"

"I did, thank you."

He deposited the box and held up the bag. "Do you like Thai food?"

Surprised, she nodded and smiled. "You offering dinner?"

He nodded, but his smile wavered when he noticed the empty Red Rock Cola bottle in her hand. "There's a Chardonnay in there that'll compliment it much better than Red Rock, though. This is the best Thai food in town."

She turned toward the house. "Then why don't you open the wine while I set the table?"

Jonas quickly opened the wine then excused himself. He ran upstairs, and she could hear him moving about. By the time the table was set he was back wearing faded jeans, a New York Yankees tee shirt and running shoes.

"Yankees?" Sissy said.

"Don't tell me you're a Mets fan."

"OK, I won't tell you," Sissy said, and neither of them had much to say for the next few moments as they ate. The silence was relaxed and comfortable. By the time both were ready for second helpings, they both were ready for conversation.

"This is excellent food," Sissy said. "Thank you, though I don't know how you knew that I was nearing the starvation point or, wardrobe notwithstanding, how you knew I'd been for a run."

"I saw you out on the road. And projection," Jonas said. "When I'm starving, I think everybody must be, and when I feed myself, I'm usually inclined to feed whoever is close at hand. Today, that happened to be you."

"And suppose I didn't like Thai food? Then what?"

"I'd have eaten it all, and you could have raided the 'fridge. There's lots of food in there."

"I noticed," Sissy said. Then she had another thought. "You don't live here, do you?"

He shook his head. "I live in Belle City, but I've got a room here—my childhood room, as a matter of fact. I spend the odd night or weekend here with Grandpa—" He caught himself speaking in the present tense, and she watched the emotions dance across his face. "I'm sorry…"

"No need to apologize, Jonas. I understand. I've been doing the same thing. It really is difficult to speak or think of them in the past tense."

"I had no idea it would be this way." He emptied his wine glass in three large gulps to force the lump in his throat back down. He wiped his eyes with his napkin and poured them both more wine.

"You loved him very much, yet you don't seem to have known him very well. Why?"

Jonas gave her a long, speculative look. "He wasn't an easy man to know. Or to like, my grandfather. He was stubborn, cantankerous, opinionated, and...he didn't like me very much. I was a disappointment to him."

Sissy had observed a sufficient number of families during their bereavement to realize the effort required for this man to make such an admission. She also could tell from his tone of voice that he didn't really understand why his grandfather hadn't liked him, though, after having read the old man's letter to her grandmother, and having listened to almost ninety years worth of her reminiscences about him, Sissy thought she had some idea why. But she asked anyway, and he pointed to the box that he'd brought in with him, and nodded permission for her look. She got up from the table and slowly approached the box, not knowing what to expect, and opened the flaps.

"Good Lord," she exclaimed; she recognized almost instantly what the box held.

"You and Richard," he said, not quite able to keep the anger from his voice.

"This is extraordinary. From 1917 to what, a month before he died? This is a treasure trove." She looked at him then and was surprised to see in his face the anger in his voice. "Why are you angry?"

"How can you ask me that?"

"It's not just about this house. There's more to it."

He got up so forcefully that he knocked over his chair. The clatter seemed to shake him back to some rational place, for he stopped and picked up the chair, placed it neatly at the table, and apologized. "I feel like I'm down the rabbit hole. Or lost with Gulliver in some strange place or time where people see and feel things differently than I do. We all see the same things, but I have a different reaction or response and yes, it makes me angry."

"Because your response is different, or because of how the others respond?"

"You're one of them. What you just said about Grandpa's journals: A treasure trove you called them. And your excitement. You reacted exactly the way Richard and Margaret did."

"Who's Richard? And Margaret?"

"He's my law partner, my business partner. Margaret's his wife and the head of the CC historical society. Richard was crazy about Grandpa—I knew that—but I didn't know until after the old man died that Richard used to come over here and sit and talk to him. About everything, he said, but knowing Grandpa, it would have been about the past. They love that stuff, Richard and Margaret: Anything to do with the past gets their juices flowing."

"And you don't have much use for the past?" And when he shrugged, she snapped at him, "You are so full of crap, Jonas Thatcher!"

He felt the same way he'd felt when Richard yelled at him. "What are you talking about? And where do you get off saying such a thing to me?"

"You drive a thirty-year-old car, your suit and shoes are handcrafted, you still wear your college class ring, and I'm guessing your watch is at least fifty years old, unless it's a replica, which I doubt. And you shrug your shoulders at the past? Who are you kidding?"

Jay tried several times to respond but couldn't make any words leave his mouth. Then he laughed. Really and truly laughed. "He would've liked you."

"I think I would have liked him, too. Grandma certainly did."

"He more than liked her, as you'll see when you read those," he said, pointing to the box of journals.

"You've read them, then?" She opened one and turned its pages without reading them.

"I started today after I left you. I'd given them to Richard to read, which he did, from first to last. So did Margaret, both of them staying up until the wee hours. They live not far from here—that's how I saw you running—I was leaving their house." He paused, and she watched as he gathered his thoughts. "I lived with him most of my life, since my parents died, and I never truly knew him. I learned a lot today." He pointed again toward the box of journals. "I wish I knew more, enough so that I could at least begin to understand…"

Sissy returned the journal to the box and walked toward the solarium, beckoning Jay to follow. She took Jonas's letter to Ruthie from her briefcase and gave it to him. He began to read and had to sit down after just a few sentences. He had stopped breathing at some point, and he exhaled noisily when he finished reading.

"The past is how we understand the present and plan for the future, Jonas. If you'd known the history of this house and the land it sits on…"

"I wouldn't have made such a damn fool of myself. Here I am talking to him about my great idea for a development project, and he knows the whole time that it'll never happen. He must have really enjoyed watching me dig the hole that'll likely bury me."

"You think he enjoyed watching you embark on a course that ultimately would cause you pain? Is that the kind of man he was?"

"He could have stopped me."

"Would you have listened?"

He looked again at the twenty-year-old letter. "I wish I'd always listened. I wish I'd known when I brought you here this morning that this truly was your house, that it had always been your house."

"You know that I can't allow you to destroy it." It wasn't a question.

"I know, Ruthie, and it's all right. Really it—" He stopped talking because she was looking at him so very strangely. "What?"

"You called me Ruthie."

He looked momentarily confused, then realized that he was talking to her as if she were her grandmother. "I…I'm sorry…your name is…"

"Ruth Barnett Nelson. Sissy to my family and friends, RB or Barney to my colleagues."

"Barney? Like you're some ugly purple thing?" They both laughed. "I'll never call you Barney, and I can't call you Sissy."

"Does that mean you won't consider me a friend?"

"You've been calling me Jonas, which nobody ever has, but which I like hearing."

"What do your friends—Richard and Margaret—what do they call you?"

"They call me Jay, but I like you calling me Jonas. It makes me think there's a chance I could be something like him one day."

"And, while it will take some getting used to, I think I like having you call me Ruthie. It makes me think maybe I could be half the woman my grandma was." Her eyes misted, and she turned away for a second. "So, what shall we do with this house and the land?"

"You ask that as if I had some say in the matter."

"You do have some say in the matter. For instance, how flexible are your design plans? Since you haven't laid any foundations, could you re-route roads, build in different locations?"

His eyes narrowed. "What are you thinking?"

"There are three immoveable objects here."

432

"Three? There's one. This house."

She was shaking her head, and he felt his stomach drop. "The small building out there—"

"That's where the live-in housekeeper lived until she retired."

"That was the one-room school for the Colored children of Carrie's Crossing. There was no public school for them so my grandfather built one. He also was the only teacher."

Jonas covered his face with his hands. "OK, go ahead, drop the other shoe. What else don't I know?"

"Somewhere—and I'm not sure exactly where, though it's close— there's a Colored burial ground. My great-grandmother is buried there, and it's just possible that it was a burial ground for slaves too."

"What are you proposing?" he asked, his face still buried in his hands.

"That we leave this house and the school intact. I'll give them to the historical society if you'll incorporate them into your development. Make them the centerpiece. You could claim all kinds of historical significance."

"Don't you think it would make potential buyers a bit uncomfortable, the association with slavery and all?" He looked at her then, and wished he hadn't.

"Not as uncomfortable as it was for the people who were slaves."

He nodded, properly chastised, and she watched him think, which meant she watched him get up, pace a few steps, sit back down, and run his hands through his hair, standing it on end, then smoothing it back down. "What about the cemetery, the burial ground?"

"Not sure. We have to find it first. If it's far enough away from where you'll be building, we just leave it alone. Have it declared an historical site and preserved, and leave it alone."

"And if, and this is a big if, it's under a building site?"

"Then the bones must be excavated by archeologists, anthropologists, studied, cataloged and removed." And the way she spoke, the words left no room for argument.

"I can guarantee that not a single shovel will go near the burial ground."

"But you don't know where it is," Sissy said.

"Don't care," he said. Then, suddenly his expression changed.

"What?"

"We're talking about my building on land that I don't own."

She paced a few steps, then turned to face him. "You own lots of property?"

He nodded. "I do."

"Any apartment buildings in Belle City?"

"Yes. Why?"

"Any of 'em high enough off the ground that I wouldn't hear all that wretched traffic?"

Jonas thought he knew where she was going, but he wouldn't let himself fully give in to the hope. "Old or new construction?" he asked, though he expected he knew the answer.

"Definitely old," she said with a wry grin, as they both remembered her recitation of his classic belongings. It would take one to know one.

"I've got a penthouse in foreclosure in a pre-war on Belle City Drive. Sixteenth floor. Heart of the city, near everything, including the subway."

"That's not a subway," she snapped, and he laughed. "What's it cost?"

"The mortgage is one-point-six."

"And this land you just mentioned, that you don't own: What's it worth?"

"At least twice that," Jonas said, hurrying to add, "but I've got rental properties worth—"

She waved away whatever he was about say and stuck out her hand. They shook on it. She had just given him his development dream in exchange for a penthouse apartment that was one of the most beautiful in the city— and a permanent monument to the former Black slaves of Carrie's Crossing. "Margaret'll be happier than a duck in the rain. Richard too," he said.

"But you're somewhat less than happy, I take it."

He gave her a bemused look. "There's so much stuff going on inside me that I don't know what I am. Perhaps not happy, but not unhappy, either, and certainly no longer angry, no longer feeling abused and put upon—"

Her laughter stopped him. "Abused? Put upon? You'd have been right at home in the Drama Department instead of wasting your time in the law school."

"I was a star of the Moot Court, I'll have you know." He struck a dramatic pose before going to get the bottle of wine and their glasses from the dining room table. He poured and held his glass out for a toast. She stood, extended her glass, and waited. He looked at her, then shifted his gaze past her to the view outside, to the truth and the history now invisible but forever whispered by the rustling of the tree leaves and the babbling of the creek. "To Ruthie and Jonas," he said, thinking that she probably was the most beautiful woman he'd ever seen.

About the Author

Penny Mickelbury is the author of ten mystery novels in three successful series: The Carole Ann Gibson Mysteries, the Mimi Patterson/Gianna Maglione Mysteries, and the Philip Rodriguez Mysteries. Mickelbury is also an accomplished playwright and was a pioneering newspaper, radio and television reporter based primarily in Washington, D.C., an experience which provided the basis for her richly drawn characters and their myriad experiences. She is a fifth generation Georgian.

CPSIA information can be obtained
at www.ICGtesting.com
Printed in the USA
FSOW02n1125111216
28435FS